Taking it in the Rear
The Vietnam War's Rear Echelon

By:

Sherman Lynch

Cadmus Publishing
www.cadmuspublishing.com

INTRODUCTION

For each man fighting in the jungles of the Vietnam War, there were twelve in rear echelon units providing the ammo, food, medical, transport, communication and air support making it possible. This is the personal account of a rear echelon Soldier who served in the Vietnam's Theater of War from 1968 to 1969 with the First Signal Brigade, which included Thailand. As a member of SEATO, Thailand allowed US Air Force bases in its country for bombers and fighter jets to support the ground forces in South Vietnam, and also sent two Divisions to fight there. But, for National Security reasons, those serving in Thailand could not document or disclose any combat action they saw or heard of in Thailand, because the US Government did not want its people, many who violently protested against the Vietnam War, to know there was a second front being fought in Thailand.

This book is not an account of tense combat action with bullets zinging through the air and bombs exploding on battlefields strewn with bodies, blood, guts and gore (though there were some firefights), but an anecdotal account of the inane and insane situations endured in the support units for frontline troops. In previous wars, rear echelon troops have been ironically portrayed in books, like "MASH" in the Korean War, and "Good Morning, Vietnam". Such is this book, which also depicts young American Soldiers and Airmen, raised on the American values and ideals of womanhood, clashing with those of Asian cultures, where women are second-class citizens and young, teenage girls, whose marriage dowry or pay from menial jobs did not repay the cost to raise them, was often cause for them to be sold into prostitution by their fathers to recoup the expense. Though the names are changed to protect the identity of individuals, those who were there may identify themselves and their brothers-in-arms.

TABLE OF CONTENTS

CHAPTER 1

WHAT GOES AROUND COMES AROUND

This was it. The time had come for me to do my duty for God and Country.

Since the Indian Wars in the 1600s and 1700s to defend our thirteen colonies, every generation of my family had fought for our freedom, because freedom isn't free. Like my patriot ancestors in Revolutionary War, and War of 1812, my great-grandfathers in the Civil War, and my grandfather in World War I, the Great War, my parents and their siblings of the Greatest Generation in World War II, and Dad also in the Korean War, it was now my generation's turn in the Vietnam War stopping Communist aggression.

It was a pleasant and warm afternoon, with a clear, blue, sky over the San Francisco Bay on August 1, 1968, as I stepped off the Oakland City Bus before the Main Gate sign of the Oakland Army Depot in California. This was the place my transfer orders to the Vietnam War said to go. I looked again at my transfer orders to report here subsequent to my 14-day precombat leave after graduating from seven months of training at Fort Monmouth, New Jersey, as a Microwave Radio Repairman with the 26L20 MOS[1], and two more months of training to repair the new LRC-3 microwave with the 26V20 MOS. There it was, in the middle of the twenty-eight names listed:

LUNCH, SHERMAN A. SPEC-4 RA19860451 MOS 26L20, 26V20
With the order transferring all twenty-eight of us to:
1st SIG BRGD, 442 BN (LL)[2] NOKHON RATCHASIMA, THAILAND

Except the name in white capital letters on the black plastic name-plate above the right breast pocket of my U.S. Army khaki uniform read LYNCH, not LUNCH.

I was dressed in my U.S. Army, short-sleeve, Class-B khaki uni-form, with highly shined black shoes. The uniform was cardboard stiff from the starch applied when I pressed it that morning at my grandpar-ent's home in Modesto, about a hundred miles away.

Worn proudly, above the left breast pocket, was the 1¼ -inch wide, red ribbon, with a ¼ -inch wide vertical yellow stripe in the middle for the National Defense Medal awarded to me in bootcamp the year before at Fort Lewis, Washington, for enlisting during a time of war.

On the pocket flap below the ribbon was the Expert Marksman Badge with the M-14 Rifle bar dangling below it for qualifying at boot-camp with the Korean War era M-14 rifle. But the U.S. Army was now issuing the M-16-A2 assault rifle, which I was shown how to use at a week-long combat course at Fort Monmouth before I was transferred.

On each sleeve of my uniform was the embroidered gold spread eagle on a dark-green patch to show my rank as a Specialist Grade 4, or Spec-4. This was a meritorious promotion for graduating in the top ten of ninety in my class. I thought this was quite an achievement, as most of my class had been to College, and I had enlisted straight out of High School. The top student in my class had been promoted to Spec-5, which surprised no one, as he had an Associate's Degree in Electrical Engineering. At the upper edge of my left sleeve was the diamond-shaped, Signal Corps-Or-ange patch of the School Brigade at Fort Monmouth. On my head was my dark-green garrison cap.

---

1   Military Occupation Specialty
2   First Signal Brigade, 442nd Signal Battalion (Long Lines)

As the Oakland City bus pulled away, I walked to the guard shack behind the Oakland Army Depot Main Gate sign. In my right hand, I carried, by its canvas handle, my 3-foot long, 18-inch diameter, OD[3] duffel bag, crammed full of my basic military issue of clothing from bootcamp, two civilian shirts and pants, my toilet kit, two packs of cigarettes, and a large manilla envelope, containing my personnel, medical and financial records. At the airline check-in counter, it had weighed 96 pounds; four pounds under the hundred-pound limit.

Clutched in my left hand were my transfer orders and my green military ID card.

At the Main Gate guard shack, I showed the lone MP[4] Private on duty my ID card and transfer orders, and set my 96-pound duffel bag on the ground beside me. After examining my ID card photo and then my face, he appeared satisfied that this was, in fact, my ID card. Then he compared the name on my ID card with the list of twenty-eight names on my transfer orders, and said, "I'm sorry, Specialist Lynch, but I don't see your name on these orders, so I can't pass you through the gate."

I politely asked, "Can't you see the name Lunch on the order is obviously a typo for my name, Lynch, as all the other info is the same?"

He replied, "Sorry, Specialist, but I can only grant access for those whose names are on the Base Roster or on a transfer order, and your name, Lynch, is not on this order."

I argued, "But the rest of my name and service number are."

He responded, "True, but your last name is not, so I can't pass you."

Again, I argued, "But can't you see it's an obvious typo?"

He answered, "the only thing obvious to me, Specialist, is your name is not on this transfer order."

In exasperation, I asked, "Even if the rest of my name and service number on my ID card are the same as on this transfer order?"

He explained, "Look, Specialist, this is a secure military base. With all the hippy crap going on here, my orders are not to pass anyone who does not have papers to match their ID card. If you haven't noticed what's been on the news, then I suggest you take a look across the street, because I have to put up with that shit all day long."

---

3   Olive Drab, a greenish brown color used in the armed forces as camouflage

4   Military Police

Yes, I had seen on the news the violent anti-Vietnam War demonstrations across the country for the last year. Some of it up close and personal, with the riots in Newark, New Jersey, when some of us from the School Brigade at Fort Monmouth were deployed to riot control duty one weekend last spring. And now, looking across the street, I saw a few dozen long-hairs in bell-bottom jeans and tie-dyed T-shirts, carrying signs with "Stop the War," and "Kill the Baby Killers," and other such slogans.

Seeing this, I asked, "Whoa, dude, and you're the only one guarding this Main Gate?"

He replied, "Nah, there's a whole platoon of MP's armed with tear gas, rifles and riot gear in that building just behind here. The Provost Marshall figured that a low-profile here, with one Private, isn't enough to provoke a violent protest, or to bring out a TV news crew to record a non-violent protest. And, then just seeing one or two guys in uniform going through here doesn't seem to be enough to antagonize them to any major violence. Once in a while, they toss a beer can or soda bottle and swear at you guys on the way to the Vietnam War. Otherwise, it's fairly quiet."

I asked, "Just the same, you're telling me that you will not let me through the gate to report for duty to the Vietnam War because of an obvious typo on my transfer orders?"

He replied, "I don't know if it's a typo or not. All I *know* is your name is not on this transfer order. And, until you show me an order with *your* name on it, I can't allow you onto this base. I don't have the authority to pass no one, not even a bird-colonel, onto this base without a transfer order with their name on it. And, this transfer order doesn't have your name on it."

I hotly asked, "Well then, Private, if you don't have the authority, then who does?"

He replied simply, "The Provost Marshall's Office."

"I requested, "Then, could you please call the Provost Marshall's Office so I can straighten out this SNAFU?[5]"

The MP Private then turned and walked into the guard shack. From behind me, a half-empty beer can whizzed past my head and

---

5   Situation Normal, All F***ked up

splatted off the guard shack's walls as I heard "Baby killer!" shouted from across the street.

I thought, "They might be a bunch of lousy hippies who hate the Vietnam War, but one of them has a good throwing arm. The irony is, I'm on my way to that war to defend with my life their Constitutional right to protest it."

I heard the MP Private identify his post, give his rank and name, and say, "There's a Spec-4 here with a transfer order that don't have his right name on it… Yes, Sergeant," and handed me phone.

I took the phone and said, "Specialist Lynch here. I have orders transferring me to the First Brigade, via the Oakland Army Depot."

As I said this, I watched the MP Private walk to the front of the guard shack, retrieve the, now empty, beer can, and toss it into a large trash can inside the guard shack, already half full of such cans and bottles, and heard him muttering as he did so, "Damn long-haired, fascist, pinko, maggot freaks don't have any respect for tradition or noth'n. It's just hate and discontent they believe in. Dadburn perverts."

I then heard a stern voice on the phone's receiver announce, "This is SFC[6] Snyder, the Provost NCOIC[7]. What's the problem Specialist Lynch?"

I explained, "They misspelled my last name on my transfer order, Sergeant, and your Private won't let me through the Main Gate to check in for deployment to the Vietnam War."

SFC Snyder said, "First, Specialist, the Private is following his orders to not let anyone onto the Oakland Army Depot without proper ID and documents. And second, this sort of thing happens all the time, and is usually fixed easily. Just give me your full name, service number, the unit of origin for your transfer order, and the Telex number on the order."

I laboriously provided SFC Snyder with the information requested, with numerous repeats for accuracy. "Last name is Lynch; first name and middle initial are Sherman A."

SFY Snyder asked, "Is that L-I-N-C-H?"

I answered, "No, it's L-Y-N-C-H, as in, hung by the neck without due process of law."

---

6   Sergeant First Class
7   Non-Commissioned Officer in Charge

Once SFC Snyder was satisfied that he had all of the required information relayed correctly, he said, "Okay, Specialist Lynch, please stand by while I check this out with the Personnel Office at Fort Monmouth."

While waiting for SFC Snyder to call back, I reached with my right hand between the two bottom buttons of my stiff khaki shirt and withdrew my open pack of cigarettes. Gently tapping the open end against my left hand, I caused the end of a cigarette to protrude past the opening of the pack. Lifting the pack to my mouth, I grabbed the protruding cigarette with my dry, pursed, lips, and then replaced the pack to its place beneath the stiff front of my shirt. Reaching into the right front pocket of my stiff khaki pants, I took out my silver Zippo lighter with the crossed semaphore flags on it, emblematic of the U.S. Army's Signal Corps. I flipped the lighter open and rotated the flint striker wheel with my right thumb to produce a spark that lit the kerosene-soaked wick with an inch high flame. I then lit the end of the cigarette protruding between my pursed lips, and took a deep pull of nicotine laden smoke into my lungs. As the nicotine in my blood provided the desired effect on my nervous system, I gave a deep sigh of relief.

As I enjoyed my cigarette, I saw other Soldiers in their Army Class-B khaki uniforms arriving in the occasional taxi cab, or on the Oakland City Bus, exit and walk up to the MP Private, present their green military ID card and their transfer orders. After some scrutiny, the MP Private would hand them back their documents and allow them to pass onto the Oakland Army Depot. This was done amidst the heckling shouts, and thrown cans and bottles from across the street.

After waiting about fifteen minutes, watching this parade of Soldiers having their transfer orders verified and passed through the Main Gate by the MP Private, I heard the guard shack's phone ring. I listened as the MP Private picked up the phone and declare, "Main Gate." After he listened for a moment, he said, "Understood, Sergeant Snyder," and hung up the phone.

Turning toward me, he said, "Okay, I've been instructed that you are cleared to pass through, and that you are to go directly to the Deployment Processing Office, which is two blocks down this street, then turn and go down two more blocks. On the right-hand side of the street, you'll see a large, white, sign that says: Deployment Processing Office. You can't miss it. Have a nice day."

I folded my transfer orders in half twice and slid them with my green military ID card into my front left pants pocket. I then reached down with my right hand to my OD duffel bag, put my right hand between the bag's two-inch wide shoulder strap and the duffel bag, and grabbed the bag's canvas hand-grip. With an experienced lift, I swung the 96 pounds of all my worldly possessions over my right shoulder. Once the shoulder strap was snug against my neck and under my right armpit, I gave a little hop to comfortably place the heavy duffel down the middle of my back.

Walking past the Main Gate, I crossed to the left side of the street and proceeded onto the Oakland Army Depot. I saw that each side of the street was lined with the ends of a long, white, two-story, wooden buildings, typical of World War II construction. Between these buildings was an asphalt driveway to a parking lot half full of cars. Around each building were neatly clipped, green, grass lawns, with white signs on stakes driven into the middle of each grass lawn, stating: "KEEP OFF THE GRASS."

I walked on the 6-foot wide, concrete, sidewalk, with curb and gutter running along the left side of the street. From the end of each two-story white building was a four-foot wide, concrete, walkway to the sidewalk. Between the edge of every green grass lawn and the edges of the concrete sidewalk and walkway were the typical, football-sized rocks with multiple layers of white paint on them.

I thought, "If the Army wants you to stay off their grass lawns, then why do they always line their white concrete walkways and sidewalks with white painted rocks, that someone could easily stumble over and fall onto their grass lawn?"

These white, two-story, buildings, with their white rocked edges, lined both side of the street. In front of some buildings was a white sign, edgewise to the street, proclaiming it as Company HQ[8] for some numbered Battalion of Engineers, Transportation, Medical, Supply, Military Police, Signal Corps, or other type of unit. Protruding at a 45-degree angle at the street end of each white sign was a Company's colorful guidon flag, with HQ below the Battalion's number. Their

---

8   Headquarters

colorful fluttering in the breeze from the San Francisco Bay broke up the white and green monotonous repetition.

Obviously, those white, two-story buildings without the large white signs and their fluttering, colorful, flags were the barracks housing those Soldiers living on base, and would be identical to the white, two-story-building I lived in for my Army bootcamp training a year ago at Fort Lewis, Washington.

For me, Army bootcamp at Fort Lewis in the Summer of 1967 was a snap for the most part. Having been a Navy brat for the first twelve years of my life and living on a series of Navy bases, then the regimentation of military life was nothing new.

When Dad retired from the Navy after twenty years in April of 1961, we moved to a farm in Oregon. So, having played football, wrestled, and ran the mile in track for my Junior and Senior High School teams, and spent the summers bucking 75-pound bales of hay, then I was in good physical condition for the strenuous exertion required for Army bootcamp. Also, I was an Eagle Scout, where hiking, camping, going to a rifle range, and attending merit badge classes at week-long Boy Scout summer camp was little different than doing the same sort of things at Army bootcamp.

I thought, "You know, other than Army bootcamp being eight weeks longer than a week-long Boy Scout summer camp, the main difference between Boy Scout Summer Camp and Army bootcamp is that the Boy Scouts of America required adult leadership."

The only real problem I had with Army bootcamp was that, when I left home I was 6-foot tall and weighed 155 pounds. Graduating from bootcamp nine weeks later, I was 6-foot-2, and weighed 175 pounds, and none of my civilian clothes fit me anymore. Plus, being taller and more muscular, and with the Army's bootcamp buzz cut removing my wavy hair, my family barely recognized me.

Also, I now smelled like a chimney. Having been a rebellious teenager, I had sneaked the occasional cigarette. But, at Army bootcamp, where we were in the field much of the time, we were issued a pack of four cigarettes in our C-Ration meals. And, as we were trained to immediately obey every order given by our DI[9], then when the DI

---

9   Drill Instructor

bellowed, "Take five, smoke 'em if you got 'em," when we were given a short break from training, I would immediately light one of my Army issued cigarettes. So now, Army bootcamp had trained me to be a chain-smoker.

The only interesting thing I saw walking down two blocks of this street was at the end of the street, when a black railroad switch engine with US ARMY in large yellow letters crossed in front of a huge, white warehouse, pulling several OD boxcars, with US ARMY in large black on their sides. The huge, white warehouse was one of many I could see. And beyond them, I saw huge cranes lifting large, steel, shipping containers high in the air, a sure sign this was an active Army storage facility, of which I was about to become just one more item stored for a short time before being boxed up and shipped to the Vietnam War.

When I came to the end of the second block and made the left turn as instructed, I saw that the right side of this street was lined with the identical, white, two-story, wooden, buildings, with neatly trimmed, green, grass lawns around the building, with white painted, football-sized rocks lining the borders of the street's sidewalk and the walkways to the buildings. But there was not a myriad of large, white signs, with colorful guidon flags flapping in the breeze. Only one large white sign, two blocks down the street. Even at this distance, I could see DEPLOYMENT PROCESSING CENTER in black letters on the white sign.

I thought, "Two blocks is time enough to enjoy another smoke," as I reached between the two bottom buttons of my stiff khaki shirt and withdrew my open pack of cigarettes.

Crossing to the right side of the street, I pulled a cigarette from the pack with pursed lips, replaced the pack back under my shirt front, and lit the end of the cigarette with a flame I had struck with my silver Zippo lighter.

As I reached the opposite corner, I made the left turn to walk on the right side of the street, and slipped my Zippo lighter back into my right, front pants pocket.

Walking on the concrete sidewalk to the right of the street, I saw there were no cars parked in the asphalt parking lot behind the white, two-story buildings. Only groups of two or three Soldiers, standing or walking about, wearing their pickle suits.[10] However, on the left side of the street, I saw it was in stark contrast to the uniformity of the right side. There were no green grass lawns, or borders of painted, white rocks. Only black asphalt parking lots in front of a white chapel with a cross on top of its pointed steeple, a Post Exchange, or PX, that a Soldier could buy any items he needed, and a large, tan colored Post Bowling Alley, that would also contain a fast-food area. At the far end was a large, white, one-story building with ENLISTED CLUB across its front in large red letters.

The Post Bowling Alley was of particular interest to me, as at Fort Monmouth, I had been a member of my School Company's 4-member bowling league team, which was the Enlisted Bowling League Champion team. Not only did each team member receive a trophy for being on the champion team, but each had also been awarded a trophy for individual excellence. My second trophy was for High Score With a Handicap. Of course, the fact that our Team Captain was on the League Trophy Committee had nothing to do with this outcome.

I thought, "Now I have a place to go in any spare time, while I wait for my flight to the Vietnam War."

Approaching the Deployment Processing Office building, I thought, "It's going to be irritating if I have to go through the same rigmarole I had at the Main Gate about Lunch being erroneously typed on my transfer orders, instead of Lynch. Heck, I'm not even sure it was a typo. More likely, it was some bored clerk who typed it as a practical joke, thinking that it would be funny if I were called 'Specialist Lunch, the lunch special.' All the guys in my class thought it was funny when I made the mistake of pointing out the typo to them. At meal times afterwards, someone would inevitably ask, 'So, what's today's lunch special, Specialist Lunch?'"

When the others in my LRC-3 repair classed received their orders, all but one read: TRANSFER TO 1ST SIG BRGD, 442D SIG BN (LL), NOKHON RATCHASIMA, THAILAND. The one other order in my LRC-3 repair class read: TRANSFER TO 1ST SIG BRGD, TANSON-HUT, SOUTH VIETNAM.

---

10   An Army Soldiers' slang for their OD Battle Dress Uniform, or BDU

The first question everyone asked was, "Where the heck[11] is Thailand?" Then, "What the heck is Nakhon Ratchasima?" And, "Why the heck are we going to Thailand instead of Vietnam, like everybody else?" Not that we had our hearts set on going to South Vietnam. After all, who really wants to go into a war zone?

Someone found a map of Southeast Asia and spread it out on a table in the classroom. We soon found that Thailand was smack dab in the middle of Southeast Asian, bordered on the north and east by Laos and Cambodia. Also, that South Vietnam was hundreds of miles from any Thai border. It took a few more minutes before we could locate Nakhon Ratchasima, the capital of the Nakhon Ratchasima Province, which was hundreds of miles west of Cambodia and Laos, and therefore, at least four-hundred miles from the war in South Vietnam. Our last question was answered by the class instructor.

The members of our 20-man class to learn to repair the new LRC-3 microwave radio were from the top ninety men in our Microwave Radio Repairman class. Our instructor explained, "As you know, LRC-3 stands for Long Range Communication, version 3, used for long distance microwave radio communications. Also, that microwave radios are the most secure form of radio communications, but are strictly limited to line-of-sight, or LOS, as the curvature of Earth's surface limits LOS to a maximum range of sixty miles, which makes normal use of microwave radios unsuitable for secure communication between the ground combat units in South Vietnam and the air support from the U.S. Air Force bases located in Thailand. But scientists have found that a very high powered and focused microwave beam can be bounced off the troposphere layer of Earth's atmosphere and received up to six-hundred miles away by a 50-foot diameter, parabolic antenna, which can reflect and focus the bounced signal to a 4-inch by 2-inch waveguide[12] receiver. This method eliminates the need for at least a dozen repeater microwave radio relay stations to cross the hundreds of miles of hostile territory to have secure communications between the combat units on the ground in South Vietnam and our Air Force's com-

---

11   In radio communications, the use of foul language is forbidden.

12   An electrical conductor consisting of metal rectangular tubing, used for the conduction of microwaves.

bat support aircraft located in Thailand, which is a SEATO[13] ally of the United States and South Vietnam, and had sent two Infantry Divisions of its own to fight in South Vietnam. As it is, all but one of the LRC-3 radios in the Vietnam War's Theater of War are in Thailand, which is why most of you are being transferred to the 442d Signal Battalion in Thailand. The one other LRC-3 radio is in Tansonhut, which is why one of you is going there."

My name was not on the transfer orders for the others in my class going to Thailand, as I'd opted out of the 30-day pre-combat leave for those transferred to the Vietnam War, on the advice of my dad, which I had earlier learned was invaluable. From his 20-year experience in the Navy, he advised me not to take any 30-day leave offered, as it would put me in debt leave-wise with the Army. Then, if an emergency leave situation arose later, it would be an excuse for my CO[14] to deny me the requested emergency leave I needed to take. Also, accrued leave was like money in the bank, and be extra money when I was discharged at the end of my 3-year enlistment, which would be handy for going to college until my GI Bill allotments started.

The most valuable advice from my dad was to turn down any offer made in bootcamp to go to OCS, Officer Candidate School.

He said, "Son, you were smart enough to have been offered a full NROTC[15] Scholarship to Oregon State University to major in Electrical Engineering. Though I was disappointed you turned it down, because you were tired of going to school, I do respect your decision. But, going to OCS is a very different matter. First, they'll tell you that you'll be a Second Lieutenant in ninety days. But then they'll ship you to the Vietnam War as an Infantry Officer to be the Platoon Leader in a Rifle Company, where your life expectancy is about two months. Second, they'll have you waive your enlistment contract for Microwave Radio Repair School. But, once you have waived your enlistment contract, the Army can then decide not to send you to OCS and send you to any training of their choosing."

And that is exactly what happened. After two days of taking aptitude tests at bootcamp, they offered to send me to OCS if I waived my

---

13   Southeast Asia Treaty Organization
14   Company Commander
15   Naval Reserve Officer Training Course

enlistment contract. When I declined, I had to write a Letter of Refusal to explain why I did not want to be a Commission Officer in the Army.

When I arrived for radio school at Fort Monmouth, I found out how sage my dad's advice was. There were 18 men who arrived at Fort Monmouth several weeks before I did, who had accepted the Army's offer to go to OCS, and had waived their enlistment contracts. But, when they arrived for OCS training, they were told the OCS class was full and were transferred to Fort Leonard Wood, Missouri, for their nine weeks of bootcamp and then eight more weeks of training to be Combat Engineers, which is the most dangerous job in an Infantry Company.

Fortunately, these new recruits and their families had organized a letter-writing campaign to their Congressmen. An investigation revealed that the U.S. Army had a shortage of Combat Engineers and was using OCS as a ploy to fill those empty billets in the Infantry Companies in South Vietnam. After the Congressional Investigation exposed this scam, the Army then renewed their enlistment contracts.

When I arrived at the Deployment Processing Office sign, I turned right and walked up the concrete walkway lined with the white-painted, football-sized rocks, to the white, two-story building. I climbed the two steps up to a grey-painted, 10-foot wide wood porch, that was six feet across. There were two doors before me. One the right-hand door was stenciled ENTRANCE in large, black, letters. The left-hand door had EXIT stenciled on it.

I thought, "There's no confusion here as to which door to use."

To the right of the Entrance door was a 2-foot tall, bottom half, of a 10-inch diameter bomb casing standing on its four tailfins and filled with sand to about two inches from the top edge. It was painted fire-engine red, and in 3-inch stenciled white letters, it read BUTTS ONLY. In the sand of this ostentatious butt can were dozens of cigarette butts. However, as I looked beyond the butt can, I could see a large number of cigarette butts lying in the otherwise pristine green grass.

I thought, "These are the last defiant gestures of many before they surrendered their brief freedom back into the idiocy of the Green Machine that is the United States Army."

I then removed the smoking cigarette from my pursed lips with my right hand and flipped it ceremoniously onto the befouled green grass to join these other symbolic gestures of defiance and individualism of the Green Machine, and thought, "Now some lowly Private will be detailed to police those up."

From behind me, I heard a booming voice of command order, "Now, Specialist, get your dumb ass down there and police up those butts and dispose of them properly."

I turned and saw a large Soldier in an Army Class-B khaki uniform, with several rows of ribbons above his left breast pocket, with the coveted CIB[16] above them, and the three chevrons and one rocker stripe of an SSG[17] on his sleeves. On his back hung a large OD duffel.

Immediately rolling my heavy OD duffel bag off of my back and set it on the porch, as I said, "Right away, Sergeant," and jumped off the porch and onto the grass.

As I rapidly began picking up the offending cigarette butts, I heard the entrance door open and a loud laugh from the SSG, and then saw a burning cigarette land on the grass at my feet. Hearing the door close, I said, "Asshole lifer."

Having picked up a large handful of smelly cigarette butts, I stepped up onto the porch and dumped them from my left hand into the red, bomb case, butt can. As I slung my 96-pound duffel bag over my right shoulder and onto my back, I saw two PFC's[18] flip their cigarette butts past the red butt can onto the grass.

In my own command voice, I ordered, "Okay, Privates, now you can get your dumb asses down there and police up those butts and dispose of them properly."

They immediately dropped their heavy duffel bags on the walkway and said, "Right away, Specialist."

As I walked through the entrance door and into the Deployment Processing Office, I heard the PFC's say in unison, "Asshole lifer," and I said to myself, "What comes around, goes around, but in the Army, it's in a downward direction."

---

16   Combat Infantry Badge
17   Staff Sergeant
18   Private First Class

CHAPTER 2

You Have Your Priorities in the Right Order

As I entered the Deployment Processing Office with my 96-pound duffel bag slung on my back, I reached up, removed my dark-green garrison cap[19], and tucked half of the cap between the black, web belt around my waist and the top of my stiff khaki pants.

Looking around the interior of this World War II era building, I thought it was originally a Company HQ, because, beyond the open area of the front half of this first floor, there was a 6-foot wide hallway in the middle of opposite wall, with several doors on either side of the hallway into office spaces. The floor was covered by a ubiquitous, well-worn, dark-brown linoleum. To my right was a wood stairway with a banister.

On each side of this open room were two 8-foot long, wooden tables, with space enough for the two chairs between each table and the sidewalls. On the front of each table hung a white cardboard sign, with

---

19   A soft military cap without a visor or brim, also called an overseas cap.

the black, stenciled, letters of A-F and G-L on those to the left, and M-R and S-Z on those to the right. On the left end of each table was a black telephone, and on the right end of each table was a six-basket stack of paper bins. In the two chairs behind each table were two Soldier in their OD BDUs, with each holding a clipboard.

Walking to the G-L table on my left, I fished my folded transfer orders and green military ID card out of my left, front pocket. When I reached the table, the Solder to my left said blandly, "Orders and ID card," which I handed to him, and then swung my duffel bag off of my back and stood it on its bottom end so I could work the combination padlock that secured its top end closed.

As I worked to unlock the padlock and open my duffel bag to remove the large manila envelope containing my military records, I heard a familiar voice from the table behind me laughingly say, "You should have seen how I punked some dumb Spec-4 into policing up all those butts on the grass."

As the Soldier on the left flipped through the pages on his clipboard, he said, matter of factly, "Oh yeah, Specialist Lynch, we just received a phone call from Sergeant Snyder at the Provost Marshall's Office to let us know that there was a small SNAFU with your transfer order. Ah yes, here it is. First Signal Brigade. We've already corrected the Lunch typo to Lynch. Could you pass me your manila envelope containing your military records, Specialist Lynch?"

Having removed the padlock from the 4-inch long, heavy-gauge wire loop that held the top end of the duffel bag together, I unclipped the large, spring-loaded, metal clip at the end of the 2-inch wide shoulder strap from the wire loop. This allowed the three 1-inch diameter metal eyelets around the top edge of the duffel bag to be slid off the wire loop that held the top of the duffel bag closed.

From the now opened end of the duffel bag, I removed a thick, large manilla envelope that contained my military passport and all of my military records, and handed it to the Soldier, who then handed back to me my military ID card. He also then passed me copy of my transfer order to the second Soldier seated to my right.

As the first Soldier unwound a red string wrapped around two brown cardboard buttons on the envelope's flap and just below the flap that held the envelope closed, the second Soldier was copying information from my transfer orders to a form on his clipboard. After the first Soldier had opened the large manilla envelope, he slid its contents onto the table's wood top.

When the second Soldier finished copying the information onto the form, he said in a monotone voice, "Okay, I'm ready," and started to hand my transfer orders to me. But then he snatched the orders back, looked at it again, and in an animated voice said, "Hey, wait a minute, Specialist. These orders say you're being transferred to Thailand, not to South Vietnam. Is that true?"

I answered, "Well, yeah, that's true. Is that a problem?"

He replied, "No problem. I just think you're one lucky dog," as he handed my transfer orders to me.

I responded, "Do you really think so?"

He replied, "Hell yes. All the others coming through here are just cannon fodder for the Vietnam War. I should know, since I just returned from that hell-hole. But while I was there, I went to Thailand for my 2-week RNR[20]. All I can say is that you're pretty much going on a 1-year, all expenses paid vacation to the Land-of-Smiles[21], full of lovely and lovably little Asian girls. I'd love to have your duty assignment."

Then, looking back down at his clipboard and resuming his tired, monotone, voice, he asked the first Soldier, "Military Passport?"

The first Soldier picked up from the pile of documents on the table before him a red-brown passport, opened it, and said "Military Passport confirmed," before laying it face down on the table to his right.

The second Soldier then made an X in a box on the clipboard's form, and asked, "DD-201 Personnel Record folder?"

The first Soldier picked up a folder, and said, "DD-201 Personnel Record folder confirmed," before laying it face down on the Military Passport.

The second Soldier then made and X in the second box on the clipboard form, and asked, "Medical Record folder?"

The first Soldier picked up a different folder, and said, "Medical Record folder confirmed," before also laying it face down on the Personnel Record folder.

---

20   Rest and Recreation
21   Because the Thai people are always smiling, it's called the Land-of-Smiles

The second Soldier then made an X in a 3ʳᵈ box on the clipboard's form, and asked, "Financial Record folder?"

The first Soldier picked up the last folder, said "Financial Record folder confirmed," and laid it face down on the Medical Record folder.

The second Soldier then made an X in the fourth box on the clipboard's form and said to me, "Let's see your dog tags."

I removed a long, metal, ball-linked chain from around my neck with my right hand. Dangling from the long chain was a 1-inch by 2-inch metal plate with a small hole in one end, through which the long chain was connected. On this metal plate was imprinted LYNCH, SHERMAN A., RA 19860451, SPECIALIST E-4, ROMAN CATHOLIC, BLOOD TYPE A-POS. There was also a shorter chain attached to the long chain, from which dangled a second, identical, metal plate, except this metal plate had a quarter-inch notch in it. When we were issued our "dog tags" in bootcamp, we were instructed, when a Soldier was killed in combat, the dog tags were removed and the dog tag on the long chain was forwarded to graves registration. Then, the second dog tag with the notch in it was crammed between the teeth in the upper and lower jaws, and the notch was to prevent the dog tag from slipping past the teeth when this was done.

I handed the chains with their dog tags to the second Soldier, who then compared the information on the dog tags with that on the form on his clipboard, and then made an X on the fifth box on the form.

Handling the tags on the chains back to me, he asked the first Soldier, "What's his bunk assignment?"

The first Soldier picked up his clipboard, flipped over its top several pages, and answered, "Building CW-307, first floor, bunk number 14. Group Leader is SSG Williams."

Picking up my document folders and passport, he slipped them into the large manila envelope, and refastened its flap closed with the red string. When he'd finished, he handed the envelope back to me, and I put it in the top of my duffel bag. I then proceeded to close the top of the duffel bag by sliding the 4-inch long metal loop through the three large metal eyelets around the top edge of the duffel bag and rehooked the large, spring-loaded, clip on the end of the shoulder strap through the metal loop. I secured the end of the duffel bag by reattaching my combination padlock into the metal loop.

When I'd finished, the second Soldier handed me a slip of paper and said, "This is your bunk assignment, Specialist Lynch. Building CW-307 is to the left as you exit from this office, and is the second building on the left. Also, sick call is at 0800, and is located down that hallway to your right, the first door on the left. If you go to sick call, don't forget to bring your Medical Record."

With that said, he removed the filled-out form from the clipboard and placed it in the bottom bin of the stack, which had an L on it.

I said, "Thanks, guys," as I reached down between the shoulder strap and the duffel bag to grab the bag's canvas handle with my right hand. With a firm heft upward on the canvas handle, I swung the 96-pound duffel bag over my right shoulder and onto my back. With the shoulder strap firmly against my neck and under my right armpit, I gave a little hop to center the heavy duffel bag down the middle of my back. Then, folding my transfer orders into quarters, I slipped it with my ID card into my left, front, pants pocket, while keeping the slip of paper with my bunk assignment in my left hand.

Thus ready, I turned to my left to proceed to the door labelled EXIT, and noticed behind me, there were two more Soldiers in their Army Class-B khaki uniforms, with their large, full and equally heavy OD duffel bags on the floor to their right side, waiting their turn to proceed to the same wooden table and engage in the same monotonous in-processing rigamarole I'd just endured. No wonder the two Soldiers behind the wooden table were bored, having to repetitiously interview an endless line of Soldiers, with a reiterated dialogue of and checking off the same set of documents. I pitied the daily grind of those poor cogs in one of the many wheels to the Army's great Green Machine.

Proceeding out of the exit door, I removed my dark-green garrison cap from my black web belt with my right hand, opened the bottom edge, and placed it squarely on my head. As I did so, I met two more Soldiers in Army Class-B khaki uniforms with heavy OD duffel bags on their backs, climbing up the steps to the porch where they defiantly flipped their cigarette butts into the green grass past the audacious, fire-engine-red butt can made from the tail end of a bomb case.

I started to say something, but thought, "Being called an 'asshole lifer' once already today was one too many times for me."

Putting this abominable thought out of my mind, I went through the automatic motions of retrieving a cigarette from beneath the stiff front of my shirt and lighting it with my Zippo lighter, then taking a deep pull of nicotine laden smoke into my lungs. I gave a deep sigh of relief as I felt the nicotine's effect on my nervous system.

Now that the rigmarole of in-processing was done, I proceeded down the white rock-lined walkway to the street in front of the Deployment Processing Office, turned to my left per my instructions, and walked on the concrete sidewalk between the black asphalt covered street and the ubiquitous white painted rocks that bordered the green grass lawns with their KEEP OFF THE GRASS signs.

To my right, across the street, I saw the Post Bowling Alley and looked forward to using it for some seriously relaxing exercise from rolling a 16-pound bowling ball down one of its many bowling lanes, and then hear the satisfying crash of the ball striking the bowling pins as I watched the round, 15-inch tall, white-enameled wooden pins fly around, knocking each other down.

I looked over my left shoulder at the corner of the Deployment Processing Office building and saw affixed there an 8-inch high, 18-inch long, white sign, with CW-311 stenciled in black. By military design, all buildings on the north or east side of a street are numbered with odd numbers, and those on the south or west side of a street are numbered in sequence with even numbers. A preceding letter designation indicated in which grid of a base's layout a set of buildings are located. The progression of the number's sequence indicated the direction from which the series of the numbers on the building on the street are located relative to Building One on a military base.

On all U.S. Army posts, Building One is the main flagpole for the post, as the flagpole is the first thing built on an Army post. Also, on top of Building One is a "truck," a small, hollow, metal ball painted gold. And in this truck is a .45 caliber bullet, so that an Army post will never be able to say it surrendered because it was out of bullets.

I learned these trivia facts from test questions given during the five-week basic electronic repair course everyone had to pass at Fort Monmouth, such as: "Where is Building One located?" "How many trucks are on Fort Monmouth?[22]" "What color are the trucks at Fort Monmouth?" And, "How many .45 caliber bullets does a truck carry?"

---

22   There was only one truck, as all others were called vehicles.

These, of course, were trick questions, as none of this information was taught in any class.

Walking past the one-lane, asphalt, driveway between Buildings CW-311 and CW-109, I saw the asphalt covered parking lot behind Building CW-109 was devoid of cars. Instead it contained numerous Soldiers, mostly in groups of two or three, standing or walking around. Beyond the edge of the asphalt was a 5-foot high wooden platform, painted dark-grey, on the edge of a large, mown, grass field about a hundred yards wide. In bootcamp, these were called PT stands, because a Drill Instructor would lead us in regimented calisthenics from on top of such platforms for our PT or Physical Training. On the other side of this 100-yard wide, mown grass field, were other asphalt covered parking lots behind a row of identical, white, two-story wooden buildings. But, unlike this parking lot behind Building CW-309, those distant parking lots contained numerous cars. Obviously, those distant, two-story buildings housed the permanent party personnel who worked on the Oakland Army Depot. For those Soldiers who worked in the Deployment Processing Office, this would at least be a relatively short walk to and from work every morning and afternoon.

Approaching Building CW-107, I saw my lit cigarette had burned down to an inch long. As there was no butt can nearby to deposit my cigarette butt, I began to field strip the butt. Holding the cigarette butt between my thumb and forefinger of my right hand, I began to roll it between them. This loosened the packed tobacco in the paper cylinder enough for it to fall out onto the concrete sidewalk. Dragging the sole of my shiny, black shoe over the still burning tobacco, I made sure it was no longer a fire hazard. The now empty paper cylinder, I rolled into a small paper ball between my thumb and forefinger. The process only took a couple of seconds. I then dropped the ball of paper into my front, right pants pocket.

Reaching the concrete walkway on the left to Building CW-107, I turned and proceeded between the two rows of white, painted rocks, up the two steps to the wooden porch, and crossed the six feet to a pair of closed screen doors. To my right, I saw there was a fire-engine-red bottom of a bomb case, standing on its four tail fins, identical to the one on the porch in front of the Deployment Processing Office.

Emptying from my pocket into this butt can the several small paper balls from cigarettes I'd smoked, I thought, "They must've had a big sale on used bomb cases sometime after World War II at an Army surplus store."

Opening the righthand screen door, I entered Building CW-107. Removing my garrison cap from my head, I placed it between my belt and pants, and found myself confronted with a row of bunk beds about ten feet from the doorway. On either side of the two doorways, I saw that the doors were swung all of the way to the walls. Looking to my left, there was another row of bunk beds endways against the left side-wall of the room that were spaced five feet apart. On the end of each bed was a large black number on white cards sequenced top to bottom and left to right, beginning with the number "1". Between these two rows of bunk beds was a 5-foot wide aisleway. Looking to my right was a 3rd row of bunk beds endways against the right sidewall of the room, which were similarly spaced and numbered. Also, to my right, was a stairway that rose up behind me to the second floor.

Holding up the slip of paper in my left hand, I saw I was assigned to bed 14 on the first floor, and that the name for our transfer group was a SSG Williams.

I yelled out, "Is Staff Sergeant Williams here?"

From the back left of the room, I heard, "Yes, back over here."

I turned to my left and walked to the end of the aisleway between the two rows of bunk beds, where I met a smiling-faced Soldier wearing a pickle suit, with the shirt sleeves rolled above the elbows. On each sleeve were the four yellow stripes of an SSG. He was of medium build, in his mid-twenties, and about 5-foot-9, much shorter than my 6-foot 2. Over the right pocket flap of his shirt was an OD cloth strip with WILLIAMS embroidered with black thread.

He greeted me with a happy, "Welcome to the sardine factory."

I smiled and said, "I'm Specialist Lynch, and was told you're our group leader," as I thought, "to call this place a 'sardine factory' is apt, as we were being packed in this room as tight as a can of sardines, and not even enough room to swing a cat."

He responded, "Ya got that right. Give me a sec to find your name," as he lifted a clipboard in his left hand and began to run his right index finger down a list of names.

I said, "They misspelled my name on the transfer orders. Someone typed Lunch instead of Lynch."

He laughed and said, "Oh yeah, I see it. Some practical joker probably did that for shits and giggles. I'll just correct that on my list. I see your name tag spells Lynch, with a Y. Is that right?"

I answered, "Yes, Sergeant. Lynch, as in hang by the neck until dead without the due process of law."

With another laugh, he said, "Hey, that's a good way to remember how to spell it. By the way, I'm not much on formality, so you can call me Steve when we're not in the company of lifers. Anyway, I have you listed as assigned to bed 14," and with a jerk of his right thumb over his shoulder, he added, "That's just across the aisle from my bed, which is number 28."

As I followed Steve down the aisleway, he pointed and said, "Yours is the last bottom bed on the left by a window. You lucked out there by getting a bottom bed by a window, as you'll get plenty of fresh air and you won't have to climb over somebody to get onto your bed. Also, you can sit on the edge of your bed to tie your boots."

When we reached the end of the aisleway, he stopped, turn around, and continued. "As you can see, there are no wall lockers to stow your gear in. So, you'll be living out of your duffel bag and have to store it on the floor beneath your bunk. I suggest you keep your duffel bag padlocked at all times, and leave nothing out on your bed, as I have no doubt that there are barracks thieves around here.

"As for the POD[23], the uniform of the day is BDU. Reveille is at five o'clock. The Mess Hall is open from 5:30 to 7:00. Your meal card will be your copy of the transfer orders, which you'll need to show when you enter the Mess Hall for meals. In fact, you'll need to keep your transfer orders on you at all time to verify you're authorized to be on this base.

"Morning formation is in the parking lot behind the barracks at 7:00. At that formation, the names of those who have been scheduled a departing flight are called. At which time, they immediately fall out of formation to get their gear from the barracks and report in front of the barracks to board busses that transport them to the departure assembly area.

---

23   Plan of the Day

"After they've called out the names of those leaving for the departure assembly area, they start dividing those who're left into groups to be assigned for KP[24] duty, laundry duty, Latrine and barracks cleaning duty, or to police the grounds for trash and cigarette butts. I'm telling everyone in our 28-man transfer group to form up behind me in three columns. Then, as soon as they've finished calling out the names of those immediately leaving for deployment, I'll call our detail to attention, order an about-face, and march all of us across the street to the Post Bowling Alley, which opens at 7:30. I suggest that everyone saying in the Post Bowling Alley for at least an hour. If there's one thing I firmly believe in, it is to protect the men under my authority from the stupidities of the Army's Green Machine as much as possible. Also, I suggest that you don't leave the immediate Departure Processing area to do any exploring. Most of the Oakland Army Depot are restricted areas patrolled by the Depot's Security Police. If you're detained by the Security Police, you could end up in the stockade[25], which could cost you a stripe and/or be fined under Article 15[26] of the UCMJ[27]. Do you have any questions?"

I replied, "Yes. What time is lunch and dinner, and where is the Mess Hall?"

Steve answered, "The Mess Hall is the building just past the Deployment Processing Office. Lunch is 1100 to 1300, and dinner is 1700 to 1900. I see that you have your priorities in the right order, Lynch."

---

24 Kitchen Police
25 The Army's term for a military jail.
26 The authority for Non-Judicial Punishment, or NJP, of any minor infraction.
27 Uniform Code of Military Justice

CHAPTER 3

ANOTHER DAY OF HURRY UP AND WAIT

My bed was the old Army type, with each end made of 1-inch metal tubes shaped like an upside-down U that could be folded flat under its bedframe. The 30-inch wide bedframe was a 6½-foot long rectangle made of 1-inch angle iron. Inside the bedframe was a mattress support composed of connected metal wires in a 2-inch by 3-inch rectangular pattern. The inside edge of the angle iron frame had a series of quarter-inch holes spaced every three inches along its sides, and every two inches along its ends. Each hole in the edge of the bedframe had one hooked-end of a 3-inch long, half-inch diameter coiled spring in it, with the other hooked-end through a hole in the end of the mattress' support wires. Bolted to the top of each leg of the bed's U-shaped ends was a 16-inch long, 1-inch diameter metal pole fitted into the bottoms of the leg of an identical to bed.

On one end of every other bottom bed along the aisleway was a 2-inch thick, cloth covered, mattress rolled into thirds. On top of the rolled mattress was a stack of folded bedding, consisting of a white mattress cover, a wool, OD-colored blanket, two white sheets, a pillow, and a pillowslip. On the opposite end of the top bed was an identical stack of a folded mattress and bedding. This gave a checkerboard appearance to the rows of bunk beds.

In the sidewall were wood-framed, 2-foot wide by 4-foot-high window openings two-feet above the floor. In each opening, were two 2-foot square window frames, containing six 8-by-10-inch glass panes in a two high by three wide pattern of wood slats. The two window frames in each opening were in offset groves that allowed them to slide past each other. Every window opening had an outside window screen. The bottom window frame was raised up all the way and supported with a half-inch piece of wood.

I thought, "Clearly these windows are fully up to allow plenty of fresh air to circulate in for the forty-two crammed in Soldiers that could occupy this room."

Also, these open windows reminded me of the very large barracks rooms at Fort Monmouth that comfortably housed fifty-six men, each with their modern, 4-foot wide double bunk that had a 4-inch thick mattress, and their double-wide lockers used as walls to separate the bunk areas, where the windows were always open at least six inches. There was an Army-wide standing order that every window in a barracks had to be open at least six inches year-round to allow fresh air to circulate in. This was because some U.S. Army bases had spinal meningitis epidemics that had killed numerous Soldiers.

Though this open-window policy was comfortable in the spring, summer and fall months in New Jersey, but the winter months were a whole different scenario. Fort Monmouth was near the Atlantic Ocean, where there was a cold, off-shore wind during the winter. With all of the barrack's windows open, it was like living in a walk-in freezer. Though Fort Monmouth's hospital reported no cases of spinal meningitis, it had admitted numerous cases of pneumonia.

I thought, "Obviously, the Army's inane plan to keep Peter from getting spinal meningitis at Fort Lewis in Washington and Fort Leonard Wood in Missouri, was resulting in Tom, Dick and Harry to be hospitalized for pneumonia at Fort Monmouth in New Jersey."

Steve pointed to the wall behind him and said, "Down that hallway on the left is the shower room, and on the right is the Latrine." Pointing to the bottom bunk across from mine, he added, "My bunk is right here, so if you have any questions, just ask. Other than that, your time is your own until morning formation at 0700. May it be ever so humble, this sardine can is our home for the next day or so."

I then unslung my 96-pound duffel bag and stood it upright beside my bed. Sitting down on the angle-iron edge of the bedframe, I began to open the combination padlock that secured the end of my duffel bag. Removing it from the 4-inch long metal loop, I then unclipped the large, spring-loaded, clip of the shoulder strap from the loop, slid off the three large, metal eyelets in the top edge of the duffel bag, and took the thick manilla envelope that was at the top of the open duffel bag and laid it on the wires of the mattress support.

Having planned ahead, I'd packed last in the top of my duffel bag a pair of my spit-shined, black combat boots; a pair of OD wool socks in one of the boots; my OD Army issued ball cap; another black web belt with a black metal belt buckle; and a set of my freshly starched OD BDU's.

I then stood up and removed from beneath the front of my stiff khaki shirt the open pack of cigarettes. From my front pants pockets, I removed my folded transfer orders, military ID card and silver Zippo lighter, and then my black leather wallet from my right rear pocket. All of these items I had placed on top of my large manilla envelope.

Having removed everything from my Army Class-B khaki uniform, I stripped down to my dog tags, skivvies and bare feet. After neatly folding my khaki uniform, I placed it, my dark-green garrison cap, my shiny black shoes with my dirty, black nylon socks in them, and then my manilla envelope into the top of my open duffel bag. When I'd closed the top of my duffel bag and secured it with my combination padlock, I dressed in my pickle suit, put on the OD wool socks and spit-shined, black, combat boots, and then laced the boots to their tops and tied the laces into a large bow knot, of which I tucked the ends of into the boot tops.

Unbuttoning the left breast pocket, I withdrew a pair of elastic blousing strings with a metal hook on each end, replacing them with the open pack of cigarettes lying on the manilla envelope. After buttoning the breast pocket closed, I reached down and hooked around each boot an elastic blousing string and rolled the bottom of each pant leg under the blousing string until it was at the top of the boot. Now, the bottom of each pant leg appeared to be "bloused."

In bootcamp, we were required to blouse the bottoms of the pant legs by neatly folding them tight around the ankle and then tying the boot top over the folded pant leg. I always thought this was a real pain in the butt, because there was always a pant leg that worked its way out of the boot's top, requiring me to stop and reblouse the erroneous pant leg. The elastic blousing string eliminated this problem once I'd graduated from bootcamp.

While I'd been changing from my Army Class-B khaki uniform into my OD pickle suit, I asked, "Hey Steve, have you been deployed through the Oakland Army Depot before?"

Steve answered, "Yeah, on my way to the First Signal Brigade in Vietnam in '65 as a PFC. I made Spec-5[28] by the end of my 1-year tour, and was transferred back to MIT[29] for instructor duty. While in Vietnam, I took my 2-week RNR in Thailand at a beach-side resort called Pattaya, which was absolutely gorgeous, and full of beautiful Thai women. When it came to the end of my enlistment and liking what I was doing in my MOS, I took the $4,000 re-enlistment bonus they offered and requested to be transferred to the 442d Signal Battalion in Thailand. I figured from my 2-week RNR in Thailand, that a tour of duty with the 442d would be like a 1-year, all-expense-paid vacation. To make it even better, I was promoted to Staff Sergeant because there are so many E-6 billets needed to be filled in my MOS."

I commented, "Hey, Steve, that's exactly what the guy who in-processed me at the Deployment Processing Office told me, that my tour of duty with the 442d in Thailand will be like a 1-year, all-expense-paid vacation. Well, Steve, I'm ready to go check out the Latrine, and then see what's happening outside."

Steve said, "I'll catch you later, Lynch."

With that, I grabbed my OD ball cap off the mattress support wires and stuck it under the backside of my pants. Walking to the hallway at the back of the room, I turned left and proceeded down it. Halfway down the hallway, there was a door in each of its sidewalls. On the left-hand door, stenciled in 2-inch black letters, it read SHOWER, and on the right-hand door, I saw LATRINE. Not hearing running water,

---

28   Specialist Grade E-5

29   Monmouth Institute of Technology, a euphemism by Signal Corps Soldiers for Ft. Monmouth.

I opened the shower door, entered, and saw that no one was in it, but all around the walls were silver showerheads on 6-inch long, half-inch diameter iron pipes, located six feet above a grey painted concrete floor that gently sloped down to a 6-inch diameter drain cover. Halfway between the showerheads, there were metal, 2-prong coat hooks mounted on the walls.

I commented to myself, "Well, no surprise here, is there?"

Turning around and closing the shower door, I crossed the six-foot wide hallway, opened the Latrine door, and saw it was also unoccupied. But the far sidewall was lined with white porcelain toilets with raised black plastic toilet seats spaced a couple of feet apart. Behind each toilet, there was a 2-inch diameter stainless-steel pipe with a flush handle fixture in it. Also, the strong smell of pine-oil cleaner filled the air. Closing the Latrine door behind me, I walked straight ahead to the nearest toilet, unbuttoned the fly of my pants, and gratefully relieved my rather full bladder.

After rebuttoning the pant fly and flushing the toilet, I turned around and saw to the left and right of the Latrine door, there were, lining the wall, white porcelain sinks spaced about two feet apart, with a 12-by-16-inch mirror in a metal frame above each. Between the mirrors were metal paper towel dispensers, with a great trashcan beneath it. I walked to the first sink to the left of the door and washed my hands. Grabbing two paper towels from the dispenser, I wiped my hands dry and tossed them into the trash can. Opening the Latrine door, I exited the over-fragrant Latrine. Closing the Latrine door behind me, I turned to my right and proceeded to the right-hand screen door at the end of the hallway with EXIT stenciled in black above it.

In route to the Exit screen door, I reached back with my right hand, seized my OD ball cap, and placed it squarely on top of my head, with the cap's bill low over my eyes. I saw at the end of the hallway the two white wood doors were swung open to the wall on either side. The door to my right had EXIT stenciled in black, and the door to my left had ENTRANCE stenciled in black. I pushed open the spring-loaded Exit screen door and walked down two wood steps onto the black asphalt surface of the parking lot. Walking away from the building, I heard the screen door loudly slam shut and give a little wobbling sound before it slammed shut again.

A short distance to my front, three Soldiers in pickle suits walking across my front to the left gave a quick look towards the sound of the slamming screen door, then they looked at me with no sign of recognition. They continued on, engaged in their briefly disturbed conversation.

Turning to my right, I began to walk around the parking lot, looking for anyone with the diamond shaped, Signal Corps orange patch of the Signal Corps School Brigade on the left sleeve of their uniform, thinking "as birds of a feather flock together, then anybody I see with the orange School Brigade patch will be a member of my group transferring to the 442d Signal Battalion and we'll have something in common to talk about."

It did not take long before I saw two Soldiers in pickle suits with the diamond shaped orange patch on their left sleeves. It took only a minute to meet up with them, as they were walking in the opposite direction, and we were soon caught up in an animated conversation about who we each were, where we were from, what our particular MOS was, our mutual gripes about the Army, and our expectations and imaginations about our 1-year tour of duty with the 442d in Thailand, especially after I told them that I'd twice been told it would essentially be a 1-year, all-expense-paid vacation.

At 5:00, I heard the broadcast bugle call for Mess from the PA system on the backside of Building CW-307. Everyone in the parking lot immediately turned in the direction of the Deployment Processing Office and walked to the Mess Hall I'd been told was in the building on its other side. I saw in the parking lot behind Building CW-109 more than fifty Soldiers there, also walking towards the Mess Hall. I looked behind me and saw across the street adjacent to Building CW-107 three more white, two-story, wood barracks buildings with asphalt covered parking lots behind them, full of Soldiers walking toward me, and thought, "Those must be Buildings CW-101, 103 and 105, with hundreds of hungry Soldiers that will trample anyone that was in the way of their going to the Mess Hall."

I then said to my two compatriots, "I think we should walk as quickly as possible to the Mess Hall before we are trampled by that hoard behind us."

They both looked back and then said in unison, "You're right," and we all three quickened our pace to almost a run.

As we passed behind Building CW-109, I saw a street adjacent to the Deployment Processing building, and on the other side of that adjacent street was the side of a very large, white, one-story building with a large loading dock behind it. I thought, "There is no doubt in my military mind that that is the Mess Hall and it is the magnet for this unrelenting sea of OD pickle suits swarming towards it."

On reaching the street adjacent to the Deployment Processing Office, my compatriots and I veered to the left as we hurriedly crossed the street to the far street corner where we were immediately confronted with a long line of Soldiers extending to the doorway in the center of the Mess Hall's front. There, I saw Soldiers progressing in two separate lines to some steps and climbing into the Mess Hall. As my companions and I joined the single-file line to the Mess Hall's doorway, I saw there was another single-file line of OD clad Soldiers coming from the opposite direction, who must be from other, two-story barracks buildings beyond the Mess Hall. I thought, "Well, this explains the second line of Soldiers entering the Mess Hall."

The single-file line of Soldiers to the Mess Hall's doorway was progressing at a steady, but slow pace. As we approached the steps leading up to the doorway, I saw there were four doors in the Mess Hall's doorway. The outer two doors were open, allowing the steady stream of Soldiers to enter in rapid succession. The center two doors had EXIT ONLY stenciled in 8-inch red letters on each door. Mounting the steps, I reached into my front left pant pocket, withdrew my folded transfer orders and my military ID card, and then unfolded the transfer orders.

Just beyond the two Entrance doors on either side of the Mess Hall's front doorway was a table with two Soldiers sitting behind each table. When it was my turn in line, I showed my transfer orders and my ID card to the first Soldier, who looked at my ID card photo, then at my face, and then at my transfer orders before he said, "Okay," and the second Soldier then pressed a lever on a silver device in his right hand to count each Soldier as they passed by.

Turning to the right as I passed the end of the table, I joined the end of the chow line along the sidewall of the Mess Hall. I saw from the chow line that the Mess Hall dining area was at least 180-feet across to the other chow line, and at least 50-feet wide from the front doorway to the food service line. There were about a half dozen rows of 10-foot long tables with a bench on each side of a table, and several feet between the 10-foot long benches. Between the ends of the tables was a space of about four feet. I also saw that the rows of tables were gradually being filled with Soldiers carrying silver trays full of food, and thought, "Boy, I hope there's a place left to sit down and eat by the time I get my chow."

Soon, I was at the head of the chow line, where there were two stacks of stainless-steel meal trays on a wheeled cart, with a second wheeled cart behind it with two more stacks of stainless teel trays. I saw as I picked up a meal tray from a stack that it was the typical meal tray, about 18-inches wide and 12-inches across, with 1-inch deep impressions to separate the items of food. In the middle was a large impression for the entre, with two smaller ones on either side for side dishes of vegetables, dessert, and a drink glass or mug.

To the left of the meal tray stacks were three large, grey plastic bins containing stainless-steel table knives, forks and spoons, of which I picked up one of each. Then, holding the meal try by its side edges with both of my hands, and my right hand holding my stainless-steel flatware, I was ready for the food service line, which consisted of large stainless-steel pots of food sitting in large, deep cutouts in a long, wide stainless-steel counter, with several inches of hot water to keep the food in the pots warm until it was served by KP food servers wearing full-length white aprons.

The first two large, deep pots contained a choice of ½-inch thick slices of roast beef or fried chicken. Then there was a large, deep pot of mashed potatoes with two half-sized deep pots with white gravy for the fried chicken or brown gravy for the roast beef. Beyond these were several large, deep pots of cooked peas, carrots, green beans, broccoli, and cauliflower. Then there were large stainless-steel trays of fresh fruit, cookies, sheet cake, and glasses of milk. As I hurriedly moved down the food-service line having my meal tray filled with a large slice of roast beef that was smothered in mashed potatoes and brown gravy, then green beans, broccoli, an apple, several cookies, and a large glass of milk, I thought, "There's no doubt the U.S. Army wants to keep its Soldiers well fed before they were deployed to the Vietnam War's meat grinder."

Though nearly all of the tables were full of Soldiers hurriedly chowing down on the food-laden trays before them, the first rows of tables were beginning to be emptied and wiped clean by several KP's.

The three of us located the nearest empty table to sit at, and as soon as we sat on the benches on either side of the table, the benches quickly filled with five more Soldiers. With little conversation beyond, "Hey, could you pass the salt and pepper," we each hurriedly consumed a very filling meal.

The three of us hurriedly finished eating our meals at almost the same time. Standing up from where I was sitting on the bench, I then lifted my used meal tray, flatware, and milk glass, and moved toward the Mess Hall's front wall, where there were three carts tended by several, white-aproned KP's. The 1st cart had three large plastic bins to put each of our knives, forks and spoons. The 2nd cart had plastic racks to place the milk glasses in. And the 3rd cart had a growing stack of used meal trays. Behind each of these three carts was a second cart to replace a cart when it became full and was wheeled away by an apron-clad KP to be cleaned. I then waited in line to deposit my used eating utensils.

As we hurried out the two Exit doors between the two Entrance doors with lines of waiting in line to be hurried through to wait in the show long to be served chow, then say at a table to hurriedly eat the chow, then wait in line to hurriedly deposit your eating utensils, then hurry through the Exit doors to wait for whatever activity the Army had planned to do, I said to my two companions, "Have you ever noticed that most of our time in the Army is to hurry to wait in a line to do something in a hurry, then wait in another line to do something else in a hurry?"

My friend to the left said, "Yeah, since the Recruiting Office hurried me to enlist, then waited for an opening to go to bootcamp, where we ran to a training area, waited until the boring class was over, then ran to the next training area to wait for the next boring class."

My friend on the right commented, "Even at Fort Monmouth it was hurry to a class, then wait for the instructor to start the class, then hurriedly smoke a cigarette before the next class was to start, where we waited on the next instructor to start his class."

Then I said, "I had hurried to the Oakland Army Depot to make sure I wasn't late to be in-processed, and then spent fifteen to twenty minutes waiting at the main gate for the Provost Marshall's Office to straighten out a SNAFU with my transfer orders before I could hurry to the Deployment Processing Office to wait for two bored Army clerks to slowly verify my military documentation. Then I hurried out so the next shmuck could have his documents checked. Then I waited in the barracks area to hear the bugle call for Mess, where we all hurried to the Mess Hall to wait in a line to get into the Mess Hall, where he then had to hurry and eat to make room for those waiting in the chow line to have a place to eat."

My friend to my left agreed. "You're right, Lunch. Life in the Army is nothing but a series of having to hurry up and wait."

During this commiserating conversation, we had each retrieved a cigarette from a pack in our left breast pocket and let them with our respective silver Zippo lighters with the crossed flags emblem of the Signal Corps on them.

I then asked them, "Either of you interested in going to the Post Bowling Alley and bowling a couple of games?"

They each said, "No thanks," and headed across the street to the Enlisted Club as I walked diagonally across the street to the bowling alley. After renting a pair of bowling shoes and paying 25 cents for an assigned bowling lane, I bought a cold can of Budweiser beer, selected a 16-pound bowling ball with the right size and spacing of three drilled holes to comfortably fit my right thumb and two middle fingers. By the time I finished my first game and my beer, I found that bowling alone was very different from bowling on a team and was not fun at all. With this conclusion, I replaced my rented bowling shoes with my black combat boots, rebloused the bottom of my pant legs, returned the rented bowling shoes, headed for the raucous atmosphere of the Enlisted Club, and proceeded to get thoroughly drunk on cheap beer.

Like a Sailor three sheets to the wind[30], I later wobbled back to my assigned bottom bed, dropped the stack of bedding on the floor, unrolled the mattress onto the mattress support frame, promptly fell onto the mattress and passed out.

The next morning, I was rudely awakened by the loud blaring of the bugle call for Reveille being played through the open window by my head from the PA system on the side of the barracks building. With a splitting headache from a hangover, I slowly rose up, sat on the edge

---

30   When the three sails on the mast of a sailing ship are full and tight from the wind behind, then go loose and wobbly as the ship turns to the wind.

of the bed, and said, "Thank God I'm on a bottom bunk and still fully dressed. It'd be hell if I had to bend over to put my boots on."

I gradually got on to my feet and slowly walked to the Latrine. There, I joined the shortest line I saw and tried to wait patiently as my full bladder screamed at me for relief. After several minutes, I stood before a toilet, unbuttoned the fly on my pants, and with a sigh of relief, I was able to alleviate the pain of holding my bladder being held in check with a very strong and long stream being voided into the toilet.

With great satisfaction, I buttoned my pant fly as I walked to the sink and washed my hands. As I grabbed two paper towels from the dispenser, I looked in the mirror and thought, "Holy crap, Lynch, you look like warmed over death. What I need now is a strong, black cup of coffee."

Exiting the Latrine, I figured rather than trying to negotiate pass a bunch of guys getting dressed to get to the front exit door, I turned right and used the rear exit doorway to leave the barracks and walked to the Mess Hall, where there was hardly any line at its front doorway. On entering the Mess Hall, I pulled my folded transfer orders and ID card from my left breast pocket, which I unfolded. Showing it and my ID card to the first Soldier behind the table, he said, "Hats off in the Mess Hall."

I quickly pulled off my OD ball cap and shoved its bill between the back of my shirt and the top of my pants. As I hurriedly walked to the end of a very short chow line, I refolded my transfer orders, and place it and my ID card back into my left breast pocket.

Arriving at the head of the chow line and picking up a stainless-steel meal tray, knife, fork, and spoon, I saw at the end of the food-service line a huge stainless-steel coffee urn set up with stacks of white ceramic coffee mugs next to the urn. As my nauseated stomach had no craving for the food fare, I bypassed everything on the serving line, grabbed a white ceramic mug, and filled it with hot, black coffee from the huge, stainless-steel urn. At the nearest open place at a table, I joyfully consumed the hot, refreshing beverage.

Once the mug was empty, I quickly returned to the huge urn and refilled the mug with more coffee. This time, I saw at the table and enjoyed slowly drinking my coffee. After drinking two more mugs of coffee, I began to feel human again, and carried my unused tray and flatware to the carts at the front of the Mess Hall before exiting to return to Building CW-307.

When I returned to my bed, I pulled my duffel bag out from underneath the bed and stood is upright and opened its top end. From the open top, I removed fresh sets of OD BDU's, skivvies, and OD wool socks, which I set on the bed. I then stripped off all of my clothing and wrapped around my nude body a white, terry-cloth towel I took from my duffel bag, along with my toilet kit. After rolling up my soiled clothes together, I placed them and all of my personal effects from the pockets into the duffel bag, closed the top, and secured it with my padlock.

With my duffel bag secured, I hurried to take a hot shower, and quickly dried off before wrapping the now damp towel around my waist. Then, I hurried to the Latrine to shave the stubble of hair from my face. Fortunately, almost everyone had already showered and shaved, and had gone to eat breakfast at the Mess Hall, so I'd not have to wait in any line to shower or shave.

Feeling totally refreshed, I returned to my bed, dressed in the fresh clothes I'd laid on the mattress, and laced up my black combat boots, blousing the bottoms of my pant legs with the elastic blousing straps. Reopening my duffel bag, I took all of the items I had removed from the various pockets of my soiled BDU's and put the items in the same order of pockets in the fresh set of OD BDU's I had on. After putting my toilet kit back in the top of my duffel bag. I closed its top, and secured it with my padlock. Then, rolling my mattress back up on the end of the mattress support, I put on it the folded bedding I had tossed onto the floor last night, and laid my damp terry-cloth tower over the end of the bed by the open window to dry.

Placing my duffel bag back under the bed, I grabbed my OD ball cap and proceeded out the building's back Exit doorway to the parking lot for morning formation. I located SSG Williams to the right of the PT stand, and fell in at the end of one of the three columns beginning to line up behind him.

At 7:00 sharp, a Sergeant standing on the PT stand shouted out, "Formation, Atten…tion!" The groups of OD clad Soldiers then all stood to the position of attention, with their backs straight, heads facing forward, chins up, arms straight down their sides, heels together and feet at a 45-degree angle. Then the Sergeant yelled, "Parade …

Rest!" Everyone in sync moved their left foot sixteen inches to the side and placed their hands together in the small of their backs.

The Sergeant then instructed, "If I call your name and service number, you're to fall out, proceed to your assigned bunk, secure your duffel bag, and carry it to the front of the barracks, where you'll form a line alongside the bus parked there."

With that said, the Sergeant began to read slowly and distinctly a name and service number from a list on a clipboard in his left hand. As a Soldier would then come to attention and fall out of formation, I saw the Sergeant make a check mark on the list with a pen in his right hand and read the next name and service number.

As soon as the Sergeant lowered his clipboard and started walking toward the steps of the PT stand, I saw SSG Williams do an about-face and command, "Detail, Atten…tion! About … face! Forward … march!" All 27 of us in 3 columns came to attention, did an about-face, and in sync began to march forward with the right foot first. SSG Williams then gave the orders necessary to march our 27-man formation safely across the street to the parking lot in front of the Post Bowling Alley, where he said, "Detail … Halt! Left … face! Wait in the bowling alley until I come back and let you know that it's safe to return to the barracks without being press-ganged for some nefarious detail in the Green Machine. Detail, fall … out!"

Walking with everyone into the bowling alley, I asked generally, "Did anybody check the bulletin board to see what the Green Machine has scheduled for us to do today?"

I heard someone yell back, "Yeah, the POD uniform of the day is BDU's, reveille at 0500, breakfast at 0530 to 0700, morning formation at 0700, lunch at 1100 to 1300, dinner at 1700 to 1900, get drunk at 1900 to 2300."

Everyone laughed and I said, "Looks like another day of hurry up and wait in the Army."

CHAPTER 4

OFFICIALLY DEPLOYED

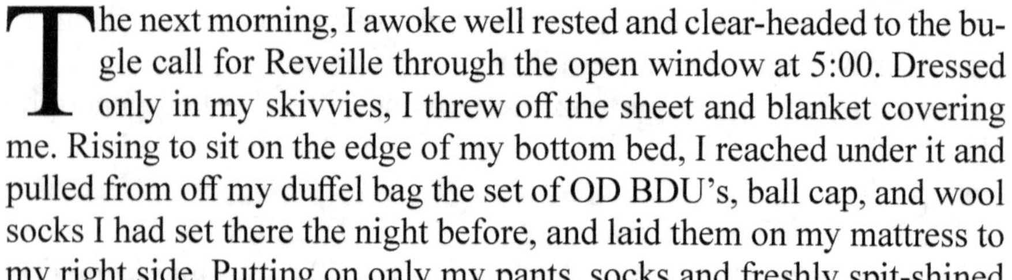

The next morning, I awoke well rested and clear-headed to the bugle call for Reveille through the open window at 5:00. Dressed only in my skivvies, I threw off the sheet and blanket covering me. Rising to sit on the edge of my bottom bed, I reached under it and pulled from off my duffel bag the set of OD BDU's, ball cap, and wool socks I had set there the night before, and laid them on my mattress to my right side. Putting on only my pants, socks and freshly spit-shined black combat boots I did not lace up, I hurried to the Latrine. Beating the rush, there was no line to wait to use a toilet, so I was able to immediately void my full bladder.

After washing my hands at a sink and drying them with two paper towels from the dispenser, I quickly returned to my bed. There, I sat on its edge, laced up my boots, and tied the laces in a large bowknot, tucking the ends into the top of each boot. Retrieving the two elastic blousing strings from the left breast pocket of my shirt lying on my bed, I quickly bloused the bottom of each pant leg. Grabbing the shoulder strap on my duffel bag with both hands, I pulled it from under my bed, between my two legs, and stood it upright before me. I quickly opened the top end of my duffel bag, removed my folded transfer orders, ID card, silver Zippo lighter, a fresh pack of cigarettes, and my black leather wallet from the top of my duffel bag, and set them to my left side on the bed.

Having closed and secured with my padlock the top of my duffel bag, I grabbed the canvas handle on its side by both hands and lifted the heavy duffel bag enough to turn it on its side to slide it between my legs back under my bottom bed. I then picked up my OD ball cap and put it on my head as I stood up. After picking up my OD shirt and putting it on, I picked up each item that I'd removed from the top of my duffel, and placed them in the usual pockets of my OD BDU uniform.

Starting for the back doorway of the barracks, I hurriedly buttoned my OD BDU shirt and tucked the bottom of the shirt under the top edge of my pants. In the hallway there was now a line of men wrapped in white, terry-cloth towels waiting to go into the shower room. Passing the open Latrine door, I saw lines of men waiting to use the toilets, and thought, "Boy, am I glad to have beat that crowd."

By the time I passed through the Exit screen door, I was fully dressed. I took the fresh pack of cigarettes from my left breast pocket, and with a quick circular motion, removed the thin red ribbon around the pack's top end, which also removed the end of the clear cellophane wrapping that kept the tobacco of the twenty cigarettes in the pack from going stale. On one end of the pack's unsealed top, I carefully removed the aluminum foil covering the cigarettes and wadded up the cellophane and aluminum wrappings I'd removed into a small ball, which I dropped into the front right pocket of my pants.

Switching the new open pack of cigarettes to my right hand, I tapped the pack's open end against my left hand. This action caused the ends of several cigarettes to protrude through the opening. With pursed lips, I pulled a cigarette from the end of the pack, put the pack back into my left breast pocket, and then buttoned the pocket's flap closed. Reaching down with my right hand into my front right pant pocket, I removed my Zippo lighter, lit the end of my cigarette, replaced the lighter into my pant pocket. With a long pull of air through the lit cigarette, I quickly felt the effect of the nicotine, and through a cloud of smoke as I exhaled, said, "Ah, nothing like the first cigarette of the day."

Behind me, I heard, "Amen to that, brother."

Looking over my left, I saw that a Soldier a few paces behind me had at the top of his left sleeve the Signal Corps orange, diamond-shaped unit patch of the Fort Monmouth School Brigade, and below that, the gold, spread-eagle patch of a Spec-4. I paused for him to catch up to me, and asked, "Mind if I join you?"

He replied, "I'd enjoy the company," and as we turned left to walk on the driveway between Buildings CW-107 and CW-109, he said, "I've been hearing a rumor that our 1-year tour with the 442d will be like a 1-year, all-expense-paid vacation in Thailand."

I responded, "Ain't no rumor, brother. I've heard that firsthand from Sgt. Williams and a clerk at the in-processing office. As they both spent their 2-week RNR from the Vietnam War in Thailand, I believe they are both reliable witnesses."

He said, "I'm glad it's not a rumor, then, and have some great experiences to look forward to while I'm in Thailand.

When we reached the street and turned right onto the concrete sidewalk, I pointed to the front of building CW-109 and asked, "Where do you think they got all of those bomb cases they've made into big, red butt cans?"

He conjectured, "Probably from outdated bombs from World War II. After all, this is an Army depot full of war material ready to be shipped to whatever war we're fighting at the time."

I responded, "Outdated bombs? Really? How does a bomb become outdated? Do they stamp a use-by date on it?"

As we smoked our cigarettes for the remainder of our walk to the Mess Hall, we discussed the various possible sources and means to obtain bomb cases and make them into butt cans.

Arriving at the rather short line to the Mess Hall, we snuffed out our lit cigarettes in the sand at the top of the large, red butt can at the bottom of the steps to the Mess Hall's front doorway. Then we each removed from our left breast pocket our folded-up transfer orders and military ID cards to show to the two Soldiers checking people into the Mess Hall. Once inside, we joined the end of a very short chow line and I commented, "The way I found, if you come here right after Reville is called, there is no long chow line to wait in for breakfast, is because yesterday morning I had a killer hangover and came here straight away to get some hot coffee. How 'bout you?"

He replied, "I also had a hangover that needed hot coffee to cure."

This time, my stomach was in need of solid substance, so I had the KP's on the food service line fill my meal tray with heaps of scrambled eggs, strips of bacon, and sausage links, some hot oatmeal, and a couple of biscuits. Then, I got a tall glass of chocolate milk and headed for a nearby table with a few empty spaces on benches where we could face each other to talk while we ate. As usual, our conversation turned to our home experiences of school, sports, cars and girls.

Having finished stuffing our faces, we stood, and picked up our trays, flatware and glasses to deposit them on the line of carts at the front of the Mess Hall. As soon as we were outside, we each lit a cigarette and continued discussing our home lives.

Returning to Building CW-307, I went to my bed, and began the process to take a shower and shave a day's growth of stubble from my face. Walking back to my bed with my white towel around my waist, I put on the fresh set of skivvies and socks I'd laid out when I opened the top of my duffel bag to secure my valuables while I showered and shaved.

Once I'd put back on my OD BDU's and black combat boots, and bloused the bottoms of my pant legs, I opened the top of my duffel bag again to retrieve my valuables and put them back in the pockets I had taken them out of. After I had put my toilet kit back in the duffel bag's top, I closed and secured its top, and slid it back under the bottom of my bed. I looked at my messy bed and said to myself, "Nobody seems to be doing any barracks inspections here, so to heck with making up this bed, and I'm ready for morning formation. With any luck they will be calling our names to leave this sardine can," and turning towards the hallway, I headed for the barracks back door to the parking lot.

At the far-right corner of the parking lot, I found some of our transfer group already forming into three columns behind SSG Williams, and contrary to the Army's no-smoking-in-formation policy, SSG Williams and others in our group were smoking while some talked excitedly about the possibility that we might be leaving this bored-out-of-your-mind place this morning, and other speculated we would be here for a couple more days as keeping Soldiers waiting was one area the Green Machine was proficient at. Joining the end of a column, I lit a cigarette and participated in discussing the various aspects of the topic.

Though there were at least fifty other Soldiers standing in groups of a dozen or more in front of the PT stand talking amongst and between groups, none had tried to join in conversation with our group. Seeing that all of these other Soldiers wore only Private or PFC stripes, I thought, "Apparently these Privates and PFC's all recently graduated from the short MOS schools that produce support personnel, like clerks, cooks, medics, and truck drivers, and were being shipped to the Vietnam War as replacements for front line or support units."

This was contrary to my group, where nearly everyone had the Spec-4 rank on their uniform sleeves. Also, we had an SSG as our group leader, who would be viewed by any Private of PFC as a major deity, because all of their DI's at bootcamp were, at least, an SSG whose main means of communication with a Private at bootcamp was by yelling with the voice of god that demanded instant compliance or suffer immediate painful punishment, like doing twenty to fifty push-ups, or running around an area with your heavy M-14 rifle held over your head for five to fifteen minutes. Also, all their instructors at their MOS schools would have been Spec-4's and Spec-5's, who these Privates and PFC's would consider to be minor deities that could order them to do some unpleasant tasks, like picking up discarded trash or cigarette butts they saw on the ground, or even to clean toilets. Yes, to them we were a group of superior beings to be avoided as much as possible. And, as they say, "rank has its privileges."

I then saw SSG Williams was talking to a Sergeant with a clip-board next to the PT stand. A few seconds later and SSG Williams was walking quickly back to our transfer group and made a quick head count before announcing, "Listen up, I've just been informed by the Sergeant we're listed for deployment. So, when you fall out to get your gear before boarding the bus, I suggest you stop at the Latrine and take a piss, because we may be on the bus for a while. I'm glad to see everyone has made it to this formation morning, as I'd hate to see that any of you missed deployment and end up in Fort Leavenworth prison for twenty years. Also, I've arranged with the Sergeant to call out our group first, so everyone face forward, cover down, and put out your cigarettes."

As I faced forward, covered down behind the guy to my front, and field stripped my cigarette, I heard, "Formation, Atten…tion! Parade … rest! If I call your name and service number, you are to fall out, proceed back to your assigned bunk, secure your duffel bag, and form a line alongside the bus in front of the barracks. Adams … Robert E … RA19765723.”

I saw a Soldier in our group come to attention, do a right face, and quickly march out of our formation. As soon as Adams had cleared our formation, I saw those who had been lined up behind Adams come to attention and March two steps forward to close up the hole Adams had left in the line, and then resume parade rest.

In alphabetical order, the Sergeant continued to call the name and service number of each Soldier in our group. When a name and service number was called and he fell out of our group's formation, then all those behind him would come to attention, take two steps forward, and resume parade rest. I thought, "This is like watching cans in a soda machine roll forward when someone removes a can of soda. Except here, it was Soldiers in lines being removed for deployment to the Vietnam War as items in the Army's Green Machine."

When in turn I heard, "Lynch … Sherman A … RA19860451," I came to attention, did a right face, marched out of our formation, and headed for the Latrine in our barracks. After voiding my bladder, I returned to my bed and pulled my duffel bag from underneath it. Sitting my duffel bag upright, I sat on the edge of my bed and opened its end. After placing my still damp white towel in the top of my duffel bag, I closed and secured it with my padlock. When I stood up, I lifted the 96-pound duffel bag onto my unmade bed, slid my right arm between the shoulder strap and the bag, which made it easier to just lift it onto my back, as I thought, "My Mom didn't raise a dummy," and then proceeded to the front exit door.

On exiting Building CW-307, I saw a large, OD color bus with U.S. Army stenciled in white letters near its front door. Leading from the bus's front door was a line of OD clad Soldiers from my transfer group with heavy duffel bags slung on their backs. At the open front door of the buss was a Sergeant holding a clipboard in his left hand and a pen in his right hand.

I watched as the Soldier at the head of the line held up his military ID card, and then the Sergeant compared the ID photo to the Soldier's face and the name on the ID card to the list on his clipboard. When the Sergeant found a match, he would make a mark on the list, and then waved the Soldier to enter the bus with the pen in his right hand. The Soldier would turn toward the bus's doorway, reach up to grab the chrome handrails on either side, and then pull himself up as he took the first step in the bus's doorway. Whereupon, the next Soldier in line would step forward and show his ID card to the Sergeant.

Walking to the end of the line behind the duffel bag of the Soldier in front of me, I removed my ID card from my breast pocket. As each Soldier entered the bus, I took several steps forward, following the duffel bag in front of me. Finally, the duffel bag swung to my right, as the Soldier carrying it turned to his left and mounted the steps in the bus's doorway. Stepping forward several steps, I showed my ID card to the Sergeant for him to compare my face to that on my ID card, and then for him to find my name on the clipboard's list of names and service numbers. While he was doing this, I was able to see ahead of this bus there was a line of at least a half-dozen busses in front of other barracks buildings with a line of Soldiers beside each bus waiting to be checked off before boarding their bus.

Seeing the Sergeant wave his pen for me to get on the bus, I placed my ID card back into my left breast pocket as I turned to my left. Reaching up to grab the chrome handrails on either side of the doorway, I also put my right foot on the bottom step in the doorway of the bus, and then pulled with my arms and lifted with my leg onto the bottom step the total weight of some 300 pounds of me and my duffel bag. Then repeating the process to gain the second step and the floor of the bus, I found myself facing a PFC in the driver's seat who said, "Please take a seat in the first available row and place your duffel bag on your lap to make room for the next guy. And, there's no smoking on the bus."

Turning to my left, I saw about two-dozen rows of double seats on either side of a two-foot-wide aisle, and that the first three rows on both sides were full of Soldiers with their large, heavy duffel bags upright on their laps. Walking to the fourth row, I saw an upright duffel bag on the lap of a Soldier sitting next to the left-hand window, I swung my duffel bag to the right off my back and onto the right-hand seat. Then turning to face my duffel bag, I bent down, reached around its middle, and with a bear hug grip, I lifted it onto my lap as I sat in the opposite seat. There, I swiveled to my right to sit squarely in the aisle seat and only able to the backside of my OD duffel that was three-inches from my nose. I said, "Boy, am I glad I took a piss before getting on this bus as this duffel bag is sure heavy on my bladder."

The Soldier in the window seat next to me said, "Same here, and I can't say much about my view either, except for the little bit I'm able to see out of the window. Any idea how long we have to sit like this?"

I answered, "I saw a half dozen busses ahead of us, and if they unload them one at a time, I would guess we'll be here for quite a while."

I saw on my left a procession of OD pickle suits carrying OD duffel bags as they filled up the seats in the row to my left, then the set of rows behind me, and then the rows of seats beyond those in succession. As I recognized the four yellow stripes of SSG Williams pass my limited vision, I thought, "Well maybe rank doesn't have privileges when it comes to deployment in the Green Machine."

Eventually, the OD parade stopped. Hearing the hiss of the bus's air breaks releasing and its diesel engine, which had been softly idling all of this time, roared loudly, the bus suddenly jerked forward. Through a piece of the window on my left that was not blocked by the head of the Soldier seated next to the window or his duffel bag inches from his nose, I saw the bus passing white, two-story buildings, then the large, one-story Mess Hall, followed by more white, two-story buildings.

Feeling the bus slow some, and I held onto my duffel bag as the bus made a right turn. Accelerating some, the bus went straight for a minute before I had to hold my duffel bag tight as the bus slowed, made a left turn, and accelerated again. After another minute, the bus slowed considerably, made a left turn, where I felt the bus rock from side to side a little and come to a complete stop, as I heard the diesel engine cease its roar from the bus's rear.

I heard a voice from the front yell, "Okay, everybody listen up. The busses will be emptied one at a time, so it'll be a few minutes before you can leave the bus."

To this announcement, I heard a lot of groans, and I said, "Yeah, let's hurry up and wait some more," and the guy sitting next to me said, "I hope we don't have to wait very long 'cause this bag is already killing my legs."

About fifteen minutes later, I heard, "Alright, it's your turn to disembark. You'll do this one row at a time, starting with the front rows. Once you leave the bus, you'll proceed to the open door in the side of the building in front of the bus. Please have your ID card ready to be shown to the Sergeant as you exit the bus. I hope you enjoyed your trip on U.S. Army Trailways Bus Line."

I thought, "This is obviously a reference to the Continental Trailways Bus Line noted for having very comfortable and spacious seats with a stewardess in attendance."

Eventually, I saw in the row ahead of the row next to mine, the Soldier in the window seat lift his duffel bag off his lap and onto the aisle seat, then stand up. I then slid my duffel bag off my lap and up right onto the aisle floor next to me. When I had stood up, I lifted my duffel bag by the top of the shoulder strap onto the seat in front of mine and stepped into the aisleway. I walked beside my duffel bag, put my right arm between the shoulder strap and bag, and positioned the bag onto my back. I was then able to easily lift the bag onto my back, and as I walked down the aisle to the front of the bus, I removed my ID card from my left breast pocket.

Exiting down the steps, I showed my ID card to the same Sergeant who had checked each of us onto the bus. As he compared my face to the ID's photo and then put another checkmark next to my name and service number, I asked him, "And where between the barracks and here did you think I could have exited the bus, Sergeant?"

He answered, "Yeah, I agree it's an inane thing to do, Specialist, but it's a required part of the powers that be in the gears of the Green Machine." He then handed me a two-by-four-inch white card tag with a white string attached that had H-13 on both sides, and said, "Tie this to the button of your left breast pocket below the flap. It's your bunk number. Keep it on you at all times."

As I followed the Soldier ahead of me, I tied the string to the button of my left breast and my ID card in the same pocket. Then, looking up, I saw the side of a huge white building with the eave of its roof fifty feet from the ground. The white sidewall must have been the length of a football field, and had large, sliding 20-foot square doors every so often along the sidewall. Toward the middle of the sidewall, one of the sliding doors was open about ten feet. On either side of this ten-foot opening were a couple of MPs in khaki uniforms, wearing white helmets, white pistol belts with white pistol holders, and white leggings.

Upon my entering through the 10-foot opening was a Sergeant in his OD BDU's about fifty feet away, organizing the entering Soldiers with duffel bags on their backs into rans of ten. On either side of the opening was an MP dressed like those outside, who directed me to join this new formation. This I did by lining up to the left of the Soldier I was following, and behind a Soldier in the first rank. As other Soldiers formed up to my left and then behind me, I looked around the interior of this huge building.

I saw that the sidewalls were a good 200 feet apart, and from end-to-end about 400 feet long. It was open to the roof that rose from the 50-foot high sidewalls to the 70-foot high center ridge beam. The ceiling beams from side-to-side were thirty feet apart. Each end of a ceiling beam, and a third of the distance from the sidewalls were four upright supports made of 12-inch I-beams. Above the 50-foot-high ceiling beams was a framework of 8-by-8-inch wood trusses bolted together in triangular configurations with ½-inch thick steel plates, all of which held up a metal corrugated roof. The two inside support I-beams formed two rows of columns about seventy feet apart. Hanging from each ceiling beam was a row of 4-foot long light fixtures, each containing four florescent light tubes. Between every other light fixture was a large rotating ceiling fan. I thought, "Wow, you could fit an entire football field in here."

After several minutes, I saw the Sergeant from the bus walk up the right side of our new formation, hand the Sergeant before us his clipboard, and say something to him. The Sergeant then asked in a loud voice, "Will Staff Sergeant Williams please come up here?"

I thought, "Obviously, it would violate Army protocol for a Sergeant to be in command of a formation containing a more senior Staff Sergeant."

As SSG Williams left our formation and walked up its left end to this Sergeant, they exchanged some pleasantries. When SSG Williams walked off to my left, the Sergeant commanded, "Group, attention! Forward…March!"

After marching about fifty feet, he commanded, "Group … Halt! Parade … rest! At this time, you are officially deployed and cannot leave this building without expressly written permission. Anyone caught attempting to leave without written permission *will* be arrested by the MPs guarding this building, *will* be charged with desertion in time of war, and faces a General Court Marshall under the UCMJ, with a maximum penalty of death. You each have a reservation on a flight to Southeast Asia, which you will board sometime in the next twenty-four hours.

"At the far end of this building to your right are telephones for your convenience. However, they do not have coin slots. You can only make free local calls or collect long-distance calls on them." To my right, I saw all across the end wall was lined with 18-inch tall, black pay phone boxes with the coin slots taped over.

The Sergeant continued, "There is no Mess Hall here. But, just this side of the phones are tables with the making for sandwiches. Also, a table with dispensers full of milk, juice and hot coffee. This chow line is open twenty-four hours a day. Also between here and the food table, there are tables and chairs for eating and smoking. You may not eat or smoke outside of this area.

"On the other side of the dining area is the door to the Latrine. There are no showers because you will not be here that long. To your left is the bunk area with beds and mattresses for you to lay on, but no bedding because, again, you will not be here that long. On your left, you will see a letter on each riser. These letters indicate a designated area for the beds. The letter on the white tag you were given corresponds to the letter of your designated area. And the number on your white tag is the number of your assigned bed in that area. You are to remain in your designated area at all times, unless you are using the Latrine, making a phone call, or are in the dining area, so you can be quickly located for your flight packet that you will get about an hour before leaving here. If you miss your flight, you *will* be charged with missing Movement and Court Marshalled. Any questions you may have can be answered by one of the permanent party. Group … Atten…tion! Dismissed to your designated area."

Everyone in this group started walking to their left where I saw about halfway up the first risers a large yellow A on the left one and a B on the right one. The next two risers had a C and a D. The following risers had an E and an F, a G and a H, an I and a J, and so on. Between all of the risers on the left and all of the risers on the right I saw a 20-foot wide aisleway that extended to the end wall of the building. I also saw from this aisleway to the sidewalls, a sea of single beds with a bare mattress on each bed.

When I arrived with the others of our transfer group, at the riser on the right with a large yellow H on it, I saw SSG Williams waving us over with a big smile and said, "Welcome to area Hotel[31]. I suggest you first find your bunk and drop your gear. If you're hungry, want a smoke, need the Latrine, or wish to make a call, then you are free to go to those areas. Otherwise, I expect you to be here in area Hotel. And, as you are now officially deployed to Thailand, your overseas pay starts as of today."

Finding my bed with a 2-inch thick mattress on it, indicated by a sign on each end with the same H-13 as was on the 2-by-4 inch card dangling from my left breast pocket button, I immediately swung my 96-pound duffel bag onto my bed, and headed to the Latrine for my much-needed relief. Walking up the 20-foot wide aisleway with a sea of men on beds to either side, I thought, "There is now no doubt in my military mind that I'm nothing more than another piece of U.S. Army equipment stored in one of many huge warehouses waiting to be bundled up and shipped off to the Green Machine's Vietnam War meat grinder. At least now, I'm officially deployed"

---

31   "Hotel" is a military verbal expression for the letter H.

CHAPTER 5

NOW, THAT'S WHAT I CALL ROOM SERVICE

Approaching the dining area, I saw it contained a dozen rows of end-to-end metal folding tables with metal folding chairs on each side. The rows of tables ran twenty feet from the building's right-sidewall across to fifty feet from a 12-foot tall, white painted wall for the Latrine area. Also, the dining area was half full of OD clad Soldiers eating sandwiches or smoking at these tables.

I saw that the 12-foot tall wall for the Latrine area was about 100 feet long and began twenty feet from the buildings 200-foot wide end wall that was lined with at least fifty black phone boxes, nearly all of which were in use by OD clad Soldiers. In the middle of the 12-foot tall wall, I saw a white wood door with LATRINE stenciled in 12-inch letters in red above the door, to which I made a beeline.

Entering the partitioned Latrine area, I saw a row of white porcelain toilets all along the building's sidewall, spaced three feet apart with a queue of two or three Soldiers in front of each toilet. I also saw on each side of the door a line of white porcelain sinks with a paper towel dispenser between the sinks. I walked to one of the shorter queues to wait for my turn.

On exiting the Latrine area, I walked in front of the phone area to the opposite sidewall where there was a chow line of ten Soldiers and joined the end of the chow line. At the head of the chow line, I saw a folding table with stacks of heavy-duty paper plates, large open boxes of white plastic knives, forks and spoons. Next to these boxes were stacks of large, red plastic cups.

Once I'd collected a paper plate, a set of plastic flatware and a red cup, I went to the end of several folding tables with 2-inch deep, 16-by-24-inch stainless steel pans full of ice, on which were trays piled full of sliced roast beef, chicken, ham, turkey, salami, and bologna, and then sliced bricks of cheddar, Velveeta, mozzarella, jack, jalapeno and Swiss cheeses also on iced trays. Next to the cheeses were 6-inch deep, large stainless-steel pots on ice full of lettuce leaves and sliced tomatoes, onions, dill pickles, and red-hot peppers. Beyond the condiments were stacks of sliced white, wheat, rye, and raisin bread. At the very end were urns full of hot coffee, cold tea, orange juice, tomato juice, white and chocolate milk.

I filled my heavy-duty paper plate with two slices of every kind of meat, cheese, and condiment. On top of this heap, I added four slices of raisin bread, which I loved. Then I filled my large, red plastic cup with chocolate milk and proceeded to the long rows of tables and chairs filled with OD clad Soldiers. When I came to a row with plenty of empty chairs, I walked to the first empty chair, set my food laden plate, plastic flatware, and red plastic cup of chocolate milk on the table, and sat in the chair. About every six feet in the middle of the tables were salt and pepper shakers, sugar and paper napkin dispensers, and white plastic spoons in jars of mayonnaise, ketchup, yellow mustard, and spicy brown mustard. Slathering two slices of my raisin bread with spicy brown mustard, I began to build a Dagwood sandwich.[32] This, I slowly savored with gusto, as there seemed to be no sense of urgency in the air.

When I had consumed my two Dagwood sandwiches and a second large cup of chocolate milk, I then liberated a cigarette from my left breast pocket, lit it with my Zippo lighter, closed my eyes while lean-

---

32   Named after the comic strip character Dagwood Bumstead (1901-1973), who made mountainous thick sandwiches with a variety of fillings, often regarded as incompatible.

ing back in my chair, and enjoyed a moment of satiated bliss. When my cigarette had burned down do its end, I snuffed it out in a glass ashtray before me, stood up with my plate, flatware, cup, and a napkin I'd used, and carried my refuse to a large, metal trashcan located at the end of the table, and then walked back to area Hotel.

Upon returning to my bed in area Hotel, I lifted my duffel bag by its canvas handle, set it on the floor, and rolled it under my bed. Then, sitting on the edge of my bed, I removed my combat boots, and laid down on the bare mattress for the favorite pass time of every young enlisted man. I went to sleep.

After several hours, I awoke feeling the need to use the Latrine, and headed up the 20-foot aisleway between the seas of OD clad Soldiers for the Latrine area. On exiting the Latrine, I walked to the end of the table with the paper plates, plastic flatware, and large red cups, as there was no one in the chow line. Picking up a paper plate, a set of flatware, and a cup, I again heaped my plate with two of everything on the food tables and filled my cup with chocolate milk. As there was hardly anyone in the dining area, I had no problem finding an empty chair. Placing my food and drink on the table, I sat down and began construction of another, thick Dagwood sandwich. After slowly consuming my two Dagwood sandwiches and two large cups of chocolate milk, I leisurely smoked another cigarette.

While I had been eating my Dagwoods and then smoking a cigarette, I'd watched a white aproned Soldier push a triple-tier cart between the tables replacing any empty jars of condiments, salt and paper shakers, and napkin dispensers. He was also emptying the ashtrays into a large, rectangular bin attached to the end of the cart.

When I'd finished my cigarette and snuffed it out in an ashtray, I stood up, gathered all my trash together and deposited it into the trash can at the end of the tables. I then noticed many of the black phones in the phone area were available, and decided this was a good time to call my parents and let them know I would be leaving on my flight to Thailand tonight. My parents, like all parents, did not like the idea of their son going to war. They did appreciate knowing my whereabouts, so I went to the nearest available phone and called them.

Upon my return to area Hotel, I joined in a game of Spades with three guys from my transfer group who had been looking for a fourth. With two guys on each end of a bed and the other two on the edge of adjacent beds, we began playing the card game. Looking around area Hotel as I sat on the edge of a bed, I saw others playing Spades, Hearts or Poker. As we played Spades, I saw every once in a while, a group playing a card game would mutually stop for a Latrine break or to go eat in the dining area, and then return to area Hotel to pick up their game where they had left off.

Occasionally, I would see a Sergeant with a stack of white business size envelopes in his hands stop at various areas and begin to call names and service numbers. As the named Soldier would approach, the Sergeant would look at their ID card and hand them an envelope. If the Sergeant still had envelopes in his hands, he would go to another area and repeat the process. Sometimes, I saw someone run up the 20-foot-wide aisle to locate an errant Soldier in the dining, Latrine and phone areas, who I would then see running back to his bunk area. After the Sergeant handed someone his envelope, there would be a flurry of activity as he prepared for departure.

About 8:00 in the evening, a Sergeant stopped at area Hotel and said, "Area Hotel, listen up, as I have departure envelopes for some of you. If I call your name and service number, then come to me and show your ID card to get your envelope. Adams, Robert E., RA 19765723."

As Adams stood up from a game of Hearts he'd been playing to get his departure envelope, everyone immediately threw in their hand, stood up, and began to line up in alphabetical order, as that would be the order in which the Sergeant would be calling out our names. Also, SSG Williams started doing a head count to make sure no one was absent. When he was done with his count, he said, "Okay, everybody is in area Hotel, thank God."

I was already standing in front of the Sergeant with my ID card ready when he called, "Lynch, Sherman A., RA 19860451." After he verified who I was, he handed me an unsealed envelope with my name, service number and H-13 typed on it.

Walking to my bunk, I removed the contents of the envelope, which were a boarding pass for Tiger Airlines, Flight 93, Seat 21-A, and a folded form letter that was an order for me to report to the Receiving/Departure area at 2115 hours, dressed in my Class-B khaki uniform, with my transfer orders and duffel bag in hand, and ready for transport to Tiger Airlines Flight 93. This meant I had less than an hour to change into my Class-B khaki uniform, fill up with chow, void my bladder and bowels, return to area Hotel, secure my everything in my duffel bag, and carry it to the departure area. Although this was plenty of time, I also didn't have any time to lollygag.

Upon returning to my bed, I retrieved my duffel bag from under the bed and stood it up on its end. Quickly, I opened the top end and removed my black dress shoes, a pair of black nylon socks, my dark green garrison cap, a black web belt with a shiny brass belt buckle, and a neatly folded Army Class-B khaki uniform, which I set on the bed's mattress. I then removed everything from the pockets of my OD BDU's, laid them on the bed, and changed out of the OD BDU's and into my khaki uniform. Once I was fully changed into my Class-B uniform, I put my folded transfer orders and ID card in my left front pant pocket, my Zippo lighter in my right pant pocket, my pack of cigarettes and the envelope containing my boarding pass under the front of my khaki shirt, and buttoned up my shirt. Grabbing my garrison cap from off the bed, I tucked it under the front right side of my black web belt as I hurried up the 20-foot wide aisle to the dining area.

Seeing the dining area was about a quarter full, with a mixture of OD BDU and Class-B khaki uniforms, I walked to the end of the chow line that had about twenty Soldiers in it, and waited for my turn to get to the food line. As I went along the food line, I filled my paper plate with my usual collection of everything, and filled my red cup with chocolate milk. Once laden with food, I located an empty chair near the end of a row of tables, sat in it, and set the paper plate heaped with the makings for my Dagwood sandwiches, plastic flatware, and red cup of chocolate milk on the table. I hurriedly built my Dagwood concoction and wolfed it down with my cup of chocolate milk, and then went to refill the cup with chocolate milk, after which I repeated the process.

When I'd finished eating and putting my refuse in the trashcan, I went to the Latrine and emptied my bowel and bladder. Then I returned to the dining area to smoke a cigarette, which would be my last opportunity to smoke until after my bus ride to Travis Air Force base eighty miles away, which was where I would board Tiger Airlines for their Flight 93 to Thailand.

Finishing my last cigarette for a while, I returned to my bed in area Hotel, where I reopened the top of my duffel bag. I then removed two fresh packs of cigarettes and placed them under my shirt front, as I figured it would be at least thirty-six hours before I had an opportunity to access my duffel bag again, where I still had two more fresh packs stored. I then crammed my used set of BDU's, dirty wool socks, and black combat boots into the top of my duffel bag. After securing the top of my duffel bag, I picked it up by the top end of its shoulder strap and hefted it upright onto my bed. Placing my right arm between the shoulder strap and the bag, I easily rolled the 96-pound duffel bag onto my back.

Making one last look around my bed and finding nothing left behind, I headed for the Receiving/Departure area. As I left area Hotel, I saw that several of the beds were devoid of duffel bags, and the remainder of our transfer group were in their Army Class-B khaki uniforms and stuffing their last items into the top of their duffel bags. After I'd walked up the 20-foot wide aisle bordered on each side with a sea of beds, I turned right at the dining area where I saw a large sign over the 20-foot square sliding door, that was now closed, which read in large, black letters RECEIVING/DEPARTURE. There were several large white cardboard signs on 8-foot metal poles, one of which read TIGER AIRLINES, FLIGHT 93.

In front of the Flight 93 sign were about twenty Soldiers in their Class-B khakis with their duffel bags standing upright on the floor to their right. They were in four columns, and as I approached, a Sergeant with a clipboard in his left hand confronted me, looked at my white tag with H-13 on it, and as he scanned down the right side of his clipboard, he asked, "May I see your ID card, Specialist?"

I reached into my left front pants pocket and withdrew my folded transfer orders and my ID card. Showing him my ID card, he then compared my face to the photo on my ID card, and my name and service number with that for H-13 on his clipboard, and then asked, "Can I see your boarding pass?" Which I removed from under my shirt and showed him, and upon his seeing my boarding pass, he said, "Okay, you can join the one of these four columns for Tiger Airlines, Flight 93, but do not leave this formation without checking with me first, and there's no smoking in the formation."

I said, "Yes, Sergeant," and proceeded forward to join the right most column, where I swung my duffel bag off my back and onto the floor in an upright position and sat on its top end, and then put my transfer orders, ID card and boarding pass back where I had them, and asked, "Hey, any of you ever hear of a Tiger Airlines?"

To this question, everyone looked at me and shook their heads, and the Private in line ahead of me looked back and said, "No, ain't nobody here ever heard of it."

As I waited in the growing formation, I eventually saw SSG Williams join it and I heard one of the guys from our transfer group ask, "Hey, Sergeant Williams, you know anything about Tiger Airlines?"

All conversation in our formation stopped as SSG Williams responded, "It's a commercial airline, but its only customer is the U.S. Department of Defense with a contract to fly military personnel to and from Southeast Asia. But it does have some lovely stewardesses for the in-flight services provided."

With that curiosity satisfied, everyone returned to their bull sessions[33] with a new topic for discussion, mostly speculating on how good looking the stewardesses might be and how bland in-flight airline meals are.

At 9:15, the 20-foot-square door was slid open by several MP's in their white-trimmed Army khaki uniforms with holstered pistols. The Sergeant with the clipboard was not standing in front of the Flight 93 sign and yelled, "Flight 93, listen up. You will proceed in single file through the doorway beginning with the right column. When you get to the doorway, sound off with the letter and number on your white tag and show me your ID card for me to check you out of this facility. When I've checked you out, you'll proceed to the back of the deuce-and-a-half truck and lift your duffel bag onto its tailgate. From there, you'll proceed to the first bus, board it, and fill the seats from back to front. When the first bus is filled, you will be directed to the second bus. There is no smoking on the busses. Okay, secure your duffel bags and let's get going."

With those instructions given, everyone slung their duffel bag over their right shoulder and onto their back. I reached into my left front pant pocket and retrieved my ID card. As I was in the right most column, I followed the OD duffel bag slowly to the open door. When I reached the Sergeant at the open doorway, I said to him, "H-13," and

---

33   An informal discussion among a small group.

showed him my ID card. He then ran the pen in his right hand down the list on this clipboard, stopped and looked at my ID card, then made a second check mark by my bed number, name, and service number, and said, "Proceed."

I stepped through the open doorway into the bright light created by large light fixtures spaced every ten feet under the bottom edge of the roof's eave fifty feet from the ground, and flooding the parking lot with light. I saw to my right, thirty feet from the building, the rear ends of three deuce-and-a-half trucks with their tailgates halfway down and two Soldiers inside. I continued to the tailgate of the truck on the left end, following the duffel bag ahead of me. When it was my turn, I swung my 96-pound duffel bag up and over the top of my right shoulder and onto the shoulder high tailgate. I then saw the two Soldiers on either end of the duffel bag lift it up and toss it end ways to the front of the truck bed onto a growing stack of duffel bags.

There were two MPs beside the tailgate who directed me to go left toward two more MPs standing to the left of the front end of a large Greyhound coach. Displayed on its destination banner above the front windows, I read, "Charter." To the right of this bus, I saw an identical Greyhound bus parked ten feet away with two more MPs standing to the left of its front end.

Following the Soldier before me to the two MPs beside the first bus, I walked to the two MPs, where one of them sternly said, "Enter the bus and go back to the last available seats. Do not smoke while you are on the bus." When I had climbed to the top of the doorway steps, I saw the interior of the Greyhound bus was fully lit, but the black shades on the side windows were pulled all the way down. The Greyhound driver sitting in his seat said, "Do not raise the window shades."

I moved down the narrow aisle between the rows of double seats. The last available seat was the window seat of the right row that was the second row from the rear. As I sat by the shaded window, I thought, "I may not be able to see anything outside the window, but I'll be able to rest the side of my head against the window to sleep comfortably on this 80-mile trip to Travis Air Force Base." Which is exactly what I did.

The next thing I knew, a Private seated next to me was shoving my right arm and saying, "Sorry, Specialist, you need to wake up. It's time to get off the bus." I opened my eyes and saw that the bus's interior lights were on, and could feel the bus was not moving. I sat up and all I could see ahead of me were the backs of heads belonging to those seated before me. Eventually, I saw those heads rise up as their owners stood and moved to the right, where they entered the narrow aisle between the rows of seats. It was then my turn to rise up, move right to the aisle, and walk to the front of the bus. Arriving at the bus's front, I turned to my right, walked down the two steps, and into the darkness outside. Just outside the doorway was an Air Force AP[34] Sergeant in an Air Force blue uniform who said, "Please walk directly to that Boeing 707 over there, and have your boarding pass ready."

About 200 feet away on the tarmac, I saw a white Boeing 707 commercial airliner with TIGER AIRLINES in large, red letters. I then saw ahead of me in the darkness a line of Soldiers walking to portable stairs with handrails that led up to the well-lit doorway in the front-end of the fuselage. I proceeded behind the Private who had sat next to me on the bus to the portable stairs, as I withdrew my boarding pass from beneath my short front. Walking to the airplane, I saw to my right one of the deuce-and-a-half trucks backed up to a well-lit cargo door in the lower side of the fuselage behind the wing, where two Soldiers were passing duffel bags to Airmen inside the plane. I thought, "Well, at least I don't have to hold my heavy duffel bag on my lap all the way to Thailand."

Climbing the steps of the portable stairs up and into the well-lit interior of the airplane, I was greeted by a beautiful, tall, blond stewardess who looked at the boarding pass in my right hand, and then said with a big, sparkling smile, "Sir, your seat A-21 is about halfway down the aisle on the right, next to the window."

I flashed my own big smile and said, "Thank you, Miss," as I turned to my right and walked down the aisle with rows of three seats on each side, looking for row 21.

From the ceiling on each side of the aisle were overhead storage compartments with labels on the side over each row providing the row number and the letter designation of the seats. Letters on the right read A, B, C, and those on the left read D, E, F. As I approached row 21, I saw that in rows 18 through 23, the Soldiers already sitting in those

---

34   Air Police

seats all had the orange, diamond-shaped patch of Fort Monmouth's School Brigade on the shoulder of their left sleeve. I thought, "Clearly, my seat 21-A was in the middle of our 28-man transfer group going to the 442d Signal Battalion." Not that I had known any of them before I had arrived at the Oakland Army Depot.

When I arrived at row 21, seat 21-B was occupied by a Spec-4. With a friendly smile, I said, "Excuse me, I'm in 21-A. Mind if I slide past you?"

Smiling as he and looked up and scooched back in his seat, he replied, "No sweat, man. By the way, I'm Thomas Meirhauser. But everyone calls me Tommy."

Facing forward, I slid past him and plopped down in window seat 21-A. Turning to my right, I extended my right hand and said, "Sherman Lynch. You can call me anything but Sherm. I hate to be called that."

Tommy shook my hand and said, "Works for me. I'm from Pennsylvania. Where are you from?"

I replied, "Oregon. What's your MOS?"

Tommy responded, "36 Delta. Communications Frame Tech. We maintain everything from the radio to the comm-lines leaving a Radio Site. How about you?"

I answered "26-Victor. I'm a Microwave Radio Repairman on the Army's new LRC-3 microwave radio, all of which are in Thailand, except for one in Tonsanut, South Vietnam."

As the seats around us filled up, Tommy and I continued to talk about our hometowns, family, and high school sports we had played. Eventually, I heard the four jet engines as they began to start with their high-pitched whine. Then the overhead PA announced, "This is your Captain speaking. Tiger Airlines Flight 93 will be departing on time from Travis Air Force Base at 12:30 am for our 6-hour flight to Honolulu, Hawaii. There, the plane will refuel and change flight crews before continuing on to Wake Island, in the Pacific Ocean, and Clark Air Force Base in the Philippines for refueling, before Flight 93 reaches its final destination at Don Muang Air Base outside Bangkok, Thailand. Thank you for flying Tiger Airlines."

Upon hearing this, I said to Tommy, "Hey, this is great. I went to first, second, and 3rd grade in Honolulu. My dad was career Navy and was stationed there from 1953 to 1957 on Ford Island, which is in the middle of Pearl Harbor. Heck, from our back porch I watched 'em raise and lower the flag over the USS Arizona, a hundred yards away. I'd be interested to see what Ford Island looks like now and if the old, wood, four-plex house we lived in is still there. I tell you, living on Ford Island as a little kid was heaven on earth, wearing nothing but a pair of shorts year-round, except when I had to wear shoes and a shirt to school or to church on Sunday, and getting to go to the pool and swim every day."

A soft, female voice came from the overhead PA system to inform everyone that the plane was about to take off, and we needed to fasten our seatbelts, raise the tray tables, and make sure our seat back was in its full upright position. Then she gave the usual speech on emergency exit locations and procedures, the oxygen masks in case of an emergency, and the Mae West flotation vest under our seat cushions. By the time she had finished, the plane had taxied to the end of the runway, where I heard the engines increase their whine to a loud roar, and then was thrust suddenly back into my seat with the acceleration of takeoff. Once the plane had levelled, I heard the roar of the engines reduce to a deep hum. Then the overhead lights and the fasten seatbelt lamp were turned off. Leaning my seat back all the way and making myself as comfortable as possible, I quickly went to sleep.

Six hours later, I woke to a female voice from the overhead PA announcing that the plane was on approach to Honolulu airport, and to please fasten our seatbelts, raise the tray table, and make sure our seat back was in the full upright position. Also, that it was seventy degrees, the skies were clear, and it was 3:20 am in Honolulu. I looked out of my window and saw it was pitch black outside, and thought, "3:20 am! Oh, that's right. Hawaii's time zone is three hours later than California's Daylight Savings Time. Darn, it'll still be dark here with the plane takes off for Wake Island, so I won't be able to see Force Island when I fly over Pearl Harbor."

Then I heard the captain on the overhead PA say, "As the airplane will only be on the ground for thirty minutes to refuel and change flight crews, there will be no passenger deboarding. Also, as they are refueling the airplane, the no smoking light will remain on."

As they had left the cabin's overhead light off, I made myself as comfortable as possible with the seat up and went back to sleep. I awoke when I heard the engines roar loudly and felt the acceleration during takeoff. When the no smoking and fasten seatbelt lamps turned off, I went to the toilet at the plane's rear. On my return to my seat, I lit a cigarette and lowered the seat back all of the way. After I had finished my cigarette and snuffed it out in the ashtray in the armrest, I went back to sleep.

A few hours later, I felt Tommy gently poking my right arm, saying, "Hey, Sherman, wake up. They're serving breakfast."

I woke up and said, "That's something I could really go for, Tommy," as I raised my seat back and lowered my tray table. Over the heads of the guys sitting in the row before me, I saw a very pretty woman with shoulder length brunette hair pushing a food cart. Stopping at each row, she passed out plastic wrapped black plastic plates with a can of tomato or orange juice to each Soldier. When I received my breakfast plate with a can of orange juice, I saw the round plate was divided equally into three parts. One for scrambled eggs, the second for two sausage patties, and a 3rd for an English muffin with small containers of jam and butter.

Tommy and I made short work of eating breakfast, and as we waited for the pretty brunette stewardess to come by with a trash cart, we each took a pack of cigarettes from beneath our shirt fronts, and lit a cigarette each with our own silver Zippo lighters. After we both made flirtatious comments with the stewardess as she collected the refuse of our breakfast, Tommy and I continued our conversation from the night before, which eventually turned to our bootcamp experiences.

I said, "Right after I took those military aptitude tests, they offered me OCS to become Second Lieutenant if I'd waive my enlistment contract for radio school. But I turned it down because I didn't want to be an Infantry Officer who would be sent to Vietnam and fragged[35] by his own men for being an idiot leader getting them killed."

Tommy responded, "Ya know, they made me the same offer, and boy, I wish I'd turned it down like you did. When I graduated bootcamp at Fort Dix, New Jersey, I was told the OCS classes were full, and they transferred me to Combat Engineer School at Fort Lenardwood. It turned out most of us in the same training cycle had the same thing happen. So, we each had our families call our congressmen and

---

35   To intentionally kill a superior, usually with a hand grenade.

tell them what happened. A congressional investigation revealed it was a scam by the Army recruiters to fill billets desperately needed by the Army, but couldn't find enough volunteers to sign up. Then, Congress forced the Army to honor our original enlistment contract."

I commented, "Yeah, I heard about you guys at radio school, but I thought it was all a rumor. So, it really did happen?"

Tommy replied, "Yeah, it really happened. It wouldn't have been too bad, but Fort Lenardwood in the summer is a horrible place to be. It had mosquitoes the size of hummingbirds."

At that time, I heard from the overhead PA, "This is your Captain speaking. We have just passed over the International Date Line, and it is now tomorrow. We will be landing on Wake Island in an hour to refuel."

After an hour, I noticed the waves on the ocean appeared much larger and heard on the overhead PA, "This is your Captain speaking. We are on approach to Wake Island and will be landing in about ten minutes."

As I saw the ocean's surface getting closer and closer, I began looking for Wake Island. I heard the mechanical noise of the wheels descending and saw the flaps on the wings extending and that we were down to several hundred feet above the waves, but still no Wake Island. The surface got closer and closer, and when it looked like we would land on the Pacific Ocean itself, I heard the screech of tires on concrete, then saw land and thought, "Thank god, we landed on land and not on water."

About thirty minutes later, after I'd watched a ground crew pump fuel from a fuel truck into the wing's fuel tank, we took off for Clark Air Force Base in the Philippines.

Several hours later, I saw the stewardess pushing the food cart down the aisle, passing plastic covered black plates of food and choice of juice. When she arrived at our row and stopped, she asked the stewardess serving from the other direction, "Do you have any more lunch meals?"

To which I heard the reply, "No, I just ran out of them."

Our stewardess looked at us in Seats 20 D, E, and F, and in row 21, and asked, "Do any of you object to having another breakfast meal, as we have quite a few of those left from this morning?"

All nine of us indicated that we had no objection to a second breakfast meal. After all, we were Soldiers and pretty much ate anything the Army served us. When the plane had landed at Clark Air Force Base to refuel and change crews, our stewardess came to rows 20 and 21 and asked, "Will the nine of you who did not receive a lunch meal please get up and follow me?"

When we reached the plane's open front door, she said, "Normally we do not allow passengers to get off and on during a refueling stop, but since each of you didn't get your lunch meal, I am giving you each a meal voucher for lunch at the Base Cafeteria. But you will only have about twenty minutes to eat."

She then handed each of us a meal voucher as we went out the doorway. At the foot of the portable stairs, an Air Force van waiting to whisk us quickly to the Base Cafeteria nearby, where we hustled in and went straight to the food service line. I chose a thick steak, baked potato, and corn on the cob. After I sat at a table with the eight others, I wolfed it all down.

When everyone was done, we rose from the table and walked quickly to the Air Force van and rode it back to the plane. A different pretty stewardess with red hair greeted us as we boarded. "We appreciate you returning so quickly to allow the plane to take off on time."

As I led the others back to our seats, I thought, "Wow, a pretty blond, a brunette and a redhead, and a complimentary steak dinner, all in one day. It can't get any better than this."

Standing in the aisle by row 21 was SSG Williams, who asked me worriedly, "Where the heck did you guys go?"

I gloatingly replied, "Just out for a free steak dinner for not getting a lunch meal, Steve," and did not mention we had a breakfast meal for lunch.

I had no sooner sat down in seat 21-A when I heard the engines spooling up, and from the overhead PA a female voice say, "Will you please fasten your seatbelts, raise your tray tables, and bring your seat backs to their full upright position?" A few minutes later, I heard the roar of the engines and felt being pushed back in my seat as the plane accelerated on takeoff. A couple of hours later, the plane landed at Don Muang Airport in Bangkok, Thailand, where we were shepherded from the plane by U.S. Air Force APs and thankfully onto big, air-conditioned Thai busses, having felt the sweltering heat of a tropical afternoon sun as I walked from the plane to the bus.

The windows of the bus were not covered, so I had a good view as the busses were driven onto a highway and on city streets directly to a very large Hotel. Enroute, I first noticed the bus was driving on the wrong side of the road as it pulled onto the left-hand lanes of a 6-lane highway. I then saw motorcycles, cars, and trucks were passing the bus on both sides at breakneck speeds with a continuous din of honking. I also saw some gruesome accidents.

After the busses arrived at the Hotel and we exited into a spacious lobby, I got into the line to the Registration Desk, where I was handed a room key and a meal voucher, and told by the very pretty Thai Receptionist with a big smile, "foucha only goot at resarant. If you eat now, you duffen bak be in you room wen finit eating, okay?"[36]

As it was about 6:00 pm local time, everyone headed for the Hotel Restaurant after they received their room key and voucher. Sitting at a table with Tommy and others in our transfer group, I saw a very pretty Thai waitress with a beautiful smile, wearing an attractive Thai style green silk dress, walk to our table and take our food orders from the menus on the table. Then she asked, "You wan picy, some picy, or no picy?" All of us asked for some or no spicy, expect for Martinez, who said, "I was raised on very spicy Mexican food, so I want spicy."

When our dishes of food arrived, Martinez put a spoonful into his mouth with a big grin. He immediately grabbed the glass of ice water before him, gulped it down, and exclaimed, "Holy Jesus, is that spicy! They don't have spices like that at home." To which we all laughed.

After dinner, I went to my Hotel room and unlocked the door. Entering the room, I saw its interior was nicely apportioned with a double bed on my right, a table and chair to my left, and a big three-drawer bureau with a large mirror on top against the far wall. In the wall to the right of the bureau was an open door, through which I saw a large white tub. To the left of the bureau was an open door to a walk-in closet. Standing upright at the foot of the bed was my duffel bag, and on the bed was a sheet of paper.

---

36   In the spoken Thai language, only the k, m, n, p, and t consonant sounds occur at the end of a syllable, and there are no v, x, z, sh, th, wh, or combination of consonant sounds like sc, sp, sr, st, etc...

Walking to the bed and picking up the sheet of paper, I saw it was a set of instructions with a meal voucher stapled to its backside. I read that the voucher was for breakfast, that the uniform of the day was Army Class-B khakis, and by 0800, I was to report to Room 220 for our in-country orientation. It also stated, if I had clothes to be cleaned, they were to be put into the laundry bag located in the bureau's top drawer and then to call valet services, and under no circumstances was I to leave the Hotel.

Opening the top of my duffel bag, I removed all of my dirty laundry from it, took off all of my clothes, and filled the laundry bag. After a nice, long, hot bath, I put on fresh skivvies and a clean civilian shirt and pants. Then I called valet services. In a few minutes, I answered a knock at the door and saw a Thai man in a neatly pressed black suit, white shirt, and black tie. He said, "I am hea fo you clo-sa to be clean. Ifa you wan pretty Thai woman, I can take you to baa to pick pretty Thai woman for fifteen dolla. You git fifteen dolla in two houwa wen I bring back laundry, okay?"

After he left with a bag of dirty laundry, I said to myself, "Just when I thought my day couldn't get any better than talking with a beautiful blond, brunette, and redhead in one day! Now that's what I call room service."

CHAPTER 6

LIVING THE LIFE OF A MUSHROOM

I had put in for a wakeup call at 6 am, figuring two hours would be plenty of time to take a nice, long, hot bath, shave, dress in my Class-B khaki uniform, enjoy eating my breakfast, and smoking a cigarette before locating Room 220 by 8 am. I wanted a long, hot bath because I figured it was doubtful there were bathtubs in up-country Thailand, especially on any military base.

As I leisurely consumed my breakfast, I greeted other members of my transfer group as they arrived for breakfast. By the time I'd finished my cigarette, several others had also finished their cigarettes, so we left together to find Room 220, which we found on the second floor of the Hotel.

Entering Room 220, I saw to the right of a door a tall, well-built Soldier in a stiffly starched Army Class-B khaki uniform with the three chevrons over two rocker stripes of an SFC. The only items above his left breast pocket were the CIB[37] and Master Parachute Wings. I

---

37   Combat Infantry Badge. All Infantrymen receive this after being in combat for the first time.

thought, "Clearly this SFC did not feel the need to wear his fruit salad[38] to show off his military expertise."

At the top of his left sleeve was a large, triangular shaped unit patch with large, white elephant tusks curving up each side to a point to form the apex of the patch. Upon our entering, he sternly commanded, "Take a seat at the front of the room. Smoke 'em if you got 'em."

Walking to a row of chairs behind the first row of tables at the front of the room, I saw that the room was 30 feet wide and 40 feet long. Across the wall at the front of the room was a whiteboard with a 24-hour clock above it. The clock had a black hour hand pointed to its "8", and a second hour hand that was red and pointing to its "21". Centered before the whiteboard was a wood lectern. To the left of the lectern was a gold-fringed American flag on an 8-foot tall wood pole. To the right of the lectern was a scroll-down map of Southeast Asia. Across the room were five rows of folding tables, and on top of the tables were glass ashtrays. Sliding across to the last empty chair in the front row, I thought, "At least I can smoke in this room," as I sat in the chair and proceeded to light a cigarette.

While smoking my cigarette, I watched as others of my transfer group came in and were ordered by the SFC to take a seat and "Smoke 'em if you got 'em." When SSG Williams entered, they exchanged a few pleasantries before he went to find an empty chair. When I saw the clock's minute hand reach the 59 mark on the clock, I heard the SFC order, "Everybody put out their cigarette." I watched the SFC then stride resolutely to the front of the room and behind the lectern, where he ordered, "Class, Atten…tion! Face the American flag!"

A few seconds later, I heard the American National Anthem played through the PA system, and the SFC commanded, "Present … Arms!" To which everyone saluted the flag. When the Anthem finished, the SFC ordered, "Ready … Two!" To which everyone lowered their hand and resumed the position of attention. He then ordered, "Ready … Seats," and everyone promptly sat down in their chair and placed both hands on the table before them.

Once the SFC saw that everyone was properly seated, he said in a monotone voice, "Gentlemen, I am Sergeant First Class Gibson, and

---

38   Slang military term for multiple of rows of multi-colored military decorations, not unlike a colorful fruit salad.

for the next two hours I'll be giving you an orientation on Thailand, its culture and customs, and the things you normally do that you should *not* do that will piss off a Thai national. At 9:00 there will be a 10-minute Latrine break, during which time you may smoke, as I permit no smoking during my presentation. Class will then resume at 9:10.

"At 10:00, you'll be dismissed for lunch, at which time I'll give each of you a meal voucher. When you have finished your lunch, you are to go to your room, change into your OD BDU's, pack your duffel bag, and report to the Hotel Lobby before 12:00 to turn in your room key at the Registration Desk. Once you have accomplished all of that, you will report to an assembly area near the Hotel's main entrance, where you will await transportation for your flight to join up with the 442d Signal Battalion at Camp Friendship, just outside Nakhon Ratchasima. You will be able to identify your departure area by this sign," and he held up a two-foot square, white sign with CAMP FRIEND-SHIP in large black letters.

He then continued, "You'll find all of the clocks in the Hotel are the same as the 24-hour clock behind me. The black hour hand is the local time in Thailand. The red hour hand in the time in Washington D.C., which is called Zulu time, and is eleven hours behind local time in Thailand." And so SFC Gibson's orientation presentation continued until 10:00, when he had a stack of meal vouchers passed to all twenty-eight of us and dismissed us for an early lunch. I found SFC Gibson's class informative and interesting, but his monotone voice was enough for everyone to nod off every once in a while, which was compounded by our jet lag.

At 10:00 I followed everyone out of the classroom and down the stairs to the restaurant. After a leisurely lunch, where I enjoyed watching all of the beautiful Thai waitresses in their colorful silk dresses until I returned to my room and changed into a freshly starched set of OD BDU's. After lacing up my black combat boots and bloused the bottom of my pant legs, I packed everything into my duffel bag except my folded transfer orders, ID card, and an open pack of cigarettes that I put in my left breast pocket, a fresh pack of cigarettes that I put in my right breast pocket, and my Zippo lighter that I put into my right front pocket. With one last look through my room to make sure I did not miss anything, I closed and secured my duffel bag, which I then slung onto my back. Picking up my OD ball cap and room key off the bed, I closed the door firmly behind me, and headed for the bank of elevators.

Arriving at the elevators, I found most of my transfer group there, each with his duffel bag on his back, which took up as much space as a person. Fortunately, there were six elevators, so it wasn't a long wait to ride one down to the Lobby. I then went to the Registration Desk to hand my room key to a very pretty and smiling Thai clerk, I thought, "Even if the Thai women up country are only half as pretty as these in Bangkok, I'm going to very much enjoy my 1-year tour in Thailand."

Arriving at the Hotel's main entrance, I had no trouble spotting the large Camp Friendship sign to its right, and joined the end of the long line of our transfer group already there. Sliding my duffel bag off my shoulder and onto its side, I sat on it and lit a cigarette in semi-comfort. When I finished smoking it, I walked to a large, metal butt can beside the entrance doors, snuffed it out, and returned to sit back down on my duffel bag.

A few minutes later, I saw a dark blue U.S. Air Force bus pull up and stop before the Hotel's entrance, at which time I stood up and slung my duffel bag onto my back. When the bus's door opened, I saw an Air Force Sergeant exit and walk through the entrance doors. Arriving at the Camp Friendship sign, I heard him announce loudly, "All of you going to Camp Friendship, listen up. When you get to the bus's door, say your name and service number so I can check it against the flight manifest. There are plenty of seats, so each of you can sit in a window seat and place your duffel bag on the floor next to you. Okay? Now follow me."

With that said, the Sergeant turned and led us to the bus, where he reached inside and withdrew a clipboard. As each of us said our name and service number in turn, the Sergeant made a checkmark by the next and said, "Next." When it was my turn, I said, "Lynch, Sherman A., RA19860451." After he said "next," I grabbed the two chrome handrails to pull myself up to climb the steps with my 96-pound duffel bag on my back. Glancing to my right, I saw at the top of the list it said in large letters FLIGHT MANIFEST, and thought, "So I'm just a piece of cargo for the Air Force to transport for the Army's Green Machine."

Reaching the top step, I saw in the driver's seat there was a Thai in the uniform of the Royal Thai Air Force with the Sergeant stripe on his sleeves. I turned to my left, walked down the aisle and found a window seat on my left, thinking, "If I remember correctly, they drive on the left here, so if I want a view of the country, then I need a window on my right."

Sitting in my chosen window seat, I shoved my duffel bag down in front of the seat next to me. When everyone had boarded the bus, I heard the Sergeant say, "In case you can't read, there are no smoking signs over the front, back, and side windows. You are not permitted to smoke on the bus."

I sarcastically asked, "And if I do smoke, then what are you going to do? Cut off my hair and send me to the Vietnam War?" And everybody laughed.

The Sergeant retorted, "No, dumbass. If you smoke, I have your name, service number, and unit. So, what I can do is file a report with your CO, who can fine you or take a stripe from you under Article 15 of the UCMJ. Nonetheless, you are being taken to U-Tapau Air Base about two hours from here. From there, you're scheduled to be flown on a military flight to Camp Friendship, your final destination."

While we traveled to U-Tapau Air Base on the 6-lane highway to the outskirts of Bangkok, I saw a repeat of the wildly driven motor-cycles, cars and trucks pass our bus as if we were on a racetrack. It appeared the first rule of the road was, the bigger your vehicle, the more right of way you had. And, the second rule was to use your horn instead of your breaks. On the streets and the highway, it was a contin-uous cacophony of honking horns and cursing voices.

I saw through my window a sign indicating we were southbound on Highway 3. Eventually, the highway reduced to four lanes and then to two lanes. By then, I saw we were travelling through a level country side with lots of trees, small farms and roadside markets. Through the opposite window, I saw a coastline with white sand beaches. Every ten miles or so, I saw through my window the town names of Chonbari, Si Racha, Pattaya and Sattahip.

When we passed through Pattaya, I saw lots of pretty women wear-ing tank-top shirts and mini-skirts, and yelled, "Hey, Sergeant Wil-liams, isn't this the place you went on RNR to from Vietnam?"

I heard SSG Williams yell from the front, "Yeah, the town isn't much to look at, but the beaches are great, and the women are beau-tiful and plentiful."

Having passed through Pattaya, I saw that Highway 3 curved east-ward to the left along the coastline. After passing through Sattahip, the bus turned right onto a road, where I saw an airport runway on my left. Then the bus made a left turn and stopped at a guard shack in the road's middle with a red and white striped barrier pole extending across the road on each side. At the side of the road, I saw a large, white sign with Thai script in black. Below the Thai script, I read, "U-Tapau Royal Thai Air Force Base."

When the bus's door opened, I saw the U.S. Air Force Sergeant stand up from the front right row, greet a U.S. AP entering the bus, and hand to the AP the manifest clipboard. Then the AP walked down the aisle making a head count. When the AP returned to the front of the bus, he gave the clipboard back to the Sergeant and exited the bus. Watching the red and white barrier pole rise in front of the bus, the bus passed the guard shack and the Sergeant sat back down.

I watched as the bus drove straight to a concrete tarmac next to the runway, where there was a one-story, glass-enclosed, small building. On the far end of this building was a 70-foot tall, 20-foot diameter, circular structure with a glass enclosed room at its top. As the bus stopped at the one-story building, I thought, "These must be the passenger terminal and control tower for the Air Base."

The Air Force Sergeant stood up, and facing us, said loudly, "This is U-Tapau Air Base, from which you will fly to Camp Friendship. When you exit the bus, you'll go directly to the passenger terminal building, where you'll set your duffel bags down on their bottom end in a row along the left sidewall. You may wait outside, but this Base is a restricted area, and you may not leave the immediate area. Also, there is no smoking beyond the red line fifty feet from the building. You may disembark now."

With that said, the bus door opened, and from the front rows, I watched as each Soldier stood, picked up their duffel bags from the floor, and set them upright on the seat before being slung onto their back. When each Soldier exited the bus, I saw the Sergeant who had remained standing in the front right row, counting them as they exited. By the time it was my turn to leave the bus, I'd already slung my duffel bag onto my back. Following those in the seats before me, I picked up my OD ball cap, stepped into the aisle, turned to my left and walked to the front of the bus, where the Sergeant counted me as I exited the bus and put my OD ball cap on.

The interior of the bus was air conditioned. Stepping out of the bus was like walking into a sauna. Even with the offshore breeze I felt, it was over ninety degrees Fahrenheit and one-hundred percent humidity. Walking into the passenger terminal, I saw it was thirty feet wide and sixty feet long, with an Airman sitting at the far end of the room behind a desk in front of a window air conditioner. Even with this air conditioner, I could feel little difference from the outside. Walking to the left sidewall to set my duffel bag down with others there, I saw the Sergeant walk to the Airman and hand hin the manifest clipboard before returning to the bus.

After setting down my duffel bag, I decided to go back outside to join the others standing in the shade of the passenger terminal and smoking cigarettes. Standing in the shade of the building, I lit a cigarette, and said, "Despite this muggy heat, that offshore breeze does make it more comfortable here in the shade."

Just then, SSG Williams came outside and said, "Okay guys, the skinny[39] from these Air Force pukes is that the C-130[40] we're supposed to fly up country in is not scheduled to arrive here for another couple of hours. I guess they bussed us down here early so our rooms could be cleaned for the others arriving in transit at the Hotel today."

To which I commented, "So, this is just another case of hurry up and wait."

SSG Williams replied, "You've hit the nail on the head, Lynch."

After we had grumbled for several minutes about the Army's penchant to have us hurry up and wait at every opportunity, the Airman from inside the passenger terminal came outside and said, "I just received a call from the control tower to tell you guys that you need to come inside right away."

I asked, "Why? Is our plane arriving ahead of schedule?"

Pointing down the runway toward the Sea of Thailand, he replied, "No. It's because of that."

Looking south, I saw about five miles away, coming from the Sea of Thailand, the black wall of a stormfront rolling in rapidly. We all then ran in a bunch behind the Airman into the passenger terminal. Moving to the window at the south end of the building, I soon saw a dark wall of rain falling so heavily that I couldn't see more than twenty or thirty feet from the building. After about ten minutes, the rain

---

39   Slang for inside or confidential information
40   A four engine, medium size, military cargo aircraft

stopped like someone on high had turned off a water faucet. Watching the flooding from the runway across the tarmac three to four inches deep, I thought, "Boy, I haven't seen so much rain since I was a kid on Ford Island in Hawaii during a hurricane and watched six inches of water flowing from the airstrip down the middle of the island a block from my home."

Then I saw a bunch of Thais running out onto the runway into the flowing water that had receded quickly to about an inch deep. Each of them had a 1-gallon tin can and a small, handheld net, with which they were scooping up things from the receding water and depositing into their tin can. As my black combat boots were waterproof, I ran outside to see what these Thais had scooped into their tin cans. Stopping the first Thai I came to, I looked into his tin can and saw swimming around the bottom lots of little fish, shrimp, and eels, and thought, "Obviously these little aquatic creatures had fallen with the rain from the sky. I've heard the expression, 'it's raining cats and dogs,' but this was actually raining fish, shrimp, and eels."

When I went back inside, I asked the Airman, "Do you know how it can actually rain fish, shrimp, and eels like that?"

He explained, "According to the meteorologist, the strong uplift of the water vapor from the warm water of the Sea of Thailand, combined with the wave tops made by the strong stormfront winds tossing into the air these small sea creatures that are carried to the surface by the churning sea, are then carried up with the water vapor. Then, when the water vapor condenses into rain, those little creatures fall with the rain."

I replied, "But this sort of thing doesn't happen very often, does it?"

He responded, "Mac, this is the height of the monsoon season, and this happens almost every day, and so regular you can almost set your watch by it."

When all the runoff had flowed off of the tarmac, I went back out to enjoy the fresh air that usually occurs after a hard rain. But the air was just as hot and humid as before. To seek some relief from the hot sunshine, I sat down in the shade of the building and leaned back against the wall. Enjoying the somewhat cooling effect of the offshore breeze, I tilted the bill of the OD ball cap down over my eyes, and went to sleep.

A couple of hours later, I awoke to the Airman announcing, "In about ten minutes, you'll see the C-130 that you'll be flying in up country, landing with some Soldiers coming in from where you're going. As soon as they get off, you'll be getting on, so you'll need to come in and get your gear."

I got up, dusted off the seat of my pants, and went inside with a dozen others who had been asleep in the shade. There, I located my duffel bag from among the others, swung it up over my shoulder and onto my back, and joined the line of Soldiers going out to the tarmac to watch for the C-130 that was about to land and then carry us up country to Camp Friendship.

In the distant, sunny blue sky, I spotted a plain flying in low over the Sea of Thailand. It was painted brown with green camouflage patters on the sides and top, and white on the underside of the fuselage and wings. From the top edge of its boxy fuselage protruded stubby wings, with two propellor engines on each wing. From either side of its flat underbelly was a set of four wheels, and two wheels under its black, bulbous nose front end. To me, this C-130 had every look of a bumblebee, which defies the aerodynamic look for flight, but can fly.

The wheels under the C-130 touched the concrete runway with a screech and a white cloud of burnt rubber. It came to a slow, lumbering roll as it followed a blue truck to about fifty yards from the passenger terminal, where it stopped sideways to the building. From beneath the high tail section, a horizontal door swung down. As soon as its descending end had touched the ground, two columns of eight Soldiers dressed in jungle fatigues and bush hats, each carrying a M-16-A2 assault rifle and loaded with combat gear ran from this rear exit to a waiting Army deuce-and-a-half truck.

Upon my seeing this, I and several others griped, "Hey Sarge, what gives? The Airman said these guys just came from where we're going, and they look like they just came from a fire fight[41]," and "Yeah Sarge, why haven't we been issued any weapons before we land in a combat zone?"

SSG Williams waved his arms overhead and said, "Hold on a minute, guys. I'm as surprised at this as you are. First, there's no armory

---

41   An intense, usually brief, exchange of gunfire between small military units.

here to issue us any weapons. Second, these guys look like they are Green Berets[42] probably returning from a FOB[43] not even close to where we are going. So just settle down before we board the C-130."

With that, we settled down a little, but I still had a nagging suspicion that some important information had been withheld. At that moment, an Air Force Sergeant in a blue flight suit approached SSG Williams and asked, "Sergeant, are you in charge of this group for transport?"

SSG Williams answered, "Yes, I am."

The Air Force Sergeant said, "Okay, I'm Tech Sergeant Yobloski, the Load Master for this C-130. I need you to get these men into two equal lines to board the plane on each side to balance the plane."

SSG Williams stepped to the front of our group and yelled, "I need you to fall in before me in two ranks."

When we had done this, the Load Master said loudly, "Okay, men, when you board the plane, sit in the last empty forward in my cargo area. Stand your duffle bag upright between your legs and hold onto it tight so it don't go flying around my cargo area if there is any turbulence. Then you're to buckle up tightly to your seat with the cross-straps, and to stay buckled until I give the order to disembark. Okay Sergeant, I need you to march them in two columns facing the rear of the plane."

SSG Williams then commanded, "Group, Atten…tion! Right … Face! Forward … March! Column left … March!"

When we were behind the C-130, I heard, "Column left … March! Okay, rout step into each side of the cargo area to a seat and strap in for the flight."

I was in the left column following the duffel bag in front of my face as I entered the rear of the plane and saw along each sidewall a series of web seats facing away from the wall. When the duffel bag in front of me swung to my right, I turned to my left and swung my duffel bag off my back, standing it upright behind me. Turning around to my right, I grabbed the top of the shoulder strap by both hands and pulled the duffel bag between my legs as I sat in a web seat. Pulling the cross-straps around me from each side and buckling it tight, I saw the web seats were close enough together that, with my duffel bag be-

---

42   A special operations unit developed in the Vietnam War.

43   Forward Operation Base

tween my legs, there was no give between my legs and those pressing against mine from each side. I also saw, except for the web seats lining the sidewalls, the interior of the cargo area was bare to the ribs of the fuselage, which arched twelve feet over my head.

A moment later, I watched the Load Master progressing forward through his cargo area giving each person's cross-strap buckle a tug to make sure it was tight and that each man had a tight grip on the shoulder strap of their duffel bag. When he pulled on my cross-strap buckle, I thought, "I'm now just another piece of cargo being checked by a Load Master to be secured in place for transit."

When he was done with his cargo inspection, he climb up to the flight deck, signaled that the cargo was ready for transport, and then strap into his jump seat. Hearing in sequence as each of the four engines would pop, chug, and roar to life, I felt the accompanying vibrations through my feet and backside. Suddenly, the C-130 lurched as it began to roll forward and taxi to the end of the runway, where I felt it swing around to the right so it could takeoff into the offshore wind, and then stop. As the four engines revved for takeoff, I saw the interior start vibrating and heard what sounded like a large demon shaking huge, metal buckets of loose nuts and bolts. There was an abrupt jolt as I was thrown to my right against the left shoulder pressed next to my right shoulder as the plane accelerated for takeoff and raced down the runway to gain enough speed to become airborne, hopefully before it reached the Sea of Thailand. As the C-130 gathered speed, the crescendo of this metal bucket of nuts and bolts became deafening.

Abruptly, the C-130's floor tilted upward as its nose aimed skyward. I knew its wheels left the surface of the runway when I felt the vibrations greatly reduce and heard the fierce shaking of this bucket of bolts and nuts lessen to a rattle. I was then thrown to my left as the plane banked for a left turn to head northward. Feeling the plane right itself, I heard the four engines continue their loud roar as the C-130 struggled to gain the altitude needed to cross over Thailand's southern mountain range to reach the plateau of northeastern Thailand where Camp Friendship was located.

Eventually, I felt the C-130 flying level and heard the loud roar of the four engines reduce to a continuous dull roar that lulled me to sleep.

I was awoken by the noise of the landing gear being lowered. Suddenly, I heard the loud screech of the wheels striking the surface of a runway, and thrown forward against the Soldier to my left from the reverse thrust of engines and breaks applied to stop the plane before it reached the end of the runway. Then I felt the C-130 swing to the left and taxi for a moment before I felt it stop moving, and I heard the four engines stop. For a second, the plane was silent before I heard the whine of the hydraulic system lower the ramp at the rear of the fuselage, and then the crunch sound as it landed on concrete. Once the ramp was down, I heard the Load Master yell, "Okay, you can unbuckle yourselves, pick up your gear, and leave my cargo area."

With no further encouragement required, I quickly unbuckled the cross-straps, lifted my duffel bag from between my legs as I stood up, and slung it over my right shoulder onto my back. Turning to my right, I followed the duffel bag in front of my face to the rear end of the C-130. Stepping off the loading ramp, I saw the lowering sun was to my right and about to set in an iridescent green sky on the other side of the runway. Looking to my left, I saw the open back end of three ½-trucks with OD canvas covers parked side-by-side fifty yards away. I also saw our two lines of Soldiers carrying duffel bags on their backs merging into single file and walking to the back of the right-hand truck, where each in turn hefted his duffel bag up and over his right shoulder onto the shoulder-high truck bed. There, two Soldiers grabbing the bag by each end and toss it into the dark cave made by the OD canvas cover. With this accomplished, each Soldier in turn proceeded to the rear of the middle truck and climbed the folded down tailgate into its canvas covered interior.

After hefting my duffel bag onto the tailgate of the truck on the right, I saw that the tailgate of the middle truck was closed and walked to the rear of the 3rd truck. From each end of the open tailgate there was a 1-foot square steel step below its bottom edge. Mounting the canvas-covered truck using the right-hand step, I reached up with both of my hands and grabbed hold of two hands reaching down to assist me into the canvas-covered cavern, where I walked hunched over to the lowered wood bench on the left side of the truck bed.

As nobody had said anything about not smoking, and I could see the glowing ends of several lit cigarettes, I proceeded to retrieve and light one of my own for a much-desired hit of nicotine. When the last of our group was aboard, I watched two Soldiers on the ground lift up the tailgate, slam it shut, and fasten it closed with steel hooks that were dangling on chains welded to the truck's sidewalls.

A moment later, I heard the truck's diesel engine turning over and them rumble to life. A second later, I heard the driver put the transmission into first gear, and the hiss of air to release the air breaks, before the truck lurched forward. Soon, I saw the two lit slits of the darkened headlights of the 2nd and 3rd trucks as they drove into line behind this first truck. I swayed forward and backward in the dark as the truck made several left and right turns. After several minutes, the truck slowed to a stop, and as soon as it accelerated, I saw to the left a guard shack with two helmeted Soldiers with rifles slung on their shoulders. After about a hundred yards, I felt the truck slow and make a left turn, slowly proceed another fifty yards, stop, and heard the engine turn off.

A few seconds later, two Soldiers unhooked the tailgate and opened it down all the way. Then I heard a stern voice order, "Get out of the truck, go to the last truck, grab a duffel bag, and take it to the Day Room. Do *not* look for yours to carry in, its too dark. They'll be sorted out once you're inside."

On each side of the dark interior of the truck, I could barely see each Soldier as they rose to a crouch and jumped out of the rear of the truck. When it was my turn, I rose to a crouch, walked hunched over to the rear of the truck, and jumped the five feet from the truck bed to the ground. Once outside of the truck, I could only see the outline of things under a starlit sky, as the sun was now down and there was no moon. Following the dark shape of the Soldier who had jumped down before me, I walked along the right side of the trucks to the rear of the last truck.

Reaching the rear of the last truck, I took onto my left shoulder a duffel bag placed there by two Soldiers on its truck bed, and followed the line of Soldiers to the lit doorway of a one-story wood building two feet above the ground. I climbed the four steps up and through the lit doorway into a room that was 30-foot wide and 40-foot long, and lit by three bulbs hanging from a 2-by-6-inch ceiling beam. Under the first light bulb was a ping-pong table, under the middle one was a card table with four folding metal chairs around it, and under the 3rd light bulb was a pool table.

Following the Soldier in front of me to the left sidewall, I rolled the duffel bag off my left shoulder, and placed it upright on the wood floor with the other duffel bags. When the last bag was deposited, the SFC began to read the last name on the side of each duffel bag, to which someone would step forward, claim it, and carry it by the canvas handle to the right sidewall. When "Lynch" was called, I walked forward, grabbed my bag by the canvas handle and carried it to the right sidewall.

Once all of the duffel bags were claimed by their owners, the SFC said, "Listen up. First, I would like to welcome you to Company C of the 442d Signal Battalion. Reveille is at 0500. The uniform of the day is unbloused BDU's. The Mess Hall, which is across the street from the Company Area, serves breakfast from 0500 to 0700. Morning formation is at 0700 in front of the Company Area, at which time you'll fall in on Staff Sergeant Williams to the left end of the Company formation with all of your military records. After morning formation, you'll begin in-processing. At this time, you'll will be assigned a bed in a transient hooch, where each of you'll be assigned a housegirl to do your laundry and make your bed each day you're there. You'll be charged fifty cents a day for this service. At this time, I'll call out eight names at a time with your hooch number and bed assignment, after which you'll follow a permanent party member to your hooch."

He then read the first eight names in alphabetical order from our transfer group's roster to go to hooch NW-546, bunks A to H, and follow a Spec-4 Collins to the hooch. He then read the next eight names from the roster to go to hooch NW-545, and as I was 14th on the roster, I was assigned to bed F, and we were told to follow PFC Mullins to hooch NW-545. As soon as the SFC started calling out names from our group's roster, I and everyone else had slung their duffel bag onto their shoulder in preparation to leave for our newly assigned hooch and bed. I now left the Day Room with the seven other who were named, and followed PFC Mullins out the back door.

Once outside, I saw what little light there was came from long horizontal window shutters along the walls of hooches that still had their lights on. Through the dimly lit, warm, humid air, I saw we were walking on a maze of connected concrete walkways between rows of wooden hooches. Along the walkways, I passed the specters of bushes and small trees between the walkways and the hooches. At one point,

I saw the dark outline of a helmeted Soldier carrying a rifle slung over his right shoulder gliding between the hooches on guard duty.

After passing several rows of hooches, the PFC turned right to the front of a hooch with NW-545 on white signs attached to each corner. As he climbed the four steps and opened the spring-loaded wood door to the front of the hooch, he flipped on a light switch just inside the doorway. Entering the hooch, I saw it was the same size as the Day Room, with four beds and a double wall locker on each side of a wide aisle way down the middle. Each bed was already made with a blanket, two sheets, a pillow and a case. On each end was a wooden T-pole with a mosquito net tied over the bed. PFC Mullins said, "Here you go, guys. Enjoy your stay at the Camp Friendship Hilton," and left.

Worn out from my long day of travel to be here, I stripped to my skivvies and climbed into my bed, as someone close to the front door switched off the three light bulbs.

About fifteen minutes later, someone flipped on the lights, yelling, "Red alert, this is no drill. Get dressed and go back to the Day Room as fast as you can. Last one out, turn off the lights."

I heard a chorus of, "Holy shit," as I leapt out of my bed, quickly pulled on my OD BDU's and black combat boots, grabbed my OD ball cap, and ran out the front door, not bothering to tie my boots. Running toward the right, I saw the lights in my hooch go out. With all of the hooch lights out, it was nearly pitch-black, so I just ran with the stream of Soldiers running to the Day Room. As our transit group was in the back row of hooches, I was among the last to arrive at the Day Room, where only the middle lightbulb was lit. The SFC was under the single light, naming individual Soldiers to get an M-14 rifle or be on a M-60 machine gun crew, and making checkmarks on a clipboard as he did so. Within minutes, only the twenty-eight men of our group and several others were left. The SFC said, "You'll need to sit tight until the all-clear sounds," and then turned out the lone lightbulb as he left.

As I sat in the hot, humid dark, I said, "Nothin' like living the life of a mushroom. Kept in a dark, humid room and being fed shovels full of manure," to which I heard, "Amen to that, brother."

CHAPTER 7

Camp Friendship, Thailand

I felt someone kicking the bottom of my combat boots and heard, "Okay, they've sounded the all-clear, you need to go back to your hooches." I opened my sleepy eyes, groggily sat up, and saw the 3 lights in the Day Room were on. As I rose to my feet and shuffled my boot laden feet to the back door, I thought, "Must've rolled onto my side after going to sleep."

With the lights on in most of the hooches, I could easily see the concrete walkway as I walked to the left of the hooch behind the Day Room. I saw it had NW-515 stenciled in black on white signs attached to it's corners. On each successive hooch was NW-525 and NW-535. When I saw NW-545 on the corner of a hooch, I could make out a dirt road behind the hooch parallel to a barely visible, 8-foot tall, chain-link fence topped with barbed concertina wire.[44]

At 5:00, I woke to the blare of the bugle call for Reveille. Getting up still fully dressed, I pulled my duffle bag from the wall locker and

---

44   So called, as the coils of wire were stretched or compressed like the bellows of the small, hand-held concertina musical instrument.

set it up right beside my bed. Opening its top, I removed a set of white skivvies, a pair of OD wool socks, a white towel and my toilet kit, and closed its top. Pulling on my combat boots, I took off my OD BDU shirt and laid it on my bed. Picking up the items I'd removed from my duffel bag, I headed for the front door thinking, "I hope the Latrine's close by, as I have to piss like a race horse."

Swinging the front door open to my left, I saw to the right of the steps an 8-inch concrete pipe partly buried at a 60 degree angle facing me with its flared end three feet above ground filled with gravel to six inches from the top. Remembering a bootcamp lecture on field sanitation, this was a "piss tube". I quickly opened my fly, and as I relieved my aching bladder, said "Thank God."

In a more comfortable mind, I walked toward the front of the Company Area looking for a shower. Seeing a guy dressed like I was, and carrying a white towel and toilet kit, I followed him as he turned left in front of hooch NW-525. I saw the concrete walkway extended past hooch NW-526, across a 50-foot wide grassy are, and between two brown, wood outbuildings. Each outbuilding was 20 feet wide on a 1-foot high concrete base, with a 1-foot gap between the base and the wall. The building to the right had a white sign with black letters read LATRINE and the building on the left had a sign that read SHOWER.

Following the guy before me past hooch NW-526, I saw halfway across the grassy area an open, rusted 55-gallon barrel on its end ten feet to the left of the walkway. Walking to the barrel, I peered inside and saw a square, rising series of 1-inch diameter, 18-inch long pipes, with right-angle elbow connectors, going to an exit hole one foot from the top of the barrel with the 1-inch pipe going to a hole in the middle of the Shower building's wall. At the bottom of the barrel, I saw a 10-inch wide ring of flames rising from an old gas stove burner, and 30 feet away, there was a white, 200 gallon, cylindrical tank with large red letters that read PROPANE, NO SMOKING WITHIN 25 FEET. From a valve on top of the tank, I saw a pipe going into ground and thought, "This is an ingenious water heating system for the Shower building."

With this bit of curiosity solved, I walked toward the Shower building with a 2-foot wide trench filled with gravel along the 1-foot high, concrete base of the Shower building, with water flowing along parts of the concrete base into the trench.

Entering the Shower building's doorway, I saw the room was twelve feet wide with an 18-inch high wood bench along the right sidewall. And, four feet above the bench were 2-by-4s with a series of 4-inch long half-inch dowel pegs protruding at an upward angle. Along the left sidewall was a horizontal pair of 1-inch pipes with six pairs of chrome valve handles connected to a half-inch pipe rising up three feet to a chrome shower-head. Beneath each shower-head was a 12-by-16-inch mirror. Under the water spraying from the farthest shower-head was a naked man vigorously lathering his body with a bar of soap.

The guy I followed to the shower building was sitting on the bench removing his combat boots. On the bench's far end, was a set of folded white skivvies next to a pile of soiled skivvies beneath a pair of OD pants and a white towel hanging on separate pegs. The guy on the bench looked up at me and asked, "You one of the replacements that came in last night?"

I replied, "Yea, that red alert last night wasn't much fun for us, stuck in the dark, not knowing which way is up, and not having a weapon. What's the deal with the shortage of weapons?"

He explained, "It's the agreement the US made with Thailand. Every military unit can only have the weapons it brought with it. Once in country, those weapons can't be increased in number or be exchanged for new models. Though the 442nd has doubled in size, it's not allowed to have additional weapons. Also, we still have the old M-14 rifles instead of the new M-16 assault rifle they've issued in Vietnam. Even the Air Force is stuck with their old F-105 fighter-bombers, though the rest of the Air Force has switched to the new F-111s. The only way they can get a new F-111 is when an F-105 is shot down. Actually, most of our red alerts are false alarms because some idiot on perimeter duty thought he heard something."

After I showered and shaved, I saw a line of guys waiting to take a shower as I went next door to the Latrine building, which was the same size as the Shower building. The bench along the length of the left sidewall was an 18-inch high, 30-inch wide wood box. On top were six hinged, 18-inch square wood lids. Next to each lid were several rolls of toilet paper. Lifting the nearest lid, I saw an 8-inch diameter hole over a steel bucket about a quarter full of feces and toilet paper. As I turned around to drop my pants, a guy on the far end said, "You'll want to check for snakes first, because there's lots of 'em around here."

Turning around, I searched the interior around the bucket. Seeing no snakes, I turned my backside to the hole, dropped my pants, sat on the hole and said, "Thanks for the heads up."

Remembering that such feces was taken out, mixed with diesel fuel and burned, I asked, "So who's detailed to burn this shit, some poor Private?"

He replied, "Naw, a local farmer has a contract to collect it, then uses it for night soil."

Having finished and pulled up my pants, I found my way back to hooch NW-545, and put on a fresh set of OD BDUs. Once dressed in the uniform of the day, I secured my duffel bag in the wall locker with my padlock, and leaving the Army khaki and OD BDU uniforms I'd worn yesterday on my unmade bed, I left to find the Mess Hall. Reaching the roadway in front of the Company Area, I saw to my right a hooch with a 50-foot flagpole and large white sign that read COMPANY C HQ, 442D SIGNAL BN in front of it. Beyond the Company C Area was a two-lane street with some traffic on it. On the other side of the street I saw a 2nd Company Area with similar wood hooches. This 2nd Company Area faced the rear row of hooches of a 3rd Company Area, and 100 yards further, this 3rd Company Area faced the front of a hooch filled, 4th Company Area.

Looking to my front across the Company C roadway, there was a football-size grassy field fronting a 5th Company Area, with a 6-foot wide, concrete walkway on the left side of the large grassy field connecting the two Company Areas. Branching to the left was a concrete walkway that led to a large, one-story building, on 6-by-6-inch wood post supporting it two feet above the ground, with steps of to a double-door entrance. Above the double doors was a large white sign that read ENLISTED MESS HALL. Just beyond the Mess Hall, to the right of the concrete walkway, was a 12-foot square, plywood outbuilding with a sign that read PX ANNEX with NW-434 below the sign.

Looking to my left, I saw the roadway ended at two 10-foot wide, 8-foot high, chain-link gates to a large, gravel-covered parking area enclosed in an 8-foot high chain link fence. To the left of this double gate was a hooch with a sign on its front that read COMPANY MOTOR POOL. Twenty feet to the right of the Motor Pool's fence enclosed parking area was 70-foot wide, 150 foot long, corrugated metal building with 30-foot high walls. In the middle of the end wall were two 10-foot wide, 20-foot high, sliding doors. To the left of this metal building was a large white sign that read SUPPLY/ARMORY, COMPANY C, 442D SIGNAL BN.

Having observed everything in my view, I thought, "I feel better now that I'm oriented to my surroundings. Now it's time to see what kind of slop they serve us for chow. I just hope the chow isn't like the rustic living conditions and rough standards of construction."

Entering the Mess Hall, I showed my ID to a Sargent in OD jungle fatigues at the entrance door. After he checked my name on a roster, I proceeded up a 10-foot wide aisle between five rows of long, wood tables and benches on each side. Beyond these, I saw a 4-foot high, plywood wall on the right half of the room, with a sign hanging from a ceiling beam that read NCO MESS E5-E9. To the left of the NCO Mess partition was a waist-high serving counter, behind which was the kitchen area with four short Thai men wearing white aprons and cooking food on large, flame heated, iron griddles.

Walking to the right end of the counter, I picked up a flat, stainless steel tray and set of steel flatware to join several OD clad Soldiers holding their trays on the counter before them. Behind the stack of trays was a Soldier in a white T-shirt who asked, "What do you want for breakfast?"

Looking to my left, I saw the Thai cooks were cooking fried eggs, omelets, hash brown potatoes, bacon, sausage patties and pancakes. To test the system, I replied, "How about a western omelet, three sausage patties and a large stack of pancakes?"

The Soldier said a Thai name, a Thai cook looked up from griddle, the Soldier rattled off something in Thai, and the cook said, "Châi dâai, krup."[45] Turning to the griddle, he poured whisked eggs onto it, and from several containers in front of him, he tossed on handfuls of shredded meat, cheese, onions, bell peppers and tomatoes.

Stepping behind a Spec-5 in the line, I set my tray on the counter next to his and said, "Short order chow in an Army Mess Hall, now that's real food service."

He replied, "Yea, these Mess Sargent's have it made in the shade. Everything is done by local Thais who work for peanuts, which is

---

45   "Yes can, Sir," or "Yes can, Ma'am" if talking to a woman.

good for you guys because there's no KP duty," as a Thai cook placed a ceramic plate loaded with food on his tray, that he slid to the end of the counter to beverage dispensers and poured himself a cup of coffee.

Behind me, an SFC set his tray on the counter, and I slid my tray along to make room for the others arriving for breakfast. A moment later, the Thai cook placed my order on the tray in a ceramic plate, that included a stack of six 6-inch diameter pancakes. The smell of my freshly cooked food wafted up to my nose and whetted my appetite, and I said to the Thai cook, "Thank you, this smells as good as home cooked."

The Thai cook's face beamed as he said, "Mâi bpén rai, krup," [46] and returned to the griddle. Sliding my tray of fresh cooked breakfast food to the end of the counter, I saw there were dispensers for coffee, tea, white and chocolate milk, grape and orange juice, and carbonated beverages. Filling three 8-ounce glasses with chocolate milk. I said, "Wow, It can't get better than this."

Next to me, I heard the SFC say, "Not only can it get better, it's a lot better. In some ways, this place is heaven on Earth. This is my second tour here, and this time I brought my wife and kids. And, if I play it right, I'll stay here till I retire. Lots of guys extend their 1-year tour to the end of their enlistment, and some then re-enlist to stay here."

Walking toward the aisle between the tables, I said, "Thanks for the info, Sarge," and thought, "Like I'm taking any advice from a lifer."

Reaching the aisle and looking for a place to sit, I saw the Spec-5 from the counter, and walking to his table, I asked, "Mind if I join you?"

He replied, "Not at all, please sit down."

Setting my tray of food and drink on the table and sitting on the bench opposite him, I asked, "How come you aren't eating the NCO Mess?"

He answered, "That's where the lifers eat, and I hate lifers. All they talk about is how great it is to be in the Army and lord their rank over everyone. Actually, I hate being a Spec-5 because it makes things awkward with my friends at work."

I responded, "Yea, I can see how that'd suck. Speaking of work, where'd be the best place to work for a Microwave Radio Repairman?"

---

46   Thai colloquial for "It doesn't matter," "That's alright," "It's not nothing," "You're welcome," etc. Literally "Not be what."

He replied, "I work in the Crypto shop, so I don't know much about where to work with radios. But, I've heard that Air Base sites are pretty laid back because their teams are squad size[47] and they live on the Air Base so there's no lifers to deal with. Also, this is a tropical zone, so leave your shirt untucked and don't blouse your pant legs. And, the tables are bussed, so just leave your stuff on the table."

Tucking in to my scrumptious breakfast, I said, "Thanks for the info."

Finishing my breakfast, and leaving the tray on the table, I untucked my shirt and headed for hooch NW-545. Arriving at the hooch, I unlocked my wall locker and removed the thick, manila envelope from my duffel bag, tossing it on the unmade bed. Sitting on its edge, I removed the blousing elastics from my pant legs and tossed them into my duffel bag with good riddance. Locking the doors to my wall locker closed, I picked up the manila envelope and left the hooch.

Arriving at the front of the Company Area, I saw groups of Soldiers gather in ranks across the roadway. Looking to the far right, I saw SSG Williams with many of our 28-man group in two ranks before him. Joining the second rank of our group, SSG Williams said to me, "I'm glad to see you got the word on tropical attire and you have your records with you, Lynch. I need everyone in two ranks aligned on the platoon to your right."

At 7:00, I saw the 1SGT walking up the roadway from my right and a Captain exit the HQ hooch. The 1SGT stopped in front of the HQ, made a left face, and in a loud voice, commanded, "Company!" to which the Platoon Sergeants before each platoon simultaneously yelled over right shoulders, "Platoon!"

The 1SGT then commanded, "Atten...tion! Dress right...Dress!" and when the platoons were aligned, "Ready...Front! Report!" which started a succession of:

"Tropo Platoon, all present or accounted for."

"Crypto Platoon, all present or accounted for."

"Headquarters Platoon, all present or accounted for."

"Motor Pool Platoon, all present or accounted for."

"Transient Platoon, all present or accounted for."

---

47   Six to sixteen men.

The 1SGT made an about face, saluted the Captain and said, "Company C, all present or accounted for."

The Captain returned the salute and said, "Dismiss the company, First Sargent," and went back into the HQ.

The 1SGT made an about face and yelled, "Platoon Sergeants, dismiss you platoons."

Then each Platoon Sergeant made an about face and said, "Platoon, dismissed for duty."

Except for SSG Williams who said, "Stand at ease, men. Smoke 'em if you got 'em. All offices on the base open at 7:30. I've been given a map of Camp Friendship, which isn't very large, as it's only one mile square and transected by two main roads. We'll march rout step[48] in two columns on the side of the road. We'll first go to the Dispensary for medical in-processing. As there are twenty-eight of us, this may take a couple of hours so when we're done, I'll take you to the PX to buy anything you need. Then, you'll be free to return to the Company Area. After lunch, we'll meet at 12:30 across the road from Company HQ and leave to in-process at Personnel and Finance.

"The word from the Tropo NCOIC, is everyone who is not Crypto will muster with the Tropo Platoon for morning formation, and then we'll go to Company Supply to be issued the unit patches. After lunch, we'll ride to the Tropo Site for an orientation on communications in this Theater of War and be assigned to our duty locations, which are spread all over Thailand. Any questions?" When SSG Williams saw there were no questions, he said, "Okay, put out and field strip your butts. Platoon, Atten...tion! Left...Face! Forward...March!"

Marching on Company C's roadway, I saw it passed over a large culvert for an 8-foot wide, 4-foot deep, dry trench that paralleled the main street. I saw a second large parallel trench on the street's other side, and thought, "What do they need these trenches for, unless their defense works for attacks?"

Between the trench and the paved main street, I saw a 12-foot wide, dirt roadside, onto which SSG Williams had our platoon make a column left and then ordered, "Rout step...March!" To my left, across the football size field, I saw behind the Mess Hall was the front of a wide,

---

48   Where the formation does not march to a cadence in lockstep.

large, one-story wood building, also on 2-foot high pillars. In front of the building was gravel covered parking area with a line of jeeps parked backwards to the building. To the left of the front door was a large, white sign that read HEADQUARTER, US. ARMY SUPPORT THAILAND.[49] Below the title was the same triangular unit patch design that I saw on SFC Gibson's uniform in Bangkok.

I also saw another entrance doorway to the Mess Hall on this end with a large sign that read STAFF OFFICER'S MESS, and thought, "This must be the Headquarters for the Commanding General of the US Army in Thailand. So, I've been basically eating the same food as the General. No wonder our chow is so good."

As we passed the 4th Company Area on my right, I saw beyond it a series of large, wood, one-story buildings on two-foot tall pillars with parking areas in front of each containing jeeps and ¾-ton trucks. Between the buildings were roadways from the main street. On a series of large, white signs before each building, I read OFFICER'S MESS, BOQ,[50] OFFICER'S CLUB, NCO CLUB, FINANCE, PERSONNEL, and POST EXCHANGE. The PX was on a corner of Camp Friendship's two intersecting main streets.

To my left, between the 5th Company Area and the intersecting main street were two large 20-foot high, concrete buildings facing each other separated by a 50-foot space. Bisecting this space between the two buildings was a 10-foot wide, concrete walkway. A large, white sign in front of the left building read CAMP THEATER, with the titles and times of the movies showing. The large, white sign in front of the other building read ENLISTED CLUB with the times it was open for each day of the week.

Stopping for the red light on a traffic signal over the intersecting streets, I saw cater-corner from us, that an entire half square mile of Camp Friendship was empty, except at the far corner was a large, 30-foot tall, light green metal building with a 50-foot diameter parabolic antenna on three of its sides. There were also two smaller two-story light green buildings and several wheeled OD vans with a 16-foot parabolic antenna near each van. I thought, "There's no doubt in my mind those 50-foot antennas are for LRC-3 microwave radios, each with a

---

49   Referred to as USAS-Thai.
50   Bachelor Officer's Quarters.

50,000 watt beam of microwave energy that would fry anything in the beam's path. This explains why there are no other buildings in this half-mile square quadrant of Camp Friendship."

I also saw an either side of the transecting main street, there were 8-foot wide, 4-foot deep trenches terminating into the two trenches parallel to the main street we had followed. Across transecting main street before us, I saw the construction of several large, concrete buildings in progress. A quarter mile to my left, I saw the front of a very large, multi-wing, one-story, concrete building, and on its sloping roofs were large Red Cross symbols. Across the front edge of its roof was a large sign, with a Red Cross on each end, that read 33RD FIELD HOSPITAL.

From the left-turn lane besides us, I watched the Thai buses that had been passing us frequently as we walked beside the main street, turn left and drove to a road fronting the Hospital. There, they made a right turn in front of the Hospital, then a right turn onto a road on the other side of the construction area, and another right turn onto the main street to drive back through the traffic light controlled intersection, and back toward Company C. I thought, "This is a good, local, mass transit system, and I won't have to worry about how to get to and from town. Also, I've now seen all of Camp Friendship, Thailand."

CHAPTER 8

THAT'S WHAT I CALL BEING INPROCESSED

Waiting for the traffic signal lights to change from red to green, SSG Williams said, "When the light turns green, you need to cross the road and make a column left onto the sidewalk." When the traffic light changed to green and our two columns crossed the main street, SSG Williams quickly walked to the front. Reaching the other side, we followed him as he turned left onto an 8-foot-wide, concrete sidewalk. Fifty yards from the 33rd Field Hospital, SSG Williams stopped, turned around raising his hand for us to stop, and said, "Okay guys, I'll need you to merge into a line and follow me into the Dispensary. But first, take a ten-minute smoke break, as there's no smoking in the Dispensary"

Merging into a single line, I saw to my right an 80 foot wide, 1-story, concrete building with two gray, metal, front doors. On the right door, stenciled in red, it read ENTRANCE, and on the left door it read EXIT. Over the two doors I saw a large, white sign with a Red Cross on each end, that read CAMP FRIENDSHIP DISPENSARY, and said, "Darn it, I was looking forward to seeing some pretty nurses at the Field Hospital, not some pock-faced zit-poppers."

Around me, I heard several agreements to my disappointed remark as I retrieved a cigarette, lit it with my Zippo lighter, and took some pleasure from the nicotine it produced. Finishing my cigarette, I field stripped it and put the wadded paper in the pocket with my Zippo lighter. A few minutes later, SSG William said, "Okay, guys, let's go on in," proceeding ahead of his 27 men into the Dispensary.

Entering the Dispensary's large entrance hallway, I saw SSG Williams directing everyone through the doorway on my left, with a sign over it that read SICK CALL WAITING ROOM. Standing at the doorway was a Medic in a white tunic collecting our thick, manila envelopes as each of us entered and saying to each of us, "Have a seat while you wait to be seen, and no smoking."

Entering the Waiting Room, I saw it was about 30-foot square with metal chairs in rows across the room between 3-foot wide aisles on each side of the room. Walking down the nearside aisle to the next available row, I moved down to the last empty chair. Eventually, I heard, "Lynch, Sherman A," called from the doorway, to which I rose from my chair and said, "Here," and proceeded to the doorway, where the white tunicced Medic said, "Follow me, please."

Exiting the Waiting Room, I saw the hallway down the center of the Dispensary was 20-foot wide, with an 8-foot wide, chest-high counter in the middle, that was 15 feet from the entrance door. Behind the counter were two other white tunicced Medics. Behind the counter, the wide hallway continued some 80 feet, with three doors on either side. Following the Medic, I entered the second door on the left.

I saw the white examination room was 20 feet wide and 30 feet long. On the right side of the room was an adjustable exam table and a 3-by-5-foot stainless steel cart. Across the far wall was a stainless-steel counter with rows of drawers beneath the counter and glass front cabinet doors 18 inches above the counter. To my left was a stainless-steel table with a Medical Officer sitting in a chair behind it.

As the Medical Officer removed my Medical Record from my manila envelope, he said, "Please, have a seat on the exam table," which I did. Opening my Medical Record, he set my Dental Record that was inside it on the desk to his left. He then looked at my yellow Vaccination Record affixed to the left, inside cover of my Medical Record and said, "Specialist Lynch, according to your shot record, you've not been vaccinated for typhoid, typhus, yellow fever or cholera?"

I replied, "It's because I'm allergic to egg serums, and each of those vaccines are made from chicken eggs. That's documented in red on the list of my allergies."

Looking at the top sheet on the right side of my Medical Record, he said, "You're right. But, no one is supposed to be deployed to Thailand without being first vaccinated for typhoid, typhus, yellow fever and cholera because those diseases are endemic here, so you're not supposed to be here."

I asked encouragingly, "Does that mean I'll be returned Stateside on a Medical?"

He replied, "No. Once you're here, you're considered exposed."

I responded, "What about my allergy to penicillin? I can't take that shot if I get gonorrhea."

He answered, "Then that sucks for you. I recommend you take all possible precautions. But, if you do, we have other medications we can use to treat it."

After being medically processed, I was returning to the Sick Call Waiting Room with my manila envelope, less my Medical Record, when I saw through the doorway across from the Waiting Room, Soldiers lining the room's wall, with a sign over the doorway that read STD TREATMENT ROOM. Sitting in a chair in the Waiting Room, I asked the guy sitting next to me, "What do you suppose they do in the STD Treatment Room?"

He replied, "I suppose they treat sexually transmitted diseases, like the clap[51] and syphilis. I've heard they have some really nasty shit here that'll rot your dick off, and strains of the clap that resistant to penicillin, which is the main treatment for the clap."

With the revolting image in my mind of my penis slowly rotting and falling off, I sat firmly in my steel chair resolving not to have any sex during my tour of duty in Thailand, and profusely praying that my brief encounter in Bangkok would not result in any STD.

When SSG Williams had been informed everyone in our group had been medically inprocessed, he went to the waiting room doorway, and said in a loud voice, "Okay, everyone inprocessing with the 442nd, you need to exit and form up on the sidewalk out front."

---

51   Slang for gonorrhea

Once we'd formed up on the sidewalk in two ranks with our backs to the 8-foot-wide trench, SSG Williams said, "Instead of going through all the B.S. to march you to the PX, I'm going to dismiss you from here. You can go to the PX on your own if you want to, or you can catch a Thai bus back to the Company Area for free, which you should be smart enough to do by yourselves. Just remember, we're to meet at 12:30 in front of the Company HQ. Platoon, Atten...tion! Dis...missed!"

En masse, we all headed to the intersection, where we each made our way to the PX cater-corner across the intersection from us. Entering the PX, I perused each of the rows to see what all was available, which included most everything from civilian clothes to uniforms, also food items, snacks, tobacco products, and alcoholic beverages. Above the alcohol beverages against a sidewall was a sign that said, "Must have a Liquor Ration Card to buy beer, wine or liquor." Over the row containing tobacco products was a sign that said, "Cigarettes sold only by the carton."

However, I found that a 10-pack carton of cigarettes cost only $1.00. Picking up a carton of Pall Mall cigarettes, I went to the checkout line, and I asked, "How is it you can sell a carton of cigarettes here for $1.00, when the Stateside PX charges $2.00, which is a lot cheaper than the $8.00 a carton cost in a civilian store?"

The clerk replied, "Because here, you don't have to pay the $1.00 Federal Excise Tax."

Outside the PX, I caught a Thai bus back to the Company Area, and found the rows of seats were too close to be comfortable for my 6-foot 2 frame because the average Thai is much shorter than the average American. Also, though the seats had Naugahyde covering, there was very little padding and I thought, "The rides to and from Nakhon Ratchasima are not going to be at all comfortable."

Exiting the bus when it stopped at the Company Area, I crossed the street and walked directly to hooch NW-545. There, I secured my carton of Pall Malls and my manila envelope in my wall locker. Turning to leave for the Mess Hall, I noticed my bed was so neatly and tightly made that it would pass a bootcamp inspection by a DI. Also, that my pile of dirty clothes was gone, along with my second pair of black combat boots and black dress uniform shoes.

Leaving the hooch, I walked through the now familiar rows of raised wooden hooches, crossed the asphalt roadway, and into the Mess Hall, where I showed the Sergeant by the entrance door my ID card. At the waist-high, kitchen counter, I looked at the kinds of food the four Thai cooks had on the hot griddle before them, and saw corned beef, large ground beef patties and hot dogs. Picking up a flat steel tray, I said to the Soldier in the white T-shirt, "I'd like two double cheeseburgers with lettuce, onions, tomatoes and dill pickle, and a large order of fried onion rings." He called a Thai name, and to the Thai cook, he rattled off a lot of Thai gibberish, to which the Thai cook replied, "Châi dâai, krup."

Waiting for my small feast to be prepared, I said to myself, "What I wouldn't give to have a nice, cold beer after lunch."

A PFC standing before me in line, looked at me and said, "You must be new here. When you leave the Mess Hall, just around to the left of the Mess Hall is a little PX Annex we call the Howard Johnson[52]. It has all kinds of convenience stuff to buy, like beer on ice."

I responded, "I thought you had to have a Liquor Ration Card to buy beer from the PX."

He explained, "That's only if you want to buy a whole 24-can case of beer. At the Howard Johnson, you can buy up to 23 cans of beer without a Liquor Ration Card. It'd really suck the big green weenie if you had to have a Liquor Ration Card to buy a can of beer, because you have to be 21 to be issued one, and most us aren't 21. Also, a can of beer only costs a dime."

I said, "You got that right. Hey, thanks for the info."

Just then, a smiling Thai cook placed on the PFC's tray a plate with a Ruben sandwich full of hot corned beef and melted cheese on rye bread, and a large pile of french fries. The PFC said, "Kup koon mâak, krup,"[53] and the smiling Thai cook replied, "Mâi bpén rai, krup."

Receiving my two large double-cheeseburgers and a pile of fried onion rings, and copying the PFC, I said, "Kup koon mâak, krup," to which the smiling Thai cook replied, "Mâi bpén rai, krup."

Proceeding to beverage dispensers, I poured three glasses of chocolate milk. Then, walking to the dining tables, I sat down and devoured my two double-cheeseburgers, fried onion rings and three glasses of milk. Leaving the Mess Hall, I went directly to the Howard Johnson.

---

52   A chain of roadside diner/convenience stores in the eastern U.S.

53   "Thank you very much, sir."

The PFC was right. The 12-foot square, plywood PX Annex had a large selection of snack items, cigarettes, and cases of Budweiser, Miller's and Pabst Blue Ribbon beer, with some in a large ice chest. Taking a One-Dollar bill out of my wallet, I laid it on the counter and said, "One Budweiser, please." The Thai proprietor took the bill, counted out 90 cents in change from a metal cash box, and handed me a cold can of Bud. I then said, "Kup koon mâak, krup," as I grabbed the can of Bud, and he replied, "Mâi bpén rai, krup."

Knowing better than to drink a can of beer openly on a military base, I quickly walked back to hooch NW-545, opened my wall locker, and removed the church key[54] I had kept in my toilet bag. Punching two V-shaped holes in the top of the beer can, I took a good swig of the cold beer, which I swished around inside my mouth, savoring this nectar of the gods, before swallowing it. Sitting around a card table playing Hearts, were four guys in white T-shirts. At the fizzing sound when I opened my can of Bud, they faced toward me and asked in unison, "Where'd you get the beer?"

Telling them about the Howard Johnson by the Mess Hall, they scrambled to put on their OD BDU shirts, and rushed out the hooch's front door. While they were gone, I took the dog tag chain from around my neck, threaded its end through a ready-made hole in the other end of the church key, and placed the chain back around my neck. Then I slowly sipped and savored every cold, refreshing drop of beer, and said to myself, "Now, this is what I call heaven on Earth, because it doesn't get any better than this."

By 12:30, our 28-man group had formed up into two ranks across the roadway from Company C's HQ with our large manila envelopes in our left hands. SSG Williams ordered, "Platoon, Atten...tion! Left...Face! Forward...March!"

When the lead element of our formation had crossed over the culvert, SSG Williams ordered, "Platoon...Halt! Rest! When the next bus stops here, I want you to board the bus from the right file first. Unless you'd rather walk to the Personnel Office in this 90-degree heat."

A few minutes later, a colorful Thai bus stopped, opened its door, and we climbed on board, with SSG Williams climbing in last. When

---

54   A device for opening cans by punching a V-shaped hole in the top.

the bus stopped across from the Personnel Office. SSG Williams stood up and yelled, "Okay, men, this is where we get off," then led us off the bus.

As the bus pulled away, SSG Williams yelled, "Lynch and Schultz post as road guards, then the rest of you run across the street and form up in two columns on the roadway next to the Personnel Office."

Running to the middle of the street, with me on the right and Schultz on the left, and stopping twenty feet apart, we each faced the traffic with our right arm extended out and hand raised up to stop the traffic. With the traffic stopped, SSG Williams told everyone else to run across the street. Passing behind me and Schultz, he ordered, "Road Guards, Recover!" and we ran to join our group on the other side.

To the right of the asphalt covered roadway was a gravel covered parking lot in front of the Personnel Office building with jeeps and ¾-ton trucks backed into the parking spaces. Across the front of the building was a 6-foot wide, concrete walkway. SSG Williams said, "In a single file from the right column, follow me to the walkway, then the first three in line will follow me into the Personnel Office, and the rest of you can take a smoke break while you wait for your turn to enter."

We followed SSG Williams in single file up the roadway, turning to the right onto the concrete walkway, and stopped in front of the Personnel Office building. Watching the first three in line follow him up the steps and into the building, I lit a cigarette and began chatting with those next to me in the line. A few minutes later, I saw SSG Williams exit down the steps, and the next in line walked up the steps and entered the building. As each person exited and the next in line entered, I saw SSG Williams had the exiting person join a line at the end of the walkway on the opposite side of the steps.

Eventually, it was my turn to the Personnel Office. Entering the building, I saw a waist-high counter across the left half of the building, fifteen feet from the two front doors, and a wall that ran the 100-foot length of the building two feet to the right of the doorway, with a door in the wall every 20 feet. Beyond the counter, I saw a series of OD steel desks facing me with a chair on the right end, ten feet from the central wall, and a 5-foot tall OD steel filing cabinet at the right end of each desk. Seated behind each desk, I saw a Soldier in a white T-shirt with a fan on the desk blowing air onto him. The shutters for the screened window in every wall was propped up to let in the fresh, hot, muggy air.

The Soldier at the first desk looked up as I approached the counter and asked, "What can I help you with, Specialist."

I replied, "Inprocessing."

Over his left shoulder he yelled, "Another inprocessing," and then to me, "Go ahead, Specialist."

The Soldier at the 3rd desk looked up and waived me to the chair next to his desk. Sitting down in the chair, I handed him my DD-201 Personnel Record from my manila envelope. Opening it, he said, "Another one for the 442nd. Boy, you guys are lucky. Because the 442nd is part of the 1st Signal Brigade in Vietnam, you're automatically awarded the Vietnam Campaign and Vietnam Service Medals. None of the rest of us get them."

As he said this, he removed a page from my record, placed it in the typewriter to his right, typed an entry on it, and replaced it into my record. He then took a form from a drawer in his filing cabinet, placed it in his typewriter, and typed some information from my record onto the form. Pulling the form from his typewriter, her turned and handed it to me, saying "This is the National Security Notification acknowledging you've been officially notified that, if you discuss with anyone or document any combat action in Thailand that you have seen or heard of, it will be considered a breach of National Security and subject to a General Court Martial under the UCMJ, and punishable with up to twenty years imprisonment and a Dishonorable Discharge. When you've read and signed the form, I'll file it in your 201-File. Any questions?"

I replied, "No. It sounds like the typical CYAF[55] bull the government likes to pull," as I signed the form.

He responded, "Sounds like you have a clear understanding of the situation. I'll file your DD-201 Record here, and you're finished here with your inprocessing, Specialist."

Once everyone had finished inprocessing with the Personnel Office, SSG Williams said, "Okay, guys, we'll just use the KISS[56] method with the Finance Office next door by following me in a single file on

---

55   Cover Your Ass First.
56   Keep It Simple, Stupid.

the walkway. When we stop, it's the same drill as before, with the first three following me inside."

When it was my turn to enter the Finance Office building, I saw it had the same layout as the Personnel Office. Being directed to an empty chair next to a desk, I sat in the chair and handed my Financial Record to guy in a white T-shirt, and asked, "So, how much is the combat pay?"

He replied, "Sorry, Specialist, but there's no combat pay here."

I responded, "But the Personnel Office just awarded me the Vietnam Campaign and Service Medals because the 442nd Signal Battalion is in the Theater of War."

He explained, "But, you have to be in a Theater of Combat to receive combat pay, not a Theater of War. You do get one benefit. Because you flew over Vietnam to get to Thailand, you will receive $50.00 in combat pay on your next Pay Day."

Finished with the finance clerk, I returned outside to the end of our exit line. As I was about to light a cigarette, a Soldier opened the door to the Finance Office and yelled, "You all better come inside, it's 2:15."

Following everyone into the Finance Office building, I looked up and saw a line of black clouds moving rapidly toward Camp Friendship. Looking out a door window a few minutes later, I saw all of the street traffic had stopped when it started to rain. Then, such a deluge fell from the sky that I couldn't see the vehicles on the street fifty yards away. Standing beside me was the Soldier who had called us in, and I heard him say, "You can almost set your clock by these cloud bursts in the monsoon season. They don't last long, but you sure don't want to be outside when they hit."

After several minutes, the deluge stopped. I noticed the 8-foot wide, 4-foot-deep trench alongside the main street was a nearly full with a raging torrent of water flowing in it, and thought, "Well, that answers the question about what those large trenches are for. They're not trenches for defensive combat positions, but large drainage canals to reduce the damage from the monsoon season's torrential rain fall. It's also why all these wood buildings are raised so high from the ground."

We rode back to the Company Area from the Finance Office on the hard, cramped seats of a colorful Thai bus. Returning to hooch NW-545, I found my uniforms cleaned, starched and pressed laying in a stack on my bed. Next to the uniforms were my skivvies and socks cleaned, pressed and folded in another stack. Also, under the edge of my bed were my highly shined combat boots and dress shoes, and I thought, "What a deal for just fifty cents a day."

Because of the heat and humidity, we decided to buy a couple cans of beer each from the Howard Johnson. Returning to the hooch, we all stripped to our skivvies to keep as cool as possible while we drank our cold beer and waited for the bugle call for Mess. As we waited to go to the Mess Hall, Tommy Meirhouser asked, "Did any of you notice the Camp Theater is showing *A Fist Full of Dollars* at 7:00. I was thinking I'd go see it. Anybody want to go with me?"

Not having anything else to do, except to play cards in a hot, humid hooch, the idea of seeing a Western starring Clint Eastwood in an air-conditioned theater was an excellent idea, and all eight of us decided to go. At 5:00, we heard the bugle call for Mess, and dressed in our more comfortable and cooler civilian clothes for dinner.

For dinner at the Mess Hall, I satiated myself with a meal of fried chicken, a baked potato smothered in creamy country style gravy, a side of peas and my usual three glasses of chocolate milk. Then we all kicked back and had a nicotine satisfying cigarette, and mutually agreed we had plenty of time to check out the amenities of the Enlisted Club, which was just across the walkway from the Camp Theater, and have a nice, cold beer in an air-conditioned building before going to see the movie.

Arriving on a Thai bus at Camp Friendship's main intersection, we exited the cramped, hard seats of the bus and went as a group of eight to the Enlisted Club. The entrance to the Club was four steel-framed glass doors, and on entering, the first thing I noticed was the air of the Club's air-conditioned atmosphere. I saw the right half of the Club was a huge ballroom with at twenty-foot ceiling. At the far wall to my right there was a stage with a loud, Thai Rock-N-Roll band trying to play the latest American hits. The rest of the spacious area was filled with round tables large enough to have eight chairs around them. Half of the circular tables were occupied with men drinking from beer mugs or from six-ounce glasses.

Just to the left of the four entrance doors, was a waist-high bar counter with a number of Thai bartenders setting up drinks on round trays for the pretty Thai barmaids, who were serving the drinks to the men seated at the round tables. Along the back edge of the counter were sets of long handles for various beers they had on tap from which the Thai bartenders were filling large, chilled mugs. Behind the Thai bartenders was a wall of shelves, several bottles deep, with a variety of hard liquors. At each end of the bar counter was a ten-foot-wide space leading to a room lined with slot machines and pinball machines.

In a line headed by Tommy, the eight of us went to one of the empty round tables and sat in the eight chairs around the table. By the time we were all seated, a pretty Thai barmaid arrived and asked, "Wat do you wan to drink?"

Tommy asked, "How much is a shot of bourbon whiskey?"

She replied, "It Happy Houa, aw witkey ten cent."

I exclaimed, "Ten cents a shot! They must have this Happy Hour only once a month! For three bucks you can buy a quart of whiskey." To the barmaid, I said, "Bring me 30 shots of Scotch whiskey."

Everyone thought this was quite the deal and each ordered thirty shots of their favorite liquor. It took three of the Thai barmaids to bring us the 48 six-ounce glasses of liquor., each containing five shots. Soon, I had six 6-ounce glasses of Scotch on the table in front of me. By the time I had consumed my 30 shots of Scotch, there were only three of us still at the table. Tommy, me and one other. The other five had left to see *A Fist Full of Dollars*, and there remained the residue of their 30 shots each.

Not wanting to waste any perfectly good booze, we poured their residue together into six 6-ounce glasses. The three of us then had two glasses each of "whatever whiskey." Finishing my ten shots of "whatever whiskey," I got up from my chair, three sheets to the wind, and wobbled out of the Enlisted Club, crossed Camp Friendship's main intersection, and caught a Thai bus back to Company C's Area. Sitting in a seat that I could not feel to be hard or uncomfortable, I said to myself, "Now that's what I call being inprocessed."

CHAPTER 9

THE BEST MADE PLANS OF MICE AND MEN

In the morning, I groggily woke to someone kicking the leg of my bed and shouting, "Hey, Lynch, you need to get up and dressed. It's almost time for formation."

In a stupor, I responded, "Okay, okay, I'm up," as I threw off the sheet covering me and quickly stood up. Before me was a house-girl with an arm load of dirty laundry, who then threw the dirty laundry in the air and ran out the front door yelling, "Chûai-dûai! Kòm-Kŭun! Kòm-kŭun!"[57]

Looking down, I saw I was totally naked, and said, "Oh crap, the shit's going to hit the fan over this."

Going to my wall locker, I tossed a set of skivvies, a pair of OD wool socks and a set of OD BDU's onto my bed, and began to dress as quickly as possible. Then, SSG Williams came into the hooch yelling, "Lynch, what's this about you trying to rape a housegirl?"

---

57   "Help! Rape! Rape!"

Sitting on the edge of my bed, pulling on my socks and combat boots, I explained, "Some of us went to the Enlisted Club, and it was Happy Hour. So, I got totally blitzed and don't remember anything after I left the club. When I got up to dress for morning formation, I found myself totally naked. Then the housegirl ran from the hooch yelling some Thai gibberish."

SSG Williams said, "Well, since you weren't chasing her through the Company Area, I'll consider it no harm, no foul. So, come on with me, since morning formation is about to start."

In the fog of my hangover, I tried to keep up with SSG Williams as he walked at a brisk pace to the roadway in front of the Company Area. Walking to the left of the Tropo Platoon, he said in a low voice to the Platoon Sergeant, "Okay, all of my men are now present," and then he joined the space left for him at the left end of the next to last rank, and I fell in at the right end of the last rank.

A minute later, I heard, "Company…" followed by a chorus of "Platoon…," then "Atten...tion! Report!" As I heard each Platoon Sergeant report "All present and accounted for," I thought through the pain of my hangover headache, "Good Lord, why do they have to yell so loud?"

When all the loud rigmarole was finished, the Tropo Platoon Sergeant ordered, "Dismissed for duty, Transient Squad, report to the Day Room for your Health and Safety lecture."

As our Transient Squad fell out for the Day Room, I heard someone say, "It's probably the same 'if you go to town, don't have an accident, and if you do, don't name it after me.'"

Entering the Day Room, I saw the ping-pong table had been folded in half against the right sidewall, and replaced by a projection screen and several rows of steel folding chairs. Also, on the card table behind the chairs, there was a slide projector with a PFC sitting next to it, and that all the window shutters were closed. Sitting in a chair in the last row to minimize any loud talking from the front, I saw standing to the right of the projection screen, there was a short, slender Soldier dressed in OD jungle fatigues with the gold bar of a 2nd Lt on his right collar and the crossed semaphore flag emblem of a Signal Corps Officer on his left collar.

I asked Tommy, who was sitting next to me, "Do you know how I ended up naked this morning in my bed, because I don't remember anything after returning to the Company Area last night?"

Tommy replied, "What I heard this morning from the guys who went to the movie last night, was they were playing cards when you staggered in and passed out on your bunk. After a while, you started yelling, "Help me, help me," and they told you to go take a cold shower. When you didn't come back after a half hour, they went looking for you and found you on your hands and knees, crawling around a bush, dry heaving. So, they took you to the shower building stripped you, gave you a cold shower, brought you back to the hooch, and put you in your bed naked."

When all of us were seated, but still talking to each other, the 2nd Lt stepped forward and ordered in a high-pitched voice, "Class, Atten...tion!" We all stopped talking and stood at attention. He then ordered, "Ready...Seats!" to which we all sat down, facing forward, and were silent.

He proceeded, "I'm 2nd Lieutenant Willis, Company C's XO.[58] I also have the collateral duties as Company C's Health and Safety, and Morale Officer, and tasked to give you a lecture on the Health and Safety Policy of Camp Friendship's STD Control Program. Under this STD Control Program, all approved local prostitutes are registered with the 33rd Field Hospital where they're all issued booklets of pink STD contact slips. All GI's, Officer and Enlisted, at Camp Friendship are issued a booklet of ten blue STD contact slips to be exchanged for a pink STD contact slip from any registered prostitute. If the woman doesn't have a pink STD contact slip, then she's not a registered prostitute. IF you have sex with that girl, then you are subject to punishment under Article 15 of the UCMJ.

"Each month, all the registered prostitutes are examined at the 33rd Field Hospital for STDs. If a prostitute tests positive for an STD, she provides the Hospital with all the blue STD contact slips she has. Then, every GI she had a blue STD contact slip for, will be ordered to the Camp Dispensary for an STD exam, at which time he must surrender his booklet of blue STD contact slips and all the pink STD contact

---

58   Executive Officer, who is second in command of a military unit.

slips he has collected. There is no punishment for contracting an STD, unless you fail to produce a pink STD for each blue STD contact slip you have signed for, but cannot account for. In which case, you are subject to punishment under Article 15 of the UCMJ. At the end of this Health and Safety class, you will each be issued condoms and a booklet of ten blue STD contact slips.

"This ends the STD Control Program portion of the Health and Safety lecture," and then we were shown projections of the usual pictures of festering canker sores on genitals, the mouth and fingers in an attempt to persuade us to use all the safe-sex practices available, if not to abstain from sex, in order not to contract an STD. At the end of Lt. Willis' lecture, we were led in single file to HQ to be each issued condoms and sign for a booklet of ten blue STD contact slips.

Entering the HQ, I saw it was essentially a hooch converted to the needs of a Company Headquarters. To the left of the front door, a wood wall ran the length of the building with three doorways in it. The first doorway, just inside the front door, led to a small 8-foot wide room with a Dutch door in the right-hand wall with a sign that read MAIL ROOM, OPEN 0700-1230, 1300-1700. The top half of the Mail Room's remaining wall was filled with cubbyholes, five inches high by three inches wide, some of which had envelopes in them.

The second doorway in the main wall of HQ had a door labeled XO, and the 3rd door was labeled CO. On the right half of the building, there was a waist-high counter eight feet from the front door that ran from the right sidewall to a 4-foot wide swinging gate with a sign that read AUTHORIZED PERSONNEL ONLY.

Several feet beyond the counter was an OD metal desk with a name plate that read PFC JAMES SCHULTZ, COMPANY CLERK. At the back of this area was a large wood desk with a name plate that read FIRST SERGEANT PACHUCIO. Between these two desks was another OD metal desk with a very pretty Thai woman sitting in a chair behind the desk. The name plate on the desk read MISS PORNTIP, SECRETARY.

Behind the waist-high counter PFC Schultz was dress in jungle fatigues, and to his right was a 9-by-11-inch box with a sign that read Condoms, Take What You Want. Reaching into the box, I took a handful of condoms, put them in my left front pants pocket, and said, "The Boy Scout Motto is Be Prepared, and I'm an Eagle Scout."

PFC Schultz asked, "Does that mean you also want to sign for more than one booklet of ten blue STD contact slips, Specialist? Some guys do go a little sex crazy when they first get here."

I replied, "No, one booklet will be enough for starters."

Handing me a booklet of ten blue STD contact slips and sliding a clipboard to me on the counter, PFC Schultz said, "Then print your name and service number next to CW-1831 to CW-1840 and sign it."

On the clipboard was a form titled CAMP FRIENDSHIP STD CONTROL PROGRAM. When I had printed my name and service next to CW-1831 to CW-1840 and signed it, I slid the clipboard back to PFC Schultz, who said, "Have fun, Specialist Lynch."

I responded, "I shall make every endeavor to do so," and exited the HQ.

Once everyone was issued condoms and booklets of ten blue STD contact slips, SSG Williams had us form up in two ranks in front of the HQ building, and commanded, "Squad, Atten...tion! Next stop is Company Supply to be issued your unit patches. Left...Face! For-ward...March!" and after fifty yards, "Squad...Halt! From the right rank, Column right...March! To the door."

Our Squad had halted by the large, white sign for Company C's Armory and Supply. To my right, I saw the Squad filing through a doorway in the 30-foot high sidewall of the 20-foot wide, 150-foot long, corrugated metal building, with the side door ten feet from the end of the building.

Entering the side door, I saw the first 30 feet of the building was an empty receiving area with a gas-powered, hydraulic forklift parked in the far-left corner. To my right, were the two 15-foot high, 10-foot wide sliding doors in the end of the building's 70-foot wide wall. To my left, I saw along each sidewall a 25-foot wide, chain-link enclosed area from the concrete floor to the roof that ran the remaining 120-foot length of the building, with a 20-foot wide aisle way in between them.

Twenty feet down the aisle way, in each chain-link wall was a Dutch door. Above the Dutch door on the left was a white sign that read COMPANY SUPPLY, and above the Dutch door on the right was a sign that read COMPANY ARMORY. Along the building's sidewall in the Company Supply area were 4-foot high, pallet sized shelves full of palletized cardboard boxes, wood crates, and various sizes of OD met-al spools of electrical and electronic wiring. The sidewall in the Company Armory area also had 4-foot high, pallet sized shelves, but containing racks of weapons and palletized OD metal ammunition cans.

Inside each enclosure, I saw a half-dozen men wearing jungle fatigues in the act of various duties. I said to Tommy, who was behind me in line, "I'll bet you donuts for Dollars that when nobody is around, they're just sitting on their butts playing cards."

Tommy laughed and replied, "No bet here, Sherman."

When it was my turn at the Company Supply Dutch door, a PFC in jungle fatigues behind the door handed me ten First Signal Brigade unit patches on a clipboard with a form and a pen on it, and said, "Specialist, here are your ten First Brigade patches. I need you to fill out the form with your name, service number and signature to document your receipt for our records."

I looked at the shield-shaped, 2-inch high by 1½-inch wide First Signal Brigade patch, and saw it was divided into three equal sized, vertical fields of orange, blue and orange, with the border edged in gold. In the center of the blue field was a vertical, lightening-bolt shaped, white sword blade with a gold handle.

Placing the ten First Brigade patches in the front right pocket of my pants, because the left pocket was full of condoms, I filled out and signed the form. Returning clipboard, form and pen to the PFC, I asked, "So, when are we issued the jungle fatigues?"

The PFC laughed and replied, "The Army only issues jungle fatigues in units actually in Vietnam. Heck, you can't even buy them at the Camp's PX. But the Air Force's Base Exchange sells the shirts and pants for twelve bucks a pop. The Camp's PX sells the U.S. Army strip for ten cents apiece, and we can have your name tag embroidered ten at a time for a buck, you just have to come back later and fill out a requisition form."

I responded, "You can bet I will. Thanks for the info."

Exiting the Supply and Armory building, SSG Williams said, "Lynch, you can take a smoke break with the Squad over there until everyone's done with supply."

Walking to the Squad by the double gate to the Motor Pool, I lit a cigarette and then said to the others, "Hey, I just got the lowdown from the Supply Clerk on how to get a set of jungle fatigues," and relayed the information to them.

When I finished my spiel, someone asked, "Any idea what they've planned for us next?"

I replied, "Hopefully, they just cut us loose till after lunch. I've a killer headache that feels like my head's going to explode wide open."

Tommy had just arrived and said, "Yea, and you're not the only one. But you know the lifers can't stand to see any of us peons sitting around with nothing to do. They'll find something, even if it's just trimming the grass with a pair of scissors."

Several in our group chimed in, "Yeah, been there, done that."

When everyone had finished with Company Supply, SSG Williams said, "I've been told by the First Sergeant that when we're done with Supply, I was to take you the Motor Pool, so just follow me through the Motor Pool's, gate."

Following him through the gate to the back, right corner of the chain-link fences enclosing the Motor Pool, he led us to a huge pile of sand. To its right, I saw an OD water buffalo[59] with POTABLE WATER stenciled in white on the sides and ends. To the left of the sand pile, I saw a 1-ton OD trailer. Standing by the trailer was another SSG who said, "So, you're the volunteers I was promised for the sandbag detail. In the back of the trailer are sandbags and entrenching tools.[60] Divide up into 2-man teams, one to hold open the sandbag while the other shovels the sand into it. If you get thirsty, there's plenty of water in the water buffalo. When you hear the bugle call for Mess at 11:00, you're dismissed for lunch."

SSG Williams added, "After lunch, you need to be back here, in the Motor Pool, at 12:30 for our transport to the Tropo Radio Site," as they both walked away.

Turning to Tommy, I asked, "You want to team up with me?"

Tommy replied, "Heck, yeah."

Walking to the back of the 1-ton trailer, I grabbed a bundle of burlap sandbags and Tommy took an OD entrenching tool. At the sand pile, Tommy unwound the holding ring on the handle, unfolded the shovel blade to be straight with the handle, and wound the holding ring to firmly keep the shovel blade in position. I then turned the sandbag

---

59   A 250 gallon tank on a trailer with spigots to fill canteens or drink water from.

60   A short wood handle with a foldable shovel on one side and a fold-able pick on the other side to dig fox holes and trenches.

bundle on its edge and Tommy used the sharp edge of the shovel blade to break the twine holding the bundle together.

As I sat down holding the sandbag open and Tommy sat opposite me putting a shovel full of sand lethargically into the sandbag, he asked, "So, how many of these are we supposed to fill?"

I replied, "The way I figure it, we're paid by the month and not by the bag, and I'm in no rush."

Tommy responded, "Neither am I. How about we take a water break and have a smoke after we fill this bag? My head's killing me, and being under this hot, humid sun isn't helping, either."

I replied, "Sounds like a plan to me. Hey, I was talking to a Spec-5 at breakfast yesterday about where the best place to work is. He told me, it would at an Air Base because they're squad-sized teams with no lifers to deal with. How about we team up and try to get one of those Air Base sites together?"

Tommy answered, "Sounds great to me. As soon as they ask for two guys to be assigned to an Air Base Site, we'll both volunteer together."

When the bugle call sounded for Mess a couple of hours later, Tommy and I hadn't even filled ten sandbags, as we dropped what we were holding and washed our hands under one of the water buffalo's spigots. Then walking to our hooch together, we changed out of our sweat-soaked clothes into fresh skivvies and OD BDUs before going to the Mess Hall for lunch.

Over lunch, we discussed our plan to be assigned to an Air Base Site together. Then we went to the Howard Johnson and bought an ice-cold can of beer each to drink when we got back to the hooch, and I thought, "Nothing like a cold beer and a short nap to help cure a hangover."

By 12:30, we were back in the Motor Pool climbing into the backs of two canvas-covered 2½–ton trucks for transport to the Tropo Radio Site. Of course, the only thing I could see was out the back of the canvas cover as we rode out of the Motor Pool onto the asphalt roadway. The truck turned left onto the main street. Stopping at the traffic light-controlled intersection, the truck then turned right onto the intersecting main street. After a minute, the truck slowed to a stop, and then turned left onto a gravel road. As the air in the back of the truck began to fill with dust, I saw we'd passed through a gated check point guarded by several Soldiers with rifles. After a quarter mile, the truck stopped, the tailgate was lowered, and I heard a voice yell, "Everybody out of the truck and follow me to the Tropo building."

Climbing down the back of the truck, I saw an OD MRC 98 microwave radio van and its 16-foot diameter parabolic antenna to the left of the gravel road. Off to my right, 50 yards away, I saw another MRC-98 van with its antenna. Turning left to follow everyone to the Tropo building, I saw a large light-green, 20-foot tall, 75-foot square metal building 100 feet from a huge, light-green, 30-foot tall, 100-foot square metal building that everyone was walking toward. Each of these two buildings sat on a 3-foot high, concrete foundation.

This 30-foot tall building was the Tropo Radio Site, because I saw on the left, right and far sides of the building the 50-foot diameter, parabolic antennas that would be used by the new LRC-3 troposphere microwave radios. To my left, I saw a 20-foot tall, light-green building on a 3-foot high, concrete foundation, fifty feet from the Tropo building. Hearing the loud mechanical sounds of engines coming from this 3rd building, I thought, "This building has the large generators to provide all of the power for the 50,000-watt microwave signal output of each LRC-3 radio and the air-conditioning required to cool the air for their operation."

Leading up to a side door to the Tropo building, I saw a set of five concrete steps everyone was using to enter the building. Entering this side door, I was immediately assaulted by the 25 degree drop in temperature inside from the hot, humid air outside. Walking into a large, 40-foot square room where everyone was gathering, it took me a moment to adjust to this radical temperature change.

To the immediate right of the side door, I saw a waist-high, 2½-foot wide, wood surface counter the length of the wall, with sets drawers over cabinet doors beneath it. In front of the counter, there were four Sergeants sitting on tall, gray metal stools. In the far wall, opposite this side door, was a door with a window in the top half. Between the far door and the left wall were a soda machine, candy machine, and a machine with bags of chips. On the full length of the left wall was a whiteboard with a large map of Southeast Asia in the center of it. In front of the whiteboard were three rows of three eight-foot long tables with folding metal chairs. This large room appeared to be in the Tropo Site's break/conference room and electronic repair shop.

Standing in front of the whiteboard was the SFC for the Tropo Platoon at morning formation. When the side door closed behind the last man of our Transient Squad, the SFC said, "Okay, Men, take a seat and you can smoke if you want. I'm Sergeant First Class Davidson, the NCOIC. Welcome to Korat Tropo, the hub of all radio communication for the Vietnam Theater of War. I'm not going to bore you men with details we don't have time for. You'll be given a short tour of this facility, and then of the Quad-C A, the Combined Combat Communication Command Agency, in the building next door. There, you'll be shown the entire communication network for the Vietnam Theater of War, of which the 442nd Signal Battalion is the keystone element. As soon as you have finished the tours, you will be given your duty assignment.

"The 442nd has been extremely undermanned. You are the second batch of replacements we've had in over six months. Three weeks ago, we received our first batch of thirty replacements. In three more weeks, we're scheduled to receive a 3rd batch of some two dozen more. Even then, the 442nd will not be fully manned. After the 3rd batch, the 442nd is not scheduled to receive any more replacements for at least four months. We anticipate it may be up to six months. During that time, a large number of men will be rotating Stateside."

I thought, "Eighteen of that two dozen will be from my LRC-3 class. But I know that Ft. Monmouth is cranking out communication repairmen by the hundreds every week. So, why is there such a shortage in the Vietnam Theater of War? The Army's motto must be Do More With Less."

The NCOIC continued, "Standing at the door to your right is Tropo's Site Engineer, Staff Sergeant Anderson. He'll lead you on a short tour of our Tropo Site, and then take you to the Quad-C A. Do not talk to anyone in the Operations Room! Neither you nor they have any time for idle chitchat. Any questions you have, you'll ask Sergeant Anderson. Is that clear?"

As one, the Squad loudly replied, "Yes, Sergeant."

He commanded, "On your feet! From the back row first, follow Sergeant Anderson to the Operations Room."

Following SSG Anderson with the Squad in single file through the door, I entered a 15-foot wide hallway. To my right, I saw a set of double, steel doors in the sidewall of the Tropo building, and in front of me was another set of double, steel doors with a sign that read

AIR-CONDITIONING ROOM. Turning to my left into a 50-foot long hallway, I saw in the middle of the right-hand wall was a Dutch door with a sign that read SUPPLY ROOM. The last fifteen feet of this wall had 4-foot high windows, four feet above the floor, and the windowed wall extended around and across the wall facing the Operations Room. Through this windowed section of wall, I saw there was a 40-foot long office area with desks, chairs and 5-foot tall filing cabinets. Across the hallway from this office area, I saw a steel door with a sign that read, ELECTRICAL ROOM, DANGER – HIGH VOLTAGE.

I thought, "With three LCR-3 radios, each with the ability radiate 50,000 watts of solid power, you better believe this electrical room has plenty of high voltage."

Entering the Operations Room, I saw it was a huge 30-foot high, 100-foot wide and 50-foot long room. On either side of the 15-foot-wide aisle that continued from hallway, I saw rows of back-to-back, 5-foot tall, 18-inch wide metal racks of electronic gear, separated by 4-foot wide passages. Walking down the wide aisle, I saw in some of the passages there were 2-man teams,[61] some in civilian clothes, with electrical test carts examining pieces of electronic gear, and that these 2-man teams were too intent on their work to even give us a cursory glance. I thought, "SFC Davidson was right, there certainly is not a chance for idle chitchat with any of these men."

I saw SSG Anderson has stopped in the middle of an intersection with a crosswise 15-foot wide aisle. On three of the four corners of this intersection, I recognized the 5-foot, gray, metal cubes of three LRC-3 radios, with their gauges, dials, switches and indicator lights. Pointing to each of these large, gray cubes, he said, "These three large items are the heart of our Tropo Radio Site. These are the LRC-3 long-range microwave radios, each producing a 50,000-watt energy beam, with one that reaches 400 miles Southeast of here to Tonsanut Air Base in South Vietnam, a second to Udon Air Base 180 miles to our North near Laos, and the 3rd to Sattahip 200 miles to our South on the coast of the Gulf of Thailand, which has an undersea cable to Clark Air Base in the Philippines. If you look around, you'll see there's no wires connecting the equipment overhead. That's because the floor beneath you is hollow."

---

61   Per Army Safety Regulations, no person is to work alone on any electrical equipment, even if it is turned off, because the capacitors can still be holding a charge.

Looking down, I saw the floor was covered with 1-foot square, white linoleum tiles. Then I saw SSG Anderson had an 18-inch-long metal bar with two 4-inch suction cups facing down on the ends, which he set on the floor, and pushed down firmly to create suction with the two cups. Then, with a firm grip on the metal bar, he lifted up a section of the floor containing four of the linoleum tiles, and I saw through the 2-foot square hole, a 3-foot deep space with various sizes of electrical wires and cables crisscrossing over the concrete floor below. When he lifted a second 4-tile section of the floor, I saw the entire floor was supported by a network of 1-inch wide, flat metal bars with 3-foot long metal pipes going down to the concrete floor beneath at each corner of the 2-foot square holes. On close inspection of floor tiles, I saw a nearly imperceptible space between the 4-tile sections of the floor.

As SSG Anderson replaced the two sections of the floor, he said, "That concludes the short tour of the Tropo building. Now, I'll lead you to the Quad-C A."

With the floor sections replaced, we followed him back up the aisle and hallway, and out the two steel doors onto an 8-foot square, concrete loading dock. Turning right, we walked down the five steps, crossed the gravel covered parking lot, full of jeeps, ¾-ton trucks and 2½-ton trucks, to the 20-foot high, 75-foot square building with five concrete steps leading to a steel door. Over the door was a sign that read COMBINED COMBAT COMMUNICATIONS COMMAND AGENCY.

When SSG Anderson reached the top step, he turned to face us and said, "Men, this is a top security facility. The only reason you're allowed entrance at this time is because you have a need to know the significance of the Quad-C A as it relates to your duties in the Vietnam Theater of War. You'll be given a short briefing by Navy Commander Schuler. At no time are you to speak or ask any questions, nor are you to reveal anything you see or hear. Does anyone have any questions?"

I asked, "Does that mean we're not to reveal to anyone that the Quad-C A even exists?"

He replied, "Except as it pertains to your duties, the Quad-C A does not exist. Does that answer that question for everyone here?"

Everyone responded, "Yes, Sergeant."

With the response, SSG Anderson turned and pushed a button in the wall next to the steel door. A 4-inch square window in the door opened, and SSG Anderson said his name, rank and service number while showing his ID card. The small window closed, and when the door swung outward to open, I saw a U.S. Marine Corps SSG with a 45-automatic pistol in a holster on his right hip and eyeballed us as he held the door open for us to enter.

Ten feet from the door was a 4-foot high, 20-foot wide, concrete wall blocking us from going any further in. Beyond the concrete wall was a 60-foot square room with a 20-foot ceiling. Across the far wall I saw a map of most of Asia, from Korea, Japan and the Philippines on the right, to Turkey on the left, with a spider web of illuminated red, amber and green lines across the map, and a 24-hour Zulu clock over each time zone. Between this huge map and the concrete wall, I saw several rows of desks facing the map, manned by men in Army, Navy, Marine and Air Force BDU uniforms. Along the left side of the room there were several doors. From a glass-fronted office to my immediate left, I saw an officer in the U.S. Navy tropical tan uniform with the silver leaf of a Commander on each collar approach us.

He stopped and said, "Men, I'm Cmdr. Schuler, the OIC of the Quad-C A for the Vietnam Theater of War. As you can see, this is a multi-service agency. Korat Tropo may consider itself to be the heart of this Theater of War, but this agency is the brain. We monitor and control all military communications from the South China Sea to the Indian Ocean. If Korat Tropo were to go down, we can reroute the most critical lines of communication to support the troop on the ground in Southeast Asia. Not only in South Vietnam, but also Cambodia, Laos and Thailand.

"To this end, your duties have top priority. If you believe anyone, regardless of their rank or position of authority, is interfering with the performance of your duty, do not argue with them, you are to contact the Quad-C A and inform this Agency immediately. Even if it's the Commanding General of USAS-Thai, because the Quad-C A has a 3-star general who out ranks him. Your priority is to keep open the lines of communication to the guy on the front-line to give him all the support to complete his mission. Know this, your chain of command may be through the 1st Signal Brigade, but at your Radio Site, the Quad-C A is your chain of command. That's all. If you have any questions, your NCOIC can answer them. Have a good tour of duty."

Cmdr. Schuler then walked away and the armed Marine opened the door for us to exit. Walking out the door, SSG Anderson yelled,

"Everyone, run back to Tropo before it rains," and leapt down the five steps at a run. Looking up, I saw the black sky overhead, and also took off at a run. As soon as I ran through the door, I stopped just past the door. As Tommy ran in, I grabbed his arm and pulled him beside me, saying, "Let's get those seats in front so when an Air Base is called, we get it."

As I sat and lit a cigarette, I heard a roar from the deluge striking the roof over head, and saw that SFC Davidson was standing before the whiteboard with a clipboard in his left hand, waiting for the roar from the deluge to cease. When the roar subsided a few moments later, he raised the clipboard and said, "Well, it must be about 2:15. I have the list of duty assignment most critical to be filled. If your MOS matches and you're interested, raise your hand and say your last name. First, we need a Microwave Repairman and a Frame Tech for Korat Air Base."

Our hands shot up and we said, "Lynch, 26 Lima," and "Meirhauser, 36 Delta."

SFC Davidson wrote on his clipboard and said, "Lynch and Meirhauser, you're assigned to Korat Air Base. If you'll join Sgt. Smith in the back, he's your NCOIC and can drive you directly there."

Tommy and I stood and looked to the back of the room, and saw a tall, slender Sgt. in jungle fatigues waiving us toward him. Sliding up past the chairs of our former Transient Squad members, I said, "Congratulations, Tommy, we got an Air Base together, far from these lifers at Camp Friendship."

We followed Sgt. Smith out the door to a ¾-ton truck, where he climbed behind the driver's wheel. As we entered from the passenger side and sat on the truck's bench seat, Sgt. Smith said, "No military formalities at the Korat Air Base Site, so just call me Jim."

I asked, "Okay, Jim, how far is the Korat Air Base Site from here?"

He laughed and replied, "As the crow flies, exactly 1.86 miles. The Korat Royal Thai Air Force Base is right next to Camp Friendship."

I thought of the old saying, "Even the best made plans of mice and men can go awry."

CHAPTER 10

AT LEAST THE PAY IS THE SAME

I said, "Wait a minute, Jim. When we flew up from U-Tapau Air Base, we landed at Nokhon Rachasima, and it was a short ride to Company C. How is it Korat Air Base is so close to the Tropo Site?"

Jim replied, as he drove from Tropo's parking lot, "Simple, Korat is the Isaan name for the capital of the Nakhon Rachasima Province. Isaan is the region of Thailand bordering Cambodia and Laos. For centuries, control of Isaan, which is a vast fertile plateau, has been fought over by Thailand, Cambodia, and Laos, and now belongs to Thailand. Locally, the city of Nakhon Rachasima is called Korat, hence the name Korat Air Base.

Tommy asked, "I saw all the grass in front that MRC-98 radio antenna is brown and withered for some distance in front of it. Why is that?"

Jim explained, "Microwave is at the high end of the electromagnetic radio waves used by radars and radios, and operates between 25 to 28 gigahertz. Billions of cycles per second. I've seen guys tie a string on a piece of meat, toss it over the top of an antenna, and when they pull it back several seconds later, it's cooked all the way through.

The guys call it microwave cooking. I once saw a bird fly in front of a MRC-98 antenna and a short distance later, fall to the ground. That's why the Tropo Site is so far from the rest of Camp Friendship. Also, the Tropo Site, even though it's next to the perimeter, believes it's safe from attack because anyone within 200 yards will be fried by the 50,000 watt microwave output from those Tropo antennas. After seeing what 5,000 watts did to that bird in a couple of seconds. I'd say that strategy is pretty sound."

Passing through the gate to the Tropo Site, I saw the four guards were all Thai Soldiers armed with the old 30 caliber M-1 carbine from WWII. I asked, "What's with the Thai guards? Don't we have any U.S. Army Infantry to guard Camp Friendship?"

As Jim turned the truck to the right onto the Camp's main transecting street into the left lane, he replied, "In our treaty with Thailand, only Army support units under USAS-Thai are permitted, so no line units like the Infantry or Artillery. The only exception is the 442nd. Originally the U.S. Air Force was to operate all of the radios in Thailand, as most of the radios were on Air Bases. But, the Air Force realized they didn't have enough signal personnel for the mission and dumped it on the Army, which the Signal Corps can mass produce. But, the Signal Corps' mass production can't provide enough signal personnel due to the massive troop build up in South Vietnam. As a result, we have a huge shortage of personnel in the 442nd. The Korat Air Base Site is suppose to have nineteen men, and with you two, we have eight. If wasn't for the civilian Tech Reps from the Philco Company, who built the Radio Sites, we'd be in a world of shit."

Approaching the Camp's main intersection, Jim pointed at the traffic light and said, "That's the only traffic light in Northeast Thailand. The Engineer Company CO, who built the Camp's roads, missed seeing any traffic lights in Korat, which he thought was uncivilized, so he personally paid to have this traffic light installed. The Thai bus drivers don't know what to make of it, and if a vehicle is not already stopped, they'll just blow right through it.

With the green light, Jim turned left into the left lane of the main street toward Company C and said, "Turning into the left lane from a left turn is easy to learn. It's when you make a right turn that'll get you. Most of the accidents are from someone forgetting on a right turn to get in the left lane and crashing head on into a vehicle."

Driving 100 yards past Company C's roadway on our right, Jim stopped at a guard shack in the middle of the street with a sign on its roof that read KORAT ROYAL THAI AIR FORCE BASE, where there were two Thai guards and two U.S. Army MP's. A Thai Sargent looked at Jim's ID card and waved us past, while the U.S. Army MP's ignored us. I asked, "Aren't those Army MP's interested in who's leaving Camp Friendship?"

Jim replied, "We call them the STD Police. Their duty is to check that all Army personnel leaving the Camp on a Thai bus have the blue STD booklet and a condom. If they don't, they're escorted off the bus and a report is sent to their CO for punishment under Article 15 of the UCMJ. It's the same thing at the gate on the other side of the Air Base, except it's the Air Police checking all the Airmen."

Driving onto the Air Base, I saw to my right a large, one-story, wood building landscaped with trees and bushes around it. Between the road and the building was a manicured lawn with 3-foot tall letters across it that spelled "Ka-Boom Club."

Tommy asked, "What the heck is the Ka-Boom Club?"

Jim replied, "That's the Air Force Officer's Club. They believe they're God's gift to the Vietnam War and Ka-Boom is the sound of their bombs hitting the ground. We say it's the sound of their outrageous stories when they fart them out their bottoms."

I saw a half mile up the road, it ended at the edge of a wide, concrete tarmac beside the runway. There, the road teed with a road that paralleled the tarmac. Approaching the tee, I saw to my left a 20-foot tall, large concrete building with four steel-framed glass door in front. On the roof, were 3-foot tall letters that spelled "NCO CLUB." To my right, I saw a collection of white, one-story, wood buildings.

When the truck stopped at the teed intersection, I saw 100 yards to my left, the end of a series of large, aircraft hangers along the tarmac. Jim then turned right into the left lane of the road fronting the tarmac, and turning right again onto the first road to the right, he continued the right turn into a gravel covered parking lot. Driving to the far left corner of the parking lot, he stopped in front of a sign on a 3-foot tall post that read, "Reserved, 442nd Sig. Bn."

Exiting the truck, I saw we'd stopped in front of a 15-foot high, 40-foot wide, light-green building on a 3-foot high, concrete foundation. In the middle of the wall, I saw a steel door with a sign in red letter that read, RESTRICTED ACCESS, AUTHORIZED PERSONNEL ONLY. Leading up the side of the concrete foundation to the door were five concrete steps with a 4-foot square, concrete porch in front of the door.

Tommy asked, "Why isn't there a sign over the door that says Korat Air Base Radio Site?"

Jim explained, "First, we don't want anything on the building to associate it with the Air Base Comm Center next door for them to think they can come traipsing in any time they want to use our top secret facility. Second, we want to keep as low a profile as possible so nobody knows what we really do here because it raises too many questions. If anyone asks, say we're the Army Liaison for the Air Base, which isn't actually a lie."

I asked, "As we drove here, I didn't see the large, parabolic antenna for a microwave radio?"

As Jim walked to the left side of the building, he said, "Follow me," and rounding the left side, he pointed up and said, "There's your microwave antenna."

Looking up at the end of the building's 80-foot long sidewall, I saw a 50-foot tall, 1-foot square, white tower with a white, 3-foot diameter, parabolic antenna mounted at the top, aimed at the Korat Tropo Site. I asked in surprise, "That dinky antenna is our radio link to the Tropo Site?"

Jim replied, "Remember, I told you the Korat Air Base Site is only 1.86 miles form the Tropo Site, so we don't need a large antenna to beam a signal that short of a distance. Plus, the output power is only 50 watts, as more than that will burnout the receiver at the Tropo Site. This radio link cost the military 5.6 million Dollars, which makes our radio link, in Dollars per mile, the most expensive in the military."

Jim then pointed to his left and said, "That building is our generator shed, providing power only to our Radio Site with double redundant, 60 kilowatts of power 24/7. We don't use the local 50-cycle, 120-volt power, which is not only incompatible with our gear, but also very unreliable."

Looking to Jim's left, at what he called a shed, I saw a 20-foot wide, 40-foot long, light-green metal building on a 1-foot high concrete foundation, that was twenty feet from the Radio Site building. In the side of the building, I saw three open 10-foot wide roll-up doors with a large, light gray generator behind each open doorway.

Jim continued, "Actually, this Radio Site is conveniently located in the middle of everything you'll need, considering a 3rd of your 1-year tour in Thailand will be spent inside this building. Across this parking lot, behind you, is the Base Exchange, which is a lot more convenient than going to the Camp's PX. To the right of our Radio Site is the Air Base Comm Center and very handy to troubleshoot any local outages we have. On the other side of the Comm Center, is the Air Force NCO Club, which you can join because they consider Spec-4s to be NCOs, unlike the Army. Behind our Radio Site is the Base Library and then the Base Mess Hall, which we can use when the gate is closed between Camp Friendship and the Air Base during a Red Alert. Across the road from the Mess Hall is the Base Theater, and just past that is the Base Enlisted Club. The road ends at the boundary fence with Camp Friend-ship, but to the right of the road's end is the NCO Club Annex, which is like a small Bar-N-Grill that's open 24/7. And finally, across the road from the parking lot is the Base Bank. Plus, the Thai buses to Korat stop on the road behind the Base Exchange, so from here, you won't be stopped by the STD MPs on your way to Korat. Basically, this is your home away from home. Okay, let's go inside."

When Jim reached the top concrete step, he opened the door back over the concrete porch with his right hand and directed us in with his left hand, quickly closing the door behind him. Entering the building, I was again assaulted by the 25 degree drop in the temperature and asked, "Jim, does anyone get pneumonia from going in and out of these air-conditioned buildings?"

Jim replied, "A few do, but after a couple of weeks you get used to it."

I saw we were in an 8-foot wide, 30-foot long hallway, leading to the Operations Room, and all the walls and doors were the same light-green color. There were 4-foot long fluorescent light fixtures and 20-inch air ducts hanging from the 15-foot high ceiling, with 18-inch air vents in the bottom of the air ducts. The floor was covered with 1-foot square, white linoleum tiles. I stomped on the floor with a solid thump and thought, "There's no hollow space under this floor."

Jim opened a steel door to our right with a sign that read, AIR-CON-DITIONING ROOM, and led Tommy and I into a 14-foot wide, 16-

foot long room containing two large machines, with the one closest to the door turned on. The two machines were light-gray in color and filled the room, except for a 4-foot space in front and the 2-foot wide spaces along the walls and between the machines. The machines were 7-foot tall with a 20-inch air duct rising to the horizontal air duct hanging form the ceiling. On the front of each machine was a set of red and green buttons, a chronometer, several gauges, and a pair of vertical, 1-inch copper pipes. On the operating machine, one of the two pipes was white with frost and had several soda cans wedged behind it.

Jim said, "This is our Air-Conditioning Room to maintain the temperature in the Operations Room at 70 degrees, plus or minus 2 degrees. If the temperature in the Operations Room rises above 80 degrees, some of our electronics gear will go out of tolerance and begin to fail. That's why we have two of them. As you can see, these machines also double as coolers for our soda cans. Other than to wedge your soda can behind the frozen pipe, you do not enter this room. It's strictly under the control of the Generator Operators. Understood?"

We both replied, "Understood."

We left the Air-Conditioning Room and crossed the hallway to a Dutch door with a sign that read SUPPLY/REPAIR ROOM. Entering a 15-foot wide, 16-foot long room, I saw the length of the left wall had a waist-high, wood counter, 2½-feet wide, with sets of drawers and cabinet doors, and three 3-foot tall, metal stools in front of it. Two feet above the counter, and on the other two walls, was shelving full of bins and cardboard boxes. Jim said, "This is our Supply and Repair Room. It contains all the spare parts and tools to repair or replace every piece of gear we have in-house."

Leaving the Supply/Repair Room, Jim led us back across the hallway to a door in the middle of the right-hand wall with a sign that read ELECTRICAL ROOM, DANGER HIGH-VOLTAGE. Jim stood before the door and said, "As you're not electricians, you are not to enter the electrical room, if there are any electrical problems, there is an alarm in the generator building that'll alert them to any electrical problems. You are never to enter the electrical room at any time. Understood?"

We both replied, "Understood."

Jim then led us to the 3rd, and last, right-hand door in the hallway, with a sign that read LATRINE. He said, "Outside I told you we didn't want our Air Force neighbors to come traipsing in to use our top secret facilities. Well, this is it, and you're to promise you won't breathe a word to anyone about what you see in here."

We each said, "I promise."

With our promises made, Jim opened the door. Entering the 8-foot wide, 16-foot long, sparkling clean room with white tiled walls, I saw to my right a white porcelain sink with stainless steel fixtures. To its left, was a stainless steel shelf with a stack of neatly folded, white towels and to the sinks' right was a laundry hamper behind the door. Above the sink was a 16-by-24-inch mirror. To the left of the towels was a porcelain, flush toilet. And, in the far right corner was a frosted-glass encased shower stall. Along the left wall was a row of sixteen single-wide, full-height, wall lockers. Many of the wall lockers had names on them, but none had a padlock securing the handle.

I heard Tommy give a low whistle and say, "Sweet Mother of God, never again am I going to use that outhouse Shower or Latrine again."

I said softly, "Amen to that, brother," and thought, "It doesn't get any better than this."

Jim said, "Welcome to our top secret facilities. This is the only air-conditioned, full service Latrine on Korat Air Base. If those Airmen in the Comm Center found out about this Latrine, especially the shower, they'd be traipsing into here all the time. The only reason we have the shower, is because the Tech Reps who oversaw the construction of the Radio Site paid the contractor to install it. The shower was never drawn on the blueprints of the building, so nobody, except those who've worked here, knows we have a shower here, and we want to keep it that way. We have a Thai janitor, named Cat, who comes in every morning to clean everything and launder the towels, and every one chips in 40 Bhat, or $2.00, every pay day for his services.

"As for the wall lockers, you will each be assigned one to keep your personal stuff in, except no booze or drugs. To be caught with either will be cause to transfer you to Tropo, and I know neither of you want that. Also, you are not to padlock your wall locker. Most of the guys keep a set of civilian clothes in there so they can leave from here to go to Korat."

I responded, "Now I know why you called the Radio Site our home away from home."

Jim said, "Okay, it's time to tour the Operations Room, the salt mine you'll be spending a 3rd of your tour of duty in Thailand."

Leaving the Latrine for the Operations Room beyond the end of the hallway, I saw across the hallway a 16-foot square room, enclosed on two sides with 4-foot high windows, four feet above the floor, and a steel-framed windowed door with a sign that read SITE OFFICE. In the Site Office, I saw a Spec-5 and a Thai sitting at the desk looking at a schematic, several other steel chairs before the desk, three 5-foot tall filing cabinets along the left wall, and a large map of Southeast Asia on the wall behind the desk.

Entering the 40-foot wide, 50-foot long Operations Room, I was confronted with the backside of a 7-foot tall row of 18-inch wide steel racks full of electronic equipment. To my left, I saw this row of racks ended six feet from the left sidewall. I also saw in the left sidewall a steel door to the generator building outside.

Following Jim to the right, I saw there was an 8-foot space between this tall row of steel racks and the right sidewall. Rounding the end of this row, I saw a facing second 7-foot tall row of 18-inch wide, steel racks full of electronic equipment that was four feet from the first row. Also, I saw beneath each stack of 18-inch square racks, there was a 1-foot square hole in the floor through which bundles of wire and cables ran to and from the equipment in the racks.

Looking down, I saw very small gaps between groups of four of the 1-foot square, white floor tiles. Stomping of my foot, I thought, "Yep, the floor is hollow under the Operations Room."

I saw back to back with the second 7-foot tall row of racks was a 5-foot tall row of racks. And four feet from this row of racks, were to back to back 5-foot tall rows of racks with a fourth 5-foot tall row of racks, four feet from them.

Against the right sidewall, facing the 4-foot wide space between the two 7-foot tall rows, I saw a gray, metal desk with four swivel chair on casters and two metal chairs in front of it. On top of the desk was a black phone, a large glass ashtray, with several cigarette butts in it, and across its back edge an array of various technical manuals between two gray metal bookends.

On the sidewall above the desk hung a 4-foot square, laminated, white chart with lines of information divided into four columns, listing in each column the ID code and data of all the hundreds of comm channels handled by the Korat Air Base Radio Site. Above this chart was the ubiquitous 24-hour Zulu clock showing the local time relative to the 11-hour time difference with Washington, D.C.

Jim had stopped at the desk with Tommy and I behind him. From the end of the first row of racks. I heard the rapid staccato of metal tapping sounds. Looking at the first row, I saw in its first stack of racks three teletype machines stacked one above the other, each with a Qwerty keyboard[62] attached to its front. In the next stack of racks, was another set of three teletype machines with keyboards. On the front of the top two machines were labels that read AP and UPI, and the middle two machines were labeled TTRS and AFN. Also, in each machine was a roll of 9-inch wide, yellow paper exiting out of their tops and down their fronts.

I asked, "Jim, what's with the teletype machines?"

Jim explained, "They're used for troubleshooting the teletype channels that pass through our Radio Site. We also use them to monitor the news feeds from the Associated Press, United Press International and Armed Forces News to AFTN, our local Armed Forces Thailand News Radio Station that broadcasts to all of Thailand. The one labeled TTRS, is a direct link to the Tonsanut Tropo Radio Site in South Vietnam. They let us known if they're abandoning their Radio Site when they're under mortar attack. Then, we announce that over the audio order wire monitored by all the Radio Sites in Thailand. If that machine starts printing out gibberish, then the Tonsanut Tropo Site is off the air and we notify the Quad-C A first and then announce it on the order wire. Then all hell breaks loose and we become busier than a one-armed paper hanger on a hot-tin roof in July."

With that said, Jim yelled to the back of the Operations Room, "Hey, Bob and Frank, where are you?"

I saw two head pop up from behind the third 5-foot tall row of racks and one said, "Over here, Jim. We're trying to isolate where that 12-volt ghost originates from. Roger said to check all the grid-leak resistors to see if one is out of tolerance. Pfizer and Pramoon are going through the schematics in the Site Office to locate all of those resistors in this row of breakout circuits."

---

62   A keyboard having the order of keys on a typewriter with the Q, W, E, R, T and Y keys at the typewriter's upper left.

Jim responded, "We've been trying for two weeks to locate the source of that 12-volts ghost. Since it hasn't affected the performance of any in-house circuit, then I need you two to take a break from that and meet our two replacements."

From between third and fourth rows of 5-foot tall stacks, a tall, skinny man in a short-sleeve blue shirt and brown pants, and a tall, well-built Spec-4 in jungle fatigues. Jim Said, "Bob Greer and Specialist Frank Howell, meet Sherman Lynch and Tommy Meirhauser. Sherman is the Microwave Repairman, so he'll be joining your team, Bob. Tommy is a Frame Tech, so he'll be joining Bill's team tomorrow morning. Frank, I'll need you to take Sherman and Tommy to the Motor Pool after formation tomorrow to get their Military Driver's Licenses for the jeep and ¾-ton truck. I know it's your day off, but they need to have them by tomorrow to drive on their meal runs. Meanwhile, I'd like you two to give them a quick tour of the Operations Room, then bring them to the Site Office, okay?"

Bob replied, "Mâi bpén rai, Jim."

As Jim turned to leave, Bob said, "Tommy, the women are going to love your name. In Thai, 'tom' means 'humble' and 'mii' means 'have.' So literally it means 'to be humble.' As for Sherman, the Thais can't pronounce it. There's no 'sh' or 'er' sounds in Thai, and 'man' means 'it'. As for Lynch, the 'ch' sound only occurs at the beginning of a word, and becomes a 'k' sound at the end of a word, so Lynch becomes 'link.' But, there's 'nk' sound in Thai, and 'nk' become 'nq' and 'ling' in Thai means 'monkey.' If I were you, Sherman, I'd get a name the Thais can say, unless you like the name 'it monkey.'

I responded, "When I was little, my Mom's family in Texas whose grandfather was in the 14th Alabama Regiment of the Confederacy, were not partial to the name Sherman. Because I liked to play in the sandbox and was always covered in sand, they called me Sandy."

Bob said, "In Thai, 'san' means 'extremely' and 'dii' means 'good,' so 'sandii' literally means 'extremely good,' it also means 'to be kind', and suggest you use you nickname when you meet a Thai."

I responded, "Thanks for the heads-up. So, what does Bob mean?"

Bob replied, "In Thai, a 'b' at the end of a word becomes a 'p,' so 'bob' becomes 'bop,' which means 'worn out.' My tîi-lók[63] calls me 'prá-eek,' which means 'movie hero.'

I asked, "You seem to speak Thai pretty good. So, how long have you been in Thailand?"

Bob replied, "I came to 442nd as a PFC in '66, extended my tour to the of my enlistment and made Spec-5, I then contracted as Tech Rep and have been here ever since. But enough chitchat, Frank and I need to give you two a tour of the Operations Room.

"To begin with, a microwave beam can carry up to five groups consisting of twelve audio circuits each, and an audio channel can carry a tone-pack containing sixteen teletype circuits. The Korat Air Base Radio Site handle 252 audio and teletype circuits, which are displayed on this chart on the wall. Each audio circuit has a 4-letter name, and each teletype circuit has a 4-letter name with a number. These are each listed on the chart with its priority level from A to E with a number from one to four, with A-1 being the highest priority. Each priority level has an allowable outage time for service to be restored. For instance, an A-1 must be restored to service within ten minutes from the report of the outage, and if it isn't, the Quad-C A must be informed as to why with an estimated time for restoration.

"The chart also shows the origin and destination of each circuit in the group an audio circuit is carried on, or the tone-pack a teletype circuit is carried on. As you can see, a lot of the audio circuits are tone-packs, and most of the teletype circuits come in one tone-pack and out in a different tone-pack. Okay, any questions about the information on this chart?"

I was overwhelmed with the idea of keeping track of 252 circuits to have any questions. Besides, my job was to keep the microwave radio up and running, not keep track of 252 circuits. I heard Tommy say, "Looks straight forward enough for me."

Then, Bob walked Tommy and I between the rows of racks containing stacks of electronic equipment that Tommy was familiar with and I had mostly never seen before. But, then my job was to maintain the microwave radio, not all of this other comm equipment. After Bob and

---

63   Thai for sweetheart or darling, but an American euphemism for a live-in lover.

Frank finished explaining to us the functions of the comm equipment in the rows of racks in which they were housed, there was on vital piece of equipment I noticed we were not shown and I asked, "Bob, where's the microwave radio I'm supposed to maintain?"

Bob replied, "Oh yeah, Sandii, I nearly forgot about that. It's in the back left corner of the Operations Room. Come on and I'll show it to you," and leading Tommy and I to the left rear corner of the Operations Room, Bob pointed and said, "Sandii, there's your microwave radio, the FRC-109."

I was totally taken aback. A foot from the back wall in the corner was a pair of red 4-inch channel iron risers from the floor to the ceiling, 18 inches apart. Fixed between the red risers, five feet above the floor was an 18-inch wide, 12-inch high, 12-inch deep gray metal box with a red digital light display, two numbered dials, a chronometer, and a red over green colored POWER ON/OFF buttons. There was a red sign with white letters on the box that read DANGER-RADIA-TION HAZARD. Rising from the top of the box was a silver, 1-by-2-inch rectangular wave-guide[64] in 4-foot segments going up between the two risers to the ceiling. I though, "Okay, this box must contain the Klystron[65] and the wave-guide will be going to the 3-foot diameter, parabolic antenna at the top of the 50-foot tower and transmitting the 50-watt microwave radio beam to Korat Tropo."

I saw descending from the gray metal box a ½-inch diameter, black coaxial cable to the backside of a set of three 18-inch wide, 8-inch high racks containing numerous 1 to 3-inch wide removable cards in vertical slots that were held in place by a thumbscrew at the top and bottom of the card. Each card had a gray metal facade containing small green, amber and red lamps, a RESET button, and an ON/OFF toggle switch. From a 1-foot square opening in the floor two feet below the bottom rack, were bundles of insulated wires rising up to the back of the removable cards. And I thought, "These removable cards must contain the multiplex circuitry for transmitting and receiving simulta-

---

64   A metal tube, gold plated on the interior surface, for the directional transmission of microwaves.

65   An electron tube using electronic fields and resonant cavities to bunch electrons into a uniform stream to generate and amplify microwaves.

neously the multiple signals over the carrier wave to the Klystron, but I've never seen anything like this before."

Bob continued, "To us, the FRC-109 is a black box[66] of transistor-ized components that nobody here knows how to repair. Every hour, someone is to come back here to check and make sure all of the lights on the removable cards are green, and that the Klystron frequency displayed by the red digital lights reads 26.985 gigahertz, which is documented on the clipboard hanging on the hook.

"If the amber light is on, then you push the reset button. If the amber light goes off, then life is good again. If the amber light doesn't go off, then you write the part number for the card on the clipboard, to go the Supply/Repair Room, find a box with that part number, and bring it back here. When you remove the new card from the box, check to make sure the part numbers on the cards match. After you switch cards and flip the On/Off switch to On, if the green light is lit, then you're good to go, and you put the bad card in the box, label it 'bad,' and put the box on the desk in the Site Office.

"If the FRC-109 goes off the air, an audio alarm sounds and you run back here to see on which card the red light is lit. You press the reset button next to the lit red light. Even if the red light goes off, you'll still need to replace the card because it'll likely fail again. If the red light for the Klystron is lit, then the Klystron box must be replaced. But, the Klystron box can only be replaced by a Microwave Repairman, which is your job, Sandii. As far as I know, the Klystron for a FRC-109 has not been reported to have failed. Therefore, Sandii, your work here will be mostly to help the Frame Tech. That wraps it up for the Operations Room and I'll take you two back to Jim."

As Bob led Tommy and I up the 6-foot wide passageway between the rows of racks and the sidewall to the Site Office, I thought, "Because I've had no training to repair transistorized circuits to work on the FRC-109, and the only specialized work I can do as a Microwave Radio Repairman here is to change the Klystron box on the FRC-109 if it fails, and it has never failed, then basically I'm as worthless here as tits on a bull, except to be a toolbox carrier for a Frame Tech. A lot

---

66   Anything having a complex function that can be observed but whose inner workings are unknown.

of good that nine months of training to be a Microwave Radio Repairman has done me. Well, at least the pay is the same."

Chapter 11

Hearts and Spades Are Kid's Games

Arriving at the Korat Air Base Radio Site Office, Bob opened the door for Tommy and I, and said to us, "I don't suppose you two have met Spec-5 George Pfizer, our Site Engineer, or Mr. Pramoon, our Site Liaison with CAT, the Communication Authority of Thailand, who has a Bachelor Degree in Electrical Engineering," and as George and Pramoon stood to shake hands with us, "George and Pramoon, meet Spec-4s Tommy Meirhauser and Sherman Lynch. Sherman's family nickname is Sandii, which his much easier for a Thai to say."

Pramoon laughed and said with a Thai accent, "Sandii is a very goot nickname. Even I, who speak goot Englit, would hap proplem saying your name. Goot to meet you, Sandii and Tommy."

Jim said, "This is the Site Office, and the only time either of you should come in here is if you're told to do so or in line with your duties. Thanks, Bob, for giving them a tour of the Operations Room."

As Bob left the Site Office, Jim said, "Let's all sit down and I'll go over the POD," and when we had all sat around the desk, he continued, "The 12-hour day shift starts after the morning formation and ends at

1900. The 12-hour night shift starts at 1835 in front of the Day Room, where you get the Site vehicle from a day shift member, and drives it to the Radio Site to relieve the day shift. Every two days we rotate shifts. After working two 12-hour day shifts, you'll work two 12-hour night shifts, then you'll have two off days. However, because this is a Theater of War, on your two off days, you'll still have to make the 0700 morning formation, where you are subject to be assigned to a company work detail. It happens occasionally, but not often, so don't make any concrete plans for your off days."

I thought, "Darn, just when it looked like I would have a regularly scheduled 48-hour pass to go see the sights in Thailand, the Army pulls its Theater of War card to trump that idea. I mean, how can I go to spend several hours seeing an exotic place and be back from in one day?"

Jim continued, "Lunch meal runs are at 1055, 1140 and 1235, which gives you 45 minutes to drive the one mile to the Motor Pool, eat lunch in the Mess Hall and drive from the Motor Pool back to here. Dinner meal runs are at 1655, 1740 and 1835. On the 1835 meal run, you hand off the vehicle to the night crew in front of the Day Room. The night meal runs are at 2255, 2340 and 0035. And, the breakfast meal runs are at 0455, 0540 and 0635. On the 0635 meal run, you hand off the vehicle to either George or me in the Motor Pool. When the vehicle's gas gauge is down to one-fourth full, whoever makes to 1235 meal run, will drive the vehicle to Camp Friendship's POL[67] and fill the gas tank.

"As I told you on the way here, the staffing for this Radio Site is suppose to be 19 men. A Warrant Officer as the OIC, a Staff Sergeant as the NCOIC, and two Sergeants as the Operations NCO and the Site Engineer. Then three 5-man squads, with a Spec-5 Team Leader, a Frame Tech, a Microwave Repairman, a Generator Repairman and an HVAC[68] Repairman. As it is, we only have eight Army personnel. If it wasn't for the four Tech Reps, and three civilian and three Thai Generator/HVAC Repairmen on contract with the company, we'd be up Schitt's Creek without a paddle with two crews working a 12-hour day or night shift seven days a week.

---

67   Petroleum, Oil and Lubricant.
68   Heating, Ventilation and Air-Conditioning.

"Tommy, after you get your Military Driver's License, you'll start work on tomorrow's day shift with Red, the shift's Tech Rep, and Jack. Sandii, you'll start on the night shift tomorrow with Bob and Frank, meeting the Site's vehicle in front of the Day Room at 1835 hours. In the mean time, company HQ called and said you two are to move your gear from your transient hooch to hooch NW-525 as permanent party tonight. Also, that Miss Porntit has already assigned you housegirls to care for your personal gear. So, you'll ride back to the Company Area on the 1655 meal run to move your gear."

I said, "Wait a minute, Jim. If I remember right, her name plate read Miss Porntip not Miss Porntit?"

Jim laughed and replied, "Sandii, you read her name right. But, everyone in the company calls her Miss Porntit, even to her face, because she's a snobby, little witch, who's the honcho over the housegirls and gets a $1.00 from them on pay day for each Soldier they take care of."

I thought, "You have to love a country where Porntit is a woman's name."

At 1655, as Tommy and I rode with Frank to the Company Area on his meal run, I asked, "So, Frank, do you live in hooch NW-525, too?"

Frank replied, "No. Like a lot of guys, I have a bed assigned to me, but I live off base in a bungalow with a my tîi-lók, who I call Mii-kâa. Means 'precious' in Thai. I met her a couple of months after I got here in October of '67. So, we've been together for eight months. I got the clap my first month here, and didn't want to go through that again, so I decided to get a tîi-lók, a lover, to live with. When I met Mii-kâa, she was a waitress I flirted with in a cafe I went to. She agreed to see a movie with me, and after we dated a couple of weeks, she talked to me about living together because she liked me and being a waitress doesn't pay much, just room, board and tips, half of which she had to give her father. She told me, that for 1,000 Bhat, $50.00, she could rent a bungalow and pay all of her monthly expenses, including 100 Bhat to her father. That solved all my worries. Also, as she spoke very little English and I spoke very little Thai, we've been teaching each other English and Thai.

"Believe me, it's much easier my learning Thai than her learning English, as English has too many sounds that don't exist in Thai, which you've already seen. Also, English has so many words with multiple meanings, like the word 'come,' which has 24 meanings depending on how it's used, where Thai may have some words with two or three meanings depending on how it's used. Plus, there's few words that mean anything's bad, even the word 'bad.' If you want to say it's bad, you say it's 'mâi dii,' which literally means 'not good.'

"The real problem with Thai, is it's a tonal language. Depending on the accent, the same sound has a different meaning. For instance, the sound 'my.' If you ask, 'Máai mài mâi mâi mái?' it means, 'New wood doesn't burn, does it?" But, if you ask, 'Mâai măi mâi mâi mái?' it means, 'Widow's silk doesn't burn, does it?' Also, instead of a verb being said before a noun, it's said after a noun. For instance, you don't say 'It's a red car,' you say 'It's a car red.'

"One other thing, don't call a housegirl, 'mama-san.' That's what a madam for prostitutes is called. If you don't know her name, then call her 'mây-bâan,' which means housekeeper. Literally it means 'mother of house.' If she is older, you can respectfully call her 'maan-daa,' which means mother. So, remember, 'mây-bâan' is housekeeper and 'maan-daa' is mother, so you don't accidentally insult her."

When Frank stopped the ¾-ton truck in front of the Day Room, he said, "Okay, I'll see you two at morning formation."

Exiting the truck, Tommy and I walked to the Mess Hall for dinner. Once we'd finished eating dinner and smoking a cigarette, we walked around the corner of the Mess Hall to the Howard Johnson and each bought a cold can of beer before walking to hooch NW-545. En route, I saw that the hooch we were moving to, NW-525, was just two rows in front of hooch NW-545, and pointing this out to Tommy, I said, "At least we don't have to carry our heavy duffel bags very far."

Entering hooch NW-545, we each punched two V-shaped holes in the tops of our cans of beer with the church key we each had on our dog tag chains. While we drank our beer, we each packed our freshly laundered clothing laying on our beds into our duffel bags. Then hefting the heavy duffel bags onto our backs, we carried them the short distance to the back door of hooch NW-525.

Entering the back door of the hooch and seeing no one there, Tommy said, "I guess everyone's at work, at chow or gone to town."

I responded, "I reckon you're right. We just need to find two empty wall lockers and unpack our duffel bags."

I saw that hooch NW-525 was laid out just like our last hooch, with eight made beds, eight double wall lockers, and a folding card table in the middle with four chairs around it. Walking through the hooch looking for an empty wall locker, I saw signs of permanent occupancy. Most of the beds had a rug on the wood floor beside it with a fan on an improvised table made from a wood crate or a cable spool nearby. Then, I saw a white, 3-foot tall, 2-foot wide mini-fridge to the left of the hooch's front door and yelled, "Hey, Tommy, there's a mini-fridge by the front door."

Tommy responded, "That's great. How about we get some beer from the Howard Johnson before it closes so we can have a cold beer when we've finished unpacking?"

I replied, "Sounds great. Let's go."

Walking to the Howard Johnson, I said to Tommy, "It's only 6:00 and the sun is about to set. Back home in Oregon, this time of year, the days are sixteen hours long and we'd have three more hours of daylight left. But, Thailand's in the Tropics and the day don't get much longer or shorter than twelve hours. Not that I'm complaining. With all this heat and humidity from the sun, it's nice for it to cool down earlier. Even better, when we're working during the heat of the day on the day shift, we'll be in an air-conditioned building."

Tommy responded, "You've got that right, Sandii. Hey, I see the Howard Johnson guy is getting ready to close the shutters on his shop. It figures he'd want to close by sundown, as I don't imagine he'd want to be a lit-up target when it's dark here. So, it's a good thing we came when we did to get beer, because I'll enjoy knocking back a couple of beers when I've finished emptying my duffel bag into the wall locker."

I said, "As will I, Tommy."

At the Howard Johnson, we each bought two 6-packs of beer, and walking back to our new hooch, Tommy said, "I like calling you 'Sandii.' It's better than calling you 'Sherman,' which sounds so formal and stuffy, in my opinion. And saying 'Lynch,' it raises some rather gruesome images."

I responded, "When I was a kid, I didn't like being called 'Sandy' because the other kids teased me that it's a girl's name. So, I insisted everyone call me 'Sherman.' Later, I learned 'Sandy' is a Scottish nickname for 'Alexander,' and is a man's name, and my middle name is Alexander. Now, I think to be called 'Sandii,' has come full circle. Besides, haven't you ever noticed that in lots of Westerns on TV and in movies, many of them have a guy called 'Sandy' because he has blonde or sand colored hair?"

Tommy replied, "Now that you mention it, I do remember that."

Entering the hooch, we each placed one of our 6-packs in the mini-fridge. Finding the first wall on the left side of the hooch was empty, I put my other 6-pack of beer in it and saw the locker had a bunch of wire hangers on the bar at the top of the wardrobe area. Seeing Tommy had found an empty wall locker 3rd down on the right of the hooch, I yelled, "Hey, Tommy, this wall locker has a lot of hangers in it, do you need any?"

Tommy yelled back, "This one has a bunch, too, so I good."

Sorting my gear from my duffel bag into my wall locker, I saw two guys enter the hooch. One went to the wall locker across the aisle form me, the other to the wall locker just beyond mine, and I said, "We're your two new hooch-mates. I'm Sandii Lynch, and that guy yonder is Tommy Meirhauser. We've just been assigned to the Korat Air Base Radio Site. I'll be starting the night shift there tomorrow and Tommy will start the day shift."

The guy across the aisle from me responded as he opened his wall locker and tossed a set of OD BDU's onto his bed, "Hi, Sandii, I'm Dick Kawalski and that's Dan Swenson. We both work at Korat Tropo tonight on the night shift. As soon as we're changed into our BDU's, we have to leave for the front of the Day Room to catch our ride to the Tropo Site, so we don't have time to get acquainted right now. But, we have the next two day off, so maybe tomorrow."

When we had finished stowing everything in our wall lockers, Tommy said, "It's Miller time," and fetched a can of beer for each of us from the mini-fridge. As he handed me my can of Budweiser, and we walked to the table to enjoy our beer and smoke a relaxing cigarette he said, "You know, it wouldn't be too bad over here, if it wasn't for all the heat and humidity, and the idea of being shot at."

Finishing my Bud, I saw three guys wearing jungle fatigues enter the hooch's front door and each grab a can of beer. Looking toward Tommy and me, a skinny, tall, blonde haired guy said with a distinctive Texas twang, "Y'all must be two of the newbies. I'm Glen Milton from Texas. This muscle-bound idiot on my right is Ronnie Dempsey from Colorado, and on my left is David Stone, a damn-Yankee from the Bronx we call Stony. We just got off the day shift at Korat Tropo."

I responded in the Texas twang I had learned from my mom, "I'm Sherman Lynch, but y'all can call me Sandii, and I'm from Southern Oregon, but was born in Shelby County, Tennessee. This he'ah is Tommy Meirhauser, a damn-Yankee from Pennsylvania. We've been assigned to the Korat Air Base site."

Tommy chimed in, "I start there on tomorrow's day shift, and Sandii starts there on the night shift. And, Sandii, just what do you mean by calling me a damn-Yankee?"

I replied, "T'ant nut'in personal, but on both sides of my family I've grandfathers who fought for the Confederacy in the Civil War. My mom told me it wasn't until she joined the Army in World War II, that she found out that 'damn-Yankee' was two words. Once, I heard her mom tell someone who asked her why Southerners drawl, reply 'Why Southerners don't drawl, it's just those damn-Yankees chop the words off.' In my family, and I'm sure it's the same in Glen's family, everyone from North of the Mason-Dixon line[69] is referred to as a damn-Yankee, with no offense intended. Right, Glen?"

Glen affirmed, "Right, Sandii. You should hear George Moore talk. He's from Macon, Georgia, and is always telling me, 'Hang on to your Confederate money, boy, for the South shall rise again!' He swears he ain't got a drawl, just that damn-Yankees talk in a hurry. George works at the Tropo Site, too. It's his day off, so I'm sure he's in Korat get'n drunk and laid. But, you'll see him at tomorrow morning's formation."

As Tommy opened the mini-fridge and retrieved a can of Bud for me and a Millers for himself, he asked, "Any of you up for a game of Hearts or Spades?"

Stony replied with a Bronx accent, "Hearts and Spades are kid's games. The only card game most of us play is Double-Deck Pinochle. Usually, we play for a penny a point, quarter a set and fifty cents a game, just to make it interesting. Either of you play, because we're looking for a fourth player? And, if you don't know how to play, we can teach you how."

Tommy and I indicated we were willing to learn. But, we were both soon befuddled by the fact a deck for Double-Deck Pinochle had eighty cards, using four of each 10, Jack, Queen, King and Ace of each

---

69   Boundary line between PA and MD surveyed by C. Mason and J. Dixon, regarded as separating the free states from the slave states before the Civil War.

suit in a deck of playing cards. Also, that there were several steps taken to play each hand of one game.

First, after each person was dealt twenty cards, you had calculate the total number of meld points in your hand from the combinations of certain cards.

Second, there was a bidding process for the top bidder to name the trump suit. During the bidding, you tried to indicate to your partner how many meld points were in your hand by how you bid with no cross-talking allowed.

Third, after the bidding and the trump suit was called, the meld cards were shown and the points counted, and the difference between the meld points and bid determined how many trick points had to won in order to make board and not go set.

Fourth, when the hand was played, each team was to take as many point cards, the 10s, Kings and Aces, as possible by the highest valued card played, with the 10 as the second highest card in a suit.

And fifth, to count the number of point cards taken by the bid winning team to see if they made board and have their points added to their total, or if not, the were set and were penalized fifty points. Also, if the other team made twenty points, to have their meld and points added to their total score. The team who had 500 or more total points, won the game.

Tommy and I spent the entire evening drinking beer, smoking cigarettes and learning the intricacies of playing Double-Deck Pinochle. By the end of the evening, I thought, "Well, compared to Double-Deck Pinochle, it's obvious that Hearts and Spades are kid's games."

CHAPTER 12

SPIKE IS A VICTIM OF THE PETER PRINCIPLE

Hearing the bugle call for Reveille at 5:00 the next morning, I got up and dressed in my OD BDU pants and combat boots. After using the piss tube, I picked up my white towel and toilet kit to shave in the Shower outbuilding, thinking, "I hope I can wait till I get to the Air Base Site tonight before I need to have a bowel movement."

Exiting hooch NW-525's front door, I looked to my left and saw a line of guys at the Shower outbuilding and said to myself, "To heck with this, I'm not missing breakfast so I can be clean shaven at formation," and went back into the hooch. There, I saw in front of the 3rd wall locker on the left a husky guy, 5-foot 9, who looked like a fullback for a football team. Walking over to him, I said in the Alabama drawl of my maternal grandmother, "Y'all must be George Moore from Macon, Georgia?"

George turned toward me and drawled, "I am. And who do I have the pleasure of addressing?"

I drawled in reply, "I'm Sandii Lynch, born in Shelby County, Tennessee, but of late from the State of Jefferson, and a replacement at the Korat Air Base Site, where I start on the night shift tonight."

Looking puzzled, George asked, "And just where in tarnation is the State of Jefferson?"

I explained, "In 1939, the three most Southwestern counties in Oregon and the two most Northern counties in California declared their secession from Oregon and California and applied for statehood as the State of Jefferson. Many contend it's named after Jefferson Davis, the President of the Confederate Sates of America. To this day, the locals still call it the State of Jefferson."

George commented, "Sounds like a Southern State to me. We'll have to talk more about the Confederacy later. How come y'all ain't shaved yet, Sandii?"

I replied, "too long of a line at the Shower building."

George offered, "Then how about y'all use my electric razor? Wouldn't want any Southern boy looking like a ragamuffin at morning formation."

As George handed me his electric razor, I replied gratefully, "Well, thank you kindly for treat'n me as good as white folk."

After shaving, I returned the electric razor and said, "George you're a lifesaver. The next two things I'm buying at the PX are a fan and an electric razor."

George said, "You'll also need a 50-cycle/120-volt to 60-cycle/110-volt conversion plug. Part of the Army's contract with the Thai government is that Camp Friendship's power be provided by the local power company, which is not only unreliable, but also a 50-cycle/120-volt system. That's why the Tropo Site and the Air Base Site have their own generators, I see you still have the School Brigade patch on your shirt. If you set all of your shirts and jackets on your bed with a First Brigade patch for each, then your mây-bâan will sew them on for you and return the old patches."

I responded, "Good to know, George," returning to my wall locker to lay my shirts and jackets on my bed with a First Brigade patch for each.

Walking with George to the Mess Hall, we swapped family folklore about our great-grandfathers in the Confederacy during the Civil War, our grandfathers in WWI, and our fathers in WWII. While we ate a scrumptious breakfast together and talked, I thought, "It's amazing how every generation finds something to go to war over. Heck, I even had ancestors who fought the Indians in the 1600s and 1700s when Virginia, the Carolinas and Georgia were colonies, and in the Revolution and War of 1812 against England."

When George and I finished breakfast and a relaxing cigarette, we were ready to face our generation's Vietnam War, and left to join the Tropo Platoon for morning formation. I found Jim in the last rank of the Platoon organizing the Air Base Squad, to his left were Spec-5 Phizer, a Spec-4 I didn't know, and Tommy. Falling into the left of Tommy, he said, "Good morning, Sandii, I see you've hit it off pretty good with the Georgia Rebel."

I responded, "You know how birds of a feather flock together,"

Tommy replied, "But I though we are birds of a feather."

I explained, "We are, Tommy, but we come from such a hybrid society that we're each covered with a variety of feathers, and our birds of a feather are on our heads."

Tommy responded, "That sounds reasonable to me."

Just then, Frank fell in to my left and said, "Sàwàtdíí, Sandii. That's the universal greeting in Thai for both 'hello' and 'goodbye.'

I asked, "So 'sàwàtdíí' works the same as 'aloha' in Hawaii?"

Frank replied, "Exactly."

Speaking with Frank, I saw past him in the 2nd Company Area across the street from ours, formations of helmeted Soldiers holding M-1 carbine rifles in both hands across their chests at port-arms, and what appeared to be an Officer side-stepping from man to man inspecting their rifles. I asked, "Hey, Frank, what's with that company across the street having a rifle inspection?"

Frank explained, "That's the Thai Infantry Battalion responsible for the defense of Camp Friendship's perimeter having their weapons inspected before mounting their guard positions. I've made friend with some of their NCOs and was shown some of their Battalion Area. It's basically the same as our Company Area, but instead of 8 men to a hooch with single beds and double wall lockers, they have 24 men crowded into a hooch with double beds and single wall lockers. Most of their Privates speak no English and are reluctant to speak with any of us when we're in uniform because they have a strict, no fraternization rule between their Privates and NCOs, who treat them pretty severely. Most of their NCOs speak a passable broken English and are fun to interact with. But, all of their Officers speak pretty good English as they are all at least College graduates, where English is taught all four years."

I heard yelled, "Company!" followed by a chorus of "Platoon!" then, "Attention!" and I faced forward and came to the position of attention, as did everyone else. Then I heard "Platoons Report!" and in sequence, each Platoon Sargent reported, "all present and accounted for." After which I heard, "Platoon Sergeants, take charge of your Platoon," and saw SFC Davidson make an about face and yell, "Tropo Platoon, dismissed for duty."

Jim said, "Okay, Frank, take Tommy and Sandii to the Motor Pool to get their Military Driver's License, and then show Tommy how to get to the Air Base Site on a Thai bus. The rest of you, let's go to the Motor Pool to get our truck and ride to the Air Base Site."

Tommy and I followed Frank to the Motor Pool building adjacent to the left of the chain-link gates to the Motor Pool's parking lot. On the front door of the hooch-size Motor Pool building was a sign that read *MOTOR POOL OFFICE, AUTHORIZED PERSONNEL ONLY*. The shutter over the window-framed space to the right of the Office door was open above an eight-foot wide porch across the front of the building that was supported on 18-inch high, concrete pillars.

Stepping onto the porch, I saw there was an 18-inch wide counter across framed window space along the back edge of this wall. Several feet beyond the counter was an OD metal desk with a fan on its left end, a stack of 2 wood bins marked *IN* and *OUT* on the desk's right end, and in the middle was a nameplate that read *SGT PETER POTTS, PARTS AND SUPPLY NCO*. Behind Sgt. Potts' desk was a swivel, metal chair with padded arms. Halfway to the back wall was a second OD metal desk with the same items on it and a nameplate that read *SSG ANGELO CORLINO, MOTOR POOL NCOIC*. In the right corner, behind the NCOIC's desk was a full-size refrigerator. Against the back wall, to the left of the refrigerator, was a credenza holding a large, steel coffee urn on its left end, and to the right of the urn were several plates with cookies, muffins, and donuts.

Leaning back against the right sidewall, in a swivel chair with arms behind the second desk, was the skinny SSG who directed us to fill the sandbags. In his right hand was a mug of coffee and in his left hand a donut. He was engaged in a jocular conversation with the First Sargent sitting across from him, who was a burly man with a square, heavy, jowled faced that looked much like a British Bulldog.

Against the front wall, on the other side of the door, were several 5-foot tall, OD filing cabinets. Along the left sidewall, I saw steel shelving with bins and boxes of automotive parts, assorted large mechanic's tools, and at the far end were numerous large, OD toolboxes with a large, red number stenciled on the end. Entering the back door was a line of Soldiers in grease-stained, OD BDUs leading to the toolboxes. I thought, "These must be the mechanics who slave over hot, greasy engines all day in this tropical heat and humidity. Am I glad to work in a clean, air-conditional building."

On the floor between Sgt. Potts and a mechanic, was an open large, OD toolbox with its tool-holding bin being held by the mechanic. In Sgt. Potts' left hand was a clipboard with a form on which he was checking the inventory of the tools.

Frank yelled, "Hey Pete, I've a couple of new guys here who need Military Driver's Licenses,"

Pete looked over his right shoulder with an irritated look on his face to make sure he wasn't about to yell at an Officer or Senior NCO for interrupting his inventory of the toolbox's contents. With a big smile of recognition, Pete said, "Mâi bpén rai, Frank, just have them fill out these forms and see John Williams. He's working on a deuce-and-a-half in stall 2," as he handed Frank two forms from the top drawer of the nearest file cabinet.

The form was a Military Driver's License Application requiring my name, rank, service number, unit in formation, work location, phone number, and if I have a State Driver's License, the State I'm licensed in, and then my signature. Below the lines for this information were check boxes for the vehicle type tested on, with a line for the name and signature of the tester.

When Tommy and I had filled out our Application forms, Frank led us through the Motor Pool gates, around the Motor Pool building to our left, and to the rear of a 2½-ton truck in the 2nd repair stall under a 20-foot high, corrugated metal roof. Under the raised hood of the truck, I saw a set of legs kneeling on the truck's left front fender. Frank yelled, "Hey John!"

I heard a frustrated voice from under the truck's raised hood yell, "What'd ya want?"

Frank replied, "Sgt. Potts said you were to check these two new guys out on a jeep and a ¾-ton for a Military Driver's License."

The frustrated voice responded, "sure, no problem. Just give me a sec to remove this valve cover."

Frank responded, "No rush. When you get to a stopping point will be fine."

The voice replied, "Thanks, I'll be with you in a sec."

A moment later, I saw a man, stripped to his waist with his hands and arm covered in black grease to his elbows, climb up from behind the hood and down the front of the truck to the ground. He then walked to a 55-gallon barrel of solvent, and dipped his hands and arms in it to remove the grease. After which he washed the solvent off with soap and water at a water trough next to the barrel of solvent. Walking towards us and drying himself with a red shop towel, I asked tentatively, "John, are you from Oregon?"

He replied, "Yep. In fact, I'm from the State of Jefferson."

I added, "And do you have a sister named Linda?"

John looked puzzled and asked, "Yea, how do you know that?"

I replied, "Linda and I had Geometry together our Sophomore year and I came to your home several times to help her. And you were a year ahead of us."

John smiled and said, "Oh yea, I remember you. You're the Math geek she called Sherman, right? You know, she's still dumb as a rock. How'd you get here?"

I explained, "Enlisted right out of high school in '67, went to Radio Repair School, and was just assigned to the Korat Air Base Radio Site. How about you?"

John replied, "Graduated in '66 and drafted January of '68. Because I had two years of auto shop in high school and was working as an auto mechanic, when I finished bootcamp, the Army luckily sent me to this paradise as a mechanic."

Frank stepped between us and said, "Okay, enough of the hometown reunion. You two can continue this later. But right now, John, you need to certify that Lynch and Meirhauser can drive a jeep and a ¾-ton truck for their Military Driver's License, okay?"

John replied, "Sorry, Specialist. I was carried away with the moment. Just let me have your Applications and follow me to the Office."

Handing our Applications to John, the three of us followed John to the front porch of the Motor Pool Office, where I saw Pete was now sitting behind his desk with a mug of coffee and donut on a paper towel on his desk, and smoking a cigarette while reviewing the toolbox inventory forms on a clipboard. I also saw the skinny SSG and bulldog-faced 1SGT still enjoying their gabfest at the back of the office.

John leaned on the counter and said, "Hey, Pete, I need Trip Tickets for a jeep and a ¾-ton."

Pete responded, "Mâi bpén rai, John," as he set down the clipboard and walked to a file cabinet. From the top and second drawers, he removed from them a clipboard with several forms on each. Closing the drawers, he walked to the counter, set the clipboards down on it, and said, "There you go, John, a jeep and a ¾-ton."

John said, "Thanks, Pete," as he printed his personal information and signed each Release Authorization Form. I saw the forms were already filled out with the vehicle's information. Removing the two forms, John handed them to Pete, who filled in his own information on the two forms and placed them in the *OUT* bin on his desk. Meanwhile, John filled in his information on the two Trip Authorization Forms, and when John had signed these two forms, Pete countersigned them and said as he gave the two clipboards back, "John, please teach them to drive properly in the left lane without crashing into anything."

John laughed and responded, "I shall make every effort," and to Tommy and me, "and that's how you get a trip ticket. Now, we'll see which hunks of junk you'll be driving."

Frank said, "There's only room for 3 in the cab of a ¾-ton, so I'll stay and pester Pete for a while."

John said, "Mâi bpén rai," as he led Tommy and me back to the Motor Pool's parking area.

Walking across the gravel parking area, I saw in its middle a line of several jeeps parked side by side with a similar line of ¾-ton trucks just beyond the jeeps. But, it was the first jeep in the line that caught my eye and I asked, "John, what's with the jeep that has chrome wheels, whitewall tires, and Tuck-N-Roll black leather seats?"

John laughed and explained, "That's the CO's jeep. He had is brother ship him the custom made chrome wheels with whitewall tires and

Tuck-N-Roll black leather seats from Stateside. It even has a custom made, solid oak steering wheel. Really pissed off Sgt. Corlino when he was ordered to have that stuff installed on the CO's jeep, but, RHIP, rank has its privileges, right?"

John found the jeep with the matching ID number on its hood ad said, "Okay, Sherman, you drive first."

Climbing into the jeep's driver seat, I found the starter button on the floor next to the clutch and started the engine, as John climbed into the passenger seat and Tommy hopped over the side onto the bench seat in the jeep's rear. John then said, "drive slowly out to the main road, and make a left turn into the left-hand lane. At the traffic light, turn left into the left-hand lane to the Hospital. When you get to the road in front of the Hospital, make a right turn into the left-hand lane. Then drive around the block on the right, staying in the left lane. When you've circled around back to the traffic light, drive through it and return here, where you'll park the jeep and turn off the engine. Any questions?"

Putting the jeep into first gear and releasing the clutch slowly to drive slow out of the parking area, I replied, "Sounds simple enough, John."

Having driven the prescribed route and parked the jeep, I understood why John repeatedly said, "into the left-hand lane." Every time I made a turn, my ingrained tendency was to turn into the right-hand lane, and I had to concentrate to make sure to turn into the left-hand lane. As Tommy and I changed places, I said, "Tommy, when you make each turn, it's really tricky not to drive into the right-hand lane and drive into the left-hand lane instead."

As Tommy started the jeep's engine, he said, "Thanks for the heads-up, Sandii."

John turned in his seat toward me and asked, "Sherman, why did he call you 'Sandii?'"

While Tommy drove the prescribed route, I explained to John the how and why Tommy had called me "Sandii." Then John said, "makes sense to me. Besides, I always thought 'Sherman' was kind of stuffy, so I much prefer calling you 'Sandii.'"

When Tommy had driven the circuitous route and had parked the jeep, John led us to our ¾-ton truck. With Tommy as the first driver and John sitting between us on the truck's bench seat, Tommy and I drove the same route as we had in the jeep with the truck. When I'd parked the truck, John then led us back to the Motor Pool Office, where he handed Pete the two clipboards with the Trip Tickets filled out. Then John gave Pete our Applications with the boxes for the jeep and ¾-ton truck driving test checked and signed, saying, "passed with flying colors."

Pete took the two clipboards and two Applications from John, and handing Tommy and I our Military Driver's Licenses, he said, "You two are now authorized to drive a jeep or a ¾-ton truck, but only on a military base. To drive any vehicle on civilian streets, you will need a Thai or International Driver's License."

Frank then said, "Great, now you can each drive to and from work. Sandii, I suggest you go straight to bed and get some sleep before it's too hot. Then, be in front of the Day Room by 6:35 to pick up our truck and drive to work. Tommy, you come with me and I'll show how to get to work on a Thai bus."

Turning to walk to my hooch for some shut eye, I saw the skinny SSG and the bulldog-faced 1SGT still sitting at the back of the Motor Pool Office having a gabfest. I thought, "Well, First Sargent Pachucio seems to be a pretty amiable fellow."

Walking to hooch NW-525, I said to myself, "it must already be 80 degrees and it's only 8:00. Soon as I get back to my hooch, I'm stripping to my skivvies and hitting the sack."

I woke to someone kicking my bed and yelling, "Get up, you lazy piece of shit." Looking up through sleep-blurred eyes, my vision was filled with the bulldog face of the 1SGT yelling into my face. "This company paid good money to put these fridges in all your hooches so you can keep your beer cold. Well, there ain't no beer in your fridge, so get your lazy ass up and go get a case of beer for your fridge. When I come back later, if I don't see a full case of beer in that fridge, I'm putting your dumb ass on report. You got that, puke-face?"

Jumping up to my on my OD BDUs, I said, "Yes First Sargent. Right away, First Sargent," as I thought, "What happened to the friendly First Sargent I saw in the Motor Pool Office that put a bug so far up his butt?"

Approaching the Howard Johnson, I passed a guy carrying a case of beer in the opposite direction and saw there were only 23 cans of beer in the case. Joining several guys lined up at the PX Annex's counter, the last one in the line was a PFC who said to me, "I see Spike got to you, too. Heck I was coming over here later to buy some beer to get me through the hot afternoon, anyway. The problem is, most of us aren't 21 and can buy only 23 cans of beer at a time, so I'll have to make a second trip to buy the 24th can of beer to fill the case."

I asked, "Who the heck is Spike?"

The PFC laughed and said, "Spike's what we call the First Sargent because that's what the CO calls him."

As the PFC bought his 23 cans of beer, I asked, "Can you hold up a sec while I buy my 23 cans of beer and explain, as we walk back to the Company Area, why the CO doesn't like Spike. But I have to admit the name fits."

The PFC explained, "The CO is Signal Corps and our previous First Sargent was Signal Corps as this is a Signal Corps company. Spike was a Transportation Corps SFC and the Motor Pool's NCOIC. But, SFC was as high as Spike could go in the Motor Pool. When our First Sargent was to rotate home, it turned out Spike had gone to bootcamp with the Battalion CO, and as Spike had been an excellent Motor Pool NCOIC, the Battalion CO did his old bootcamp buddy a favor and promoted him to be our new First Sargent.

"But, Spike doesn't know anything about communications and is totally incompetent to discuss anything with the CO on how to administer his Signal Corps Company to fulfill its mission. The only thing Spike knew about was being a vehicle mechanic, so the only thing cared about was the Motor Pool, and began to send guys on their off days to work details in the Motor Pool. This pissed everyone off, and now every morning the CO can be heard yelling, "Spike, get your ugly gear-head out of my HQ." So, Spike goes to visit the Motor Pool NCOIC to talk about the good old day for couple of hours before wandering around the Company Area to make our lives as miserable as his. At lunch, Spike goes to the NCO Club and spends the rest of the day in its air-conditioned space talking with his lifer buddies."

I responded, "Sounds like Spike is a perfect example of the Peter Principle."

The PFC asked, "The Peter Principle? What the heck is that?"

I explained, "The idea that a person in an organization will be promoted to his level of incompetence, and Spike is a victim of the Peter Principle."

CHAPTER 13

This is the Perfect Place to Work

Entering my hooch, I saw the five others in the hooch were all asleep in their beds with their fans oscillating back and forth, gently blowing cool air over their skivvy covered bodies. Quietly closing the door behind me, I went to the mini-fridge and silently placed the three 6-packs of Budweiser beer, each held together by a plastic holder, on the bottom shelf of the fridge, and the fourth plastic holder with five cans of beer on the top shelf, beneath the freezer compartment, where they could chill faster.

Closing the fridge door and quietly leaving the hooch to get the 24th can of Bud, I thought, "Having a bed at the front of the hooch near the fridge might be handy, but not worth the price if Spike is doing a beer inspection every morning. This trip, I'm buying another 23 cans of Bud and store some in my wall locker to put in the fridge tomorrow morning to beat Spike to the punch. Heck, it won't be a waste, it'll be an investment, as I'll be drinking them eventually."

Returning with my second 23-can case of Bud, I quietly set the three 6-packs of Bud in the bottom of my wall locker. Then I placed the 5-can pack on the top shelf of the fridge next to the other 5-pack, from which I removed a slightly chilled can of Bud and opened it with the church key hanging from around my neck. Sitting on the edge of my bed and drinking my beer, I looked at my wristwatch on the left wrist and thought, "heck, it's almost 10:00 and too warm to try getting any more sleep now. Might as well go to the PX and buy a fan, an electric razor and the power converter before lunch. Besides it's cooler now than it'll be after lunch, and I'll avoid being caught in that 2:15 torrential monsoon rain."

Finishing my can of Bud, I walked across the Company Area to the main street, where I boarded a Thai bus and sat crosswise on one of its hard bench seats. Exiting at the traffic light, I looked both ways when the light turned green to make sure a Thai bus was not close enough to drive through the intersection against the light to run me down. Once I was safely across the street, I entered the Camp's PX, where I located and bought a fan, an electric razor, a power converter to change the local 50-cycle/120-volts to the 60-cycle/110-volts required for the electric razor, and a carton of Pall Malls.

Returning to my hooch laden with my booty, I saw my five hoochmates were now up and each drinking one of my Budweiser beers. I heard Glen say, "Hey Sandii, thanks for the morning brew. It's nice to have a cold one when you get up from a hot, sweaty bed. And don't worry, we'll replace them after lunch. By the way, the guy across from you is Dick Kawalski from San Francisco, and the guy next to your bunk is Dan Swensen from Wisconsin. Dick and Dan, that's Sandii Lynch from Oregon, newly assigned to the Air Base Site. So, Sandii, what do you think of your first encounter with Spike?"

Opening the box to remove the fan, I replied, "As I see it, Spike is the perfect example of the Peter Principle."

Looking up, I saw questioning expressions on their five faces, and related what I'd learned from the PFC and the definition of the Peter Principle. After my explanation, they all laughed in agreement, and Ronnie asked, "I'm starved, how about we go to lunch, and then spend the afternoon drinking beer to stay hydrated and teaching Sandii the finer points of finesse in Double-Deck Pinochle?"

Having put everything in my wall locker, I said, "Sounds like a plan to me," and the six of us left for the Mess Hall. Then after lunch, we went to the Howard Johnson, where they each bought two 6-packs of beer, and a cold can of Budweiser to replace the ones they borrowed from me.

Returning to the hooch, I put four of the five cans of cold Bud in my wall locker and opened the fifth can with my church key, while they put one of their 6-packs in the fridge and removed a cold can of beer they'd each put in it before going to lunch, which they opened with their own church keys. After they'd put their other 6-pack in their wall lockers, then the four of us sat around the card table, with one sitting behind me on the end of a bed to Kibitz as we played and the sixth man-out watching.

When the last hand of a game was played, we'd take a piss break and get another can of beer. Then, I'd sit down to play the next game and the other five amicably rotated positions, so each would have a turn to play, giving me a diversity of strategies from other Kibitzers. By dinner time, I'd a well-rounded understanding to effectively play Double-Deck Pinochle.

At one point, I saw three house girls enter the hooch with arm loads of freshly laundered, pressed, and folded clothes. The first to enter was a skinny, older woman with red-stained teeth, several of which were missing. The second woman was in her twenties, taller, with a medium build, and a round, pockmarked face that would have been pretty, except for the scars. The 3rd woman was a teenager, very short and petite, with a cute, heart-shaped face. Each of them had long shiny black hair.

I saw Glen, who was then the man-out, walk to the older woman, make the wâai with the palms of hands together before his face, perform a low bow, and say, "Sàwàtdii, Maan-daa."

She responded in kind and said, "Sàwàtdii, lûuk-chaai[70] Glen."

When Glen rose up, he turned to me and said, "Sandii, you need to come and meet our hooch mother and our other mây-bâan."

Setting my cards facedown on the table, I stood up, walked to the older woman, and minicking Glen, made the wâai, bowed low and said, "Sàwàtdii, maan-daa."

Turning back to Maan-daa, Glen said, "Pûu-châai chûu, Sandii[71]."

The three women bowed and said, "Sàwàtdii, Sandii."

---

70 Means "Son."
71 "Man name, Sandii."

Then with a nod of the head to each, Glen said, "Sandii, this is our hooch mother, Maan-daa, which means 'mother,' and she treats each of us as a son. This is Súmat, and, this is Nit-nòi, which means 'a little bit,' because we can't wrap our tongues around her real name."

Returning to the Double-Deck Pinochle game, I watched in disappointment as Maan-daa set some of the clothes she was carrying on my bed and thought, "I'd rather have Nit-nòi as my mây-bâan."

Watching Sumat put some clothes on Tommy's bed, I thought, "now I can tell him who his mây-bâan is."

When they had left, I asked, "Glen, how come Maan-daa's mouth and teeth look like they've been bleeding?"

Glen explained, "From chewing beetlenut. It's a local remedy to numb the pain caused by tooth decay and gum disease. You'll see lots of older people using it.

At 5:00, I heard the bugle call for Mess. Finishing the hand we were playing, our beer, and our cigarettes, we went to our wall lockers to dress for dinner. Unlocking my wall locker, I saw that nobody else, except Tommy, had any laundry lying on their beds, like I did. Across the aisle from me, I asked, "Hey Dick, when did you put your laundry in your locker?"

Dick replied, "I didn't, Maan-daa did. If you give her the spare key to your padlock, she'll put everything away for you. Also, you don't have to worry about being ready for one of those inspections the lifers like to give, as she'll keep in perfect military order for you. And she won't dare steal anything from your locker because, not only will she lose her job, but Porntit will also file a criminal complaint. Then she'll have a criminal record and be called a'kîi-gìat', which literally means 'shitty honor,' a stigma no self-respecting Thai wants to be called. But don't leave anything laying out when you're gone, as a Thai sees it as something you don't want and can take it without considering it as stealing."

I said, "But mine is a combination lock."

Dick replied, "Then give her the combination. She won't forget it, even if you do."

Opening my wall locker, I began placing all the shirts and jackets on hangers I'd left on my bed with the First Brigade patches to replace my School Brigade patches. I saw each sported the First Brigade patch at the correct place on the left sleeves. Looking close, I saw the hand stitches looked almost machine done. Having hung up my shirts and jackets, I put on a fresh set of OD BDUs to wear for dinner and to work. Seeing the First Brigade patch on my left sleeve, I thought, "now I'm definitely a member of the 442nd and nobody will be able to see I'm a newbie."

I asked, "Hey Dick, I've had a 6-pack of beer since lunch and don't even feel a buzz. Why's that?"

Dick explained, "We sweat so much in this heat, the beer keeps us hydrated, so the alcohol in the blood is not only denatured by your liver, it's also sweated out through the skin. I think that's why they sell it to us so cheap. Did you notice when Glen introduced you to our mây-bâan, he didn't point with his finger but nodded to each with his head?"

I replied, "Yea, they told us at our orientation in Bangkok never to point at a Thai with your finger or sit with the bottom of your foot toward a Thai, as it's interpreted to mean they're equal to your finger or foot, and is an insult."

Dick said, "At least some of you were paying attention."

I asked, "So, are you and Dan going to Korat tonight?"

Dick replied, "No. I'm a one-digit midget,[72] and so short that I need a stepladder to tie my boot laces. I've orders transferring me to the Army Presidio in San Francisco next week for my discharge, as San Francisco is my hometown. With all the rioting Stateside, I extended my tour of duty here to the end of my enlistment, which is next week. I've been here nineteen months, and it's been great. But for the last two months, I haven't been going to Korat to get laid, because I want to be clean when I get home. That's what a lot of guys do before going home. Looks like everyone's ready to go to dinner."

Returning to the hooch after dinner, I saw it was nearly time to meet Tommy with the truck on his 1835 meal run. Rolling up my toilet kit and a set of skivvies in a towel, I heard Dick say, "looks like you plan on shaving at the Air Base site to avoid the crowd in the morning here."

I responded, "That's the plan. Live and learn," not adding the plan included a shower.

---

72   The number of digits in the number of days someone has left in the country.

By 6:35, I was waiting in the dim light of dusk at the front of the Day Room with Glen, Ronnie, and Stony, and several others who worked at the Tropo Site. A minute later, I saw the dimmed headlights of a ¾-ton truck turning onto Company C's roadway from the direction of the Air Base. Recognizing Tommy's smiling face behind the truck's steering wheel, we waved at each other as he stopped in front of the Day Room. As he opened the door, I asked, "How was your first day, Tommy?"

He replied, "Very busy. Fortunately, I'm already trained on the equipment and troubleshooting the circuits but getting a handle on those 252 in-house circuits is going to take a while. I don't envy you having to do that and cross-training as a Frame Tech, too."

Responding as I climbed into the driver's seat and closed the door, "Yea. It looks like I'll be getting a crash course on being a Frame Tech. At least Bob and Frank already know all that stuff, so there won't be a rush for me to cross-train. By the way, I met your mây-bâan this afternoon. Her name is Súmat, in her twenties, and would be pretty if it wasn't for the pockmarks on her face. Also, if you give her the spare key or combination to your padlock, she'll keep your locker inspection ready."

Tommy replied, "Thanks for the info, Sandii, and I hope the night goes good for you."

Driving toward the Motor Pool, I said, "Mâi bpén rai, Tommy," and made a U-turn to the right. Passing the Day Room on the left side of the roadway, I saw a 2½-ton truck stopped before it with the Tropo Site's day shift crew climbing out of its cab or down its tailgate, as the night shift crew waited to climb in and go to work. Turning right into the left lane of the main street, I drove the 100 yards to the Korat Air Base gate, stopped, and showed the Trip Ticket and my ID card to the AP at the gate. After he gave them a cursory look and waved me through the gate, I drove to the street's end at the tarmac, and turned right into the left lane of the frontage road. At the first road to the right, I turned right into the left lane and continued to my right into the Base Exchange's parking lot, stopping the truck in the reserved spot for the 442nd Sig. Bn.

Exiting the trucks, I saw a covered light above the door illuminating it and its steps. Mounting the steps and opening the door. I entered the hallway with my towel wrapped bundle in my left hand. Even though it was dark outside, I still felt the physical assault of the

20-degree drop in temperature from outside to inside. Also, having enter from the darkness outside, my eyes were assaulted by the bright florescent lights inside.

Walking to the last door on the right at the end of the hallway, I entered the Latrine and placed my bundle on the top shelf of the locker with my name on it. Exiting the Latrine, I saw in the Site Office across the hallway, Jim, Bob, and two other men in civilian clothes. Also in the Office, I saw a nice-looking woman, 5-foot 7, with brown hair and a medium build, who was standing to the left, watching the men talk. Proceeding to the Operations Room, I saw Frank and the Spec-4 I'd seen at formation standing by the desk.

Frank saw me and said, "Sandii, this is Jack. He's the Microwave Repairman for the team we're relieving. He was telling me how impressed he and Bill were with Tommy, today. Jack, this is Sandii, your counterpart on our team."

Jack said, "Glad to meet you, Sandii. And don't worry about cross-training as a Frame Tech. With all the electronics we were taught at Microwave School, I had no problem learning it, and I'm sure you won't either. If you can read a schematic, then the equipment is pretty straightforward. Well now that my counterpart is here, my tîi-lók is waiting at home for me, see you later."

As Jack hurried away, I asked, "Frank, I just saw a woman in the Site Office. Is she the Tech Rep, Bill?"

Frank laughed and replied, "as far as I know, there are no female Tech Reps, and her name is Judy, not Bill. She's Jim's wife, and works part-time at the Base Exchange. She schedules her workdays to be on the days Jim works, so they can have lunch together at the Base NCO Club, and ride a bus home together to the Jomsurang Hotel in Korat. It's where most of the families live for men stationed at Camp Friendship and Korat Air Base."

Seeing Bob walk around the corner of the first row of racks, I said, "Sàwàtdii, Bob." And he responded, "Sàwàtdii, Sandii. Glad to see you found your way safely here. Hey, Frank, Jim wants to see you in the Site Office."

I asked, "Does that usually happen? Tommy and I were told to go directly to the Operations Room and relieve our counterpart when reporting for work. That only the Team Leader was to go to the Site Office for Shift Change Report."

Bob replied, "You're right, Sandii, and this is not usual. I can only say that Frank is getting good news that's bad news to him. So how'd your day go? Did you get some sleep before it got too hot?"

I frustratedly replied, "Spike, our First Shirt, literally kicked me out of my bed and ordered me to buy a case of beer to put in our mini-fridge. Because I'm not 21, I can only buy 23 cans, and had to make two trips to the PX Annex. So, no, I didn't get any sleep before it got too hot, which really pissed me off. But, I had a good afternoon drinking beer and learning to play Double-Deck Pinochle."

Bob responded, "Yea, I've heard others complain vehemently about Spike. I'm surprised nobody has fragged him. But, I've heard rumors the guys rotating home next week have some payback planned."

Just then, Frank returned saying, "Damn lifers are having me promoted to Spec-5 to replace Dick Kawalski as a team leader at Korat Tropo when he's discharged from the Army next week. Not that I mind being promoted, but I hate the idea of having to work with all those lifers there. I was figuring I'd be promoted in four months to replace Phizer when he leaves. But, Jim did arrange it so I won't have to start there for two more weeks, when the new group of replacements arrive, as it will be a safety issue. Plus, Sandii will need to be brought up to speed as the newbie won't know anything about our in-house circuits."

Bob responded, "Sandii, I told you it's good news that's bad news to him. But, that means we'll need to get cracking if we only have two weeks to bring you up to speed on all 252 of our in-house circuits. We'll put the training on the breakout circuits to the back burner and can OJT[73] Sandii on that gear while we're troubleshooting it and focus on the circuit interface racks in the Grand Canyon. In the meantime, Sandii, anytime we're not teaching you something, I want you sitting at the desk memorizing all the data on that chart above it. Any questions?"

I asked, "What do you mean by the 'Grand Canyon?'"

Frank replied, "Sandii, you see the space between those two tall rows of racks?"

I answered, "Yes."

---

73   On the job training.

Frank explained, "Well that's our Grand Canyon, and it's where we do 90 percent of our work in our Operations Room when one of our 252 in-house circuits is reported out to see if the source of the outage is in-house and our problem, or not in-house and someone else's problem.

Bob said, "Frank, why don't you continue with Sandii, while I start the log for this shift."

Frank responded, "Mâi bpén rai, Bob. Come on, Sandii, and I'll get you started on how we work in the Grand Canyon."

I followed Frank to the 3rd stack of racks on their right, where stopped, pointed to the top of the stack, and asked, "Do you see the 4-inch speaker at the top of this stack?"

Looking up at a round, 4-inch speaker in a 6-inch high rack, I said, "yes."

Frank continued, "That monitors the Order Wire for all the Radio Sites in Thailand and is where we usually first learn of a problem with our 252 in-house circuits. Think of it as a party phone line where nobody hangs up. Eventually your ear will become so attuned to most of the ID codes for our circuits, that you'll be half asleep and the mention of one of those 252 ID codes will wake you.

"Now, on either side of this rack are, ironically, two Lynch phones. The left one is labelled 'Order Wire' and is for us talk on the Order Wire. The right one is to talk on any audio circuit coming through our Site. Any questions?"

Looking at the two Lynch phones, I saw they were black handsets, hanging vertically from handset hooks at elbow height. I also saw in the racks between the two handsets, at shoulder height, were five 2-inch racks with twelve ¼-inch jack holes, equally spaced across the 18-inch racks. Above each jack hole was a label with a circuit ID code. To the right of these five racks was an identical set of five 2-inch high racks with twelve jack holes similarly labelled. I thought, "Okay, these are the send and receive pairs of the sixty audio circuits."

Looking to my left, I saw in the two stacks of racks adjacent to the six teletype machines, were two other matching sets of racks with jack holes. But these were twelve 2-inch high racks, each with sixteen labelled jack holes across each rack, and thought, "okay, these are the send and receive pair of 192 teletype circuits, which totals 252 circuits."

Then facing Frank, I said, "I remember from microwave school, each microwave signal can have up to five carrier groups, and each group twelve audio channels, and each audio channel can contain a tone pack with sixteen teletype channels. In these two stacks with the Lynch phones, there are five sets of twelve audio circuits, which would be five groups of twelve audio channels that would be 60 of our 252 in-house circuits. On the other side of the Grand Canyon, next to the teletype machines are 12 sets of 16 teletype circuits, which would be the 12 tone-packs with the 16 teletype channels each that account for the other 192 in-house circuits. Am I correct in this deduction?"

Frank yelled, "Hey Bob, this is one bright guy for a microwave jockey. He's already figured out the breakout configuration of our 252 in-house circuits."

Bob turned in his swivel chair and said, "that's great, Frank. Then we shouldn't have any problem bring Sandii up to speed by the time you have to go to Korat Tropo in two weeks, if he can get a handle on each of our 252 in-house circuits."

For the next several hours Bob and Frank explained to me in detail, each piece of test equipment in the racks of the Grand Canyon and how they were used to troubleshoot any outage of an audio or teletype circuit. Several times I heard amongst the frequent chatter on the Order Wire speaker, "Korat Base." Then we'd stop and I'd watch Bob or Frank talk on the Order Wire handset, and the other make notes in a spiral bound notebook, as they worked together with various patch cords between the test equipment and a pair of audio or teletype jacks to resolve an outage. Several times we took a smoke break and I'd study the date on the chart over the desk.

On each end of the various lengths of patch cords used to connect the ¼-inch jack holes of the circuits with the ¼-inch jack holes in the test equipment, there was a ¼-inch diameter, 1½-inch long probe with a 2-inch plastic grip. Each probe had a tip, ring and sleeve. The metal tip to receive the signal from the in-house breakout equipment, the metal ring connected to the ground for the signal, and the metal sleeve to send the signal on to the customer. Between each metal part was a plastic insulator.

Just before I left on my 10:55 meal run, Frank took me to one of many hooks between the racks in the Grand Canyon holding the patch cords. There, he selected a four-foot long patch cord, and said, "Sandii, our test to determine if you've spent enough time in the Grand Canyon to be certified Frame Tech is when you can do this."

Then, holding one end of the patch cord in his right hand, he flipped the other end up into the air, and when it fell back down, I saw there was a knot in the patch cord.

Frank then said, "And you'll be an Expert Frame Tech when you can do this," as he flipped the patch cord again and I saw a 2nd knot, "and a Master Frame Tech when you can do this," as he flipped the patch cord again made a 3rd knot.

I asked, amazed, "how long did it take you to learn that?"

Frank replied, "To get the first knot, it took a couple of months, and a while longer to get the 2nd and 3rd knot. Now that you have that challenge to look forward to, you can go to midnight chow."

Arriving at the Company Area, I saw the Tropo Site's 2½-ton truck parked in front of the Day Room and parked behind it. Quickly exiting my truck, I entered the Mess Hall, and saw Glen standing at the counter. Picking up a tray, I looked to see what was cooking on the griddles, and saw it was a mix between breakfast and lunch, and there were only two Thai cooks, instead of four. I said to the T-shirted Soldier sitting on the stool, "I'll have two double-cheeseburgers with lettuce, tomato, pickle, onions, and mustard with fried onion rings."

Sliding my tray next to Glen's, I said, "Hey Glen, I found out Frank Howell is being promoted to Spec-5 to replace Dick as Team Leader when he leaves next week, and is he pissed."

Glen looked at me and said, "Hey Sandii, I can believe that. Frank hates lifers, and I know he loves working at the Air Base. That'll leave you short on your Team. Any word who the lucky dog is from Tropo who'll replace Frank, because I'd love to work there?"

I replied, "They plan to let him stay at the Air Base until the new batch of guys arrive in a couple of weeks and replace him with a newbie."

As Glen received his order of a Western omelet, sausages, and pancakes, he responded, "Isn't that going to leave your team short of an experienced Frame Tech at mealtime?"

I replied, "They're rushing my cross-training to have me pretty much up to speed, having me focus on memorizing our 252 in-house circuits. Sounds like a lot, but I already have a handle on how to do it."

Following Glen as I received my order, he said, "well, if you learn all those circuits as fast as you've learned to play Double-Deck Pinochle, then I believe you can do it."

Arriving back at the Operations Room, as Frank left on his meal run, Bob led me to the back, lifted a two-foot square section of the floor, and said, "I know you didn't get any extra sleep this morning and you look plenty tired to me, so help me pull this out from under the floor."

Looking down through the hole in the floor, I was surprised to see a rolled-up mattress. Helping Bob pull it up onto the floor, he said, "Frank and I talked it over and agreed that after you get a couple of hours sleep, you won't be dosing off while you're trying to cross-train enough in the two weeks before Frank leaves to be effective as a Frame Tech. And, before you leave on your 6:35 meal run, we want you to have a nice, hot shower so you won't have any problem getting some sleep before it gets too hot. But, this time, make sure there's plenty of beer in the fridge, okay?"

I replied, "This is really thoughtful of you two, because I'm bone tried. And don't worry, I already have three 6-packs of beer in my locker to remedy that issue with Spike," and thought, "even if it's close to those lifers at Korat Tropo, this is the perfect place to work."

CHAPTER 14

I LOVE YOU, OVER.

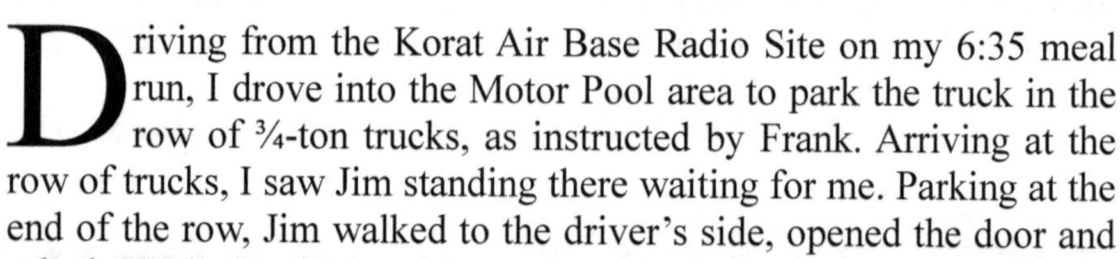

Driving from the Korat Air Base Radio Site on my 6:35 meal run, I drove into the Motor Pool area to park the truck in the row of ¾-ton trucks, as instructed by Frank. Arriving at the row of trucks, I saw Jim standing there waiting for me. Parking at the end of the row, Jim walked to the driver's side, opened the door and asked, "Well, Sandii, how'd your first night shift go?"

Handing Jim the Trip Ticket clipboard, I replied, "Aside from Frank's tirade about being transferred to Tropo in two weeks, things went pretty good. Bob and Frank think I'll be up to speed to work on the in-house circuits by the time Frank's replacement arrives."

Jim responded, "Glad to hear that. I need to check the fluid levels before formation, so I'll see you tonight."

Turning for my walk to the Mess Hall, I saw Jim unlatch the hood-clamps to open the hood. At the Mess Hall's counter, I picked up a tray and ordered a Western omelet, sausages and pancakes. When my breakfast order was placed on my tray, I said to the Thai cook, "Kup koon mâak, krup," and filled three glasses with chocolate milk. Sitting at a table, I quickly ate my delicious meal, and then lit a cigarette to smoke on the way to my hooch, as I wanted to hit the sheets and get as much sleep as possible before it got too hot.

Arriving at my hooch, I took two 6-packs of Budweiser out of my wall locker and put them in the fridge to foil Spike's animosity to the Signal Corps. Then stripping to my skivvies, I drew back the blanket on my bed, turned on my fan sitting on the floor, and thought as I lay on the white sheets, "I need to find something to put my fan on."

Waking several hours later to the 11:00 bugle call for Mess, I found myself on sweat-drenched sheets, despite the cooling breeze from my fan, my mouth and throat were parched. Rising form my wet sheets, I padded barefoot in my skivvies to the fridge, where I removed a cold can of Bud and punched two V-shaped holes in its top with my church key. Quenching my parched mouth and throat, I walked to the front door and opened it enough to aim a stream at the piss tube.

Turning toward my bed, I saw Dick standing behind me in his skivvies with an open can of beer, waiting his turn for the piss tube. I said, "Sàwàtdii, Dick. Say, where can I find a crate to put my fan on?"

Dick replied, "Sàwàtdii, Sandii. Heck, I'm so short, I have to look up to see a snake, so you can have mine if you want. Just give me some time to clear my stuff from it. Yea, finding a good crate takes some scrounging around. Besides, mine already has a shelf in it to put books and magazines on."

I responded, "Kup koon mâak, Dick. You know, Frank is really pissed he'll be replacing you as a Team Leader at Tropo, even with the promotion to Spec-5."

Dick said, "So I've heard. Believe me, between being short-handed and the lifers riding my butt to get things done while they sit in the Site Office drinking coffee, being a Team Leader at Tropo is no picnic. And the pay difference doesn't come close to make up for all the hassle."

I commented, "Heck, Dick, the way you act with us, I didn't even think you were a Spec-5."

Dick responded, "Only lifers power trip on their rank, and I'm no lifer. Heck, when I was promoted, they wanted to move me to a 4-man, NCO hooch, because they think it's a breach of good order and discipline for an NCO to live and fraternize with his men. But, I told them where to stick it, because I like living with my friends. Not like that Snooty Pfizer you have at the Air Base. That's who they should send to Tropo instead of Frank. But, I wouldn't wish that brown-noser as Team Leader on anybody. You ready for lunch, Sandii?"

I answered, "Ready as I'll ever be," as I thought, "It's good Pfizer works in the Site Office, if he's half the lifer Dick says."

Exiting the front door, Dick asked, "Mind if we stop at the Mail Room on the way to the Mess Hall? I'd like to check for mail."

I replied, "Mâi bpén rai, Dick, I'm in no rush."

Walking into Company C's HQ, we made the quick left through the Mail Room's doorway. As Dick checked his mail slot, I saw several slots to the right of his, a label that read LYNCH, SHERMAN over a mail slot. Seeing no mail in the slot, I thought, "Not unexpected as it'll take a week before anyone I wrote to Stateside receives the letters with my address for here."

Looking to my left as we exited the Mail Room, I saw PFC Schultz and Miss Porntit working at their desks. Turning to my right and walking out HQ's front door, I asked, "Dick, today is Saturday, so why are Schultz and Porntit at work?"

Dick explained, "This is a Theater of War, and there's no day off from a war. The closest Camp Friendship comes to a day off is Sunday, when things slow down. But we still have morning formation, like any other day. All nonessential personnel work a 9-hour day, six days a week, but the offices never close. There's always somebody on duty to man the phones. During non-business hours, members of the Headquarters Platoon stand Charge of Quarters, or CQ duty in the HQ. If we were working a Radio Site Stateside, we'd be divided into four teams working an average 42-hour week, not three teams working an average 56-hour week, plus being subject to work details on our off days. If we need gas for our trucks on Sunday, Camp Friendship's PLO is open."

Leaving the Mess Hall after a good tongue wag with Dick over lunch and a cigarette, Dick asked, "How about we each get a couple of 6-packs of beer from the Howard Johnson on our way back?"

I replied, "I've never turned down an opportunity to buy beer."

Returning to the hooch with two 6-packs of Budweiser to put in my wall locker, I found Glen, Ronnie and Stony looking for a fourth to play Pinochle. As Dick said he needed to pick up two suits from a tailor in Korat, and Dan was not in the hooch, then I happily agreed to be Glen's partner. As the cards were being dealt, Glen asked, "Sandii, you ready to test your ability and play for a penny a point, quarter a set and fifty cents a game?"

I responded, "Glen, if you're willing to take a chance on me as your partner, then I'm ready to play for real."

Playing cards all afternoon, drinking beer to stay hydrated and taking piss breaks between games, the hot afternoon past quickly. When I heard the bugle call for Mess at 5:00, Glen and I were down less than a dollar, and the score had teeter-tottered all afternoon. Getting up from the table to go to dinner, Glen motioned me aside and said, "Sandii, you were a great partner. How'd you like to be my regular partner? As regular partners, we'd eventually read each other's playing style well enough to win against any other team on a regular basis."

I replied, "Win, lose or draw, I enjoy having you as a partner. So, heck yeah. I think we can give those damn-Yankees a run for their money."

During the afternoon, when our mây-bâan had entered the hooch with our clean laundry, I excused myself from the table for a minute to greet Maan-daa and hand her a piece of paper with my combination on it. Opening my wall locker later to take out a fresh set of OD BDUs to wear for dinner and work, I saw all my clothes on hangers were equally spaced and in proper military order. Sliding open the two bottom drawers, I saw every item was precisely folded in place. Locking my wall locker, I thought, "Very good, Maan-daa. Even my bootcamp DI would be hard put to find any fault inspecting this wall locker."

The four of us left for the Mess Hall, and after a delicious dinner and relaxing cigarette, we returned to our hooch to get ready for work. Retrieving a set of skivvies, socks and toilet kit from my wall locker and rolling them up in a towel, I joined the others at front door to walk to the front of the Day Room by 6:35 for our rides to work. When Tommy drove up in the truck, I asked, "So, how'd it go today, Tommy?"

Exiting the truck, Tommy tiredly replied, "Way too busy this morning. I think everybody and his brother Stateside was sending last minute orders before going home for the weekend. Made me realize they're a half day behind us. I mean, it may be Saturday morning here, but it's late Friday afternoon there. Even Jim and Roger had to pitch in and help for a while because a few of the outages were in-house with the breakout gear. But it's been a quiet afternoon, which gave us a chance to catch up. So, you should have a pretty quiet night. Oh, yeah, there was a lot of chatter on the teletype news wires about protests and riots in San Francisco, L.A., Chicago and Boston. But that's nothing really new, is it?"

I replied, "It does sound like a rerun of old news. See ya tomorrow, Tommy," as I started the truck.

Arriving at the Radio Site and putting my towel wrapped bundle in my Latrine locker, I again saw Jim's wife in the Site Office as I walked to the Operation Room. Entering it, I saw Frank and Jack by the desk laughing and asked, "What's the joke?"

Jack replied, "That, if those hippies rioting Stateside ever found out what's happening in Thailand, they'd rush to Washington, D.C., and burn down the White House. As it is, their riots are so routine, they're becoming humdrum. If it wasn't for the liberal press keeping it on the front page, they'd stop. Instead, their riots against the Vietnam War just keep going on and on. The irony is, without the support of the riots by the press, North Vietnam would've seen it can't possibly win against the might of the U.S. military, and would've packed up and gone home after the failure of their all-out Tet[74] offensive that severely depleted the NVA."[75]

I responded, "Yea, Tommy told me how the news wires keep chattering on about the same old riots Stateside. I can certainly see the irony that it's our own press that's fanning the flames of this war and not Ho Chi Mihn[76] in Hanoi. Well, nothing is better for the press than a war to report on. Tommy also told me how busy you guys were this morning, but how it quieted down in the afternoon."

Jack complained, "Quiet for him and Bill. But, since Bill was going over with Tommy how we locate circuit outages, I had to spend the afternoon logging our outages from the morning. Enough shoot'n the bull, I need to get home or my tîi-lók will accuse me of being a butterfly."[77]

As Jack hurried from the Operations Room, Frank said to me, "Talking about logging outages, now is as good a time as any to in-

---

74   Vietnamese Lunar New Year's festival, celebrated late January or early February.

75   North Vietnam Army.

76   Chairman of the Communist Government of North Vietnam.

77   Chasing women like a butterfly flits from flower to flower.

troduce you to our Site Log. So, pull up a chair next to me and I'll go over it with you."

Sitting down in the straight chair next to Frank, Bob sat in the swivel chair in front of the desk, and I watched as Bob opened an 8½-inch wide, 1-inch long by ½-inch thick, OD canvas covered book titled, "Korat Air Base Radio Site Log, 1968 Log Vol. II," with a bookmark between two of the pages. I saw at the top corner of each page was printed with a sequential number in red. Also, each page had ¼ -inch spaced, horizontal blue lines and a vertical red line one inch from the left edge. The left-hand page already had entries with Zulu times written in the left margin with a corresponding entry noting what happened at the time.

Frank explained, "Sandii, this is our Site Log to record every in-house circuit outage with the Zulu time it began, the circuit ID and its priority. Then the Zulu time service is restored, the circuit ID, the symptoms, the location of the outage, and action taken to restore service. If the circuit is a tone-pack, record the circuit ID of just the tone-pack, not the IDs of the teletype circuits it contains. If any of the teletype circuits are not returned to service with the tone-pack, which often happens with the crypto circuits, then the time and reason for the delay of returned service is recorded. Each entry is initialed by the person making the entry.

I then saw Frank pick up an 8½-by-11-inch, spiral bound notebook with many of its pages torn out, and he said, "This is our Temporary Log we take notes in during the circuit outage. When we have time later, the notes are written into the Site Log, and then torn out and thrown away. Initially, you'll make notes in the Temporary Log, while Bob and I work on the circuit outages.

"The Site Log is not just to document circuit outages. It also provides continuity from shift to shift, and is a troubleshooting and preventive maintenance tool. If you're having a problem locating the source of an outage, you can look back for the same symptoms and what was the solution. Also, if the same part in other equipment has failed, then you can schedule PMs for Preventive Maintenance on related equipment to avoid future outages. I suggest you not only read today's entries when you get an opportunity, but the entire Site Log for a feel of outage cycles. For instance, this morning's outages were not a fluke, but happens every Saturday morning when everybody Stateside sends a flood of messages Friday afternoon before their weekend. Also, on Monday evenings here when they go back to work Monday mornings responding messages received over the weekend. Any questions?"

I replied, "Sounds reasonable to me. I'll add reading the Site Log to memorizing the chart over the desk," as I saw Bob arriving from the Site Office. He said, "So, what have you two been up to while I've been hobnobbing in the Site Office?"

Frank answered, "I've been explaining to Sandii our Site Log and the use of the Temporary Log, and telling him why we have a spike in outages on Saturday mornings and Monday evenings."

Bob responded, "Good job, Frank. Why don't you focus with Sandii on using the patch cords to isolate an outage? And, Sandii, I was talking to Roger about inviting you to our compound in Korat tomorrow night for us to be better acquainted in an informal setting. Four of us Tech Reps have our homes in a gated compound where we live with our tîi-lóks. If you drink before you get there, it's okay. But don't bring any booze with you because Jim Horn, from Tropo, considers it such a serious breach of etiquette, as to have you barred from the compound. What do you think?"

I replied, "Sounds great, but I haven't been to Korat, so how will I find your compound?"

Bob asked, "How about you, Frank, could you bring Sandii?"

Frank replied, "It'd be a real hassle to ride a bus from Korat to here, pick up Sandii and then ride back to Korat, don't you think? I'm sure some of the Tropo guys will be going who could bring him. Sandii, do you know anyone at Tropo working the night shift tonight?"

I answered, "There's three guys in my hooch who're working the night at Tropo. I'm sure at least one of them can take me to the compound."

Bob responded, "Great. Now that's sorted, Frank, you show Sandii how to use the patch cords to isolate outages, while I start the entries in the Site Log for our shift?"

Frank said, "Come on Sandii. Let's get you acquainted with using the patch cords?"

Following Frank into the Grand Canyon, I watched as he picked up the Lynch phone not used with the Order Wire, and showing me the jack plug on the loose end of one of the two Y-cords plugged into the bottom of the handset, asked, "Do you know what kind of plug this is?"

I replied, "It's a tip-ring-sleeve plug used for stereo headsets," which confused me because the plug for a handset usually had a 2-wire tip-sleeve plug, not a 3-wire tip-ring-sleeve plug.

Frank responded, "Very good. As you pointed out yesterday, each of these two sets of five racks have twelve jack holes in each rack for the audio circuits. The five racks on the left are from the breakout circuits for the receiver side of the microwave radio, and the five racks on the right are to the breakout circuits to the transmit side of the microwave radio.

"Each jack hole has two wires to the breakout equipment and two wires to the customer. When you put a plug into a jack hole, it opens the contacts between the two sets of wires, and the circuits are close-looped through the three wires going to the handset. By putting one plug from the handset into a receiving audio jack hole and the other plug from the handset into the corresponding transmit audio jack hole, you can listen and talk to the customers on both ends of the audio circuit. You understand so far?"

I replied, "Okay, I've got the picture. But what if you only want to talk with the customer here or on the other end?"

I watched as Frank selected two other Y-connected patch cords, and showing me the plug on one of them, he said, "If you look at the plug on this patch cord, you see it has the ring and sleeve, but no tip. Using this patch cord, it allows you talk or test the circuit with the local customer and see if there's a problem between the local customer and us, while blocking the signal to the breakout circuits."

Then Frank held up the plug on the other Y-patch cord and said, "If you look at the plug on this patch cord, you see it has the tip and sleeve, but no ring. Using this patch cord, it blocks the circuit with the local customer, and allows you to talk or test the signal to the breakout circuits to determine if the problem is with our breakout circuits, the customer at the other end, or somewhere in between. Does that answer the question?"

I replied, "Very clever. But if you're not careful, you could cross-connect two circuits."

Frank responded, "That's true, you do have to be careful not to cross-connect two circuits. But sometimes we get orders from Quad-C

A to do that when they need circuits rerouted to bypass a Radio Site that has gone off the air. But now I want to point out the terminal ends of our five groups. If you look at the label beneath each row of jacks, you'll see they read from top to bottom; Group 1, Korat Tropo; Group 2, Korat Tropo; Group 3, Tansanut Tropo; Group 4, Sattahip Tropo; and Group 5, Udon Tropo.

"The audio channels of the two groups to Korat Tropo are broken out and terminate with their customers on Camp Friendship, or broken out and rerouted into groups to their three MRC-98 microwave radios to other Air Base sites in Thailand. The other three groups do not breakout at Korat Tropo, but are re-transmitted as groups to Tonsanut, Sattahip and Udon, where they are broken out. This saves Korat Tropo from having too many through circuits to deal with by dumping them on us at Korat Air Base to give us something to do in our spare time," to which Frank laughed.

Until I left for my 10:55 midnight meal run, Frank had me practice and then tested on using the various types of patch cords, not only between the audio receive and send circuits, but also the teletype receive and send circuits, and the various kinds of test equipment in the Grand Canyon.

Arriving at the Mess Hall, I saw Glen was also on the 10:55 meal run. Sitting across from Glen with my meal tray, I said, "Glen, it's good to see you're also on the 10:55 meal run."

Glen responded, "Hey, partner. Yeah, I always try to make the 10:55 run. So, how's it going with you?"

I replied, "Frank's been showing me how to use the patch cords."

Glen said, "Yeah, those can be a real spaghetti-fest sometimes."

I asked, "I've been invited to the Tech Rep's compound tomorrow night, and wondered if you're planning to go, so you could show me how to get there?"

Glen replied, "Sure thing. I never miss a chance to go to their compound and relax in a non-military environment. In fact, we can make a day of it after lunch and show you some of the sites. But, I need to warn you, we always hang out at Jim Horn's, and he has four house rules that if you break, you'll be banned from his home. On your first visit to this home, you're shown where the refrigerator is and you're welcome to anything in it, but never ask again. Second, do not bring your own booze, he's got plenty to drink. Third, no shoptalk, to include the military. And fourth, don't pick the roses, and he does have a beautiful rose garden."

I responded, "Yea, they told me about not bringing any booze, but thanks for the heads up on the other three rules. And, that'll be great if you show me around Korat so I can get an idea of its layout and some landmarks."

Returning to the Air Base, I told Bob, "Glen Milton at Tropo said he'd be happy to show me how to get to the compound. While Frank's on his meal run, I'll start copying onto a piece of paper the info from the chart. I've found it's the best way for me to memorize things."

Bob removed a spiral bound notebook and a clipboard from the desk's bottom drawer, and handing them to me, he said, "Here, Sandii, you can use these, so long as it doesn't leave the building, as that information is classified Top Secret."

I said, "Thanks, Bob," as I sat in the straight chair by the desk and began copying the info on the 252 in-house circuits.

Several minutes later, I heard the phone on the desk rind and picking up the handset, Bob said, "442nd Signal Battalion, Korat Air Base, Bob Greer speaking." Then, "Well hey, Ted, how's the PBX[78] world goin? ... Excellent. Which circuit? ... Thank, Ted. How'd you enjoy the Scotch? ... Great. I'll talk to you later," and hung up the phone.

Turning to me, Bob asked, "Sandii, how'd you like to call your family or girlfriend Stateside for free?"

I replied, "Thanks, Bob, but I tried one of those MARS[79] calls once and found having to say, 'I love you, over,' to be very irritating."

Bob explained, "This is not a MARS phone call. It's an actual phone call you'd pay $4.00 a minute for, but it's free. That was Tech Sgt. Ted Mosby at the Base Telephone Exchange next door. He has a friend, Rosie, who works at the WATS[80] exchange in St. Louis, Missouri, and will make phone calls for us on the WATS lines when the phone traffic is slow there. Ted uses one of the two audio circuits we have in the Sat-

---

78   A telephone exchange system in a building with outside phone lines.

79   Military Auxiliary Radio System. An organization of Ham Radio operators with equipment that connects their radio to their telephone to make local calls for military personnel from other MARS stations on military bases all over the world.

80   A telephone service that ties into a long-distance network so that toll-free calls can be received from defined areas.

tahip Tropo Group that connects to Clark Air Base in the Philippines, where Ted knows a guy who will put calls through to Hickam Air Base in Hawaii, who in turn patches the call to Rosie. As you'll learn, most what gets done in the military is based on who you know more than on what you know. So, are you interested?"

I replied, "A free call home? You bet I'm interested. Dad was career Navy, so he taught me about the key three C's; cooks, clerks and corpsmen.[81] The people who feed you, keep your records straight, and make sure your Shot Record doesn't get lost, as it is the Enlisted and not the Officers who get things done in the military."

Bob responded, "Glad to hear you know how things actually get done in the military. By the way, there's a 3-second delay, so you'll have to wait three seconds before you respond, and vice versa, or you'll be talking over each other."

A few minutes later, the phone rang again and Bob answered it. After a brief conversation, he hung up and said, "Follow me, Sandii, and I'll show you how to patch in for your phone call."

Following Bob to the audio jack racks, I watched as he selected a tip-sleeve Y-patch cord, inserted the middle plug into the bottom of the Lynch phone, and then insert the two end plugs into the corresponding receive and send audio jacks in the Sattahip Group. Passing the handset to me. Bob said, "Say hello to Rosie."

Placing the handset to the right side of my face, I said, "Hello, Rosie. I'm Sherman Lynch at Korat Air Base in Thailand," and gave the phone number for my girlfriend, Linda, in Madison, New Jersey. I thought, "Is Linda going to be surprised. And while I was taking a hot shower last night, I was saying that it can't get any better than that. Boy, was I wrong about that."

I heard Linda's father answer the phone, and after required three seconds, I quickly asked, "This is Sherman. I'm fine, but could you please put Linda on, so I can surprise Linda with a 'Happy Birthday' greeting?"

A moment later, I heard Linda's sweet, little voice ask, "This is Linda, to whom am I speaking?"

---

81   Medical Corpsmen, the military's enlisted medical personnel.

Again, I waited three seconds before I replied, "Happy Belated Birthday, Linda! This is Sherman. You'll need to wait three seconds to respond because it takes three seconds for our voices to travel between New Jersey and Thailand. Also, you don't have to say 'over' as this is not a radio call, but a regular phone call. So, how's my Itty-bitty doing?"

"Itty-bitty" was my pet name for Linda because she was only 4-foot 11 and weighed 90 pounds. She was so petite, she bought most of her clothes in the girls department, as she had to take in even the smallest women's dress sizes. And, she bought kid's shoes because in women's size shoes, she wore a 4 size quad-A shoe, which had to be special ordered. Also, try as she might, she couldn't get her weight up to her goal of 95 pounds. She'd stuff herself at dinner, race upstairs to the bathroom scales to check her weight, and come back disheartened at weighing 92 or 93 pounds, much to the chagrin of her mother and older sister, who had a weight problem.

In fact, her whole family was diminutive. Her father, a Marine in WWII, was 5-foot 2, her mother and sister were 5-foot, and her older brother, a Benedictine monk, was 5-foot 3. In their home, at 6-foot 2, it felt like I was in Munchkin Land from the "Wizard of Oz." After dinner, they'd have a shot of Scotch whiskey, and was how I developed a taste for Scotch. But, before I could date Linda on a regular basis, the family had the tradition that a suitor must walk barefoot across the living room on fresh eggs. Luckily, we'd raised chickens on my family's farm, so I knew how to arrange the eggs in groups to do so and not break any.

I met Linda at a YWCA[82] dance in Newark, New Jersey. Monthly, the YWCA brought two bus loads of GIs up from Ft. Monmouth, 70 miles south of Newark, to a Friday night dance party. Linda had been coerced by her sister and some friends to go to the dance. I had just been dumped by a girl who, unknown to me, had been waiting for her fiancé to return from the Vietnam War, and I was also coerced by friends to go to the dance. At one point of the dance, the shortest guy in our group, who was 5-foot 4, began fast dancing with a 6-foot tall girl on a dare. The guys laughingly dared me to ask this very short girl in

---

82   Young Women's Christian Association

an unflattering purple shift to dance next to the other mis-sized couple, which I did. One thing led to another, and by the end of the evening, we agreed to meet at noon the following Saturday for lunch in Morristown, New Jersey, which was near her hometown that was not on the local bus route from Newark.

At the time, I was a PFC making $113 a month, so I couldn't afford a car, nor did I have much to spend on a date. Luckily, persons in a military uniform with an ID card could ride the New Jersey Transit buses for free. But, to ride the 70 miles from Ft. Monmouth to Newark, and then the 50 miles to Morristown, took at least three hours. When I arrived in Morristown, Linda was waiting in her car to pick me up. We'd had such a good time together as we walked and talked in a local park after lunch that day, that she invited me to dinner at her family's home, which I quickly accepted.

However, unknown to Linda, her sister, Mary, had made a date with a guy she'd met at the YWCA dance, provided she had a friend to double date with his friend. Mary knew that Linda had made no date with anyone for that evening and would be available to go out with his friend. So, Mary had invited them both to dinner at her family's home to meet Linda. Needless to say, dinner proved to be very awkward, and the two men were quite angry with Mary for the SNAFU.

The next month, I was promoted to Spec-4, which raised my pay to $200 a month and able to take Linda on actual dates. We even made several day-trips to New York City. But, Linda knew I would be going to the Vietnam War when I finished my training at Ft. Manmouth, and did not want to consider our having a committed relationship until after I returned. So, after dating for four months, I was in Thailand missing her and she was in New Jersey missing me, which we repeatedly said during our 15-minute phone conversation. As we said goodbye to each other, I thought, "Thank God we don't have to say 'I love, over' when we hang up."

CHAPTER 15

LUCK IS PASSED TO THE NEXT GENERATION

After Linda and I finished our phone call, I heard on the handset, "This is Rosie, Mr. Lynch. Would you like to place another call?"

I replied, "Yes, please, to my parents in Oregon."

As I was having a conversation with my very relieved parents, two sisters and younger brother, I saw Frank enter the Operations Room and Bob asked, "Frank, do you want to call home? We have a line Stateside."

Frank replied, "I just talked with them last week, so I'm good."

I saw Bob pick up the phone on the desk's receiver and say, "Hey, Ted, we're about done with Rosie here, so be ready to take the line when we unplug."

Indicating to Bob when I was done, I saw him quickly pull the two plugs from the audio jacks, and say as he left the Operations Room, "Okay, I'll be at the NCO Annex for my meal break if you need me. And, Sandii, you can go back to copying the in-house circuit info from the chart."

For the rest of the night, I worked on memorizing the information for the 252 in-house circuits. When Bob returned, he and Frank resumed their search for the source of the elusive 12-volt ghost in the breakout circuit racks. A couple of times, I heard on the Order Wire speaker, "Korat Base," and I would stop to pick up the Temporary Log and record the Zulu time, circuit information and problem, while Bob and Frank ran tests in the Grand Canyon on the circuit, as I observed. When they determined the problem was not in-house, I recorded the Zulu time, circuit ID and the location of the problem. Then, Bob would make an entry in the Site Log from the notes I'd made in the Temporary Log, and we would each return to what we'd been doing.

At the end of our 12-hour shift, I made the 6:35 meal run and drove the truck to the Motor Pool, where I saw Spec-5 Phizer standing at the end of the row for ¾ -ton trucks. Exiting the truck, I gave him the Trip Ticket as he asked, "How'd the night shift go, Specialist Lynch?"

I thought, "What a lifer. He doesn't even call me 'Sandii' like everyone else," as I replied, "Nice and slow, Specialist Phizer. Have a nice day."

Walking across the Motor Pool area toward the Mess Hall, I heard him release the hood-clamps and open the hood, presumably to check the truck's fluid levels. Exiting the Mess Hall after eating breakfast and lighting a cigarette, I saw morning formation was over, with half the Tropo Platoon walking to the Motor Pool for their rides to work, and the other half walking to the hooches to get some sleep or to the main street to catch a Thai bus to Korat. This was confirmed when I saw Jack among those walking to the street.

Arriving at the hooch, I walked back to the 3rd bed on the right, saw Tommy getting ready to go back to bed, and said, "Hi, Tommy. I see you're going to get some more shuteye for your night shift tonight. It should be pretty quiet tonight, as it's the middle of the weekend. But, I want to give you a heads up that tomorrow evening will likely be busy, as that is when those Stateside will be returning to work Monday morning and replying to the messages they received from Vietnam over the weekend." And moving closer, I whispered, "And

FYI,[83] there's a mattress under the floor in the back right corner of the Operations Room to nap on if you get sleepy tonight."

Tommy responded, "Now that's some info worth knowing, and thanks for the heads up. You have anything planned for your two off days?"

I replied, "I've been invited this evening to a compound in Korat where four of the Tech Reps live. Glen's taking me sightseeing in Korat this afternoon before we go to the compound."

Tommy said, "Sounds great. Too bad we're on different shifts. We hardly see each other, except in passing. And speaking of passing, I need to pass out and get some sleep before it gets too hot."

I responded, "Me too, Tommy. Sweet dreams."

Walking to my bed, I saw Glen as he came through the front door, and as we passed, I asked, "Glen, we still on for this afternoon?"

Glen replied, "For sure, but we need to get some sleep first."

I responded, "En route to do so."

Checking first to make sure there was plenty of beer in the mini-fridge, I went to my bed, turned on my fan that was now sitting on the wood crate Dick gave me, and turned back the blanket to expose the white sheets. Stripping to my skivvies, I placed my cigarettes, Zippo lighter, wallet and toilet kit on the crates wood shelf. Then, laying on the cool, white sheets, I went promptly to sleep.

Waking to the 11:00 bugle call for Mess, again lying on sweat drenched sheets, and with a parched mouth and throat, I went through my routine to getting a cold can of Bud to drink as I used the piss tube. Opening my wall locker, I dressed in my civilian blue shirt and brown pants, black nylon socks and black dress shoes. As I put my cigarettes, lighter and wallet in my pockets, I saw that my pile of laundry and boots were gone, and thought, "Good old Maan-daa, she is efficient," as I heard Glen say, "Looks like you're ready to get some lunch, Sandii."

I responded, "Ready as a hog at the food trough."

Walking to the Mess Hall, Glen asked, "Have you had a chance to change any of your Dollars to Bhat, the Thai currency?"

---

83 For Your Information

I replied, "No. I hadn't thought of that, and it's Sunday, so all the banks are closed."

Glen responded, "Mâi bpén rai, Sandii. I've plenty of Bhat in my wall locker from Pay Day. We're paid in Dollars, but they have a table for exchanging Dollars to Bhat at the going rate of 20 Bhat to the Dollar. Also, while we're in Korat, I see we need to find you a tailor."

I asked, "A tailor sounds expensive. Why not go to a store?"

Glen laughed and said, "Sandii, there aren't any stores like that in Korat. To buy clothes, you have to go to a tailor shop, where they'll make whatever you want at very little cost. Heck, they'll make you a tuxedo for 15 bucks. You have to go back for a fitting. So it takes a few days. See this blue silk shirt I'm wearing? Two bucks. It's the same for shoes. You got to a cobbler, they make a mold of each foot, and then make a shoe to fit each mold."

Feeling the smoothness of Glen's silk shirt, I responded, "That's amazing. I'll have to do that this afternoon."

Returning to our hooch after lunch, we each grabbed a beer from the mini-fridge and opened them with our church keys. Following Glen to his wall locker as I drank my Bud, I watched as he opened it, stood on the shelf above the drawers, and retrieved form the back of the shelf above his hanging clothes, a cigar box that rattled as he set it on his bed. When Glen opened the box, I saw it contained blue and red Thai paper currency, and several sizes of coins.

Picking up a blue Thai bill, Glen explained, "This blue one is a 20-Bhat bill that I think of as a One-Dollar bill. The larger red ones are 100-Bhat bills, called a 'Loi Bhat,' that I think of as a 5-Dollar bill. These quarter-size, silver coins are 1-Bhat coins, Thailand's base currency, that's 5 cents American. Like we have 100 pennies to a dollar, they have 100 sá-taang to a Bhat. This tiny brass coin is 5 sá-taang, worth a quarter of a penny. The brass coins the size of a dime are 25 sá-taang worth slightly more than a penny. And the brass coins the size of a nickel are 50 sá-taang, worth 2½ cents.

"You don't have to know how to count in Thai, as all shopkeepers can count in English. And if needed you can use your fingers to show how much. Also, all sales are negotiated. If you don't try to argue a price down, they're offended, as it says to them you don't think they're worth talking to, and you deserve to pay their outrageous asking price.

The usual rule of thumb[84] is the price you should pay is at least half the asking price. And, if you're persistent, you can get the price down to a third or even a quarter the asking price. Also, the more Thai you know, the better price you'll get, as you'll have shown an effort to learn their language and will like you for that.

"The two main phrases in Thai you should know when shopping are: 'tâo-rái Bhat,' which is 'how much Bhat;' and 'geng-bpai Bhat,' which is 'too much Bhat.' Also, one technique to use is to act like you're not that interested, which makes them argue that you are really passing up this bargain. Another method, is to act like you're walking away and say 'geng-bpai,' and they'll make a lower offer."

I said, "I really appreciate the economics lesson, Glen."

Glen responded, "Mâi bpén rai, Sandii. Before we leave, you already know you'll need a condom and your blue STD booklet to leave Camp Friendship. Also, that you can ride a Thai bus for free on the Camp and the Air Base. But, it'll cost you one Bhat to ride bus past the Air Base's Main Gate to Korat, which the driver collects from each person when he stops at the Main Gate. In any case, I can exchange 400 Bhat for 20 Dollars."

Removing two 10-Dollar bills from my wallet, I handed them to Glen, and watched as he counted into my right hand three red 100-Bhat bills, four blue 20-Bhat bills and twenty silver 1-Bhat coins. He then said, "That should be more than enough for our daytrip to Korat, even if you want to get drunk and laid."

I responded, "I've no plans for that, so 400 Bhat will be plenty."

Glen added, "Just for comparison, that's a month wages for a Thai. So be careful, as there's plenty of pickpockets in Korat. I always carry my wallet in a front pants pocket. And, don't carry any Dollars in your wallet, though the Thais prefer them."

I said, "Thanks for the tip and the currency exchange. Give me a sec to put my cash in my wall locker and get my STD stuff, and I'll be ready to go."

Exiting the front door, we walked to the street at the end of our Company's roadway and crossed to the other side, where we boarded a Thai bus. Stopping 100 yards later, I watched the MP walk up the bus's

---

84   A method of estimating that is practical but not precise, from the old English law that a man could not beat his wife with a stick thicker than his thumb.

aisle, and held up my ID card, a condom and my blue STD booklet, alike the others on the bus. After he walked by, I placed the three items in my wallet, which I placed in my front right pants pocket with my Zippo lighter, as the left pocket was bulging with twenty 1-Bhat coins.

As the Thai bus was mostly empty, Glen and I had each taken a hard bench seat across from the other near the front of the bus so Glen point things out to me. At the tarmac, the bus made a right turn onto the frontage road. Pointing out the right-hand window, I said, "See the green building across the parking lot form the Base Exchange? Well, that's the Air Base Radio Site."

Glen replied, "All the times I've been past here, I never knew what it was. I mean, there's no sign or any big antenna, or that it's so close."

I explained, "If you look at the top of the tall, white tower behind it, you'll see a 3-foot diameter antenna, which is only 1.86 miles from Tropo. There's no sign that says 'Korat Air Base Radio Site,' as it would then look like it was part of the Air Base Comm Center and be an excuse for them to come in any time they want. If anyone asks, we just tell it's the Army Liaison to the Air Base."

Glenn responded, "Very clever. Now, look to our left at the end of the runway. See how the last fifty yards slopes up? Well, the runway was built by the Japanese in World War II, and the slop up was to help the planes clear the jungle on take-off."

Rounding the end of the runway to the left, I saw that its end rose up about thirty feet into the air and thought, "What a rush for the fighter-jet pilot on takeoff when that slope tosses him up into the air."

When the bus turned left at the other side of the runway, I saw the Royal Thai Air Force had its own flight line and hangers. There, the bus turned right and stopped at the Main Gate, where an American AP boarded the bus to check the Airmen for their condoms and blue STD booklets. Behind him, the bus driver followed collecting a 1-Bhat coin from each passenger.

Watching as the bus passed through the Air Base Main Gate, I was surprised to see Thai Soldiers in camouflaged BDUs walking among elevated wood building surrounded by grass lawns like those on Camp Friendship. I asked, "Glen, I didn't know there was a large Thai Army Base here, too?"

Glenn replied, "Yea, this is the headquarters for the Royal Thai Army's Second Army over all of Northeast Thailand, it's also the home of their Black Panther Division, currently deployed to South Vietnam, as a member of SEATO, the Southeast Asia Treaty Organization, which includes the U.S., Japan, South Korea, Australia and New Zealand. Yea, this Army Base is huge. They even have their own Horse Racing Track and Polo Grounds, and they provide for Camp Friendship's security with an Infantry Battalion."

I responded, "Yea, Dick told me about their Battalion Area across the street from our Company Area."

Riding across the Thai Army Base, I saw its streets also had deep, wide drainage canals next to them. And further on, I saw a half mile to my right an array of large bleachers, and heard Glen say, "That's the Second Army's Horse Race Track."

I also saw the bus made frequent stops on the Thai Army Base and that each Thai Soldier paid the driver a 50 sá-taang coin as they boarded. I asked Glen about this and he explained, "The Thai military only pay half-fare. As you can see, they're all in uniform because they're on duty and ready for action 24/7. It's the same with their Police force, who carry their holstered pistols 24/7. And, you don't want to argue with their Police if they detain you, as they will shoot you for 'resisting arrest.' Just a word to the wise."

Passing through the Thai Army's Main Gate, I saw on both sides of the road the same deep, wide drainage canals. Over these canals were narrow bridges, made of wood planks, leading to raised paths between raised bungalows with gardens. In the space beneath the raised bungalows, I saw lots of chickens in the shade avoiding the hot sunshine. At a couple of stops, I'd watch an American exit the bus and briskly cross a narrow, wood bridge to a path for some bungalows, and thought, "Obviously a GI or Airman going home to his tîi-lók."

After watching rows of bungalows with gardens and chickens, and smelling the decay and feces form those gardens and chickens, I heard Glen say, "Look, Sandii, Korat City. We'll exit at the end of the line, near the Chainarong Gate on the South edge of the moat that surrounds Korat. The Chainarong Road leads directly to the Làk Muang, which is a pillar that marks the center of Korat City. Làk Muang literally means 'Pillar City,'"

Looking through the bus's front window, I saw a one-mile expanse of white, three and four story buildings. I also saw a berm before the city supporting train tracks. Crossing over the train tracks, Glen said,

"A quarter mile to our left, you can see the Chira Train Station. There, you can catch trains for day trips to many of the sights near Korat to the north, east and west of here. Maybe we can do that on some of our off days, as I've heard of some interesting sights and festivals within a couple hours of Korat."

I also saw the two-lane road we were on had become a much wider street lined with two-story buildings with shops on the bottom floor. About 200 yards past the train tracks, the bus turned left onto a wide street fronting a 50-foot wide moat, across which I saw the three and four story buildings of Nakhon Ratchasima, the Provincial Capital.

Exiting the bus onto a sidewalk a foot above street level, I followed Glen to the corner of the intersection, where I saw the name of the street fronting the outside of the moat was Tanon Ratchanikan, Glen said, "Tanon is Thai for a street, road or avenue."

We walked across Ratchanikun Road to a 200-foot wide area between two ends of the moat. On the other side, I saw a large, white ceremonial gate with a wood structure on top and a sign that read, 'Pratu Chainarong,' Glen said, "Pratu is Thai for door or gate. This is the Chainarong Gate to the Chainarong Road."

I remarked, "Does that mean this is the wrong gate and road for people from China to enter?"

Glen laughed and replied, "It just might be."

Passing the Chainarong Gate, I saw a 40-foot wide strip of land fronting the moat in both directions, and then a two-lane street in front of the multi-storied, white buildings with a sign on the corner that read, Tanon Kamhaeng Songkhram. Looking across this road, I saw a large, wood building with an open front, and elevated on posts five feet above the ground. Up the middle were steps leading to a chest-high counter with several uniformed men standing around it. Lining the inside walls, I saw a series of barred cages and asked, "Is that raised, wood building the Korat Zoo?"

Glen laughed and said, "It's kind of a zoo, but for people not animals. That's the Korat Jail. But, the locals call it 'bâan ling,' which means 'monkey house.' Anyone arrested by the police are jailed there, and they provide no food, water or bedding, only a small hole in the floor as a toilet. And, it's open 24/7 for public viewing, like monkeys in cages. The Thai culture is very family oriented, and if you don't have family or friends who care enough to bring you food and water, then to the police you're a kîi-giat, literally 'shit-honor,' and whether you live or die means nothing to them.

"I heard about a guy from Camp Friendship who was in there, and his NCOIC had to send him a blanket, and then bring him food and water three times a day. Can you imagine how pissed your NCOIC would be if he had to that? Plus, the CO would slam you with an Article 15."

As we crossed the road when a policeman directing traffic from the middle of the intersection had stopped the traffic, I replied, "I imagine Jim would be very pissed having to ride an uncomfortable bus to and from Korat three times a day, plus his lost time at the Radio Site, and people having to fill in for me. So, where do we go to first, Glen?"

Glen answered, "To a cafe to get a cold soda, first. Then to find a tailor shop for you to order some clothes."

Walking on the sidewalk on the left side of Chainarong Road, I saw the first floors of the multi-story buildings were bars or shops of some kind. At the first cafe Glen and I came to, we entered and was greeted by a very pretty, smiling waitress wearing a white blouse and black skirt. After exchanging sàwàtdiis, she led us to a square table with a chair on each side. Sitting down opposite each other, I saw Glen raise two fingers and said, "Tâo-rài Bhat săawng Pepsi yen, mâi mii náam-kăng?"

The waitress gave a big smile and replied, "Nŭng Bhat ták Pepsi," and Glen said, "Dii mâak."

As the waitress walked away, Glen explained, "I asked 'how much Bhat two Pepsi cold, not have ice? And she said 'one Bhat each.' So, a nickle each. That's about the extent of my Thai. I ordered no ice, as the water, even though Korat treats their's, it can make you sick, including the ice. But, some of the major Hotels have their own water treatment facilities. It's interesting there's no Thai word for ice? 'Náam-kăng' literally means 'liquid-solid.'"

After we finished our Pepsi's, I handed the waitress a 1-Bhat coin, but I saw Glen gave her a 50 sá-taang tip with his 1-Bhat coin and she said, "Kup koon mâak, ká. Koon dii mâak pûu-chăai."

Exiting the cafe, Glen said, "She called me 'a very good man,' I thought she was very pretty, and would like to have dinner here before we go to the compound, so I can flirt with her, as I'm looking for a tîi-lók that's not a prostitute. That work for you, Sandii?"

Continuing our walk up Chainarong Road, I replied, "Okay by me. You know, when Frank met his tîi-lók, she was a waitress."

Passing a couple of store fronts, I saw a tailor shop. As we entered, a man wearing a Sikh turban turned from a waist-high counter along the left side of the shop and greeted us with an India accented, "Ah, gentlemen, how may I help you today?"

Telling him I wanted some silk shirts and cotton pants, he led me to a table with stacks of catalogs and magazines and said, "Please sit and look. When you see the style of shirt and pants you want, I'll make it for you from the cloth of your choice," pointing to a large selection of cloth bolts on shelves covering the sidewall behind the counter. Leaving Glen and I to search through the catalogs and magazines, he returned to talk with an Indian woman and girl behind the counter.

While Glen and I flipped through the pages, I began to hear a deluge of rain outside. Looking out the window behind me, I saw a torrent pouring down and water rushing several inches deep between the foot-high curbs lining Chainarong Road to Korat's moat, and thought, "It must be about 2:15."

Finding in a fashion magazine the style of shirt and pants I wanted, I took it to the counter. There, the Sikh tailor helped me select the colors for three silk shirts and two cotton pants. After he measured me, we agreed on 40 Bhat for each shirt and 60 Bhat for each pair of pants, for a total of 240 Bhat. Giving him a red 100-Bhat bill and a blue 20-Bhat bill for the deposit, he said they'd be ready for a fitting tomorrow afternoon, and I thought, "All that for twelve bucks, which would have been the cost of one of those silk shirts Stateside."

Leaving the tailor shop, Glen and I proceeded up Chainarong Road for the City Pillar. On my right, I saw swarming around the few cars and trucks on the road, lots of motorcycles, scooters, bicycles, and tricycles with a deep, padded seat for two people behind the peddling driver. Glen pointed to a tricycled vehicle and said, "They're called 'Sǎawm-law,' which means 'three-wheel.'"

Watching the traffic, I saw the road was black asphalt, but there were no painted lines to mark lanes for the traffic. Though the traffic stayed mostly to their left, I often saw motorcycles and scooters make a race around to the right of vehicles that had slowed or stopped.

Approaching a wide cross-street, I saw a policeman standing on a 2-foot high, 3-foot square, white concrete block in the center of the intersection, waving his hands and arms around, directing traffic. Amazingly, the chaotic mass of vehicles obeyed his signaling, and I thought, "They probably obey his signals, as the alternative is to be shot by the policeman."

Reaching the intersection, we waited for the policeman to stop the traffic so we could cross safely. Glen said, "This is Mahat Thai Road, but west of Korat's moat it becomes Jomsurangyat Road and leads to Korat's main Train Station three miles from here."

Crossing Mahat Thai Road, I saw 200 yards ahead, another major intersection with a large, bronze pole on top of a tall, white concrete base in its middle. Arriving at this intersection a few minutes later, Glen explained, "To our right is Chomphon Road that goes to the Phonian Gate at Korat's east moat. To our left, it goes to the Chomphon Gate at Korat's west moat and the Monument to Thao Suranari, Korat's heroine. When Laos invaded Thailand in 1826, she convinced the women to seduce the Laos Soldiers so the men could launch a surprise attack and saved the city. Across the way is Prajak Road that goes to the Phonsean Gate and the north moat."

I asked amazed, "How do you know all this?"

Glen replied, "My first off day, I spent exploring Korat. Heck, it isn't all that big. It's less than a 3-mile walk around the moat, and the new part of the city extends about a mile past the west moat. You ready to head back to the Chainarong Gate to check out the market place before dinner?"

I replied, "Lead on, McDuff."

Crossing to the other side of Chainarong Road, we walked the third of a mile back to the Chainarong Gate, where Glen led me to the left onto Kamhaeng Songkhram Road. About a hundred yards ahead, I saw in the 40-foot wide space between the road and the moat, there were rows of little booths that looked like a flea market selling all kinds of items, mostly food. After we trolled the booths for an hour, Glen said, "Once the sun goes down this place is packed with Thais buying food to take home and eat. It seems Thais aren't much on home cooked meals. And speaking of meals, let's go back to that cafe for some dinner before we go to the compound."

I added, "And to flirt with the pretty Thai waitress."

Entering the cafe, I saw it was more than half full of people, all Thais, and the two white bloused, black skirted waitresses busily serving customers. The one who served us earlier looked up, and seeing us, I saw a big smile cross her pretty face as she almost ran to Glen and said, "Sàwàtdii, dii mâak pâu-chăai. Maa nâi na, chan mii dtí pâa koon."[85]

Glen replied, "Sàwàtdii, sŭai mâak pûu-ying. Kup koon mâak, krup," as she led us to a table.

Sitting down at the table, Glen said, "Pŭm puut nít-nòi Thai. Koon chûu à-rai, krup?"

She replied, "Chan chûu, Sùpa. Koon chûu à-rai, ká?"

Glen said, "Pŏm chûu Glen, dĭao diao, Sùpa," then to me, "I said she was a beautiful lady, that I speak a little bit Thai and asked her name. She said her name is Sùpa and asked my name. I said my name is Glen, and to wait a moment. Sandii, how would you like to try some chicken fried rice?"

I replied, "Sounds good to me, Glen."

Facing Sùpa again, Glen asked, "Sùpa, táo-rài Bhat kăao-pàt núa-gài gàp Pepsi?"

Sùpa replied, "Sìi Bhat, Glen."

Glen responded, "Rao ao săng kăao-pàt núa-gài gàp Pepsi."

As Sùpa walked away, Glen faced me and explained, "She said the chicken fried rice with a Pepsi is four Bhat, and I told we wanted two of them."

I responded, "Twenty cents for a sit-down meal, that's really cheap. But, you've been here only a month. How'd you learn so much Thai?"

Glen replied, "I only know a handful of phrases. But, Camp Friendship has an Education Center with Thai language classes that hands out a 100-page manual with lots of conversational phrases. It's just past the Enlisted Club, across from the Dispensary. So far, it's taught me enough to meet people, order food and get directions. I still have a lot to learn, as what I said with Sùpa, is about all I know."

I responded, "I'm going there tomorrow and signing up. Are you going to be able to come with me to the tailor shop tomorrow?"

Glen replied, "And have an excuse to see Sùpa again? You bet!"

After we ate our kăao-pàt núa-gài, that was very spicy but good, we put our 4 Bhat each for the meal on the table, with Glen leaving a gen-

---

85   "Hello, very good man. Come here, I have a table for you."

erous 2-Bhat tip, and left the cafe. Outside, Glen hailed a săawm-law, and after a heated exchange for a minute, an agreement was reached, and we climbed into the rear seat beside each other.

As the driver peddled us away, Glen explained, "I asked him how many Bhat to go to the Sing Hăi Beer Warehouse, which is across the road from the compound, and he said 20 Bhat, which is way too much. Usually, it's 3 Bhat, but because there are two of us, we agreed on 5 Bhat."

Watching the driver peddle us up Chainarong Road, I saw he turned left onto Mahat Thai Road. Passing Korat's west moat, I saw the name of the road had changed to Jomsurangyat Road. A quarter mile further, he turned left onto a two-lane road named Buarong Road, and 200 yards later, he stopped in front of a large, corrugated metal building on the left with a large sliding door. Above the door was a big sign with Thai script that read in English below it, "Sing Hăi Beer Warehouse."

Exiting the săawm-law, I gave the driver five 1-Bhat coins, and saw across the road an 8-foot high, 200-foot long, concrete wall with glass shards sticking up from its top. In the middle of the wall, there was a 10-foot wide, sliding metal gate with a door in its right end.

Following Glen across the road, I watched him knock on the door in the gate. When the door opened, I saw a Thai with a rifle slung on his right shoulder motion us in, and thought "They take their security seriously here."

Entering the compound, I saw there was a 40-foot wide, gravel parking area, between the exterior wall and a 6-foot high wall across the compound with four equally spaced wrought iron gates. Behind each gate was a 30-foot wide, two-story, concrete house. Following Glen to the 3rd gate from the left, he yelled, "Hey, Horn, this is Glen with the new guy form the Air Base Site. Okay to come in?"

Through the gate, I saw a concrete walkway to a set of steps for a porch across the front of the house with a 2-foot high wall around the porch. Sitting in a chair on the porch to the left of the front door, I saw a man in his fifties yell back, "As long as you ain't got any booze with you."

Following Glen through the gate, I saw neatly trimmed rose bushes along the interior wall and a 20-foot wide, well manicured lawn be-tween the rose bushes and the porch on either side of the 4-foot wide walkway. Sitting on the wall around the porch, I saw Bob, Frank, Ronnie, Stony and one other guy I didn't know. Approaching the porch, Glen said, "Jim Horn, this is Sherman Lynch who just started at the Air Base Site, but everyone calls him Sandii. Sandii, this is Jim Horn,"

I saw Jim Horn get up from his chair and say, "Come on, Sandii, and I'll show you where the fridge is."

Following him into the house, I saw at a table to my right four pretty Thai women sitting and chattering in the sing-song sound of Thai. Beyond them was a waist-high counter and a gas stove. In the middle of the back wall was a door, and to my immediate right was the foot of a staircase along the sidewall to the second floor. At the far end of the alcove under the stairs was a large, white refrigerator. When Jim Horn opened it, I saw it was half full of brown quart bottles labeled "Sing Hăi Beer," and he said, "Now you know where fridge is so you can get what you want without me having to show you again."

Watching Horn return to the front, I grabbed a quart bottle of Sing Hăi Beer, used the bottle opener hanging from a string on the side of the fridge to open the bottle, and took a swig. As Glen also opened a bottle of beer, I said, "Wow, this is some potent beer."

Glen responded, "Yea. The Thais didn't know anything about brewing beer, so they contracted a German brewery to build one for them. Basically, what you're drinking is German beer. So, take it easy on drinking it."

Exiting the front screen door, Glen said, "Sandii, this is Tom Lewiston, my Team Leader. Tom, this is Sandii."

Before me was a bespectacled, round faced, slender man, about 5-foot-9, in his mid-twenties, who said, "Glad to meet you, Sandii," as I shook his hand and replied, "A pleasure, Tom."

Behind me, I heard Jim Horn ask, "Did you say your name is Sherman Lynch?"

Turning to face him, I answered, "Yes, Sherman Lynch the Third, to be exact."

Horn responded, "So, your dad's name is Sherman Lynch, Junior. Was he in the Navy in World War II, and is he also called 'Buddy'?"

I replied, "Yea. He enlisted in the Navy, July 1941, and was an Aviation Electronics Technician. Did you know him?"

Horn answered, "Well, I'll be hog tied. We were shipmates at the Battle of Okinawa on the USS Curtis, V-4, a seaplane tender. I was a Signalman in the Radio Division. We used to swap sea stories in the

Petty Officers Mess. I tell you, he was one lucky son-of-a-gun. Darn near had his head tore off when we were hit by a Kamikaze. The shrapnel killed everyone in his gun crew but him, with one piece ripping open his forehead and killing the guy next to him. Actually, he was supposed to have been in the Ships Library that morning, as it was his habit to check out a couple of books to read during his gun-watch in the afternoon. But, he got into an argument with the Chaplain, who ran the Ship's Library, over some books he wanted to check out. To not be tempted to go to the Library, he changed his afternoon gun-watch to the morning. The Kamikaze that had hit amidship, not only killed the others in Buddy's gun crew, it also killed everyone in the Ship's Library that morning. Buddy always claimed, if it wasn't for the miraculous intervention of the Chaplain, he'd have been killed, too."

"Yea, I remember him telling me that at the beginning of the War, he was assigned to a PBY[86] Squadron in Adak, Alaska that went on a mission to bomb a Japanese invasion fleet heading for the Aleutian Islands. Out of the Squadron's 21 planes, his was the only one to return, and on just one engine. Then he was transferred to a Marine Forward Observation Team to call in Naval Aviation attacks from Japanese held islands before the Marines landed on the island. He was told their life expectancy was two months. He made three pre-landing sorties before he was transferred to the USS Curtis. Heck, he even lucked out after the Kamikaze attack, because the Ship's Surgeon did plastic surgery and was able to put his shrapnel-ripped face back together afterwards as good as new.

"All I can say is, Buddy was one, very lucky guy, and I hope some that luck was passed to his next generation."

I gratefully responded, "Jim, Dad told me very little about his War experiences, and I appreciate what you told me," as I thought, "Dad's Grandfather survived fighting with the 33rd Tennessee Infantry Regiment in the Civil War that suffered 40 percent casualties in it its first battle and 90 percent casualties in Pickett's Charge on Cemetery Ridge at Gettysburg. And his father survived being in the Army during WWI. Also, Dad's younger brother, Robert, told me he was a Navy Hospital Corpsman on a destroyer at the battle for Guadalcanal, where so

---

86   A type of long-range seaplane.

many Navy Corpsman with the First Marine Division had been killed, they pulled the Corpsman from the ships to the beach. Now, there's a Hospital Corps Memorial at the Camp Pendleton Marine Corps Base in California, depicting a Marine holding a dead Corpsman, with the caption, 'Where Angels and Marines Fear to Tread, There You Will Find a Corpsman Dead. Guadalcanal, 1942.' Later, his destroyer sank in a typhoon, and he was one of the few survivors. So, hopefully some of that luck is passed to the next generation in this Vietnam War."

CHAPTER 16

What Goes Around, Comes Around

After Jim Horn finished his sea story about my dad's luck in World War II, I asked, "Frank, why are the four women inside, instead of out here with us?"

Frank explained, "In Thai society, women are second-class citizens. At any social gathering, women sit separately from men. And, there's no PDA, public display of affection, between men and women. My tîi-lók, Mii-kâa, won't even hold my hand in public, and walks behind when we go anywhere. Even a wife walks behind her husband in public. Only prostitutes will walk beside or hold hands with a man in public, and then only if the man insists. However, PDA among men is common, and not seen as a homosexual act, but a show of manly comraderie.

"When Mii-kâa and I went on our first date, she insisted at least one other couple go with us. Our first date was actually a triple date, with the three girls walking behind me and two Thai men. I nearly crawled out of my skin when the two Thai's locked arms with me on either side. Luckily, I had seen it before and told myself it was the custom for Thai men to do so. It took a little getting use to, but now I'm okay with it. Even though Mii-kâa and I live together, she'll not go any-where socially without another couple along. Tom's tîi-lók, Renu, is the same way."

Glen asked, "Frank, Sandii told me that when you met Mii-kâa, she was working as a waitress. This afternoon, when Sandii and I arrived in Korat, we first stopped at a cafe to get a cold Pepsi. The waitress was really cute and showed some interest in me, so I tipped her 50 sá-taang. We came back later for dinner before coming here. She seemed happy to see me, and we flirted some, so I tipped her 2 Bhat. How do I figure out if she'll be my tîi-lók?"

Frank replied, "First, I have to say you certainly are a big tipper, and you got her attention. Second, your name stinks, literally. In Thai, it means 'odor' or 'smell,' so you'll want to modify it to 'glin-dii," and be a 'good smell.' Third, a waitress usually works for room, board and tips, so be careful with how much you tip her. Also, you don't want to come across as a big spender. In Thai society, to boast or show off is bad form. Fourth, when you go there again and she's not there, tip the other waitress less, as it shows it's her that you're interested in. And, believe me, she'll find out, especially if you ask for her by name. Fourth, go there in the mid-afternoon when things are slow so you can talk with her, then find out what she likes to do and her work schedule, so you're not going there when she's not at work. Fifth, when you ask her out to some place she'd like to go, usually dancing or a movie, not a bar, make it a double date to show you respect her.

"When you ask her out, if she doesn't have a girlfriend to double date with, I'm sure Tom or I could go with our tîi-lók. But, it would be best if we were to meet her first. You don't want to be on a double date and then find the girls don't get along. Also, it's best if it's her idea to live together. But, be prepared to find out she's only flirting you for the big tips."

Glen responded, "Thanks for the info, Frank. It's good to know the cultural differences I'll have to deal with."

Looking down, I noticed what appeared to be a burning spiral of incense, eight inches in diameter, lying on a ceramic plate. I asked, "Bob, what kind of incense stick is that on the plate? I've never seen a spiral one."

Bob replied, "It's not incense, Sandii, it's a mosquito repellent, and it works pretty good. Normally at dusk, there's lots of mosquitoes. But, as you can see, there are none."

I asked, "Where do you buy them? I'd like some for the hooch."

Bob answered, "I don't know where you'd buy them. The girls get them when they shop. Besides, I don't think they're for indoor use, as they never light them indoors."

At 9:30, Frank said, "You four need to head back to Chainarong Gate to catch a bus back to Camp Friendship before they stop running at 10:00."

Standing up from where I was sitting on the porch's wall, I said, "Sàwàtdii" to Bob and Jim, and thanks Jim for sharing his stories about how lucky my dad was to survive WWII. I heard Frank say through the screen door, "Maa nîi na, Mii-kâa, way-laa bpai kǎawng-rao bâan."[87]

As Glen, Ronnie, Stony and I walked to the compound's sliding gate, I saw Frank and Tom climb onto motorcycles. When they had started their motorcycles, their tîi-lóks climbed on behind them and held on tight before they roared out the now open gate. I asked, "Glen, how come and Tom don't ride their motorcycles to work?"

Glen replied, "Because no civilian vehicles are allowed on the bases, except for the Thai buses and delivery trucks."

Walking through the open gate, we turned left onto the darkly lit Buarong Road walking four abreast on its right side, I asked, "Why do the buses stop running at 10:00?"

Ronnie explained, "Because the COs want their troops at least half-way functional by reveille in the morning. They don't have bed checks or a curfew because many of us work night shifts. The troops are more likely to be in their racks by 11:00, if the last bus from Korat leaves at 10:00. Also, there are several buses that make the last run at 10:00, so guys can't say there wasn't enough room to ride the last bus. The buses start running again at 3:00 for those who work in the Mess Halls to have the chow lines ready to start at 5:00 for reveille."

I responded, "But, that doesn't make any sense. It doesn't stop, or even slow down a guy from getting drunk all night because he knows there's busses after 3:00 he can ride to be back in time for morning for-

---

87   "Come here, Mii-kaa. Time to go to our home."

mation at 7:00. In fact, it sounds counter-productive in two ways. First, a guy may know he's reached his alcohol level by 11:00 or 12:00, and be ready to return then. But, he'll just keep drinking because there's nothing else to do, and end up passed out in some gutter, miss formation and not be at work, which'll threaten the unit's mission. Or second, having reached his alcohol limit by 11:00 or 12:00, and looking for something to do till 3:00, will be enticed by a prostitute and get an STD. Nope. As I see it, whoever thought up this inane policy, didn't think it through."

Stony responded, "I agree, Sandii, as I know of guys that's happened to. But, as they say, ours is not to reason why, ours is to do and die."

Reaching Jomsurangyat Road, we crossed to a large building on the right with a sign that read, "Chaophaya Inn," and a line of săawm-laws in a queue waiting for fares. Crossing the road, Glen yelled, "Hâa Bhat pûa săawm-law bpai Bprà-tun Chainarong gàp sŏng pûu-chaai,"[88] and said to us, "That'll save having to bargain with the first driver in the line."

I saw the drivers look to the one at the head of the line, and when he hesitated, three drivers jumped forward. Glen then motioned with his hands for the two drivers closest to the head of the line, and they quickly pushed their săawm-laws to us. As Glen and I climbed into the seat behind the first driver, Glen said, "nothing like a little competition to speed up the bargaining process."

Riding up Jomsurangyat Road, I saw some old pickup trucks with Thais sitting on facing bench seats in the back and asked, "What are those pickups carrying people in the back?"

Glen replied, "They're called 'sŏrng-tăa-ou,' Korat isn't big enough for large city busses, so they've converted those pickup trucks to travel between Korat's main train station and the east moat on the three main roads, and between the Phonsaen Gate and the Chainarong Gate, north and south. It only costs 25 sà-taang to ride, which is cheaper than taking a săawm-law, but not as convenient."

Pointing to our right at a medium size building, Glen said, "That's the Maha Viravong National Museum. It's kind of small and costs 20 Bhat to

---

88   "Five Bhat for 3-wheeler go to Gate Chainarong with two men."

go in, but contains ancient pottery, with a variety of old Buddha images. Also, they'll let you look at what's stored in the back. So, it's a nice place to visit."

About 200 yards past the museum, the driver turned left at the end of the moat onto Ratchanikum Road. Two minutes later, he stopped near the Chainarong Gate. Climbing out of the săawm-law, I gave the driver five 1-Bhat coins before we crossed the wide road to board a Thai bus going to the military bases. Riding back in the full bus on cramped, hard bench seats was boring as there wasn't any outside lights to see anything by until we arrived at the Air Base. Even there, the only things lit up were the hangers.

Arriving finally at the Company Area, I was more than ready to exit the bus. Entering our hooch, I was surprised that Dick was not there packing for his trip home in the morning. Looking to my left, I saw Dan on his bed with headphones over his ears, singing loudly the Beatles' Sargent Pepper's Lonely Hearts Club Band song. When he stopped singing, I asked, "Dan, do you know where Dick is?"

Taking off his headphones and looking toward Dick's bed, Dan said, "Heck, I don't know. Last I saw, he'd laid out his stuff and was putting it in his duffel bag. He'd mentioned he'd be meeting with the others, as they had a project to finish before leaving."

Joining my three compatriots at the fridge and removing a cold can of Bud, I said, "I thought Dick would be packing his gear to go home tomorrow. But, Dan said that Dick and the others leaving for home have a project they're working on that'll be finished tomorrow."

Ronnie responded, "Yea, I've heard rumors, but nobody knows what they're up to. As for me, I'm too tired to care. Besides, every-one knows that 1-digit midgets get crazier the shorter they get, so a no-digit midget is beyond comprehension. So, I'm going to bed and get some sleep, then in the morning we'll all find out what crackpot trick they've been up to, and hope it doesn't blow up in our faces, be-cause they won't be here for the consequences."

Finishing my beer, I stripped to my skivvies, and leaving the clothes in a pile on the floor by the bed, I turned back the blanket, lay down on the sheet and was asleep in no time.

Waking to the 5:00 bugle call for Reveille, I sat up on the edge of my bed, and seeing Dick also sitting on the edge of his bed, I said

"Sàwàtaii, Dick. Didn't see you when we got back from Korat last night. Did you finish your project?"

As Dick got a beer from the mini-fridge, he laughed and replied, "Sàwàtdii, Sandii, it's a great day for a Pollock to go home. And, yes, we did finish our project and it's a humdinger. So, how'd your first trip to Korat go?" as he headed for the piss tube.

Replying as I followed his lead, "Great! Glen gave me a tour of Korat, helped me order three silk shirts and two pair of pants at a tailor shop for 240 Bhat, and after we had dinner at a cafe, he showed me how to get to the Tech Rep's compound. It turns out that Jim Horn and my Dad were shipmates in the Navy during World War II. You going to tell me about your humdinger?"

As Dick finished with the piss tube and walked to his wall locker, he laughed again and said, "Seeing is much better than telling, and would steal its impact. Besides, you and the entire Company will see it soon enough. Heck, everyone passing the Company Area will see it and become the talk of Camp Friendship."

As I finished with the piss tube and opened my wall locker, I responded, "Then it must be a real humdinger if it'll be the talk of Camp Friendship. Is it in the big field across from the Company Area?"

Dick replied seriously, "Whoa, we're crazy, not insane. To put something in the middle of that field would've gotten us busted for sure, and we're not doing anything to prevent our going home today."

Putting on my OD BDUs, I responded, "I don't know about that. I've heard you no-digit twidgets can become incomprehensible. So, I hope it's not over the top."

As Dick finished putting on his Class-B Army khaki uniform he'd wear home, he replied, "Oh, it's over top, but discreet. Looks like you're ready to head for the Mess Hall. Mind if I join you for my last meal here? My flight from Korat Air Base is scheduled for 9:00, and the truck carrying us to the flight line leaves from the Day Room right after formation."

Walking out the hooch's front door, I replied, "It'll be an honor and privilege to enjoy the company of your last meal here. Besides, I may need you to point out or explain your humdinger to me?"

Dick laughed and said, "Sandii, if I have to point it out to you, then you're in need of glasses. And if I need to explain it to you, then you haven't watched any TV for the last few years."

As we walked on the walkway between the two hooches in the row to the front of ours, I saw two Soldiers walking ahead of us between the Day Room and HQ, point up and over HQ, then double over and nearly fall to the ground laughing. I also heard Dick start laughing as I looked up and over HQ's roof, and seeing what Dick's humdinger was, also began to laugh hysterically.

In the dawn light, on the 50-foot flag pole, in front of HQ, I saw hanging by the neck a full size replica of Spike. Trying not to fall over in laughter, I gasped, "You hung Spike in effigy. That's perfect."

Rounding the front of HQ, I saw the head was an exact replica of Spike's head, and below it a large sign read "R.I.P. SPIKE." Wiping tears of laughter from my eyes, I asked, "Where did you get a head that looks just like Spike?"

Dick explained, "One of the guys used a telephoto lens on his camera to get close-ups of Spike during morning formation. Then took the photos to a potter in Korat who makes statues of the Buddha, and paid him 100 Bhat to make the bust, saying it was for father's birthday."

Entering the Mess Hall, I heard lots of applause and saw Dick raise up both hands in front, saying with a German accent, "I know nutting," in imitation of Sargent Schultz from the TV sitcom "Hogan's Heroes," which brought a round of laughter.

Picking up our trays loaded with breakfast, Dick and I were walking to a table, when I heard another round of applause and saw two others dressed in their Class-B Army khaki uniforms entering the Mess Hall. As they passed us on their way to the counter to order breakfast, Dick said, "Sàwàtdii, Charlie and Mike. I didn't know everyone would be so happy to see us go."

One of them responded, "Sàwàtdii, Dick. Yea, it makes a fella feel down right unwelcome."

There was a festive air in the Mess Hall as others who had finished their breakfast came by to say, "Excellent job," "Thanks for the farewell gift," "That hit it on the nail's head," and other such congratulatory remarks.

Leaving the Mess Hall to return to our hooch, I saw Spike's effigy was still hanging high and said, "Dick, I bet if anyone tried to take it down, they'd be crucified by the Company."

Dick responded, "Ain't nobody gonna touch it. Even the lifers despise Spike, and that include the Motor Pool NCOIC. I've heard some other gear-heads say he's started to complain about Spike coming around every morning for a couple of hours to bend his ear repeatedly about their 'good old days' in the Motor Pool, while he has other things needing his attention in the Motor Pool. No. Nobody's taking down but Spike, himself."

Just then, I heard hooting and hollering from the main street and saw a Thai bus heading into Camp Friendship with heads poking out the open windows and arms pointing at Spike's effigy. Turning to Dick, I said, "This isn't going to be just all over Camp Friendship. I'll bet it'll be all over the Nakhon Ratchasima Province by tomorrow."

Dick responded, "And I'd bet it'll be a month before he shows his face in the NCO Club."

Returning to our hooch, I watched Dick check his wall locker one last time to make sure he hadn't missed anything. Then taking out his wallet, he removed a red 100-Baht bill, and handing it to me, he said, "I settled my mây-bâan tab with Porntit last Saturday. But, I want you to give this to Maan-daa and tell her it's from Dék-chaai. It means 'boy child,' which is what she always called me because 'dic' in Thai means 'dictionary.'

Taking the red bill from Dick, I said, "It'll be my pleasure to do so."

Watching Dick heft his heavy duffel bag onto his back, he said, "I know you're a good guy and am sure you'll do that for me. Now, I have to get this load of crap to the Day Room so it'll be ready to put in the truck that's taking us to the Air Base."

Holding the hooch's front door open for Dick, we left for the Day Room, where he set the duffel bag down against the right sidewall. Leaving the Day Room, we crossed the roadway to where the Tropo Platoon was gathering, and as Dick joined the members of the Platoon, they laughed and joked with him, while I went to be with the Air Base Squad.

After several minutes, I saw the four Platoon Sergeants leave HQ, and watched SFC Davidson walk toward us. When he arrived, he ordered, "Platoon, Atten...tion! Dress Right...Dress!" and when everyone was aligned, "Ready...Front! Parade...Rest! Now, listen up. You will remain at Parade Rest. When the First Sargent arrives in a few minutes, there will be no sniggering, coughing or chuckling in the ranks. Anyone who does, will have extra duty on your next two off days. I and the other Platoon Sargents have met with the CO, and have agreed there will be no repercussions for this college prank, even though we know who they guilty parties are. But, we don't know how the First Sargent will react, and we don't want him provoked, by anyone, especially the instigators. And, if you think your orders to fly home can't be canceled, then you're gravely mistaken."

With that said, SFC Davidson made an about face and stood at Parade Rest, too.

A minute later, I saw from the corner of my right eye, Spike arriving with his usual brisk step and eye his Company. But when he looked the flagpole, I saw Spike stop in his tracks and his jowled, bulldog face became beet red. Then, he ran banty-legged to the flagpole, where he grabbed the end of the hoist line tied to the cleat on the side of the flagpole to remove his effigy.

But, Spike did not untie the hoist line to remove his effigy. Instead, he came to attention, made a left face, and with a sinister grin on his lips, he growled, "Company…," with which each Platoon Sargent called, "Platoon," and Spike ordered, "Atten...tion! Present...Arms!" I saw the entire Company give a hand salute, and thought, "Spike's making us render honors to his effigy."

After a full minute of being forced to render honor to Spike's effigy, Spike commanded, "Order...Arms! Platoon Sargents, detail two men from your platoon to report front and center for burial detail."

I saw each Platoon Sargent make an about face, point at individuals in their Platoon, and say, "You and you, report front and center for burial detail." Then watched eight men form a rank in front of Spike, salute and say, "Reporting for burial detail," and Spike order, "Lower the body."

I watch the eight men form a circle around the flagpole, and as two of them untied the hoist line from the cleat, Spike ordered, "Company, Present...Arms!" faced the flagpole and saluted, while his effigy was slowly lowered into the waiting hands of the other six men. When the effigy was in their hands Spike commanded, "Order...Arms! Carry the body into HQ, lay it on the counter, and return to your Platoon."

I saw the CO, who had been standing on the top step to his HQ watching the whole affair, open HQ's door for the burial detail to carry Spike's effigy into the HQ. But instead of having a somber look on his face, I clearly saw he was laughing at the entire process.

When the eight men returned to their Platoons, Spike faced the Company and ordered, "Platoon Sargents…Report!" As the Platoon Sargents went through the rigmarole to report, "All present or accounted for," I clearly saw the CO trying to keep a straight face. When Spike saluted and reported to the CO, "Company all present and accounted for, Sir," the CO returned the salute, ordered, "Dismiss the Company, First Sargent," and quickly ran into his HQ, where I then heard peels of laughter.

I saw Spike make an about face and order, "Company, you will return to your quarters, change into your Class-A Summer Green uniform, and reform here by 0730. Sargent Potts and Specialist McFee, I want to see you now, before you change. Platoon Sargents, take charge of your Platoons."

SFC Davidson made an about face and said, "Except for those with transfer orders to depart today, all of you are to go to your hooches, change into your Class-A uniforms and report back here. Dismissed."

Along with everyone else, except those being transferred, I returned to my hooch. Upon entering, I saw everyone grab a can of beer and open it with their church key, and I followed suit. As we stood in a circle, Stony raised his can and said, "Ain't no lifer going to deprive me of my morning can of brews. Here's to Dick and Company, and their safe flight home." And joining the others, I raised my can of Bud, said, "Here, here!" and took a swig.

Going to my wall locker, I removed a tan poplin shirt, black tie and nylon socks, and dark green Class-A jacket, pants and garrison cap, laying them on my bed. Then I quickly dressed in the items I'd laid on my bed as I drank my beer. Once we were all dressed and gathered at the hooch's front door, I saw in the 3rd bed on the right that Tommy had slept through all of this, having worked the night shift, and pointing him out to the other four, I said, "Looks like Tommy's missing all the fun."

Dan responded, "I imagine George and the rest of the night crew are not only going to be really pissed about missing the fun, but also at having to work the extra time and the sleep they'll miss before it gets too hot."

Exiting the front door, Glen said, "At least they don't have to attend this inane funeral."

Arriving at the assembly area across the roadway from HQ, I saw everyone was laughing as they formed up. Standing with Air Base Squad in the Tropo Platoon's last rank, I saw Spike walk from the direction of the Motor Pool wearing his Class-A green uniform with several rows of fruit salad above his left breast pocket. When he arrived at the flagpole, Spike faced the Company and ordered, "Company, Atten...tion! Burial Detail, front and center."

I saw the 8-man Burial Detail leave their Platoons and form a rank in front of Spike. But this time, there was a ninth man in his Class-A uniform, who was carrying bag pipes. Spike then ordered them to retrieve his effigy form the HQ. When they returned, I saw the effigy was on an OD stretcher with four men carrying it on each side with Spike leading them on the roadway toward the main street, with the bagpiper following the Burial Detail playing a funeral dirge.

Watching this procession make two left turns at the far end of the Company formation to pass in review before the Company, I saw as the effigy passed each Platoon in turn, the Platoon Sargent ordered, "Present...Arms! Order...Arms!" When the effigy had passed before the Tropo Platoon, I heard the CO yell form the front of HQ, "Spike, when you're done with this farce, report to my office."

Once the Burial Detail was past the Company, I heard each Platoon Sargent order, "Platoon, Right...Face! Forward...March!" and follow the Burial Detail through the 20-foot wide space between the Motor Pool's fence on the left and the Supply/Armory building on the right. Emerging past the Supply/Armory building, I saw fifty feet beyond it, a 30-foot square, windowless, concrete building with a sign on the door that read, "Co. C. 1SGT," and thought, "So, this is Spike's doghouse."

Beyond the Motor Pool's perimeter fence, I saw a large field with large piles of sand, gravel and rocks. And, 25 feet past Spike's doghouse, there was a large, scooped out hole in the ground with the Burial Detail stopped before it. Just past the hole, I saw Sgt. Pott's sitting in the driver's seat of a large Caterpillar tractor with a front end loader.

After Tropo Platoon passed the hole, I heard Spike order, "Company...Halt! Right...Face! Present...Arms! Burial Detail, lower the body." I then saw the eight men lift Spike's effigy off the stretcher, carry it into the hole, set it on the ground and then climb out of the hole. I then heard the bagpiper start playing *Amazing Grace*, while Sgt. Potts filled in the hole with the front-end loader.

Once the hole was filled in and Sgt. Potts had turned off the trac-tor, I heard the bagpiper cease playing and Spike command, "Order... Arms! Platoon Sargents, take charge of your Platoons." Then I heard SFC Davidson order, "Tropo Platoon...Dismissed!"

Returning with all the others to our hooches to change out of our Class-A green uniforms, I thought, "Fortunately for you, Spike, I don't have a bomb, or I'd blow you and your doghouse sky-high. But for now, it sounds like the CO is going to rip you a new one for this waste of man-power with this farce. Just remember, Spike, there's only one of you and over one-hundred of us, and what goes around, comes around."

CHAPTER 17

HOW DO I GET IN GOOD WITH A BOMB LOADER?

Walking back with Dan, Glen, Ronnie and Stony to our hooch, there was a sense of victory, defeat and revenge in our discussion. Victory, as now Spike was the laughing stock of Camp Friendship, and soon all of Korat. Defeat, in the way Spike had turned things around with his funeral farce, forcing the entire Company to render military honors to his effigy. And revenge, as I lamented to them my earlier thought, "Man, if only we had a bomb, we could blow Spike and his doghouse sky-high."

Dan retorted, "A bomb? That's not going to happen. They keep a pretty tight count on all the ammo that's issued here, even during a Red Alert. Plus, they won't issue us hand grenades because we're Signal Corps and afraid we'll blow ourselves up by accident. Otherwise, we'd have fragged Spike long before now."

I responded, "Well, Tommy was tricked into going through Combat Engineer School before he went to Ft. Monmouth to be a Frame Tech. And, I know they're taught to handle demolition material there."

Glen exclaimed, "For real? Well, it wouldn't hurt to talk with him about it."

During the remainder of our walk back to our hooch, we excited-ly discussed various ways and times to break into Spike's doghouse, speculated on where would be the best place to put our bomb, and determining how big it should be. By the time we returned our hooch, the only two things we decided on was to let Tommy sleep while it wasn't too hot to do so, and to have a cold can of beer to celebrate the inception of our planned revenge.

Entering to our hooch, we each quietly opened a can of beer from the mini-fridge so as not to disturb Tommy's needed sleep. Standing by the front door drinking our beer, I said to Glen in a low voice, "I'm going to the Education Center this morning to sign up for a Thai lan-guage class as you suggested, so I can get one of those Thai language manuals you talked about. I may even take the class to see how good it is. You still on this afternoon to go with me to the tailor shop?"

Glen quietly replied, "Heck yeah. I think we should wait until after the two o'clock downpour. That way we'll have time to talk with Tom-my after lunch about this bomb idea of yours. Then, after we go to the tailor shop for your fitting, we can go to Sùpa's cafe early enough to beat the dinner crowd so I can flirt with her while we eat before going to the compound. What do you think?"

I answered quietly, "Sounds like plan that works for me," as I went to my wall locker to change.

Changing into my civilian clothes, I saw Dan rapidly putting on the jungle fatigues he'd worn to morning formation. As he worked the day shift, he had to quickly get to the Motor Pool to ride Tropo's $2\frac{1}{2}$-ton truck to work and relieve the night shift. Seeing this, I thought, "George is going to be madder than a wet hen at having to miss out on most of the sleep he'd need to get this morning."

Leaving for the Education Center, I walked between the hooches so as not to be caught up in the 8:00 flag raising ceremony at the flagpole in front of HQ. Catching a Thai bus heading into Camp Friendship, I road crosswise on one of its cramped, hard bench-seats until the bus stopped across the street from the Camp's Dispensary.

Across the 8-foot wide drainage canal adjacent to the street where the bus stopped, I saw a 70-foot wide, one-story, concrete building set back twenty feet from the sidewalk with a roadway to its right side. Over a windowed, metal framed door in the center of its front, I saw a sign that read, "Camp Friendship Education Center." Using the road-way beside the Education Center, I crossed over the canal to it.

Opening the windowed door, I entered a 30-foot square, air-conditioned reception area to the right of door, with a waist-high counter across its middle. Lining the front wall, I saw several steel-framed couches with thick cushioned seats and backs. Walking up to the counter, I said to the Spec-4 sitting at a desk behind it, "Excuse me Specialist, I arrived here last week and was told you offer classes to learn Thai. Could you tell me how to enroll in one?"

Rising from behind the desk, he walked to the counter and said, "No problem. If you'll just fill out this form for us, I can get you registered," as he handed me a clipboard with a chain-attached pen and an Education Registration Form on it.

I said, "Thank you," and taking the clipboard, I sat on the middle couch. Hunched over the clipboard, I began to fill in my name, rank, service number, unit and education level on each field of study listed. Filling out the extensive form, I thought, "They must offer a lot more than classes on Thai," and finishing the form, I asked, "What sort of other classes do you offer here?"

He replied, "Mostly, we provide correspondence courses from High School through College. A lot of guys here aren't High School graduates because you only need to have an eighth grade education to enlist in the military. Also, many have started work on College credit courses. Most do it for promotion points. Up to 25 percent of your points for promotion can come from courses you've completed, and the Army reimburses you for the cost of the books and tuition, if you pass the course."

I responded, "Really? I didn't know that. But right now, I'm interested in taking a Thai language class."

He went over the options they offered. Luckily, they had a flexible two-day-a-week evening class on Monday, Tuesday or Wednesday, and Thursday, Friday or Saturday at 8:00 on "Thai for Beginners." I signed up for that class, as it fit perfectly with my work schedule. Then, I caught a Thai bus in front of the Education Center, and seeing it was only 9:30, I decided there was plenty of time to go to the Air Base Site's Top Secret Facility for the proverbial three S's, to "shit, shower and shave" before lunch.

Exiting the bus at the Company Area, I went to my hooch, where I rolled up my toilet kit and a set of skivvies in a white towel. Returning to the main street, I caught a Thai bus to the Air Base. When the bus stopped at the Air Base Gate, I removed my blue STD booklet and a condom from my wallet, which I now habitually carried there, and showed them with my ID card to the STD MP. When I exited the bus across the road from the Base Exchange, a guy asked, "Where you going with that towel bundle?"

I answered, "To the Air Base Swimming Pool."

He exclaimed, "The Air Base has a swimming pool?"

I replied, "Sure, just past their Mess Hall," exiting the bus.

Walking across the gravel parking lot, I entered the Air Base Site and went strait to the Latrine. After I finished with my three S's, I decided to leave my toilet kit in my wall locker, and rolled the skivvies in my wet towel. Going to the Operations Room, I found the two Spec-4s I'd seen before at morning formation, with a short, slender, red haired civilian working between the first two 5-foot tall rows of racks, with one of the racks slid out. The civilian asked, "Who are you?"

I replied, "I'm Sandii Lynch. I just started on Bob and Frank's Team last weekend as the microwave guy."

He responded, "Glad to meet you, Sandii. I'm this Team's Tech Rep, David Solomon, but everyone calls me Red. This is Larry," pointing to a tall, skinny guy with curly blonde hair, freckles and a hooked nose, "and John," pointing to a medium built guy with thick black hair combed straight back. "I suppose you're here to use our shower and crapper?"

I replied, "Indubitably, and I was hoping one of you will be making the 10:55 meal run to catch a ride with."

Larry exclaimed, "Is it that time already?"

I answered, "Close enough for government work."

Red responded, "Okay, Larry, you can go to lunch and take Sandii with you. If things are still slow after lunch, we can get back to tracking down this 12-volt ghost."

Following Larry out to the ¾ -ton truck, I asked, "Still looking for that elusive 12 volts?"

Climbing into the truck, Larry griped, "Actually it's their 12-volt ghost. I'm the Team's microwave man and feel worthless as a fart in a hurricane around their breakout circuits. To them, I'm just a glorified toolbox carrier. The only microwave repair I've done so far is push the Reset button when I saw an amber lamp on for one of my hourly checks on the FRC-109. Something a first-grader can do.

As Larry drove out of the gravel parking lot, I responded, "I hear you, brother. So, what'd you think of Spike's funeral?"

Larry laughed and replied, "It's the dumbest thing Spike has done so far. I'm sure if they could've got hold of a hand grenade, they'd have much preferred to frag Spike, then there'd have been a real funeral we'd have all enjoyed. Fortunately, Sgt. Davidson gave Tropo a heads-up that shift change would be delayed and why, which they passed to Bill and Jack here, as Tommy had already made the 6:35 meal run. Jack was glad to be here rather than having to render honors at Spike's funeral farce. But, he'd seen Spike hung in effigy when he made the 4:55 meal run, so he didn't miss that. In fact, most of the chatter on the Order Wire this morning was about Spike being hung in effigy and his funeral farce. By now, everyone in the 442nd has heard about it, and by tonight, the story will have spread to every Air Base in Thailand, as this is the funniest thing anyone is Thailand has ever heard of, Spike'll be the laughingstock of the military in Thailand."

I responded, "Not only the military. With all of the Thais who saw Spike hung in effigy as they rode to work this morning, and how life-like the effigy was, it'll be all over the Province that we actually hung our First Sargent. Spike isn't going to be able to anywhere on or off Base without being pointed out to others and laughed at, especially the story that his effigy buried with full military honors. I mean, the only thing missing was a 21-gun salute."

Larry laughed and added, "And Spike would've had that too, if he had a key to the Armory. Did you see how pissed the CO was about the funeral farce?"

I replied, "Yea. I heard how the CO yelled at Spike to report to his Office when the funeral farce was over. I'll bet that's the first time in a long time the CO has wanted to see Spike in his HQ. As I heard it, the CO kicks Spike out of his HQ every morning.

Larry answered, "Come on, Sandii. You know full well it's the Company Clerk who actually runs any Company. The only thing the CO and First Sargent contribute is the power of authority and their stamp of approval for what the Company Clerk does. They may make some decisions about what should be done, but it's the Company Clerk that gets it done. And, in our case, it's PFC Schultz."

I asked, "Any word on what was done to the guys who hung Spike in effigy? Did they make their flight, okay?"

Larry laughed and explained, "Yea, they got off scot-free. Jim had us stop by the flight line on the way to work and saw them before they boarded one of those old C-130s to fly out of here. They told us SFC Davidson escorted them to the Day Room to get their duffel bags, and told them to walk between the hooches and catch a bus to the Air Base. The STD MP hassled them about not having their blue STD booklet. But when they showed their transfer orders Stateside to him, and as he'd seen them get on the bus at the Company Area, he laughed and said, 'I bet you're the guys that hung the First Sargent in effigy. Kudos to you,' and let them pass. So yea, they made their flight, okay."

Turning left onto our Company Area roadway, Larry stopped the truck in front of the Day Room and said, "I'll drop you off here to avoid any inquiries as to why you were at the Air Base Site in civilian clothes and carrying a wet towel. You have a good day and I'll see you at morning formation."

Returning to my hooch, I saw George, Glen, Ronnie and Stony standing around the 3rd bed on the right talking with Tommy, who was sitting on the edge of his bed getting dressed in civilian clothes. I ran up and asked, "So, Tommy, what's the word?"

Tommy replied, "Sandii, the word is 'no.' As much as I'd love to help you build a bomb and blow up Spike in his doghouse, I don't know how to build a bomb, even if we had the materials, which we don't. Building and blowing up bombs is something EOD[89] does, and those guys are crazy to begin with. The only thing they taught about demolition in Combat Engineer School was how to slap a plastic explosive on something, put a blasting cap in it and hook it to a detonator. Unless you can get those things, there's nothing I can do to help you, because I wasn't taught how to make any of those things, only how to use them. But, I have to admit it was a good idea at the time. And talking about good ideas, I've heard the bugle call for Mess, and I'm hungry enough to eat a horse."

---

89   Explosive Ordinance Disposal

Leaving with the others for the Mess Hall, I thought, "The only place around here with bombs is the flight line on the Air Base. And the only people with ready access to those bombs are the Air Force bomb loaders who work on the flight line. Now, how do I get in good with a bomb loader?"

CHAPTER 18

WHAT AM I FIGHTING FOR HERE?

The only talk I overheard in the Mess Hall during lunch was about hanging Spike in effigy and his funeral farce afterward, even at the table where the others from my hooch were eating. Later, when the conversation at our table turned to our plans for the afternoon, I asked, "Glen, now that this bomb idea is a bust, do you want to go with me to the tailor shop in Korat for my fitting right after lunch or wait until the monsoon rain has passed?"

Glen replied, "After it rains, as the only other thing I want to do before we go to the compound is go to Sùpa's cafe for dinner so I can get to know her better."

Tommy interjected, "Wait a minute, Sandii, did you say you're going to a tailor for a fitting. After Jack told me how cheap it is to have clothes made here, I was planning on going to Korat and find a tailor shop. Mind if I tag along with you two this afternoon? That way, I can learn how to get to Korat and not have to wander around looking for a tailor shop. Plus, I can be back here in plenty of time to go to work tonight."

I replied, "Fine with me. That okay with you, Glen?"

Glen answered, "It's okay with me, as long as Tommy doesn't hit on Sùpa while I'm trying to talk with her."

Tommy said, "No problem there, as the only two things I know in Thai is 'sàwàtdii' and 'mâi bpén rai.' So, what do we do between lunch and the rain this afternoon?"

George chimed in, "The same thing we do everyday when there's nothing to do or too broke to go to Korat, play Double-Deck Pinochle, drink beer and smoke cigarettes. As Tommy needs the practice, I could partner with Tommy, since we're on the same shift, and you four can rotate." With all six of us in agreement, we went back to our hooch, and for the next couple of hours, we sat around the card table, played Double-Deck Pinochle, drank beer and smoked cigarettes.

At one point, I saw Maan-daa, Súmat and Nít-nòi enter the hooch with arm loads of clothing. Being the odd-man-out at the time, I approached Maan-daa as she put my freshly laundered clothes in my wall locker. Performing the wâai and bow, I said, "Sàwàtdii, Maan-daa."

Maan-daa responded in kind and said, "Sàwàtdii, Sandii."

Taking from my wallet the red 100-Bhat bill Dick gave me earlier and handing it to Maan-daa, I said, "Dék-chaii say Maan-daa dii mâak mây-bâan give Lói Bhat to Maan-daa."

Maan-daa looking surprised, replied, "Kup koon mâak, dék-chaai dii mâak pûu-chaai."

I made the wâan, bowed and responded," Mâi bpén rai, Sàwàtdii, Maan-daa," and returned to the card table.

When the hand was finished, Glen asked, "What was that about, Sandii?'

I replied, "Dick wanted me to give Maan-daa a Lói Bhat from him as a tip for being his mây-bâan."

Glen responded, "That's a might big tip Dick gave her. Do you realize that's a week's take home pay for her? That's the same as a 50-Dollar bill to us."

Hearing the deafening sound of the monsoon downpour begin on the roof, I watched as the Double-Deck Pinochle cards were collected, divided into two piles and put in the two boxes they came in. As Glen, Tommy and I walked to the fridge to get a can of beer each to drink before we left, I said, "Glen you might explain the Thai currency system to Tommy before we leave for Korat, and if you can manage it, sell Tommy ten bucks worth of Bhat to him."

Glen responded, "Good idea, Sandii. How about it, Tommy, would you like me to explain the Thai currency system to you, and sell you enough for your little trip to Korat? If you need more Thai currency you can go to the Currency Exchange at the Air Base Bank located across the road from your Air Base Site, which is very convenient for you two."

After Glen gave Tommy the explanation on the Thai currency and sold Tommy 200 Bhat for $10.00, the three of us walked to main street and boarded a Thai bus for Korat. As there were few people riding the bus to Korat in the afternoon, we were each able to sit sideways on a hard bench seat close together near the bus's front, where Tommy could see the sights on the way to Korat.

When the bus stopped at the nearby Air Base Gate, we each showed the STD MP our ID card, condom and blue STD booklet. As the bus proceeded to Korat, Glen and I pointed out and explained the sights we could see through the bus's window. Exiting the bus when it reached the end of the line near the Chainarong Gate, we crossed Ratchanikum Road, walked between the moats bordering the south edge of Korat, and passed the Chainarong Gate. Passing the agate, I pointed out to Tommy the city jail, and explained to him the locals called it the "bâan ling," or "monkey house," and why they called it that, as we crossed Kawhaeng Songkhram Road and walked up Chainarong Road.

Walking up the left side of Chainarong Road, Glen pointed to the cafe where Sùpa worked as a waitress, and that we'd eat dinner there after we were finished at the tailor shop. He also explained how he met Sùpa by flirting with her, and today hoped to talk some more, with the expectation she'd become his tîi-lók. When I told Tommy it only cost 4 Bhat for a meal of chicken fried rice and a Pepsi, he exclaimed, "Four Bhat! That's only 20 cents. How can they make any profit with such a low price?"

Glen explained, "I had that question, too. Thailand is a major exporter of rice. I took a day-trip to Phimai, about thirty miles northeast of Korat, to see the restored Angkor-era temple complexes there. En route, I saw miles of rice paddies and found the rice was sold for a few Bhat a bushel. Also, you saw on the way to Korat how many chickens are raised around people's home. I figure it costs the cafe owner less than a Bhat to make a serving of chicken fried rice, plus the waitresses work for room, board and tips. The owner's largest expense is the cost of the building. Tommy, you need to realize the cost of living here is very low. The average Thai laborer earns 15 Bhat a day. That's only 75 cents a day, so 20 cents for a meal is quite a bit of money."

Approaching the tailor shop where I was to have my fitting, I said, "Okay, here's the tailor shop."

Entering the tailor shop, I saw the tailor wearing a Sikh turban at the back of the shop, and heard the Indian woman behind the counter to my right say loudly the back, "Sing, customer." Watching the tailor hurry toward me saying, "A thousand pardons, Mr. Lynch," he picked up a stack of clothes the Indian woman handed him and said, "Please, this way to the changing room."

I responded, "Before we do the fitting, I'd like you to meet my friend, Tommy, who's interested in buying some clothes."

I watched as he greeted Tommy, and asked Tommy and Glen to sit at the table with catalogs magazines to look for the designs he liked. When I'd finished with the fitting, I explained it would be three days before I could return, which was okay with Mr. Sing. Then turning his attention to Tommy, I watched Tommy order three silk shirts and two cotton pants for 240 Bhat, the same as I was charged. As Tommy gave Mr. Sing a red 100-Bhat bill for a deposit, I saw Glen was chomping at the bit to talk with Sùpa at the cafe and said, "Now, Let's go to the cafe and get some dinner."

Entering the cafe, I saw there were only a few occupied tables, but the pretty waitress in the white blouse and black shirt was not Sùpa. She came directly to us, said with a gracious smile, "Sàwàtdii, ká," and led us to a table. As we sat at the table, Glen asked with a smile,

"Sùpa tîi-nǎi?"

The waitress replied, "Sùpa mâi mii tam-ngaan wan-nii," and Glen said, "Mâi bpén rai, rao ao sǎawm kâao-pàd núa-gài gàp Pepsi, krup."[90]

As the waitress left to get our order, Glen smiled and said, "Now I know Monday is Sùpa's day off, and I can show through this waitress it's only Sùpa I'm interested in and am not a butterfly."

When we'd finished our dinner, I saw that with the four 1-Bhat coins we each left by our plate to pay for the meal, we each left a 50 sá-taang coin as a tip, and I thought, "Not a bad tip, but half as much

---

90   "Supa where?" "Supa not have work today." "No problem, we want 3 fried rice chicken with Pepsi."

as Glen left for Sùpa, and a clear message that will be past to Sùpa by this waitress."

Tommy said, "I'll have to remember that 'kâao-pàd núa-gài.' I thought it was a pretty good meal though a little spicy. Thanks for showing me how to get to Korat and the tailor shop. I'll be back for the fitting tomorrow, but right now I need to go back and get ready for work."

After we said goodbye to Tommy, Glen hailed a săawm-law driver and argued him down to 5 Bhat for a ride to the Sing Hăi Beer Warehouse. Arriving at the Warehouse, I counted five 1-Bhat coins into the driver's hand, and we crossed Buarong Road to the walled compound, where the armed guard allowed us to enter through the door in the sliding gate. Walking across the gravel parking lot to the wrought iron gate for Jim Horn's home, I saw the same array of parked motorcycles as the evening before, and said to Glen, "It looks like Frank and Tom are already here with their tîi-lóks."

Glen laughingly responded, "I doubt those two girls would let them go out at night alone. It's as bad as being married," and then yelled through the gate, "Hey, Horn, it's Glen and Sandii. Okay for us to come in?"

Horn yelled back, "As long as you ain't got any booze with ya."

Opening the gate, Glen led the way to the porch, where we said, "Sàwàtdii, Jim," As we passed him and entered his home through the screen door. Passing the four tîi-lóks sitting at the table, we exchanged sàwàtdiis before opening the refrigerator, where we each removed a quart bottle of Sing Hăi Beer. Opening the bottles with the bottle opener on the fridge's side, we took a swig of the strong brew, and then headed for the front porch, where I heard lots of laughter.

Exiting the screen door, I saw besides Jim Horn, Bob, Frank and Tom, that my NCOIC, Jim Smith, was there. He explained, "Yea, I know, I don't normally come here because Mary doesn't like to. But, since it's only a short walk from the Jomsurang Hotel, I just had to come tonight and share this morning's fiasco of hanging Spike in effigy and his funeral farce. I found out while Mary and I were having dinner at the Hotel, the CO tried to give Spike an Article 15 and demote him back to the Motor Pool for misappropriating military material for personal use. But, Spike complained to his buddy, the Battalion CO, who countermanded the Article 15, which is too bad, as SFC Davidson would have been promoted to be our new First Sargent.

"Everywhere I go in the Hotel, people are asking if it's true our Company hung the First Sargent in effigy and afterward he held a military funeral to bury his effigy. Most of the lifers there think the effigy hanging was a breakdown of 'good order and discipline,' and the CO should have held the funeral in support of his First Sargent. But, since Spike held the funeral in revenge, then his action justifies the effigy hanging and has made Spike a joke even to them."

During Smith's explanation, Ronnie and Stony arrived, each retrieving a bottle of Sing Hǎi Beer from the fridge. For the next couple of hours, different parts and personal views of the effigy hanging and funeral farce were told to Bob and Horn, and we'd all laugh heartily at each telling. At 8:00, I heard from the gate, "Hey, Horn, this is Red and Sùda. Okay if we come in?"

Horn yelled back, "As long as you ain't got any booze with ya."

Watching as Red entered through the gate with a very beautiful Thai woman behind him, I saw everyone raise their bottles of beer toward them and say with jocularity, "Sàwàtdii, Red and Sùda." to which Red responded, "Sàwàtdii, everyone," and Sùda made the wâai, bowed and said, "Sàwàtdii, ká."

Proceeding across the porch and into the home, I heard Red say, "Sàwàtdii, krup," with female voices replying, "Sàwàtdii, ká," followed by lots of female chatter in Thai. Bob said to me, "Red and Sùda live next door at the end house."

When Red returned with a bottle of Sing Hǎi Beer, everyone began to tell him about Spike being hung in effigy and the funeral farce. But, Red held up both hands and said, "Hold on fellas. First, John and Larry were both there and told me all about it. Second, you guys haven't been to work since Sunday morning. Bill and I have been reading a lot that's been coming across the AP and UPI news wires about disturbing things happening Stateside, and I need to share it with you." As Red said this, he pulled handfuls of yellow teletype paper strips form both of his pant's pockets.

Red continued, "So you'll know this is not bullshit, I've brought these AP, UPI and AFN clippings for you to read. As you know, in two weeks the Democrats will hold their National Convention to select their nominee for President and create their national platform on the issues. It's normal to have demonstrations at Presidential rallies before a National Convention. But, at the rallies this weekend, the demonstrations have been much larger, more militant and very diverse in their demands at what needs to be put in the Democratic Party Platform.

"The college students are demanding an immediate and total removal of all troops from the Vietnam War. Also, for federal laws that students have administrative control over every campus that receives federal funds, which is nearly all of them. And since Martin Luther King, Jr. was killed last April, the Black movement has become more militant, demanding stronger federal laws on Civil Rights, Equal Education, and Remuneration for descendants of slaves. Plus, the Hispanic migrants are pushing Federal Minimum Wage laws and to improve their living conditions. Also, since Bobby Kennedy's assassination, the White communities are demanding large increases in the National Guard for a race war that might be started by Black militants."

Bob responded, "But, we've been reading on the news wires about campus demonstrations and Blacks rioting in the streets of big cities for a long time. And, the Hispanic migrants are all foreigners and can't even vote. This isn't anything new."

I chimed in, "Heck, last spring at Ft. Monmouth, we were given riot equipment and crowd control training to deploy against the Blacks rioting in Newark, New Jersey. But, it stayed mostly in the Black neighborhoods, where they burned down black businesses. There was a big scare it would turn into a race war, but nothing like that happened."

Red responded, "Yea, I know about those demonstrations and riots at college campuses and on city streets. But, now the press is on a feeding frenzy that these are now at Democratic Presidential rallies since the Republicans have made that war hawk Nixon their candidate for President, and predicting things will come to a head at the Democrat's National Convention. Also, the military's AFN news wire is telling the AFTN in Thailand and the AFVN in Vietnam not to release any of the news from the AP and UPI news wires available to them. Yes, I know that our AFTN has always watered down the bad news of what's happening Stateside. But, this is different. AFTN is being told to black out this news to the troops."

I felt a sober mood come over the previous jocular atmosphere of our group a few minutes ago and thought, "Heck, half of us here are under 21 and can't vote, so what's it matter to us who's running for

President. There's nothing we can do but watch history happen, or at least the part we're told about."

For the next hour, before Glen, Ronnie, Stony and I left to catch a bus back to Camp Friendship, no more was said about Spike's effigy or its funeral. But, there was lots of talk as the slips of yellow teletype paper were passed around and read, and what it meant for the Democratic National Convention to be held at Chicago in two weeks.

When we left for our walk to the Chaophaya Inn and hired săawm-laws for a ride to the Chainarong Gate, Jim Smith left with us. Seeing he had slips of yellow teletype paper in his left hand, I asked, "Jim, what are you going to do with those news clippings?"

Jim replied with a steely voice, "I'm going to share this news that the military doesn't want any of us to know about what's happening Stateside with the others who live at the Jomsurang Hotel. Maybe those who live there and have the horsepower, will be able to lift the news blackout intended to deprive us of our Constitutional Right of access to the freedom of the press," which enjoined us with Jim in a discussion that, even though we were under the control of the military, we still had our Constitutional Rights. At the Chaophaya Inn, Jim parted ways with us, as Glen used the same ploy to hire two săawm-laws for 5 Bhat each for a ride to the Chainarong Gate. There, we caught a Thai bus to Camp Friendship.

The next morning, I saw the process of our morning formation was performed with the same banality as if the events of the previous morning had never happened. When we were dismissed and I was walking to the Motor Pool with Jim, Frank and Phizer, I saw Spike didn't go to the Motor Pool Office as usual, but was walking outside the Motor Pool's fence to his doghouse. Pointing this out to the others, I said, "Looks like Spike's going to be living a monastic life a while."

At the Air Base Site, I relieved Jack so he could go home to his tîi-lók, and spent the rest of the day continuing my Frame Tech cross-training, making the fruitless hourly checks on the FRC-109, and when necessary, taking notes in the Temporary Log while Bob and Frank worked to restore any outage to our in-house circuits. Occasionally, I heard the "ding, ding, ding" on a AP or UPI teletype machine, indicating urgent news requiring the attention of some news pundit who'd put whatever spin on it the editors required. I would then see Bob go read whatever some newshound had decided was urgently newsworthy. But throughout the day, which was Monday night Stateside, there was very little on protests at political campaign events.

I also saw Jim periodically come from the Site Office, read printouts monitoring the AP, UPI and AFN news wires to the Air Base's AFTN Broadcast Site. Watching Jim tear off the yellow printouts, which he took back to his Site Office, and I thought, "AFTN may have orders to censor the news, but we don't."

On my 6:35 meal run, I drove the truck to the Day Room, where I met John and Larry ready to drive the truck to the Air Base Site for their night shift, and I went to the Mess Hall for dinner. Returning to my hooch, I drank a cold can of Bud while I changed into my civilian clothes before leaving for my 8:00 Thai language class at the Education Center.

While changing my clothes, I saw Glen, Ronnie and Stony return form their day-shift at the Site. I told what little news had come over AP and UPI news wires, and how I saw Jim periodically tear news copied on the AP and UPI teletype machines to take back to his Site Office.

Ronnie said, "Good for Jim, This censorship by the military to keep from us what's actually happening back home just isn't going to work. And it never does, because there's always a leak in the system somewhere. In this case, it's Jim."

I responded, "It's like what my Mom says, 'It's impossible to make something foolproof, because fools are so ingenious.'"

Leaving the hooch, I heard Glen yell, "Hey, Sandii, wait up," and as we walked to the main street, he said, "Thought I'd pop into Korat to see if Sùpa's working tonight and see how that goes, since yesterday was her day off. What about you?"

I replied, "That's quite a ways to go just to 'pop in.' I've go that 'Thai for Beginners' class at 8:00 in the Ed Center and see how that goes. At the least, I'll get their Thai language manual. You think you might have some time to help me with the inflection of the words? Frank told it's as much how you say a word that gives it the meaning as the sound itself."

Glen answered, "Be glad to help you, partner. Whenever we're off and don't have something else planned, like after lunch when we work the night shift or on our off day."

As Glen crossed the street to catch a Thai bus to Korat, I responded, "That'll be perfect, and good luck with Sùpa," and heard Glen say,

"Sàwàtdii, Sandii, and good luck at the Ed Center," as I waited on my side of the street for a Thai bus to the Education Center.

Arriving at the Education Center, I found the "Thai for Beginners" class in the first classroom on the left. Entering a 30-foot square classroom, I saw by the clock on the wall that I was fifteen minutes early. The teacher was busy writing on the whiteboard across the front of the room, and I saw him glance over his right shoulder and say, "Go ahead and grab one of the blue lesson manuals on the desk, then have a seat, preferably in the front row so I don't have to yell to the back of the room."

Following his instructions, I picked up from a stack on the desk, one of the light-blue manuals titled "Thai for Beginners, Produced by USAS-Thailand," and had the USAS-Thai unit patch design on the cover page. Sitting in the middle of the front row, I scanned the contents while waiting for the class to begin.

At 8:00, I heard the teacher say, "I'm Specialist Jackson, one of the Thai translators assigned to USAS-Thai. As a collateral duty, we're assigned to teach the Thai language to anyone assigned to Camp Friendship who wants to learn Thai, so I'm not the only person that'll be teaching this class." He continued to explain, "Since Thai is a tonal language, it's best to study how it's written to understand the length and inflection of each syllable made by the different characters used in Thai script. There are 44 letters in the Thai script, all of them consonants, and 38 other symbols arranged around a consonant, or set of consonants, to indicate not only the vowel sound, but also the length and one of the five inflections for the vowel's sounds."

I quickly realized that learning to read Thai was a lot more complicated than just learning to speak Thai, which was my primary objective. I patiently waited while Jackson droned on about consonant, vowel and accent symbols, and the placement of vowel and accent symbols around the consonant symbols, and decided self-study with Glen was my best option to quickly learn to speak Thai.

Later that evening, while trying to make sense of the symbols of the four accents marks printed over English approximations of vowel sounds in the Thai language, I saw Glen enter the hooch, grab a can of beer from the fridge and open it. Sitting next to me on my bed, he said with frustration, "The one good thing is Sùpa was working tonight, but the cafe was so busy that I didn't have a chance to talk with her. I guess the only times I'll have to talk with her at the cafe will be on the after-noons I work nights and on my off days. So, how'd the Thai class go?"

I replied with some frustration of my own, "The class is setup to teach how to read Thai so you can better learn to speak Thai. But, the written Thai is so complicated, I decided to just use their manual to learn to speak Thai. Now, I find the symbols and spelling they use in the manual are also a problem. So, I'm really going to need your help with pronouncing the words."

Glen responded, "I figured that would happen as I had the problem. Luckily, I had Dick to help me. Now, I guess turnabout is fare play. How about we do it in the evening after we work the day shifts, and right after lunch on the days we work the night shifts and on our off days? But, not tonight as I'm too tired from riding those cramped bus-es to and from Korat."

I said, "Sounds good to me, and we'll start tomorrow night."

The next day at work was much the same, and spending the eve-ning with Glen helping me use the Thai language manual was very productive. As were the following Thursday and Friday after lunch, before we left at 1:00 for Korat to spend the slow afternoons at the cafe so Glen could talk with Sùpa. Then, we'd have dinner and leave for Camp Friendship to work our night shifts. This also gave me a chance to hear and speak actual Thai, and to go to the tailor shop to pick up the clothes I ordered.

On the news front, at the Republican political rallies, things were fairly normal with some anti-Vietnam War protests. But, the political rallies for those vying for the Democrat Party's ticket for President had larger anti-war protest, and huge protests for more social, civil rights and college administration reforms, with the news pundits forecasting major protests over the weekend.

Saturday and Sunday were off days for Glen and I. We spent the mornings after formation sleeping while it wasn't too hot to do so. Af-ter lunch, Glen helped me with my Thai studies till 1:00, when we rode a Thai bus to Korat and the cafe to arrive before the monsoon down-pour hit after 2:00. Then, during the slow afternoon at the cafe, Glen would talk with Sùpa, while I listened with the benefit of tuning my ear to the sing-song rhythm of spoken Thai, expanding my vocabulary, better my pronunciation of words and the variations in Thai grammar. When more customers began to arrive for dinner, we ate dinner and then walked to the compound, taking our time to window shop along the way. Arriving at the compound, we'd each sip on a bottle of Sing Hăi Beer liberated from Horn's well-stocked refrigerator and spend the evening in friendly discussions.

On Sunday evening, Jim Smith showed up with his morning take from the AP, UPI and AFN news wires on his way home from morning formation. Though protest activities at the various rallies for the Democrat Presidential contestants had been mild during the week, those held on the weekend, had become violent at several of the rallies, according to the AP and UPI news clippings that Jim Smith showed us. He also showed us clippings from the military's AFN wireservice to AFTN and AFVN, broadcasting to all the troops in the Theater of War, to quash this disturbing news being set out by the AP and UPI news wires.

Through the narrow window of news provided by the AP and UPI news services, it was hard to grasp the total and actual size or significance of what was happening Stateside. Of more concern to us was the fact our military was censoring this vital information, and if it wasn't for the fact that the Korat Air Base Radio Site was the only place in Thailand the tonepack from Stateside carrying this teletype information was broken out before it arrived at the AFTN broadcast radio station, then none of us, including the local military commands in Thailand, would know what was happening to the election process in the races for the Presidency of the United States. On this issue of censorship, there was a lot of heated discussion, as it was bad enough the American people were being denied information on the combat action in Thailand for alleged National Security reasons, but this censorship was violating our First Amendment Right to Freedom of the Press.

Glen and I continued our new routine to study Thai in the evening after we worked the day shift on Monday and Tuesday, and then to study Thai in our hooch after lunch before going to the cafe in Korat at 1:00 to practice our conversational Thai with Sùpa. When we worked the night shift on Wednesday and Thursday, I'd read the news while at work from the AP and UPI news wires, which I shared with the guys in my hooch. The news showed there was a growing intensity at the rallies for Democrat Presidential Candidates during the week before their National Convention in Chicago.

As Friday and Saturday were my off days, then it was in the evenings at the compound, that we were able to continue receiving news about the day's activities Stateside. After Glen and I studied Thai in our hooch and practiced speaking Thai with Sùpa at the café, Jim Smith now was in the habit of showing those in the compound every evening his takes from the AP, UPI and AFN teletype machines. He also told us the Senior Officers living at the Jomsurong Hotel were also angry at the censorship by the military to deprive them of this vital information, as the news showed there was an expanding intensity at these growing demonstrations to the flashpoint of violent riots on Friday and Saturday's rallies.

Though the news I read on the news wires as I worked the day shift on Sunday and Monday showed rapidly growing tensions over the weekend before the Democrat National Convention started in Chicago on Monday, August 26th, it paled in comparison to the total chaos that erupted when the Convention started. As I worked the night shifts on Tuesday and Wednesdays, I read on the news wires where large numbers of National Guard troops had to be called up to support the Chicago Police and Illinois State Police trying to hold the perimeter barricades around the Convention Center where the Democrat National Convention was being held.

By this time, Sgt. Smith, with permission from Cmdr. Schuller at Quad-C A, had set up a feed from the AP and UPI circuits at the Air Base Site to all the Radio Sites in Thailand and Vietnam. This "let the cat out of the bag,"[91] and I thought, "When whole segments of American society is trying to tear apart the United States Government, then what am I fighting for here?"

---

91   To let a secret be found out.

CHAPTER 19

SKIP WILL MAKE LIFE HERE A HOOT-AND-A-HALF

As usual after a night shift, my Thursday morning meal run was at 6:35. Driving the Air Base's ¾-ton truck into the Motor Pool, I saw Jim waiting at the end of the row for ¾-ton trucks. Exiting the truck, Jim said, "Good news, Sandii. Last night, the 32 replacements arrived. I'll be letting Frank know at shift change this morning that he's worked his last shift at the Air Base, and right after Shift Change, he's to report directly to the CO's office for his promotion to Spec-5. Then tomorrow morning he'll start on the day shift at Tropo as the new Frame Tech Team Leader for its crew.

"This also means, when you start your day shift on Saturday, you'll have a new Frame Tech on your team to replace Frank. Bob and Frank say they're impressed with the progress in cross-training you've made, so I can rest easy in that regard. Also, I'll consider you to be the senior enlisted man on your shift, which means you'll be in charge of the Air Base Site on the night shift when Bob isn't present in the Operations Room. So, if the crap hits the fan while Bob's taking a crap, then it's your butt that's on the crapper to get things back on line," Jim said with a laugh as he un-clamped the hood latches to check the truck's fluid levels.

Walking to the Mess Hall, I recognized beyond the Headquarters Platoon, the slender, black haired Spec-5 with the orange, diamond shaped unit patch of the Signal Corps School Brigade on his left sleeve, organizing the new Transient Platoon for Company C's morning formation. I thought, "That's Tim Reynolds, who was promoted to Spec-5 for graduating at the top of our 90-man class. It'll be interesting to see who in that Platoon will be the new man on my team, as it will surely not be one of the 18 guys from my LRC-3 microwave radio class, but an unknown Frame Tech."

Not wanting to miss breakfast, and as it'll be likely I'll see them at lunch, I went into the Mess Hall. After a delicious breakfast, I walked to my hooch, drank a cold Bud as I stripped to my skivvies, and turned on my fan. Leaving my clothes in a pile on my combat boots, I laid down on my bed's white sheets and fell asleep.

Waking to the 11:00 bugle call for Mess in my sweat-soaked bed, I went through my routine to get a cold Bud from the fridge to drink while I used the piss tube and then got dressed. By the time I'd put on a wonderfully smooth, green silk shirt and brown cotton pants, everyone in the hooch was gathering to go to the Mess Hall for lunch at the hooch's front door wearing a plethora of colors, except Dan, who was working the day shift. I thought, "What a sight the six of us will make in the Mess Hall to the newbies who arrived last night and will be dressed in their drab OD BDUs."

Entering the Mess Hall in our flamboyant array of colors, I saw 18 familiar faces with expressions of surprised recognition when they saw me comfortably ensconced in this established group. They were sitting collectively at a couple of tables as I walked up to them with open arms and said, "Hey, guys, welcome to Thailand, the Land of Smiles and Heaven on Earth."

They all laughed and responded, "Hey, Sherman, it's great to see you again."

I said, "Let me get some chow and I'll join you."

Returning with a breakfast laden tray, I saw they were pointing to an empty place in their middle. Setting my tray on the table, before I could even sit down, the first question I heard was, "Rumor is, you hung the First Sargent in effigy. Is that true?"

I laughed and replied, "It's no rumor. Two weeks ago, several guys rotating Stateside hung Spike in effigy early in the morning that they left. 'Spike' is what everyone in the Company calls the First Sargent, and for good reason."

I then gave a brief history of how he became the First Sargent and some of the things he did to cause such ire from the troops. When finished, I quickly said, "Before you ask me another question, there's a suggestion I want to make first. Today, you'll finish all your inprocessing, and tomorrow, you'll be given your duty assignments. They'll start by asking for volunteers for various Radio Sites. Try to be assigned to an Air Base Site because they're squad-sized units with no lifers. I know you're all LRC-3 trained, but the Battalion is very short-handed and there's only three Radio Sites in Thailand with the LRC-3, Udon Tropo to the north near Laos, Sattahip Tropo to the south by the Sea of Thailand, and Korat Tropo here at Camp Friendship, and all the Tropo Sites are run by lifers. Oh, and Korat is the local name for Nakhon Ratchasima. Most of the radios in Thailand are MRC-98s, which we were taught how to repair at Ft. Monmouth. But, try to get an Air Base Site. Now, what else do you want to know?"

For the next half hour, most of the questions focused on girls, bars and booze, a Soldier's first priorities. Basically, I replied there are lots of pretty girls, but the Army had a stringent anti-STD policy, and showed them my blue STD booklet. That I hadn't been to any of the plentiful bars full of prostitutes, but described the local jail and how the police can shoot you for resisting them in anyway. And, the local Sing Hǎi Beer is aptly named, as it's a potent German beer. When asked about my silk shirt, I told them it was not store bought, as there are no ready made clothing stores, only tailor shops, but so cheap that my silk shirt only cost me 2 Dollars.

Soon, Spec-5 Reynolds decided it was time to break up their reunion with me and leave to finish their in-processing, and I said, "One other thing, nobody here calls me 'Sherman' or 'Lynch' as they're unpronounceable for Thais. Everyone here calls me 'Sandii,' which means 'very good' in Thai."

After parting ways with them in the Mess Hall, I returned to my hooch to join Glen for our study of the Thai language. Entering the hooch, I grabbed a can of Bud from the fridge as Glenn said, "So, Sandii, it looked like you had quite a reunion."

I responded, "Yea. Those are 18 of the guys in my LRC-3 class at FT. Monmouth. Mostly, they just wanted the lowdown on the basics of life here; girls, bars and booze. I'm sure several of them will end up at Korat Tropo. None of them will go to Korat Air Base, as the shortage there is for a Frame Tech to replace Frank. The reason I didn't arrive with them, is I didn't want to take the 30-day pre-deployment leave they offered. And now, I'm glad I didn't, as I wouldn't be working at Korat Air Base, which is the best place to work in Thailand."

Glen responded, "No argument there, as I wish they'd transferred me there to replace Frank. Besides, I'm also glad you didn't' take the 30-day leave, or I wouldn't have such a great Double-Deck Pinochle partner or someone to study Thai with."

Just then, Stony passed us on his way to the fridge and I asked, "Hey, Stony, why don't you join us in learning Thai?"

Stony replied piqued in his Bronx accent, "I don't want to learn any of their foreign gobbledygook. If they have anything to say to me, they can say it in English."

As Stony returned to his Double-Deck Pinochle game, Glen Said, "As I understand it, Stony started to learn Thai, but they couldn't understand Thai spoken with a Bronx accent. George has the same problem speaking Thai with a Southern drawl."

Glen and I spent the next hour practicing Thai phrases from the "Thai for Beginners" manual. At 1:00, we each drank another can of beer, then walked to the main street and boarded a Thai bus for Korat. Exiting the bus near the Chainarong Gate, we walked the short distance on the left side of Chainarong Road up to the cafe where Sùpa worked. Entering the cafe, I saw Sùpa standing by the entrance door and her face light into a big smile as she said, "Sàwàtdii, Glìn-dii lé Sandii."

Glen had asked Tom to find out from Renu what brand of cologne Thai women liked the most, and Tom said straight out it was English Leather. A week ago, Glen splashed on some English Leather before we left. When Sùpa met us at the door and smelled the fragrant cologne, she said, "Glen, Koon mii glìn dii, ká," and Glen had responded, "Bâang-tii koon rîak pŏm chûu bpé Glìn-dii, Sùpa."[92] Thereafter, Sùpa called him 'Glìn-dii.'

While we leisurely drank our Pepsi, we both chatted with Sùpa, who would occasionally correct our grammar or the way we said a word. This took some convincing on Glens part for Sùpa to correct us, as in the Thai culture, it's impolite for someone to publicly criticise another, especially for a woman to correct a man. At one point, Glen asked Sùpa, "Koon chôp tam à-rai?" and she replied, "Chăn chôp bpai roong-pâap-pa-yon saa-maa-rai yii-bpùn."[93]

We instantly realized we had no idea what "roong-pâap-pa-yon saa-maa-rai yii-bpùn" meant. Then Sùpa said, "Nâng hên saa-maa-rai yii-bpùn," as she pantomimed sitting in a chair and swinging a two-handed sword. I knew "nâng" meant "sit" and "hén" meant "see," and Nipon was Asian for Japan, and said to Glen, "Sùpa is saying she likes to sit and see Samurai Japan movies."

Glen had prepared for this moment by asking Tom how to ask a girl in Thai to go on a group date. When Glen asked Sùpa in Thai if she would go on a group date with him, she excitedly replied in Thai that she did. As Glen and I worked the night shift on Monday, and as Sùpa said she had Mondays off and a girlfriend who was available to go with a tall, handsome American, then we agreed to meet at noon on Monday for lunch in the cafe before going to a matinee of a Japanese Samurai movie at 1:00.

When the numbers of customers began to increase about 4:00 and Sùpa became too busy to talk with us, we had chicken fried rice for dinner and left for compound. Though it was a quarter mile longer distance to the compound, we walked up Chainarong Road to Korat's center at Làk Muang. Turning left, we window shopped down Chomphon Road to the Thao Suranari Monument. There we crossed Rajedmnern Road to Phoklang Road passing the Jomsurang Hotel, where Jim and Mary lived. At Buarong Road, we turned left toward the Sing Hăi Beer warehouse, and passed several walled compounds before crossing Jomsurongyat Road to the Tech Reps compound.

Passing through door in the compound's sliding gate that was opened by an armed guard, and then receiving permission to enter Jim

---

92   "Glen, you have smell good." "Sometime you call my name is Glìn-dii."
93   "You like do what?" "I like go theater Samurai Japan."

Horn's home, I saw not only Horn, Bob, Frank and Tom on the porch but also Jim Smith, and they were engaged in an animated discussion. Entering the house, we exchanged sàwàtdiis with the four tîi-lóks sitting at the table before we each retrieved a bottle of Sing Hăi Beer from the refrigerator.

Exiting to the porch, I congratulated Frank on his promotion to Spec-5, as we greeted everyone on the porch. Then Smith told me and Glen, "I stopped by the Air Base Site on my way home and picked up the teletyped news on yesterday's activities at the Democrat National Convention, which I've been sharing here before I leave to give a briefing at 7:00 in the Hotel's dining room. Long story short, they decided Hubert Humphrey will be their Presidential Candidate, which has angered the mobs to greater rioting, as he's not the strong liberal for an immediate pullout of troops from Vietnam nor in favor of major civil rights reforms. It appears the Democrats nominated him for some Party Platform deals to beat Nixon. And so ends day three of their convention."

He then turned to me and said, "Sandii, I know there's not to be any work related talk here, but if you don't mind, I want to talk with you about your newbie for a minute," and taking me aside, he said, "Tomorrow's suppose to be our off day, but I'll be going to the Tropo Site after lunch to pick up your new Frame Tech. What I need is you to be ready after Saturday's morning formation to take him to the Motor Pool to get his Military Driver's License. I've made arrangements with Sgt. Potts to have someone standing by to do the driving test. I'm giving you the heads-up now, as there'll be plenty of confusion tomorrow with the large number of replacements joining the Tropo Platoon for morning formation. Any questions?"

I replied, "No, and thanks for the heads-up, Jim."

Returning to the gathering on the porch, deep in discussion about the worsening events at the Democrat National Convention, Jim said his goodbyes and left for his briefing at the Jomsurong Hotel. Shortly, Ronnie and Stony arrived, reigniting the discussion as they were updated on the latest news from the Convention.

At 9:30, Glen, Ronnie, Stony and I walked to the Chaophaya Inn, and hired two săawm-laws to take us to the Chainarong Gate. As Glen and I rode in our săawm-law to the the Chainarong Gate, I explained the reason Jim took me aside. Glen responded, "Yea, he knows full well it's taboo to have any work related talk. But, it's good he gave you a head-up now, as I remember the confusion when you transient group joined Tropo Platoon for morning formation.

"While Jim was having his powwow with you, I told Tom about our double date for Monday with Sùpa to see a Japanese Samurai movie. He said the Thais are as fanatic about those Samurai movies as we are about our Westerns, but to be prepared, as they're dubbed in Thai, and have subtitles in other languages all around the edges."

Arriving at the Chainarong Gate bus stop, we paid the two drivers 5 Bhat each and boarded a Thai bus for the uncomfortable ride back to Camp Friendship. Returning to our hooch, I saw Dan getting ready for bed and asked, "Hey, Dan, did you hear the Democrats nominated Humphrey as their Candidate for President, and the rioters are not happy about it?"

Dan replied, "Yea. They've two teletype machines hooked up to the AP and UPI feeds from the Air Base, and are very annoying, as every few minutes I'd hear a 'ding, ding, ding' from them and a bunch of guys would run over to see what the urgent news was. I'll be glad when they're disconnected, as it's interfering with work. Also, did you know tapping into those news wires is illegal as only AFTN is contracted to receive them?"

I replied, "Maybe. But, AFTN's censorship of the news from AP and UPI is also illegal, as it's violating our First Amendment Right to Freedom of the Press, so tit for tat. I guess you heard Frank was promoted to Spec-5 and will be starting as you Team Leader at Tropo tomorrow?"

Dan answered, "It's about time. We've really been hamstrung with the Microwave Team Leader trying to fill in, but he doesn't know squat about breakout gear. I need to get some sleep, so I'll see you in the morning."

At breakfast the next morning, I again sat with my 18 former classmates and was asked a myriad of questions, mostly about where the other Radio Sites were located and what it was like there. Thought I knew their names and general locations, I didn't know what it was like there, as I hadn't been anywhere other than Korat, only that they were great places because there wasn't a large Army presence like Camp Friendship and had no lifers.

Morning formation proved as hectic in the Tropo Platoon as expected with the addition of over two dozen transients. Plus, as all Army plans are subject to change, SFC Davidson had decided the new troops were to be transported, after Lt. Willis' Health and Safety lecture, to the Tropo Site for their orientation and assignments, instead of sitting around all morning doing nothing. Jim told me after we were dismissed, "Sandii, as you've just heard, the timing has changed. John will bring your newbie to the Motor Pool on the 10:55 meal run, and I want you to meet them there at 11:00. By then, I'll have arranged with Sgt. Potts to have someone standing by to give him the driving test. It won't take long, so you'll have plenty of time to see that he gets lunch and is in the Motor Pool to ride back with Larry on the 12:35 meal run. Any questions?"

I replied, "Sounds good, as long as the powers that be don't change things again. Besides it'll give us a chance to get acquainted over lunch before we start working together tomorrow."

Jim responded as he walked to the Motor Pool, "Good, I'm glad we have this part settled," as I headed for my hooch to get some sleep before my day's activities began.

Walking at 10:00, before my bed was drenched with sweat, I drank a can of Bud as I put back on the OD BDUs I'd worn to morning formation. I thought as I did so, "It's too bad Pay Day isn't till Tuesday next week because Labor Day is Monday, as I'm looking forward to buying two sets of jungle fatigues. Which reminds me, I need to stop by Company Supply and order some name tags for the fatigue jackets. Luckily, I still have two First Brigade patches left from the ten I was issued."

At Company Supply, it took several minutes to fill out the request forms and give the Supply Clerk a One-Dollar bill to order the ten OD name tags, which was the minimum I could order. Then, walking across the roadway to the Motor Pool Office, I saw Sgt. Potts had a Military Driver's License Application and two clipboards with Trip Tickets for a jeep and a ¾ -ton truck ready for me. Handing me the two clipboards, Sgt. Potts said, "Sorry, Lynch, but I don't have anyone I can spare to give the driving test. However, I can overlook that, and let you give the driving test," as he added with a laugh, "if you promise not do anything dumb and wreck one of my vehicles."

I responded by raising my right arm to the square and made the three fingered Boy Scout sign, and said, "On my honor as an Eagle

Scout, I'll not wreck your vehicles," as I thought, "This is just another SNAFU as I predicted."

Signing the Release and Trip Ticket forms for both vehicles, Sgt. Potts countersigned them. Retrieving the two clipboards, I walked into the Motor Pool Area and found the jeep I had signed for and checked the fluid levels. I then did the same for the ¾-ton truck and waited for John to arrive with my new team member.

A few minutes later, I watched John drive into the Motor Pool and park the Air Base Site's truck next to me at the end of the ¾-ton truck's row. I saw exiting the passenger side, a skinny, 5-foot-9, PFC with thin, curly, reddish hair, and a narrow, humped nose over a big, friendly smile, who said, "Hi, I'm L.L. Kranowitz, a Jew from Cleveland, Ohio, but everyone calls me, Skip. You must be Sandy."

John said, "Sandii, here's your newbie," and laughed as he added, "It's a good thing everyone doesn't call him, Red, as one 'Red' at a time is all I can handle. Have fun you two."

As John walked toward the Mess Hall, I said, "Actually, my name is Sherman Lynch, but Thais can't pronounce it, so I'm called, Sandii, which means 'very good' in Thai, and the Thai spelling is with two 'I's, one for each side of my nose."

Skip laughed and responded, "That's a good mnemonic, Sandii. So, where are you from?"

I replied, "I'm a Catholic from Southern Oregon. So, at least we believe in the same God. As far as I know, you're the first Jew I've ever known. How about you?"

Skip laughed and answered, "Oh, I know lots of Jews."

I laughed and said, "I love your sense of humor, Skip. I think we'll get along great. I hope you know how to drive a stick."

Skip replied, "I've been driving my shtick[94] brother crazy for years. I also can drive a stick shift."

I responded, "Good. So, let's start with the Army's version of a sports car, the jeep."

Leading him to the jeep I'd signed for, I climbed into the passenger seat, as Skip walked around and climbed into the driver's seat. Describing the same route I'd taken for my License, I repeatedly stressed

---

94   Yiddish slang for an attention-getting person.

turning into the left lane on every turn. Pointing out to him the starter button next to the clutch pedal, I also cautioned him to drive slowly while in the Motor Pool Area. Skip drove the described route and stayed in the left after each turn in the jeep and the truck. Taking him to the Motor Pool Office, Sgt. Potts issued him a Military Driver's License, and as we walked from the Office, I asked, Skip, "There's an empty bed in my hooch, you want to move to it?"

Skip replied, "Sounds great. At least I'll know one person to where I'm moved to."

Leading Skip to the HQ, I walked up to the counter, and seeing Porntit sitting at her deck, I politely said, "Sàwàtdii, kon Porntip. Kâaw-toat, pŏm châawp pûut dûai koon dǐao, na."[95]

I saw her look up, and rising from her desk, she said, "Sàwàtdii, ká. You speak pretty goot Thai. How may I hep you?"

I replied, "PFC Kranowitz has just been assigned to the Air Base Radio Site to be on my Radio Team. As there's an empty bed in hooch NW-525 where I live, could you be kind enough to have him assigned to that bed, please?"

She said, "No pra-pa-lem. May I see you tran-sa-fo papaw, PFC?"

After Skip gave her his copy of the transfer orders, she returned to her desk and made a note on a clipboard. Returning to the counter and handing the orders back to Skip, she said, "Okay, PFC, you now assign to NW-525."

I responded, "Kup koon mâak, kon Porntit."

Turning to leave the HQ, I said to Skip, "Okay, it's all set with Porntit for you to move into the same hooch as me. In fact, your bed is right in front of the mini-fridge where we keep our beer cold, directly across from mine. Also, three of the guys in our hooch work the same shift we do at the Tropo Site. How about we move your gear now to your new home now? Then we can get some lunch before you ride back to the Air Base Site with Larry."

Skip replied, "Sounds perfect to me, Sandii. But, did you just call that Thai woman, Porntit?"

Turning left to walk between the Day Room and HQ, I laughed and replied, "Yea. It's actually Porntip, but everyone calls her Porntit."

---

95   "Hello, Miss Porntip. Ask pardon, I like speak with you a moment, please."

Skip laughed and said, "You gotta love a country where Porntit is a woman's name."

I laughed and responded, "My sentiment exactly," and thought, "Just when I believed things couldn't get any better, I get this fun guy for a teammate. Spending the next year working and living around Skip will make life here a hoot-and-a-half."

CHAPTER 20

It's More Entertaining Than a Spaghetti Western

G rabbing an end of Skip's duffel bag to help him carry it from the transient hooch to my hooch, Skip asked, "What about my clothes that are out being cleaned?"

I replied, "Mâi bpén rai, Skip. By the time you get back from the Air Base for dinner, they'll be on your bed. In case you don't already know, 'Mâi bpén rai' means lots of things in Thai, from 'I'm sorry' to 'Thank you.' Mostly used to say 'no problem.' Also, the universal greeting is "Sàwàtdii,' and also used for 'goodbye.'"

Carrying the duffel on the walkway to my hooch, Skip asked, "How long have you been here to know so much Thai?"

I laughed and said, "Three weeks."

Skip exclaimed, "Only three weeks! How's that possible?"

I explained, "I signed up for a class at the Education Center called, 'Thai for Beginners,' where they hand out a manual. I only went the one time to get the manual, as there's another guy in our hooch, Glen, who's also interested in learning Thai, and we spend a couple of hours a day practicing. Plus, we go to a cafe in Korat every afternoon we have off, where there's a waitress Glen knows that we talk with in

Thai. In some ways, Thai is easy to learn, but it's tricky because it's a tonal language. So, how you say a sound, can give it different meanings. Like the sound 'my.' To say 'Máai mài mâi mâi, mái,' means 'New wood doesn't burn, does it?' But, to say 'Mâai măi mâi mâi, mái,' means 'Widow's silk doesn't burn, does it?'"

Skip responded, "Wow! It all sounds the same. But, if I'm with you, you can translate it for me, right?"

I replied, "Actually, all you need to know is about a dozen phrases to buy things, get laid or drunk. Even then, most shopkeepers and the girls who work in the bars know enough English for you to get what you want. It just depends on how much you want to learn about the Thai culture while you're here."

Arriving at the back steps to hooch NW-525, we carried Skip's duffel bag up and through the back door to the front of the hooch, where we set it on his new bed, and I said, "This calls for a beer." Going to the mini-fridge, I retrieved two cans of Budweizer, punched two holes in the top of each, and handing one to Skip, I asked, "Hope it's okay for Jews to drink beer on Friday?"

Skip laughed and replied, "Only till sundown," as he took the can, raised it up, and said, "Mazel tov."

Finishing our beer, we went to the Mess Hall and had a fun lunch, talking and telling anecdotes about our lives. After we ate lunch, I took Skip around to the Howard Johnson, where we each bought two 6-packs of beer. Arriving at our hooch, we each put a 6-pack in the fridge and our wall lockers. I saw everyone who lived in the hooch was there, except Dan was at work, and introduced Skip around. Several offered him a cold beer, but he declined and said, "Thanks, fellas, but I don't think showing up at the Radio Site half blitzed would go over big with Sgt. Smith."

I responded, "Talking of Sgt. Smith, I need to get Skip to the Motor Pool so he doesn't miss his ride back to the Air Base Site."

As we left, Skip thanked everyone for their warm welcome. And, on the way to the Motor Pool, I said, "Sorry, Skip, but I won't be here this evening. Glen and I usually leave at 1:00 and go to a cafe in Korat where Glen's girlfriends works to practice speaking Thai with her. Then we have dinner before we go to a compound where four of the Tech Reps live, and won't be back till about 10:30. So, I probably won't see you again until reveille tomorrow morning."

Spotting the Air Base Site's truck parked in the Motor Pool, we went and stood by it. While waiting for Larry to arrive and drive Skip back to the Air Base Site, I explained to Skip that Saturdays were usually very busy because it was Friday afternoon Stateside and there was lots of orders going out before the people there went home for the weekend. I suggested he learn as much as he could from Red, John and Larry about how things worked in the Operations Room this afternoon, as he'll have to hit the ground running in the morning.

Skip responded, "So, you're giving me a heads-up that my first day at work will be a Baptism of Fire, as you Catholics would say?"

I replied, "Exactly. But, things usually quite down by the afternoon. Also, Sundays are typically slow, so it balances out. And, one other thing. You'll want to bring a towel, your toilet kit and a change of skivvies to work with you tomorrow after lunch. You'll see why this afternoon."

Skip looked at me quizzically and asked, "Does this mean after my Baptism by Fire there'll be a Baptism by Water?"

I laughed and replied, "Yea, something like that. You know how sneaky we Catholics are." And seeing Larry walking towards us, I said, "Sàwàtdii, Larry. I know Skip is a Frame Tech, but please take good care of him anyway. After all, he does have other redeeming qualities."

Larry laughed and responded, "Mâi bpén rai, Sandii. We'll not burn him at the stake then, even though he's a redheaded Jew. Hope you have fun at the compound tonight. Let's get going, Skip, we don't want to be late getting back and have Spec-5 Phizer on our backside about it."

Returning to the hooch, I grabbed another can of Bud from the fridge to drink as I changed out of my OD BDUs and into civilian clothes before Glen and I left for Korat. When the mây-bâan entered the hooch with the clean laundry, I exchanged sàwàtdiis with Maandaa and told her she had a new dék-chaai named, 'Skip.' I then explained to her that another mây-bâan had Skip's laundry, which transient hooch and bed he had been in, and could she get his cloth for him, to which she replied, "Mâi bpén rai," and continued with putting her clean laundry away.

Glen then said, "Sandii, it's really good the way you look after Skip."

I responded, "Someone has to look after Skip. As a Jew, I don't want him wandering around Camp Friendship for forty years looking for his laundry."

Glen and I then left to catch a Thai bus for Korat to talk with Sùpa at the cafe. Mostly, we talked about our plans for Monday's group date for lunch and to see Japanese Samurai movie, which Sùpa told us was playing at the Roong-pâap-pa-yon Gaan-grà-tam[96] on Wacharasrit Road, that was two blocks west, down San-Prasit Road. When I asked Sùpa about her girlfriend who would be going with us, Sùpa said her name was Jintana[97], she worked as a mây-bâan at the Sri Pattana Hotel, and that she was, "taa-pii hâi-giat" woman, which I understood to mean that she was a pretty, honorable woman.

Leaving the cafe after eating dinner, Glen and I agreed to walk past the theater and see where it was. As per Thai custom, we were to walk in front of the two girls, which meant we'd be leading the way there, and we didn't want to look like a pair of lost idiots on our first date with two women we were trying to impress.

Walking up Chainarong Road, we turned left onto San-Prasit Road, which passed right in front of Korat's Police Station. A short distance past the Police Station, there was a 100-yard wide, rectangular lake that extended all the way to Kamhaeng Songkram Road. Two-hundred yards beyond the lake, we crossed Wacharasit Road. To the right of the intersection, I could see a theater on the other side of Wacharasit Road. Walking to the theater's marquee, which only had Thai script on it, I saw on either side of the entrance doors, encased in glass showcases, were poster showing fierce-faced Samurai engaged in sword fights.

Glen said, "This is obviously the right theater, and it looks like Thais sure like blood-thirsty movies."

I responded, "Like movie posters of our Westerns don't show cowboys gunning each other down, or cavalry massacring Indians? Remember, Tom said Thais think of Japanese Samurai movies like we thing of our Westerns."

Glen laughed and replied, "You have a point there, Sandii. And I'm sure that like our Westerns, these Samurai movies are more about the action than the dialogue."

---

96   Theater Action.
97   Means "imagination" or "thought" in Thai.

Continuing up Wacharasit Road, I saw there were several cafes and bars around the area of the theater. Reaching the wide Mahat Thai Road, we crossed over to explore what else was on Wacharasit Road. On our left, I saw we passed the Wat Bueng compound, and Glen explained, "'Wat' is Thai for 'Temple,' and the compound not only contains the Temple, but also living quarters and classrooms for the monks who live and study Buddhist scriptures there. The monks range in age from eight to eighty, and all Buddhist males were expected to spend at least one year of their life as a monk, who are easy to spot as they all wear distinctive orange robes."

Just past the Wat Bueng, we crossed the wide Chomphon Road, and saw that Wacharast Road was now Chakkri Road. After 200 yards, we arrived at the wide Assadang Road, and looking to my right, I saw across another small road 80-yards away, a large, five-story brown building, that was newer and quite different than the four-story, white buildings lining Assadang Road. Across the top of this building, in large white letters it read, "Korat Hotel."

Turning to the left down Assadang Road, I saw these four-story, white buildings had the same kinds of shops, cafes and bars on the first floor as all the other roads I'd seen, and I commented to Glen about this. Glen explained, "The floors above the first floors contain living quarters for families and employees, or rooms rented to workers who live in the area. The rooms above the bars are for the girls who work there to serve their clients."

I responded, "Between the Air Force Base and Camp Friendship, there must be at least 6,000 Airmen and Soldiers as clients for them to serve. That surely explains why there are so many bars in Korat."

Glen said, "And you know how much nature abhors a vacuum."

When Assadang Road ended at Chomphon Road, I saw the large Thao Suranari Monument 200 yards to my left, and to my immediate right a white building that resembled an old fortification. Pointing to this building, I asked, "Glen, what's this building?"

Glen replied, "That's Suranari Hall. It's a museum of sorts with a cool diorama and even cooler sculpted mural creatively depicting the famous 1826 battle led by Thao Suranari, the heroine of Korat."

Crossing over Rajadamnern Road, I saw Assadang Road became Suranari Road, and on the corner to my left, there was a large five-story, white building with large letters at the top that read, "Sri Pattana Hotel," and said, "Hey Glen, that must be where Sùpa's friend, Jintana, works."

Glen responded, "Well, now you know where to find her."

The first road past the Sri Pattana Hotel was Buarong Road, where we turned left towards the Sing Hai Beer warehouse. After crossing Phoklang and Jomsurangyat Roads, we soon came to the compound's gate, where the armed guard let us in. Receiving leave from Horn to enter his home because we brought no booze, we quickly made to his refrigerator to get a cold bottle of Sing Hai Beer as we exchanged sàwàtdiis with the 3 tîi-lóks sitting at the table.

Emerging on to the porch, I saw why there were only 3 tîi-lóks at the table. Frank wasn't here as this was his first day being a Frame Tech Team Leader on the day shift at the Tropo Site. But, Jim Smith was there and said, "Yesterday was the last day of the Democrat National Convention, and I'm sure the people of Chicago are ruing the day they contracted to hold it there. As I was just showing Bob, Horn and Tom, the copies from the AP and UPI new wires, things went very bad there again with rioting and burning in the streets around the Convention Center, and reports of numerous injuries to the police and National Guard fending off attacks by the rioting mobs. Now, the news pundits are predicting that riots will likely happen at many of the Presidential Rallies around the country.

"I've received orders from the Quad-C A to pull our plugs into the AP and UPI news wires for the other Radio Sites as it's having an adverse effect on restoring outages in a timely manner."

I responded, "Yea, Dan Swenson was complaining about that when we returned to our hooch last night. He said that every time one of the teletype machines would go 'ding, ding, ding' for some urgent news report, guys were going to read what the urgent news was. Said he can hardly wait for the plugs to be pulled on the news wire taps. He also said the wire taps were illegal, despite the fact the military news blackout violates our First Amendment Right to Freedom of the Press."

Horn state, "All this news crap from Chicago is putting a real damper on social drinking, so I ban all political discussions from my house from now on. If you want to talk politics, then you'll have to take it elsewhere."

Bob said, "Here here. No more political talk here or my place. With that decided then, Sandii, what do you thing of our new Frame Tech?"

I replied, "He's called, Skip, and for a redheaded Jew from Cleveland, I think he's got a great sense of humor and is fun to be around. In fact, I sweet talked Porntit in Thai into moving him to my hooch."

Tom laughed and asked, "Now how did you sweet talk that witch, Porntit, into anything?"

Bob exclaimed, "You've only been here three weeks! How'd you learn enough Thai to get Porntit to do anything?"

Glen responded, "Sandii already speaks five other languages, besides English, and we spend two hours a day practicing Thai from the 'Thai for Beginners' manual the Army issues. Plus, we go to a Thai cafe in Korat and talk with Sùda, a waitress I know there. And speaking of Sùda, she and her girlfriend have agreed to a double-date on Monday afternoon to see a Japanese Samurai movie."

Tom asked, "Do either of these girls speak English?"

I replied, "Sùpa speaks very little English. We haven't met her friend, Jintana. But, she works as a maid at the Sri Pattana Hotel, so I imagine she speaks a little English. Sùda described her as pretty and honorable."

Bob asked, "Do you remember what words Sùda used?"

I answered, "She said 'taa-pii hâi-gíat.' I know 'giat' means 'honor,' 'taa' means 'she,' and 'pîi-sûa' means 'butterfly,' which is something pretty. So, I just figured it meant 'she pretty honor.'"

Tom said, "Sandii, 'tay' means 'she,' not 'taa.' So hold on a second," and he asked through the screen door, "Renu, à-rai 'taa-pii hâi-giat' pûut na?"

I heard a female voice reply, "It say 'beautiful lady give honor,' ká."

Tom said, "Sandii, though your Thai is a little off, I'd say your translation is spot on. Sùpa may have exaggerated her friend's qualities so you'd go on this blind, or you've hit the jackpot."

Jim Smith stood up and said, "This has been interesting, but I have to go back to the Hotel for that briefing at 7:00 about yesterday's activities in Chicago. So, I'll see most of you tomorrow. Sàwàtdii."

The five of us spent the rest of the evening discussing the foibles of blind dates and proper etiquette for a group date with Thais. I wanted to talk with Bob about Skip's duties at work tomorrow, but house rules forbid any talk about work.

When Glen and I arrived back at the hooch about 10:30, we found everyone on their beds asleep, except George and Tommy, who were working the night shift. Soon, I was also asleep on my bed.

Waking at 5:00 to the bugle call for Reveille, I began my routine of getting a can of Bud from the fridge to drink, as I used the piss tube and dressed for breakfast. Saying, "Sàwàtdii, Skip," as he got up and followed my lead. I went to my wall locker, and removed a fresh set of OD BDUs and socks, which I laid on my bed. Seeing Skip also beginning to dress in his OD BDUs, I asked, "So, Skip, did you get your clothes back okay?"

Skip replied, "Yea. They were already hanging in my locker when I unpacked my duffel bag."

I responded, "Good. I asked our mây-bâan, that's Thai for 'maid,' to get them from the other hooch for you. We all call her Maan-daa, which is Thai for 'mother,' as she's an older woman who treats us like her sons. How was your orientation?"

Skip answered, "Very good. The Operations Room has the same equipment and set up as one of our classrooms at school, so that's easy enough. The main thing I'll have to learn are the 252 in-house circuits, which is just a matter of time. Also, I now understand why I should bring my personal gear with me after lunch. You're definitely right that the Korat Air Base Radio Site is the best Radio Site in Thailand to work at. How was your day, yesterday?"

I replied, "Great. Glen's girlfriend, Sùpa, has set me up with a blind date to go with them to a Japanese Samurai movie on Monday afternoon. Her name is Jintana, and she works in-housekeeping at a large local Hotel. Sùpa described her as a beautiful, honorable lady. But, you know how girlfriends tend to exaggerate, so I'll have to wait and see for myself. You ready for breakfast, Skip?"

Skip replied, "Do bagels have holes? Because this bagel has a hole the size of a basketball."

I laughed as we left the hooch and said, "Now that's one I haven't heard before."

Skip asked, "Why is the chow so good in this Mess Hall?"

I explained as we walked to the Mess Hall, "Our Mess Hall has two sides. The Enlisted side, where we eat, and the Officer's side for the USAS-Thai Headquarters' Officers. So, we basically eat the same food as the General."

Skip responded, "So, not only do I work at the best Radio Site in Thailand, but I eat at a General's Mess Hall, too? Man, it doesn't get any better than this."

Entering the Mess Hall, I laughed and said, "You haven't seen the half of it, so far. I also used to say 'it can't get any better than this,' and then it got better. You'll see. Even having you for a teammate has made it better."

As Skip and I ate breakfast and talked together, I saw Spec-5 Reynolds enter, and as he passed, I asked, "Hey, Tim, what assignment did they give you?"

Tim stopped and replied disgruntled, "The lifers at Tropo decided to keep me here working straight days, four on and two off, for a couple of weeks to groom me as a Microwave Team Leader to replace a guy who's leaving in a month. Most of the other guys were sent to Air Base Sites, which is where I'd rather be. Plus, I'll be put in charge of guys who've already been working on the radios for awhile, who'll resent having a newbie telling them what to do. Makes me wish I'd never been promoted to Spec-5 when we graduated. How about you, Sandii?"

I replied, "You know, Tim, living the dream. Sorry to hear about your assignment."

Tim responded, "Thanks for the sympathy. I'll talk with you later, as I need to get some breakfast before formation."

After formation, Skip and I rode on the fold-down seats in the back of the ¾-ton truck, as Jim drove and Phizer sat in the cab. Arriving at the Air Base Site, Skip and I went directly to the Operations Room, while Jim and Phizer entered the Site Office, where I saw Bob and Bill waiting to do the Shift Change Report. In the Operations Room, I introduced Skip to Jack as our new Frame Tech on my Team. Tommy had already left on the 6:35 meal run, and as soon as Jack stood relieved, he quickly left the Radio Site for his tîi-lók in Korat.

A moment later, I saw Bob walk up to Skip and say, "Welcome to the Team, Skip. I'm Bob, the Tech Rep and Team Leader. But, before we get organized here, Jim wants to see you in the Site Office."

Skip responded, "Glad to meet you, Bob. Guess I better go see what the Boss wants."

As Skip left, Bob turned to me and said, "Sàwàtdii, Sandii. I wish we could have talked last night, but Horn has his House Rules for a reason and we must abide by them. Things here were pretty quite last night, as expected, but I'm sure things are going to get very busy here soon. Since you're now familiar with our in-house circuits for the most part, I want you to assist me with testing the outages in the Grand Canyon and Skip taking notes in the Temporary Log. If we trace an outage to the breakout racks, then I want Skip to help me there so I can check his knowledge and skill level for repairing breakout circuits. If that happens, then I want you remain in the Grand Canyon to monitor the Order Wire, and Jim or Phizer will come out to help check any our circuits if an outage is called in. You OK with that plan?"

I replied, "Mâi bpén rai. It's pretty much what I thought."

Just then, Skip returned form the Site Office with a big smile and said, "Jim told me, since I'm filling the billet of a Spec-4, he's requesting I be promoted to Spec-4, and it may happen in a couple of weeks."

Bob and I both congratulated Skip on his promotion, and I said, "I told you it'll get better and there's more to come."

Bob explained to Skip his plan and the procedures for the Temporary Log. Soon, we began to receive reports of outages and Skip had his Baptism by Fire. After lunch, thing quieted down as usual, and I began orienting Skip to the dynamics of our in-house circuits, as Bob transcribed the notes in the Temporary Log to the Site Log. Things went smoothly for the rest of the day with only a few outages traced to some other Radio Site. Occasionally, the AP and UPI tele-type machines would "ding, ding, ding," but we ignored them as they were about more riots at political rallies, which we were burned out on hearing about.

After work, Skip spent the evening learning to play Double-Deck Pinochle with George, Tommy, Ronnie, and Stony, mainly because it was the end of the month and they were broke, which was cause for them and Glen to bum beer and cigarettes from me. Meanwhile, Glen and I spent the evening practicing Thai phrases from the "Thai for Beginners" manual that we could use for our double date on Monday.

The next day was Sunday, and pleasantly quiet as it was Labor Day weekend Stateside. The quiet was only interrupted by the "ding, ding, ding" from the AP and UPI news wires. I spent the morning with Skip helping him learn our 252 in-house circuits, which fairly cemented my knowledge of them. In the afternoon, I worked in the Grand Canyon monitoring the chatter on the Order Wire, while Bob tested Skip's knowledge of the breakout circuits. After work, we all spent the evening doing what we had done the evening before.

Monday was Labor Day, which made no difference to us, as in a Theater of War there are no holidays. Glen and Tommy were at work, and everyone else asleep, when Glen and I got up at 10:00 to prepare for our double date with Sùpa and Jintana. By 11:00, when I heard the bugle call for Mess, I'd been to the Howard Johnson and bought beer and cigarettes for everyone else, who were not getting up until lunch. Glen and I then walked across the Company Area to the main street and caught a Thai bus for Korat. We had figured the half hour bus ride would allow us to meet at the cafe for our noon rendezvous a little bit early.

Entering the cafe, I saw on the left side of the cafe, facing Glen and I, Sùpa sitting at a table and sitting to her right was a stunningly beautiful Thai woman wearing a pink dress. As we approached the table, the two women stood, made the wâai, bowed low and said, "Sàwàtdii, ká." I saw that Jintana was 5-feet 7 and understood why she wanted to meet a tall American, as she was taller than the average Thai man.

Glen and I responded in kind and said, "Sàwàtdii, krup."

Sùpa then said, "Glìn-dii lé Sandii, jaa pûu-ying kaawng dì-chan pûak chûu Jintana."

I replied, "Pŏm chûu Sandii. Yin-dii tîi dâai rúu-jak, Jintana."

Jintana responded, "Chên-gan, ká."[98]

As we ate lunch and I gazed at Jintana sitting across from me, I was amazed at how beautiful and graceful she was, and thought, "Sùpa, you did not exaggerate when you described Jintana as a 'beautiful lady that gives honor'."

Though mostly we spoke in Thai, Jintana did try to impress me that she spoke some English, but not enough to express herself. Besides, I enjoyed the sing-song sound of her voice speaking Thai more than the guttural sound of English. I found that, besides being a mây-bâan at the Sri Pattana Hotel, she also belonged to a dance troupe performing the traditional Thai Ram dances at local festivals in the Province, and I thought, "No wonder she is so graceful in her movements."

---

98   "Glen and Sandii, meet woman belong my friend name Jintana." "My name Sandii. Rejoice at can acquaint with Jintana." "Same here."

Finishing the meal, I left a blue 20-Bhat bill on the table and thought, "Lunch for 4 people with a large tip for a Dollar is very inexpensive, plus my generosity should make a 'san-dii' impression that doesn't belie my name."

Leaving the cafe, the two girls naturally exited behind Glen and I, and followed a couple of steps back as we walked up Chainarong Road and turned left down San-Prasit Road. A quarter mile later, we crossed over and then turned right up Wacharasit Road. When we stopped beneath the theater's marquee, hoping it was the correct theater, we were rewarded as I heard the two female voices behind us say, "Dii mâak, Glìn-dii lé Sandii."

Glen walked to the ticket window and asked in Thai, "Four tickets, how much Bhat," and the vendor replied in Thai, "Four Bhat." When Glen had the four tickets, he gave two to Sùpa. Then Glen and I entered the theater together, with the two girls behind us.

Entering the theater, I saw it was a 50-foot square room with rows of fold-down wood seats and no armrest between them, facing a large, white screen. Glen and I decided earlier that I would find four seats together, about a 3rd of the way form the screen, then lead the way into the row to ensure he and Sùda sat next to each other. As I did this and turned to sit down, I was pleasantly surprised to see Jintana was right behind me, followed by Sùpa and Glen, and I thought, "The men might choose the seats to sit in, but the women choose the sitting order."

I'd decided earlier to make no attempt at holding Jintana's hand during the movie to honor the no PDA culture of the Thai culture. This was totally alien to me, as Stateside, if a girl refused to hold my hand on a date, then that was our last date. However, during the first sword-fighting blood bath, I felt the long slender fingers of both Jintana's hand reach around the left sleeve of my silk shirt and squeeze my bicep. I then felt her lovely hands remain there until the lights came on at the end of the movie, which I really enjoyed.

As Glen and I were walking back to the cafe, with the two girls walking the socially expected two steps behind us, I asked, "Did you notice anything familiar about that Samurai movie?"

Glen laughed and replied, "You mean that it was just like watching that Clint Eastwood spaghetti Western,[99] 'A Fist Full of Dollars,' except they were fighting with swords instead of pistols?"

I laughed and answered, "Exactly. I think we should ask Sùpa and Jintana to go see another Japanese Samurai movie again next Monday when Sùpa is off. It didn't matter that it was all dubbed in Thai and had all those subtitles around the edges, I knew exactly what was being said. Actually, I think these Samurai movies are more entertaining than a spaghetti Western."

---

99   A Western that was filmed in Italy.

CHAPTER 21

NOW THIS IS WHAT I CALL A PAY DAY

Walking back to the cafe from the theater, Glen and I agreed not to talk about our date in case Jintana understood enough English to get the gist of anything we said. Arriving in front of the cafe, Glen explained in Thai to Sùpa we didn't have time to eat dinner with them because we had to work that evening, not because we were broke. When Glen asked if they both would like to see another Samurai movie with us next Monday afternoon. I saw Jintana touch Sùpa's arm and nod her lovely head with a big smile on her beautiful face when Sùpa looked at her. Sùpa then told Glen with her own big smile that they would like that very much. With that decided, we exchanged parting sàwàtdiis, and the two girls entered the cafe.

Walking from the cafe down Chainarong Road to the bus stop, Glen exclaimed, "Wow! Sandii, I can't believe a girl as beautiful and graceful as Jintana isn't already married. You certainly hit the mother lode with her."

I responded, "Yea, I was totally blown away with her grace and beauty. But, I'm not surprised she isn't married. You saw how tall she is. Even by American standards, she's taller than the average woman. Don't get me wrong, I like that she's tall. But, I doubt any Thai man would like having a tall wife."

Glen agreed, "You're right about her being too tall for a Thai man. Just the same, she is gorgeous."

Boarding a Thai bus, I saw it was nearly empty because all of the Americans were flat broke, as this was a rare fifth weekend of a month, and most of them are broke by the fourth weekend. In fact, I was down to my last couple of Dollars, and had paid for the meals as Glen had been down to his last handful of 1-Bhat coins. We had agreed I was to pay for the meals so he could save face buying the movie tickets.

Riding the bus back to Camp Friendship, Glen and I sat sideways in adjacent rows so it would be easier and more comfortable to talk. Most of our talk was relating our favorite movie scenes to how they compared to the same scene in *A Fist Full of Dollars*, and how insolent it was for the Japanese to copy it scene for scene in their Samurai movie. Even though we agreed that the sword fights lasted longer and caused a more visceral response than watching one cowboy just shoot it out with two or more other cowboys, which didn't show much, if any bloodshed.

When Glen and I exited the bus, it was still an hour until we could go to the Mess Hall for dinner. So, we swung by the Howard Johnson, where I spent my last two Dollars on three 6-packs of Budweiser and two packs of Pall Mall. Entering our hooch, Glen and I grabbed a cold beer each before I put the three 6-packs into the nearly empty fridge.

Walking toward the card table, I saw Dan and Skip where partnered against Ronnie and Stony, and were so engrossed with the hand being played in their Double-Deck Pinochle game, that nobody looked up when we entered the hooch. When they had finished the hand, I asked, "Well, Skip, how's your game going?"

Skip replied, "It's better than Hearts or Spades, but a lot more complicated. How was your double date?"

I answered, "It went really good. Jintana was really nice and the Samurai movie was fun to watch, but exactly like seeing a remake of *A Fist Full of Dollars*, except with swords, and bows and arrows instead of pistols and rifles."

Glen cut in and said, "What Sandii's not telling you is that Jintana is an absolute fox.[100] And, he has a second date with her to see another Samurai movie next Monday with Sùpa and me."

Ronnie interjected, "Really? Sandii's landed a gorgeous Thai woman?"

Glen extolled Jintana's grace and beauty till the 5:00 bugle call for Mess. I felt, if I said anything positive about Jintana, then it would sound like I was bragging. When pressed, I humbly said, "Yes, she's very pretty, but also very talented."

At dinner, I spent the time going over with Skip how different working the night shift was than the day shift in order to deflect any talk about Jintana. In some ways, I was now feeling conflicted, as I did have a girlfriend Stateside I had strong feelings about, even though Linda insisted ours was not a committed relationship. And, it wasn't like I'd set out to find someone to date, but to help Glen have a date with Sùda. But, I had to admit that being with Jintana had an intoxicating effect on me.

When Tommy stopped the truck in front of the Day Room on his 6:35 meal run, I asked, "How was work today?"

Tommy replied, "Quiet as a graveyard. We found that 12-volt ghost. Turned out the bug[101] was an actual bug shorting out the bus bar[102] to the frame. How was your blind date, Sandii?"

Skip interjected, "Sandii won't admit it, but Glen said she's an absolute fox and is one of those traditional Thai dancers at festivals you see pictures of."

Tommy accusingly asked, "For real, Sandii? A total fox?"

I replied, "Well, she is very pretty and talented. But, we can talk about her later. Right now, Jack is waiting for me to relieve him so he can go home to his tîi-lók."

Tommy responded, "Okay, Sandii. Sàwàtdii, you two."

When Skip and I arrived in the Operations Room, Jack said quickly, "It was a quiet day, and should be quiet tonight. So, have a nice evening and I'll see you tomorrow night."

---

100   Slang for a woman who is sexually attractive.

101   A defect or imperfection in a machine.

102   A non-insulated conductor that carries a current to many electrical circuits.

As Jack quickly left, Skip said, "Boy, is he in a hurry to leave. Didn't even introduce himself to me. Justa wham, bam, and not even a thank you ma'am."

I responded, "You'll just have to excuse Jack. He's always in a hurry to get home to his tîi-lók."

Bob entered the Operations Room and said, "Looks like it's going to be a quiet night, guys, as it's Labor Day Stateside. But, we'll be busy just the same. I guess you've heard our 12-volt bug was an actual bug, and Jim wants us to do PM on all the racks in the Operations Room by pulling open every rack and vacuum them out by tomorrow morning, which will take a few hours. Sandii, I want you to go to the Supply Room and get the vacuum cleaner. Skip, you get the flat tip screwdriver from the desk drawer and begin to loosen all the screws on the racks so Sandii and I can quickly go along and pull out each rack to vacuum it. When you've loosened all the screws, then go back and tighten them as we finish vacuuming each rack. If we do this right, then we'll get this done quickly. While you're getting started, I'll start the entries in the Site Log. Any questions? Good, then let's get going."

Bob's plan worked smoothly. It took two hours to methodically slide out each unscrewed rack, run the circular bristle attachment over the electronic equipment in each rack, and then shove the rack back into place before sliding out the next rack. Bob and I were amazed at the number of bugs we were finding as we went from rack to rack, as we thought the Radio Site building was sealed from the outside and hadn't seen any insects flying around the Operations Room. It was a mystery to us how they were getting into the equipment, and thankful none had shorted out a power supply, which could have started a fire.

When Bob and I had vacuumed out the last rack, and Skip had tightened the last screw, which he had been doing right behind us as we finished a stack of racks, I put the vacuum cleaner in the Supply Room. Changing the used collection bag for a new one, I saw the used bag was nearly full of bugs and dirt and showed it to Bob and Skip. Bob then took it to the Site Office to be shown during Shift Change Report in the morning.

When Bob returned to the Operations Room, he said, "Sandii, now let's all sit for awhile as I want to hear all about the 'taa-pii hâi-giat' woman you had a blind date with."

As we all sat in chairs in front of the Operations Room desk, I said, "Bob, it seems I hit the jackpot with Jintana. She is indeed a beautiful lady that gives honor to any man she would be with, except for one flaw from a Thai man's point of view. She's 5-foot 7, which is why Sùpa said she wanted to go out with a tall American. Also, she's a Thai Ram dancer with a troupe that performs at local festivals, so her every movement is very graceful. And, she does speak a little English, but not much.

"What surprised me the most, while she was sitting next to me watching the Japanese Samurai movie, was during the first bloodletting sword fight, she grabbed hold of my arm with both hands and didn't let go until the light came on at the end of the movie. I thought Thai custom didn't' allow any PDA between a man and woman in public."

Bob responded, "That depends on where and how she held your arm. Were her hands around your arm, over the shirt sleeve?"

I replied, "Yea. Why?"

Bob explained, "It's socially acceptable for the woman to touch her man publicly in some situations, as long as there's no skin contact, and for protection is one of them. Since being protected from watching violence can be on of those situations, then I think Jintana took advantage of this exception, but only because she really likes you for some reason. The only other situation it's allowed, that I know of, is with Western style dancing, but only when required as part of the dance. No bear hug dancing is allowed. In Thai dancing with men and women, there is no contact.

I responded, "Well, I think she really likes me, as she wanted to go on a second date with me to another Samurai movie next Monday. But, I think it's because I'm a tall American."

Bob laughed and said, "It may also be your nose."

I asked, "My nose? What about my nose?"

Bob answered, "It's the size of your nose. It's longer than a Thai man's nose. Thai women believe the size of a man's nose is directly proportional to the size of his penis."

I responded, "Really? You're kidding."

Bob replied, "No kidding, Sandii. Mix that with being tall and American, and she'll find you very attractive."

I pointed at Skip and laughed, "Then, with that big Jewish nose of yours, Skip, you're going to be very popular with the women in Korat."

Skip laughed and responded, "That may be true, but I already have a Jewish princess[103] waiting in Cleveland."

Bob added, "If you think being with Jintana will become serious, then having her as your tîi-lók is a simply between you two. But marriage to a Thai woman, especially the caliber of Jintana, is a whole other matter. Girls are considered the property of the father. To marry a Thai girl, you'll have to pay the father a dowry, which is based on how much it cost him to raise her, and any intrinsic value she may have, like her age, her looks, and if she's a virgin. For a plain looking, farm village girl, the dowry could be as little as $1000. If she's pretty and has a university degree, it could be as much as $25,000. Just thought you should know how that works in Thailand. So, Sandii, what'd you think of the Japanese Samurai movie?"

I replied, "It was a knockoff of that spaghetti Western with Clint Eastwood, *A Fist Full of Dollars*, even though the action in the Samurai movie was more intense."

Bob responded, "Sandii, you've got that backwards, *A Fist Full of Dollars* is an Italian knockoff of a Japanese Samurai movie. So are *A Few Dollars More* and *The Good, the Bad, and the Ugly*, as well as the Yul Brenner movies *The Magnificent Seven* and *Sapata*.

I exclaimed, "You're kidding!"

Bob explained, "I'm not kidding. It started when Yul Brenner took all the money he made from the musical he starred in, *The King and I*, and bought the rights to a popular Japanese movie about seven rogue Samurai who are hired by a village to drive out a large band of other rogue Samurai that have been terrorizing the village. Yul Brenner not only became famous for starring himself in the movie, but the all-in gamble also made him very rich. So, the Italians have been buying the rights to other Japanese Samurai movies to make knockoffs as American Westerns, like those Clint Eastwood movies, which I'm sure are the first of many.

"Okay, enough chit-chat about spaghetti Westerns. Even thought it's a quiet night, we still have work to do. Sandii, I want you to keep working with Skip to get up to speed on our in-house circuits, as tomorrow evening will be busy with all the traffic from Stateside with

---

103   To the Jews, any pure blood Jewish woman is considered a Princess.

people coming back to work Tuesday morning after their three-day weekend for Labor Day, and we won't have any of the Site Office honchos here to back us up. Meanwhile, I'm popping over to the NCO Club for dinner before they close. If you need me, you can call me there through the Base's telephone exchange and I can be back here in a minute. Then, after your midnight meal runs, I'll continue checking Skip out on our breakout gear."

When Bob left, I said, "Skip, remember my telling you working here keeps getting better?"

Skip replied, "Yea, but I don't see how."

I responded, "Well, just follow me," as I led him to the back of the Operations Room. Using the double suction cup device, I lifted a 2-foot square section of the floor. Showing Skip the mattress stored there, I explained, "Sometimes, when it's slow in the middle of the night, Bob'll allow you to take a nap for an hour or so. But, don't mention this to Jim or Phizer."

Skip responded, "You're right, things keep getting better."

I worked with Skip in the Grand Canyon until Bob returned from the NCO Club and took Skip back to the breakout racks to check him out on the breakout circuits. Meanwhile, I monitored the Order Wire until it was time for my 10:55 meal run, and met up with Glen in the Mess Hall. Telling Glen about Bob setting me straight on how the Japanese Samurai movie plots were actually the basis for the spaghetti Westerns, Glen responded, "Tom told me the same thing. It only goes to show most of what we call Western Civilization, originated in the Orient and came to us through Italy, like gunpowder, the printing press, flying kites and hot air balloons, and our spices. Even the spaghetti came from China."

I responded, "Now that you mention it, I remember learning in High School that astrology, algebra and our religions came from the Middle East. It's a good thing tomorrow's Pay Day, or we wouldn't be able to go to the cafe and talk with Sùpa. Listening to the girls talk as we walked to the theater, I could only make out a phrase here and there, and really need to practice more with Sùpa. Even then, it doesn't seem to be enough. I think I need to find a group I can learn by immersion with."

Glen said, "That sounds good, but the only immersion I'm looking for is with Sùpa."

Arriving back at the Air Base Operations Room, I saw Skip standing in the middle of the Grand Canyon talking excitedly on a Lynch handset, and heard Bob say, "Ted called awhile ago to say he had a line up with Rosie, and Skip's been busy talking with his Jewish princess and family ever since. Do you want to make a call Stateside, Sandii?"

I replied, "Heck yea. It's been three weeks since I called on my first night shift."

When Skip finished and gave me the handset, he said, "If you tell me it gets better than this, I'll call you a liar."

While I made my phone calls to Linda and my parents, Skip made his meal run. When Skip returned, I took a two-hour nap as Bob went over the breakout circuits with Skip, because today was Pay Day and the pay line started at 8:00, which would cut into my morning sleep time. After I got up, Skip took his two-hour nap. While I sat at the Operations Room desk and listened to the Order Wire, Bob went into the Site Office to sleep on the cushioned chairs he arranged as a bed, since he had to pick up his paycheck at the Tropo Site.

Making the 5:40 meal run, I then waited while Skip left on his 6:35 meal run for the day shift to arrive after the 7:00 morning formation to relieve me. When the Shift Change Report had been made in the Site Office, then Jim drove me back to the Company Area. Entering my hooch, I saw everyone changing into their Class-B Army khaki uniforms. Once I'd changed into my Class-B khaki uniform, Skip and I looked over the other's uniform for discrepancies, so we'd appear as sharp as possible in front of the CO when we reported for pay.

By 8:00, everyone in my hooch headed for the Day Room to be paid, except George and Tommy, who were working the day shift. Turning left onto the walkway towards the Day Room, I saw the line to the Day Room's front door was already extending across to the front of the HQ. So, I turned right behind the HQ to walk up the other side. Reaching the front of the HQ, I was able to join the pay line's end with the five others from my hooch. Seeing the pay line was moving at a reasonable pace, I decided there wasn't time to smoke a cigarette. Besides, if I took out a pack of cigarettes, it would be quickly emptied by those standing in line around me, who would bum a cigarette from me.

Approaching the Day Room's front door, I looked back along the pay line around me and saw one Soldier who stuck out like a sore thumb. I asked Glen, who was standing behind me, "There's a guy dressed in a rumpled pickle suit in the pay line. Doesn't he know you have to be in your Class-B uniform to be paid?"

Looking back down the line, Glen then faced me shaking his head with a sad expression and replied, "That's PFC Brown, the Company's only lineman and a real hard luck case. His life was all set with his own business, a wife and two kids when he was drafted into the Army at age 28. When he arrived here after nine weeks of bootcamp and eight weeks training to be a lineman at Ft. Gordon, Georgia, his business went bankrupt and his wife divorced him. When that happened, he said he'd been screwed enough by the Army, and if anyone needed him, they knew where he lived in Korat with tîi-lók. The only other time we see him is when he shows up on Pay Day.

"Fortunately, for him, he's the only lineman in the Company, and if we need his expertise, then they send someone to get him. Some lifer tried to put him on report once for being AWOL,[104] but a bunch of guys made it clear that if anyone messed with Brown, then they'd be taken out. Even the CO has given him a pass, so long as he does his job. I've heard he has extended his tour to the end of his enlistment and partnered with a local phone company to put in landline services for them."

I thought, "Well, that's one way to screw the Army when the Army has screwed you."

Entering the Day Room's front door, I saw the fold-up Ping-Pong table and pool table were moved to the right sidewall, and the card table, with several others, were now aligned down the left half of the room. The pay line ended eight feet from the first card table, where the CO and a Paymaster from Finance were seated. At the second card table I saw the XO and Spike, the next one had Porntit and PFC Schultz, and the last one had a Thai man with banded stacks of blue 20-Bhat bills and red 100-Bhat bills, and rolls of 1-Bhat coins.

When it was my turn, I marched the eight feet to the first table, halted, made a left face, presented my ID card with my left hand, saluted with my right hand and said, "Specialist Lynch, Sherman A., reporting for pay, Sir." To which the CO returned my salute and said, "At ease, Specialist Lynch," as he searched down a copy of the Company Ros-

---

104 Absent With Out Leave

ter, found my name and said, "Lynch, Sherman A., two-hundred-seventy Dollars and no cents."

As the Paymaster counted $270.00 from a large metal lockbox, the CO turned the Company Roster toward me, handed me a black ballpoint pen, pointed to my name and said, "Sign here for your pay, Specialist Lynch." Once I signed my name, the Paymaster counted thirteen 20-Dollar bills and one 10-Dollar bill into my left hand. Then, I came to attention and saluted the CO with my right hand. The CO returned my salute and said, "Dismissed." Making a right-face to proceed to the next table, I thought, "Being paid $50 in Combat Pay for the few minutes to fly over South Vietnam at 35,000 feet is sure going to come in handy."

At the second table, the XO asked "How much in U.S. Savings Bonds do you wish to buy, Specialist Lynch?" and I thought, "This is such a scam. The Army expects every Company CO to have 100% of the troops he commands to buy at minimum a $10 Savings Bond for $7.50 to help the military to pay for the war effort and the Soldier's monthly pay. But, the $10 Savings Bond can't be redeemed for $10 until it has 'matured' in seven years. So, why am I buying a U.S. Savings Bond? Because, if I don't, then the Army enters into my DD-201 Service Record that I'm opposed to the war effort, which affects my chance for promotion," as I handed the XO my 10-Dollar bill.

Taking my 10-Dollar bill, I saw the XO find my name on his copy of the Company Roster and write "$10.00" next to my name. When Spike hand me the $2.50 in change I put it in my left front pants pocket and walked the few steps to the 3rd table.

There, I showed Porntit my ID card and handed her a 20-Dollar bill. I watched as she found my name on her copy of the Company Roster, made a checkmark next to the "$8.00" written by my name, and handed the 20-Dollar bill to PFC Schultz, as I thought, "$8.00 a month for Maan-daa to launder my clothes, keep my wall locker inspection ready, spit shine my boots and shoes, and make my bed every day is a great deal. Not that she'll see the $8.00, as Porntit keeps a $1.00 kickback."

When PFC Schultz gave me the $12 in change, I proceeded to the fourth table where Dollars were exchanged for Bhat. I had already decided my first purchase was to buy two sets of jungle fatigues at the Air Base Exchange for $48, then cross the road to the bank and open a savings account with the $50 I received in combat pay, which would leave me $150 and change. Figuring a pack of Pall Malls and a 6-pack of Budweiser per day came to $21 a month, plus $25 for other expenses, left me at least $100 to spend in Korat. So, I handed the Thai man five of my 20-Dollar bills and said, "I'd like two rolls of twenty 1-Bhat coins, eighteen 20-Bhat bills and sixteen 100-Bhat bills."

After he handed me the 2000 Bhat in exchange for the $100, I exited the Day Room. Returning to my hooch, I put the $154 in my wallet, and hid my 2000 Bhat in pipe tobacco can I'd found and kept on the top shelf in my wall locker for this purpose. Then, I retrieved a can of Bud from the mini-fridge. Drinking the beer, as I stripped off my Class-B Army khaki uniform prior to going to bed and get some sleep before it got too hot, Dan, Ronnie and Stony each handed me a 5-Dollar bill as they returned from the pay line.

When I asked, "What's this for?" Dan replied, "For the beer and butts we bummed from you when we were broke."

I responded, "But, this is more than what you bummed cost me."

Ronnie replied, "Then think of it as paying you in advance for when we're broke at the end of the month."

I responded, "Well thanks, guys," as they walked to their wall lockers, and thought, "Who says kindness doesn't pay. But, what I can't figure is they're planning to be broke before the next pay day. We get paid ten times what a Thai makes, and everything is so cheap, it beats me how they can blow through $200 in a few weeks. Guess it's because my family didn't' have much money while I was growing up on the farm and watched my parents plan for every penny, and learned from them the value of being frugal. Heck, when I was paid $78 a month in bootcamp, I thought it was a lot of money."

Waking at 11:00 to the bugle call for Mess, I found myself lying on my sweat soaked sheets as usual. I went through my routine of getting a cold Bud and using the piss tube before going to my wall locker to take out a silk shirt and pair of cotton pants to wear for lunch. Opening my wall locker, I saw Skip doing the same and said, "Sàwàtdii, Skip."

Skip responded, "Sàwàtdii, Sandii. I'm amazed at how sweaty my bed was when I got up. I can understand why everyone went to bed as soon as they returned from the pay line."

I said, "It's like this every morning, Skip. You'll soon be in the habit of getting as much sleep as possible in the morning when you work the night shift and on your off days. Even with a fan, there's no way to sleep in the afternoon with all the heat and humidity."

When we'd finished dressing in our civilian clothes and drinking our beer, Skip and I left for lunch at the Mess Hall. After lunch, we caught a Thai bus to the Air Base, where we exited when it stopped behind the Base Exchange. As we each selected two sets of jungle fatigues in the BX, Skip asked, "If it's so cheap to have clothes made by a tailor in Korat, why is it they don't make jungle fatigues for a lot less than the 12 bucks each we pay here?"

I replied, "Maybe the military has cornered the market on the OD stop-rip cloth they're made with. Next time I see my tailor, I'll ask him."

Skip asked, "Speaking of tailors, could you take me to Korat with you tomorrow to see your tailor so I can have some clothes like yours made?"

I answered, "Don't know why not. Besides, then you can have another 'it can't get better than this' experience."

Skip exclaimed, "In Korat? What part of working at the Air Base Site is in Korat that can make it so much better?"

I replied, "I don't want to spoil it for you, so just trust me."

After we bought the jungle fatigues, and Skip bought a fan, I asked Skip to wait at the Air Base Site while I went to the bank, where I opened a savings account with a $50 deposit. At the Radio Site, we hitched a ride with Tommy in the truck on his 12:35 meal run to the Company Area, where he dropped us, and all of our loot, in front of the Day Room.

Returning to our hooch, as I was putting my new jungle fatigues in my wall locker, I saw Maan-daa setting her cleaned laundry on my bed. After she was unburdened, we exchanged sàwàtdiis, I asked in Thai if she would like to meet her new "Dék-chaai." Leading her to Skip's bed, I said, "Excuse me, Skip, I'd like you to meet Maan-daa, your mây-bâan."

As Maan-daa left us to put her laundry away after meeting Skip, he saw Nít-nòi putting an arm load of laundry on Ronnie's bed and asked, "Why can't she be my mây-bâan?"

I laughed and replied, "Because Maan-daa has promised to keep Nít-nòi away from horny, young Jews like you."

After introducing Skip to Maan-daa, it was 1:00 and time for Glen and I to catch a Thai bus to Korat to spend the afternoon talking with Sùpa before the dinner crowd began to arrive. Then we'd eat our own dinner and returned to Camp Friendship to get ready for working the night shift.

Entering the cafe, I was totally surprised to see Sùpa talking with the exotic Jintana sitting at the table near the left sidewall. When Jintana looked at me and paid me a dazzling smile, I thought, "Now this what I call a Pay Day."

CHAPTER 22

JINTANA

Watching Sùpa quickly approach Glen and I at the cafe's entrance, I saw Jintana's dazzling smile evaporate to a frown as she quickly stood up behind the table, made the wâai before her face, and bowed very low from the waist. As we approached the table, I heard Jintana say slowly so I could understand, "Kăaw tôat. Dì-chăn mii kwaam-sâo-jai kàt-jung-wà kaawng bpai-yîam gàp Sùpa."[105]

I didn't catch everything she said, but I did get the gist and realized my surprised expression was mistaken for one of disappointment that she was at the cafe uninvited. I also made the wâai, bowed from my waist very low, and replied slowly as I tried to remember the words, "Mâi bpén rai. Pŏm săan sùk nai hŭa-jai hĕn Jintana. Pŏm bprà-làat-jai hĕn koon tîi-nîi."[106] And was happy I had been spending so much time learning to speak Thai.

As I rose, I gave the largest smile I could to Jintana. Watching her slowly rise from her supplicant position, I saw she had tears from her

---

105   "Ask forgive. I have sorrow interrupt belong visit with Sùpa."
106   "No problem. I extremely happy in heart see Jintana. I surprised see you here."

eyes, but her dazzling smile had returned. I added, "Kăaw-tôat, pŭa sâo kaawng pŏm nâa jaak bprà-làat-jai. Sà-rà-naa káo-rûam pûak-rao."[107]

Jintana bowed her head and said, "Kup koon mâak, ká," as she gracefully wiped the tears from her face.

Then Jintana, Glen and I sat down at the table together, I asked in Thai what she would like to eat. When she politely said she was not hungry, I asked Sùpa to bring three plates of chicken fried rice and bottles of Pepsi. While Sùpa went to get the food, Jintana said there was little work to do at the Sri Pattana Hotel because very few guests were there and her supervisor had given her the rest of the day off. I said this was because the men had no money, but today they received money, that the Hotel would be full tonight, and she'd have much work there tomorrow.

Jintana asked if I liked "Ngaan-dtén-ram." I knew "ngaan" meant "work," "dtén" meant "dance" and "ram" meant "formal dance." I extrapolated this meant "ballroom dance," and asked if she meant "waltz" and made the 3-4 tempo sound for a waltz.

She responded, "Châi pûut, jang-wà-wáawm,"[108] as she pantomimed doing a waltz, and I said that I did like "ngaan-dtén-ram."

Of course I could ballroom dance. My parents loved to dance. In fact, that's how they met. In 1946, Dad was picked by Fleet Admiral "Bull" Halsey, the Chief of Naval Operations, to fly to the Naval Air Stations across the U.S. to inspect the electronics on Naval aircraft. Then, only daylight flights were allowed, and he often had to land at a Naval Air Station before dark and wait till the next day to fly again. Once, he'd landed at the Corpus Christi Naval Air Station in Texas, and looking for something to do, he went to the local USO[109] dance, where he met Mom. From then on, every time he flew across the U.S., he directed his plane to layover at Corpus Christi so he could dance with Mom. Eventually, he convinced Mom, who was a WWII widow, to marry him.

Mom was from Texas, where it's traditional for teenage boys and girls to learn to ballroom dance for the cotillions[110]. When I and my

---

107   "Ask forgive for sad belong my face from surprise. Please join us."
108   "Yes. Speak waltz."
109   United Service Organization that support men and women in uniform.
110   A formal ball, especially one at which debutantes were presented to society.

sister, who was a year younger, were in Junior High School, our parents taught us how to ballroom dance. Though I resented it then, I later learned from my sister when we were in High School, the girls liked for me to ask them to dance because I knew how to dance, unlike the other boys. So, I told Jintana that I very much liked to ballroom dance.

When I said that, I saw Jintana's eyes light up as she told me that every Thursday night she went with a group of friends to a "nai-klàp" where they would ballroom dance. I thought this was great for four reasons. First, I'd see Jintana more often than Mondays on a double date with Glen and Sùpa to a movie. Second, I didn't have to arrange for another couple to have other dates with Jintana. Third, I would be able to hold Jintana in my arms as we danced. And fourth, I'd be with a group of Thais so I could learn and perfect my Thai language skills.

Jintana told me the night club was north of the Sri Pattana Hotel, just off Rajadamnern Road, on Vatmung Lane. And that everyone met there at "Săawng tŭm." Literally, two hours after sundown, or 8:00. The Thai method of telling time is based on the four parts of the day, "dtii" from midnight to 6:00 AM; "châao" from 6:00 AM to noon; "baai" from noon to 6:00 PM; and "tŭm" from 6:00 PM to midnight.

I thought, "Since the last bus to Camp Friendship leaves Chainarong Gate at 10:00, then I'll have to leave the night club by 9:30, which will only give me an hour and half to dance with Jintana, or I have to find a place to spend the night. I can talk to Bob about this tonight at work."

Establishing with Jintana that I would meet here in the night club at 8:00, Glen and I struggle with describing to the two girls how the Italians, "chaao-ì-dtaa-lii," copied Japanese Samurai movie plots to make "a-maa-ri-gaa kaao-baawi" movies. We also confirmed the four of us were going to another Japanese Samurai movie next Monday afternoon, much to the relief of Glen and Sùpa, who could not go without Jintana and I.

Once the dinner crowd began to arrive at 4:00, Glen and I said our sàwàtdiis and left to catch a Thai bus to Camp Friendship. When we returned to the hooch, I grabbed a cold can of Bud from the minifridge. Opening my wall locker, I found both sets of jungle fatigues pressed and hung up, and that Maan-daa had sewn the First Brigade patches correctly on the left sleeves and my Spec-4 patches on each sleeve. Changing into a set of my new jungle fatigues, I saw Skip walk up to me, turn around with outstretched arms, and ask "How do I look?"

I replied, "Nobody will guess you've been in country less than a week. How's the Double-Deck Pinochle going?"

Skip responded, "Pretty good. Dan thinks I can try playing for money, so that's a good vote of confidence. How was your trip with Glen to see his girlfriend?"

I answered, "You mean Sùpa? It was fantastic. Jintana surprised me by also being at the cafe, which almost mucked things up because she thought I was angry with her for being there uninvited. But we straightened it out, and she invited me to meet her with some friends Thursday night at a night club to ballroom dance."

Skip exclaimed, "That fox asked you to go on a date! Well you suave devil."

Playing it down, I said, "Can't exactly call it a date, as it's what she does with a group every Thursday and we'll arrive separately. She may just want someone tall to dance with for a change."

Skip called down the hooch, "Hey, Glen, do you think Jintana asked Sandii to meet her at a night club as a date or because she wanted someone tall to dance with?"

I heard Glen laugh and yell from his bed, "From where I sat, it looked like Jintana wants to date Sandii more often, and to ask him to go dancing was as good excuse as any."

Skip laughed and scoffed at me, "You must think I'm a putz if you think I'd fall for that line."

I responded defensively, "You know as well as I do that a man never knows what's going on in a woman's mind. If Jintana wants me to dance with her at a night club only because she likes to dance, but is too tall for a Thai man to ask her, makes sense to me. And to assume she wants more only invites disaster. You know what happens when you assume anything?"

Skip replied, "Yea, It can make an 'ass' out of 'u' and 'me.' But don't you consider the other possibilities of Jintana wanting to dance with you?"

I answered, "If I considered any other possibilities, it would be futile. I learned long ago, when it comes to having a relationship with a woman, its the woman who decides what it is, and what the man decides means nothing. Even when Glen and I went to the movie with

Sùpa and Jintana, we had decided on the seating arrangement. But they had decided otherwise, and it didn't matter one bit what we'd decided. And Frank, the man you replaced, told me it was his woman who asked if he wanted to live with her, not him asking her. And it's the same with Glen, who wants Sùpa to be his tîi-lók, but knows it's Sùpa who decides. No, Skip. It doesn't matter what kind of relationship I want with Jintana, because it's her who will decide. The only decision I'll have is to accept or reject it. When it comes to dealing with women, it's the KISS method that works best."

Skip laughed and responded, "Yea, I know, Keep It Simple Stupid. And you're right. Even in the male dominated Jewish society, where the man makes the decisions as the head of the family. But the wife, who's the neck, decides which way head is facing when he makes a decision. So, what's your plan with Jintana at the night club?"

I laughed and replied, "To keep it simple, stupid. To enjoy dancing with her as much as she decides." Hearing the bugle call for Mess, I added, "So, how about I put on my new jungle fatigues and we get some chow before we go to the Day Room for our ride to work?"

Donning my new jungle fatigues, I found the stop-rip material was airier, lighter and cooler to wear in the heat and humidity of tropical Thailand than the heavy, thickly woven cotton of the close fitting, Army issued, OD BDUs. Skip and I then headed to the Mess Hall for dinner, after which we each bought two 6-packs of beer at the Howard Johnson. Returning to our hooch, we each rolled up a clean set of skivvies in a towel before leaving to stand in front of the Day Room with those who were gathering in wait for their rides to the Tropo Site.

I commented, "Skip, I'm glad we ride in the cab of our ¾-ton truck verses riding in the back of a canvas-covered deuce-and-a-half truck to choke on the dust raised on that gravel road to the Tropo Site."

Skip responded, "Once was plenty for me, too. Can you imagine doing that six times a day?"

I replied, "Don't even want to imagine it, and once was enough for me, too. Okay, here comes Tommy with our truck?"

As Tommy stopped the truck in front of us, I asked through the open window, "How'd work go today, Tommy?"

Exiting the truck, Tommy replied, "Everything was quiet till an hour ago, then it started to get busy. You will want to brace yourselves for a very busy night," adding with a laugh, "and pray there are no bugs."

Climbing in the driver's seat as Skip walked to the other side, I responded with a laugh at the double entendre, "Why, are you jealous of the number of bugs we found in the racks last night? Must've set a world record."

Tommy laughed and said as I drove the truck away, "I'm sure it did."

Entering in the Operations Room, I found things were busy enough that Jim was helping Jack in the Grand Canyon, and I saw Rodger with Bob in the second aisle of the breakout racks. I said, "Skip, you go see if you can relieve Roger so he can go home, and I'll relieve Jack."

Walking into the Grand Canyon, Jack saw me and said, "Sandii, thank the Great Buddha you're here so I can leave this mad house," and he look at Jim asking, "Okay if I go home now?"

Jim laughed and said, "Sandii and I have this mad house under control, so you can go home and cool your jets," and to me he calmly said, "I have an Alpha-1 crypto outage here, but it's on their end as the square-wave test signal's amplitude is good and in sync. They're in the process of inserting a new crypto card now. So, I'd like you to check SLAB-7 and TALS-6 to see if the square-wave signals going through our house are within tolerance, or if the problem is in-house. No rush there, as they're both Charlie circuits. Right now Bob and Roger are tracking down a problem with SNAP-2 in the breakout circuits, and it's a Bravo circuit."

I replied, "Right, Jim. I already sent Skip to help Bob and Roger."

Jim responded, "Good thinking, Sandii," as I selected two tip-ring-sleeve patch cords to connect to two of the rack mounted oscilloscopes in the Grand Canyon to monitor SLAB-7 and TALS-6 simultaneously. In a few minutes, I told Jim both circuits looked good in-house, and was waiting for a pause in the rapid Order Wire chatter to tell Sakon Nakon Air Base that SLAB-7 looked good from here and tell Taklii Air Base that TALS-6 looked good from here. While I was waiting, I heard on the Order Wire, "Korat Base-Warin, check WMAL-2," which I knew was a Bravo-1 circuit and one step below the critical Alpha circuits, and responded, "Warin-Korat Base, will check WMAL-2." As I scribbled down the information in the Temporary Log, I thought, "Tommy was right, this is going to be a very busy night."

Things began to slow down about midnight, when Jim sent Skip and I to the Mess Hall together, while he and Roger continued to help Bob with a couple of remaining outages. When Skip and I returned,

I saw Jim and Roger asleep on the chairs in the Site Office. Bob said, "There are no current outages, so I'm taking the truck to the NCO Annex for a hamburger and fries. And do not disturb Jim or Roger unless the building is on fire."

Skip and I waited for another onslaught of outages while Bob was gone. But, while we listened to the chatter on the Order Wire, we thankfully heard no call for "Korat Base." When Bob returned 15 minutes later with a basket of fries and a hamburger, I happily reported there had been no report of outages to us. As Bob sat at the desk to eat, he began copying data from the Temporary Log to the permanent Site Log, which he did for the next couple of hours while Skip and I put things away and monitored the Order Wire.

At 4:00, Bob went in the Site Office to wake Jim and Roger, so they could catch a Thai bus home to Korat. As Jim left, he told me, "Tell Phizer I won't be at morning formation, and Roger won't be back until noon," and I thought, "That means Phizer will be in charge of our Radio Site from 7:00 till noon because he's the Site Engineer. I pity John, Larry and Red if he tries to order them around."

Things were still quiet when Skip left for his 4:55 meal run. I felt it was a good time to get Bob's advice in private about Jintana, and said, "Bob, there's been some new developments with Jintana that I'd like to talk about with you."

I saw Bob swivel in his chair from the desk to face me in the chair I was sitting in and ask, "New developments with Jintana? I thought you wouldn't be seeing her again until next Monday to see another Japanese Samurai movie. What happened?"

I related to Bob everything that happened at the cafe when Glen and I went for our usual visit with Sùpa. When I'd finished, I asked, "What do you make of Jintana showing up unexpectedly at the cafe to ask me if I'd like to meet her at a night club with her regular group to dance. Is it just because she wants a tall man to dance with, or do you think it could be more?"

Bob shook his head as he chuckled and said, "The fact she would show up at the cafe without being invited is very unusual for any Thai to do. As a Buddhist, to do anything to make another person uncomfortable is just not done. In fact, the Thai phrase, 'sà-baai dii mái,' which we take to mean 'how are you,' literally means 'are you comfortable?' For her to show up uninvited, tells me it was an act of desperation. And either, she is desperate to have a tall man, like yourself, to dance with her in a regular group where none of the men like to dance with a tall woman, which is very unlikely, or she's afraid you'll find another girl to be with during the week before your next date, since it is Pay Day and you now have lots of money to spend on other women, which is more likely.

"The inscrutable Oriental mind can be difficult to understand in the best of circumstances and that of the Oriental woman is unfathomable irregardless. If she's afraid you'll be looking for another woman to be with, I'd be very cautious because she has set her sights on you for whatever purpose, which could still be to have a tall man to dance with, as she clearly enjoys dancing. If you really like her, then go with the flow and see what she has in mind. Otherwise, you need to break it off now before your in too deep. Remember the old adage, 'hell hath no fury like a woman scorned.' All in all, if what you've told me about Jintana is accurate, then she is a person who focuses on what she wants and is not afraid to do what it takes to get it. After all, it takes years of practice and determination to belong to a Thai Ram dance troupe for the Thai festivals."

I responded, "I really appreciate your insight, Bob. Now, do you know anything about this night club where I'm to meet her?"

Bob replied, "I know where it is, and it's not a bar. It's a place where middle income Thais go to socialize and dance. Not the high society types, but mostly for the younger set, so its mores tend to be less stringent than general Thai society. The attire is not black-tie, so your silk shirt, slacks and black dress shoes will be fine. The cost of drinks is a little more, but you're not going to be guzzling down the booze, so one or two drinks will be plenty. Also, it'll close at midnight on weekday nights because most of the customers have to be at work the next morning. Anything else?"

I replied, "On the subject of the closing time, as you know, the last bus for Camp Friendship leaves at 10:00, which means I'd have to leave by 9:30, or plan on spending the night somewhere. As the Sri Pattana Hotel is the closest to the night club, do you know anything about it?"

Bob answered, "It's one of the better Hotels in Korat, but not set up for Westerners like the Jomsurang Hotel. The rooms have ceiling fans, unheated water, squat toilets, and are priced at 50 Bhat per night. Also, the front desk people speak fair English. But, if you want air-conditioning and a hot shower, you'll need to find another Hotel."

I responded, "Well, it'll be at night, so having just a fan is okay. And, I'll have already showered and had a BM. Also, $2.50 a night is affordable, since it's close by."

Bob said, "Then it sounds like you're set to go dancing with Jintana."

A moment later, Skip returned from breakfast, so I had a quick shower and shaved before I made the 6:35 meal run. Arriving at the Motor Pool, I saw Spec-5 Phizer waiting there. I explained to him, "Jim and Roger both spent the night at the Site because we had a lot of circuit outages, and they didn't leave till 4:00 this morning. So, Jim won't be at formation this morning, and Roger said he'll be back by noon. But, when I left everything was pretty quiet."

Phizer responded, "I guess that leaves me in charge till noon. Thank for the report, Lynch."

Walking to the Mess Hall, I thought, "What a butt hole. He still doesn't call me Sandii like everyone else."

After breakfast, I went to my hooch, where I found Skip stripping to his skivvies and drinking a beer. Grabbing a can of Bud from the mini-fridge to drink as I readied for bed, I said, "Skip, you have a good sleep because you're going to have a busy night with Glen and I."

Skip laughed and responded, "I hope it's a different kind of busy than we had last night."

Laughing in kind, I said, "I assure you, it'll be a very different kind of busy."

After lunch, Glen and I had our usual Thai practice session, while Skip partnered with Tommy in Double-Deck Pinochle against Ronnie and Stony. Tommy had told me, "After work, George charged out of here like a ram in rut last night and this morning after formation, now that he has a hand full of Bhat to spend on the pûu-ying[111]. I imagine we won't see him again till 6:00 to change for work."

I laughed and said, "And what about you, Tommy?"

Tommy laughed and replied, "I figure most of the guys at Camp Friendship and the Air Base were hitting the bars and the pûu-ying last night, and since I wouldn't be getting to Korat till 8:00, that I wasn't

---

111   A girl or woman.

interested in picking from the left overs or sloppy seconds. What I need is a real fox like you. How's that been going?"

I answered, "It's progressing. We're supposed to meet at a Thai night club tomorrow night for ballroom dancing, and I'll let you know how it goes."

When I heard the monsoon rain hit, Skip finished his hand of Double-Deck Pinochle and joined Glen and I in getting ready to leave for Korat. I double checked with Skip to make sure he had a condom and his blue STD booklet. At the main street, the three of us boarded a Thai bus for Korat, which made the usual stop at the Air Base gate for the STD MP to check us before allowing us to leave Camp Friendship. Since it was mid-afternoon, the bus was less than half full and we had no trouble finding three empty rows together that we could comfortably sit sideways in as Glen and I pointed out points of interest to Skip.

Exiting the bus when it stopped in Korat, I pointed to and explained to Skip Korat's "bâan-ling," and its inhospitable nature, as we walked the short distance past the Chainarong Gate to the tailor shop. Once Skip had selected a design and choices of cloth for three silk shirts and two pair of cotton pants, and paid the 120 Bhat deposit, we then walked the few dozen yards back down Chainarong Road to the cafe.

Entering the cafe, I saw Sùpa was standing near the door waiting for us. We made the wâai, bowed our sàwàtdiis before Glìn-dii introduced Skip to Sùpa, which she pronounced as "sá-kip." I was relieved that Jintana was not there, as I didn't want Skip drooling all over her, not because I wouldn't want to see her.

Though I could see Skip was annoyed that Glen, Sùpa and I were speaking Thai, he very much enjoyed the chicken fried rice and Pepsi, and was surprised it only cost 20 cents. He was also impressed with how pretty Sùpa was, and asked, "Can you guys ask her if she has a sister or another pretty girlfriend who would go to the movie with me when you go next week?"

Glen and I laughed as Glen pitched Skip's request to Sùpa. She laughed as she replied in Thai that she had many pretty girlfriends who would like to be with a "jà-mùuk yài" man. Glen and I laughed as Glen translated, "Sùpa said she has lots of pretty friends who would like to go out with a 'nose big' man."

Skip eagerly said, "Châai dâai, krup."

Sùda laughed and told Glen that tomorrow she will have a pretty friend in the cafe at noon, and if Sá-kip didn't like her, then she'll have a second pretty friend in the cafe at 4:00. When glen translated this, Skip said, "That's great. Then I won't have to go on a blind date like Sandii."

When we left the cafe, Glen and I showed Skip the way to the theater on Wacharasrit Road where we saw the Japanese Samurai movie, so he'd know where it was. We then continued to Mahat Thai Road, where we turned left and went to Chomphon Road, and crossed it onto Jomsurangyat Road as we passed the moat on our left. Reaching Buarong Road, we turned left and walked to the Sing Hăi Beer Warehouse, where we stopped. Pointing at it, I said proudly, "Skip, this is the Sing Hăi Beer Warehouse."

Skip exclaimed, "This is the it-doesn't-get-better-than-this surprise?"

I turned Skip around to face the compound across the road and said, "No, Skip. That is. It's where Roger, Bob and Red live, and a crazy Oklahoma Indian named Jim Horn, who works at the Tropo Site." As we crossed the road, I added, "This is where we come in the evening to relax, drink free beer, and have good conversation that's not work or military related. That's one of Jim Horn's four house rules. The other three are, don't bring your own booze, beer is strictly self serve, and don't pick the roses."

As the guard passed us through the door in the gate, Skip said, "You're joking?"

Crossing the gravel parking area, I replied, "It's no joke."

When we reached Jim Horn's gate, Glen yelled, "It's Glen, Sandii and the new guy, Skip. Is it okay for us to enter?"

I heard Horn reply, "As long as ya don't have any booze with ya."

Skip followed Glen and I as we paraded down the walkway, up the steps, across the porch, through the green door and to the refrigerator, where we each grabbed a quart bottle of Sing Hăi Beer, pausing briefly to make the wâai, bow and exchange sàwàtdiis with the three tîi-lóks sitting at the table. Passing back through the screen door to the porch, Skip said, "Sandii, you're right, it can't get any better than this to be working at the Air Base Site," and I thought, "famous last words, Skip, but I'm sure it will get better than this for you."

I then introduced Skip to Jim Horn and Tom Lewiston. After an hour, Ronnie showed up and told us Stony was looking for a different distraction tonight. About 8:00, I heard a motorcycle's rumble and the crunch of gravel as it crossed the parking area. I then saw Frank and his tîi-lók enter through the gate. After Frank had led her into the house and returned with a bottle of Sing Hǎi Beer, I introduced him to his replacement at the Air Base, Skip. Until 9:00, there was considerable frivolity amongst the eight of us. Then, Glen, Ronnie, Skip and I left for the Chaophaya Inn to hire sǎawm-law drivers for 5 Bhat each to carry us to the Chainarong Gate for a bus ride to Camp Friendship.

The next morning, after breakfast at the Mess Hall and morning formation, I went back to bed and slept until I heard the 11:00 bugle call for Mess. After lunch, I rolled up a clean set of skivvies in a white towel, and caught a ride with Larry to the Air Base Site to perform the three Ss in preparation for my date with Jintana. Returning to the hooch, I remembered Glen was to take Skip to the cafe at noon to meet Sùpa's friend to see if she was pretty enough to take to the movie on Monday, or to opt for the girl "behind door number 2." So, I played Double-Deck Pinochle with Tommy as my partner against Ronnie and Stony for money, all the while drinking beer and smoking cigarettes until dinner at 5:00. For Tommy and I, it proved a profitable afternoon, as we came out nearly $3.00 ahead.

Straight from the Mess Hall after dinner, I caught a Thai bus to Korat. It was crowded with Soldiers also going there, and became very crowded as it picked up Airmen while crossing the Air Base. Enduring the cramped, hard seats and the swaying of men holding handrails hanging from the ceiling, after a half-hour, I was grateful when I exited the bus, and decided riding at peak hours was a bad idea.

At the Chainarong Gate, I was only to argue a sǎawm-law driver down to 4 Bhat for a ride to the Sri Pattana Hotel. There, I entered a nicely decorated, wood-paneled lobby and walked to the Reception Desk. Speaking Thai to the Thai Receptionist, though I knew she spoke English, I rented Room 325 for 50 Bhat, asked for a wake up call at 4:00 in the morning, and rode the elevator to the 3rd floor, where I easily located Room 325.

Using the room key I was given, I entered Room 325 and saw it was 20-foot square, with a double bed against the right sidewall beneath a large ceiling fan. Against the left sidewall, I saw a 3-drawer bureau next to a table and chair. Seeing a door in the sidewall beyond the bed. I walked over, opened it, and saw across an 8-by-10-foot bathroom, with a squat toilet to the right of a curtained shower stall. To the right of the door was a sink in a mirrored vanity.

Stripping to my skivvies, I laid on the bed to relax under the cooling breeze of the ceiling fan until 7:30. At that time, I went into the bathroom to relieve my bladder and splash water from the sink onto my face to freshen up. By 7:45, I was dressed again and left for the night club.

Leaving the Sri Pattana Hotel, I turned right at Suranari Road and walked to the corner, where I turned left to cross the road, and followed Rajadamnern Road a hundred yards to the left to Vatmung Lane. There, I saw 50 yards down the lane a large, two-story high building with large Thai script in blue neon lights over a double-door entrance. Walking to the entrance, and looking at my watch as I entered the night club, I saw it was precisely 8:00.

To the left of the club's entrance, I saw a maitre d' standing behind a lectern. And to his left, I beheld the tall, beautiful Jintana dressed in a ¾-sleeved, light blue silk dress with the skirt hemmed just below her knees. We each made the wâai, bowed and said our sàwàtdiis. Jintana led me to the top tier of three tiers with large, half-circle booths with eight thickly padded chairs in a half circle around a curved, candle lit table. There, I saw all of the people in the night club were Thais. The booths on each of the three tiers faced a large, wood dance floor in front of a stage with an 8-piece, string orchestra on a band stand. Between every other booth, I saw a set of red carpeted steps leading down to the dance floor.

Having followed behind Jintana's graceful walk to the table with three smiling Thai men sitting to the left of the table and three smiling Thai women on the right, where she proudly announced, "Tis is my boyfaren, Sandii." I made the wâai, bowed and said, "Sàwàtdii, krup." They all did the same, but to my chagrin, they all said, "Nice to meet you, Sandii." As I sat down in the empty chair between two of the men, they all introduced themselves and started asking me questions in heavily accented English. I then realized they mostly wanted to practice their English language skills on me, and that my expectation for this evening to be an immersion into the Thai language was dashed. I was buoyed up with the success of my other three expectations; to see Jintana more often than on double dates with Glen and Sùpa on Mondays, to not have to arrange for another couple for us to date more often, and best of all, to hold her graceful elegance in my arms as we ballroom danced. But, now I thought, "What did it mean for Jintana to declare I was her 'boyfriend' to her friend?"

Since English was the language spoken at the table, when I heard the band begin to play Viennese waltz, I nodded my head to Jintana, who was seated across from me, and asked, "Please, Jintana, will you dance with me?" To which she vigorously nodded her beautiful head and said, "Ye-sa, tang-ká you."

Leaving the table, Jintana properly followed behind me to the dance floor, where I found an open space to dance. Turning to face Jintana, I presented my arms and hands in the position to dance a waltz. I was very pleased when Jintana had properly placed her right hand on my raised left hand without clinching it, then stepped into the circle of my right arm where her waist pressed lightly against my right hand. Then, laying her left arm on my right arm to establish the "frame" to dance a waltz, with her thumb and forefinger making a V-shape beneath my right deltoid muscle, I happily thought, "Now this is a woman who knows how to waltz."

Jintana felt light as a feather in my arms as she followed my every lead indicated by the slight pressure or change in angle of my hands for a turn or twirl or dip. Mom taught me a man has two jobs when ballroom dancing. First, to make the woman look good with every movement. Second, as he leads her around the dance floor, to make sure she doesn't bump into anyone else. This required constant vigilance on my part as to where and what the other dancing couples were doing. Sometimes I was able to glance at Jintana's lovely face and be rewarded with a dazzling smile from her elation and joy with my dancing abilities.

We danced beautifully together to every waltz, cha-cha, tango and fox trot the orchestra played. Jintana also taught me to dance to the Thai music, where the men and women danced in separate, concentric circles with elegant arm and hand movements. The only time we stopped was to get a drink of Pepsi to quench our thirst.

At 11:00, I said, "Jintana, I need to go to the Sri Pattana Hotel to sleep. I have to get up at 4:00 to go to the Army Camp to eat and be ready for work by 7:00."

Jintana responded cheerfully, "You dit not say you sa-tay at Sri Pattana. Where room you sa-tay?"

I answered, "I'm in Room 325."

Jintana replied as we climbed the steps to our booth, "I saw-ry cannot go wit you to Sri Pattana aw-lone. I mut be wit frien to go. Wen do you an Glìn-dii see Sùpa again, maybe see you at ca-fay. Okay?"

I answered with a big smile, "We will be at the cafe Sunday at 3:00 to see Sùpa. Yes, I would like to see you there, too."

Jintana responded happily, "I see you wit Sùpa at ta-ree on Sunday."

At the booth, I told the group, "I have to work early tomorrow morning and must go to my room at the Sri Pattan Hotel to get some sleep. It was nice to meet you and hope to see you next week."

One of the men said, "It not propa you go in dark to Sri Pattana alone. I can go wit you."

Immediately, the other two men said, "We go wit you, too." Then everyone in the group stood up and we left together, with the three Thai men walking arm in arm with me, followed by the four women walking arm in arm. When we reached the entrance of the Sri Pattana Hotel, I thanked them for a wonderful evening, that I would see them again next week, and said my goodbyes there, even to Jintana, as I entered the Hotel.

As I rode the elevator to the 3rd floor, I thought, "The one thing that would have made this evening perfect was if I could have kissed Jintana good night."

Entering Room 325. I quickly stripped before I went to bed. About 15 minutes later, I heard a loud knock on my door and a perfunctory female voice say loudly through the door, "room sa-bit."

I got up thinking, "This must be some mistake," and said, "One moment, please," as I pulled on my pants. Opening the door, I saw Jintana standing in front of the doorway wearing the black frock and white apron of a housekeeper, and holding a short stack of towels over her left arm. She then quickly pushed past me, saying "I hat tow-en you o-da."

As I stared in amazement, Jintana pushed the door closed behind her, dropped the towels on the floor, and grabbing my face with her long delicate fingers, she gave me a kiss with her mouth full on mine. I thought, "It can't get better than this," as I wrapped my arms around her, pulled her lithe trembling body against my broad, bare chest, and returned the passion of her kiss.

CHAPTER 23

A Quagmire For Me Up to My Neck with My Hormones

At 4:00 in the morning, I woke to a knocking on my room's door and the sound of a male voice through the door saying, "Way-kup caw, way-kup caw." Rolling from my right side onto my back, I said loudly, "Kup koon mâak, krup."

Seeing Jintana was not beside me, I asked softly, "Jintana?"

With no answer, I pulled on my boxers, went to the bathroom door, and opening it slightly, I asked softly again, "Jintana?"

Again with no answer, I pushed open the door, and seeing she was not there, I said to myself, "Smart girl. Not only did you get the idea to use your housekeeping clothes as a ruse to get into my room without arousing any suspicion, you were smart enough not to spend the whole night with me and caught leaving my room this morning. I'm sure it's Hotel policy to fire any staff caught with a Hotel guest."

Wishing to wash the crud from last night off my body, I decided to take a shower, cold water or not. Pulling off my boxers, I saw some dried blood around my pubic area. Going quickly back to the bed and drawing off the top bedding, I saw some blood smears on the bottom sheet and softly asked myself, "Oh crap, what have you gotten yourself into with Jintana?"

Going back to the bathroom to take a cold shower, which I now needed in more ways than one, my mind ran rampant with what I'd been taught in Catholic High School about virgins and what a man who has lain with a virgin was obliged to do, and did those same values apply in Thai culture.

My Catholic High School education in my Senior Year Marriage Class, taught by the Priests in an all boy class, as the girls were in a separate class taught by the Mother Superior, was instructed in three parts. First, the religious view that marriage was a Holy Sacrament ordained by God as a sacred, lifetime commitment to a woman, and a duty for the procreation of children. Second, though taught the biology of male and female reproduction, that sex was only to be performed in the sacred bond of matrimony between a man who had been celibate and a woman who was a virgin, and any man who lay with a virgin was, in the eyes of God, already married to the woman. Also, any sex outside the sacred bond of matrimony was a mortal sin deserving of eternal damnation to Hell. And 3rd, the financial duty of a man to provide food, clothing and shelter for his wife and children.

I thought, "What I need is a cold shower to help clear my head and think this through rationally, and not through the guild-ridden lens of the Catholic Church."

With that thought focused in my mind, I braced my body for a "cold" shower. When I felt the spraying water in the shower with my hand, I found it wasn't cold. It just wasn't hot. I thought "Thailand is a tropical country where the water is not naturally cold, it is tepid. Though not as relaxing as a hot shower, it will allow my mind to unwind from its guilt-trip as I clean my body."

By the time I finished the tepid shower, I'd gained a more rational state of mind to deal with this added complexity of Jintana as a woman. Deciding not to ponder this quagmire until I'd talked with Bob, I dressed to leave. Before leaving the room, I rolled the bedding into a large ball, setting it by the door with the idea the housekeeper would be too busy to notice and have something to gossip about, which would surely be heard by Jintana.

Leaving the room key on the table, I exited the Hotel, and was able to quickly argue in Thai a săawm-law driver down to 3 Bhat for a ride to the Chainarong Gate. Catching a Thai bus before 5:00 that was half full of Americans, I was able to make it to my hooch by

5:30. As everyone had already left for breakfast, I was not inundated with questions about my date with Jintana, as I dressed in a fresh set of jungle fatigues and went to the Mess Hall for breakfast, lingering until it was time for morning formation. Joining the left end of the Air Base Squad, which comprised the back rank of the Tropo Platoon, Skip changed positions to stand next to me and asked, "Sandii, how it go with Jintana at the night club?"

I replied, "It was great. Dancing with Jintana was like dancing with an angel, both beautiful to see and light as a feather. She really knows how to ballroom dance. Plus, she introduced me to her friends as her 'boyfaren.' I don't know exactly what that means in the Thai culture, but I'm sure it was to make clear to the girls in her group that I was strictly hands off to them. How'd it go at the cafe with choosing a date for Monday's movie?"

Skip replied, "The first girl was beautiful, but I'm sure not as beautiful as Jintana. Plus, she seemed very into me. So I decided on her, rather than 'a pig in a poke.'[112] But, she doesn't speak much English, so Glen had to translate everything."

Just then, I heard Spike yell from the front of the formation, "Company…," which stopped any further talking in the ranks.

After formation, as Skip and I walked to the Motor Pool, and then as we rode in the back of the ¾-ton truck to the Air Base Site, he pumped me for more information on my date with Jintana. When I told him I spent the night at the Sri Pattana Hotel, where Jintana worked, he asked, "So, did you ask her up for a night cap?"

I replied indignantly, "Certainly not. If she went to my room, she'd have been fired instantly. I didn't even try to kiss her goodnight because it would have been socially unacceptable by her friends, who escorted me to the Hotel."

When we arrived in the Operations Room, Jack was raring to go and said, "Nothing to report, so I stand relieved," as he rushed to go home. A few minutes later, Bob appeared and said, "Sàwàtdii, Sandii and Skip. There's nothing to report from the night shift, so while I start the Site Log entries and review what's happened while we've been off,

---

112   To purchase something before it is seen.

Sandii, I want you to work with Skip on learning our in-house circuits. By the way, Sandii, how'd it go at the night club with Jintana?"

I replied, "She dances like a dream. But, I'd like to talk with you later about some cultural differences, especially the meaning of her calling me her 'boyfriend.'"

Bob responded, "Is that literally what Jintana called you?"

I answered, "Literally."

Bob said, "I'll have to think about that and talk to you later."

As I led Skip to the Grand Canyon, I responded, "Sounds great to me," and spent the rest of the morning with Skip in the Grand Canyon going over the in-house circuits. A few times we had a call to check an in-house circuit, but Bob just sat back to see how I handled it with Skip, and thought, "Bob must be evaluating how well I can handle in-house circuits outages and how well Skip and I work together."

At 10:55, Skip left on his meal run, and Bob sat me down next to him at the desk and said, "Jim told me how impressed he was with your handling the circuit outages during the chaos here Tuesday night. After watching you this morning. I've no doubt when we work the night shift, I'll have nothing to worry about when I'm out for my night meal. And Skip has shown he can handle routine outages in the break-out racks. Also, it's obvious that you two not only enjoy each other's company, but you work well together, which means I have a good team working with me and will report as much to Jim, who writes your Quarterly Fitness Reports.

"As to what it meant to Jintana in the Thai culture to call you her 'boyfriend.' The Thai word 'faan' not only means boyfriend or girl-friend, but also a loved one, fiancé, husband or wife. Where 'boyfriend' Stateside can mean anything from a casual relationship a woman has with a man, to a committed relationship. The question is whether Jin-tana meant it in our American context or in its Thai context."

I responded, "There were six others at our table, besides me and Jintana, and everyone insisted on speaking English, so she may have meant it in the American context. But, based on what happened later, I think she meant it in the Thai context."

Bob had a puzzled look and asked, "Later? What happened?"

I told Bob how Jintana used her housekeeper uniform as a ruse to come into my room, and what I'd found when I got up in the morning, concluding, "So, I don't know what it all means, as I was taught in

Catholic High School that when a man has sex with a virgin, then they are married in the eyes of God. So, in the Thai culture, can Jintana think of me as her husband, as the word 'faan' can mean?"

Bob laughed and replied, "For a woman to be a virgin in Thailand doesn't have the value it has in Western Cultures. Here, its only intrinsic value is in figuring the price of dowry the father can ask for. Remember, in the Thai culture a woman is a second class person. Young girls are often sold to a bordello or bar to be prostitutes. How old is Jintana?"

I replied, "I'm not sure. Maybe 18 or 19. Why? Are there statutory rape laws?"

Bob laughed again and said, "Relax, Sandii. As far as I know, Thailand has no statutory rape law. I've seen girls as young as 12 and 13 sold into prostitution. Usually they're 14 due to Thailand's mandatory eight years of education law. So you're safe there, Sandii. I just wondered if you knew Jintana's age. Most girls don't receive an education past the 8th grade, and begin working as housekeepers, waitresses or other unskilled work at age 14. You might want to discreetly find out how old she is, that's all.

"As for being her first sexual encounter, she may see you as a man of the world who was best able to initiate her sexuality. As much as she might see you as a tall dance partner."

I asked, "Several times last night she called me 'tîi-lók.' Could that mean she wants to live with me as my tîi-lók?"

Bob laughed and replied, "We Americans have corrupted the meaning of 'tîi-lók' to mean a lover. The Thai words for 'lover' as we mean it are 'kon-lók,' a 'love person,' and 'chûu-lok' that refers to extra-marital relations. No, 'tîi-lók' means 'in love,' and is a term of endearment, the same as our saying 'dear,' 'darling' or 'sweetheart.' Now if Jintana were to say 'Chán lók koon,' which literally means 'I love you,' or said 'Lók koon kâo layo,' meaning loosely 'I have fallen in love with you,' then you have a problem, unless you're looking for a permanent relationship.

"But, with most of us having a 'tîi-lók' relationship, the girl knows from the outset that any love interest is temporary and mutually satisfying, and that someday you're returning Stateside without her. My advice is the same, 'to go with the flow.' If she wants to live with you as your tîi-lók, she'll tell you. If all she wants is to have you as a dance partner that she can satisfy her sexual needs with, you'll figure that out soon enough. But, if she wants to be your wife, she'll simply say, 'Yàak dtàng-ngaan gà koon,' which literally means 'Want marriage ceremony with you,' and take you home to meet her father for permission."

Just then, Skip came in and asked, "So, what've you two been jawing about?"

I replied, "Bob was saying what good work we've been doing, that we make an excellent team, and he's confident we can handle any problem that comes up when he's gone to get something to eat."

Bob added, "Plus I've been having to hear about how wonderful Jintana is to dance with. So, Sandii, when will you see Jintana again?"

I replied, "I'll see her on Sunday at 3:00, the next time Glen and I'll be having dinner at Sùpa's cafe. Then again Monday afternoon when we all go to see a Japanese Samurai movie."

Bob responded, "You really have me curious if Jintana is as beautiful as you claim. Since we're off Tuesday, maybe she'll agree to come to the compound if she's willing double with us to travel there."

I replied, "That's a very generous offers. I suppose it won't hurt to ask. But now, I need to make a meal run."

When I returned 45 minutes later, I found Bob and Skip with a breakout rack pulled open, taking measurements with probes from the portable test cart between them. Bob looked up and said, "Sandii, you might as well come over and see how we do this as part of your Frame Tech cross-training."

Joining them as a toolbox carrier, I held open a schematic of the circuits they were troubleshooting to begin my Frame Tech cross-training. From then on, whenever there was an in-house outage in the breakout circuits, I was learning how to find and repair the problem, which wasn't any different than doing it with a microwave radio, as electronic schematics all basically had resistors, capacitors, diodes and tubes. Things were just arranged differently.

After work, I spent the evening sitting at the card table playing Double-Deck Pinochle with Glen as my partner, drinking beer and smoking cigarettes till 9:00, when we were all too tired to play any longer and went to bed to get eight hours of sleep before reveille sounded at 5:00 in the morning. Glen had only asked, "How'd your date with

Jintana go?" When I gave a brief description about how good she was to dance with, she wasn't mentioned again.

The next day was Saturday, and work that morning presented the usual mass of outages, so it was good for me to spend a couple of hours drinking and smoking as we played cards before I went to bed at 9:00 wondering what reaction Jintana would have when I asked her to double date to the compound on Tuesday when we met tomorrow for a 3:00 dinner at the cafe.

Sunday morning was like any other day I didn't work the day shift. Breakfast, formation, then sleeping till the 11:00 bugle call for Mess, and after lunch my practicing Thai with Glen. As we began our practice session, I asked, "Glen, do you know how old Sùpa is?"

Glen replied, "Actually, it's never come up. Why?"

I explained, "It's something Bob asked me about Jintana the other day. When I said I didn't know, he advised I might want to know, as most Thai girls start working at 14. But, I don't want to ask Jintana straight out how old she is because she might think her age will be an issue for me."

Glen exclaimed, "If Sùpa's only 14, it'll be an issue for me! If she becomes my tîi-lók, I wouldn't want to be thought of as a cradle robber, or worse, a pedophile."

I responded, "Well, neither would I. Bob said there are no statutory rape laws in Thailand, so we'd be safe under the law."

Glen asked, "How about I ask Jintana how long she's worked at the Sri Pattana Hotel, which is a benign question, then you can add 14 to that and it'll give you some idea how old she is?"

I replied, "Yea. And I can ask Sùpa how long she's worked at the cafe, and give you some idea how old she is. I don't think either of them are 14, but they could easily be under 18."

Glen responded, "I'm 20, so having a 16 or 17 year-old tîi-lók would be acceptable."

I asked, "Then you agree we should ask the other girl how long she's been working?"

Glen replied, "It's a deal."

Glen and I figured out to say, "Koon tam ngaan tîi-nîi gìi bpii," which means, "You do work at here how many years," and to say "Koon tam ngaan tii roong-ram sii paw-taw-naw gìi bpii," which means, "You do work at Hotel Sri Paltana how many year." Then we practiced saying the questions with the correct intonations so when we asked it would sound as casual as possible.

After the monsoon rain stopped, Glen and I left for the main street and caught a nearly empty Thai bus for Korat. It made a short stop at the Air Base gate for the STD MP's check before continuing across the Air Base, stopping to pick up several Airmen. Then it crossed Thailand's Second Army Base, picking up a few Thai Soldiers. When the bus made its final stop by the Chainarong Gate it was nearly 3:00, so we hurried the short distance up Chainarong Road, arriving at the cafe on time.

Entering the cafe, I saw Sùpa sitting on the other side of a table, chatting with Jintana. Seeing the movement at the door catch her eye, Sùpa said something to Jintana, and they quickly stood up and walked toward us, both wearing expressions of joy. I saw that Jintana was wearing a bright yellow blouse tucked into the top of a Thai style, straight skirt extending to the mid-calf with 2-inch wide, horizontal sea green and black stripes, and a 2-inch wide black belt that accentuated her slender waist and shapely hips. I was again taken aback by her stunning beauty and grace, and thought, "Will she always have this effect on me?"

I quickly glanced at Glen to my right and saw he was having trouble trying to keep his eyes focused on Sùpa, though a very pretty, nicely shaped woman, she looked almost dowdy walking next to Jintana.

They both stopped six feet in front of us, and simultaneously made the wâai, bowed and said, "Sàwàtdii, Glìn-dii lé Sandii." To which Glen and I responded in kind and said, "Sàwàtdii, Sùpa lé Jintana." The girls waited as Glen and I walked around them so they each could walk properly behind their man to the table and sit at the table after their man decided where he would sit. Jintana surprised me when she sat next to me instead of across from me as before.

I ordered four meals, so that Sùpa could eat with us because there were no other customers in the cafe. When Sùpa returned with the four plates of chicken fried rice and four bottles of Pepsi. I invited her to sit and eat with us. When Sùpa said it would be improper, I told her it would be against the teachings of the Great Buddha for me to allow her to be uncomfortable while we sat and ate in front of her. She agreed to sit and eat with us until someone entered the cafe, and thanked me profusely for my kindness, as I thought "Since it's Sunday

and most of the shops were closed, it's unlikely there'll be other customers for a while."

When Sùpa sat down and we had each picked up a napkin to place
on our laps, I felt Jintana place her left hand briefly on my right thigh
under the guise of putting the napkin on her lap, and I thought, "This
is a sign from her for my kindness to her friend."

As we talked gaily and ate our meals together for over a half hour,
because no other customers came in, I asked Sùpa casually if she liked
working in the cafe. When she said it was a good place to work as the
owner was kind to his employees, I asked, "Koon tam ngaan tîi-nii gìi
bpii, na," and she answered proudly, "Săawm bpii." I saw Glen give a
slight grin as I thought, "Three years, so Sùpa is 17."

I then heard Glen casually ask, "Jintana, koon tam ngaan tîi roong-
raam sii paw-taw-naw gìi bpii, na," and heard Jintana answer, "Sŏng
bpii." I saw Glen make a small shrug with his shoulder as I thought,
"Two years! Jintana is only 16! Good thing there's no statutory
rape laws."

When I saw Sùpa quickly get up, I looked over my right shoulder
and saw two young couples entering the cafe. Looking at Jintana and
speaking in Thai, I asked, "I ask you if like go on group date to party
at night on Tuesday at house belong friend?"

I saw Jintana's eyes light up and nod her head as she asked, "I like.
Where house belong friend?"

I answered, "On road Buarong near warehouse Sing Hăi Beer."

She asked, "What time?"

I replied, "Six hour afternoon, Where meet you?" Knowing we
could not meet where she worked.

She thought a moment and answered, "At Monument Thao Suranari. Will you stay Sri Pattana again?"

I answered, "Stay, yes. Maybe floor level same," and she said,
"Good much."

I looked at Glen's puzzled face and said in English, "I'll explain later."

When Sùpa finished serving her new customers, Glen explained to
Sùpa that we had to leave for work, but we would see them at noon
tomorrow to go to the theater. When we all stood to leave and Sùpa
began to lead us to the cafe's door, I saw Glen put a blue 20-Bhat bill
on the table. I also put five 1-Bhat coins by Jintana's left hand, saying
"For săawm-law to Sri Pattana," and saw her quickly put the coins in

a skirt pocket and say, "Thank you very much," As she followed us to the cafe's door.

Arriving at the door, we all made the wâai, bowed and said our sàwàtdiis.

As Glen and I walked to the Chainarong Gate to board a Thai bus back to Camp Friendship, I explained, "Bob is curious if Jintana is as beautiful as we say she is, so he wanted me to ask if she would go on a double date to the compound on Tuesday night. I didn't want to ask in front of Sùpa and hurt her feelings to think she was not being included, so you understand why I didn't have that conversation in front of Sùpa. Jintana said she would like to go. I'll still come with you on Tuesday here to have dinner and go to the compound with you before I go with Bob and his tîi-lók to pick up Jintana at 6:00."

Glen responded, "I appreciate your considering Sùpa's feelings. Also, this might pave the way for Sùpa to go with us to the compound next Monday. I think if she talks with the other tîi-lóks and sees their lifestyle, then she might get the idea to be my tîi-lók. Otherwise, I'm going to start looking for someone else. I'm just too horny to hold out for nothing."

I said, "I know what you mean. Do you know what time Sùpa gets off work at night? If it's early enough, maybe you and Sùpa could go dancing at the night club on Friday night with Jintana and me. It costs only 50-Bhat to stay at the Sri Pattana, which is close to the night club and cheaper than paying for a pûu-ying at a bar. Anyway, it's an idea," and I thought "It'll also be another night I can go dancing with Jintana."

Glen replied, "That's an excellent idea. I'll have to ask her tomorrow when we go to the movie."

When we returned to the hooch, I changed into my other set of jungle fatigues before going to dinner at the Mess Hall. There, Glen and I found Skip feeding his skinny body with a large mound of roast beef and potatoes. We soon joined him with the same fare, and talked about our triple date, and explained to Skip how the girls will walk behind us as we lead the way to the theater. As for the seating arrangement, we told him that was up to the girls.

That night at the Air Base Site, work was much the same as the night before. When Skip made his 10:55 meal run, I gave Bob a run down on what had happened at the cafe, including my reference to

Buddha to persuade Sùpa to sit and eat with us, and how Jintana had discreetly touched my leg. Also, that Jintana agreed on the double date to the compound, and to meet her at 6:00 in front of the Thao Suranari Monument. Then, Glen would like to bring Sùpa to the compound next Monday, and maybe get the idea from their tîi-lóks to become Glen's tîi-lók.

Bob commented, "What you did for Sùpa, especially referencing the Buddha, had certainly made you more appealing as a person to Jintana. And, that she took a chance to physically show her appreciation for your kindness to Sùpa says even more. I think it was a very clever way you used to get some idea of their ages, and I'm not surprised that Jintana may be 16. Are you okay with the age difference?"

I replied, "When I was a Senior in High School, I took a 14-year-old Freshman from another High School to our Senior Prom who was prettier and had a better figure than any other girl there. If I was okay dating a girl three years younger than me two years ago, dating one four years younger now isn't a problem."

The next morning, Glen, Skip and I slept till 11:00 after working the 12-hour night shift. After dressing in civilian clothes, we went directly to the main street to board a Thai bus for Korat to arrive at the cafe by noon. There, I met Glûaimàai, Skip's very pretty and petite date for the movie. But Skip's reaction to meeting Jintana showed he was clearly impressed with her grace and beauty. As we ate lunch, I asked Glûaimàai in Thai, because she clearly spoke very little English, where she worked. She said at a cafe on San-Prasit Road as a waitress. When I asked how many years she had worked there she had replied, "Only five month." I saw Glen almost choke on a mouthful of chicken fried rice, as I thought, "Glen has come to the same conclusion I have, that Skip is dating a 14-year-old girl, and Skip, you are totally clueless."

As we walked to the theater after lunch, Glen and I put Skip between us, while the three girls walked behind us, arm in arm, and chittering away in Thai. I heard Glen say, "Skip, do not turn around when I tell you this, but we think your date may only be 14 years old, 15 at best."

When Skip exclaimed, "How do you know that!" I explained our process of deducting a girl's age, and because she'd only been working as a waitress for five months. Then I asked, "What do you think?"

Skip replied, "She's way too pretty to kick to the curb. I'll see how this date goes, but my first thought is to drop her like a hot potato. So, how old are Sùpa and Jintana?"

Glen answered, "Respectively, 17 and 16."

Skip asked, "And, Sandii, you're okay with dating a 16-year-old?"

I replied, "Would you kick a total fox like her to the curb just because she's 16?"

Skip laughed and said, "Not on your life."

Arriving at the theater just before the movie started at 1:00, I selected a row with six empty seats together, and slipped across to the last empty seat. Turning to sit down, I saw Jintana was sitting next to me, as expected. The order behind her was Skip, Glûaimàai, Sùpa and Glen, and thought, "Looks like Sùpa decided she'd rather not have her Glìn-dii sitting next to Jintana or Glûaimàai. Smart girl."

As the house lights went off and movie started, I saw Jintana's elegant, long fingers were properly intertwined on her lap. But, as two Samurai confronted each other on the screen, I felt those long fingers gently encircle my upper left arm over the sleeve of my silk shirt, and thought, "Jintana's jumped the gun. Last time she didn't grab my arm until the bloodletting started, and then she'd clinched my arm."

Watching the movie, though distracted by Jintana's caress of my arm, I saw nothing in the action scenes related to our usual cowboy movie plots. There, the hero cowboy meets a girl, girl meets the bad guys, bad guys capture the girl, cowboy beats up all the bad guys to rescue the girl, and cowboy rides off with the girl. This was more like the good guy enters town, sees a bunch of bad guys bully the people, good guy tells the bad guys to stop, bad guys scoff at the lone good guy, good guy spends 15 to 20 minutes fighting and killing all the bad guys with his sword, and the good guy walks away alone.

As we walked back to the cafe with the three girls behind us chatting away in their sing-song voices, I heard Skip comment, "It had lots of good action, but it wasn't like a regular cowboy movie plot with a damsel in distress being rescued."

I heard Glen laugh and respond, "And neither do those cowboy movies that are so popular now that are copies of Japanese Samurai movies. Think about it, in those Clint Eastwood and Yul Brenner movies, there are no starring woman's role. The good guy rides in alone, kills all the bad guys, and rides off alone."

Skip laughed and said, "You're right, Glen, there are no women glamming onto the hero in those movies. But, I did like it when that pretty Glûaimàai. grabbed my arm."

Returning to the front of the cafe, we each made wâai, bowed and said our sàwàtdiis before Glen, Skip and I walked to the Chainarong Gate to catch a Thai bus back to Camp Friendship. Riding the bus, we favorably critiqued the movie's scenes, discussed the girls, and how we looked forward to seeing another Samurai movie with them next Monday, despite Glûaimàai possibly being a 14-year-old. Skip rationalized that he had a Jewish Princess back home and wasn't looking for someone else to love.

That night at work, Skip excitedly told Bob all about how great the movie was, how pretty and fun Glûaimàai was, leaving out our suspicion she was only 14, and how incredibly beautiful Jintana was, though she was a little tall for his taste in women.

Bob responded, "Now, I <u>have</u> to see this Jintana for myself."

I replied, "And you will tomorrow night."

The next afternoon at 1:00, Glen, Skip and I left for Korat. Skip was going to pick up his clothes from the tailor shop to have something "decent" to wear to the compound with Ronnie, as Stony was going to the bars to get drunk and chase pûu-ying. Meanwhile, Glen and I figured the lunch crowd would be gone so we could chat in Thai with Sùpa before we had dinner at 4:00 and then leave for the compound.

While we talked with Sùpa, Glen asked her when the cafe closed. When she replied it closed at 8:00, Glen asked if she would like to go dancing Friday at a night club with him, Jintana and me after work. I saw her eyes go wide, and she smiled big as she said, "Really truly?" in Thai, and Glen replied, "Really truly." I thought Sùpa would jump from her skin with joy as we made plans for Friday night.

Walking toward the compound, when we reached Rajadamnern Road, I told Glen, "I need to go to the Sri Pattana to make final arrangements for Jintana's visit to the compound tonight. So, I'll see you there soon."

Glen responded, "I'll be sure to save you a cold Sing Hǎi for you," as he walked on.

A few minutes later, I walked up to the Reception Desk and said in Thai to the pretty clerk behind the desk, "Want take bedroom on 3rd floor. How much for four nights?"

She replied in Thai, "100 Bhat."

Handing her a red 100-Bhat bill, I said, "Thank you very much. I take for four nights," and thought, "Ten bucks for four nights is half price, and is great as I'll need the room tomorrow night if thing go well for Jintana with the tîi-lóks at the compound tonight, as well as for Thursday and Friday night."

Arriving at the compound ten minutes later, I walked up to the porch, exchanged sàwàtdiis with Bob, Jim Horn, Tom and Glen, and said, "Okay, Bob, everything is set for Jintana's visit."

Bob responded, "Great, we'll leave in ten minutes, which gives us plenty of time to walk to the Chaophaya Inn to hire two sǎawm-laws to ride to the Monument and pick up Jintana. Gùlaap will ride by herself behind us so Jintana can ride with her back here. By the way, Glen has been telling us that he and Sùpa are going to double date to the night club Friday night with you two. I think it's great they'll finally go on an actual date."

Ten minutes later, I heard Bob say to Gùlaap through the screen door in Thai it was time to go get Jintana. When Gùlaap exited onto the porch and made the wâai and bowed to the men there, I saw she was a young, very pretty woman, dressed in a dark blue blouse and a horizontally striped light-blue and pink Thai skirt that extended to her mid-calf. Walking up Buarong Road to the Chaophaya Inn, she followed behind Bob and I in the Thai tradition. After Hiring two sǎawm-law for three Bhat each to take us to the Thao Suranari Monument and then to the Sing Hǎi Beer Warehouse, Gùlaap rode behind us to the monument.

Approaching the Monument, I saw Jintana shining radiantly in the red glow of the setting sun she was facing as she stood enshrined by the monument's base behind her. She was wearing bright yellow silk blouse and the same Thai style skirt as Gùlaap, except Jintana's had light-gray and light-green stripes.

I heard Bob gasp, "Is that Jintana in front of the monument?"

I replied proudly, "Yes. That's Jintana."

Bob responded, "She looks amazing. Sandii, you lucked out with that beauty."

As I climbed out of the sǎawm-law when it stopped, Jintana made the wâai, bowed and said, "Sàwàtdii, Sandii, I happy to see you."

I replied in kind, "Sàwàtdii, Jintana, your beauty gives me great honor," and moving to stand to Jintana's left, I continued, "Please meet my friend Bob, and Gùlaap, Bob's faan."

After everyone said their sàwàtdiis, Jintana gracefully boarded the săawm-law, and the two women began to talk gaily as we returned to the compound. When Gùlaap and Jintana crossed the porch, Horn, Glen and Tom stood to exchange sàwàtdiis with the two women. As the four of us entered the house, I heard Tom quietly exclaim, "Glen, you're totally right. She's absolutely gorgeous, but very tall for a Thai woman."

Inside the house, as the other two tîi-lóks stood up from the table, I saw they were each wearing a colorful silk blouse and the same Thai style skirt as Gùlaap and Jintana, and I thought, "Obviously, they'd heard that their guest was supposed to be a beautiful Thai lady, and had worn their best clothes so they would not be completely out done by this newcomer."

I watched as Gùlaap made introductions around the table, and with a glance from Jintana, I saw the four of them sit at the table, and begin talking and laughing together like long lost friends. Being completely ignored, Bob and I each grabbed and opened a cold Sing Hăi Beer from the refrigerator and exited this woman's inner sanctum.

On the porch, we discussed the pros and cons of having a very beautiful woman in a man's life. When Ronnie and Skip arrived and then returned to the porch with their Sing Hăi Beer, Ronnie exclaimed, "Sandii, she's not a total fox, she's a fox and a half." And, when Frank arrived with Mii-kâa at 8:00, I saw she too was brightly attired in a traditional Thai dress. When Frank returned to the porch with his Sing Hăi Beer, he said, "Wild horses couldn't have kept Mii-kâa away from meeting Jintana, but if I had taken a second look at her, I think Mii-kâa would have scratched my eyes out. However, Jintana seems to be getting along really well with the girls, probably because they don't see her as a threat since she's here with Sandii and being introduced as Sandii's faan."

At 9:00, the two gatherings broke up, and as all the girls exited past the porch, I discreetly said to Jintana that I was in Room 319. Gùlaap and Jintana walked behind the men as we all went to the Chaophaya Inn to hire săawm-laws. As the săawm-law Bob and I were in approached the Sri Pattana Hotel, we stopped 50 yards from the Hotel for me to walk the rest of the way, while the two girls rode past us to let Jintana off at the entrance.

Entering Room 319, I saw it was identical to Room 325, and went into the bathroom to relieve my bladder. Then, stripping to my waist, I took a bird bath in the sink to freshen up for Jintana. A few minutes later, I heard the expected knock at the door and Jintana's voice behind it say, "Room sa-bat." Opening the door, I saw Jintana in her uniform holding several towels as she quickly stepped into the room, shut the door behind her, drop the towels on the floor and give me a passionate kiss, as I then held her close to my bare chest. After a minute long kiss, she tilted her beautiful face back and said, "I go cra-sy at paw-ty way-ting to kit you. Women aw nite to me, say okay come to paw-ty to-maw-ro night."

I responded, "I'm very happy to hear that. Friday night, Glìn-dii and Sùpa will go to the night club with us if you like."

She laughed and replied, "You know I lai-ká dan-sa wit you baa-ry mut."

I said, "Good because I have this room four nights."

She responded, "Fo-ra night with you be baa-ry goot," as she kissed me passionately again.

At 4:00 in the morning, I woke to the knock on the door and a male voice saying, "Way-kup caw." After a tepid shower to wash the crud off my body, I quickly dressed, and taking the room key with me, I left to hire a săawm-law for a ride to the Chainarong Gate. Returning to the Company Area, I went straight to my hooch, dressed in a fresh set of OD BDUs before going to the Mess Hall for breakfast and then to morning formation.

After morning formation, I slept till the 11:00 bugle call for Mess. After lunch, Glen and I practiced speaking Thai. When our three mây-bâan entered, I exchange sàwàtdiis with Maan-daa, and then asked her in Thai, "Nít-nòi work very good, how long she work as mây-bâan?"

Maan-daa replied, "One year. You speak Thai very good, Sandii" and went back to putting the cleaned clothes in the wall lockers.

Glen looked at me and exclaimed, "My mây-bâan is fifteen!"

I laughed and said, "Looks that way, Glen. Maybe you should stop hitting on her?"

Glen said defensively, "I don't hit on her. Besides, I have Sùpa."

At 1:00, Glen and I left to spend the afternoon with Sùpa. When I told Sùpa that Jintana would be able to double date with us to the night club, she was elated. Then Glen told her that he would be staying at the Sri Pattana, and offered to her that she could spend the night there, too, if she didn't want to ride alone in a sǎawm-law back to the cafe. Sùpa had a sly smile when she replied that to spend the night at the Sri Pattana was better than riding alone home.

Glen and I left after we ate dinner at 4:00 and walked to the compound together. At 5:45, Bob, Gùlaap and I repeated the same process to pick up Jintana at the Thao Suranari Monument. As we began our ride from the Chaophaya Inn to the monument, Bob said, "Sandii, I think you may be up to your knees in a quagmire with Jintana. Gùlaap told me that Jintana thinks you're a Buddhist because last Sunday you cited the Buddha to persuade Sùpa to sit and eat with you at the cafe. And, that you would make a good husband for a Thai woman. Just to be clear, Gùlaap made sure for me to understand that Jintana would not say that she was planning for you to be her husband, just the implication that you would be a good husband for her as a Thai woman."

I responded, "Well, Jintana has not said, or even hinted, that she's in love with me or made any reference she's interested in getting married, but thanks for the back channel information," as I thought, "You're right, Bob, I may be in a quagmire with Jintana at least up to my knees. So far, she's made no indication she wants more than to dance and have sex with me as her boyfriend, which is fine with me. But, just the same, she is so enticing to me when I see her, I know that Jintana is a quagmire for me up to my neck with my hormones."

Chapter 24

How To Get A Bomb

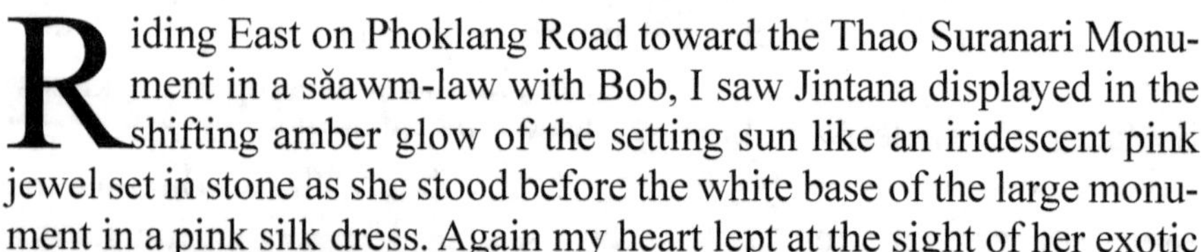

Riding East on Phoklang Road toward the Thao Suranari Monument in a sǎawm-law with Bob, I saw Jintana displayed in the shifting amber glow of the setting sun like an iridescent pink jewel set in stone as she stood before the white base of the large monument in a pink silk dress. Again my heart lept at the sight of her exotic beauty, and my loins began to ache with anticipation of the delayed gratification I must endure for endless hours until we can be alone.

"Damn," I thought, "my hormones are in a quagmire up to my neck at the very sight of this exotic woman."

As the sǎawm-law Bob and I were in crossed over Rajadamnern Road to its left lane, followed by Gùlaap's sǎawm-law to stop in front of the monument, I saw Jintana's radiant smile and the joy in her eyes with her own longing for me. Then, I saw her lovely shaped legs begin to eagerly step toward me. But she caught herself, and quickly walked to Gùlaap, where the two beautiful women made their wâais, bowed and exchanged sàwàtdiis before Jintana gracefully slid into the seat beside Gùlaap. When the two sǎawm-laws began to move down

Rajadamnern Road, I said, "Bob, we are lucky men to have such beautiful women in our lives."

Bob responded, "Yes we are. I know exactly how you feel because when I met Gùlaap two years ago, my heart lept at the sight of her beauty, and she, too, was then 16. My mother used to say, 'Marry a young woman and teach her to meet your needs before she becomes set in her ways.' My heart still leaps at her beauty when I see Gùlaap. And I saw it in Jintana's eager eyes for you. But, if it's love or lust that she has for you, the resulting benefits are the same, right?"

I laughed and replied, "My Mom use to say the same thing, and she would know because she married a man five years younger than her, so it works both ways. And you're right, whether its love or lust, the benefits are the same."

That evening, in the insulated world of Horn's home, it was as relaxing as the other evenings spent with the men drinking beer and talking about their topics of interest, while the women sat in their inner sanctum, where I could hear their lilting, sing-song voices as they gaily talked.

At 9:00, the comradery ended as usual, and Bob, Gùlaap, Jintana and I used the same method to reach the Chaophaya Inn. But this time, Jintana said it was okay for her to ride alone behind me to the Sri Pattana. And though we rode in separate săawm-laws, I still stopped before reaching the Hotel so she could arrive alone.

Waiting in Room 319 for Jintana's knock on the door, I had gone to the bathroom to relieve myself and freshened up in the sink for her. Hearing her knock and her melodic voice say, "room saa-bit," I quickly opened the door, stood back to let her in, I closed the door as she dropped the towels on the floor. Putting my hands around her I slender waist, pulled her lithe body to my bare chest, and said in Thai, "I like room service you give me very much."

She laughed and replied in Thai, "I like to give you room service very much. I miss you and want to be with you around the clock, darling," and gave me a passionate kiss.

The night then progressed at a slower, gentler pace than the previous two nights of rampant passion. And though she often called me "Darling" and said, "like everything about you," but she didn't say, "I love you."

Before Jintana left, we showered together to mutually wash the crud off our bodies. I told her that I had to work till 7:00, and should not wait by the night club's entrance door, but would meet her at the table with her friends. After she left, I thought, "It looks like Jintana's satisfied with me as her boyfriend to dance with and for our mutual sexual pleasure, and not to live with me as my tîi-lók, nor has plans to marry me. But, I need to find another Hotel for our meeting, because eventually someone will discover our trysts here and she'll be fired."

The next morning, I left as usual after the 4:00 wake up call to return to my Company Area. Changing into a fresh set of jungle fatigues in my hooch, I saw Glen approach me and say, "After I saw how well Jintana gets along with the tîi-lóks, I'll ask Horn at work for his permission to bring Sùpa to his home next Monday with you and Jintana."

Skip overheard this and said, "That sounds great. Think I could bring Glûaimåai, too?"

I replied, "Do you really want to bring a 14-year-old girl to a party with tîi-lóks? Then, what if she gets the idea you want her to be your tîi-lóks?"

Skip frowned and responded, "You're right. I didn't think about that."

We then left for the Mess Hall to have breakfast. After morning formation, as we walked into the Motor Pool's parking area to get our ¾-ton truck, I pointed to the first jeep in the row and said, "Hey, Jim, what happened to the CO's jeep? The chromed wheels, white wall tires and Tuck-N-Roll leather seats are gone."

Jim laughed and replied, "I heard that Spike went crying to his buddy, the Battalion CO, and complained our CO's modifications violated Army Regs. So, the Battalion CO ordered they be removed and replaced with the original parts. But, those parts were used to replace the worn-out parts on other jeeps that were then thrown away. So, all new parts were ordered to replace the CO's custom-made parts. Then, our CO sold those parts to the Battalion CO, who then ordered the Motor Pool Sargent to have them installed on his jeep. R.H.I.P."

The work on the day shift was a little busy, and Bob had Skip and I work on our in-house outages as he made the notes in the Temporary Log. Then, Skip and I took turns copying the data from the Temporary Log to the permanent Site Log. With this to keep me busy, time flowed by and distracted me from my anticipation of a very enjoyable evening dancing with the graceful Jintana.

While Skip was on his 10:55 meal run, I asked Bob, "I'm concerned that eventually Jintana will be caught with our trysts at the Sri Pattana and be fired. Do you know of another Hotel I could stay at?"

Bob replied, "You might try the Korat Hotel on Assadang Road. It's similar to the Sri Pattana."

At 2:00, Jim called Skip to the Site Office. When Skip returned, he yelled in celebration, "I've been promoted to Spec-4. After tomorrow's morning formation, I'm to report to the CO's Office to get my promotion order. I'll have two hours to get my issue of ten Spec-4 patches from Supply, then to go to Personnel for a new ID card and dog tags, before going to Finance to have my pay increase recorded. So, I may not get to work until 9:00. Can you two survive without me till then?"

Bob and I congratulated Skip on his promotion, and told him take as long as he needed to get the paperwork done, as we had Jim and Phizer for backup. Then I said, "But when you get back here, I'm looking forward to tacking those stripes on each sleeve."[113]

At the end of the day, I made the 6:35 meal run so I could leave for Korat as soon as I ate. When John and Larry took over the ¾-ton truck, I told them about Skip's promotion. John replied, "Great. It's been a while since I've tacked on some stripes. You can bet Larry and I will be practicing tonight to make sure we don't miss those skinny arms of his."

I responded, "And I'll make the 6:35 run to make sure Skip's there when you get to work."

Going to the Mess Hall, I wolfed down my meal, then quickly changed into my blue silk shirt and white cotton pants before catching a Thai bus to Korat. Exiting the bus at the Chainarong Gate, I looked at my watch, saw it was 7:40 and knew I had plenty of time to get to the night club by 8:00. I had no problem in quickly arguing down the price for a ride to the night club down to 3 Bhat, since I now spoke decent Thai.

---

113   A military tradition where those of equal or higher rank hold the new stripes to the arm where they are to be sewn on the sleeve and punch it with their fist.

Arriving in front of the night club, I paid the driver 3 Bhat, and another 2 Bhat to the maitre d for the cover charge. Climbing the stairs to the 3rd tier, I quickly spotted Jintana in a red silk dress sitting with her six friends. On reaching them, I made the wâai, bowed and said, "Hello, my friends. How are you tonight?"

As they replied in kind, a waiter appeared at my right and I ordered a bottle of Pepsi. Sitting in a chair the men had saved in their midst, they began in turn asking me conversational questions with their strong Thai accents. When the waiter had returned, I paid the 3 Bhat for my Pepsi and took a large swig to quench my thirst. Setting the bottle on the table, I set my eyes on Jintana, and being enthralled by her beauty, I thought, "She is a rose among daisies in that form-fitting red dress."

Seeing Jintana looking at me expectantly with those captivating, almond shaped eyes, I said, "Jintana, would you honor me with a dance?"

She replied, "It is my honaa to dan-sa wit you," as we both stood up from our chairs.

Leading her to the capacious dance floor, I heard the orchestra begin to play a tango and thought, "Perfect. A tango. The sexiest form of ballroom dance."

Assuming the standard ballroom position, on the first down beat I thrust my right leg between her legs. On the second down beat, I put a little pressure with the heel of my right hand against her waist to signal she was to go straight back as my left foot stepped forward with her right leg moving backward. Repeating the steps on the 3rd and fourth down beats. I then pulled her close, made a slight pull with my finger son the small of her back and pushing her extended right hand back with my left hand, I signaled she was to turn clockwise. On the following four quick beats, I swung her around 180 degrees, ending with a deep dip with her back shoulders nearly touching the floor, for which she perfectly counter balanced her weight on her left leg. On the next two down beats, I sensuously raised her up to the ballroom position for the next dance move.

Glancing up to our table, I could see the three women's mouths were open with astonished envy at my opening move, and I thought, "Okay, you three guys, beat that if you can."

I soon saw the three men and three women paired up on the dance floor trying to copy my moves. After several minutes of watching them fail, I danced Jintana to them and slowly went through them as they mimicked my moves. Soon, they were able to perform the maneuver reasonably well. When Jintana and I took a break to drink some Pepsi, I could see the other three women with eager looks that I may ask one of them to dance, though Jintana had clearly staked her claim on me.

During the rest of the evening, I saw that the three men were changing dance partners and realized there were not three couples, but six friends who liked to ballroom dance on a regular basis.

At 11:00, they all escorted me to the Sri Pattana Hotel with the men walking beside me practicing their English, with the women behind us. That Jintana was there was purely incidental to them. As we made our goodbyes at the Hotel's entrance, I saw Jintana give me a knowing look as she slipped in before I did.

Entering Room 319, I quickly relieved and freshened myself in the bathroom, and then waited for Jintana's knock. After she entered the room and gave me a passionate kiss as I held her against my bare chest, she said in Thai, "You are a sexy dancer and make me want you all the time. Chest hair belonging to you give tickle to me."

I asked, "You don't like my chest hair?"

She replied, "Oh, I like your chest hair very much. Thai men don't have chest hair," as she lowered her hands and unbuttoned the top of her uniform. She then grabbed two handfuls of my chest hair and pulled them gently to her two perfectly formed breasts. As she gave me another passionate kiss, I thought, "So much for verbal foreplay."

Later, as we mutually washed the crud from each other's bodies in the shower, she said in Thai, "I like very much you are a tall man, sexy, and ballroom dance very good."

I responded, "And I like to see your beauty very much, and give me happiness to be near you," and thought "This clinches it, she likes me, but only for dancing and mutually gratifying sex, which is fine with me."

Before Jintana left, we arranged to meet at the Gài Yâang Sâang Thai restaurant on Rajadamnern Road, just North of Vatmung Lane, at 7:30 for dinner before we went to the night club. I also gave her 5 Bhat for a sǎawm-law to take her to the restaurant and to order a soft drink while she waited.

At 4:00, I heard the wake-up call through my door, to which I quickly got dressed and left for the Company Area. Going directly to my hooch, I change into a fresh set of jungle fatigues before going to the Mess Hall for breakfast. Meeting up with Glen, we went over the plans for he and Sùpa to meet Jintana and me at the night club. With everything set, we then left for morning formation.

After the formation, I rode alone in the back of the ¾-ton truck to the Air Base Site, while Jim and Phizer rode in the cab. At the Air Base Site, John and Larry bragged how ready they were to tack on Skip's Spec-4 stripes at shift change that night. In the Operations Room that morning, work was slow and gave me time to talk with Bob while Skip went through the rigmarole for his promotion.

I gave Bob a run down on my evening with Jintana, to which Bob laughed as I described the effect my opening Tango move had on her six friends. Also, that it was easier now to talk with Jintana in Thai than in English with her limited vocabulary. When I finished, he said, "I think your assessment of what Jintana wants from you is accurate. It makes since she'll want to have as much fun as possible before she's married to someone else, or even to you."

When Skip arrived, I saw Maan-daa had sewn a set of Spec-4 patches on his jungle fatigue jacket, and I promptly tacked each on with hard punches. For the rest of the day, Skip and I did all the work under Bob's supervision. Half way through the afternoon, Bob sent Skip and I to the nearby Air Force NCO Club to join and receive NCO Club Cards, as we couldn't join Camp Friendship's NCO Club because the Army didn't consider Spec-4s to be NCOs, though Corporals were.

Skip returned early from his 5:40 meal run to avoid a bunch of guys from tacking on his Spec-4 patches, which allowed me to leave at 6:30. Luckily, John and Larry were waiting in front of the Day Room. Exiting the truck, I said, "You two have fun tacking on Skip's stripes," as I left quickly for my hooch. Changing quickly into a silk shirt and pair of cotton pants, I left for Korat. Exiting the Thai bus, I quickly hired a săawm-law for 3 Bhat to the Sri Pattana Hotel, where I told the driver I'd give him 2 more Bhat if he waited to take me to the Gài Yâang Sâang Thai restaurant. I then rented a room for Glen and Sùpa.

Entering the restaurant, my heart lept in my chest as I saw the exotic Jintana in her bright yellow silk blouse, sitting at a table. And on seeing me, I then saw a dazzling smile graced her face as she stood to greet me. After exchanging sàwàtdiis, we sat down across from each other, and a waitress came to the table asking, "How you wan chicken? Sa-picy, lit-ta sa-picy, no sa-picy?"

I said, "Little spicy," and when she quickly returned with an entire barbecued chicken on a platter and a plate for each of us, I thought, "Now I know why its named 'Chicken Barbecue Make Thai'."

And when I paid 15 Bhat for the chicken and two Pepsis, I thought, "75 cents for an entire chicken that can easily feed four people is a good deal."

At 8:00, Jintana walked behind me the 200 yards to the night club, where I paid the 4 Bhat cover charge to the maitre d', and then to a table on the 3rd tier, where she sat opposite from me as I ordered two bottles of Pepsi. A few minutes later, I saw Glen and Sùpa enter the night club. Excusing myself, I quickly went to greet them in the Thai manner. As Sùpa followed behind us, I said to Glen, "Pepsi is 3 Bhat a bottle, but I don't know what they charge for beer or liquor." Glen laughed and said, "I'm here to feel Sùpa in my arms, and don't want it dulled by alcohol."

As Glen ordered two Pepsis from the waiter who appeared at his elbow, he sat opposite from Jintana. When Sùpa sat next to Jintana, I saw her beauty was greatly enhanced. She was wearing a form fitting, light green dress that shimmered in the table's candle light that accented the curves of her ample breasts, her slender waist, and her round hips and tight buttocks, and thought, "Sùpa, there's nothing dowdy about you now and I understand why Glen wants to feel your body in his arms when he dances with you tonight."

I then saw Jintana was not pleased that my gaze had lingered momentarily on Sùpa, and I quickly asked her to dance with me. Soon, I saw Glen walk onto the dance floor with Sùpa following, as the orchestra played a waltz, and I experienced a flood of joy from the lightness of Jintana dancing in my arms.

As Jintana and I gaily danced around the floor, I saw Glen was having difficulty dancing with Sùpa. Knowing Glen was from Texas, where he surely learned to ballroom dance at Texas cotillions, it must be that Sùpa didn't know how to ballroom dance. I showed this to Jintana, and for the rest of the evening, the three of us taught Sùpa the basic moves and rhythms for the waltz, cha-cha and tango. By the time the night club closed at 12:00, I saw Sùpa enjoyed being in the experienced arms of Glen.

As Sùpa and Jintana followed Glen and I to the Sri Pattana Hotel. I passed him the key to Room 307 and told him about the 4:00 wake-up call. As we crossed Suranari Road to the Hotel, Jintana quickly passed me to enter the Hotel before I did. When Glen, Sùpa and I exited the elevator at our floor, and we began to walk in opposite directions to our rooms, I said, "Sàwàtdii, koon naawn kuun-nîi dii mâak, châi dâai?"

Sùpa laughed and replied, "Naawn kuun-nîi dii mâak, châi dâai. Sàwàtdii."[114]

Entering Room 319, I went to the bathroom and had a birdbath to freshen up for Jintana, and then waited for her knock on the room's door, to enter the room. When she entered and held my face for a passionate kiss, I held her close to my bare chest. She then lowered her face to my chest, and as she nuzzled my hairy chest, she said in Thai, "I love you have much hair chest to give me tickle."

As she playfully nuzzled the hair on my chest, I unbuttoned her uniform to expose her round, perfectly formed breast. And as she gave me another passionate kiss, I felt their firmness as they nuzzled my chest hair.

After we took a tepid shower to wash the crud from each other, I told her that I worked Saturday and Sunday night, but Glen and I would be at Sùpa's cafe from noon to 4:00 for lunch and to practice Thai with Sùpa, and could she join me there. She said she had to work Saturday, but was off Sunday and would meet me there. I then took a blue 20-Bhat bill from my wallet and said it was for the săawm-law to and from the cafe.

After the 4:00 wake up call, I met Glen in the hallway and asked, "Did you sleep good last night?"

Glen laughed and replied, "Sùpa kept me too busy for any sleep."

I responded, "I got some sleep because Jintana can't spend the night. But, I hope to fix that by staying at another Hotel. She told me she has Sundays off, and will meet at the cafe at noon."

Exiting the Hotel, we hire a săawm-law for a ride to the Chainarong Gate, and rode a Thai bus to the Company Area. After breakfast and formation, I stripped to my skivvies and slept until 11:00. Then Glen and I rode a Thai bus to Korat to spend the afternoon talking with Sùpa in Thai. But, during the afternoon, I rode a săawm-law to and from the

---

114   "Goodnight. You sleep tonight very good, yes can?" "Sleep tonight very good, yes can. Good night."

Korat Hotel for 5 Bhat, and found it had the same type of rooms for the same price.

Returning to the Company Area, I changed into my OD BDUs. And after dinner, I waited with Skip in front of the Day Room for Tommy to arrive with the ¾-ton truck. Arriving at the Operations Room, I relieved Jack so he could go home to his tîi-lók, and we waited for Bob to finish the Shift Change Report. When Bob came into the Operations Room, he told us, "Jim wants us to begin a scheduled PM to replace the tubes in the breakout circuits. This is a lengthy process because it requires notifying the users on both ends and the intermediate Radio Sites of the circuit's outage."

At 9:30, Ted called from the PBX building to tell us he had a line to Rosie, and did any of us want to call Stateside. Skip quickly said he did so he could tell his Jewish Princess and his parents about his promotion. As he talked to them for a half hour, Bob and I continued doing the PM. When Skip was done, I spent a half hour talking with Linda and then my parents, while Bob and Skip continued with the PM. And when I was done, Bob talked with his parents, as Skip and I did the PM. By the time Bob notified Ted we were done with the line, it was time for Skip to make the 10:55 meal run.

While Skip was gone on his meal run, I told Bob how Glen, Jintana and I had fun giving Sùpa a crash course on ballroom dancing. Bob commented, "While boys and girls are given lessons in Grade School to perform traditional Thai dances, they're taught nothing about Western dance. They may later learn to Rock-N-Roll at pop dance clubs, but ballroom dance classes are held at schools for higher education, which is where Jintana's friends at the night club probably learned to ballroom dance."

I responded, "That makes sense. And, last night, Sùpa wore a very enticing dress, which was quite different from the white blouse and black skirt she wears for work, or the simple clothes she wears when we go to the movies. I'm sure Sùpa was trying to give Jintana a run for the money to keep Glen's focus on her, as she certainly got my attention briefly. Also, this afternoon, I went to the Korat Hotel and found its pricing was the same as the Sri Pattana, and will stay there instead. So, thanks for the tip."

When I made the 6:35 meal run and delivered the truck to Jim, immediately after breakfast, I went to my hooch, stripped to my skivvies, turned on my fan, and fell instantly asleep on my bed. A couple of hours later, I awoke to the sound of someone kicking Skip's bed and yelling, "Get out of that bed you lazy maggot and get a case of beer to put in your fridge. This Company didn't buy that fridge for decoration. And, I'll be back later to check. You got that, slime ball?"

Hearing the front door slam shut, I quickly got up and saw Skip at his wall locker and said, "Skip, I'm sure between all of us, we have a case of beer to put in the fridge."

Opening my wall locker to take out a 6-pack of Budweiser, I saw Glen, Tommy, George, Ronnie and Stony walking in a row to the front of the hooch, each carrying a 6-pack of beer. When we opened the fridge's door, we saw there were a dozen cans of beer already there, and I heard George yell with his Georgia drawl, "I'm gonna hang that damn-Yankee from the flagpole myself, and it ain't gonna be no effigy this time."

As we filled the fridge with our 6-packs of beer, we all agreed Spike needed to be stopped from this return to his vindictive behavior, and wondered what had happened to embolden Spike to do so. Then we all returned to our beds to get more sleep before it was too hot.

At 11:00, I woke this time to the bugle call for Mess. By the time I'd dressed and was ready, Glen was waiting at the hooch's front door for us to go board a Thai bus for Korat and meet our girlfriends at the cafe.

Entering the cafe, I saw they were both standing near the door, and making the wâai, they bowed and said together, "Sàwàtdii, tîi-lók." After Glen and I responded in kind, and had all stood upright, I saw that Jintana was wearing no bra under a form-fitting, white silk blouse and her nipples pressing against its front. As I felt my blood rush to my loins, I thought, "You vixen. The way Sùpa was dressed last night made you jealous when my attention was momentarily drawn from you. And now, you want to make sure my eyes are only on you, and now you're pleased because I haven't taken my eyes off the front of your blouse."

As Glen and I walked past the girls for them to follow us to a table of our choice, I saw that Jintana's appearance didn't effect Glen because he'd been focused on the enticing look of desire Sùpa had for him. Sitting at a table with my back against the wall and Glen to my right, I watched mesmerized by the small jiggles of Jintana's firm, round breasts beneath her tight, white blouse and thought, "You have to know watching your breasts is driving me mad with desire for you."

We all were looking up at Sùpa as I placed an order for four chicken fried rice meals and asked her to eat with us. When we each placed a napkin on our laps, I felt the long, graceful fingers on Jintana right hand not just touch my left leg in appreciation, but give my upper thigh a squeeze to get my focus back on her, which I did. Looking at her with longing desire, I said in Thai, "I went to the Korat Hotel yesterday and decided it's a better place for us to stay the night."

I saw Jintana's eyes light up as she said, "Really truly, darling?"

I replied, "Really truly, darling of mine."

Eating our lunch, we discussed our plans for tomorrow's lunch, going to see the movie, and my recommending to have dinner at the Gài Yâang Sâang Thai restaurant, before going to the compound. When several people entered the cafe a few hours later, Glen and I left to return to the Company Area, while Jintana remained to chat with Sùpa. As we walked to the Chainarong Gate, I asked Glen what he thought of Jintana not wearing a bra and said, "Sandii, the only tits I have eyes for are Sùpa's."

When Skip and I arrived at the Air Base for work, we found out why Spike was back to his vindictive ways. Bob told us, "The Battalion Operations Officer has orders to return Stateside in a couple weeks, and your CO has been chosen as his replacement. Since your XO is only a 2nd Lieutenant and cannot be your CO, and Battalion has no other Senior Company Grade[115] Officers available, then USAS-Thai is loaning an Infantry 1st Lieutenant to the 442nd to be your CO until a Senior Company Grade Signal Corps Officer is transferred to the 442nd. Spike's elated to have an Infantry CO to whip his Signal Corps Company into line and off its high horse."

Skip and I both groaned and said, "Well, there goes the neighborhood."

We then spent the rest of our night shift doing the scheduled PM on the breakout racks. At one point, Ted called to let us know he had a line up to Rosie, but we declined as we had just called last night. By the end of our night shift, we'd only finished the PM on half the breakout

---

115   Lieutenants and Captains.

circuits. At 6:35, I made my meal run, delivered the truck to Jim before eating breakfast, and then blissfully slept the morning away.

Waking at 11:00 to the bugle call for Mess, Glen, Skip and I quickly dressed for our noon rendezvous with our three girlfriends for lunch. Entering the cafe, I thankfully saw that Jintana was wearing a bra. After lunch and the movie, we left Skip and Glûaimàai at the cafe, while Jintana and Sùpa rode in a săawm-law behind Glen and my săawm-law to the Gâi Yâang Sâang Thai restaurant, where we feasted on a whole barbecue chicken.

En route to the compound in săawm-laws, Glen and I agreed for me to go to the Korat Hotel to rent for each of us a room for four nights, and gave me a red 100-Bhat bill to pay for his. After we gained permission from Horn to enter his home, the four of us exchanged sàwàtdiis with Horn, Bob, Tom and Skip before entering the house where Jintana gaily introduced Sùpa to the three tîi-lóks. Being summarily ignored by the five women, Glen and I each retrieved and opened a Sing Hǎi Beer from the refrigerator, and left the women's inner sanctum for the men's domain on the porch.

After I'd drunk some of my Sing Hǎi Beer, I excused myself to make the one-mile trip to the Korat Hotel, where I rented Rooms 214 and 215 for four nights and requested 4:00 wake-up calls for each morning. By the time I returned, Ronnie and Stony had arrived, and I gave Glen the key for Room 214.

At the end of the pleasant evening on Horn's porch, the parties broke up at 9:00. Jintana and Sùpa then walked behind our 5-man phalanx to Jomsurangyat Road, where we hired two săawm-laws at the Chaophaya Inn. When Glen, Sùpa, Jintana and I entered the Korat Hotel, we walked to the elevator. When the elevator door closed, I felt Jintana's two hands grasp my upper left arm possessively. Looking past Glen to my right, I saw Sùpa also had a firm grip on Glen's upper right arm.

Exiting the elevator, Jintana didn't loosen her grip on my arm until we were in Room 215, where she gently pulled me around to face her and said in Thai, "You're the most wonderful man in the world," and I responded, "And you're the most desirable woman in the world."

I saw the layout for Room 215 was identical to those at the Sri Pattana, as I led Jintana to the bed and we laid down on our sides facing one another. For a while, we talked about how good it was to spend the day and evening together, and finally be able to spend the night together side by side. As we talked looking happily into each other's eyes, I began to feel Jintana's hands slowly unbutton my shirt and then slide her hands up under my T-shirt, running her sensuous fingers through my chest hair, where she used them to gently pull me on top of her.

At 4:00, I woke to the wake-up call, and was happy to feel Jintana snuggled in my arms. When I went to the bathroom for a shower to wash the crud from my body. Jintana was right behind me to enjoy the shower with me. As I left for Camp Friendship, she said, "I'll return at 3:00 when I finish work."

I joined Glen in the hallway, and then shared a săawm-law to the Chainarong Gate. Sitting together on the Thai bus, we extolled the beauty and virtues of our women the entire time. After breakfast and morning formation, we returned to the Korat Hotel for uninterrupted sleep. Glen said he was going to spend the afternoon with Sùpa before coming to the compound, and then return to pick her up when she got off work at 8:00. I then said, "Jintana will be here at 3:00 when she gets off work. Then after dinner, we'll go to the compound, so I'll see you there."

At 3:00, Jintana returned to my Hotel room and taking me by the hand to the bathroom, she shared her pent-up lust for me in the shower. Over dinner she discussed with me inviting Glen and Sùpa to go dancing with us tomorrow night again. When we went to the compound that night, I invited Glen to bring Sùpa to the night club for dancing, which he happily accepted. That night, Jintana and I enjoyed each other thoroughly, especially since she didn't have to leave my side in the middle of the night. When I left for work in the morning, I left the room key so she could reenter the room when she left work at 3:00.

Returning at 7:30, I found Jintana dressed enticingly in her light-blue silk dress, and felt my hormones surge with anticipation as we left for the night club. Surprisingly, Jintana said it was okay with her to ride in a săawm-law with me to and from the night club. At the night club, Glen and I thoroughly enjoyed the sensation of holding our women in our arms as we danced. Halfway through the evening, I heard Glen yell, "Hallelujah!" and I saw Glen bring Sùpa over to Jintana and I, where he said, "Sùpa has decided that she wants to live with me as my tîi-lók."

As Jintana and I rode to the Korat Hotel, I half expected her to say she also wanted to live with me as my tîi-lók. She didn't, but I did feel her built up passion from dancing, as she stroked my thigh with her long, slender fingers. And I thought, "Mom was right when she said, 'There is no greater foreplay for a woman than ballroom dancing'," which proved to be true when we returned to Room 215 and Jintana began to passionately kiss me as she fumbled to quickly remove my shirt.

The next evening at 7:30, when I returned from work, I found Jintana looked breathtaking in her form-fitting, bright yellow blouse and sea-green skirt with a black belt that accentuated her round breasts and shapely hips. I thought, "She's going to make everyone's eyes at the night club pop out of their faces looking like this," as I said, "Your beauty gives me great honor." And after a thrilling evening with her dancing in my arms, and having eyes only for her, I again experienced a woman with unbridled passion when we returned to Room 215.

The next day, after morning formation and again after lunch, I went to bed and slept to recover from four days and nights of being with Jintana, and thankful my Friday night shift was a quiet one. On Saturday, as Sùpa no longer worked at the cafe and Jintana was working, I had no reason to go to Korat. So, I spent the afternoon playing Double-Deck Pinochle with Skip, Ronnie and Stony, as we drank beer and smoked cigarettes. Also, Saturday was another quiet night at work, and as I was returning from my 10:55 meal run, I saw two men walking toward the Air Base trying to hitch a ride, because there was no bus service after 11:00. Stopping beside them, I asked, "Need a lift?"

They yelled, "Heck, yea." Running to the passenger door and climbing in, one of them asked, "What's an Army truck doing going to the Air Base this time of night?"

I replied, "I work the Radio Site at the Comm Center."

The other one responded, "No kidding. Can we take a look?"

I answered, "I've been told no visitors. But what the heck, it's the middle of the night, why not?"

Entering the Radio Site, I heard Bob yell, "Hey, Sandii, Ted's gotta line up Stateside, want to call home?"

I replied, "Just a sec, Bob," and turning to the two Airmen, I asked, "Either of you want to call home for free on a WATS line?"

They responded, "No kidding? An actual phone call for free?"

I replied, "No kidding," and as they followed me up the hallway, I yelled, "I don't, but I've a couple of friends here who would."

Passing Skip as he left on his 11:40 meal run, I saw Bob's mouth drop open as I walked into the Operations Room with two young men in civilian clothes and asked, "Is it all set up?"

Bob replied, "Yea, it's all setup," and said nothing as I walked into the Grand Canyon, took the handset from its hook, and handing it to the Airman behind me, said, "Just say hello, Rosie."

As the Airman gave his information to Rosie, Bob motioned me to the desk and asked, "You want to tell me what's going on?"

I replied, "Just being kind to two Airmen I picked up hitchhiking from the Camp. They wanted to know why an Army truck was driving to the Air Base. I told them I worked at the Radio Site, they asked if they could take a look, I said what the heck why not, and here they are making free phone calls home, for which they will be eternally grateful."

When the two Airmen had finished their phone calls and I was leading them to the Radio Site's front door, they both enthused their gratituted and said, "Man, if there's *anything* you need, just name it. And if we've got it, it's yours with no question asked."

I responded, "Really? Anything? No question asked?"

They replied happily together, "Yea, man. That's right. If we've got it, it's yours."

I enquired, "Where do you guys work?"

One of them answered, "On the flight line. We're bomb-loaders on the F-105's."

I whispered, "Can you get me a bomb, no questions asked?"

They looked at each other and shrugged their shoulders, as one said to the other, "Well, we did promise him anything with no questions asked." Then looking at me, they nodded their heads, as one said, "Sure. But we'll need to borrow your truck for a while. And then, you must forget you ever saw us."

I responded, "Deal," as we shook hands, and I thought, "And that's how to get a bomb."

CHAPTER 25

NOTHING LIKE EASY MONEY ON A SURE BET

Just as the two Airmen were exiting the Radio Site, I saw Skip return from his 11:40 meal run and park the ¾-ton truck in the 442nd BN Reserved Parking space. Passing the Airmen as he entered the Radio Site, he asked, "What did those two guys want?"

I laughed and replied, "What those two guys want is to borrow our truck for a couple of hours to bring us a bomb so we can blow up Spike."

Skip exclaimed, "What?"

I replied, "I'll explain while Bob's on his meal run," as we walked to the Operations Room, where Bob said, "I'm going to go to the NCO Club. So, no shenanigans while I'm gone, guys."

As soon as I heard the front door of the Radio Site close, I gave Skip a complete rundown on what had happened with the two Airmen, and made Skip promise not to talk with anyone about the bomb, especially Bob, as this was a "need to know" operation.

Skip said, "My lips are sealed. I only wish I could go with you."

I then checked for an open audio channel that broke out at Korat Tropo, and then said over the Order Wire, "Korat Tropo, Korat

Base." I then heard Glen's voice respond, "Korat Base, Korat Tropo. What you need, Sandii?" I replied, "Korat Tropo, Korat Base. Meet me on TRVA-2."

Using a tip-sleeve patch cord, I then blocked TRVA-2 to my customer and was able to talk directly to Glen on my handset without anyone else able to listen in. When I heard Glen's voice on my handset, I said, "Glen, please don't say anything or react to what I'm about to tell you, okay?"

Glen replied calmly, "Okay, I understand."

I explained, "In a couple of hours, I'll have a bomb delivered to me that we can use to blow up Spike. When I call you on the Order Wire, I want you to have it arranged for you, Ronnie and Stony to meet me in front of Company Supply. Then we'll get George and Tommy to help carry the bomb to Spike's hooch so Tommy can detonate it. Hows that sound to you?"

I head Glen laughed and say, "It sounds just like what the doctor ordered. Okay, if there's a problem on this end, I let you know on the Order Wire."

A couple of hours later, I heard a knock on the Radio Site's front door. I saw Bob and Skip were working in a row of breakout racks. When I opened the door, one of the Airmen was there and said, "No questions asked, your 200-pound bomb is on a cradle under a tarp in the back of your truck. Just don't blow yourself up," and shut the door.

Returning to the Operations Room, I asked, "Hey, Bob, okay with you to go get a burger at the NCO Annex?"

Bob replied, "Mâi bpén rai, it's quiet."

I then went to the Order Wire and said, "Korat Tropo, Korat Base." When I heard Glen respond, "Korat Base, Korat Tropo," I said, "I checked the circuit and it's good to go." I then heard Glen say, "That circuit's good here, too."

I quickly left and drove the truck to the Company Area, where I backed it up between the Motor Pools fence and the Company Supply/ Armory building, turned off the engine and exited the truck. A minute later, Glen arrived in a 2½-ton truck with Ronnie and Stony. Then the four of us went to our hooch, where we roused George and Tommy, who were very willing to blow up Spike with a 200-pound bomb.

Once George and Tommy were dressed in their OD BDUs, which are nearly invisible in the dark, the six of us went to the ¾-ton truck and took off the tarp. With three of us on each side gripping hands under the bomb as a human bomb cradle, we easily lifted the 200-pound bomb off its bomb cradle. Then sidestepping to the side of Spike's doghouse, we carefully set the bomb on the ground next to it. Then everyone looked at Tommy expectantly.

I saw Tommy look around at the expectant faces and then say, "Hey, I told you guys before that I don't know anything about bombs. That's an EOD thing. So, unless one of you want to hit the bomb's head with a hammer, I don't have any other ideas."

Since none of us had any other idea on how to detonate the bomb, and nobody volunteered to do that, then we agreed the best thing to do was to get the red shop rags from the two trucks, and wipe the bomb clean of fingerprints and leave it next to Spike's doghouse.

Returning to the Air Base, I located a large dumpster to put the bomb cradle in before going back to the Radio Site. There, I found Bob and Skip still putzing around in the row of breakout racks. I decided the innocent thing to do was sit at the desk and read through the record of outages in the Site Log. I later made my usual 6:35 meal run and turned the truck over to Phizer, who was waiting in the Motor Pool parking area.

Walking across the Motor Pool's parking lot toward the Mess Hall, I resisted the urge to walk to the left corner of the Motor Pool's chain-link fence to peer through it and see if there was any activity around the bomb. In the Mess Hall, I quickly ate breakfast as I kept glancing at the time on my watch. Not wishing to miss the show, at 6:55 I left to stand on walkway in front of the Mess Hall. As I lit a cigarette and waited to see what happened, I saw the backside of Company C's four Platoons lined up in formation across the roadway form the Company's HQ.

A minute later, I could hear to my right a man yelling, "Bomb! Bomb!" Then, I saw Spike running bantam-legged with terror on his face, yelling, "Bomb! Bomb!" I also saw confusion in the formed ranks as they watched Spike run into the HQ still yelling, "Bomb! Bomb!" It became quiet, except for the murmuring of questions in the ranks about what to do. It was all I could do to keep a straight face as people exited the Mess Hall asking what was going on, and I said, "It sounded like Spike was yelling about a bomb as he ran into the HQ."

Shortly, I heard to my left sirens from a jeep with flashing blue lights, marked MILITARY POLICE, and carrying four MPs, followed by sirens from a red fire truck with flashing red lights, both turning onto the roadway to the Company Area. Then I saw Spike run out of the HQ waving at the vehicles to follow him. At this point, the organized ranks of the Platoons collapsed as everyone mobbed behind the vehicles as they went toward the Motor Pool.

Moving down the walkway, I watched the progress of this circus and saw the MP's jeep with an MP on either side blocking the 20-foot-wide space between the Motor Pool's fence and the Supply/Armory building, and Spike leading the other two MPs to his hooch. Deciding there wasn't much else to see, I past behind the bedlam to my hooch. There I found Glen, Dan, George and Tommy laughing and drinking beer in celebration. As I joined them, I thought, "Too bad Skip, Ronnie and Stony are stuck at work missing the action. Luckily, it's Sunday, so there won't be much work to do until they're relieved."

Finishing our beers, Dan, George and Tommy, not wanting to miss formation when it was finally held, went back to the chaos, while Glen left for Korat to set up house with Sùpa. But, Glen assured me they would be at the compound tonight. Then I stripped to my skivvies to get some sleep before going to meet Jintana for lunch at the Korat Hotel and rent a room there for four nights.

Waking to the bugle call for Mess at 11:00, I began my routine of opening a can of Bud and taking a piss, before dressing to go to Korat. As I dressed, I heard Skip laugh and say, "Well, Sandii, your plan didn't go off as you intended, but it did cause a big bang just the same. I didn't get relieved until after 8:00. Jim told us the Army's CID[116] has started an investigation and wanted to interrogate everyone in the Company, but the CO told them that most of our jobs were mission critical to the Vietnam Theater of Combat. And, if the CID cannot find any tangible evidence to tie a member of his command to the bomb, there won't be any interrogations unless they get authorization from the Quad-C A. The CO believes the Thai Cong[117] were trying to blow up the Company's Supply Room to disrupt our ability to support our ground forces in South Vietnam.

---

116   Criminal Investigation Division.
117   Thailand's equivalent to Vietnam's Viet Cong.

"So, are you and Jintana going to be able to meet me and Glûaimàai at Sùpa's old cafe to see a Samurai movie with us?"

I replied, "Absolutely. We love to see those movies," and thought, "Besides, Glûaimàai can't go with Skip, unless we're along, too."

When I arrived at the Korat Hotel, I went to the Reception Desk and paid 100-Bhat to rent a room for four nights. Then entering the Hotel's Restaurant, I saw Jintana sitting at a table looking astonishingly beautiful in her form-fitting pink dress and a radiant smile that made my heart jump for joy, as my loins ached with anticipation from our two-day hiatus.

Approaching the table, I saw Jintana stand to greet me in the Thai fashion with her form-fitting dress displaying every luscious curve of her body. Exchanging sàwàtdiis, my eyes drank in the desire flowing from her lovely, almond-shaped eyes as I told her how much I missed her. As we sat at the table, she told me she would like to have the Hotel's "som tum"[118] for lunch.

When the pretty waitress in a white blouse and a Thai style skirt with red and black horizontal stripes came to our table, I ordered the "som tum" for Jintana, and the "laab muu"[119] for myself from the menu, with a Pepsi for each of us. The menu showed our meals cost twice as much as the cafe, but still less than a Dollar.

I asked Jintana in Thai, "Is there anything special you want to do today?"

She replied, "The only thing special I want to do today is be with you."

Finishing our lunch, we went to our room, and after a fevered, passionate interlude that satisfied each of our anticipations, she comfortably spooned the luscious curves of her body within the embrace of my arms, and we passed into exhausted slumber. A few hours later, I woke to find her sensuous body still curved against my body within my embrace, and the feel of her tantalizing buttocks against me reignited my desire for her, to which she responded in kind.

After a playful, tepid shower, we dressed and went to the Hotel's Restaurant for a delightful dinner before our one-mile walk in Thai tradition to the compound. When we arrived at Horn's home and re-

---

118   An unripe papaya salad flavored with chili, lime, garlic and peanuts.
119   Finely chopped pork mixed with chili, lime, roasted rice and herbs.

ceived his standard response to my request for entrance, we then made our sàwàtdiis to the four men on the porch. As Jintana joined the four tîi-lóks, of which Sùpa was now a member, I retrieved and opened a bottle of Sing Hăi Beer from the refrigerator and joined my amiable friends on the porch.

Shortly, we were joined by Skip, Ronnie and Stony. Amazingly, during our discussions, the topic of the bomb found by Spike's hooch did not come up, and I thought, "Those of us who participated may want to claim bragging rights for the bomb, but certainly are smart enough to not do something so stupid. As for the others, it's a military topic, which house rules forbid."

When the social gatherings broke up at 9:00, Sùpa and Jintana again walked behind the 5-man phalanx to Jomsurangyat Road, where everyone went to the Chaophaya Inn to hire săawm-laws. Arriving at Korat Hotel, we entered our room where Jintana impatiently spun me around, threw herself into my embrace and kissed me passionately. After a moment she leaned back into my arms to look at my face, and I saw the desire in her beautiful, almond-shaped eyes as she said in Thai, "All the time I walk behind you, I see your tight butt that I like to hold when you're between my legs," as she reached down with both hands, grabbed my buttocks, and pulled me to her undulating hips.

Later, we showered to remove the crud from our bodies. I was washing her well-shaped backside, when she sensuously leaned forward and gyrated her perfectly rounded buttocks against my groin, rousing my lust for her, and I thought, "You certainly are making up for the 61 hours we were apart."

The next morning, as I left for morning formation, I asked, "Jintana, would you like to have lunch with Skip and Glûaimăai today, and then see a Samurai movie?"

She replied, "That will be fun, but everything about you is fun."

After morning formation, I told Skip that we were on for lunch and a movie, as I changed into fresh clothing before returning to the Korat Hotel. Entering our room, I stripped to my skivvies, and crashed on the bed. Waking to a gentle knock on the door and hearing Jintana's sweet voice say, "Darling, it's Jintana," I jumped up from the bed and opened the door. Watching her enter our room, I saw her gracefully appear in a sensuous form-fitting, blue silk dress and heard her ask, "Can we ask Skip and Glûaimàai to go to the night club tonight? I miss dancing with you very much."

Overwhelmed by her sensuality, I replied, "I belong to you, so we'll do anything you want."

She responded, "I only want you to be happy."

I quickly dressed to leave for the cafe, and we arrived there in a sǎawm-law 10 minutes later.

As I told Skip our invitation to go dancing at the night club with us, I heard Jintana tell Glûaimàai the same thing, and saw her eyes open wide with excitement. When Skip saw her reaction, he said, "She'll kill me if I don't accept. Besides I'd love to dance with her, too."

At the theater, naturally the girls sat between Skip and I, and as soon as I saw one Samurai quickly slash open three others who had attacked him, I felt Jintana grab my left arm with both hands. Glancing across the two girls, I saw Glûaimàai had the same two-hand grip on Skip's right arm. Awhile later, I saw Glûaimàai had slid her left hand down the inside of Skip's arm and was resting on his thigh. And 15 minutes later, I saw her hand was now between his thighs, and thought, "Skip, you are in a quagmire up to your butt with this beautiful little woman."

Walking Glûaimàai to the cafe she worked at on San-Prasit Road, we agreed to pick her up when she got off work 8:00. Then Jintana and I returned to the Korat Hotel in a sǎawm-law, and went to our room. As we began to kiss passionately, I felt her unbutton my silk shirt and then her hands slide up under my cotton T-shirt, gliding her sensuous, long fingers through my chest hair. Then shrugging off my shirt and pulling my T-shirt off over my head, while she fondled my chest hair, I thought, "Why should she have all the fun?"

I then unzipped the back of her silk dress and skillfully unhooked her bra. As they slid from her sleek shoulders, I gently spun her around. Cupping her firm, round breast in my hands, I kissed her on the nape of her long, slender neck. As I heard her moan with pleasure, she then turned and lustfully kissed me as I felt her fumbling hands trying to quickly remove my pants, and I thought, "So, you've decided we've had enough foreplay and it's time to ride the rodeo."

After our shower, we dressed and went to the Hotel's Restaurant for a nice dinner. Then we rode a sǎawm-law the mile to the compound, where we socialized with our respective genders until 7:30. As we walked to the Chaophaya Inn to hire two sǎawm-laws for our tandem ride to Glûaimàai's cafe, Jintana decided it was okay for us to walk arm in arm, since it was dark and nobody was around.

When we entered the cafe, I saw Skip sitting at a table drinking a Pepsi, while waiting for Glûaimàai. As we sat at the table with Skip, I saw Glûaimàai enter through a door at the cafe's back dressed in a white silk, form-fitting dress that accentuated every womanly curve of her petite body. I saw Skip gape in awe. I immediately set my gaze on Jintana to make sure she knew my eyes were only for her, as I thought, "Glûaimàai might only be 14, but she appears every bit a full grown woman."

As Skip and I rode in a săawm-law in front of our women's săawm-law, I said, "It looks like Glûaimàai went all out to give Jintana a run for the money, even though she knows she's not in Jintana's league. So, do you know how to ballroom dance?"

Skip replied, "I hope it's all show intended for Jintana, because the way she looks tonight added to her natural beauty, it's driving me crazy. As for ballroom dancing, it was part of the PE curriculum in Junior and Senior High School. I may not be top notch, but I'm pretty good."

Arriving at the night club, I paid the 8-Bhat cover charge for the four of us, as the host of our foursome. With the girls in tow, I then led Skip, with the girls in tow, to a table on the 3rd tier, paying 12 Bhat for the four Pepsis I ordered from the waiter. When we each had a swallow of Pepsi, Skip and I then led our women to the dance floor as the orchestra struck up a Waltz. Although it was obvious Glûaimàai had not waltzed before, she was a quick study and soon was gaily dancing in Skip's arms, while I thoroughly enjoyed the elegance, grace and beauty of Jintana in my arms as we danced.

Since Glûaimàai had been on her feet all day at work, I saw by 10:00 she was beginning to fatigue, and suggested, as I had to be up at 4:00, it was time to leave. When Glûaimàai said it was okay with her to ride with Skip alone so I could get to bed sooner, I thought, "I'm as good excuse as any for you to ride with Skip."

As Jintana road beside me to the Korat Hotel, I felt her hand caress my thigh in anticipation. I decided this time to beat her to the punch with my own desire for her, and entering our room, I quickly pulled her to face me, planted a full on passionate kiss to her mouth, as I unzipped her dress, unhooked her bra, and slid them over her shoulders to the floor. Still passionately kissing her, I lifted her lithe body by her slender waist and carried her to the bed. Laying her back on the bed, I sucked her right breast wholly into my mouth as I quickly unbuttoned my shirt. After I pulled my T-shirt off over my head, I then sucked her left breast wholly into my mouth as I quickly removed my pants and heard her moan with anticipation.

Jintana's reaction to my passionate initiation at first was surprise and then total enthusiasm. As we later lie entwined, she said, "You make me feel the most desired woman in the world," and I thought, "You are the most desirable woman in the world," as I went to sleep.

Showering together after the 4:00 wake-up call, she said, "I wish we could be together every day, and every day was as perfect as yesterday. I'll be happily waiting for you when you finish work today."

After morning formation, as Skip and I rode in the back of the ¾-ton truck, I asked, "How was the ride to the cafe with Glûaimàai?"

Skip replied morosely, "Glûaimàai said she wants to be my tîi-lók, like Sùpa is tîi-lók for Glìn-dii. I knew she was up to something at the movie when she gradually slid her hand between my legs. I thought it was to say she wanted to have sex. And when she came out in her white dress, I was totally ready to, but there's no way I'm going to bed with a 14-year-old girl. I tried to explain she was too young, but she doesn't speak enough English to understand. All she knows is that I won't see her again. Maybe Sùpa can explain it to her, since they're good friends."

At work, things were busy, so I arranged over the Order Wire with Glen to take the 10:55 meal run. Over lunch together, I explained to Glen everything that happened between Skip and Glûaimàai, and asked if Sùpa can explain it to her. Glen responded, "I'll try, but it's going to be hard for them to understand, as to them a 14-year-old girl isn't too young to be a tîi-lók and is considered a full grown woman in Thailand. They'll think that Skip doesn't want her for a tîi-lók because he doesn't like her. But, I'm sure Sùpa will talk to her, if for no other reason than to console her."

Returning to the Air Base Site, I passed on to Skip what Glen told me, and Skip said, "I don't see what's so hard to understand, but at least Sùpa will talk to her about it."

Making the 6:35 meal run, I found John and Larry ready in front of the Day Room, and happy to hear that after a busy morning, things had slowed after lunch. I then hustled to the Mess Hall for a fast dinner before going to my hooch and quickly change to go dancing with Jintana. By 7:00, I was on a Thai bus headed for Korat, and according to my watch, I entered the Hotel at 7:40.

Entering our room, I saw Jintana enticingly dressed in a form-fitting, white silk blouse and a royal blue skirt with a red belt that perfectly enhanced her lovely round breasts and the contours of her womanly hips, and thought as I felt my arousal for her, "Having your clothes tailor made certainly allows a woman to wear form-fitting clothes to augment the shape of her body."

I was prepared for Jintana to give me her usual passionate kiss. Instead, she gave me a hug around my waist with her left cheek against my chest as I put my arms around her shoulders and held her close. After a moment, she leaned back and looked at my face. I saw a tear in the corner of each beautiful, almond-shaped eye glistening like a diamond, as she said, "I now know you desire me more than anything in the world and it fills my spirit with comfort," and dropping her arm, she added, "We can now dance with our hearts content." As I followed her to the door, I wondered, "What was that all about?"

We arrived at the night club five minutes before Glen and Sùpa, and I had already ordered a Pepsi for each of us. As Sùpa approached us behind Glen and passed through the candlelight of the table next to ours, I saw she was stunningly attired in a form-fitting, low-cut, hot pink dress with a black belt that accentuated her slender waist, deepened the low-cut cleavage of her breasts, and showed the sensual roundness of her undulating hips as she walked. When I quickly looked back to Jintana, she said across the table, "It's okay for you to see her beauty, because I know the desire of her heart is only for me."

As Jintana and I gaily danced away, I saw the look in her eyes no longer had a lust for me, but a contented passion from her heart. I also saw a difference between Glen and Sùpa as they danced joy fully together, satisfied to be in each other's presence, and I thought, "Sùpa, your low-cut attire to keep Glen's focus away from Jintana is wasted effort, as the only tits he's interested in are yours."

As Jintana and I rode back to the Hotel, I saw her pent-up passion from our dancing together in the impatient caress of her hand on my thigh. But, when we entered our room, she allowed me to initiate my passionate foreplay as I did before, and the movements of her body and the sounds that now emanated from her, showed a greater sexual satisfaction. When we later washed each other in the shower, she subtly invited me to initiate foreplay with her. When I felt our lovemaking culminate in orgasmic shudders from her writhing body, and I thought, "After all our passionate, sexual encounters, this is the first time she's had an orgasm."

When I woke to the 4:00 wake-up call, it was such a pleasure to feel Jintana snuggled in my arms that I almost went AWOL to stay in this heaven with her. But decided it was best to depart now so I could enjoy her anticipated passion on my return.

At morning formation the CO stated, "The CID has officially determined the bomb found beside Spike's hooch was a terrorist act by the Thai Cong to destroy our Company Supply and Armory, as Air Force records show the bomb was released from an F-105 last week. Case closed," and I thought, "But, Spike knows he was the target of men from this Company, and if he continues to piss us off, the next bomb will be exploded."

Work was slow at the Air Base Site when I saw Bob tear off a long piece of yellow paper from the AP teletype monitor. He then called Skip and I over to the desk and said, "Read this."

After reading it, I said, "So, it's just another bunch of Black college students demonstrating at San Francisco State that was put down by the police and National Guard. The only thing I see interesting, it's that Dick Kawalski, who was a Team Leader at Tropo and discharged a month ago, is supposed to be a student there now."

Bob responded, "I've been following this story for a couple of weeks, as this demonstration is different. Normally, Blacks demonstrate at Colleges for discrimination against Blacks in their admission policies. S.F. State has no such admission policy and there's a lot of Black students there. What these Black students demand is to have Black professors and classes on Black History, Black Culture and U.S. History course material to not be literally 'white washed.' And now Black students at some of the other prominent Universities are also demanding the same changes. No, I don't think this is just another student demonstration. You just wait and see."

I replied, "The only first-hand knowledge I have with College demonstrations, is that in my Senior year in High School, a handful of long-haired students demonstrated against the local College's administration. And, when a bus load of long-haired students from U.C.

Berkeley joined them, the football team broke practice, gave them all free shaves and hair cuts, put them back on their bus, and then escorted the bus out of town."

After work, I made the 6:35 meal run and skedaddled for Korat. Entering our room, I was again enthralled by Jintana's natural exotic beauty. That she was wearing a form-fitting, white silk blouse conformed to the contour of her tantalizing breasts, and a red skirt with a black belt that augmented her slender waist and heightened the sensuality of her hips, only enhanced my desire for her. But, when she saw the physical arousal she affected on me, she quickly grabbed my arm and led me back out to the hallway. I then knew she wanted the desire we had for each other now to be increased by the foreplay from an evening of ballroom dancing.

Arriving at the night club, I quickly spotted Glen and Sùpa at a table on the 3rd tier waiting for us. As I mounted the steps with Jintana following and approached the table, they both rose to greet us in the Thai style. As Sùpa bowed, the top of her red silk blouse was cut so low to show the tops of her breasts, that the view now exposed the areolas of her nipples, and I thought, "There is no doubt in my military mind that the only tits Glen will be looking at tonight will be yours, Sùpa," as I saw Glen was also staring at her exposed areolas.

As the evening progressed, whenever Jintana and I danced to a Tango, every time I thrust my right leg between her legs, I would press my thigh against her mons pubis. Or, when I stepped back with my left foot for a reverse dip, which forced her right foot to step between my legs as I rolled her to my left for a deep dip with her left leg wrapped around my right leg and my right knee pressed against her mons pubis, then when I raised her back up to the ballroom position, I held her in such a way that I would slide her mons pubis seductively up the length of my right thigh.

When we rode back to the Hotel, I saw my ballroom foreplay had aroused Jintana to such a height of sexual frustration, that I could feel her hand slide over my crotch with longing. As soon as we entered the room, I initiated my previous passionate foreplay that placed her on the bed wearing only her panties and her right breast sucked into my mouth, as I removed my shirts. Sucking her left breast into my mouth, I could feel on my bare abdomen the crotch of her panties sliding in anxious desire, as I lay between her inviting legs and removed my pants to gratify her with my own aroused passion. Then I slid her panties from her undulating hips and down her long, well-formed legs. As I made love to her, I slowly changed my position until I heard her frantically yell, "Tîi-nán, tîi-nán,"[120] and felt her whole body in an orgasmic shudder, and then continued to gyrate against my groin until she felt the explosion of my climax.

As we lay together in exhausted euphoria, I realized I'd be working the next two nights while she worked her day shifts, and we wouldn't be together again like this for almost 70 hours. So, when we showered later, I again initiated foreplay as I had done in the shower the night before, and was rewarded to feel her body shudder with her second orgasm that night. Drying each other off afterward, I said, "I hope that keeps you satisfied until Saturday evening."

She laughed and replied, "It won't, but now I have something amazing to look forward to."

Walking to the 4:00 wake-up call, I could feel the sensuous form of Jintana in my arms snuggled against me. Though I felt my hot blood flooding my groin in response, I decided that after 2½ days of anticipation, the gratification will be more intense later, than to have a quicky right now, and got up to go to morning formation and then some much needed sleep.

When I woke at 11:00 to the bugle call to Mess on sweat-soaked sheets, I renewed my routine of getting a can of Bud to drink as I used the piss tube and dressed before going to the Mess Hall for lunch. But there, my routine changed because Glen was now living with Sùpa and all I had to look forward to in the afternoon was playing Double-Deck Pinochle, as I drank beer and smoked cigarettes. While I dressed, I heard Skip ask, "Do you think Sùpa can ask one of her friends to go on a double date to the movies on Monday with me?"

I replied, "I doubt it after the way you dumped Glûaimȧai. But, you'll have to talk with Glen about that, since Sùpa is his tîi-lók. Besides, for the next two Mondays we're on the day shift. However, I could talk to Jintana about it."

Skip responded, "Thanks, Sandii, you're a pal," as we left for the Mess Hall together.

---

120   "There, there."

After lunch, Skip and I swung by the Howard Johnson and bought a couple of 6-packs each for our afternoon of playing Double-Deck Pinochle. While Skip and I partnered against Ronnie and Stony for money, the two of them started to bum beer and cigarettes from me, which was expected because they had paid it forward to me last Pay Day. It turned out Skip and I made good partners because we'd spent so much time working together at the Air Base Site, and by dinner time we were a few bucks ahead.

Work that night wasn't too busy as it was Thursday. When Skip and I weren't working on circuit outage calls and making Site Log entries, Bob had us going over our electronic circuits with schematics. But not just on the breakout circuits, as we were also responsible for maintaining all of our electronic test equipment, too. And though we had been trained at Ft. Monmouth to repair the test equipment as part of our courses, that had been many months ago and much had been forgotten.

After I finished the night shift, my Friday was a repeat of Thursday, except that after lunch, instead of buying two 6-packs of beer, I bought three, plus a carton of Pall Mall cigarettes. And though I was keeping busy at work or playing cards in my hooch, I was continuously thinking of Jintana and anticipating our reunion at 3:00 on Saturday.

The Friday night shift was much the same as Thursday night's, except after Bob's meal break, I kept seeing Bob walking over to look at the teletype machines monitoring the news-wire services. At 4:00, watch Bob rip off a strip of yellow paper from one of the machines and heard him say, "Okay, that clinches it. You two come over here."

When Skip and I were standing by Bob, he asked, "You guys ready to make some easy money?"

Skip and I replied, "Sure."

Bob held up the strip of yellow paper and explained, "The Detroit Tigers and the St. Louis Cardinals will be playing in the World Series, and this is their game schedule. The first game is October 2nd, next Wednesday, the day after our Pay Day. As the games are being played Stateside in the afternoon, which is after midnight here, then AFN sends a live feed of the play-by-play action our local AFTN to be recorded and rebroadcast by AFTN at 8:00 in the morning. As you know, our Radio Site is the only one in Thailand that monitors the news feeds to AFTN. So, aside from the guys at AFTN, we're the only ones who will know the final scores of each World Series game before its rebroadcast by AFTN to all of Thailand at 8:00. That give you time to make bets at the Mess Hall in the morning and make 20 to 30 Dollars in easy money for each game. The one thing you don't want to do is make large bets, because that will raise suspicions. Unless some fool insists on making a big bet. Also, avoid giving point spreads."

I responded, "Nothing like easy money on a sure bet."

CHAPTER 26

This Is A Disaster

After making the 6:35 meal run to deliver the truck to the Motor Pool, and had breakfast in the Mess Hall, I went straight to my hooch, stripped to my skivvies, turned on my fan, and fell asleep on my bed's sheets. Waking to the 11:00 bugle call for Mess lying on sweat-soaked sheets, I grabbed a cold Bud from the mini-fridge, pissed, and dressed in a fresh set of skivvies and civilian clothes. Then, I went to the Mess Hall with Skip for lunch. After lunch, we went to the Howard Johnson and I bought three 6-packs of Bud and a carton of Pall Malls. I then gave Skip $1.20 to buy for me two more 6-packs of Bud. Returning to our hooch, I set the six 6-packs and the carton of Pall Malls on the card table. I told Ronnie and Stony, "These are for you and Dan. It'll have to last you till Monday, when I can buy more."

Leaving to catch a Thai bus to Korat, I then walked the short distance from the Chainarong Gate to the cafe on San-Prasit Road where Glûaimàai worked. Entering the half-empty cafe, Glûaimàai exchanged sàwàtdiis in the Thai style with me. She was wearing the usual loose-fitting white blouse and a black skirt reaching halfway below the knees of 4-foot 11-inch tall, very petite body, which reminded me of my Linda in New Jersey.

She showed me to a table, where I ordered a Pepsi. When she returned with the Pepsi, I gave her a big smile and said in Thai, "Glûaimàai, I am your friend and angry at what Skip did to you. I think he 'has no brains'[121] not to have you as his tîi-lók as you are a beautiful woman. It is sad his people think a female under 18 years is a girl and not a woman. Skip can only see you as a friend."

She responded with a very engaging smile on her beautiful face, "So Skip not think I'm 'not pretty,'[122] and is a man with no brains to not want me for his tîi-lók. I am very happy you are my friend to explain this confusion to me."

Leaving the cafe, I put two 1-Bhat coins on the table. One for the Pepsi, the other as a tip. I then hired a sǎawm-law for the ¾-mile ride to the Korat Hotel, where I'd reserved the same room for four nights, and paid the receptionist 100 Bhat. Entering the room, I took a shower to wash the dried sweat from my body, and then lay on the bed wearing only my boxers, and fell asleep.

Waking to a knock on the door and a female voice saying in Thai, "Darling, it is your girlfriend," I rose from the bed and opened the door. I was enthralled by Jintana's ethereal beauty and aroused by the curves in her form-fitting, red silk dress.

I saw Jintana smile with delight as she watched the effect in my boxers that she desired. Entering our room quickly, I wrapped my arm around her and gave her a passionate kiss, as I lifted and carried her to the side of the bed. Unzipping the back of her dress, I was pleased to find she had no bra on. When I slipped the dress from her shoulder and it fell to the floor, I was more aroused to see she had no panties on either. Lifting her by her slender waist, I lay her back onto the bed and sucked her breast fully into my mouth. Lying between her long sensuous legs raised invitingly into the air as I removed my boxers, I felt her lusting crotch sliding on my abdomen with desire, and thought, "She's not wasting any time to make up for the 2½ days we've been apart."

With Jintana already fully aroused, and my knowing the position to be in to elicit her climactic response, I soon heard her yell with

---

121   There is no word for "stupid" in Thai.
122   There is no word for "ugly" in Thai.

satisfaction as I felt her body convulse from orgasmic spasms. Then I felt her crotch grind with desire against my groin until she felt my explosive release as I thrust deep into her. Rolling off her in gratified exhaustion, Jintana rolled with me straddling my groin and said, "I've waited too long to let go of you now," and she continued to undulate her hips, massaging her crotch on my groin. Reaching up, I cupped both of her firm breasts and messaged them with my fingers, until I saw her face contort with ecstacy and felt her body shudder again in orgasm. Then falling on my chest in sexual exhaustion, still holding me in her, I heard her say, "My darling boyfriend, I will never let you go," and we both fell into contented sleep.

Waking a couple of hours later, I found her still lying on my chest holding me inside her. Feeling ravenous for food, I said, "My darling, we must eat." Gently rolling her off my chest, I felt her legs tighten, reluctant to my sliding out of her.

As we cleansed the crud from our bodies in the shower, I felt aroused washing her desirable breasts while she washed my loins. Turning her around as if to wash her back, I cupped her firm breasts in my hands, puller her against my chest, and kissing the nape of her neck sensuously, I heard her moan with desire. Feeling my rising arousal, she leaned forward in lust, presenting her desirable, round buttocks to me. Shortly, I felt her body shudder with orgasmic release, then continue undulating her sensuous hips until my climactic thrust distended fully into her.

Jintana had brought a bra and panties in her handbag, and wore them when we went to the Hotel's Restaurant for dinner. After we ate a delicious dinner, I hired a sǎawm-law for a ride to the compound. At 7:45 Glen, Sùpa, Jintana and I left for the night club. As Glen and I walked before our women, I told him about my encounter with Glûaimǎai.

Glen responded, "Yea, I know. Sùpa and I had dinner there to console her. Sùpa said your kindness to her has earned you merit with the Buddha, and your explanation that Skip 'has no brains,' has made her happy."

After an evening of my seductive ballroom foreplay with Jintana, she was so aroused that she removed her bra and panties in the ladies room with anticipation just before we left the night club. As the sǎawm-law bounced on the road while we rode to the Hotel, I watched her enticing breast jiggling in her form-fitting red silk dress, sliding against the fabric.

Entering our room, Jintana was so aroused, it resulted in an immediate encore of our afternoon lovemaking, and our lying contentedly in the afterglow of our orgasmic release, falling into blissful sleep. Then, she had another orgasm while we showered together after my 4:00 wake-up call.

After morning formation, I returned to our room and, except for lunch in the Hotel's restaurant, I spent the entire day sleeping only in my boxers until 3:00. Waking to Jintana's knock on the door and hearing her say, "Darling, I'm ready for you," I felt aroused as I went to open the door. When I saw Jintana's stunning beauty in her form-fitting, blue silk dress, and again without her bra or panties, my arousal lept from my boxers and Jintana yelled with delight. Our Sunday afternoon was an orgasmic encore, and she again kept me in her as we slept in sexual exhaustion with her head lying on my chest.

As we showered before dinner, I was enticed as I washed her sensuous body, and initiated foreplay that culminated in our mutual orgasms. When we had dressed, I stood behind her, and sliding my hands over all her womanly curves, said "You are the sexiest woman in the world and will never stop making love to you."

I then felt her butt undulate against my groin in response and heard her say, "And I will never stop wanting you in me."

After dinner, we again rode a săawm-law to the compound, and I reveled in the feel of her sensuous body next to mine. At the compound, I saw that Skip, Ronnie and Stony were already there. When Jintana had joined the four tîi-lóks, and I'd joined the men on the porch with a bottle of Sing Hăi Beer in my hand, Glen asked, "Is Jintana going to become your tîi-lók?"

I replied, "So far, the subject has not come up. She seems completely satisfied with only dancing and having sex. But, she was completely frustrated when we couldn't be together on my last two night shifts with her having to work days, so that might change her mind."

Glen laughed and said, "I know what you mean about dancing and sex. Now that Sùpa and I are living together, every time we go dancing, she can hardly wait for us to get home to bang my brains out."

I laughed and responded, "Same thing with Jintana."

After a pleasant evening of camaraderie, the parties broke up at 9:00. Sùpa and Jintana walked and chatted behind our 5-man phalanx to Jomsurangyat Road. There, Glen, Sùpa, Jintana and I crossed over to the Chaophaya Inn to hire sǎawm-laws, and the three men turned right walking to the Chainarong Gate because they were nearly broke. While Jintana and I rode in our sǎawm-law, she told me how Sùpa thought it was very good of me to explain to Glûaimàai how Skip had no brains for not wanting her to be his tîi-lók.

Entering our room, I initiated my sexual foreplay slowly because Jintana was not already fully aroused as she had been before. While removing her dress and bra, I sucked one whole, firm breast into my mouth for half a minute, then switched to her other breast. Lying her back onto the bed, I hissed down the mid-line of her abdomen, as I continued manipulated her breasts with my fingers. Reaching her mons pubis with my kisses, and her hips now undulating with desire, I slipped her panties from her butt, and kissed her naturally hairless nether region. Sliding her panties up her raised, lovely long legs, I continued kissing up her spread inner thighs, listening to her moans of anticipation, and saw her writhing in lust to receive me.

With Jintana fully aroused, and my groin fully engorged and aching to satisfy her, we began our passionate lovemaking, with my goal to feel her body convulse in orgasmic ecstacy and then her pleasure to feel the distending thrust of my orgasm. Rolling onto my back, she rolled with me, straddling my groin to achieve another orgasm. Collapsing onto my chest in exhaustion, she lay there as we slept through the night.

Walking the next morning to the 4:00 wake-up call, we showered together washing the crud from each other. As I began to be aroused by the site and feel of her exquisite body, I thought, "A quicky in the shower before I run to morning formation just cheapens the experience for both of us. It's better to wait and have the anticipation for our dancing foreplay tonight."

As it was Sunday night Stateside, Monday's work was slow and gave me a chance to read the Site Log for the two days I was off. On my 11:40 meal run I went to the Howard Johnson after lunch and bought three 6-packs of Bud and a carton of Pall Malls. Entering my hooch, I saw Dan listening to his stereo system, and George and Tommy playing Double Solitaire.

Stopping at Dan's bed, I handed him a 6-pack of Bud and a pack of Pall Malls, to which he said, "You're a lifesaver, Sandii," as I walked to the back of the hooch, and set on Ronnie and Stony's beds a 6-pack of Bud and a pack of Pall Malls each. When George saw me do this, he drawled, "Hey, Sandii, you wouldn't have any brew and a butt for a fellow Rebel, would you?"

Walking to the card table, I handed him and Tommy each a pack of Pall Malls and drawled, "Anything for a fellow Rebel. I'll check and see how much brew I have in my locker."

Finding two 6-packs of Bud in my wall locker, I returned to the card table, gave a 6-pack to each, and said, "Guess you'll have to settle for some Bud until tomorrow."

Tommy laughed and said, "Beggars can't be choosers. You're a godsend, Sandii."

I laughed and responded, "According to Jintana, I'm a Buddha-send. See y'all later."

Walking to the Motor Pool, I then drove back to the Air Base Site, and spent a quiet afternoon as Bob went through the schematics on the test equipment with Skip and I. Leaving on my 6:35 meal run, I handed the truck over to John and Larry, as I hurried to the Mess Hall for a quick dinner before I changed clothes to leave for the Korat Hotel.

At 7:40, I knocked on our door, and when Jintana opened it, she looked absolutely ravishing in her bright yellow, form-fitting, silk blouse and blue skirt with a red belt showing every desirous curve. As she gave me a passionate kiss, I was aroused with her body pressing and moving sensually against mine. Then she forcefully stepped back from me and said breathlessly, "I want you to take me now, but we must see Glìn-dii and Sùpa at 8:00. Then, we'll leave at 10:00 for you not to be too tired from working all day for us to have lots of making love."

I responded, "Sounds very good to me," as we left our room.

Arriving at the night club before Glen and Sùpa, we went to an empty table on the 3rd tier, where I ordered four Pepsis. By the time the Pepsis arrived, I saw Glen and Sùpa enter, with her wearing a very provocative, form-fitting, low-cut, sky blue dress. Rising to greet them, Jintana said, "Sùpa told us she wears low-cut dresses because Glìn-dii likes to see her breasts, and when they get home from dancing, his lovemaking is very vigorous."

Watching Glen and Sùpa while they danced, I saw Glen feasting his eyes on the exposed parts of her breasts, and when the opportunity provided, Sùpa would bend forward so he could see down her cleavage. I thought, "Sùpa's problem is, like most Thai women, her breasts are smaller than American women, so she has less to work with to entice Glen. As for me, I'm a leg man, and that I can suck one of Jintana's breasts fully into my mouth fits my maxim, 'anything more than a mouthful is a waste.' Meanwhile, I'm focused on arousing Jintana by pressing my leg against her mons pubis as often as possible."

Just before 10:00, Jintana told Glen and Sùpa, "I'm tired and will be leaving now. Also, I'm unable to go dancing tomorrow night."

Then, Jintana went to the ladies room, and when she came out, I saw her bra had been removed. And, as we rode in a sǎawm-law to the Hotel, I watched her breasts jostle against her silk blouse. Entering our room, and before I could initiated any foreplay, Jintana said, "No! I'm ready for you now! You just take off your clothes."

Quickly removing my silk shirt and T-shirt, I saw Jintana unbutton her bright yellow blouse in front of me and provocatively wiggle her exposed breasts at me as she slipped her blouse sensuously off her shoulders onto the floor. By the time I'd pulled my T-shirt off and was fumbling to quickly remove my pants and boxers, I saw her belt and skirt were on the floor and stared with fascination as I watch her perfectly formed, long legs walk enticingly to the bed beneath her undulating round hips. When I finally had my pants and boxers off, she was lying on her back with her luscious legs raised and spread invitingly. Feeling my groin fully engorged with lust as I moved toward her. Seeing she was fully ready to receive me, I thought, "You weren't kidding when you said, 'I'm ready for you now.'"

After Jintana had laid contented on my chest caressing my chest hair for a half-hour, she sat up on my groin, placed my hands on firm, round breasts, and began undulating her hips, saying, "I want to feel the joy of heaven rush through me again."

Feeling my arousal for her beginning to flow to my groin, and the wetness of her arousal flow warmly onto me, she said, "Dearest, I'm ready for you again."

When she collapsed in exhaustion the second time on my chest, we went happily to sleep.

Waking to the 4:00 wake-up call, we went to take our usual shower together. After a couple of minutes, Jintana turned from me and placed my hands on her breasts. As she pressed her undulating hips against my groin and felt the rising of my arousal, she said, "Oh, yes, please let me feel your desire for me before you leave. Yesterday, you didn't and I was afraid all day I was no longer desirable to you."

As she leaned forward and I thrust into her, I asked "Forgive me. If I left right after I made love to you, wouldn't it make you feel cheap?"

Moaning with pleasure, she replied, "Every time you make love to me, I feel rich with your desire for me," as we began our first lovemaking rodeo of the day.

Today was October 1st, Pay Day and at 9:00, I rode in the truck with Jim to the Motor Pool. After he parked the truck, we walked to the Pay Line at the Day Room. As we worked the day shift, we were on the list for head-of-the-line priviledges and we didn't' have to be in our Class-B Dress khaki uniform. Reporting to the CO for pay, I was paid $220. After I paid $7.50 for a $10 U.S. Savings Bond and $8 for my mây-bâan, I had $202.50, of which I exchanged $100 for 2,000 Bhat.

When Jim and I returned, then Skip, Phizer and Bob left to be paid. While Skip and Phizer were being paid in the Day Room, Bob drove the truck to the Tropo Site to get his paycheck. Making the 11:40 meal run after lunch, I went to my hooch and found Tommy waiting to hand me $40, $10 each from Dan, Ronnie and Stony, and $5 each from George and Tommy. Going to my wall locker, I put $50 and 1,600 Bhat into my tobacco can, and then drove back to the Air Base Site.

At 2:00, I went to the bank across the street and deposited $50 into my Savings Account. After a moderately busy afternoon at work, I made the 6:35 meal run, turning the truck over to John and Larry before going to the Mess Hall for a quick dinner. In my hooch, I quickly changed for my trip to Korat, and decided that tomorrow afternoon I'd go to my tailor and order three more silk shirts and two more pairs of cotton pants for 240 Bhat.

Arriving at the Korat Hotel, I had the Reception Desk change my wake-up call to 3:30. Going up to our room, I knocked on the door and said, "Darling, I'm home."

When the door opened, I saw Jintana's beautiful face leaning from behind the door and her exotic, almond-shaped eyes sparkling with joy. Entering the room, she closed the door, revealing a full view of her statuesque body. My arousal was immediate as she held my face with both hands, and arching her lithe body, pulled my mouth to her firm right breast, which I sucked fully into my mouth, and heard her moan of ecstacy.

Lifting Jintana by her slender waist, I stood upright as I sucked her left breast into my mouth and carried her to our bed. Laying her sensual body back onto our bed, I pulled my shirts off. She then grabbed my head with both hands and pushed my face to her naturally hairless mons pubis undulating between her raised legs. I heard her gasp with pleasure as I slid my mouth and tongue around her nether parts, while I removed my pants and boxers, and smelled the sweet aroma of her womanly nectar. With my engorged manhood released, I began to pull myself over Jintana's inviting body, and felt her legs arch back and spread wide to receive me for our 2nd lovemaking rodeo today.

After achieving the climaxes we desired, I laid in euphoria with Jintana's head on my chest and her desiring hips straddling my groin, and we fell blissfully asleep.

I woke to the arousal of Jintana's undulating sensuous hips on my groin. Feeling my blood flowing hot to my loins, I rolled her over beneath me, and felt the flow of her womanly nectar in response to my rising desire expanding inside her. As I began my rhythmic response to her craving, she moaned, "Oh, yes. I want to feel your desire for me as much as possible before we are apart for three days," and I thought, "So, this is why you told Glen and Sùpa you were too busy to go dancing tonight."

When we had accomplished the climaxes of our 3rd rodeo ride, we both fell asleep in euphoric exhaustion. A couple of hours later, I woke aroused to Jintana's undulating hips and happily enjoyed the lust of our 4th rodeo ride. Waking to the 3:30 wake-up call, I had plenty of time to express my parting desire for Jintana's succulent body as we again made love in the shower, and to enjoy the view of her fully revealed body desiring me when we passionately kissed goodbye and I left to catch a Thai bus to Camp Friendship.

After breakfast and morning formation, I spent my morning in exhausted sleep recovering from the repeated fulfillment of the desire Jintana and I had for each other. After lunch, I stopped at the Howard Johnson and bought two 6-packs of Bud, one of which I put in the mini-fridge as I retrieved one to drink before leaving.

Arriving at Korat's Chainarong Gate it was a short walk to the tailor shop. At the shop, I ordered three silk shirts, white, green and dark blue, and two pair of cotton pants, black and brown, all for 240 Bhat. With my 120 Bhat deposit, I received assurance they would be ready for a fitting by 2:00 tomorrow. Returning from Korat, despite 90 degree heat and high humidity, I stripped to my skivvies and went back to sleep under the full-blast of air from my fan.

Things that night were slow at the Air Base Site, so Bob continued to go over the test equipment with us. After our meal runs, Bob put the World Series game on a speaker to hear while we sat at the desk chatting. By 4:00, we heard the St. Louis Cardinals had beat the Detroit Tigers 4 to 0. Skip made the 4:55 meal run to the Mess Hall for his bets against the Tigers, and I made the 5:40 meal run for my bets against the Tigers. Then, Skip made the 6:35 meal run to deliver the truck to Jim in the Motor Pool, while I waited for shift-change after 7:00 and Tommy to give me a ride to the Company Area.

At lunch, I collected $23 from my bets, and then played Double-Deck Pinochle till 1:30, when I left for Korat to have my fittings at the tailor shop. After the fittings, I decided to go to the cafe where Glûaimàai worked to drink a Pepsi and see how she was doing.

Entering the nearly empty cafe, I watched Glûaimàai's beautiful face light up when she saw me. When we exchanged sàwàtdiis, she said in Thai, "I'm very happy to see my good friend," as she led me to a table. I ordered a Pepsi, and when she returned, we gaily chatted about what was happening in our lives. When I left, I put two 1-Bhat coins on the table.

Thursday night at the Air Base Site was very much like Wednesday's, and in the morning, we learned the Tigers had beat the Cardinals 8 to 1. This time I made the 4:55 meal run to make bets against the Cardinals, and Skip made the 5:40 meal run to make his bets. Then, after sleeping all morning, I went to lunch and collected $25 from my bets.

After lunch, I left for the Korat Hotel, where I paid 100 Bhat for four nights in the room I'd reserved, and requested wake-up calls for 3:30. Entering our room, I took a shower, put on the fresh boxers I'd brought, and then lay on our bed waiting for Jintana's arrival.

At 3:00, I heard a knock on the door and heard Jintana say, "Darling, I'm ready for you." Opening the door, I beheld Jintana's rapturous beauty and felt my arousal watching her firm breasts jiggling against her form-fitting, bright yellow silk blouse as she quickly entered our room. As I began to give her a passionate kiss, she grabbed my left hand, and guiding it up under her skirt, between her spread legs, she placed it on her hot, wet crotch, and said, "I Told you 'I'm ready for you, and now your desire is ready for me," as she looked down at my engorged manhood.

Jintana quickly slipped her clothes off as she walked seductively to the bed with me close behind. Then turning around, she threw herself onto the bed, spread her legs up into the air, and giggled as she said, "I'm hungry for you sausage."

After our hunger for each other was fed, I held her to my chest as her loins held onto my groin, and told each other how much we missed and desired the other while we were apart. After awhile, I held her up by her lovely shoulders, looked desiringly at her breasts, said, "And now my lips are hungry for you," and sucked her left breast into my mouth. Hearing her moan in delight of my desire for her, I thought, "And so begins the second course of our feast."

When our exhaustion had assuaged, I said to the top of her head resting on my chest, "Darling, would you enjoy some dessert in the shower?"

Reluctantly lifting my grasp of her loins, she giggled, "I would love for you to serve me dessert in the shower."

As we washed each other's bodies and began to feel my arousal for her delectable body, I turned Jintana around and cupping her firm breasts, I pulled her back against me and felt her hips undulate in contact with my groin. As she felt my desire for her rising as I became engorged, she leaned forward and I felt her love canal swallow my manhood completely. Then holding her rapidly undulating hips tight against my groin, I soon felt her entire body shudder in an orgasmic shudder, and when my desire for her culminated in an orgasmic thrust distending deep into her, I gasped, "Dessert is served."

After dinner in the Hotel's Restaurant, we rode in a săawm-law to the compound. At 7:45, Glen, Sùpa, Jintana and I walked to the Chaophaya Inn and hired two săawm-laws for a ride to the night club. Arriving at the night club, I said to Jintana, "I told Glìn-dii we were leaving at 10:00," and she giggled, "You know how much I like to feast on your sausage."

At 10:00, Jintana went to the ladies room, and when she came out, I saw she had removed her bra and panties, and while we rode a săawm-law to the Hotel, I watched as her braless breasts jostled against the silk fabric of her blouse. Walking down the hallway to our room, I loosened my clothes, and as we enter our room, I released my pants and heard Jintana squeal with delight as my pants dropped to the floor showing her I was fully aroused. Removing my shirts, I watched her clothes fall from her sensuous body as she ran to our bed, threw herself backward onto it, spread her lovely legs into the air as she reached down and pulled open her love canal to receive my rapidly advancing lust for her.

At midnight, the flames of our desires were again fanned to a hot frenzy of lust culminating in orgasmic exhaustion. And at 3:30, as I demonstrated in the shower my parting desires for her sensuous body, I thought, "Will my hormones ever fail to rage at the site of her exotic beauty?"

After morning formation on Saturday, I returned to our room at the Hotel and slept until noon. Deciding this was a good time to pick up my new clothes, I walked the one mile to the tailor shop, paid Mr. Sing the 120 Bhat that was due, and left his shop with my new clothes in a shopping bag.

I then walked the short distance to the cafe on San-Prasit Road where Glûaimàai worked. Entering the cafe, I saw Glûaimàai standing by the door and beheld a stunning smile appear on her beautiful face as we exchanged sàwàtdiis and said in Thai, "I'm so happy to see my special friend," as she led me to a table. When she brought my order of chicken fried rice and a Pepsi, she lingered and asked in Thai, "Sometimes in the afternoons, when the cafe is not busy, can you help me learn to speak English so I can get big tips like the other waitresses?"

I replied, "As your friend, I would love to, my next afternoon off is Tuesday," and I thought, "This is great, because I miss the practice speaking Thai in the afternoons with Glen and Sùpa since they started living together."

After paying 4 Bhat for the meal, I left Glûaimàai a 1-Bhat tip, and walked back to our room at the Hotel. There, I took a refreshing shower, and lay on our bed in my boxers waiting for Jintana.

Hearing a knock on the door and Jintana's voice say, "Darling, I'm ready for you," I felt my instant arousal, stripped off my boxers, opened the door and said, "And I'm ready for you."

Jintana cried out in delight as she ran to our bed, shedding her clothes from her sensuous body with me close behind her fully aroused. Throwing herself on the bed with her luscious legs raised open and eager to receive me, she moaned with satisfied desire as I quickly filled her with my lust.

Our passion, lust and desire for one another was as intense as it was on Friday, and our Saturday afternoon, evening and night, and our parting in the morning was a delightful repeat in every way. And as I left in the morning, I thought, "Why can't every day be as wonderful as these last two days. Heck, Jintana, if you were my tîi-lók, or better yet, my wife, they would be."

I exited the Thai bus at the Air Base Site and found the Cardinals had beat the Tigers 7 to 3. As I ate breakfast in the Mess Hall, I made my bets against the Tigers, and when I made my 11:40 meal run, I collected $32 in bets.

Sunday was quiet day at work, and was able rest up in anticipation of spending the night with Jintana. Making the 6:35 meal run, I passed the truck to John and Larry, ran to the Mess Hall for a fast dinner, raced to my hooch to quickly change, before running to catch a Thai bus for Korat. As I waited for the bus, I thought, "I bet this is why Jack is always in such a rush to go home to his tîi-lók."

Walking down the hallway to our room, I unbuttoned my shirt and unfastened my pants, and knocking on our door, I said, "I'm ready for you," feeling fully aroused with my desire for Jintana.

Entering our room when the door opened, I saw Jintana's sumptuous body fully exposed to me, and felt my hormones exploded through my body intensified my engorged desire for her. Dropping my pants, she saw the full extension of my desire for her and grabbing me by my waist, she pulled me to the floor with her legs wide with desire and her wet love canal lusting to receive me. As I thrust deeply into her, she gyrated her hips fiercely against my groin as I reciprocated with unbridled lunges deep into her.

I soon saw the arch of her lithe body and heard the cry of her ecstacy as her orgasm raged through her convulsing body, and then my own explosive thrust distending fully into her. With her legs wrapped in desire around me, I lifted her bodily form the floor and carried her to the bed, where I lay on my back as she continued the passionate undulations of her hips until I felt the shudder of her second orgasmic convulsion.

An hour later, my desire for Jintana was aroused by the undulations of her sensuous hips against my groin. Rolling her over beneath me, I began my rhythmic response to her desire for me. Finishing our climaxes a second time, though not as intense as the first, we passed into euphoric sleep. With the 3:30 wake-up call, I again enjoyed expressing my parting desires for Jintana in vigorous lovemaking as we showered. While dressing to leave, I thought, "Tonight I'll again heighten your desire for me as we dance."

Stopping at the Air Base Site, I found the Cardinals had squashed the Tigers 10 to 1. After going to the Mess Hall for breakfast and to place my bets against the Tigers, I went to my hooch and dressed in a fresh set of jungle fatigues, before I left for formation and to go to work. At lunch I collected $26 from my bets against the Tigers.

As Monday was slow at the Air Base Site, I rested in anticipation of dancing sensuously with my exotic Jintana on our double date with Glen and Sùpa at the night club. On my 6:35 meal run, my anticipation drove me through a quick dinner in the Mess Hall, a fast change into my new clothes, and a run across the Company Area to catch a Thai bus to Korat.

Arriving at our room, I knocked expectantly on the door, but it didn't open. As Jintana had the room key, I knocked for five more minutes with the idea Jintana was in the bathroom getting ready to go dancing. I then went to the Reception Desk and asked if there were any messages for my room and was told there wasn't any. In desperation, I ran the 900 yards to the Sri Pattana Hotel and asked the Receptionist if Jintana was available. The Receptionist replied, "I'm sorry, but Jintana quit this morning and went home with her father. Would you be Mister Sandy?"

I answered, "Yes, I am. Why?"

She said, "Very good, because Jintana left this envelope for you," and handed me an envelope addressed, "To Mister Sandy."

I responded, "Kup koon mâak, krup," taking the envelope. I quickly opened it to find a sheet of Sri Pattana Hotel stationary. But, the writing was in Thai script.

Running to the nearby night club, I paid the 2-Bhat cover charge. Spotting Glen and Sùpa waiting at a 3rd tier table, I ran up the steps toward them. I then saw Glen get up, run to meet me, saying, "What happened, Sandii?"

I replied breathlessly, "Jintana's gone and left me this letter. But, it's in Thai script, so I need Sùpa to read it to me."

I followed Glen to their table and heard him say, "Sùpa, Jintana's gone and you need to read her letter to Sandii," and I handed the letter to Sùpa.

I watched as Sùpa read through the several lines of Thai script, and then I heard her exclaim in Thai, "What a pity! It reads: My Darling Sandii, I love you so very much and want you for my husband. I am very sad to tell you my father has accepted a dowry for me to marry a rich Thai man. I will miss you very much and love only you all of my life. Jintana."

I asked, "Sùpa is there a way to stop the marriage?"

She replied, "No. A daughter belongs to her father. When a father accepts a dowry for marriage, the daughter must marry the man, even if she is tîi-lók for another man."

I collapsed into a chair and said morosely, "This is a disaster."

CHAPTER 27

TRADING ONE FOR TWO IS GREAT

I heard through my anguish Sùpa say, "I'm too sad for our friends to dance. We must comfort Sandii and take him safely to his room."

Then Sùpa and Glen walked with me the ¼-mile to the Korat Hotel. There, Glen got the spare key to my room and they escorted me to my room. Entering alone, I walked to the empty bed in a daze, fell across it, and cried myself to sleep.

Waking to my 3:30 wake-up call and not finding Jintana in my arms, I then remembered last night, and the passionate love I had for my exotic Jintana became a passionate rage against the man who sold her into servitude to a rich man she probably didn't even know.

Leaving our heaven on Earth for the last time, I walked the mile in the early morning temperate air to the Chainarong Gate and assuaged some of my passionate rage. By the time I exited the Thai bus at the Air Base Site, I'd applied my Mom's old adage, "If you can do something about it, do it, and if you can't do anything about it, let it go," and I began to let Jintana go.

In the Air Base Site, I learned the Tigers had beat the Cardinals 5 to 3. With the Cardinals up 3 games to 1 in the World Series, I had no problem finding takers for my bets against the Cardinals in the Mess Hall before morning formation. As the Tropo Platoon organized for formation, there was lots of speculation as to what changes the Infantry Officer would effect in our Signal Corps Company. The general consensus was that whatever they were, we weren't going to like them.

When the Company was called to attention by Spike, I saw our CO standing to the right holding our Company Flag and an Infantry Officer standing to the left. After Spike read the order transferring command to the Infantry Officer, the Officers faced each other and our new CO saluted the departing CO, who presented the Company Flag to our new CO. Then, our new CO passed the Company Flag to PFC Schultz as our former CO entered HQ.

With the Change of Command ceremony concluded, Spike went through the rigmarole of taking Report from the four Platoons. Then Spike faced our new CO, saluted and reported, "All present or accounted for, Sir."

Our new CO returned Spike's salute and said loudly, "Men, I'm Second Lieutenant Price, your new Commanding Officer. I'll keep this short as many of you have mission-critical duties to attend to. Suffice it to say, I'll command this Company according to Army Regulations. I have an open door policy, provided you follow your chain of command. I'll make every attempt to know each of you by name, and will tour the Company Area with the First Sargent after this formation. Every Friday after morning formation, I'll conduct a Standby Health and Welfare Inspection. In conclusion, allow me to say it is an honor to command this Company. First Sargent, dismiss the Company."

At the words, "Standby Health and Welfare Inspection," I heard a collective groan in the ranks and thought, "I've been in this Company for two months and there hasn't been an inspection of any kind, except Spike inspecting the fridges for beer. And, as our mây-bâan keep everything in inspection order, then it's a waste of my sleep time standing around waiting for him to walk through."

When we were dismissed, I explained to Skip what had happened to Jintana as we walked to our hooch, and he responded, "That's a tough break, Sandii. What are you gonna do?"

I replied, "I'm sure Sùpa won't have any problem fixing me up with one her girlfriends to go to the movies and dance with. It's just that I was so happy being with Jintana."

When we entered the hooch, I grabbed a cold Bud from the fridge to drink, stripped to my skivvies and went to sleep.

Waking at 11:00 to the bugle call for Mess, I dressed in a new silk shirt and cotton pants, went to the Mess Hall for lunch, and collected $36 in bets from guys who were sure the Cardinals, with a 3 to 1 game lead, would win. Returning to my hooch to put my winnings in my tobacco can, I drank a cold Bud as I looked in my Thai lanugage manual on how to say "bookstore" in Thai, which was simply to say the Thai words for "store" with "book." I figured it would be easier to teach Glûaimàai English with a textbook.

When I exited a Thai bus at the Chainarong Gate, I paid a săawm-law driver to take me to a bookstore he said was on Mahat Thai Road. Fortunately, the store owner spoke good English and had no problem locating a Thai textbook on first year English for 120 Bhat, $6.00. I also bought a Thai-English/English-Thai dictionary for 60 Bhat, $3.00.

After a short walk to San-Prasit Road, at 1:30 I entered the nearly empty cafe where Glûaimàai worked. I saw a big smile grace her beautiful face as we exchanged sàwàtdiis. After bringing me a Pepsi, she told me how sad it was to hear what happened to Jintana and me. As I told her, "Bad things happen to good people, and life must go on," I thought, "Boy, bad news travels fast in this city."

Glûaimàai was ecstatic when I laid the textbook on the table and explained I could tutor her on my afternoons off, which would mostly be teaching her how to say the words she learned from the textbook. I then said, "Jintana and I used to meet with a group of friends at the night club on Thursday nights to dance, and I know you like to dance, so maybe you'd like to dance with us."

I saw her lovely, almond-shaped eyes open wide with excitement as she responded with enthusiasm, "I have to work late on Tuesday, Thursday and Saturday. Maybe we can go tomorrow or Friday?"

I replied, "I work tomorrow night, but we could go with Glen and Sùpa Friday night."

With that planned, we spent an hour going through the textbook together, and when I left, I said, "I'll talk with Glen tonight about Friday and see you tomorrow afternoon."

That night at work, I told Bob what happened with Jintana, and he said, "That's too bad, but it's one of the problems in a relationship with a Thai. Her father can marry her off at any time, unless you marry her, or have an agreement with the father, like I have. I pay him a monthly fee for Gùlaap to be my tîi-lók."

I responded, "You're kidding."

Bob laughed and said, "No. I rent Gùlaap for 100 Bhat a month, which is more than he would get with her working as a waitress. I think of it as tîi-lók insurance."

I arranged for Glen to meet me on the 10:55 meal run. When we met at the Mess Hall, Glen asked, "How are you doing without Jintana? Do you want Sùpa to set you up with one of her pretty girlfriends?"

I replied, "It is what it is. I was crushed, but it wasn't her choice, so I just have to put it behind me. But, that's not what I wanted to talk with you about. You know I'm helping Glûaimàai learn English, and when she went dancing with Skip, you saw how quickly she took to ballroom dancing. Well, she wants to know if she can go dancing with us Friday night."

Glen responded, "Fine by me, and Sùpa is always looking for an excuse to go dancing and then bang my brains out when we get home. Besides, she and Glûaimàai are friends. So, yea, we can double-date with you Friday after we meet at the compound."

After breakfast the next morning, I slept till the 11:00 bugle call for Mess. I dressed in a silk shirt and cotton pants while drinking a cold can of Bud, then went to lunch with Skip. When we returned to our hooch, I shot the bull with the guys about the World Series and how impossible it would be for the Tigers to win three straight games to win the Series. At 12:30, I left to see Glûaimàai at the cafe, and didn't tell Skip, thinking it was none of his business since he had dumped her.

When I told Glûaimàai that Glen, Sùpa and I would pick her up at 8:00 Friday night to go dancing with us, she said joyfully, "It'll be so much fun to dance with my very special friend. You make me very happy. Thank you very much."

I spent the next two hours helping her pronounce the words she had memorized and how English grammar was different from Thai grammar. It was enjoyable for me to watch her lovely lips try to say consonant sounds that didn't exist in Thai or didn't occur at the end of syllables in Thai.

At work that night, we listened to the 6th game of the World Series, and possibly the last. When the Tigers trashed the Cardinals 13 to 1, we cheered. Not because we cared who won the World Series, but because there would be a 7th game we could make sure bets on.

When I made the 5:40 meal run, I found the betting heavily in favor of the Cardinals, and had no problem finding guys taking my bets against them. In the Mess Hall at lunch, I collected $42 in bets. While I slept after breakfast though, I'd woken to the sound of Spike entering our hooch to check on the amount of beer in our fridge, and was thankful we now kept it well stocked.

I left for Korat after lunch, and exiting the Thai bus at the Chainarong Gate, I then leasurely walked the mile to Sri Pattana Hotel as it was the closest to the night club I'd be dancing at for the next two nights, and rented a room for two nights. I then walked the mile to the cafe on San-Prasit Road to tutor Glûaimȧai in English, which was a pleasure as she is such a natural beauty. While tutoring her, I asked, "Glûaimȧai, you're so beautiful, why aren't you married?"

She replied sadly, "I wish I was married like most of my classmates are. But I'm too small. Thai men want a wife with large hips to have many sons. Many small women, like me, die in childbirth. But, maybe an American man will marry me if I speak good English."

At 4:00, I had dinner before I walked to the compound, where I spent a pleasant evening talking and drinking a bottle of Sing Hǎi Beer. At 7:30, I left and walked the half-mile to the Sri Pattana Hotel. After a refreshing shower, I put on a fresh set of skivvies before I dressed, and then left for the short walk to the night club.

Entering the night club, I paid the cover charge and spotted the familiar faces at a table on the 3rd tier. Approaching the table, I saw the group was composed of three men and four women, and thought, "At least I won't cause someone to be the odd-man-out."

At the table, I made the wâai and bowed, saying, "Hello, my friends, may I join you?" and they all responded in kind and said, "Hello, Sandii, please do." As the men moved to empty a chair for me to sit in their midst, a girl sitting across from me asked, "Where's Jintana?"

I replied, "Jintana's father arranged for her to be married and she left last Monday."

The girl said, "What a pity. You need to dance with a pretty girl and be a happy man," as she gave me a come-hither smile on her pretty face.

I responded, "You're a pretty girl. Will you give me the honor to dance with you?"

She replied excitedly with a receptive smile, "The honor will be mine."

When we rose form our chairs, I heard her say, "My name is Julii," and saw she was 5-foot-2 and wearing a form-fitting, sky-blue dress hemmed six inches above her knees, revealing her firm, round breasts, a very slender waist, a tight sensuous butt, and shapely legs.

As she walked behind me to the dance floor, I heard her sweet voice say, "I watched with envy when you danced with Jintana because you're a very sexy dancer."

The orchestra struck up a Tango as we assumed the ballroom position. On the first down beat, I pulled her close as I thrust my right leg between her legs, pressing my thigh firmly against her mons pubis. Then my left leg stepped passed her right leg, forcing her to step back. When I thrust again between her legs, the force of my thigh against her mons pubis pushed her back, I heard her gasp and felt her left hand clinch my right arm from the arousal. Stepping back with my left foot, I dipped backward, forcing her mons pubis to slide down my thigh onto my knee, which I ground into her mons pubis. As I slid her mons pubis up my thigh to resume the ballroom position, I asked, "You mean sexy like this?"

She gasped, "Oh, yes! Very much like this."

As we danced, I found Julii to be very responsive to my leads. She was enthusiastic, sensuously light in my arms, and very desirable to watch. While we danced, we asked questions about each other. When I asked where she worked, she replied, "I don't have a job, I'm a 3rd year student at Suranari College," and I thought, "She's a junior in college, so she's 20 and not some teenage girl."

When we stopped to quench our thirst with some Pepsi, one of the other girls eagerly said, "You look fun to dance with. Maybe you would like to ask me to dance," and I did.

As we returned after a couple of dances, I saw Julii staring at me longingly, and she grabbed my arm and said, "My turn to dance with you."

While we were dancing a slow waltz, she asked if I was still staying at the Sri Pattana Hotel, and when I told her I was, she asked with longing in her lovely, almond-shaped eyes, "Would it be okay if I came with you and we had a nightcap there?"

I thought, "This is a 20-year-old woman, who wants to have sex with me, and who I find very sexually desirable," and I replied, "I would like that very much."

I saw her eyes sparkle with delight as she responded, "That is very good. I will go to the ladies room for several minutes and then you say it's time for you to go while I'm in the ladies room, and I will meet you across the lane, okay?"

When the waltz finished, Julii followed me up the stairs. While I finished my Pepsi, I watched as she took her purse and walked with swaying, enticing hips to the ladies room. Feeling my arousal from watching Julii, I told those at the table it was time for my return to Camp Friendship. Leaving the night club, I walked across Vatmung Lane and waited in the dim light from the night club. A few minutes later, I saw Julii leave the night club, scurry across the lane, and giving me a hug, say, "I'm ready for that nightcap now."

As she walked beside me on my right side by the lane in the dark, she pulled my right arm around her and placed my hand on a bra-less breast, and said, "I'm all yours tonight."

When we turned right onto the well-lit Rajadamnern Road, she slipped under my arm and walked behind me in the Thai style all the way to my room at the Sri Pattana Hotel.

Entering my room, she gave me soft, sensuous kisses as I felt her anxiously unbutton my shirt and ask, "Is it true American men have chest hair?"

In reply, I pulled my shirts off over my head, and as she ran her fingers up through my chest hair, she said desirously, "Oh yes, it is very sexy," and I felt my lust for her growing in my loins.

As I unzipped the back of her dress, she lowered her hands and unzipped my pants. I felt my pants slide down my legs as her dress slipped off her shoulders onto the floor exposing her enticing breasts. Holding her with my hands around her slender waist, I lifted her petite body up, and sucking her left breast entirely into my mouth, I heard her moan with desire as I felt her shapely legs wrap possessively around me and vigorously grind her crotch against my chest.

Carrying Julii's aroused body to the bed, I sucked wholly her right breast into my mouth, and then pulled the top covers on the bed back.

Lying her lusting body on the bed's sheet, she lowered her legs to my sides as I pulled her panties from her undulating hips, and I stood to slide them off her well-shaped legs. Taking off my boxers off, I saw Julii look desirously at my engorged shaft and said, "You're such a large man and I'm a small green woman, please be gentle with me," as she raised her lovely legs into the air and spread them wide for me to mount her.

With Julii's enticing legs spread wide, eagerly ready to receive me, I saw she was a small woman. Holding my swollen shaft to guide its head slowly into her hot, wet love canal. Rhythmically pushing into her tight love canal as it adjusted to my size, I heard her moans of desire. Gently pushing deeper into her, I saw her lovely face contort with pleasure and her hips undulate with lust to have more of me. When I'd filled her, her hips began to undulate vigorously with her lust. Matching my powerful, rhythmic thrusts with the undulations of her lusting hips, she began to cry out, "Dâai! Dâai!"[123] repeatedly.

Soon, I felt her body shuddering with orgasmic convulsions. As I continued my rhythmic thrusts, Julii cried out, "Oh yes, my darling, give me more," and again I felt her hips undulate vigorously with her lust for me. And when my orgasmic thrust distended deep into her, I heard her gasp, "I knew your lovemaking with me would be wonderful." As I lay exhausted on her sensuous body, I felt her lovely legs wrap desiringly around my waist.

When we had regained our breath, Julii began to describe what she enjoyed about our foreplay and lovemaking. As I began to lift myself off her, I felt her legs clinch around my waist, and seeing her arch her back and push her lovely, firm breast upward, she said, "Please stay in me and suck my breasts into your mouth again."

Taking Julii's enticing left breast into my mouth, I massaged it with my lips. Feeling her hips begin to undulate with lust, I became fully aroused again for her lusting body. When I began my rhythmic thrusts deep into her, I heard her moan, "Oh yes, my darling, give me more of your love for me."

When we had both climaxed and lay in the euphoria of our lovemaking, Julii asked, "Can I stay all night with you, my darling?"

---

123   "All right! All right!"

I replied, "My darling, it would make me happy if you did, but I have to get up at 4:00 to shower and go to Camp Friendship," as I rolled onto my back. Rolling her desirable body with me so she could sleep with head on my chest with me still inside her, she responded, "This is perfect, my darling."

At 4:00, we showered together, washing Julii's succulent breasts, I felt my arousal as she washed my groin. And when Julii saw my desire for her fully aroused, she squealed, "Oh yes, my darling," turned around, bent over and presented her tight, sensuous butt to me. As I began to rhythmically push into her small love canal, she moaned, "Gently, my darling, I'm still sore from last night."

I asked as I gently pushed deep into her, "Why sore from last night?"

She moaned as I rhythmically pushed, "It was my ... first time ... lovemaking ... and you made it ... perfect ... my darling," and I thought, "How was I to know she was a 20-year-old virgin."

As we dried each other off, Julii asked, "When can I dance with you again, my darling?"

I replied, "Is Saturday night okay? I have to work, but I could meet you at 8:00 in the night club."

She responded, "That would be very okay, my darling."

Julii's sumptuous body was standing nude before me as I was about to leave, and as I passionately kissed her, I slid my hands desiringly over her womanly curves, and then said, "I am so looking forward to dancing with you Saturday night, my darling," and she placed my right hand on her crotch saying "As am I, my darling."

Before leaving the Hotel, I stopped at the Reception Desk and paid 50 Bhat for two more nights. Riding the bus from Korat, I exited at the Air Base Site and found the Tigers had won the World Series 4 to 1. Returning to my hooch, I quickly changed into a fresh set of jungle fatigues and went to the Mess Hall. Since most were convinced there was no way the Tigers could win three games in a row against the Cardinals, I again had no problem making bets against the Cardinals.

After morning formation, everyone in our hooch, except Dan who was working, were standing by their open, spotlessly clean, wall locker, wearing freshly pressed jungle fatigues, highly shined black combat boots, with our beds perfectly made. The mây-bâan had taken great pride in preparing our hooch for their first standby inspection. It wasn't long before our new CO entered our hooch by the front door and I yelled, "Atten...tion. CO's in the hooch."

We had practiced after formation, and everyone came to attention at the same time. As all inspections begin on the left, Lt. Price marched to me first. When he stopped at attention before me, with Spike behind him, I said, "Specialist Lynch, ready for inspection, sir." He looked around briefly and said, "Very good, Lynch," as he made a right face and marched past Dan's area to George. After he inspected Skip last and marched to the front door, Lt. Price said, "Excellent work men," and then to Spike, "Whoever said the Signal Corps weren't' Soldiers, didn't know what he was talking about," and that was our last standby inspection. Later, we each gave our mây-bâan a blue 20-Bhat bill tip.

Waking at 11:00 to the bugle call for Mess, I got up, drank a cold can of Bud as I dressed in a silk shirt and cotton pants, and went to the Mess Hall for lunch, collecting $48 from some dour men. As I traveled to Korat, I stopped at the Air Base Bank across the road from the Radio Site, and exchanged the $48 for 960 Bhat. When I exited the Thai bus at the Chainarong Gate, I walked to the tailor shop and asked Mr Sing where I could find a good cobbler, and he directed me to one on Mahat Thai Road to the left of Chainarong Road.

Walking up to Mahat Thai Road, I turned left and found several shop doors the cobbler's shop. The cobbler told me it would cost 100 Bhat, $5.00, to make a cast model of each foot and lower leg, which he would store in his shop and use to make me custom made boots and shoes. I gave him a red 100-Bhat bill, and he put a plaster cast to the knee on each foot and leg. While I waited fifteen minutes for the cast to set, I selected from a catalog the picture of the type I wanted for some brown suede shoes. He said they would cost me 120 Bhat, $6.00, and would be ready on Wednesday, for which I gave him a 60-Bhat deposit.

Leaving the cobbler shop, I walked the short distance to San-Prasit Road. Entering the cafe, Glûaimàai flashed me a large, glowing smile on her beautiful face as she greeted me and led me to a table against the wall. Then, she quickly returned with a Pepsi and the textbook, and sat adjacent to me with her back to the wall so she could see all of the cafe. We chatted for a few minutes before she opened the textbook and I be-gan to help her with the pronunciation of the words she'd memorized.

After an hour, when the cafe was empty of customers, she stopped and asked in Thai, "Sandii, you're my very special friend, my teacher and you think I'm beautiful, yes?"

I replied, "Yes I am and yes I do."

She then said, "Sùpa told me Jintana talked to her about how you were a very good man, a very good and sexy dancer, and a very good lover, who taught her how to have the best sex and was her first lover. I am a small, green woman, and I would be honored if you were my first lover and taught me how to have the best sex as my very special friend. I'm not asking to be your tîi-lók, I'm asking you so I can be very good tîi-lók for an American man. Will you do this for me, please?"

I replied, "Glûaimàai, as your very special friend, I will be honored to teach you what I know about sex. And tonight, after we dance, I will give you the first lesson because dancing is part of the best lovemaking. Okay?"

With a very happy smile on her beautiful face, she replied, "Yes, very okay. But now we study English," and I thought, "If she is as small, or smaller, than Julii, then I better get some K-Y Gel lubricant on my way to the Hotel."

At 4:00, I ate dinner in the cafe, and as I walked along Mahat Thai Road to the Sri Pattana Hotel, I stopped at a drug store and bought a tube of K-Y Gel lubricant. Arriving at my room, I put the tube of lubricant in the top dresser drawer, took a shower, put on a fresh set of skivvies and dressed before walking to the compound. There, I drank a bottle of Sing Hǎi Beer while we talked about the World Series.

Glen, Sùpa and I left the compound at 7:30. As we walked in the dark to the Chaophaya Inn, Sùpa was in between us, and I told them how I had bought a textbook for Glûaimàai to help in her study to learn English and how well she was doing. At the Inn, we hired two sǎawm-laws to take us to the cafe. In the cafe, we waited a few minutes before I saw Glûaimàai walk from the cafe's back looking stunningly beautiful in the same white, form-fitting dress she'd worn dancing with Skip.

As we rode to the night club in sǎawm-laws, the two girls rode together behind Glen and I. When we arrived, Glen and I led the girls to a table on the 3rd tier, where they sat opposite us, which was fine with me as I enjoyed seeing Glûaimàai's beautiful face and the low-cut view of Sùpa's breasts. Soon after our order for four Pepsis arrived, the girls followed Glen and I to the dance floor. Our first dance was a

Waltz, and as I led Glûaimàai in some basic waltz moves, I watched her glide through them smoothly and beautifully.

The next dance was a Tango and I said, "This is a very sexy dance," and took every opportunity to press my right leg against her mons pubis at the apex of her lovely legs. When the Tango ended, Glûaimàai pulled me against her and moaned with arousal, "Oh, it is a very sexy dance. Makes me want you to teach me sex right now."

At 10:00, Glûaimàai told Glen and Sùpa she was tired from working all day, and we left the night club. Walking the short distance to the Sri Pattana Hotel, she followed me to my room.

Entering my room, I looked down at Glûaimàai's beautiful face and saw her longing desire for me in her exotic, almond-shaped eyes. Placing my hands around her very slender waist, I lifted her small body up effortlessly to eye level and tenderly kissed her enticing lips. She responded with a passionate kiss, wrapping her arms possessively around my neck, and her attractive legs wantonly encircled my waist grinding her lusting crotch against my abdomen.

Returning the passion of her kiss, I unzipped the back of her dress and unhooked her bra as I carried her writhing body to the bed. Shrugging her shoulders forward and lowering her arms, I slipped the top of her dress and bra off, exposing her succulent, danty breasts. Placing my hand under her tight round butt, I raised her enticing breasts level with my mouth, and sucking her left firm breast into my mouth, I heard her moan with desire as her hands pulled my head against her gyrating chest.

Sucking her right breast into my mouth, I carried her to the bed. Quickly removing my shirts, pants and boxers, I saw her stare desiringly at my engorged shaft as she rapidly pulled off her dress and panties. Lying back onto the bed, Glûaimàai raised up and spread her enticing legs wide to receive me, and I saw the smallness of her love canal. I tried gently to slide my two middle fingers to widen her enough to receive me, but without success.

Retrieving the tube of K-Y Gel, I squeezed a liberal amount onto the fingers of my right hand. Pushing the lubricant into her love canal, I felt the tips of my two fingers begin to slide into Glûaimàai. As I gently worked my fingers in deeper, I lay between her spread, upraised legs to suck her dainty, firm breasts into my mouth in turn. I heard her moan with delight as I worked to widen her love canal with my two fingers working deeper into her, and felt her rapidly undulating hips lusting to have me in her. When I felt my fingers sliding fully into her, I removed them, applied K-Y Gel to the head of my shaft aching with lust. Holding it with my right hand, I began to push it rhythmically into her widening love canal, and heard Glûaimàai start yelling, "Daai! Daai!" as I thrust in deeper and deeper.

Soon, her love canal was wide enough to fully receive me. I felt her undulating hips vigorously sliding her love canal along my shaft as I made love with her. Suddenly, I saw Glûaimàai's head and back arch and heard her yell, "Chai-yoo!"[124] as I felt her small body shudder with orgasmic convulsions.

As I continued my rhythmic thrusts lusting for her enticing little body, Glûaimàai renewed the vigorous gyrations of her hips, yelling in Thai, "Yes, my darling, don't stop. I want all of you, my darling." Soon, I felt my orgasmic release distend deeply into her, and heard Glûaimàai gasping, "Oh, my darling, your lovemaking is perfect."

I rolled onto my back, easily rolling her on top of me, with her small love canal taut around my shaft. When Glûaimàai laid her head on my chest, she quickly sat up on my groin and exclaimed, "You have hair all over your chest!" Then sliding her dainty hands through my chest hair, she said, "Oh-ho, it feels so luxurious," and as she playfully wiggled her sensuous hips on my groin, she added, "And you are a most sexy man."

In response, I reached up cupping her desirable, dainty, and firm breasts in my hands, and said, "And you are a most sexy woman, my darling."

When she laid her beautiful face on my chest hair, she continued to slide her little hands through my chest hair, she asked lovingly, "My darling, when will I see you again?"

I replied, "I work Sunday. If you like, I can pick you up after work and bring you here."

She responded, "Yes. I would like that very much, my darling."

I said, "This morning, I won 900 Bhat on a baseball game. On Monday, I will buy you two new dresses for when we go dancing on Wednesday and Friday."

---

124   "Hurray!"

She sat up quickly on my groin again and exclaimed, "Really, Truly! On Monday, you will buy me two new dresses for dancing? But, that's very expensive."

I replied, "My darling, you are the beautiful woman I dance with and make love to, and I want you to be my most beautiful woman when we dance."

Then laying her head on the mat of hair on my chest, we went to sleep.

When I woke to the 3:30 wake-up call, I found Glûaimàai still on top of me with her sensuous hips straddling my groin and her exotic, almond-shaped eyes looking desirously into mine. As she sat on my groin lustfully undulating her hips to arouse me, she placed my hands on her enticing breasts and said, "You are my sexy man and want you making love to me."

Feeling my arousal for Glûaimàai growing rapidly inside her, I rolled her over beneath me and felt her luscious legs lift up and spread wide lusting for the rhythmic strokes of my shaft in her love canal. Soon, I heard Glûaimàai yell "Daai! Daai!" and felt her vigorous undulating hips join wantonly with my rhythmic driving thrusts lusting for her sensuous body. Soon, I saw her enticing breasts lift up with the arching of her beautiful face and back from her orgasmic convulsions, and heard her joyously yell, "Chai-yoo!" As I continued my lusting, rhythmic thrusts, she yelled with delight, "Yes, my darling, more, much more," and again felt her vigorously undulating hips lustfully stroking my engorged shaft. Then, my orgasmic thrust distended deeply into her, and I heard Glûaimàai satisfyingly moan, "Your love for me is perfect, my darling," and I responded, "and your beautiful small body is perfect for my love, my darling."

Work at the Air Base Site on Saturday mornings are usually very busy. But Friday had been Columbus Day, and the beginning of the three-day weekend Stateside, that began Thursday. So Friday morning had been very busy and Saturday was a nice, slow day.

While Skip was on his meal run for lunch, I told Bob how I met a 20-year-old woman named Julii at the night club Thursday night, that she asked to come to my room for a "nightcap," and said she was a "green woman" just before we had sex. I asked Bob, "So, what did Julii mean when she said she was a 'green woman'?"

Bob replied, "Probably that she was a virgin. In Thai, there's no word for 'virgin,[125]' and no stigma in Thai culture for a girl who's had sex, as there is in Western cultures. In fact, most girls have sex within a year or two after they've graduated Grade School at 14. A girl who has not had sex is said to be a 'green fruit.' So the question I have is, how did you know this girl is 20?"

I answered, "She said she was a Junior at Suranari College, which makes her 20."

Bob laughed, "In Thailand, their College is what we call High School. She's 16."

I took the 6:35 meal run for dinner. After changing clothes, I caught a Thai bus to Korat, and arrived at the night club before 8:00. Paying the cover charge and not seeing Julii, I went to a table on the 3rd tier and ordered two Pepsis.

At 8:00, I saw Julii enter the night club and went to greet her. I saw she was wearing a very becoming, form-fitting, pink silk dress showing not only the enticing curves of her womanly body, but short enough to display her shapely legs, and said, "You look very desirable, Julii."

She responded, "My darling, I want to be very desirable to you as we dance," as I led her to our table.

As we gaily and sensuously danced together, I enjoyed how desirable she looked and the desire in her eyes she had for me. By 10:00, we were both so aroused with lust that we went to my room, where we passionately released the lust we had for each other in orgasmic explosions.

While Julii lay on my chest fondling my chest hair with me firmly held inside of her taut love canal, we discussed how much we looked forward to dancing together on Thursday and Saturday next week. As our lust and desire was again aroused, we made passionate love before we fell asleep with her head on my chest and her possessively holding me tight inside her love canal.

After the 3:30 wake-up call, as we showered together, Julii sensually washed my loins, and when I was fully aroused, she turned around, leaned forward, and enticed me with her sensuously undulating hips.

---

125   For example, the Thai version of The Book of Mormon translates "virgin" as "female Brahma single lady,"1 Nephi 11:13.

Sliding into her tight love canal of desire, we vigorously satisfied the lust we had for each other.

As she stood nude before me, passionately kissing me goodbye, Julii asked desirously, "My darling, are you my boyfriend?" and I desirously replied, "Only if you're my girlfriend."

Riding the Thai bus to my Company Area, I thought, "I may have lost my exotic Jintana, but I've been seduced by two other beautiful women who desire dancing with me sensuously and then satisfy our pent-up lust passionately with vigorous lovemaking. Trading one for two is great."

CHAPTER 28

Lt. Price Just Had An Attitude Adjustment

As Skip and I rode in the back of the ¾-ton truck to the Air Base Site Sunday morning after formation, Skip asked, "I haven't seen you around the hooch all week. I could understand it when you were with Jintana, but why are you gone all day and night now?"

I replied, "In the afternoon, I go to this place to tutor English, which helps with my Thai skills. At night, I go to the night club and dance."

Skip responded, "Sounds better than sitting around the hooch all day playing Double-Deck Pinochle, or going to the bars spending all your money drinking, chasing pûu-ying, and getting the clap."

Being a Sunday, work at the Air Base Site was comfortably slow. Because the Air Force flew combat missions 24/7, the Base Exchange was open Sunday afternoons. So after lunch, I went to the BX, and bought a carton of Pall Malls and two tubes of K-Y Gel to use until Glûaimàai's small love canal adjusted to my size. These I put in my Site wall locker for my 6:35 meal run, and thought, "Since I'll been seeing Julii or Glûaimàai almost every day or night of the week, it might be cheaper to rent the Hotel room by the month. Something to check into tonight, as I'll be with Glûaimàai all day tomorrow."

Exiting the Thai bus at the Chainarong Gate at 7:35, I hired a săawm-law to take me to the Sri Pattana Hotel and then to the cafe on San-Prasit Road. At the Hotel, I found their monthly rate for a room was 675 Bhat, $33.75, and promptly extend my stay for 30 days. At the cafe, I found my beautiful little Glûaimàai ready to leave, wearing a pink cotton blouse and the mid-calf long black skirt she wore for work. I thought, "She must have spent most of her income on the form-fitting, white silk dress to go dancing with Skip," as I saw her face brighten with a beautiful smile of relief at seeing me, and a desiring look in her exotic, almond-shaped eyes.

After we exchanged sàwàtdiis, Glûaimàai followed me outside, where she stood back and watched as I skillfully bargained in Thai a săawm-law driver down to 3 Bhat for our ride to the Sri Pattana Hotel. Arriving at the Hotel, she followed me to my room in the Thai style.

Entering my room, I turned and saw Glûaimàai had unbuttoned her blouse in the hallway and now quickly removed it. Only her bra concealed her enticing, danty breasts as she held her arms up expectantly with desire in her lovely, almond-shaped eyes. Feeling my desire for her aroused, I swiftly lifted and passionately kissed her, as she wrapped her lusting legs around my waist. She then removed her bra, exposing her lovely breasts, as I carried her to the bed and became fully aroused by her sexual longing for me.

Setting Glûaimàai down beside the bed, I watched her rapidly slide off her skirt and panties, as I drew back the bed covers. Watching her lie back on the bed, raising and spreading her luscious legs, I speedily undressed, lusting for her small, sensuous body. I then pulled a tube of K-Y Gel from my pants pocket. Squeezing a large amount of the gel onto the fingers of my right hand, I pushed the gel into her love canal with my middle two fingers, as I lay between her lusting legs and sucked her enticing left breast into my mouth.

After using the same method to expand her small love canal with my two fingers, I then rhythmically began to push my engorged shaft completely into her tight her love canal. Feeling her sensuous hips undulate vigorously with lust to receive me, I heard Glûaimàai yell, "Daai! Daai!" with passionate desire.

When we had consummated our lust with orgasmic release, I rolled onto my back with her small, desirable body easily rolling on top of me, straddling my groin and possessively holding me in her taut canal.

After talking about the desire we had for each other while we were apart and her desire for lovemaking many times with me while we were together tonight and tomorrow, Glûaimåai then propped up her beautiful face on her hands and elbows, with her dainty, firm breasts distending enticing from her chest, and listened intently as I began my lecture on what an American man would want from his tîi-lók.

I explained that American men fell basically into three categories. There were "breast" men like Glìn-dii, which is why Sùpa wore low-cut dresses to show the bare tops of her breasts for him to see. There were "butt" men, some of which liked small tight butts like hers, and others who liked large, round butts. Then there were men, like myself, who were "leg" men and enticed by shapely, muscular legs, like hers and Jintana's. But, all American men were attracted to a pretty face, which Thai women seemed to have in abundance. For a while, we discussed how a woman could use her clothes to best display or enhance the attributes of her body.

After a while, Glûaimåai sat up on my groin, placed my hands on her firm breasts and asked, "You like my small breasts, my darling?" as she began to undulate her sensuous hips.

I replied, "My darling, I love to see them and the way they fit in mouth," as I leaned up and sucked one into my mouth, and Glûaimåai moaned, "Chai dâai,"[126] as I felt her hips undulate vigorously on my groin. Rolling over to place Glûaimåai beneath me, I felt the gush of her womanly nectar flowing from her love canal, and as I rhythmically made long, thrusting strokes, I heard her yell, "Daai! Daai!"

When we had satiated our sexual lust for each other with orgasmic release, we fell exhaustedly to sleep, with Glûaimåai's head on my chest and her hips possessively holding me in her taut love canal.

Waking to the 3:30 wake-up call, I felt Glûaimåai arousing me with her undulating hips against my groin. Lifting her from my chest, I began sucking on her firm, danty breasts until I felt the flow of womanly honey wetting my groin. Leaving Glûaimåai on top, I encouraged her to slide her wet love canal on my engorged shaft, which she did vigorously until I saw the orgasm raging through her body, to which I added my firm upward thrusts into her love canal and my orgasm exploded

---

126   "Yes do it."

into her. As she collapsed onto my chest, she gasped, "I love this new lovemaking you teach me, my darling."

While we showed together, I explained how I had to be at a gathering of everyone in my Company at 7:00, and would be back by 8:00, to which she said, "And maybe you desire me enough for lovemaking when you return, my darling."

I responded, "My darling, I'll always desire you enough for lovemaking."

When I returned from morning formation, I found Glûaimàai asleep, curled up on the bed nude. Stripping off my clothes, I lay on the bed to spoon with her. As I did, her sensuous butt snuggled against me and she cooed, "My darling, you feel so good and warm." With her enticing butt rubbing against me, I became aroused and she said, "I'm so happy to feel your desire for lovemaking with me."

After several minutes of passionate foreplay, I felt her hot nectar flowing. Rolling onto my back with Glûaimàai on top, I held my engorged shaft up as she worked it into her expanding love canal.

When we had fully satisfied our desire for each other, we washed the crud from one another in the shower, got dressed, and went to the nearby Ming Ter restaurant on Rajadamnern Road for breakfast. As we chatted, Glûaimàai told me the location of her clothier on Mahat Thai Road where she had her white silk dress made. When I asked her who made the white blouse and black skirt for work, she replied, "I can't afford to buy my work clothes, so the cafe provides them. That's why they they're too big for me."

I responded, "My darling, it's the clothes that makes the woman desirable. The likely place you'll meet an American who will have you be his tîi-lók is at work. That's how Glen met Sùpa."

After breakfast, we walked the short distance from Ming Ter to the clothier's shop, where I put five red 100-Bhat bills in her hand and said, "You are to order two beautiful dresses for dancing, two silk blouses and two skirts to wear other places with me, and two white blouses and two black skirts for you to look desirable at work. If this is not enough money for the deposit, I'll pay the rest when I return. I'm going shopping and will be back soon, my darling," and walked away before she could protest.

Walking to the bookstore a few shops further on, I bought an English version of the Kama Sutra, the Hindu book on sex. Returning to the clothier shop, I sat in a chair and watched Glûaimàai happily selecting colors of silk for new clothes with the shop owner. When it came to the bargaining on the price, I watched as she vehemently argued the price down, and then saw her hand three of the red 100-Bhat bills to the owner.

When I saw Glûaimàai pay the deposit, I stood and walked out of the shop with her following me. As she walked behind me in Thai style to the Hotel, I heard her happily chattering about what she had ordered, their colors, and that one of the dresses would be ready for a fitting tomorrow morning so she could wear it when we went dancing Wednesday night.

Glûaimàai followed me back to room, and turning around after we entered, I saw her pink blouse falling on the floor and her leaping up into my arms. Wrapping her arms and legs around me, she said, "I love you so much for all the clothes you bought me, and I must be a 'butt' woman as watching your firm butt as we walk made me lust for your lovemaking," as I unhooked her bra and carried her to the bed.

Quickly stripping off my clothes, I saw Glûaimàai slip off her skirt and panties, and then lie back on the bed, raising and spreading her luscious legs wide for me to mount her. But this time, I seized her sensuous hips, and lifting her, I rotated her body onto her hands and knees. Then holding Glûaimàai by the hips, I induced myself into the opening of her wet love canal, and began to rhythmically push into her, causing her love canal to expand as I thrust deeper in. As I did so, I saw her hips undulate vigorously and heard her passionately yell, "Châi dâai! Châi dâai!"

When our lust for each other was fulfilled, I heard Glûaimàai gasp, "I love your desire for me, my darling, and every way you teach me lovemaking."

After we had washed the crud from us, I showed her the Kama Sutra book I bought and said, "This is a textbook for lovemaking. When you see a position you like, then the next time we make love, we'll do it. But now, we must eat lunch before we meet Glìn-dii and Sùpa at the theater."

Bringing the book to the Ming Ter, she picked a position as we ordered lunch. Then, we discussed how to do it as we ate our meals.

Leaving the Ming Ter, we walked to the theater, where we saw Glen and Sùpa. After we exchanged sàwàtdiis, Glen saw the book in my hand and asked to see it. As Glen and Sùpa flipped through the pages, Glen laughed and said, "Sùpa told me how you were teaching sex to Glûaimàai along with English and dancing, preparing her to be a good tîi-lók for an American. Hey, I need to get one of these. Where'd you buy it?"

Entering the theater, I told Glen where the bookstore was located. As we watched the Japanese Samurai movie, I felt Glûaimàai's hand caressing my inner thigh. I was in such lust for her when we left the theater, I paid a săawm-law driver 5 Bhat to take us to the Hotel as fast as he could.

In the room, we stripped off our clothes, and Glûaimàai lept to her hands and knees on the bed, to present her lusting love canal for me to enter. Once my rhythmic thrusts had expanded her love canal fully, we shifted to the Kama Sutra position she'd selected in the book. When our lust had culminated in orgasmic release, we showered together before going to the Ming Ter for dinner.

As we ate dinner, Glûaimàai selected another position from the book. Discussing how to make love in this position, I said she could spend the night in my room while I was at work, and when I returned by 8:00, we would try our new position before she left for her dress fitting at 9:30. Leaving the Ming Ter for work, she told me how much she was looking forward to her sex lesson in the morning as I left her the room key.

Arriving at my hooch, I changed into my OD BDUs, and walked with Skip to the Day Room to wait for Tommy to arrive with the truck. Because it was a Monday night and everyone Stateside was returning from a three-day weekend, things were very busy at the Air Base Site responding to numerous circuit outage calls. When I returned from my 10:55 meal run, I brought with me a silk skirt, a pair of pants, my black dress shoes, two sets of skivvies, and all the Bhat I had stored in my tobacco can. Making the 5:40 meal run for breakfast, I told Skip he'd need to make the 6:35 meal run, as I was now renting a room at the Sri Pattana Hotel by the month and going to Korat directly from the Air Base Site.

After I was relieved by Jack, I caught a Thai bus for Korat. Returning to my room, I knocked on the door. When I entered the room, Glûaimàai, without a stitch on, jumped up into my arms, kissing me passionately, as she wrapped her arms and legs around me, and said, "My darling, I ached for you all night and am so happy to be in your arms."

Lifting Glûaimàai up higher, I hungrily sucked each of her enticing breasts into my mouth in turn, and heard her squeal with delight at my desire for her as I carried her to the bed. While I quickly removed my shirts, she rapidly unzipped and pulled my pants and boxers down, releasing my engorged shaft. Seizing my large shaft with one of her hands, I saw her pick up an open tube of K-Y Gel and squeeze a liberal amount on its head. As she lay back on the bed, raising and spreading her legs wide to eagerly receive me, Glûaimàai said, "My darling, I ache for you to be in me."

Leaning on my hands with my body between her enticing legs, I began my rhythmic thrusts to push deeper into her love canal, as I felt Glûaimàai's luscious hips undulate vigorously to relieve the ache she had for me. When I felt the head pushing against her cervix, we shifted into the position we had studied in the Kama Sutra.

After satiating our lust for each other, we showered to clean the crud from our bodies. Then, we both lay nude on the bed as Glûaimàai chose from the book the position she wanted to try in our next encounter. This we discussed until she dressed to leave for her dress fitting at 9:30. As soon as we'd passionately kissed goodbye and she left, I fell exhausted across the bed and went to sleep.

A couple of hours later, I woke refreshed and walked the mile to the cafe on San-Prasit Road for lunch. There, I saw Glûaimàai's glowing smile on her beautiful face. When we had exchanged sàwàtdiis, she led me to a table by the wall, and brought me a plate of chicken fried rice and a Pepsi. By the time I'd finished my meal, the lunch crowd had cleared out and we began our English studies.

As I was leaving to return to the Hotel to change into my OD BDUs, Glûaimàai smiled sensuously and asked, "Is it okay if I come to your room tomorrow morning for my next lesson my darling?"

I eagerly replied, "It's very okay, my darling."

From the Hotel, I went to the Chainarong Gate, where I walked to the market on Kamhaeng Songkram Road and bought a cotton shopping bag for 2 Bhat. This I'd use to carry my clothes and other items inconspicuously to and from the Hotel. I then boarded a Thai bus to the Company Area, where I had dinner in the Mess Hall before changing into a fresh set of OD BDUs. Then I lay on my bed and went to sleep.

An hour later, Skip roused me up and laughingly said, "Sandii, I know that coming to work isn't as fun as coming in girls, but we need to get to work."

Fortunately, things were dead slow after the midnight meal runs, and I was able to get a couple of hours sleep on the mattress at the Air Base Site. On my 4:55 meal run for breakfast, I put two changes of clothes and skivvies in my shopping bag with my black dress shoes to take to the Hotel. After I was relieved at Shift Change, I rode a Thai bus to Korat in my OD BDUs, carrying my shopping bag. Returning to my room, I was completely stripped when I heard Glûaimàai's knock at the door.

Craving for Glûaimàai when I heard the knock, she cried out in delight when she saw my aroused desire for her. As she pulled off her pink blouse and dropped off her black skirt, I saw she was not wearing a bra or panties. When she was on her hand and knees on the bed, I applied some K-Y Gel to my engorged shaft and began to enter her lusting love canal. I found she was expanding more readily to my rhythmic thrusts, and soon we were making love in the erotic sexual position she had chosen.

When we had both achieved orgasmic satisfaction, Glûaimàai gasped, "All night I dreamed of having you in me, and tonight, it will not be a dream, my darling."

I responded, "And I will be very happy to be in you after I see you dancing in your beautiful new dress."

After we showered, Glûaimàai selected a new position from the book, which we discussed until she left at 9:30 to pick up her new dress. Then, I crashed onto the bed for a couple hours before walking to the cafe for lunch and to tutor her in English. When I left the cafe after eating dinner, I walked to the cobbler shop, where I paid the 60 Bhat due. Then I walked to the Hotel wearing my new, brown suede shoes, that fit my feet like a pair of gloves, while carrying my black shoes in a shopping bag

Leaving the black shoes in my room, I walked the half-mile to the compound, where I drank a bottle of Sing Hăi Beer and showed everyone my new shoes, while chatting with the usual gang on the porch. At 7:30, Glen, Sùpa and I left to pick up Glûaimàai at the cafe.

When I saw Glûaimàai enter from the back of the cafe, the room glowed from the bright red, form-fitting, low-cut dress showing the tops of her delectable, dainty breasts, that enhanced her desirable, womanly figure. Also, her shapely legs were displayed beneath the hem swirling around her mid-thighs, and I thought, "Darling, you sure know how to catch my eye."

I heard Glen give a low whistle and say, "Sandii, whatever you paid for that dress was worth every Bhat."

Then I saw Sùda run to Glûaimàai, give her a hug and say, "Nung-saao,[127] I'm so proud of the way you look tonight."

When we went outside to hire two sǎawm-laws to take us to the night club, I saw the heads of several Americans turn to gawk at Glûaimàai. Hearing one of them give a wolf whistle, Glen remarked, "Sandii, if she walked down this street dressed like that, she'd be someone's tîi-lók before she reached the end of the block. Luckily, she has eyes only for you."

I turned my head to look and saw Glûaimàai exotic, almond-shaped eyes looking desiringly at me and thought, "Yes, my darling, and I desire you too."

When we entered the night club, I saw many of the women look enviously at Glûaimàai, and any man who stared too long, was brought back to reality from a remark by his woman. After a couple of hours dancing gaily and sensuously together, we made our excuses and walked to the Hotel, where we quickly stripped and copulated vigorously with wanton lust for each other in the position Glûaimàai had chosen from the book.

With our lust satiated in orgasmic release, I rolled to my back with Glûaimàai possessively holding me inside of her. With her head lying on my chest, I heard her say affectionately, "I love you being inside of me," as we went to sleep.

With the 3:30 wake-up call, I lifted Glûaimàai by her shoulders, and leaning forward, I sucked her left breast into my mouth. Pressing my gyrating groin desirously against her loin, I felt her respond in kind with her sensuous, undulating hips. Moving my mouth to her right breast, she moaned with desire and I felt her nectar gush onto my groin. Then her wet, taut love canal began stroking the length of my shaft voraciously.

---

127   "Little sister." An affectionate term for a younger woman.

While we laid in the afterglow of our orgasmic satisfaction, I heard Glûaimàai say, "I love you so much, and will be waiting hungry for you after your meeting, my darling."

I responded, "And I desire your hunger for me, my darling."

After we showered together, I dressed in my OD BDUs, and gave Glûaimàai a passionate goodbye kiss, as she stood naked before me. When I returned, we again made vigorous, passionate love to satiate our lust for each other. After we showered, we lay side by side on the bed, as she selected another position from the Kama Sutra and we discussed how to achieve it. When she had to leave for work, I gave her a passionate kiss in the nude, and then watched her desire for me as she exited the room.

I slept for a couple of hours before leaving to have lunch at the cafe and tutor Glûaimàai in English. At 4:00 I had dinner and told her I would miss her very much until I picked her up on Friday evening to go dancing. Instead of going to the compound as usual, I decide to return to my room to get some much needed sleep before I met Julii at the night club that night.

After walking the short distance to the night club, I spotted my group of dance friends on the 3rd tier. Approaching their table I saw Julii's longing look and her desire for me in her lovely, almond-shaped eyes. When I exchanged hellos with everyone and sat among the men, I saw only Julii was leaning eagerly toward me and thought, "Julii has made it clear to the other three girls that I'm her 'boyfriend' in the Thai meaning."

Julii and I then danced gaily and passionately, expressing how much we missed each other since last Sunday morning. At 10:00, she went to the ladies room and I made my excuse to leave for Camp Friendship. When she ran across the lane several minutes later, I saw her enticingly firm breasts jiggle in her form-fitting, yellow blouse. As we walked in the dark to Rajadamnern Road, I put my right arm across her shoulders and my hand inside her blouse, cupping her bare left breast, and heard Julii moan with desire.

Approaching the well-lit road, I removed my hand and Julii followed me to my room. In the hallway to my room, I had unbuttoned my shirt, and as we entered my room, I quickly pulled my shirts off over my head and turned to face Julii. Seeing she had already dropped her blouse and skirt to the floor and was panty-less, I reached down, grabbed her bare tight butt in my hands and lifted her up high enough to suck her right breast in my mouth, as I felt her legs wrap around me and her wet crotch grind on my abdomen.

Carrying Julii to the bed, I laid her on her back and rapidly removed my pants and boxers. When Julii saw my lust for her protruding before me, she exclaimed, "Chai dâai!" as she lifted and spread wide her enticing legs, anxious to received me. Instead, I seized her sensuous hips, rolled her onto her hands and knees, and induced the head of my lusting shaft into the opening of her small love canal, where I was able to push it in a little ways.

Grabbing Julii by her luscious hips, I pulled them in rhythm with my thrusts, and with each deepening thrust into her love canal, she would yell, "More!" When her love canal was accepting my full length, we began to vigorously make love with my full length deep into her lusting love canal. Soon, I heard Julii yell, "Daai! Daai!" and then felt her orgasmic convulsion.

Continuing my long, vigorous thrusts into her sensuous body, Julii yelled, "Yes, give me more. I love you filling me with your desire for me." When my orgasmic thrust distended into her, she yelled, "Don't stop, my love, I need more of you." Repositioning us, with me on my back and Julii on top, her luscious hips undulated vigorously against my groin until her second orgasm raged throughout her body.

After Julii collapsed onto my chest, she gasped, "I love how you made love differently, my darling."

I responded, "Variety is the spice of life. In the morning, do you want more spice?"

Julii replied, "I love the variety you've given me, my darling, and if you give me more spice in the morning, I'll love you even more."

Roused by the 3:30 wake-up call, I happily found Julii on top with me in her taut love canal. After we had fully aroused our lust for each other, I shifted Julii to one of the Kama Sutra positions I had practiced with Glûaimâai. When we had consummated our lusts with orgasms, she gasped, "My darling, I love you more than I did last night."

I responded, "Then Saturday after we dance, you'll love more and then even more gain."

When we showered together, Julii smiled at me with desire as she sensuously washed my groin. As I became fully aroused, she cooed, "I love you so much, my darling." Turning around, Julii bent forward and enticingly presented her butt to me. Entering her love canal, I vigorously made love to her, as I watched her sensuous hips undulate rapidly with desire. Then, hearing her yell, "Daai! Daai!" I saw her luscious body shudder with orgasmic convulsions. When my orgasmic thrust distended into her, Julii breathlessly moaned with satisfaction, "I love you so very much, my darling."

Leaving dressed in my OD BDUs, I kissed her passionately goodbye. Desirously sculpting my hands over the skin of her luscious nude body, I said, "I will ache for you until I'm with you again Saturday night," and Julii added, "when I'll feel your love for me."

Walking briskly to the Chainarong Gate to catch a Thai bus to my Company Area, I thought, "Variety is indeed the spice of life."

Returning to my hooch, I changed into a fresh set of jungle fatigues before going to the Mess Hall. After formation, I rode with Skip in the back of the truck to the Air Base Site, and worked through a comfortably busy Friday. When John and Larry relieved me at 6:45, I was off in a flash to catch a Thai bus for Korat in my jungle fatigues.

Exiting the bus at the Chainarong Gate, I hired a săawm-law to take me to the Sri Pattana Hotel. In my room, I changed into a silk shirt, cotton pant and my brown suede shoes. Having plenty of time, I leisurely walked the mile to the cafe on San-Prasit Road.

Entering the cafe, I saw Glûaimàai waiting for me near the door looking stunning in a form-fitting, low-cut, light blue silk dress with the hem at her mid-thigh. Viewing her beauty and her enticing body displayed sensuously by her revealing dress, I felt my hormones rush through me. Leaving the cafe to hire a săawm-law, I saw the many passing Americans look desirously at Glûaimàai and thought, "Eat your hearts out guys, this sexy woman has eyes only for me."

Arriving at the night club, Glûaimàai followed me up to the table on the 3rd tier where Glen and Sùpa were waiting for us. As we exchanged săwàtdiis, I saw Glen look down Glûaimàai's enticing cleavage at the top of her dainty, firm breasts, and when we stood up, he winked and said, "Her tits look perfect and they belong to you."

After Glûaimàai and I had happily and sensuously danced together for two hours, we made our excuses and walked to my room at the Hotel. There, we passionately copulated our pent up lust for each other in the position she had selected from the book. With our orgasmic release, I positioned her sensuous small body on top of me with her possessively holding me in her tight love canal, and Glûaimȧai asked as she caught her breath, "Oh, my darling, can we do that position again in the morning?"

I gasped in reply, "With pleasure, my darling," and after the 3:30 wake-up call, we satisfied our passionate desire for each other using the same position.

After we enjoyed our shower together, I saw Glûaimȧai watch me longingly as I dressed in my jungle fatigues for work. When she stood enticingly naked as I passionately kissed her goodbye, she cooed, "When can we be together again, my darling," and I desiringly replied, "Sunday morning at 8:00."

Saturday morning at the Air Base Site was chaotic as usual, before it settled down for a quiet afternoon. When I was relieved at 6:45 by John and Larry, I was gone like a shot in my jungle fatigues to catch a Thai bus for Korat. After I walked the mile from the Chainarong Gate to the Hotel and changed into a silk shirt, a pair of cotton pants and my brown shoes, I was easily at the night club before 8:00.

When Julii arrived at 8:00, I was aroused at the sight of her desirable body in a form-fitting silk blouse and short skirt that revealed her womanly shapes, curves and well-formed legs. As Julii danced sensuously with me, I saw the lust building in her revealed in the increasingly enticing moves of her body. When we walked along the darkened lane, as I slid my right hand under her blouse and cupped her bra-less breast, I felt Julii slide her left hand under the front of my pants, and running her fingers along my stiffening shaft, she said, "My love for you aches to feel you inside me, my darling."

Entering my room, I rapidly stripped and watched Julii shed her blouse and skirt as she ran to the bed. Climbing onto her hands and knees, she began undulating her hips enticingly and moaned, "I need to feel you loving me, my darling."

When I had pushed deep into Julii's wet love canal, I shifted her body into a Kama Sutra position I had learned with Glûaimȧai. While was thrusting voraciously into Julii, I heard her yell, "Daai! Daai!" and felt her luscious body convulse with orgasmic pleasure. Feeling her body writhing with lust, I heard Julii gasping, "I need your love so much, my darling." When I had my own orgasm, she again yelled, "Daai! Daai!" and convulsed with an orgasm as my orgasmic thrust distended deep into her love canal.

When I had positioned Julii on top of me, with her luscious hips possessively hold me in her love canal, she said emotionally, "I love you more than ever, my darling," as she pressed her desiring hips against my loin.

I spent my next seven days, when I was not at work, happily feasting daily on the desire and lust that Glûaimàai and Julii had for me, with Julii benefiting from my practice with Glûaimàai in the different Kama Sutra positions, and both declaring their increasing love for me.

The next Saturday, I was working the night shift with Skip and Bob, when Bob said, "There's supposed to be a really good floor show in the NCO Club across the street at 9:00 I'd like to see. Since it's quiet right now and I'm confident you two can handle any outage that may occur, then I'll be leaving at 9:00 to see the show. If anything comes up that you can't handle, then have them page my name, and I'll be right back. Any questions?"

Skip and I looked at each other, then shook our heads in response, and Bob left at 9:00 for the NCO Club.

About 9:30, we had a phone call form the Air Base Comm Center's Crypto Section that KEG-6 was down and their tests showed the problem was not in their house. Since KEG-6 was classified as an A-1 circuit, then Skip and I had ten minutes to find and fix the source of the outage. As we were hooking patch cords between KEG-6's monitor jacks and our test equipment in the Grand Canyon, I heard the front door to the Air Base Site slam shut and said to Skip, "Sounds like Bob wasn't impressed with the floor show."

A few seconds later, I heard, "May I have you attention, men?"

As it wasn't Bob's voice, I snapped without looking, "Look, Bud, we're too busy to give you any attention."

I heard, "Is that any way to address your Commanding Officer?"

I looked up and replied, "No, Sir. But, with all due respect, we're too busy right now, Sir."

Lt. Price retorted, "Too busy to give your CO a tour of this Radio Site?"

I replied, "With all due respect, Sir, I'm too busy to even talk to you, as I have an A-1 priority circuit out."

Lt. Price responded, "Specialist Lynch, I came here to be given a tour of this Radio Site, and I order you to stop fiddling around with that equipment and give me a tour of this Radio Site."

Exasperated, I said, "Excuse me, Sir," walked past Lt. Price to the desk, picked up the phone and said into it, "Ted, put me through to Quad-C A, it's urgent," and when I heard, "Quad-C A, Commander Schuler," on the other end, I said, "This is Korat Base, Sir, I've a problem here."

Cmdr. Schuler responded, "You certainly do. You have an A-1 line down."

I said, "That's not the problem, Sir. My CO is here ordering me to give him a tour of the Site," and heard, "You don't have time for that nonsense. Put your CO on the line."

I handed the phone to Lt. Price and said, "Navy Commander Schuler wants to talk with you, Sir."

Lt. Price took the phone and said into it, "This is… Yes, Sir… No, Sir… Yes, Sir," and then said to me, "I apologize for interfering with your critical duties, Specialist Lynch," and then into the phone, "Will that do, Sir?… 0800 tomorrow in your office… Yes, Sir… Right, Sir… Good night, Sir," and hanging up the phone, he turned around and briskly left the Operations Room.

Walking back to Skip in the Grand Canyon, I saw he had continued working on the KEG-6 outage, and had a big grin on his face. When I heard the Sites front door slam closed, I laughed and said, "Skip, I think Lt. Price just had an attitude adjustment."

CHAPTER 29

Now That's What I Call An Attitude Adjustment

When Bob returned from the floor show at the NCO Club at 10:00, I told him what had happened with the CO and how he was ordered by Cmdr. Schuler to report to his Office in the Quad-C A at 0800 in the morning. Bob laughed and said, "I'm sure Schuler will give Price quite the attitude adjustment. One of the Senior NCOs that works there, lives just down the road from me, I'll give him a visit and find out what happened at that meeting. So, what's the scoop on KEG-6?"

Skip replied, "Took us a couple of minutes, but we traced it to a wonky tube in the breakout circuits."

Since it was a Saturday night, Bob had no problem finding an un-used audio circuit to talk with Jim Horn about what had happened with the CO's visit to the Air Base Site. When Ted called from the Air Base PBX to let us know he had a line up with Rosie to use the WATS for free phone calls home, he told us the call to the Quad-C A had been on an unsecure line and now everyone at the Air Base Comm Center knows how Cmdr. Schuler had jacked up an Army Infantry Officer and gave him a lube job. By Sunday noon, Lt. Price was the joke of the military signals community in Thailand.

Making the 6:35 meal run, after breakfast I went to my hooch and removed from my wall locker five 6-packs of Budweiser and five packs of Pall Malls to put on Dan, George, Tommy, Ronnie and Stony's beds. Being the week before Pay Day, I knew they'd be broke and had stocked up on beer and cigarettes while working the day shift on Thursday and Friday to see them through to Wednesday, when I worked the day shift and could buy more for them to have till Pay Day on Friday.

Once they'd been provisioned for the day, I put fresh clothes in my shopping bag to take to my Hotel room. Arriving at my room, I stripped to my boxer's and laid on the bed waiting desiringly for Glûaimàai's knock on the door at 8:00.

Hearing Glûaimàai's knock on the door, my arousal was Pavlovian to her passionate lust I'd receive when I opened the door. And opening the door, I saw the beautiful Glûaimàai with the look of desire and love she had for me, and her bra-less tantalizing breasts exposed and aching to be sucked into my mouth.

Entering my room, Glûaimàai lept into my arms, giving me a passionate kiss as her arms and legs wrapped possessively around me. Feeling her, bare crotch rubbing wantonly with the desire she had for me, I carried her lusting body to the bed, where her blouse and skirt fell to the floor. Positioning herself on her hands and knees to present her luscious hips and desiring wet love canal to receive me, I had little difficulty pushing into her tight love canal, as she had acclimated to my size from our frequent lovemaking.

My desire and lust for Glûaimàai had not assuaged with our frequent lovemaking, but had intensified because each time we were using different Kama Sutra positions, or repeating a position that had been very enjoyable. It was the variety in our lovemaking that brought the spice to the lustful hunger we had for each other.

Also, my frequent tutoring of Glûaimàai in English was at the level where she insisted we speak in English, or at least a pigeon English. And though I often corrected her grammar, syntax or pronunciation, she was an apt pupil and was learning quickly. As was her ballroom dancing skills, where she easily followed my lead with the subtle pressure of my hand or fingers to the small of her back, or the movement of my left hand holding her right hand.

Glûaimàai also had taken her white silk dress back to the clothier and had it altered with a low-cut top and the hem raised to her mid-thigh, and now she looked as provocative in her white silk dress when we went dancing, as in her red and blue silk dresses, and drew the same admiring looks form the passing American men when she stood in front of the cafe while I negotiated the price for a ride to the night club.

With the 3:30 wake-up call, our desire for each other reignited our lust, and when our lust had culminated with orgasmic release in a new sexual position, Glûaimàai cooed in her sing-song Thai accent, "I lo-ba you so muk, my belo-bat, to wake wit you desi-ra fo me. I am happy we can ha-ba lo-bamaking aw day an aw night, to go to mooby wit Glìn-dii an Sùpa, an tat you dan-sa sek-sy wit me tonight."

I responded, "I love you so much, too, my beloved, and to be with you all day and all night, But, now we have to shower together before I go to my meeting at Camp Friendship."

After we showered, Glûaimàai lay on the bed desiringly nude, happily looking through the book and choosing our next position for when I returned, while I dressed in me OD BDUs for morning formation. Then I lay beside her tantalizing body to discuss for several minutes how to do it before we passionately kissed goodbye, as I left for Camp Friendship to go to formation, and to pass out the beer and cigarettes to the guys in my hooch.

When I returned, Glûaimàai gave me a passionate kiss before she urgently helped me strip for our vigorous lovemaking in the new position to satisfy our mutual lust in orgasmic release. Then we took a quick shower together before going to the Ming Ter for breakfast. There, Glûaimàai selected a position from the Kama Sutra book for our next lovemaking experience.

Returning to my room, we tiredly undressed, then Glûaimàai spooned in my arms on the bed as we slept for a couple of hours. Waking to her sensuous kisses and desiring caresses, we assumed the Kama Sutra position to vigorously make love again, before showering and going back to the Ming Ter for lunch. After lunch, we walked to the theater and met with Glen and Sùpa. Before entering the theater,

I pulled Glen aside and asked, "What do you think if were to bring Glûaimàai to the compound tonight?"

Glen laughed and replied, "Sandii, if you don't, you'll have some explaining to do to Sùpa and Glûaimàai. You've been buying her clothes and having sex with her for two weeks. She might be your student, but she's also your woman and deserves the social recognition. And, the tîi-lóks already know about you two and are curious to meet her. Plus, it'll let that idiot Skip see what he's missing out on and get some razzing from the guys for turning down Glûaimàai's offer to be his tîi-lók."

Returning to the girls, I said, "Sùpa, I'll be bringing Glûaimàai to the compound tonight, so you might tell her what to expect."

Sùpa laughed and replied, "Sandii, you aw a si-lii man. Sii know about compoan an ang-ry if you not take her becau-sa sii loo-sa fa-sa."

And Glûaimàai added, "If you not take me, it say you not lo-ba me, but I know you lo-ba me."

As I watched the movie, Glûaimàai did not sensuously stroke my inner thigh to arouse me like before. At the end of the movie, she told me, "Wen we get home, I wan to ha-ba fun fo-play firt, be-for you 'bang my brain out,'" and laughed.

When we returned to my room, I sensuously and slowly undressed Glûaimàai, enticingly kissing the nape of her neck then down to her danty breasts, sucking each of them into my mouth in turn, while I removed her blouse and bra. Continuing to kiss her desiringly down her abdomen, I slowly loosened her skirt and caressed her firm butt, as it slid down her legs to the floor. Laying her on the bed, I kissed her temptingly around her mons pubis, before kissing alluringly down her inner thighs and smelling the sweet nectar of her desire flowing from her love canal. Slowly sliding her panties down her trembling legs, I heard her passionately moan, "Chai dâai."

While seductively undressing Glûaimàai, I'd also removed my own clothes. Finally slipping her panties from her feet, I heard her yell, "Dâai! Dâai!" as her legs lifted up and spread wide to receive me. Rising up, I saw her luscious body writhing in lust and her arms out stretched desiring me. Pushing my engorged shaft into the full length of her wet love canal, I began to shift her into the Kama Sutra position we'd discussed. Wrapping her legs around me, she grabbed me with her hand, and yelled, "No, lo-ba me like tis!" as her lusting hips undulated vigorously to my rhythmic thrusts.

When our lust was orgasmicly satiated, Glûaimàai held me on top of her heaving body with her arms and legs wrapped possessively around me, and said in Thai, "My darling, I love you more than all the world."

I responded, "My sweetheart, I love you also, and want to always make you happy," and thought, "Jintana said she was too tall for a Thai man to want her, but a Thai man married her. You say you're too small for a Thai man to want you, but a Thai man may want to marry you because you are so beautiful. No, my dearest, I was burned once. I love you, but I'll not be burned twice."

After a long while talking in English of our love for each other, our desires when apart, and what meeting the tîi-lóks of my friends might be like, we took a sensuous shower together and copulated again, before getting dressed for the evening.

Glûaimàai had brought her blue silk dress to the compound, as the red dress would have been over the top for a social gathering and Skip had already seen the white dress, though not with the alluring alterations. It seems I was the only one who had not known I was bringing Glûaimàai to the compound tonight.

We walked the short distance to the Ming Ter for dinner, but I decided after dinner to hire a sǎawm-law and ride to the compound. After we said our sàwàtdiis to the men on the porch, Glûaimàai said in English, "It iss nice to meet you. An Sá-kip, it iss goot to see you again," before she went into the house and was warmly welcomed by the four tîi-lóks. When I returned to the porch with my bottle of Sing Hǎi Beer, Skip was being razzed about turning down an offer by such a beautiful, little fox to be his tîi-lók. That it was because she was only 14 made as much sense to them as it did to Sùpa.

At 7:30, the four of us walked to the Chaophaya Inn and hired two sǎawm-laws for a ride to the night club. As we danced, Glûaimàai said, "I am happy Sá-kip not wan me for tîi-lók, so now you lo-ba me."

By 10:00, we all left the night club, and when Glûaimàai and I entered my room, we quickly stripped to release the pent-up lust we had for each other from dancing, and vigorously made love in the position Glûaimàai had passed on earlier. With the 3:30 wake-up call, we again devoured our sexual desires in another Kama Sutra position. And when I returned from formation, after distributing the beer and cigarettes to my five hooch-mates, we satisfied our passion at a slower pace because we knew we wouldn't be in each others arms again for a day and a half, though I'd see her at the cafe for lunch and her English lesson.

After Glûaimàai left at 10:30 for work, I slept a couple of hours before walking to the cafe for lunch and to tutor her in English. When I'd finished my dinner at 4:30, I walked back to my room for some sleep before my 8:00 meet with Julii at the night club.

When Julii entered the night club at 8:00, I saw she was wearing a very enticing light green blouse and a leg revealing, dark green, short skirt. Going down to meet her, I saw her beaming smile and the look of desire she had for me in her exotic, almond-shaped eyes as we exchanged hellos. Arriving at the table on the 3rd tier, Julii asked, "Darling, my father thinks it would be good to meet my boyfriend. When would be a good day for you to have dinner with my family?"

Sounding like a reasonable request, I replied, "I work till 7:00 tomorrow and Thursday, but I could eat dinner at your home at 5:00 on Friday or Saturday. Would that be okay, my darling?"

As Julii gave me a 3×5 inch card with an address, directions and a map on it, she said happily, "I love you so much, my dearest. Saturday at 5:00 will be perfect. Now I want to dance with you."

Dancing happily and sensuously together, I felt the desire and lust we had for each other growing. A 9:30, Julii said desperately, "My darling, I love you so much and I've not been with you for a week. Please, I want to go to your room right now, okay?"

I replied eagerly, "Very okay. The sooner the better."

Julii followed me from the night club directly to my room. Walking down the hall, we loosened our clothes. Entering my room, I saw Julii's clothes fall from her luscious body and her mount the bed on her hands and knees, presenting her wet, lusting love canal to me. Grabbing her sensuous hips with my hands, I pulled on them as I thrust my engorge shaft all the way into her tight love canal, and heard Julii moan with satisfaction, "Oh yes, my love, it feels so wonderful to have you deep inside me again."

As I began to shift her writhing body into a Kama Sutra position, I heard her yell, "The spice, yes, more spice. I love the spice you give me, my love." Once we were in the position, our bodies gyrated vigorously in our wanton lust until I heard Julii yell, "Dâai! Dâai!" and felt her luscious body shudder in orgasmic spasms. And when my orgasmic thrust distended deep into her love canal, she gasped, "I love you, my dearest, I love you forever!"

Repositioning Julii on top of me, her sensuous hips gyrated vigorously on my groin, as I massaged her enticing breasts with my hands until I felt her body convulse in orgasmic release. As she fell sexually exhausted on my chest, she gasped, "I love you so very much and missed you more than words can say."

Julii talked for a while about how much she ached for me when we were apart, and that she loved me with all her heart, mind and spirit. Then we made vigorous, passionate love in a different position before falling asleep with her on my chest and holding me inside her. After the 3:30 wake-up call, we again made vigorous, passionate love. And though I was sexually spent as we showered together, Julii's sensual enticements aroused me to copulate with her voluptuous body again.

Leaving for work in my OD BDUs, we passionately kissed goodbye, as I slid my hands over the luscious curves of her nude body, and said, "I love you, my dearest, and will miss you very much till we dance again Thursday night."

Julii responded with tears in her eyes, "As will I, my love."

When I arrived at the Company Area, I went to my hooch and changed from my OD BDUs into a fresh set of jungle fatigues. I'd found, though the light weight, airy jungle fatigues were great to wear in the heat of the day, they were too light-weight to wear in the Air Base Site at night when the temperature in the air-conditioned building dropped to 68 degrees Fahrenheit.

After breakfast in the Mess Hall and formation, Skip and I were riding in the back of the truck when he asked, "So, is Glûaimàai your tîi-lók now?"

I laughed and said, "No, she's not my tîi-lók. I'm helping her learn English and some times I take her dancing with Glen and Sùpa. I'll admit she'll make some lucky guy a really good tîi-lók, but after I was burned with Jintana, I'm not in the market for a tîi-lók."

When we arrived at the Air Base Site, I relieved Jack, and within fifteen minutes, I had an excruciating headache on the left side of my head. I said to Bob, "Hey, I have a killer headache. Can I go outside for a minute?"

Bob replied with concern, "Sure, Sandii," and from the desk's top drawer he handed me a bottle of aspirin and added, "Here, take a couple of these."

Walking to the front door, I stopped at the air-conditioning room and grabbed my can of Pepsi wedged behind the frosted pipe. Exiting through the front door, I stood on the small concrete porch, shook a couple of pills from bottle, popped them into my mouth, and swallowed them with some Pepsi. After ten minutes, I'd finished the Pepsi and the pain had subsided.

Returning to the Operations Room, I gave the bottle of aspirin back to Bob and said, "Thanks, I feel much better now."

Within ten minutes, it felt like I'd been knifed in my left temple. Feeling a wave of nausea, I grabbed my head between my hands and sat in a chair. I felt Bob seize me by my left arm, and pulling me up form the chair, he said, "Let's go back outside." As we passed the Site Office, Bob opened the door and said, "Hey, Jim. I think Sandii has Radio Sickness," as we went out the front door.

In a minute, Jim joined us and asked, "What's going on?"

Bob replied, "I think Sandii has Radio Sickness."

I said, "No, I'm okay now. I'm not sick any more."

Jim said, "Yep, I agree Bob, he has Radio Sickness. Come on, Sandii, I'm taking you to the Field Hospital."

I resisted and said, "I don't need to go to Hospital. I'm fine now."

Jim grabbed me by my right arm, and pulling me to the truck, explained, "You might feel fine now, but as soon as you return to the Operations Room, you'll be in pain again. We call it Radio Sickness. It happens occasionally. Usually a filling that's in tune with a high frequency generated by the radio equipment. Now get in the truck. I'm taking you to the Hospital."

Arriving at the 33rd Field Hospital, Jim parked the truck, led me to the Reception Desk, and said, "I have a man here who needs to see a Dentist."

A Spec-4 in a white tunic asked, "Is he in pain, Sargent?"

Jim replied, "Yes, he is."

The Spec-4 said, "Okay, Sargent, take him to the hallway on you right, turn left, and halfway down on your right, you'll see the Dental Office."

Following the Spec-4's directions we entered the Dental Office. Jim explained to a PFC in a white tunic behind a desk my symptoms. The PFC asked to see my dog tags, and copied the information to a form on a clipboard. He then took the clipboard through a pair of swinging doors behind him. A few minutes later, the PFC returned with a Dental Officer, who said, "Okay, Specialist Lynch, tell me what happened."

After I explained what happened to me at the Air Base Site, the dentist ordered, "I want a full set of dental X-rays, STAT, and then put him in Suite 2," and left through the swinging doors.

As the PFC escorted me to their X-Ray Room, Jim said, "I'm going back to the Air Base. Have em call me if you're not coming back to work, otherwise you can ride a bus back to the Radio Site."

After they X-rayed my teeth, I was escorted to Dental Suite 2, and sat comfortably in a dental chair. Several minutes later, the dentist entered, put the X-ray negatives on a light-box mounted to the wall, and said, "Looks like the back left lower wisdom tooth has grown in at an angle into the other wisdom tooth, and is the culprit for your pain at the Radio Site. The right lower wisdom tooth hasn't erupted yet, so I can't extract it. But, I can extract the other three."

An hour later, with both sides of my jaw numb from the Novocain injections, a bottle of codeine pills, a light-duty chit, and orders to return in 48 hours for a follow-up visit, I was on a Thai bus back to the Air Base Site. I was told that 'light-duty' in a Theater of War included working on electronic equipment, even though I was under the influence of a narcotic and could be electrocuted.

Returning to the Air Base Site, I told everyone three of my four wisdom teeth were extracted, ordered to return in two days, given a bottle of codeine pills, issued a light-duty chit, and told to go back to work. Jim responded, "If you're taking a narcotic, I don't want you touching any electronic gear. During any circuit outages, the only thing you'll do is take notes in the Temporary Log. Now, everybody get back to work."

Luckily, it wasn't a busy day, so there wasn't much note taking in the Temporary Log. Skip took me on the 10:55 meal run, and even with my jaw being tender, I still had my two cheeseburgers and french fries for lunch, though I chewed a little slower. After lunch, I made two runs to the Howard Johnson for six 6-packs of Budweiser and a carton of Pall Malls, that I distributed to my five hooch mates.

Later, I asked Bob, "I told you about the College girl I've been dancing and having sex with. Though she'd told all of her friends I'm her boyfriend, and always saying how much she loves me, she's never said anything about marriage. Now, she's told me her father wants to meet me, and I've agreed to have dinner with her family Saturday evening at 5:00. What do you think?"

Bob replied, "First, don't worry about it. If he was concerned about his daughter having sex with you, he would have stopped her from seeing you already. He likely wants to see what kind of man you are and determine your potential as a future son-in-law. After all, she can't marry you without his permission. My advice is to be yourself and answer all of his questions honestly.

"Oh, I thought I'd let you know. I talked with my neighbor, who works at the Quad-C A, and he was at work the Sunday morning after you had that run-in with your new CO. Cmdr. Schuler told him loudly, and in no uncertain terms, that the Army's Signal Corps is made up from the brightest minds in the Army, that their duties are critical to lives and success of his fellow Infantrymen on the front lines in Vietnam, and if he hears of anything the CO does to negatively affect the morale or efficiency of the men in his command, then he has the influence to have him relieved of his command and put in charge of a Mess Hall in Timbuktu."

Later, I made the 4:55 meal run, and when I was relieved by John and Larry at 6:45, I was out of there like a house on fire to catch a Thai bus for Korat. Exiting at the Chainarong Gate. I hired a săawm-law to take me to the Hotel. I rested on the bed in my room for a half hour before dressing to take Glûaimàai dancing at the night club. Hiring a săawm-law for the mile ride to the cafe, I saw when I entered, that she looked very enticing and beautiful in her form-fitting, low-cut, white silk dress with its hem swirling around her mid-thighs, revealing her well-formed legs. Standing by me as I bargained the price for our ride to the night club, I again saw the admiring looks from the passing Americans.

Arriving at the night club, we met up the Glen and Sùpa, and had a fun evening chatting and dancing. Before 10:00, the orchestra played a Tango, to which Glûaimàai and I danced very sensuously. Seeing the lust she held inside for me in her beautiful face, we left for my Hotel room. After we'd satiated the pent-up lust we had for each other in orgasmic release, I held Glûaimȧai's petite body desiringly in my arms. As she lay comfortably on top of me with her luscious hips holding me possessively inside her, I heard her say pensively, "I know you lo-ba me a lot an wan me to be your tîi-lók, but afrait you loo-sa me like Jintana," and I thought, "I'm glad you understand my heart, my darling."

In the morning, we passionately made love to fulfill our desire for each other. As we enjoyed our shower together, I told Glûaimȧai that Friday was my Pay Day and wouldn't be able to see her until lunch in the afternoon. After dressing in my jungle fatigues, I picked up Glûaimȧai's nude body desiringly in my arms and passionately kissed her goodbye.

At morning formation after breakfast, I told Jim, "My jaw feels fine, so I haven't been taking any of the codeine pills and am one-hundred percent fit for duty."

Making the 10:55 meal run, I again made the two trips to the Howard Johnson to buy six 6-packs of Budweiser and a carton of Pall Malls to provide for my five broke hooch-mates. I also put a couple of changes of civilian clothes in my shopping bag to take to my Hotel room. After making the 4:55 meal run for dinner, when John and Larry relieved me at 6:45, I was gone lickety-split to catch a Thai bus for Korat.

Exiting the bus at the Chainarong Gate, I hired a sǎawm-law to take me to the Hotel, where I rested in my room for a half hour before I dressed and left to meet Julii at 8:00.

When I entered the night club, Julii was waiting for me near the entrance door. After we exchanged bows and hellos, she excitedly said, "Oh, my dearest love, I'm so happy. My father say he is glad you are to have dinner with our family at 5:00 on Saturday. He is very much wanting to meet you."

While we danced together, Julii bubbled with joy, more so than her usual happy self. Even while we danced sensuously to the Tangos, there was a pleasure in her lovely, almond-shaped eyes filled with the lust rising within her. It made me think, "There must be something more for Julii in this dinner than just meeting her father. But, whatever it is, I'm really enjoying the effect it has on her."

Even our brief sexual petting as we walked in the dark after we left the night club, had a joyfulness to it. And, when Julii had satiated her lust and desire for me in different Kama Sutra positions with multiple orgasms from our initial lust driven sex before we slept, and after our vigorous lovemaking with the 3:30 wake-up call, she said with giddy pleasure, "Oh, my dearest heart, I love you so very much, and your love for me makes me so very happy, it will live forever."

After we'd copulated in our morning shower and had passionately kissed goodbye as I desiringly caressed the womanly curves of her sensuous nude body, Julii said coquettishly, "I'm so looking forward to you having dinner with my family on Saturday."

At morning formation, after Spike had made his report to the CO of "All present or accounted for," the CO said in a loud voice, "Stand at ease, men. Today is Pay Day, the day I know you've all been waiting for. But, next Friday will be a Company Holiday with all the steak you can eat and all the beer you can drink while watching dancing go-go girls."

And a big cheer went up form the Company formation.

"Any personnel unable to attend the Company Holiday festivities due to their critical duties will be issued a case of beer. Also, the following week, I've arranged for two truck loads of plywood and 2-by-4s to be delivered for you to build partitions in your hooches. And as for you, Spike, if you don't get your act together as First Sargent of this Company, I'll transfer you to the Mess Hall. Now, dismiss my troops to the their duties."

After we were dismissed, Jim laughed and said, "Sandii, now that's what I call an attitude adjustment."

CHAPTER 30

Two Luscious Green Fruit To Grow On My Branches

After morning formation, as Skip Glen, Ronnie, Stony and I walked to our hooch, we laughed about how our new CO had kicked Spike off his high horse and our relief that we'd not have to worry about keeping the mini-fridge well stocked with beer for Spike's inspections.

Entering our hooch, we each grabbed a beer from the fridge. Making two V-shaped holes in the tops, we stood in a circle, raised our beer cans together and shouted "It's Miller time!" After our toast, we went to our wall lockers and changed into our Class-B khaki uniforms to be paid. As we stood around the front of the hooch discussing how to partition the hooch into our individual spaces with the lumber that was coming, Dan arrived from his night shift.

Dan asked, "What's all the hubbub about? The guys relieving us for the day shift were talking about a Company party, lumber to remodel hooches and Spike being sacked."

As Dan was getting a can of beer from the fridge and changing into his Class-B khakis to be paid, we all crowded around Dan talking in turns about Lt. Price's announcement at morning formation for a Company Holiday, lumber to partition the hooches, and if Spike doesn't get his act together, he'll be transferred to the Mess Hall.

When Dan had changed uniforms, we each had another can of beer before leaving for the Pay Line. Joining the Pay Line to the front door of the Day Room, where it had extended to the walkway between the Day Room and HQ, I saw it was rapidly growing longer behind us. Looking toward the Day Room, I saw PFC Brown several guys ahead of me, dressed in his rumpled pickle suit being told about the new CO's declarations at morning formation, which was the topic of discussion all along the Pay Line, and thought, "What's Lt. Price going to say about PFC Brown's appearance?"

Soon, the front door of the Day Room opened, and the Pay Line began to move up the steps and into the Day Room. Watching when it was PFC Brown's turn to be paid, I saw him salute and say, "PFC Brown, David, US 19883232,[128] reporting for pay, Sir." Lt. Price then read down his Company Roster and said, "Brown, David, PFC, US 19883232, 147 Dollars," and looking up added, "PFC Brown, if you'll meet me in the HQ, I'd like to discuss your promotion to Spec-4."

PFC Brown blurted in surprise, "I'm being promoted?"

Lt. Price asked, "You have been doing your job, haven't you?"

PFC Brown replied, "Yes, Sir."

Lt. Price responded, "Fine. If you want to be a Spec-4, be in the HQ at 1000. Next."

When it was my turn, I was paid the expected $220.00. After I bought a $10 U.S. Savings Bond for $7.50, paid the $8.00 for Maandaa's services, and exchanged $100 for 2,000 Bhat, I had $102.50 left. Returning to my hooch, I put all of my Dollars in my tobacco can. As I changed into my civilian clothes, Dan, Ronnie and Stony each stopped when they returned from being paid, handed me a 10-Dollar bill, and said, "Thanks, Sandii, for the beer and butts."

Retrieving a can of Bud from the fridge and lighting a Pall Mall, I then put a few things in my shopping bag to take to Korat, and waited for George and Tommy. After awhile, they each came in the hooch, and handed me a 10-Dollar bill, saying "Thanks, Sandii, for the beer and butt," before hurrying to the Motor Pool for their rides back to work.

---

128 "US" indicates a draftee, "RA" Regular Army, and "NG" National Guard.

With the $50 of "pay it forward" money in hand, I left to catch a Thai bus to the Air Base Bank, where I deposited the $50 in my Savings Account. Then I caught another Thai bus to Korat, where I walked to my tailor shop, ordered three more silk shirts and two more cotton pants with a fitting for Monday morning, and paid a 120-Bhat deposit. From there I walked to cobbler shop on Mahat Thai Road, where I ordered a pair of tan leather shoes that would be ready by Wednesday, and paid a 60-Bhat deposit. Then I walked to the Sri Pattana Hotel, and paid 675 Bhat for a 30-day extension for the rent on my room, which left me with eleven red 100-Bhat bills in my wallet and 65 Bhat in my pocket.

Going to my room, I slept for a couple of hours before leaving at 1:00 for the one-mile walk to the cafe on San-Prasit Road. Entering the cafe, I saw the beautiful Glûaimàai looking very appealing in her form-fitting white blouse and mid-thigh black skirt. Greeting me at the door, we exchanged sàwàtdiis. Then, as she lead me to a table near the wall, she said, "I mi-sa you so mu-cha tis mo-ra-ning, my daw-ling."

I responded, "And I missed you this morning, too. But, you look so beautiful and desirable, I can hardly wait to see you tomorrow morning, my dearest."

Glûaimàai said, "I ache for you now, but I can wait foe you, my lo-ba."

After I ate lunch and tutored Glûaimàai in English till 4:00, I returned to the Company Area. While waiting for dinner in the Mess Hall at 5:00, I saw Dan sitting on his bed listening to music by the Beach Boys from his reel-to-reel tape deck in his wall locker. Behind his tape-deck stereo system, I saw tall stacks of 8-inch reel boxes labeled with all kinds of music, and said, "Dan, I guess buying all of those reels of music set you back quite a bit."

Dan replied, "Not really. All it cost me was for the reels of blank tape. The Air Base Library has an Audio Room set up with tape decks to make copies of their audio-tape albums. All you have to do is reserve a time slot and you can make copies from any of the hundreds of albums they have. The Base Library is next to the Air Base Comm Center, so it's close to where you work. If you and Skip each buy a tape deck from the Base Exchange, then you can checkout audio tapes from the Base Library and make copies here or at work. That's what some of us at the Tropo Site do."

I said, "I'll have to check into that with Skip. Thanks for the info, Dan," as I left for the Mess Hall to eat dinner.

At work that night, I discussed what Dan told me with Skip. He thought it sounded great and would go to the Base Exchange to check on the models of tape-deck systems available, their features, and prices. Overhearing our discussion, Bob commented, "Yea, Frank and his teammate before you, both had tape decks they'd bring to work and copied lots of audio tapes from the Base Library."

When I was relieved at 6:45 by John and Larry, I beat feet to catch a Thai bus for Korat. Arriving at the Chainarong Gate, I hired a săawm-law to take me to the Hotel. Entering my room, I stripped to my boxers and rested on the bed to wait for Glûaimàai's knock on the door.

At 8:00, I heard Glûaimàai, and with my Pavlovian arousal for the desire I had for her, I opened the door and she lept into my waiting arms. Passionately kissing me with her desire for me, she wrapped her arms and legs possessively around me.

After we had vigorously satiated our lust in the Kama Sutra position we'd discussed, we showered, and then laid nude on the bed side by side looking through the Kama Sutra book. As Glûaimàai selected the position for tomorrow morning, I felt my desire for this beautiful woman welling up inside me and though, "Maybe I can work out a deal with Glûaimàai's father for her to be my tîi-lók like Bob did for Gùlaap," and asked, "Where does your family live?"

She thought for a moment, then answered in Thai, "My family live in Pak Mak, a small town in Loei Province near Laos, about 500 kilometers from Korat. My father has a friend here who arranged for me to work at the cafe. Why do you ask?"

I thought, "That's 300 miles! There's no way I could get there and back in one day," as I said, "Just want to know where you're from."

When Glûaimàai kissed me passionately goodbye as she left for work, she said, "I lo-ba you bery mut an wan to be in you awm tonight, my daw-ling."

I responded, "And you will be tomorrow night, my love."

After she left, I slept for a few hours before dressing and walking to the cafe for lunch, and then tutored Glûaimàai in English. At 4:00, I walked back to my Hotel room, took a quick shower, shaved with my electric razor, and dressed for dinner at Julii's home. I then hired a sǎawm-law to take me to her address off Yotha Road, south of Jomsurangyat Road.

I arrived a little before 5:00 in front of moderate size house in a clearly middle-class neighborhood. An affable, 5-foot-7, Thai man in a white silk shirt and black cotton pants met me at the door. I made the wâai and bowed low, making sure my was lower than his, and said, "Sàwàtdii bi-daa kâa-pa-jâao, yin-dii tîi dâai rúu-jak koon."[129]

He responded in kind and laughingly said in good English, "Hello, Mr. Sandii, and welcome to my humble home. May I say your Thai is very good, and I welcome the chance to be acquainted with you, too. Please, join us for dinner. I apologize, my oldest son is at University."

He led me to the dining room and offered me the chair to the right of his, at the head of the table, and next to Julii, who was beaming with pride. Across from me sat his slender and very pretty wife, and clockwise from her, sat Julii's other older brother and two younger brothers. I thought, "As his only daughter, then Julii is the apple of her father's eye."

After a delicious Thai dinner, which was typically spicy, and friendly conversations in English, Julii's father escorted me to his back porch. There we sat in wicker armchairs overlooking a beautiful yard, facing a lovely sunset. He offered a Camel cigarette, and once they were lit, he said, "Julii told me you're an honorable man and a very good dancer, and that she is very much in love with you. Do you love Julii?"

I emphatically replied, "Very much, Sir."

He casually asked, "And how is your sex with Julii?"

I'd prepared for such a question and replied candidly, "Lovemaking with Julii is like being in heaven. Very passionate, very vigorous and very frequent."

He laughed and said, "I often wondered if she was like her mother. Thank you for your candor. So, what are your career plans?"

I replied, "Right now, I'm a Microwave Radio Repairman in the Signal Corps. I plan on extending my one-year tour of duty in Thailand by six months, and make Sargent in six or seven months. When I'm discharged, I'll go to University in Oregon, where I'm from, and earn a Bachelor's and Master's Degree in Electrical Engineering."

---

129 "Greeting father my, welcome chance can be acquainted with you."

He responded, "Very impressive. Do you plan on working in Thailand?"

I answered, "That's over six years away, and depends on the job market."

He then asked questions about living in Oregon, and when we finished our cigarettes, he said, "I understand you must be at work by 7:00, so I'll call a taxi to take you to the Chainarong Gate."

As I rode in an old 1951 Desoto to the Chainarong Gate, I thought, "I've just been interviewed to be his son-in-law with Julii. No wonder Julii was all excited about this meeting. She wants to marry me."

At work that night, while Skip was on his meal run, I told Bob about the meeting with Julii's father and my conclusion, and Bob asked, "So, do you want to marry Julii?"

I laughed and replied, "According to her father, Julii's mother is also great in bed, so there's no wanting there if I married her. She's very pretty, as her mother still is. And, there's no doubt Thai women make great wives, so it's a possibility."

Bob responded, "I doubt her father will approve, as he wouldn't want his only daughter and his grandchildren going to America and never see them again. If you had said you would most likely return to Thailand, then he would likely approve of her marrying you."

After Skip returned from his meal run, he pulled out a bunch of brochures, one for each tape deck system sold at the Base Exchange, listing their options and cost. We spent the rest of the night discussing which would provide the best bang for the buck.

Returning to my Hotel room after being relieved by John and Larry, I was again waiting with my desires for Glûaimàai. When I heard her knock at the door, I felt my Pavlovian arousal and lust for her as I ran to the door, which were rewarded by her passion for me. I reveled in the desire and love we had for each other, as we satiated our built up lust in passionate, vigorous lovemaking in another Kama Sutra position, culminating in our orgasmic release.

I felt happy just being near Glûaimàai as we showered together and then lay nude on the bed planning our next Kama Sutra adventure. Even while tutoring her in English at the cafe, I was happy knowing that as of 8:00 that night, we would be together for a night, a day and a night sleeping, eating, socializing and dancing, with all of our lovemaking being icing on the cake. Actually for me, Glûaimàai was like a two-course gourmet meal with Julii being a sumptuous dessert.

There was a little extra spice added Monday evening. The tîi-lóks, having heard about Glûaimàai's sexy red silk dress, and wanting to see it, had persuaded her to wear it to the compound Monday evening. When she approached the front porch of Horn's home wearing the red dress, I heard all the men stop speaking and saw their eyes lock on Glûaimàai walking behind me. I then saw the four tîi-lóks assemble behind the screen door with their own admiration. When I came back out to the porch with my bottle of Sing Hǎi Beer, Skip said, "Fourteen or not, I wish Glûaimàai was my tîi-lók."

Tuesday, I pleasantly spent the afternoon at the cafe with Glûaimàai as I ate lunch, tutored her in English, and then had dinner before returning to my room for a few hours of sleep. Waking well rested, I showered and shaved before dressing to meet Julii at the night club to feast on her lust for me as my sumptuous dessert.

Arriving at the night club before 8:00, I found a table on the 3rd tier for us and ordered two Pepsis. I'd noted before why we always sat at a table on the 3rd tier. I was traditional for the honored 1st tier to be for the revered older patrons, the 2nd tier for the mature patrons, and the 3rd tier for the younger set.

Watching the entrance door for Julii's arrival, I recognized one of the girls from our Thursday night dance group enter wearing an enticing, form-fitting, red silk blouse, a short blue skirt and a white belt that enhanced the curves of her womanly figure. Watching her scan the 3rd tier, I saw her spot me and give a friendly wave, which I returned, and then walked up the steps to my table. As she approached, I stood and we exchanged hellos in the Thai manner. With a sad expression on her pretty face, she said, "You remember me, I am Sùusǐi, Julii frien. May I sit?"

I replied, "Please do, Sùusǐi."

After we sat opposite each other, Sùusǐi said, "I am saw-ry to say to you, Julii cannot come to meet you. Julii as-ká I gi-ba tis to you," and handed me a folded sheet of paper.

Unfolding it, I saw it had tear-stained printing that read: "My darling Sandii. My father say I cannot marry you because he not want his only daughter go to America and never to see me again. My father send me to live with his brother in Udon Thani to go to College there.

I love you very much and want with all my heart, mind and spirit to be your beloved wife. I will love you for all time, Julii."

I asked, "Sùusĭi, how did Julii get this to you to give me tonight?" as I thought, "How ironic, 'sùu sĭi' in Thai means 'to get good fortune.'"

Sùusĭi asked, "Can I say in Thai? My Angrit not goot like Julii."

I replied in Thai, "Yes, but speak slow so I can follow what you say."

She said in Thai, "Thank you very much. I live on the same lane as Julii and we are very good friends. She has told me all about you. How much she loves you and wants to marry you. Also, she told me how much she liked dancing sexy and then lovemaking with you. And liked your chest hair. Since you are sad, maybe it will make you happy to dance with me?"

Looking at Sùusĭi's very pretty, smiling face, the desire in her lovely, almond-shaped eyes, and how enticing she looked in her form-fitting red blouse and short blue skirt, I replied, "Yes, dancing with you would make me happy."

As we danced a Cha-cha and then a Waltz, I found Sùusĭi very enjoyable to look at and dance with. She was two inches taller than Julii. Also, her form-fitting blouse revealed her breasts were slightly larger than Julii's, and her short skirt swirled around two very shapely legs.

Next, the orchestra played a Tango, and Sùusĭi desiringly asked, "Julii say you dance very sexy Tango, can you show me?"

I replied, "With pleasure," and with every chance, I pressed or slid my right thigh against her mons pubis. Soon I felt Sùusĭi grinding her mons pubis longingly against my thigh in response. When the Tango ended, she held me close and gasped, "I like very much your sexy Tango."

After the orchestra played a couple more Waltz's and Cha-cha's, it played another Tango. After we danced another very sexy Tango, Sùusĭi asked breathlessly, "I lust for you very much. Will you show me your room and make love with me?"

I replied, "I lust for you very much, too," and as we left the night club and walked quickly to my Hotel room with Sùusĭi behind me, I thought, "Your name is now ironic, as you also have brought me good fortune."

Entering my room, we passionately kissed as we stripped off our clothes. As I fondled her voluptuous breasts, Sùusĭi reached her hands down and caressed my protruding shaft, and admiringly said, "Julii said you are a large man, and I'm very happy you are. But, please be gentle with me as I am also a small green woman."

I led Sùusǐi to the bed, where she lay on her back, spreading her enticing legs high and wide to receive me, as I opened the dresser drawer and removed the open tube of K-Y Gel. She moaned, "Chai dâai," in desirous anticipation, as I squeezed the K-Y Gel into the small entrance of her love canal, and lay between her up raised legs quivering with lust. I then rolled onto my back with her luscious hips straddling my groin.

Lifting Sùusǐi up by her slender waist onto her knees astride my waist, I held the lusting head of my shaft beneath her so he could induce it into her well-lubricated love canal. As she began undulating her sensuous hips to push the head of my shaft into her expanding love canal, her beautiful, almond-shaped eyes looked with desire into mine as she moaned, "Dâai! Dâai!"

Soon, I felt the head of my shaft pop Sùusǐi's hymen, and saw her face wince a little as she happily declared, "My darling, I am now a woman."

Sùusǐi began vigorously undulating her luscious hips to expand her love canal sheath as quickly as possible to have me fully inside her. Once she had me completely in her, she began to rapidly gyrate against my groin, and I soon heard Sùusǐi yell, "Dâai! Dâai!" as I felt her lusting body shudder with orgasmic release. I then quickly rolled her over with me on top, between luscious legs, to release my own lust for her sumptuous body with long rhythmic thrusts into her taut love canal, and heard her yell, "Yes, my darling, I want to feel your hot, sexual desire[130] squirt into me."

When my orgasmic thrust distended deep into Sùusǐi's love canal, I rolled onto my back with her on top and her luscious hips holding me tightly. As she lay happily with her head on my chest and her fingers caressing my chest hair, Sùusǐi cooed, "My darling, if you will be my boyfriend, I will not make the same mistake Julii made to tell my father I want to marry you. I want very much to dance with you, have wonderful lovemaking with you, and be your girlfriend. Would you like me to be your girlfriend, my darling?"

---

130   The Thai word for "semen" is "náam-gaan," literally, "liquid-sexual desire."

I replied, "Yes, my darling, I desire you to be my girlfriend very much. Will you stay the night with me, my beloved?"

Sùusĭi snuggled her desiring hips against me and replied eagerly, "Oh yes, my love, I want very much to sleep with you and make love with you again in the morning."

I then explained to Sùusĭi my work schedule, that the next time I could dance with her would be Saturday, and if she liked, she could meet me in my room at 5:00 and have dinner together. Also, I had a 3:30 wake-up call, to give us time for lovemaking and to shower together before I left for Camp Friendship. Sùusĭi said, "I will very much like lovemaking with you in the morning, my darling."

I thought, as we went to sleep, "The Lord Buddha taketh away and Lord Buddha giveth."

Waking in the morning with Sùusĭi on top. I lifted up her shoulders to expose her full, firm breasts hanging down like two delicious peaches before my desiring eyes. Sucking each in turn into my mouth, she moaned with delight and gyrated her hips vigorously against my groin. Hearing her yell, "Chai-yoo!" as her orgasm raged through her voluptuous body, I rolled over on top of Sùusĭi. Savoring my lusting, rhythmic thrusts between her desiring legs, deep into her taut love canal, with my distended orgasmic thrust, she yelled, "Yes, my darling, squirt your sexual desire into me!"

As we showered, Sùusĭi desiringly cooed, "I am so glad you chose me to be your girlfriend. I will try very much for you to be happier with me as you were with Julii, my beloved." And when I'd dressed, she passionately kissed me goodbye, as I desiringly caressed the sumptuous curves of her nude body, she said, "I will miss you very much until I see you here Saturday at 5:00."

At work that morning, there was continuous clatter from the teletype machines monitoring the AP and UPI news wire services with the often "ding, ding, ding" for URGENT news. I asked, "Bob, what's all the excitement on the news wires about?"

Bob replied, "The election returns. Yesterday, was Election Day. Oh yeah, you two aren't old enough to vote, yet."

Skip sourly responded, "Yea, we're old enough to die for our country, just not old enough to vote on what we're dying for."

Bob said, "That's one of the ironies of the U.S. Anyway, the Election Poles have just closed on the East Coast. It'll be another three hours before they close on the West Coast. And then, it'll take several hours to count the votes. In the meantime, all the news agencies are doing exit poles to get early projections on who's going to win. Most of us are for Nixon because he wants to win the Vietnam War to keep the Communists out of the rest of Southeast Asia, and we contractors get to keep our jobs. But, Humphrey wants to pull out of South Vietnam and let Southeast Asia go to the dogs and be taken over by the Communist insurgents, which also means shutting down all of the Air Force Bases in Thailand."

I responded, "If they close the Air Bases here, then we'll be transferred Stateside, and I like it here. In fact, I've thought about extending my tour here. Though that's mainly because I don't want to go to Ft. Huachuca, Arizona. I've heard a couple of the guys had classmates who went there and have received letters describing the conditions there. Besides being in the middle of nowhere, and literally 80 miles from anywhere, they're on Burial Detail Teams for the funerals of all the guys being killed over here, or on Riot Control Teams, which could get you killed by a fellow American. It'd be a terrible irony to survive the Vietnam War, and the go Stateside and be killed by Americans for who you've just laid your life on the line for to protect their Constitutional rights."

After a busy day working the day shift, I quickly returned to my Hotel room and changed clothes. Picking up Glûaimàai at the cafe, we rode in a sǎawm-law to meet Glen and Sùpa at the night club. As we danced together, I very much enjoyed looking at her beautiful face, watching the hem of her blue silk dress swirl enticingly around her well-formed legs, and feeling our lust grow when dancing to the Tangos.

Leaving the night club at 10:00, we then feasted on our pent-up lust in a new Kama Sutra position. When we had satiated our lust with orgasmic liberation, Glûaimàai effusively gasped, "We must do tat again in ta mo-raning, my daw-ling."

In the morning, we sensuously enjoyed the same position again. After we showered, Glûaimàai lay on the bed nude selecting our next lovemaking position as I dressed in my jungle fatigues for morning formation. We briefly discussed the next Kama Sutra position before I desiringly kissed her goodbye as I caressed her petite nude body.

Returning to my Hotel room after formation, I saw Glûaimȧai lying enticingly in the nude on the bed and she said, "I wake up wan-ting you in me. Pa-lee-sa, my daw-ling, ha-ry an make lu-ba to me."

Quickly stripping, I watched Glûaimȧai's enticing hips lustfully undulate with desire for me and felt my arousal surging with lust for her. As I pushed fully into her tight, wet love canal, and started to shift her position, she said, "No, my daw-ling, I wan see you going in me. See you eye wit desi-ra fo me. See you lu-ba fo me."

Watching Glûaimȧai's beautiful face filled with her love for me, I felt her vigorous, undulating hips lust for my shaft rhythmically thrusting into her. Soon, I saw her firm, dainty breasts lift up as her back arched with her orgasm raging through her perfect petite body, and she yelled, "I lu-ba you! I lu-ba you!" Then, I felt my distended orgasmic thrust deep into her love canal and gasped, "I love you, Glûaimȧai."

Rolling onto my back with Glûaimȧai on top, with her head on my heaving chest, she said breathlessly, "I lu-ba you, my daw-ling, I lu-ba you so mut,"

"And I love you, too, my dearest," and held her desiringly in my arms until it was time to shower before she had to dress and leave for work at 10:30.

After Glûaimȧai passionately kissed me goodbye, I dressed, picked up my shopping bag and walked to the cobbler shop, where I paid the balance for my new, tan leather shoes. Wearing my new shoes and carrying my brown suede shoes in my shopping bag, I walked to the tailor shop. Having gone for my fitting Monday morning with Glûaimȧai, I paid the balance for my new clothes, and placed them in my shopping bag on top of my suede shoes.

Returning to my Hotel room, I slept for an hour. When I woke, I walked to the cafe for lunch and tutored my beautiful Glûaimȧai in English. As we exchanged parting sȧwȧtdiis at 4:00, she said, "I look to see you in ta mo-ra-ning, my daw-ling," and I responded, "As do I."

Returning to my Company Area, I went to my hooch and changed into my OD BDUs, leaving my new clothes on the floor with my dirty clothes to be cleaned and pressed by Maan-daa tomorrow. As I ate dinner in the Mess Hall. I found the talk was all about the Company Holiday. That there were already several BBQ grills in the Motor Pool, four pallets of beer, two of which had been emptied into four ¼-ton jeep trailers to be covered with ice in the morning, and an elevated stage built for the go-go girls to dance on.

Driving the truck to the Air Base Site, the Company Holiday was all Skip could talk about. On the Order Wire, there was frequent chatter on the preparations being made, as there were men from several outlying Radio Sites that were part of Company C and driving in the morning to attend the festivities.

Being relieved in the morning by Jack, I was gone like a driven home run ball to Korat. Returning to my Hotel room, I stripped to my boxers and lay on the bed waiting with desire for Glûaimàai's knock on my door. Hearing her knock, before I was off the bed, she said in Thai, "Darling, get dressed, I have a friend with me." Dressing quickly, I heard two female voices talking outside the door.

Opening the door, my beautiful, little Glûaimàai entered, followed by a very pretty Thai girl as small as her, dressed in a form-fitting white blouse and short black skirt. After exchanging sàwàtdiis, Glûaimàai said in Thai, "Sandii, meet my good friend Lompèt. Lompèt, meet my very special friend Sandii. My darling, I must tell you for the last week, a short American man has been coming to the cafe every night for dinner and flirting with me. He say he fall in love with me when he first saw me in my white dress last week in front of the cafe. Last night, he asked me to be his tîi-lók and maybe to marry him someday, and I said yes.

"My good friend Lompèt, is a waitress and small like me. I told her how you taught me English, to ballroom dance and have sex in many positions, so I can be a good tîi-lók for an American man, as no Thai man will marry me because I'm too small. Lompèt would like very much for you to teach her to be a good tîi-lók, too. If you don't want to, it's okay and she will leave with me now."

I responded, "Thank you, Lompèt, you are a very pretty woman," and to Glûaimàai I said, "You'll be an excellent tîi-lók, and thank you for introducing me to Lompèt," and thought, "'Lom-pèt' means 'wind-spice' or 'spicy wind'."

As Glûaimàai left my room and my life, I gently took Lompèt's small left hand in my large right hand and sat on the edge of the bed. Placing my hands on her small womanly hips, I stood her between my knees. My eyes were only a little lower than her lovely, almond-shaped eyes as I asked, "Are you a green fruit?" to which she nodded her head nervously with a flirtatious smile and said, "Yes, I'm a green fruit, but I want to be picked by you."

Then putting her arms timidly around my neck slowly, Lompèt suddenly tightened her arms, pulling her lips firmly against mine, giving me a passionate desiring kiss, and I thought, "Lompèt, you are a 'spicy wind,' and the Lord Buddha has replaced the two ripe fruit that have fallen from my tree with two luscious green fruit to grow on my branches."

CHAPTER 31

It's Just the Way Things are in Thailand

Anticipating I would gently initiate Lompèt into the discovery of her first sexual encounter because of her hesitant approach to me, her sudden passionate and desirous kiss was a pleasant surprise. She then leaned back with my hands holding her luscious, round hips. Extending her arms and her hands around my neck, she looked at me with her lovely, almond-shaped eyes and said in Thai, "Sandii, you are the first man I ever kissed, but, I want you to know I want to have sex with you and am very worried about my first time lovemaking. Was my kiss okay?"

Taking Lompèt's pretty face in my hands and looking at the desire to please me in her lovely eyes, I said, "My darling, your kiss was delicious,"

Kissing her tenderly on the lips, I began to slowly unbutton her blouse. Then kissing sensuously along her neck, I slipped the blouse off her shoulder and onto the floor. Reaching behind her back, I unhooked her bra and saw it slide down Lompèt's chest, exposing her enticingly firm, apple sized breasts. Sucking her delectable left breast fully into my mouth, I heard her moan with delight as I felt her hands grab the back on my head, pulling my mouth firmly around her breast.

Moving my mouth to Lompèt's right breast, I unfastened her skirt, slipping it and her panties to the floor. Putting my strong left arm around her slender waist and lifting her as I stood up, I felt her lovely legs wrap desiringly around me. Then turning around, I lay her on the bed and reached in the dresser drawer with my right hand, grabbing the tube of K-Y Gel. As I quickly stripped, Lompèt saw my engorged, protruding shaft, and said with concern, "you're so big and I'm so small, will you fit in me, my darling?"

I replied, "your beautiful body was made for lovemaking and your love canal will expand to receive me," as Lompèt raised her enticing legs high and wide for me to enter her. Then, as I'd done with Súusîi, I squeezed a large amount of K-Y Gel into her wet love canal, and rolled her on top of me. As Lompèt sat the small opening of her lusting love canal on the head of my shaft, I held my engorged shaft with my right hand to let her expand the sheath of her love canal with the head of my shaft. This was a method I learned from the Kama Sutra.

While Lompèt undulated her sensuous hips to expand her love canal over my engorged shaft held with my right hand, I enjoyed caressing her enticing, firm breasts with my left hand. When the sheath of her love canal had stretched and taken me fully in, Lompèt moaned with delight, "my darling, you're right. My body was made for lovemaking with you. It feels very good to finally be a woman with your desire for me," and began to vigorously gyrate against my groin as I massaged her lovely breasts with both hands.

Shortly, Lompèt yelled, "Dâai! Dâai!" as her luscious body convulsed with the orgasmic release rushing through her body. Then, rolling her over beneath me, I began my long, rhythmic thrusts into her taut love canal to satisfy my lust for her sensuous, petite body, and she cried out, "my darling, I love the feel of your desire for me. Let me enjoy the hot squirt of your sexual desire."[131]

When my orgasmic thrust distended fully into Lompèt's love canal and I exploded into her, she yelled, "Yes, my darling, I feel your hot sexual desire filling me with your love!"

---

131   In Thai, the word for "semen" is literally "sexual desire".

Rolling onto my back with Lompèt on top, she lay exhausted with her head on my chest and gasped, "My darling, I am very happy your lovemaking made me a woman. The others at the cafe call me a green lime as no man wants me." Then, propping her pretty face on her arms to look me in the face, she asked, "I know you're my teacher, but can I tell them you are my boyfriend? It'll make them very envious."

I replied, "My beautiful Lompèt, I'll be your teacher and your boyfriend, like I was with Glûaimaai, until you become a tîi-lók, like she did. But first, my darling, we'll shower together before we dress, and I'll buy you some beautiful clothes to take my pretty girlfriend dancing in. Can you be here tomorrow morning at 8:00 to go for a fitting of a new dress?"

She excitedly answered, "Yes, my darling, and to have more lovemaking, too. I want to learn many positions from you."

After we showered and dressed, Lompèt properly followed me to the clothier shop Glûaimaai used. Entering the shop, Lompèt stood behind me as I told the owner I wanted two low-cut silk dressed made for Lompèt like she had made for Glûaimaai, and two silk blouses and two skirts, for the price Glûaimaai paid, with one dress ready for a fitting tomorrow morning. When the owner agreed, I took two red 100-Baht bills from my wallet and gave them to her for the deposit. Then, I chose a pale blue silk for the dress to be fitted tomorrow and Lompèt chose a hot pink silk for the other dress. After she chose the material for her blouses and skirts, the owner took her in the back for her measurements.

Outside the shop's door, I looked down into Lompèt's lovely, almost-shaped eyes and said, "You're my beautiful girlfriend. You'll tell me where you work and follow me into the cafe. I'll tell everyone you're my girlfriend, and they'll see you have a tall, handsome American boyfriend. Then I'll kiss you goodbye, okay?" and thought, "Far be it for any Thai girl to disagree with her boyfriend."

She nodded her pretty head vigorously and replied, "Very okay, my darling. I love you very much for the honor you give me to be your girlfriend. The cafe is two doors to the right."

Entering the cafe, a pretty waitress came to me, bowed and said, "Sàwàtdii, ká. How may I help you?"

I responded in kind, then stepping to my left, revealing the diminutive Lompèt behind me, I said imperiously in Thai, "The beautiful

Lompèt is the woman I love and is my girlfriend." Giving her a passionate kiss, I bowed and said, "Sàwàtdii, my heart's desire," and thought as I left the cafe, "Lompèt, no one will ever again call you an unripe lime."

Walking the short distance to the Sri Pattana Hotel, I asked the pretty Receptionist to wake me at 11:30 for lunch and was able to get an hour of sleep before I left for the Company Holiday festivities.

Arriving at the Company Area just after noon, I saw the party was in full swing in the Motor Pool. Fishing out a can of Budweiser from the ice in one of the four jeep trailers, I watched a couple of guys dumping cases of beer from the nearby pallets into the ice of another trailer. Punching two Y-shaped holes in the top of my can of Bud with my church key, I walked over to the three BBQ grills.

I saw the grills were made from 55-gallon barrels cut in half lengthwise, with the bottom half welded to 1-inch angle iron legs. The top half was hinged along the back for a lid, and a large piece of ½-inch woven-wire screen was used for the grill. Standing in front of the BBQ grills were two Thai cooks with long-handled forks.

Picking up a heavy-duty paper plate, I pointed to one of the inch thick steaks on a grill and one Thai cook speared it onto my plate while a third Thai cook ladled some pork-n-beans next to the steak. Taking a set of plastic ware from nearby boxes on a card table, I walked to the lengthwise rows of tables from the Mess Hall. Set up endwise to a raised stage were two pretty Thai go-go dancers, who didn't have a clue how to go-go dance. But they were topless, so the men were happily watching their small bouncing breasts.

Spotting two guys from my microwave class, I joined them and found they'd luckily been assigned to an outlying Radio Site. Catching up on the world they lived in, and thanking me for the tip to volunteer for an Air Base site, they told me how amazingly cheap it was to live there. Though the bars and nightlife wasn't all that good, there were plenty of pretty, Thai girls who wanted to be your tîi-lók and live with you, if you gave their father 100 Baht a month.

Asking if I had a tîi-lók, I replied, "I don't have a tîi-lók, but I'm dating a college girl I go dancing with on Tuesday, Thursday and Saturday nights and sleeps with me afterwards. Then I know a waitress who likes to dance and sleep with me the other four nights of the week, and I don't have to pay their fathers anything. Of course, they don't know about each other, and if they did, they'd probably cut my dick off. But, like they say, 'variety is the spice of life,' and my life is nice and spicy."

Returning for another can of Bud and a plate of steak and beans, Lt. Price came up to me and said, "I understand everyone calls you Sandy?"

I responded, "Yes, sir. It's because the Thais can't pronounce my name. In Thai, 'Sandii' means 'extremely good'."

Lt. Price said, "Sandii, it's the uniform you say 'sir' to, not the man, and right now I'm not in uniform, so you can call me David."

I replied, "Okay, David. Thanks for the party you're giving."

David responded, "No, Sandii, I thank you. If it wasn't for you doing your duty, instead of kowtowing to me, I'd be an Infantry Officer trying to make this Signal Company into an Infantry Company and end up being hung in effigy, or with a bomb in my hooch. And, I don't believe that cock-and-bull story it was done by the Thai Cong, which proves you guys are way smarter than any Infantry Squad to pull it off and get away with it."

"Sandii, I pulled your DD-201 file and found you're a natural linguist. Also, the word in the Company is you speak Thai and live in Korat. My wife has arrived here, and I'm hoping you can show us around Korat to do some shopping."

I said, "David, if you want to learn a language, you live among the people. And why me, as lots of guys in the Company speak Thai and live in Korat?"

David replied, "Because you're the only one that doesn't live with a tîi-lók. I understand tomorrow is your off day. Would you be able to join us for dinner at the Jomsurong Hotel, then help us do some shopping?"

I answered, "I already have dinner plans, but we could meet in the Hotel Lobby at noon and eat lunch at a Thai restaurant, which is cheaper than eating at the Hotel, and then I could take you shopping. How's that sound?"

David replied, "Sounds good, Sandii. We'll see you at noon tomorrow."

Getting another can of Bud and a plate of steak and beans, I spotted Glen at a table. Sitting across the table from him, I asked, "Quite a party, eh Glen?"

Glen replied, "Sure is, Sandii. I hope the CO does this every month so we can visit with the guys from the other Radio Sites, and I'd like to see dancers with bigger tits, but it is what it is. Sorry to hear about Glûaimaai. Súpa told me about her becoming some guy's tîi-lók, which was the whole idea. Also, that Glûaimaai fixed you up with another girl. What's she like?"

I answered, "Her name is Lompèt. She's small, like Glûaimaai, and in bed her lovemaking is like her name, 'Spicy Wind,' but only time will tell if she's as good at learning English or dancing. She has Sundays off, so would it be okay if we switched our movie matinee from Monday to Sunday? Also, could you ask Súpa to check with the other tîi-lóks to see if it's okay to bring Lompèt to the compound Sunday night?"

Glen laughed and replied, "It was Súpa's idea for Glûaimaai to set you up with Lompèt, so you better bring her to the compound if you know what's good for you. Also, as Glûaimaai and Lompèt are the same size, Súpa said Lompèt will be wearing that sexy red dress. As for the movie, Súpa has already told me we'll be going on Sunday. Sandii, you already know with these women make the decisions. They just let us think we do," and I thought, "The more things change, the more they stay the same."

I said, "Guess this party will break up soon."

Glen asked, "Why do you say that?"

I replied, "because of the monsoon rain."

Glen laughed and responded, "The monsoon season ended over a week ago, Sandii. The prevailing wind this time of year is to the South from the Gobi Desert and across the Himalayas. We're now in the dry season. There won't be any monsoon rains again until late April or May, and not only drier, but also a little cooler, at least by Thai standards, which'll make it easier to sleep some in the afternoon and not wake up for lunch drenched in sweat."

I responded, "In that case, after I drink another Bud and finish this steak, I'm going to get some shut-eye, as I didn't get much sleep this morning."

Waking to the 5:00 bugle call for Mess under the cooling breeze of my fan, I found that my sheets were not drenched in sweat, as the temperature was in the upper 80s and not in the mid-90s with 100% humidity. Fetching a can of Bud from the fridge to drink while I dressed in my OD BDUs, I then left with Skip to have dinner in the mess hall. Meeting Tommy in front of the Day Room on his 6:35 meal run with the truck, Skip and I then drove to the Air Base site to work the night shift.

After a relatively quiet night, I made the 6:35 meal run to the Motor Pool to pass the truck to Phizer for the day shift. Then, eating a quick breakfast in the mess hall and hurrying to my hooch to put my brown shoes and two changes of clothes in my shopping bag, I left to catch a Thai bus for Korat. In my Hotel room, I changed into my civilian clothes and lay on the bed to relax as I waited for Lompèt's knock on the door. Laying there thinking of Lompèt, I began to feel my arousal for her delectable body.

Hearing Lompèt's knock on the door at 8:00, I got up, opened the door and saw her happy smile become a frown. Entering my room, she said, "Glûaimaai say when you open the door, you're undressed and desiring her. Do you not have desire for me, my darling?"

Unfastening my pants, I said, "My darling, I didn't want you to think I only wanted you for lovemaking," and when my pants dropped to the floor revealing my arousal for her, I added, "as you can see, I desire you very much, my darling."

Seeing me fully aroused, Lompèt squealed, "Oh yes, my darling, your large desire for me makes me very happy with my desire for you," as she removed her blouse and skirt to show me she wore no bra or panties. As I quickly removed my shirts and picked up a fresh tube of K-Y Gel off the dresser, Lompèt ran over and leapt backwards onto the bed. Spreading her enticing legs high and wide to receive me, I saw her wet crotch as she said excitedly, "See, my darling, I have much desire for you."

Using the same technique as last time, Lompèt worked the head of my shaft up into her expanding love canal with sensuous undulating hips and happily moaned, "Châi dâai! Châi dâai!," as I enjoyed massaging her lovely firm breasts. When she had me fully inside her taut love canal, she lustfully gyrated against my groin until I felt her lusting body shudder with her orgasmic release and she yelled, "Chai-yoo."

Quickly rolling Lompèt's gasping body beneath me and her desiring legs raised around me, I began to satisfy my lust for her luscious petite body with long rhythmic thrusts, sliding into her wonderfully tight love canal as she moaned, "My darling, I love you very much. Your lovemaking makes me feel so desired."

After my orgasmic thrust distended into Lompèt's love canal, ejaculating my hot sexual desire into her, I rolled onto my back with her on top. As her sexually drained body fell onto my chest, Lompèt said breathlessly, "My dearest boyfriend, I am so happy you desire lovemaking with me. And the people at the cafe are very envious of the honor you gave me at the cafe yesterday, especially with the desire you had for me when you kissed me goodbye."

I responded, "My darling, you are beautiful, and I desire lovemaking with you very much."

After we showered and dressed, we passionately kissed before Lompèt walked behind me to the clothier. When she modelled the low-cut, form-fitting, pale blue silk dress for me as it was being fitted, I said in Thai, " You are an excellent seamstress to make my girlfriend look so beautiful in this dress you have made for her. What is your name?"

The owner replied, "My name is Mrs. Pooman. You honor me with your praise, Mr. Sandii, but your girlfriend is already beautiful. The dress will be ready Monday, and the rest ready for fitting."

When Lompèt's fitting was finished, I said, "My darling, I must return to my room for sleep as my boss honors me to have lunch with him and his wife then show them some shops in Korat. But, I will have desire for you tomorrow morning at 8:00."

Lompèt, with longing in her lovely almond-shaped eyes, responded, "And I will have much desire for you, love of my heart."

Returning to the Hotel, I told the pretty Receptionist I wanted an 11:30 wake-up call and went to my room for some needed sleep.

Waking to the 11:30 wake-up call, I dressed and walked several hundred yards to the lane off Phoklang Road that led to the Jomsurong Hotel. Entering the lobby and not seeing Lt. Price, I went to the Reception Desk and informed the two very pretty Thai Receptionists in Thai that I was waiting to meet Lt. Price and his wife. Then, chatting with them in Thai while I waited, I saw the one named Suumii was engaged when she flashed me her diamond ring. The other girl, named Dhoi, had a beautiful oval face but was bashful. As Suumii encouraged Dhoi to flirt with me, I found she was a 20-year-old widow.

Seeing Lt. Price enter the lobby with a lovely blond woman, I said, "I need to go now, but I'd like to talk with you again sometime," to which Suumii replied with a giggle, "Mr. Sandii, you can come any day to talk with Dhoi."

As I approached Lt. Price, he said, "Hello, Sandii. This is my wife, Mary. Mary, this is Sandii the brave man who fearlessly faced down his commanding officer."

I responded, "A pleasure to meet you, Mary. So, David, what would you like to eat? Thai BBQ'd chicken, Thai vegetarian, or Thai fried rice, which is much tastier than it sounds!"

David replied, "I love BBQ'd food. How about you, Mary?"

Mary answered cheerfully, "BBQ sounds great to me."

I responded, "The Gài Yâang Sâang Thai, which literally means 'chicken BBQ made Thai', and is only about a quarter mile from here, so it's an easy walk. And, I can point out a few places of interest along the way. Also, you need to know in Thai culture, the women walk behind the men, even if they're married. Only a prostitute will walk beside a man. But, since we're Americans, we can bend the rule a little, and Mary can walk between us, if she's half a step back. Is that okay with you, Mary?"

Mary laughed and replied, "Seriously? Well, I can live with that."

I added, "There's one other thing you need to know about Thai culture. There's no physical touching between men and women in public; even husbands and wives, except when dancing, in a theater, or when riding in a vehicle. When seated at a table, men and women sit opposite each other. When you ride in a săawm-law, a 3-wheeled vehicle, or on a bus together, David, do not put your arm around Mary. Men only do that with prostitutes. Also, you'll see men walking around arm in arm together. They're not gay. It's just a sign of camaraderie in the Thai culture."

David said, "Sandii, thanks for the lesson on Thai etiquette, I certainly don't want to do anything to have someone think Mary's a prostitute. So let's go because I'm starved."

From the lane to the Jomsurong Hotel, we turned right onto Phoklang Road. Pointing ahead to the Thao Suranari Monument, I told them the story of how she plotted the defeat of the invading Laos Army. Turning left onto Rajadamnern Road, I pointed left at the Sri Pattana Hotel where I stayed, then right at the Suranari Hall Museum, and then left at Vatmung Lane to the nightclub saying, "That's where I go ballroom dancing on my nights off. They have an eight-string orchestra, a 2-Bhat cover charge, and three tiers of tables. Generally, the

1st tier is for those over 50, the 2nd tier for people in their 30s and 40s, and the 3rd tier for the younger set in their teens and 20s."

Approaching the end of Rajadamnern Road, I pointed to the wall around the Phayap Temple Complex to our right across the moat, explaining it contained not only the large temple but also buildings for the monks to sleep, eat, and study in. Also, how the moat formed a 4-mile perimeter around old Korat. Pointing to our left at the end of the road, I said, "There's the Thai BBQ place. David, how spicy do you like your BBQ'd chicken?"

David replied, "I like my BBQ very spicy."

Entering the restaurant, I exchanged Sàwàtdiis with the pretty Thai waitress and said in Thai, "Table for three people, a little bit spicy chicken and three Pepsis."

The waitress led us to a table and left to get our order, as Mary sat across the table from me and David. When the waitress returned with a BBQ'd chicken on a platter, a large bowl of rice, three bottles of Pepsi and tableware for each of us, David asked, "Is this whole chicken just for us?"

I replied, "In Thailand when they cook a chicken it means the whole bird. But you don't have to eat the head, David. And anything leftover they'll put in a box for you. So, dig in."

David cut off a drumstick, took a bite and said, "Wow, this is very spicy, but really tasty."

I responded, "Good, so the next time you come here, David, be sure to order the 'little bit spicy' chicken," and Mary laughed.

As we ate, I explained, "There are no off-the-shelf stores in Korat, and all clothing and shoes are custom made. And don't pay the asking price, as it's a personal insult to the vendor if you don't argue down the price, and the asking price is at least double the expected price. Also, the more Thai you speak, the better the price, so you might check out the Thai language classes at the Camp's Education Center."

Walking back up Rajadamnern Road after lunch, I explained, "In Asian cultures, women are second-class citizens. Though education in Thailand is required for all children through 8th grade, when a 14-year-old graduates from the 8th grade, she's considered a full-grown woman but still the property of her father. As such, the father can either sell her as a bride under Thailand's dowry system, find her a menial job with half her wages going to her father, or sell her as a prostitute to a bar or brothel; unless the father is rich enough to pay for her higher education. A lot of girls try to become a tîi-lók, a live-in-lover, for an American who then pays the father $5 a month. If she's lucky, a lot of the guys marry their tîi-lók and take them home, where they make the perfect subservient wife.

"David, most of the tîi-lóks with the guys in your Company are 16 and 17, and some as young as 14. I know a guy who'd been dating a beautiful girl, and when she offered to be his tîi-lók he turned her down, as he learned she was 14. Everybody thought he was stupid to do so. Now, she's happily another guy's tîi-lók. Also, I fell in love with a gorgeous, 16-year-old woman. One day we're happily in love and thinking of getting married, the next day she was gone, sold by her father to marry a rich Thai. It's like my Mom says, 'It may not be right, but that's the way it is.' Besides, there's places Stateside where it's normal for 14 and 15-year-old girls to get married. So it's not a bad thing, it's just the way things are in Thailand."

Pointing to our right, just before we turned left to cross over onto Mahat Thai Road, I said, "That's the Ming Ter Restaurant. It's close by and has good Thai food at a good price."

On Mahat Thai road, I led David and Mary into the clothing shop. As the owner I exchanged Sàwàtdiis, she said, "I so happy to see you again, mi-sa-ta Sandii."

I responded in Thai, "Mrs. Poomsan, you honor me with your greeting. This man is an Army Officer and my boss. His wife wants to buy a beautiful silk dress. If you're good to her, she will bring her friends and buy many dresses," and in English, "Mrs. Poomsan, this is Mrs. Price. Mrs. Price, this is Mrs. Poomsan. I told her you want to buy a beautiful silk dress, and if you're happy with the dress, you may buy more dresses from her. She'll show you some magazines, from which you'll pick out the style you want. Meanwhile, there's something I want to show David."

Leaving the shop, David said, "Is it okay to leave Mary here?"

I replied, "Unless you want to be bored to death for the next half hour, she'll be fine. Besides, there's a good bookstore near here where you can buy an English-Thai dictionary."

Returning twenty minutes later with the dictionary David bought, Mary excitedly showed us the picture of a lovely cocktail dress and said, "Mrs. Poomsan can make me this beautiful dress with silk for only ten dollars."

Looking sternly at Mrs. Poomsan, I said in Thai, "You dishonor me with this expensive cost. You make beautiful silk dresses for Glûaimaai and Lompèt for 100 Baht."

She replied, "But Mrs. Price is a tall woman, so it will take more silk to make the dress."

I responded, "Okay, 120 Baht. But it must be ready for a fitting Tuesday morning."

When she nodded her head, I turned to Mary and said, "Mrs. Poomsan said, as you're a special customer, the dress will only cost six dollars and be ready for a fitting Tuesday morning."

Leaving the shop after Mary's measurements were taken and David paid the 60-Baht deposit, I said, "See, if you can speak some Thai, you can get a better price. Now, how about we stop at a cafe for a Pepsi, and I'll introduce you to a 14-year-old girl I've just agreed to teach English and ballroom dancing to, to increase her chances to be a tîi-lók for an American."

Entering the cafe two doors up Mahat Thai Road, Lompèt hurried to me with a big smile. As we exchanged Sàwàtdiis, I said, "Lompèt, this is my boss and his wife. I brought them to meet my girlfriend and have a Pepsi." Then turning to David and Mary, I said, "This is my student, Lompèt."

After they exchanged Sàwàtdiis, Lompèt quickly led us to a table and went to get our Pepsis. As we sat down, Mary said, "Lompèt's a very pretty little woman. I'd think she'd have no problem finding a Thai husband."

I responded, "That's the problem, she's a little woman. No Thai man will marry a little woman, as little women like Lompèt mostly die in childbirth. Her best option is to learn some English and American dancing and become a tîi-lók for an American. My last student just became the tîi-lók for an American man who wants to marry her."

Leaving the cafe, David said, "Now I understand when you said, 'it's just the way things are in Thailand,' Sandii. It's like they say, 'when in Rome, do like the Romans do'."

I took them to the cobbler shop, where they each had their feet cast for molds and ordered a pair of shoes. We then went to the tailor shop and David ordered some silk shirts and cotton pants. On the way back to the Jomsurang Hotel, I led them past the Action Theater and told them how they could watch Japanese Samurai movies for one Baht each, and that many of the spaghetti westerns we enjoyed watching were copied from those movies. By the time we'd returned to their Hotel, it was 4:00, and they thanked me profusely for my time and help to take them shopping. I then walked to the Reception Desk and said to Dhoi in Thai, "Sàwàtdii, beautiful lady. I will see you again soon."

Dhoi shyly replied, "Thank you very much, Sandii. Sàwàtdii," as Suumii sitting next to her giggled at her bashfulness.

Returning to my Hotel, I lay on the bed and cat-napped until 5:00, when I heard a knock on my door. Opening the door, I saw Súusîi rush into my room with her yellow silk blouse unbuttoned and her luscious breasts exposed. As I quickly shut the door, she dropped her blouse to the floor, and throwing her arms around my neck, we passionately kissed each other.

Cupping Súusîi's enticing firm breasts in my hands, I felt my raising arousal for her pushing against my pants. Reaching her right hand down and feeling my growing lust for her, she moaned in Thai, "oh, my darling, I have ached for you so much since Wednesday and I feel you aching for me, too."

When our clothes had fallen to the floor, Súusîi grabbed my left hand, pulled me willingly to the bed, and pushed me back onto the bed. Straddling my groin, she induced the head of my lusting engorged shaft into the opening of her love canal, and as the opening expanded with her undulating hips pushing me into her, she moaned, "I love you are my boyfriend and desire me so much, my darling."

After we'd satisfied the lust we had for each other in orgasmic release and she lay gasping on my chest, I breathlessly said, "Thank you for serving me desert before dinner."

Súusîi giggled in response, "Oh no, my darling. That was an appetizer. I'll serve you dessert after dinner," as she wiggled her voluptuous hips enticingly against my groin.

After enjoying our shower together, we went to the Ming Ter for dinner. As we asked each other questions over dinner, I learned Súusîi was in her second year of college, so she was fifteen and not sixteen as I thought. This also explained why her English was not as good as Julli's.

Leaving the Ming Ter, we met David and Mary as they entered. I said, "David and Mary, this is my girlfriend, Súusîi. She's a student at Suranari College. Súusîi, this is my boss, David, and his lovely wife, Mary."

Súusîi held out her right hand and said, "Bery ni-sa to meet you, Da-bit and Ma-ry."

David and Mary shook her and in turn and said, "Very nice to meet you, too, Suzy."

As they passed, I heard Mary say, "She looks a little young for college," and David chuckled, "Mary, in Thailand, College is what we call High School."

Returning to my room, I slowly seduced Súusîi with sensual foreplay, during which she desiringly moaned, "Châi dâai! Châi daai!" Then as I pushed my engorged shaft deep into her taut, wet love canal, Súusîi moaned, "Oh yes, my darling, I love you so much. Your lovemaking and desire for me make me happy you are my boyfriend."

When our vigorous copulation ended in mutual orgasmic satisfaction, and Súusîi lay contentedly on my chest with her luscious hips possessively holding me inside her, I said, "My darling, dessert is best served slowly," and Súusîi wiggled her desiring hips and giggled, "and hot."

After we playfully washed the crud from each other in the shower, we dressed and left for the night club. Entering the night club, I saw David and Mary with smiling faces waving for us to join them on the 3rd tier. As Súusîi followed me up the steps, I saw that Mary was sitting properly across the table from David. As we approached the table, they both stood to greet us, and we exchanged hellos. When we were seated at the table, with Mary and Súusîi sitting opposite David and me, David faced me and said, "Mary and I love to dance, and this is a great place for ballroom dancing. We're really glad you pointed it out to us," and with a nod toward Súusîi and a wink to me, he added, "It's just the way things are in Thailand."

CHAPTER 32

I MUST BE IN HEAVEN

Súusîi and I had a fun time with David and Mary that evening in the night club. When we took breaks from ballroom dancing, which David and Mary were very good at, Mary asked Súusîi questions about what it was like to be a woman in the Thai culture. As Súusîi's English language skills were limited, Mary used simple words and the need for me to translate were limited mostly to the complicated concepts, like Thailand's dowry and education system. By the end of the evening David and Mary had a clearer picture of the oppressive nature of Thai culture on it's women as second-class citizens, even in the middle-income families.

Most of the evening, though, I spent dancing, and enjoying the look and feel of Súusîi's enticing body in my arms. I didn't do any sexy Tango moves with her until just before 10:00, which Súusîi eagerly enjoyed. Making our excuses to David and Mary, Súusîi and I left the night club.

Walking quickly to my Hotel room, Súusîi and I wasted no time to begin vigorously venting the pent up lust we had for each other with passionate lovemaking. When our copulation was satisfied in orgasmic release, and Súusîi lay panting on my chest with her lovely legs straddling my groin holding me inside her taut love canal, she gasped, "I love you very much, my darling. Your desire for me and your love-making give me much pleasure and happiness."

I responded, "Your desire for my lovemaking makes me happy you're my girlfriend, my darling."

She asked, "Is it okay if I sleep next to you in your arms feeling surrounded by your love for me, my darling?"

I replied, "Very okay, my darling," and rolled to my right side, where Súusîi spooned in my arms with luscious butt snug against my groin. As I cuddled her sensuous body warmingly in my arms, she said, "Next weekend, there's a big festival in Phimai with long boat races, cultural performances, colorful religious processions and a light show. If you have the day off, maybe we can spend the day together there. And, if David and Mary can go, too, it would be good as we need another couple to go with us. Would you like to do that?"

I replied, "Next Saturday is an off day for me, and as Phimai is only 30 miles from Korat, then I'd very much like to do that with you. Also, I'm sure David and Mary would like to do that, too, with you to show them around and me to translate for them." And, we spent the next little while, before we fell asleep, discussing how we could get there and back on the busses that left every 20 minutes from Korat's Bus Terminal 2 to Phimai for 20 Bhat, and that it was a 1-1/2 hour trip.

Waking to my 3:30 wake-up call and feeling aroused by Súusîi's sensuous butt pressed enticingly against my groin, I began kissing her tenderly on her neck and caressing the womanly curves of her voluptuous body. I felt Súusîi's luscious hips begin undulating against my groin with desire in response to my growing arousal and seductive foreplay, as she moaned with pleasure, "It feels so good to wake up to your desire for me, my darling."

When I felt the hot nectar from Súusîi's love canal wetting my groin, I lifted her onto her knees. As I pushed fully into her from behind, she moaned, "Châi dâai! Châi daa!" and began to vigorously gyrate her luscious hips in sync with my long, rhythmic thrusts. With my distending orgasmic thrust, Súusîi yelled, "Yes! Yes! Give me your sexual desire, my darling."

Laying together for awhile, we enjoyed the feel of being in each other's arms. Later, as we washed the crud from each other in the shower, Súusîi began to sensuously wash my groin. Feeling my rising arousal for her in her hands, she cooed, "oh yes, my darling, I feel your desire growing for me and it's a long time till Tuesday night, please give me more of your sexual desire."

As she turned around and enticed me with her lusting love canal, I grabbed her luscious hips with my hands and vigorously made love with her again. When my climax distended fully into her love canal, she moaned with satisfaction, "My darling, I'm so happy with your desire for me."

When we had dried each other off, and Súusîi was helping me dress in my OD BDUs to leave for Camp Friendship, she cooed, "I love very much that I'm your girlfriend and you desire very much making love to me, that I ache very much for you when we're apart. But, feeling your sexual desire inside me makes me happy while I wait to be loved by you again, my darling."

As I passionately kissed Súusîi goodbye, I caressed the sumptuous womanly curves of her nude body, and then said with desire, "I, too, will be aching to give you my sexual desire Tuesday night, my beloved girlfriend."

After morning formation, I walked to Company C's HQ, and entering it, saw Lt. Price in his jungle fatigues talking with a Sgt. and a PFC, who I presumed was the CQ and his runner, as it was Sunday. As Lt. Price turned to leave, he saw me and asked, "Specialist Lynch, what can I help you with?"

I replied, "Sir, can I speak privately with you?"

He answered, "Mâi bpén rai. You can talk with me on the way to the bus. I presume you're on your way back to Korat."

I responded, "Thank you, Sir. Well, first, who do I see to extend my tour here?"

Lt. Price replied, "I'll have PFC Schultz put the forms in your mail slot. So, you want to stick around and enjoy the company of all these beautiful young Thai women?"

I answered, "Actually, Sir, the word coming from the guys we know at Ft. Huachuca, Arizona, is it's safer here in this Theater of War, than at Ft. Huachuca, which is where most of us with time left on our enlistment goes to from the Vietnam War."

Lt. Price responded, "Well, that explains why over half the men in this Company have requested tour extensions. What's the second thing?"

I replied, "Súusîi and I were wondering if you and Mary would like to join us on a day trip to a big festival this Saturday?" Explaining to him where Phimai was, some of the activities, and how we would travel to and from Phimai, I concluded, "and I wouldn't be fraternization as I'll be along as your translator and Súusîi will be your guide, since she's familiar with Phimai."

Lt. Price responded, "That sounds like something Mary and I would like to see. And you're right, we'll need you to translate for us, so it won't be fraternization. But, it'll depend on the Army. So, if nothing comes up, why don't you two meet us at the Jomsurang Hotel Lobby at 9:00 on Saturday morning?"

I answered, "Súusîi will be very glad to hear that when I see her at the night club Tuesday night," as we boarded the Thai bus for Korat that was nearly full of Soldiers leaving after their morning formations.

Arriving at my Hotel room, I stripped down to my boxers and lay on the bed waiting for Lompét's knock on the door. As I lay there, I thought of the previous morning, how upset Lompét was at my being dressed and not ready for lovemaking as I'd been with Glûaimâai. Also, that she hadn't worn a bra or panties, and was already wet with lust for me. With the memory of her petite body on the bed eagerly enticing me to make love with her, I began to feel my arousal for Lompét.

Hearing Lompét's knock on my door, I rose from the bed, quickly opened the door and saw her pretty, smiling face looking up at me with longing as she entered. I saw she was wearing no bra under the pretty pink blouse she wore with a black skirt. When Lompét glanced down and saw my lust for her lifting the front of my boxers, she squealed with delight, "Oh yes, my darling, I'm so happy to see your desire for me."

Dropping the large bag she was carrying in her hands to the floor, she leapt up into my arms, wrapped her arms tight around my neck and her lovely legs desiringly around my waist, and began to kiss me passionately. Returning her kiss with my own passion, I felt Lompét's wet crotch gyrating with lust against my abdomen as I carried her to the bed. Releasing her grasp from around my neck and waist, I set her down on the floor. Anxiously stripping off her blouse and shirt, Lompét said, "My darling, I woke this morning wanting to feel our desire for me," and throwing herself backward onto the bed, the raised her inviting legs high and wide, added, "Please hurry, my darling, I ache very much for your lovemaking."

Taking the tube of K-Y Gel from the dresser, I squeezed the lube into her love canal. Then repeating our previous method, Lompét straddled my groin and undulating her luscious hips, she quickly stretched the sheath of her love canal with the head of my lust filled shaft. Taking it fully into her, she moaned happily, "Oh yes, my darling, my body was made for lovemaking with you."

When our vigorous lovemaking fulfilled our pent up lust for each other with orgasmic release, and we lay on the bed sexually spent. With Lompét's head on my chest and her luscious hip straddling my groin, she cooed, "My darling, I love that we'll have all day and night together for lovemaking, to see a movie, go to a party, and learn English from you with the textbook Glûaimâai gave me. It's so wonderful to be your girlfriend, my darling."

I responded tiredly, "And I love that you're my girlfriend, also, my darling. But, I was up early this morning for my meeting at Camp Friendship, so I'll need a little sleep after we shower. You can sleep with me or study English as I sleep. Okay, my darling?"

She replied, "After being with you yesterday, I had to work late last night. I'd very much like to sleep cuddled in your arms, my darling."

After showering together, Lompét showed me that the large bag she'd brought contained the English textbook, her bra and panties, and the sexy red dress Glûaimâai had given her, which she hung up in the wardrobe next to my clothes. Then we spooned in the nude on the bed with my arms wrapped warmly around her diminutive body fitting comfortably against my torso and legs and slept for a few hours.

Waking to Lompét's sensuous little butt pressed against my groin and feeling my arousal for her, I began my foreplay, to which she eagerly responded. When our vigorous lovemaking had satiated our lust for each other, we were famished for food. After a quick shower to wash the crud off and getting dressed, Lompét properly followed me to the Ming Ter. As we ate lunch, I taught her several common phrases and the English names for items we could see, coaching her through sounds that were foreign to the Thai language.

Finishing our lunch, Lompét then walked behind me to the Action Theater. Arriving before Glen and Súpa, I continued to point out objects and give their English names until Glen and Súpa came. While we did this, I found Lompét to be a very bright and apt student.

Entering the Theater, Súpa and Lompét sat between Glen and me with our hands in our laps. At the first bloodletting by the Samurai, Lompét grabbed my left arm and hid her pretty face behind it, saying, "Forgive me, this is my first Samurai movie."

I patted her hands patiently and said, "It honors me as your boyfriend to protect you, and I like the feel of your hands on my arm," and saw Súpa smile with approval. For the rest of the movie, Lompét happily held my arm with her small hands, leaning her pretty face on it, ready to hide from any bloodletting action. At the end of the movie, I asked what she thought of it, and she replied, "It was very exciting and liked it very much, but I've not seen so much blood before. Thank you for protecting me."

Returning to my Hotel room, we again made love. With the repeated stretching of Lompét's love canal, she found it easier to take my engorged shaft fully into her. When our copulation resulted in the desired rush of orgasmic release, Lompét breathlessly moaned, "My darling, I love your desire for me to have so much lovemaking."

I responded, "My darling, the sight of your beautiful body gives me desire for much lovemaking with you."

Taking a quick, cleansing showered together, we then lay nude next to each other on the bed, and with the textbook, I showed Lompét how the English alphabet worked and the sounds each letter represented. After an hour, I went to the dresser, and retrieving the Kama Sutra book, I again lay next to her sumptuous nude body and explained, "This is the textbook for our sex lessons. You'll look through the book, pick the position you want to learn. Then we'll discuss how it's done, and after the party tonight, we'll make love in that position."

Lompét perused the Kama Sutra book, and after several minutes, she pointed to a page and said, "this looks fun, can we do this one tonight, my darling?"

Discussing how to do the position for a while, Lompét then rolled onto her back, pulled my head to her succulent firm breasts, and as I sucked them in turn into my mouth, she moaned, "My darling, all this talk of lovemaking has wet my desire for you."

Reaching down with my right hand between her widely spread legs, I felt Lompét's womanly nectar flow from her love canal, and my own lust for her enticing body rushed to my loin. Climbing between her inviting spread legs, she raised them high and wide as I began to push the head of my lusting shaft rhythmically into the taut, expanding sheath of her lusting love canal, and Lompét moaned with desire, "Châi daai! Châi dâai!"

After our vigorous lovemaking had climaxed in the rush of our orgasms, Lompét gasped beneath me, "My darling, I love you very much and the sexual desire you give me, makes me happy I'm your girlfriend."

I responded, "My darling, it makes me happy to give my sexual desire to my girlfriend."

After our quick cleansing shower, Lompét dressed in her sexy red silk dress, and I treated her to dinner in the Hotel's restaurant. When we'd finished dinner, I hired a sǎawm-law to take us to the compound, where she made quite the entrance in her red dress at Horn's home. She was also well received when Súpa introduced her to the other three tîi-lóks inside the home. Exiting onto the porch with a bottle of Sing Hǎi Beer, Ronnie asked, "Sandii, where do you keep getting these hot-looking Thai women from?"

I laughed and replied, "The Lord Buddha taken away and the Lord Buddha giveth."

After a few hours of pleasant comradery on the porch, Glen and I decided it was time to leave and told Súpa and Lompét we were ready to go. Exchanging sáwátdiis with everyone on the porch, Glen and I left with our two girls walking behind us. Crossing Jomsurang-yat Road, Glen and Súpa turn right for the Chaophaya Inn to hire a sǎawm-law, as Lompét continued to follow me up Buarong Road toward the Sri Pattana Hotel.

Entering my Hotel room, as we stripped off our clothes, Lompét excitedly said, "My darling, the party was so much fun. The women were so friendly and made me feel like one of them. They told me many things about what it's like to live with and take care of an American man, as it's very different than being with a Thai man. My darling, I'm so lucky you're my boyfriend to teach me these things. I love that my body was made for lovemaking with you, and you desire lovemaking with me so much," and throwing herself backward onto the bed with her enticing legs raised high and wide, she added, "I'm ready for you to teach me this new lovemaking position."

I rhythmically pushed into Lompét's wet, expanding love canal, as her undulating hips lustfully responded, until I was fully in. Then, I easily shifted her diminutive body into the new Kama Sutra position we'd discussed, and vigorously made love until we each experienced the rush of our orgasmic release. Laying entwined together, Lompét gasped, "That lovemaking position was wonderful with you, my darling. I can hardly wait till morning for our lovemaking in another position."

After slowly extracting ourselves, we took a playful shower together. Laying happily beside each other on the bed, I watched my very pretty Lompét as she selected the next Kama Sutra position for our lovemaking in the morning. After we discussed how to effect the position she chose, we spooned contentedly together and went to sleep.

With the 3:30 wake-up call, my lust for Lompét was aroused with the sight and feel of her sensuous body cuddled within my arms and had no problem arousing Lompét's lust for me with my enticing kisses and caresses of the luscious curves of her petite body. When I felt her womanly nectar moisten my lusting groin, I again had little difficulty rhythmically pushing into her tight love canal as her undulating hips lusted to have me fully in her. Shifting Lompét into her chosen Kama Sutra position, we commenced our energetic lovemaking. Achieving the orgasmic rush we desired, she gasped, "I love you very much, my darling, wider than the Earth is my desire for your lovemaking."

I responded, "Then after we go dancing tonight, your desire for my lovemaking will be wider than the sky."

After we showered and Lompét helped me dress in my OD BDUs, I removed a red 100-Bhat bill from my wallet. Handing it to her, I said, "This is for the dressmaker, when you pick up the blue silk dress to wear, then I take you for your dance lesson tonight. I'll pick you up from the cafe at 8:00. Until then, you'll be in my heart, my darling."

Returning to the Company Area with my shopping bag full of clothes to be cleaned, I went to my hooch. There, I drank a cold can of Bud as I changed into a fresh set of jungle fatigues. Leaving my OD BDUs on the pile of my other laundry, I walked to the Mess Hall with Skip, who said, "Glen told us that Glûaimâai is a tîi-lók for someone else. Lompét looks really hot. Is she your tîi-lók?"

I laughed and replied, "No, Skip. She's my new student that I'm teaching English and ballroom dancing to, so she can be a tîi-lók for someone, like I did for Glûaimâai. If you think she's so hot, she'd be happy to be your tîi-lók."

Skip laughed and responded, "You know my Princess is the only tîi-lók I want. So thanks, but no thanks.

After a delicious, filling breakfast and morning formation, Skip and I rode in the back of the truck to the Air Base Site. As I relieved Jack from his night shift, he said, "Workwise, it's been a quiet weekend, except for the 'ding, ding, ding,' from the AP and UPI machines with their Urgent news on the big demonstrations and riots Stateside for this 3-day Veteran's Day weekend. Makes me glad my tour extension has been approved all the way up the chain-of-command. Last week, I received the order for my tour extension."

I responded, "Yea, I talked to the CO yesterday about putting in my request for a tour extension, and he told me over half the men in the Company have extended their tours. What about you, Skip? Are you requesting a tour extension?"

Skip replied, "It's something I've considered, but I'll first have to discuss it with my Princess, Judith."

When Bob entered Operations Room, one of the teletype machines sounded its 'ding, ding, ding." Bob took the flathead screwdriver from the top desk drawer and opened the AP and UPI teletype machines. I watched as he unscrewed something in each machine and then say, "Oh my, there's a malfunction in the alarm circuits in these two tele-type machines. It's too bad we'll be busy with higher priority circuits to make repairs at this time."

After a few outage reports to break up the monotony of a quiet morning, I left on my 10:55 meal run and met Glen in the Mess Hall. I told him about the "malfunctions" of the AP and UPI teletype machines and that I was putting in a tour extension request. Glen responded, "If we still had those AP and UPI circuits tapped into us, I know some guys who'd have ripped them from their racks and tossed them out the door, by now. And, I'm going to put in my tour extension request this week, too. How's things going with Lompét? She sure looked hot last night."

I replied, "She's a pretty smart girl, and picking up on the English okay. And initially, it was difficult to have sex with her. But, with our frequent lovemaking, she's expanded enough to mount her with some ease, and she really enjoys having sex. As for dancing, I'll have to see how it goes tonight. She'll probably need Súpa to show her some of the female dance steps."

Glen responded, "Yes, Súpa said she's worked it out with Lompét last night to be at the cafe this afternoon to show her some steps as she's really afraid she'll disappoint you on the dance floor."

Walking to the Mail Room after lunch, I found the multi-page Tour Extension Request Form in my mail slot and took them with me to the Air Base Site. As I began to fill the Form out, I saw it was no simple matter. Not only did it ask for a signed statement by me as to why I wanted the tour extension, but also signed endorsements from my Team Leader, NCOIC, Company CO, Battalion CO and Brigade CO before it was forwarded to Army Personnel in Washington, DC, for final approval and the orders to be issued. I simply wrote for my reason, "To meet the manpower shortage needs for my MOS in the 442d Sig. Bn."

Getting Bob and Jim to endorse my request was easy enough. And leaving early on my 4:55 meal run, I was able to give it to PFC Schultz in HQ before he left for the day, and watched him put it in the IN Box on his desk. After eating dinner in the Mess Hall with Glen, I went to my hooch, where I packed a few clothes in my shopping bag to take with me to Korat from the Air Base Site.

When I was relieved at 6:45 by John and Larry, I told them about the "malfunction" in the AP and UPI teletype machines, to which they had a good laugh. Then, leaving quickly with my shopping bag, I returned to my Hotel room, where I changed clothes to take Lompét dancing.

Entering the cafe after my half-mile walk from the Hotel, I saw the petite Lompét standing by the front door waiting for me. She looked very enticing in the pale-blue silk dress, which flattered the color of her light tan skin, revealed the lovely tops of her apple-size breasts, and showed off her shapely legs. After we exchanged sáwátdiis, I said in Thai loud enough for the benefit of her fellow workers to hear, "I'm happy to see my girlfriend looks so beautiful in her new dress," to which Lompét gushed with pride, "Thank you, my darling boyfriend."

As I bargained with the sǎawm-law driver in Thai on the price of our ride to the night club, I saw several passing American men give Lompét approving looks and though, "It won't be long before you're some guy's tîi-lók, if I don't decide to keep you for myself."

Entering the night club, I spotted Glen and Súpa waving to us from a table on the 3rd tier. As Lompét followed me up the steps to their table, they both rose to greet us. After we exchanged sáwátdiis and sat down at the table, they told Lompét how beautiful she looked in her blue dress.

After our Pepsi's arrived and we had a refreshing drink, I led Lompét to the dance floor with the sound of a Waltz being played. Finding Súpa had done a fine job teaching Lompét the rhythm and basic steps for the Waltz and Cha, we had fun dancing those together. It was only the Tango I had to teach the rhythm and basic steps for. With the help of Glen and Súpa to show Lompét how to do the Tango as I danced with her, she caught on very quickly.

When it was getting close to 10:00 and the orchestra played a Tango, I then did the sensuous foreplay with Lompét that the Tango allowed. As the music stopped and I was holding her tight in a reverse dip, with my right knee firmly lifting her mons pubis, Lompét gasped, "My darling, I desire you very much. Can we leave right now and make love?"

I replied, "Yes, my darling, we can leave now."

Exiting the night club, Lompét followed, urging me to walk there quickly. Entering my room, she rapidly stripped of her clothes, ran to the bed, and laying on her back with her lovely legs enticingly raised high and wide, Lompét moaned, "Hurry, my darling, I ache very much for your lovemaking."

Pushing my lusting shaft into Lompét's hot, wet love canal, though it was still a tight fit, her rapidly undulating hips made sliding fully into her easier, as she moaned with passionate desire, "Châi dâai! Châi dâai!" When I began to shift Lompét into the Kama Sutra position she'd picked that morning, she yelled urgently, "This way, my darling. Quickly, I need your lovemaking this way." With her luscious hips vigorously gyrating against my groin, Lompét cried loudly, "Dâai! Dâai!" as I saw her lusting body convulse in an orgasmic rush.

As I began my long, rhythmic thrusts, Lompét moaned breathlessly, "I love you very much, my darling. And your sexy dancing filled me with so much desire for you, I thought my body would explode." And when my orgasmic thrust distended deep into her, Lompét yelled, "Yes, my darling, I feel your sexual desire filling me with your love."

When I began to roll onto my back, Lompét stopped me and moaned softly, "Please, my darling, just let me curl up beside you in your arms."

As we spooned, with her petite body snuggling against my torso and legs, and holding my arms tightly around her, Lompét cooed as she fell asleep, "Your lovemaking has filled me with so much joy and happiness, my darling, I must be in Heaven."

CHAPTER 33

No Way Any Vermin Can Escape This Better Mousetrap

Waking to the 3:30 wake-up call, I felt Lompét's petite body cuddled comfortably in my arms with the curve of her luscious, little butt snug against my loin, causing my desire for her to rush to my groin. As I began to gently kiss her neck and sensuously caress the curves of her appealing flesh, Lompét cooed with delight, "I love you very much, my darling, and the desire you have for me." Then, rolling over in my arms, she pushed her firm, apple-size breasts enticingly to my mouth and cooed, "Your reward for lifting me into heaven last night," and moaned with pleasure as I sucked each wholly into my mouth in turn.

After our energetic lovemaking in the Kama Sutra position Lompét chose the previous morning resulted in the orgasmic release of our lust, Lompét gasped, "It is so good waking to your desire for me, my darling."

As we showered together, Lompét lamented, "It's too bad I have to work late and can't go dancing with you tonight, my darling. But, I'm very much looking forward to our dancing and lovemaking Friday night. I had no idea dancing could have on the lovemaking to lift to one into heaven. Now I know why Súpa likes very much to dance with Glín-dii. Still, I am looking forward very much to our lovemaking every morning, my darling."

After we showered, Lompét helped me dress in my jungle fatigues. Then as I desiringly caressed the curves of her luscious, petite body while we passionately kissed goodbye, I thought, "I also am looking forward to our lovemaking, my darling."

Arriving at the Company Area, I walked to the Mess Hall for a delicious breakfast before morning formation. As the Tropo Platoon gathered for formation, Glen, Ronnie and Stony came over to Skip and me, and Ronnie said, "The lumber to build our partitions will be delivered this morning to the Motor Pool. Whichever of you has the 10:55 meal run, try to leave a little early to meet Dan, George and Tommy there to help carry 6 sheets of plywood, 27 of the 2-by-4s and a box of nails to the hooch. Tommy will be at Company Supply before it opens to sign out a couple of hammers and a saw. Then after lunch, Dan, George and Tommy will build the partitions while we're at work. How's that sound to you?"

I replied, "Sounds as slick as hog snot on a doorknob."

Glen laughed and said, "That's what I said, then I had to explain it to these damn-Yankees."

Arriving at the Air Base Site after formation, I explained to Bob about the lumber delivery to the Motor Pool and what needed to be delivered at our hooch to build the partitions. As things were slow that morning, Bob allowed me to leave at 10:45 on my meal run. Driving into the Motor Pool, I saw Dan, George and Tommy, among lots of other guys, pulling sheets of 1/2-inch plywood and 8-foot long 2-by-4 boards from 3 pallets of each, onto their own little pile of lumber. Parking my truck in the end of ¾-ton trucks, I saw the 2½-ton truck from the Tropo Site arrive, and Glen and Stony climb out when it stopped.

Hussling with them over to Dan, George and Tommy, we worked in pairs, each carrying two sheets of plywood to our hooch, which we set edgewise on the ground, leaning them against the hooch's front. Returning to the Motor Poot, two pairs of us then picked up the ends of ten 2-by-4s each, and the third pair picked up the remaining seven with a large box of nails, which we carried to our hooch and set on the grass next to the walkway. With that chore done, we went into our hooch, and each drank a cold can of beer before going to lunch.

While Skip was on his meal run, I discussed with Bob my upcoming day trip on Saturday to the Phimai Festival with Lt. Price, his wife and Súusîi, and how I will act as a translator and Súusîi will be our guide. Bob said, "That's a clever way to get tight with your CO without technically fraternizing. You'll have lots of fun at Phimai's Festival, as it's quite the annual event. But, I don't see how you're able to balance two girlfriends at the same time. I find having one woman keeps me busy enough."

I replied, "First, I'm not trying to 'get tight' with my CO, as he's only temporary until our new Signal Corps Captain arrives in four weeks. It's just he and his wife are needed for Súuzîi and me to go to the Phimai Festival, as she can't go without another couple with us.

"Second, Súuzîi and Lompét are from separate worlds. I think of Súuzîi as my girlfriend, because Lompét will become somebody's tîi-lók after awhile. I doubt Súuzîi's father will be selling her out from under as a bride like Jintana's father did. Besides, I can only be with Súuzîi twice a week so it's nice to have Lompét to be with on those other five days. It may sound a misogynistic, but it's more like polygamy, which I understand use to be legal in Thailand."

Bob responded, "I see your point. If I could only be with Gúlaap twice a week, I'd likely have a second tîi-lók to take up the slack. I'm not sure if polygamy is still legal, but I know 'pan-ra-yaa' means 'wife' and 'á-nú-pan-ra-yaa' means 'minor wife'."

Returning to my hooch on my 4:55 meal run, I saw it had been equally divided into eight areas with three partitions on each side. Each partition was eight feet wide by four feet high, starting from the edge of the wall locker that was edgewise to the sidewall. The 4-by-8 sheets of plywood were nailed to rectangular frames of 2-by-4s, with each upright 2-by-4 end having an extension nailed to a ceiling rafter. The 4-foot height of the partitions allowed for the free circulation of air and some privacy for sleeping. Praising Dan, George and Tommy for a job well done, I gave each one of my cold cans of Bud as I drank one before going to dinner.

Leaving for Korat when I was relieved by John and Larry at 6:45, I had entered my Hotel room by 7:30. As I stripped off my jungle fatigues, I heard an unexpected knock on my door, and quickly pulled my pants back up. Opening the door, I was pleasantly surprised to see Súuzîi enter my room. Dropping her purse on the floor, she wrapped her arms around my neck and gave me a quick, passionate kiss. Then, releasing my neck and stepping back, she said, "please forgive me, my darling, but I couldn't wait until after we danced to feel your desire for me," as she unbuttoned her light green blouse, exposing her luscious, firm breasts.

Feeling my arousal for Súuzîi, I quickly pulled off my pants and boxers. Then, following her to the bed as she slipped off her dark green skirt, I saw she wore no panties over he sensuously swaying butt. Turning to face me as she lay on the bed, Súuzîi saw my rising lust for her and cried out in delight, "I knew you've been desiring my love for you," as she enticingly raised her lovely legs high and wide to receive me into her love canal wet with desire.

Laying between her inviting legs, I pushed rhythmically into her taut, love canal as she yelled with pleasure, "Yes, my darling, I've ached for you very much." With her luscious hips undulating with lust to speed my penetration, I rapidly slid fully into her. Then, shifting her writhing body into the Kama Sutra position Lompét and I had used that morning, Súuzîi moaned with joy, "Yes, my darling, Julii said you know many lovemaking positions."

When our vigorous lovemaking satisfied our lust for each other, climaxing in our orgasmic release, Súuzîi grasped, "That was wonderful, my darling. I love your desire for me so much. Now I can enjoy dancing in your arms without aching for your lovemaking till later."

As we took a playful shower to wash off the crud, I told Súuzîi that David and Mary would go to the Phimai Festival with us, and we were to meet them in the Jomsurong Hotel Lobby at 9:00. She replied excitedly, "That's wonderful, my darling, as we'll have time to make love before then. After three days of no lovemaking, we'll be crazy with desire for each other."

We then happily dressed and left for the night club, with Súuzîi walking properly behind me. Arriving at the night club, I saw David and Mary waving to us from a table on the 3rd tier, and Súuzîi followed me up to their table, where they stood to great us. As we sat down after exchanging sáwátdii's, Mary slowly said, "Súuzîi, this Phimai Festival sounds like fun. Can you tell me more about it?"

Súuzîi excitedly replied, "It bery bik in Nakhon Ratchasima Provint," then she looked at me and said in Thai, "My darling, I don't know the English words. Can you translate for me?"

When I explained this to David and Mary, David said, "That's why you two are going with us, Sandii. Without Súuzîi, we'd get lost or not understand what's happening. And, without you to translate, we won't understand what Súuzîi will be telling us."

For the rest of the evening, when we weren't dancing, Súuzîi answered their questions in Thai, and I'd translate her answer. By the time Súuzîi and I left, after dancing a sexy Tango, David and Mary were thrilled at the prospect of what they'd experience at the Phimai Festival.

With the pent up lust Súuzîi and I had for each other from our sexy Tango dance, on entering my Hotel room, we rapidly stripped and jumped onto the bed to feast on our lust with vigorous lovemaking. Shifting Súuzîi to a Kama Sutra position Glúaîmáai especially liked, she was enraptured with the greater pleasure experienced with her orgasm. After my orgasmic thrust distended into her, grasped with delight, "Amazing, my darling. Your lovemaking is amazing, my beloved. We must make love like that again in the morning."

Rolling to my right side, Súuzîi placed herself facing me in my arms, with her pretty face snuggled on my chest, under my chin. I felt Súuzîi's firm breasts on my abdomen and her groin pressed desiringly against my right thigh, with her right leg between my legs. As we went to sleep she cooed, "I love you, my darling. Being the woman you desire so much, makes me glad to have you as my beloved boyfriend."

Waking to the 3:30 knock on my door, Súuzîi lifted her lovely face up, kissing me passionately. Feeling her firm breasts enticingly rubbing my chest and her undulating hips gyrating her loins desiringly against my groin, I reached down with my hands and grabbed her luscious butt, pulling her tight against my lusting arousal for her.

When I felt her feminine honey flow from her love canal, I rolled Súuzîi on her back, and climbing between her inviting legs raised wide to receive me, I pushed my lusting shaft fully into her taut love canal. Then arranging our wanton bodies in the Kama Sutra position she desired, we vigorously made love. After our lust for each other was satiated with the orgasmic rush of our climaxes, Súuzîi gasped, "Yes, my darling, your lovemaking is amazing."

After lying together in the afterglow of our lovemaking for a while, we rose from the bed and showered together. Súuzîi sensuously enticed me to make love to her again, and when she felt my orgasmic thrust distend into her love canal, she happily moaned, "I love the feel of your sexual desire, and looking forward to Saturday morning to feel all the sexual desire you've saved for me."

Passionately kissing Súuzîi goodbye and caressing the enticing curves of her voluptuous body, I thought, "As 'faang-ying' means both 'girlfriend' and 'wife,' then I'll think of you as my 'pan-ra-yaa' and of Lompét as my 'á-nú-pan-ra-yaa'," and said, "My darling, you're correct, Saturday is too long a time without making love with you. Can you be here at 4:00 Thursday as I don't need to leave for work until 5:00?"

Súuzîi squealed happily, "Yes, my darling. I leave school at 3:30 and can be here at 4:00 to make love with you. I love you very much, my darling," and looking into her happy, almond-shaped eyes, I replied desiringly, "And I love you very much, too, my darling," as I left for Camp Friendship.

Exiting the Thai bus at my Company Area and going to my hooch, I drank a cold can of Bud as I exchanged sáwátdiís with Skip in his newly partitioned space before going to my own space and changed into a fresh set of OD BDUs. When we were ready, I left with Skip for the Mess Hall to have a hardy breakfast before formation.

Leaving for Korat when formation was over, I returned to my Hotel room. Having stripped to my boxers, I lay on the bed and thought of my luscious, petite Lompét as I waited for her knock on my door, and began to feel my arousal for her.

Hearing her knock, I opened the door, and seeing my desire for her, she happily yelled, "Yes, my darling, I have much desire for you, too," and passionately kissed me as I rapidly removed her blouse and skirt from her sensuous body. Then, picking up her desiring nude body and carrying her to the bed, I placed Lompét on it. Laying between her enticing, upraised legs, I rhythmically pushed into her lusting love canal as she moaned with delight, "Chái dáai! Chái dáai!"

Attaining full penetration, we shifted to the Kama Sutra position we'd discussed the previous morning, and energetically made love. Experiencing the rush of our orgasms, Lompét gasped with delight, "I love very much the desire you have for my small body," then stroking my shaft with her taut love canal, "and that I was made for lovemaking with you, my darling."

I responded, "Yes, my darling, I also love that you were made for love-making with me," as I thought, "and that you're my 'á-nú-pan-ra-yaa."

After we laid on the bed side by side for awhile, selecting and discussing the Kama Sutra position for our lovemaking the next morning, we began to take a fun shower together. Seeing my arousal as I playfully fondled her apple-size breasts, Lompét moaned, "Yes, my darling, fill me with more of your sexual desire," as she turned around and enticed me with her desiring love canal.

When we'd finished our lovemaking in the shower, it was time for Lompét to quickly dress and leave for work. After we passionately kissed goodbye, I said, "I love you my darling, and look forward to seeing you in the cafe at 11:00 for your English lesson."

Lompét giggled, "I love you, too, my darling, and wish my English lessons could be as much fun as my lovemaking lessons."

After Lompét left, I slept for a few hours. Waking refreshed, I dressed and left for the cafe. Entering the cafe, I saw Lompét standing by the entrance door, where we exchanged sáwátdiis before she led me proudly to a table near the right sidewall. Taking my order for chicken fried rice and Pepsi, she soon returned with my lunch and the English textbook, and we began the English lesson in earnest as I ate my lunch.

I worked with Lompét helping her correctly say the words she had learned from the textbook. This was a real problem for her, as it was for all Thais, as English had so many consonant sounds that did not exist in Thai. At 3:30, I returned to my Hotel room, where I changed into my OD BDUs before leaving for Camp Friendship.

Entering my hooch, I grabbed a cold can of Bud from the mini-fridge. Then greeting Skip, Dan, Ronnie and Stony, who were sitting at the table in their T-shirts, drinking beer, smoking cigarettes, and playing Double-Deck Pinochle, I said, "It sure feels homier in here with these petitions up," to which everyone agreed.

When the bugle call sounded for Mess at 5:00, they finished the hand being played and put on their OD BDU shirts, except for Dan, who was dressed in civilian clothes. As we walked to the Mess Hall, I asked, "So, Dan, what've you got on tap for tonight? You going to Korat?"

Dan replied, "I'm a 2-digit midget who's going home clean. So, I won't be going to Korat, but to the Air Base Library. I heard they've got the new Mamas and Papas' album I'd like to copy to my collection. How about you? The guys say you've got a hot, new tîi-lók."

I answered, "She's not my tîi-lók. I'm teaching English and ballroom dancing to improve her chances to become a tîi-lók. Actually, I have a girlfriend I go out with. In fact, we're going on a day trip to the Phimai Festival on Saturday. She told me it's really something to see."

Dan responded, "Yea. I went last year. You'll have a lot of fun."

After dinner, everyone returned to the hooch for a last cold beer before going to the Day Room and wait for our rides to work, except Dan, who went to the Air Base Library. When Tommy arrived with our truck, he said, "Last night was really bad with everyone Stateside returning from their 3-day Veteran's Day weekend, so you'll want to read the Site Log. And, today we had to call in Brown to replace some wiring. But, your night shift should be okay."

I responded, "Thanks for the info, Tommy, and for building the partitions. They look really good."

Arriving at the Air Base Site, I relieved Jack, who laughed as he informed us the alarm circuits in the AP and UPI machines were still out, as he quickly left for Korat. While waiting for Bob to finish the Shift Change Report, Skip and I read the Site Log entries for last night, and found they were extensive. But, several of our outages showed we had a vermin issue, as some of our subfloor wiring was chewed on and had to be replaced.

When Bob entered the Operations Room, he said, "You two hold the fort for a minute, while I get a few things from the NCO Club." Several minutes later, he returned with a ceramic saucer and plate, the metal tops cut from a 16-ounce can and a 1-gallon can, and a small piece of raw meat. Setting these on the desk, he left again and returned with the test cart and toolbox from the Supply/Repair Room, saying, "And now to build a better mousetrap."

As Bob removed the cover of the oscilloscope, he explained, "As you know, the cathode-ray tube requires high-voltage and high-current, and it's the current that kills you, not the voltage."

We watched as Bob crimped large alligator clips to each end of two long pieces of heavy gauge wire. Unplugging the connector that carried the high current to the back of the cathode-ray tube to produce the energy beam for illuminating the trace on the phosphorescent screen of the oscilloscope, he clipped the end of one wire to the plug, The other end of the wire he clipped to the smaller metal lid. Then, he clipped an end of the other wire to the oscilloscope's frame and its loose end to the larger metal lid.

Pushing the test cart to the back of the Operations Room, he removed a floor section and carefully set the ceramic plate on the bare concrete subfloor. On top of the plate he set the larger metal lid, the ceramic saucer, and the smaller metal lid with the piece of meat in the middle of it. Carefully replacing the floor section, Bob turned on the oscilloscope and said, "Now we wait," as he walked to the desk and stared his entries in the Site Log.

Awhile later, I hear a loud "snap" at the back of the Operations Room. Skip and I followed Bob to the back. When he lifted the floor section I saw a dead rat lying beside the contraption. By the time I left on my 10:55 meal run, it had killed two more rats.

While working on my night shifts, I'd developed the habit of writing my weekly letter to Linda. This week, I wrote about my decision to extend my tour by six months. This would allow me to be discharged from the Army five months early to move to New Jersey and find a job as a microwave radio repairman, instead of languishing and being away from her for those five months at Ft. Huachuca, AZ.

Before the end of our shift, Bob had turned off and then disconnected the clips from the oscilloscope and reassembled it. Removing the piece of meat from his "better mousetrap," Bob replaced the floor section. As Bob pushed the test cart back to the Supply/Repair Room, he said, "We'll leave the trap there and use it again tomorrow night to make sure none of these vermin have escaped my 'better mousetrap'," and I thought, "There's no way any vermin can escape this 'better mousetrap'."

CHAPTER 34

I HAVE A PART OF YOU TO LOVE ALL MY LIFE

aking the 6:35 meal run, I quickly ate a delicious breakfast before walking rapidly to my hooch. After putting a few changes of clothes in my large shopping bag, I walked at a fast pace to the main street, where I boarded a Thai bus for Korat. Returning to my Hotel room, I stripped to my boxers and lay on the bed in wait of Lompét's knock. Thinking of how best to initiate this new Kama Sutra position she had chosen, I became aroused with my desire for Lompét when she knocked on my door.

When I opened the door, Lompét saw my arousal and squealed with delight, "Yes, my darling, I also have ached for your lovemaking," as she ran to the bed, stripping off her clothes and throwing herself backward onto the bed. She then moaned with longing, "I love your desire for me, my darling, and I desire you very much," as she invitingly lifted her enticing legs high and wide to receive me.

Instead, I seized Lompét's luscious hips with my strong hands, lifted her up and turn her petite body over onto her knees. Then, pushing fully into her tight, wet love canal, we easily move into Kama Sutra position we'd discussed, and began our energetic lovemaking. When the lust we had for each other was expended in the rush of our orgasms and we lay in the afterglow of our lovemaking, Lompét cooed, "I dreamed all night of your lovemaking, my darling, and woke aching to feel you loving me. I'll be so happy sleeping in your arms after we dance and make love tomorrow night."

After we had fun showering together, we lay on the bed next to each other, as Lompét happily selected the Kama Sutra position for our lovemaking tomorrow morning. Discussing how to perform in this position, I began to playfully caress her luscious, petite body. Lompét soon rolled on her back and desiringly moaned, "my darling, I ache for your lovemaking." Climbing between her craving legs, I had no problem sliding fully into her taut love canal, wet with her desire for me.

When our vigorous lovemaking culminated in orgasmic release, Lompét gasped, "I love you very much, my darling, and am very happy you're my boyfriend, but I must quickly dress, or I'll be late for work."

Watching Lompét clothe her shapely, petite body, I said, "you have such a beautiful body, my darling, I can't help my desire for lovemaking with you," and she joyfully responded, "and that my body was made for lovemaking with you is wonderful, my darling."

As we passionately kissed goodbye, Lompét caressed my body with her small hands, and then cooed, "your body is so big and strong, my darling, I can't help my desire for lovemaking with you, either."

After Lompét left, I tiredly went to bed and slept for a few hours. Waking refreshed, I quickly showered, dressed and left for the cafe, where Lompét served me lunch and I enjoyed teaching her English till 3:30.

Returning to my Hotel room, I stripped to my boxers and lay on the bed waiting to enjoy Súuzîi's lust for our lovemaking. Soon, I heard her knock on my door and I opened it. Súuzîi cried out when she saw my arousal for her lifting the front of my boxers, "My darling, I love your desire for me so much," as she ran into my arms, and we began to passionately kiss.

Lifting Súuzîi in my strong arms, I carried her to the bed. As I helped her to rapidly remove the clothes from her voluptuous body, she panted, "Yes, my darling, I've ached so much for the desire you have for me."

Turning Súuzîi's nude body over, I lifted her sensuous body by its slender waist, set her down on the knees atop the bed, and holding her luscious hips, pushed fully into her lusting love canal. Then, easily moving with Súuzîi into the Kama Sutra position I'd used with Lompét that morning, we vigorously made love. As she moaned with delight, "My darling, this feels so exciting," I thought, "Practice makes perfect."

When our lust was satiated with the orgasmic rush we desired and we lay in the afterglow of our lovemaking, Súuzîi happily cooed, "I love you very much, my darling, and the feel of your sexual desire shooting into me is very satisfying. I'm glad you decided to make this time to be with me and not wait till Saturday morning to satisfy our love for each other. And, the lovemaking position was so exciting."

I replied, "I'm happy you enjoy my different lovemaking positions, and you were willing to spend this short time with me before I had to leave for work."

After we playfully showered together and were dressing to leave, Súuzîi for home and I for work, she said, "Now I won't be aching for you so much till I see you Saturday morning, my darling. I'm really looking forward to being with you all day and night, and yes, I very much enjoy your different lovemaking positions, it makes me feel more loved by you than just having sex with my boyfriend. I have friends that have sex with their boyfriends and felt very loved at first, but then complain after awhile it feels like their boyfriend is just using them for sex."

When we had passionately kissed goodbye, Súuzîi followed me to the Hotel's entrance, where I hired a săawm-law to take her home and one to take me to the Chainarong Gate to ride a Thai bus to Camp Friendship. Arriving at my Company Area, I'd enough time for dinner in the Mess Hall before I needed to be in front of the Day Room for the ride to work.

At the Air Base Site, Bob left again for the NCO Club to get another piece of meat for his "better mousetrap." But that night I didn't hear the "snap" of success from the trap. As Bob disconnected the clips and reassembled the oscilloscope, he said, "I that solved our vermin problem for now. But, I'm going to set it up each month to make sure it stays that way."

The next morning, I made the 6:35 meal run to deliver our truck to Phizer for the day shift. After a quick breakfast, I walked rapidly to the main street and caught a Thai bus for Korat. Arriving at my Hotel room, I stripped to my boxers and prepared for my next lovemaking lesson with Lompét.

Opening the door when Lompét knocked on it, she happily saw I was aroused with my desire for her. After a passionate kiss, she quickly removed her clothes as she ran to the bed, and we vigerously began our lovemaking session in the Kama Sutra position we'd discussed. When we'd orgasmicly released our lust and enjoyed the pleasure of our afterglow, we happily showered together. Then, Lompét chose our next Kama Sutra position as we lay next to each other on the bed. This time, I kept my desire for her sensuous, petite body in check as we discussed how to perform the position, as having the quicky we had yesterday didn't allow us the time to enjoy the afterglow.

When we'd passionately kissed goodbye and expressed our love for each other, I laid tiredly on the bed and slept for several hours. Then, I dressed and went to the cafe, where I had lunch and enjoyed Lompét's company as I taught her English. As I wasn't going back to the Company Area to eat dinner, I dined at the cafe at 4:00, and saw Lompét happily beam when I left a 2-Bhat tip with the 8 Bhat I'd paid for the lunch and dinner.

Returning to my Hotel room, I stripped and lay on the bed to catch up on the sleep I missed working the night shift. Waking a few hours later, I showered and shaved. Then, putting on a light blue silk shirt to complement the hot pink dress Lompét would wear tonight, I left for the cafe.

Entering the cafe, I saw Lompét standing near the door wearing her hot pink silk dress that gave an enticing glow to her face and the tops of her firm, apple-size breasts showing above the low-cut of her dress. Exchanging sáwátdiis, she followed me out the front door, and as I hired a săawm-law for a ride to the night club, I saw many American eyes looking desiringly at Lompét.

Arriving at the night club, we entered, and I quickly located Glen and Súpa at a table on the 3rd tier. With Lompét following, we went to their table, and exchanging sáwátdiis, Glen said, "Lompét, in that red dress, you looked very sexy, but this pink dress makes you look very desirable, like eating fresh fruit," and Súpa added, "Yes, younger sister, you look very lively in that dress."

As I danced with Lompét, I was enticed by how lively and desirable she looked swirling around in my arms, and loving the sight of her.

When it was close to 10:00, I danced a sensuous Tango with Lompét, and when it ended, she again gasped, "My darling, I desire you very much. Can we leave now and make love?"

Returning quickly to my Hotel room, I rapidly stripped and watched Lompét hastily take off her clothes as she ran to the bed. Then, throwing herself backward onto it, with her shapely legs invitingly raised high and wide, Lompét urgingly moaned with desire, "Hurry, my darling, I ache very much for your lovemaking."

Driving my lusting shaft fully in Lompét's taut, wet love canal, and trusting in the fast rhythm of her undulating hips vigorously lusting for me as she ardently yelled, "Dâai! Dâai!" Then I saw her writhing, petite body convulse in an orgasmic rush, and she gasped, "I love you, my darling. It's more than my small body can hold when your sexy dancing fills me with so much desire for you," and when my orgasmic thrust distended into her, Lompét cried out, "Yes, my darling, I feel your sexual desire filling me with your love."

Laying on my right side, Lompét spooned against my torso and holding my arms like a warm blanket around her, she lovingly cooed as she fell asleep, "My darling, again I'm in heaven filled with your love."

With the 3:30 wake-up call, the feel of Lompét's sensuous, little butt pressed against my groin caused my arousal. Then she wiggled her butt enticingly as she happily cooed, "I love the feel of your desire for me in the morning."

Soon, we were energetically making love in the Kama Sutra position Lompét had picked the morning before. In the afterglow of our orgasmic release, Lompét purred happily, "I love you very much, my darling. Our lovemaking every morning makes me feel happy all day long."

As we playfully showered together, I explained, "My darling, I won't be able to come to the cafe today to teach you English. My boss has given me the great honor to travel with him and his wife to the Phimai Festival as his translator. But, I'll be here tomorrow morning at 8:00 filled with my desire for you."

She responded, "My darling, I'm proud of the great honor your boss gives to my beloved boyfriend."

After Lompét helped me dress in my OD BDUs, and I had desiringly caressed her luscious body as we passionately kissed goodbye, I said, "I love you, my darling, and happy you're my girlfriend," and Lompét responded, "And I love you, too, my darling, and happy you're my boyfriend."

Arriving at my Company Area, I went to the Mess Hall and had a large breakfast to prepare for my busy day before going to formation. After formation, I walked with Jim to catch a Thai bus for Korat and he asked, "Do you have anything special planned for today?"

I replied, "I'm going to the Phimai Festival with Lt. Price and his wife to translate for them. Since I've never been to Phimai before, it should be an interesting day-trip."

Jim laughed in response, "Plus some serious kudos for you."

Entering my room and stripping to my boxers, I lay on the bed and became aroused as I thought of Súuzîi and her sumptuous body. Hearing her knock on my door, I opened it and Súuzîi squealed with joy, "My darling, I'm so glad to see your desire for me," as she dropped her bag on the floor, ran into my arms and kissed me passionately.

Returning Súuzîi's passionate kiss, I lifted her with a bear hug and carried to the bed. Releasing my bear hug, I quickly pulled off my boxers as she rapidly removed her blouse and skirt, revealing she'd worn no bra or panties. Jumping back onto the bed, Súuzîi eagerly raised her shapely legs wide and moaned with want, "I've ached so much to feel your desire for me."

Lying between Súuzîi's inviting legs, I push fully into her taut, lusting love canal. Shifting her luscious body into the Kama Sutra position I used several hours earlier with Lompét, Súuzîi cried out, "Yes, my darling, I love the variety of your lovemaking." And, when our energetic lovemaking culminated in the orgasmic release we strived for, she gasped, "I love you very much, my darling, and your name is apt, as you're 'extremely good' in your lovemaking."

Playfully washing the crud from each other as we showered, Súuzîi happily said, "I'm glad we made love before our day-trip, as I'd have been distracted from the fun at the Phimai Festival with my unrequited desire for your lovemaking," and I laughed, "As it would've also been difficult for me to walk being fully aroused by the sight of your beautiful body."

Arriving at the Jomsurang Hotel at 9:00, Súuzîi entered the Lobby to meet David and Mary as I bargained with two săawm-law drivers to take us the one mile to Bus Terminal 2. By the time Súuzîi returned with David and Mary, one driver had agreed to carry us men for 5

Bhat and the other for 4 Bhat for the women, who were much lighter. Explaining to David and Mary it was Thai custom for Mary and Súuzîi to ride in a săawm-law behind David and me, we climbed on and rode them to Bus Terminal 2 accordingly.

We rode the săawm-law on the maze of roads and lanes that was the shortest distance to Bus Terminal 2 located northwest of Korat on Thailand's Highway 2. There, David bought four bus tickets to Phimai for 20 Bhat each, and Súuzîi pointed out the bus going to Phimai.

Boarding the bus first, I selected two rows of seats on the bus's left side, next to each other and near the front, explaining to David that not only were the windows facing away from the traffic side of the bus, but would also shade us as it travelled north and then west to Phimai. With David and I sitting properly in front of Mary and Súuzîi, and David and Mary sitting next to the windows, which allowed me to use the aisleway for my long legs, we waited for the bus to leave. The only problem was the bus seats were the same hard, cramped style as the Thai busses servicing Camp Friendship.

The bus soon pulled out of Bus Terminal 2 into the left lane of Highway 2. This is the main Highway from the ancient capital of Ayutthaya north of Bangkok, across the mountains eastward 120 miles to Korat, then northward 250 miles across the western part of the wide, verdant plain of the Korat Plateau, to the city of Nang Khai, across the Me Kong River from Vientiane, the capital of Laos.

Highway 2 was lined with two-story businesses, Hotels and homes, and every couple of miles a small town. Beyond these I saw miles of rice patties around farming hamlets as far as my eyes could see, which was a beautiful panoramic view from the bus.

The bus stopped every few hundred yards to let people off or to charge people as they boarded. So, the ride was slow going and took an hour to cover the twenty some miles before it turned right onto the road to Phimai. There, the bus continued to stop every few hundred yards for passengers to exit or board the bus. After another half hour of seeing the expansive, panoramic view of rice paddies surrounding farming hamlets, we covered the remaining eight miles to the bus terminal on the western edge of Phimai.

By the time we exited the bus, we were more than ready to stretch our legs on the 600-yard walk to the Khlong Chakrai, or Chakrai Canal, bordering the West edge of Phimai. Crossing the 100-yard wide canal, we walked up Anantajinda Road that led to the heart of Phimai, and the Phimai Historical Park. Súuzîi explained Phimai was a city of 25,000 people that surrounded the Historical Park, which contained the ruins of the Prasat Hin Phimai[132], a Mahayana Buddhist temple complex started in the 10th century by the Khmer King Jayavarman V and finished by his successor King Suriya Varman I in the 11th century. Also, that it's one of Thailand's finest surviving Khmer temple complexes that once stood on an important trade route linking the Khmer capital of Angkor, in Cambodia, which was the northern reaches of its realm and included the entire Korat Plateau.

Súuzîi led us along Anatajinda Road to the Phimai Historical Park's Visitor Center at the southern entrance of the Prasat Hin Phimai, which she explained was oriented south towards the Khmer capital. David paid the 80-Bhat entrance fee, and as we approached the visitor Center I saw half dozen Thai Ram dancers in their beautifully ornamented costumes gracefully performing one of the elegant ceremonial dances. When we were closer, Súuzîi pointed and called out, "Sandii, look, it's Jintana." Pointing out the tall Jintana to David and Mary, Súuzîi explained, "Jintana wa-sa Sandii girlfrient befo she get ma-rit."

Mary exclaimed, "She's absolutely gorgeous, Sandii. I can understand why you fell in love and wanted to marry her."

When the dance troupe finished their beautiful performance, they lined up in front of the Visitor Center to receive the audience, and Súuzîi led us to Jintana at the end of the line. After she exchanged sáwátdiis with Jintana, Súuzîi said, "It's so good to see you again, Jintana. We heard you are married."

Jintana replied happily, "Súuzîi, it's so good to see you here with Sandii. And yes, I'm happily married to a generous man and I'm already with child."

Súuzîi responded, "That's wonderful to hear. Your husband must be a very generous man."

As Súuzîi went to another Thai Ram dancer she knew, Jintana happily said in a soft voice as we exchanged sáwátdiis, "Sáwátdii, my beloved Sandii. It is good to see you here with Súuzîi and be able to tell you the child is yours. Now I have a part of you to love all my life."

---

132   Temple Stone Phimai

CHAPTER 35

THERE ARE NO PURPLE HEARTS IN THAILAND

Jintana's news the child she carried was mine, stunned me, and I thought, "How could this be? We were only together for a few weeks. But, Dad said that it only took once. Why didn't I use the condoms the Army gave us? Well, Jintana had come on pretty strong, and I'd so much lust for her, I couldn't think straight. Plus, the Catholic High School hammered into me that sex was for procreation and the use of any kind of birth control was a sin against God. So, now I'll have to live with the fact I've a child I'll never see."

Walking to see the Prasat Hin Phimai ruins, Súuzîi saw I was visibly upset and said tenderly, "My darling, how thoughtless of me. I know you love me now, but you loved Jintana enough to marry her and it must hurt your heart to see her married to another man, now. Please forgive me, my darling."

I smiled and replied, "I forgive you, my darling. And you're right, it's you I love, now, and your love for me makes me very happy. Besides, I'm relieved to know Jintana is happy in her marriage."

Arriving at the South entrance of the old stone wall encircling the Prasat Phinai complex, I saw the 100-yard long, ancient laterite stone, inlaid entrance causeway leading to the ruins of the 80-foot tall sandstone central tower of the Khmer sanctuary above the crumbling stone gallery surrounding it. Also, the two flanking towers of sandstone to its left and laterite to its right.

After viewing the impressive ruins from the South, we walked to the East end of the wall, crossing the wide Thai Songkhram Road to the Rabiang Mai Restaurant on the right corner with Samairújii Road. It was a semi-fancy place, and Súuzîi selected some of its Isaan food to try, making sure they weren't too spicy for our American palettes, which we found were quite tasty.

Finishing our lunch, Súuzîi directed us to turn right on Tha Songkhram Road. Passing along the 300-yard long East wall of the Prasat Hin Phimai on our left, we walked another 300 yards to the Phimai National Museum on the right side of the road and situated on the banks of the Sa Kwan, that Súuzîi told us was a 12th century Khmer reservoir. I found the museum housed a good collection of Khmer sculptures from the Prasat Hin Phimai, the distinctive black Phimai pottery that dated from 500 BC, and the many exquisite lintels and other ruins from around the lower Isaan area.

Leaving the museum an hour later, we walked West from Tha Songkhram Road, down Romsai Road, beside the 200-yard long North wall of the Prasat Hin Phimai, to the Chakrai Canal and watched the exciting long-tail boat races till 4:00. Then, walking back up Romsai Road, we went to the Vinaya Barakat Restaurant on the east corner of Mahisuan Yattra Road, and had their delicious, stir-fried egg noodles with vegetables, sesame seeds and chicken, as we saw the ruins of the Prasat Hin Phimai through its North gate.

Leaving the restaurant, we walked back down Romsai Road, past the Derm Temple complex, to Phimai's Lak Muang[133]. There, we turned left onto Wong Prang Road along the West wall of the Prasat Hin Phimai to Anantajinda Road, where we turned right and made the ¾-mile walk to Phimai's Bus Terminal. We boarded the Korat bus at 5:00, and watched the panoramic view of the other side of the highway in the lowering daylight on the 1½ hour trip. Returning to Korat's Bus Terminal 2 by 6:30, David and Mary thanked us for the

---

133   Center City

fun day-trip to Phimai's Festival before I hired săawm-laws for the rides back to our Hotels.

Entering my Hotel room, Súuzîi and I quickly stripped, and as I removed the condom I carried in my wallet, she decried, "My darling, please don't use that. I can't feel your sexual desire if you do."

I responded, "But, what if I get you with child?"

She laughed and replied, "Then I'll happily have your child. But, I doubt that will happen, as I take medicine to prevent it."

After we enjoyed our energetic lovemaking in a Kama Sutra position I'd learned with Glûaimâui, we had a pleasant shower washing each other's bodies. Watching Súuzîi's luscious body as she dressed in the fresh clothes she'd brought in her bag, I said, "You're a beautiful woman and I love you. Your love makes me very happy you're my girlfriend, my darling."

She responded as she finished dressing, "It quickens my heart to hear that, my darling. I've been afraid your seeing Jintana may have dimmed your desire for me, which your lovemaking showed me it has not lessened."

Arriving at the night club, we met up with David and Mary, and had a pleasant evening dancing and socializing. By 10:00, Súuzîi and I had our sexy Tango together. Then, quickly returning to my Hotel room, we expanded our pent up lust for each other joyfully in vigorous lovemaking, and enjoyed the afterglow of our orgasmic release as we spooned lovingly together and went to sleep.

With the 3:30 wake-up call, we enjoyed the desire we had for each other with passionate foreplay, and the lust we generated, powered our robust lovemaking and the orgasmic release we desired. Laying blissfully in the afterglow, I said affectionately, "My darling, because I work the night shift Tuesday, I won't be able to meet you at the night club. But, if you'd want to meet me after school, I'd like that."

She replied joyfully, "Yes, my darling, I'd like that very much. I'd die if I had to wait till Thursday to feel your desire for me."

After amusing each other as we showered, I dressed in my OD BDUs to leave for Camp Friendship. As we passionately kissed goodbye, I slid my hands desiringly over Súuzîi's smooth skin, feeling the luscious curves of her body. Then looking in the exotic, almond-shaped eyes of her pretty face, I said lovingly, "My darling, you're so beautiful and I'll miss you very much till Tuesday," and she cooed in return, "And I love you, my darling, and will miss your desire for me till Tuesday."

Arriving at my Company Area, I went to my hooch and drank a cold can of Bud as I changed into a fresh set of jungle fatigues. Leaving my OD BDUs on top of the laundry I'd brought from Korat, I tossed my shopping bag in my wall locker, and left with Skip for the Mess Hall. Exiting our hooch he asked, "So, how was your day-trip to Phinai?"

As we walked to the Mess Hall and during our breakfast, I told Skip all about the scenery I saw as we rode to and from Phimai, the ruins of the Prasat Hin Phimai, the things displayed at the museum, the long-tail boat races, watching Jintana dance, and her telling me she was happily married as we greeted in the reception line. I left out that she was with child, as I didn't want any wild gossip that I might be the father.

After formation, I gave Jim a brief summary of my day-trip to Phimai as we walked to the Motor Pool. As Jim climbed into the driver's seat, he said, "Mary and I went to the Festival last year, but we didn't have a translator or guide along like the CO did to explain it all to us."

At work, Bob asked, "How'd things work out Saturday with your trip to Phimai?" and laughed when I replied suggestively, "Things worked in and out very well."

Meeting Glen in the Mess Hall on my 10:55 meal run, I told him about my day-trip with the CO and wife to the Phimai Festival and seeing Jintana, leaving out her pregnancy. Glen responded, "Súpa will be glad to hear Jintana is happily married. She's worried Jintana may have married a man who treated her badly, as has happened to a few of her friends. As I've already seen the sights in Phimai, I wouldn't endure again the 3-hour, butt-numbing bus ride just to have fun watching the boat races."

After eating lunch with Glen, I swung by the Howard Johnson and bought three 6-packs of Bud on the way to my hooch. Packing a few changes of clothes in my shopping bag, I took them with me back to work. Being relieved at 6:45 by John and Larry, I left like a rabbit chased by a coyote for Korat. Returning to my Hotel room, I hung my clothes in the wardrobe, stripped to my boxers, lay on the bed, and waited for Lompét's knock on my door.

As I waited, I took the Kama Sutra book from the dresser drawer where I kept it, and began to review the position Lompét had selected. When I answered her knock on the door, she was very pleased to see I was fully aroused with my desire for her shapely, petite body. After our vigorous lovemaking in the Kama Sutra position, and spooning together to enjoy the pleasant feelings that resulted in the orgasmic release of our lust, Lompét cooed, "I love you very much, my darling, and anxious to know how the trip to Phimai with your boss and his wife went."

After I gave her a brief summary about the success of the trip, and telling her of my short encounter with Jintana, she said, "I'm so proud of you, my darling, with the success of your trip. And, I'm glad Jintana is happily married, because now I have you for my boyfriend, who makes me very happy with his desire to make love with me."

Being tired from my long day at work and from our energetic lovemaking, I contentedly went to sleep holding my loveable, petite Lompét snuggled in my strong arms. With the 3:30 wake-up call, we quickly refreshed our lust for each other, and passionately made love in the same Kama Sutra position. After having fun showering together, Lompét helped me dress in my jungle fatigues and told me how much she was looking forward to our dancing and being able to spend the night together. When we'd affectionately kissed goodbye, and I'd desiringly caressed her succulent, petite body, she cooed, "I love very much your desire for my little body."

Returning to my Company Area, I went to my hooch and drank a cold can of Bud as I changed into a fresh set of jungle fatigues. Then, I went to the Mess Hall with Skip for breakfast before formation, after which we rode in the back of the truck to the Air Base Site. As it was a Monday morning, there was an uptick in outage reports when units transmitted their Morning Reports for the actions on Saturday and Sunday. This gave us an excuse not to repair the "malfunction" to the audio alarm circuits in the AP and UPI teletype machines.

Making the 10:55 meal run to have lunch with Glen in the Mess Hall, he asked if Lompét and I were going to meet him and Súpa at the night club. I replied, "If we don't, I'll never hear the end of it from Lompét," and Glen laughed, "Same here. And I do enjoy the benefits after we've been dancing."

That evening, Lompét was again wearing her hot-pink silk dress when I picked her up from the cafe. At the night club, the four of us had fun socializing between dances. When it was close to 10:00 and the orchestra began to play a Tango, Lompét exclaimed, "Tango! Yes, my darling, I want very much to feel your sexy dancing."

When the Tango finished, we quickly left and returned to my room, where I feasted on Lompét's impassioned lust for me. As she spooned blissfully in the afterglow, wrapped in my arms, she cooed euphorically, "I love you very much, my darling, and the heaven you put me in," and fell asleep.

Lompét was in a frisky mood when we woke at 3:30. Turning over in my arms to face me, she began kissing me desiringly as she coaxed my arousal for her with the writhing of her enticing body sensuously against mine. When my lust for her was fully aroused, we shifted smoothly into our last Kama Sutra position and began our lovemaking in a frenzy. Laying in the afterglow of our orgasms, she cooed, "My darling, when I woke with your arms lovingly around me, I felt a big need for you to fill me with your sexual desire."

I responded, "And the feel of your sensuous body drives my need to fill you with my sexual desire."

After we enjoyed our shower together, Lompét chose a new Kama Sutra position as we lay on the bed, and then assisted me as I dressed in my jungle fatigues. When I'd tenderly kissed her goodbye as I stroked her lovely body, I said, "I look forward to being with you this afternoon in the cafe as I teach you English."

Exiting a Thai bus at the Company Area, I walked to my hooch, where I drank a cold can of Bud as I changed into a fresh set of OD BDUs. Then, I went to the Mess Hall for breakfast before morning formation. After formation, I joined those heading for the main street to catch a Thai bus for Korat. Returning to my Hotel room, I stripped to my skivvies and slept till noon.

Waking from my much needed sleep, I leisurely dressed in a silk shirt and cotton pants, and then strolled to the cafe, where Lompét served me lunch. After spending a pleasant afternoon teaching my pretty Lompét English, I left at 3:30 for my Hotel room and my 4:00 rendezvous with Súuzîi.

Laying on the bed wearing only my boxers, I became aroused planning which Kama Sutra position to enjoy with Súuzîi. Answering her knock on the door, I saw her pleasure at seeing my arousal for her, and we were soon engaged in releasing our pent up lust with vigorous lovemaking in the Kama Sutra position I'd planned.

When our copulation attained the climax we desired, and we then snuggled affectionately in the afterglow, Súuzîi mused, "I love you very much, my darling, and your desire for me. I wish we could be together, but I'm afraid to lose you like Julii did. If I came from a poor family, we could live together, or even get married. Just the same, I very much enjoy being your girlfriend, my darling."

I responded, "My darling, I very much enjoy being your boyfriend, and what time we're able to have together, even if it's only for an hour like today. But Thursday, we'll have all evening to dine and dance together, and then be in each other's arms all night," and she giggled, "And have lots of lovemaking in different positions. I love you very much, my darling."

After we showered playfully together, I dressed in my OD BDUs and Súuzîi in the clothes she had worn, and then we kissed lovingly goodbye before leaving. At the Hotel's entrance, I hired a sǎawm-law for each of us, and I returned to Camp Friendship.

Departing the Thai bus at my Company Area, I walked to my hooch and drank a cold can of Bud as I emptied the laundry in my shopping bag onto the floor before putting fresh clothes in the shopping bag to pick up on my way to Korat the next morning. Then Skip and I went to the Mess Hall for dinner before Tommy arrived with the truck in front of the Day Room at 6:35.

Things went smoothly on the night shift at the Air Base Site, and I wrote Linda a long letter describing my day-trip to the Phimai Festival. Leaving on my 6:35 meal run to deliver the truck to Jim in the Motor Pool, I then went to the Mess Hall for breakfast before swinging by my hooch to pick up my shopping bag on the way to Korat.

Entering my Hotel room, I readied myself for Lompét when she knocked on the door. Soon, she was making love with me in the new Kama Sutra position in enthusiastic response to my desire for her. After we cuddled happily for a while, we had fun playing in the shower together before laying on the bed side by side as she enjoyed choosing and discussing the Kama Sutra position for the next morning. When Lompét had dressed and we'd affectionately kissed goodbye, I lay on the bed and slept till noon. Then, I dressed and went to the cafe for lunch and had a delightful time teaching English to Lompét. At 3:30, I returned to my Hotel room and changed into my OD BDUs to work the night shift at the Air Base.

The night shift was again quiet, so I wrote a lengthy letter to my parents describing my day-trip to Phimai, and then was able to get a couple hours shuteye before Skip left on the 4:55 meal run. When I delivered the truck to Jim in the Motor Pool on the 6:35 meal run, he said, "SFC Davidson told me the CO wants you to report to him in the HQ right after formation for a special duty assignment. When I asked what it entailed, he said you'll be going to the Green Hill Radio Site overnight. I know it's a tough break for you, as it's your two off days, but the needs of the Army come first."

I responded, "Yea, this'll be a tough break as I've a date for dinner and dancing tonight. But, it's like my Mom always says, 'tough titty said the kitty, but the milk's still good.'"

When I'd quickly eaten breakfast in the Mess Hall, I crossed the roadway to HQ, and entering it, I saw Lt. Price talking to Sgt. Potts. When the screen door slammed close, Lt. Price saw me and hurriedly said, "That's it for now, Sgt. Potts. Specialist Lynch, I need to see you in my Office right away."

Walking through the swinging gate at the end of the counter, I followed him to the CO's Office. Closing the door behind me, he said, "Sorry to do this to you, Sandii, but the Motor Pool's having a surprise I.G. (Inspector General) Inspection this afternoon, and the NCOIC told me he has a three-quarter-ton truck that's drivable, but won't pass the inspection. You're being detailed to ride shotgun on the truck with a Thai driver to take supplies to the Green Hill Radio Site, about seventy miles from here by road. I've been up there. It's at the top to Pho Sam Ngam, which is over 3,000 feet high and fifty miles from Cambodia. It'll take you about three hours to get there, with the last twenty miles up a windy, paved road through the jungle. Then you'll ride back first thing tomorrow morning.

"At 1200, you'll report to the Armory for an M-14 rifle, combat harness, and 80 rounds of ammo. Then, you'll report to the Motor Pool Office to sign the truck out. I've picked you for this detail because you can speak Thai and the Thai driver speaks little English, and your DD-201 File shows you qualified Expert with the M-14. Also, this is your two off days. Any questions?"

I replied, "Am I restricted to Base during the interim?"

He answered, "No, as long as you report to the Armory by 1200, you're dismissed."

Leaving HQ, I quickly went to board a Thai bus for Korat. Arriving at my Hotel room, I said, "Sáwátdii, Lompét," whose expression went from very happy to perplexed, as I explained, "Forgive me, my darling, but my boss gave me a great honor to go on a special, one-day trip for him to Pho Sam Ngam this afternoon and won't be back till tomorrow."

When we'd passionately kissed, Lompét smiled and said, "I forgive you, my darling. I know the Army has many surprises. At least we can make love now for the desire I have for you," as we eagerly stripped. After the orgasmic release of the lust we had for each other with our vigorous lovemaking using the Kama Sutra position we'd discussed the previous morning, we showered happily together. Then, we dressed and passionately kissed goodbye, before we left for the Hotel's entrance, where Lompét walked on returning to the cafe.

Hiring a sǎawm-law, I rode to Suranari College at 248 Mit Rapaap Road and left a note for Súusîi that read, "I am on a trip for David and will not be able to have dinner with your family tonight. Will see you Saturday. Sorry, your friend, Sandii," then rode on to the Chainarong Gate.

Returning to the Company Area, I entered my hooch by 9:30 and saw everyone there laughing and drinking beer. Grabbing a can of cold Bud from the Mini-fridge, Skip saw me and said, "Sandii, where've you been? You've missed all the fun."

I replied, "the CO's having me ride shotgun to the Green Hill Radio Site to get a dilapidated ¾-ton out of the Motor Pool during the inspection and had to tell Lompét I'll be gone. What'd I miss?"

They all replied in turn, that after formation, or when they got off the night shift, everyone was ordered to the Motor Pool to help the gear-heads get the vehicles ready for inspection. Some were given voltmeters and told to pull the fuses and check to make sure they were good. But, since they weren't told to put them back in, they left them lying on the floorboards. Others were given 9/16th-inch wrenches and sockets with ratchets, and told to make sure the nuts and bolts were on tight and tightened them till the nuts snapped off the bolts. And some were told to drive the vehicles to the wash racks and clean them, but when they did, they spun the rear wheels, spraying dirt and gravel around the parking area. When the NCOIC pulled their Military Driver's License for violating Motor Pool rules, they just sat in the vehicles, telling him that without their license, they no longer knew how to drive. Eventually, the NCOIC kicked all the miscreants out of his Motor Pool.

Fetching another cold can of Bud from the fridge, Ronnie said, "At least on your road trip to the Green Hill Site, you'll see all the countryside south of here. I've heard the view from up there is spectacular and you can see all the way into Cambodia."

Stripping to my skivvies as I finished my Bud, I slept for an hour before the 11:00 bugle call for Mess. Drinking another can of Bud as I put on a fresh set of jungle fatigues, I left for the Mess Hall.

After eating lunch, I reported to the Armory and was issued with the M-14 rifle, a steel helmet with fiberglass helmet liner, 5 magazines with 16 rounds of 7.62mm bullets each, 2 canteens of fresh water, and a combat harness with suspenders to hold up the three-inch wide, web belt with two magazines pouch and a First Aid pouch. Adjusting the helmet liner's headband to fit my head, I placed the six-pound steel helmet and liner on my head. Once I'd adjusted the length of the web belt to my waist size and harness suspenders to fit my long torso, I attached to the web belt a canteen of water to be over each hip and the 2 ammo magazines with 16 rounds each into each ammo pouch. Then, I draped and fastened the entire rig over and around my body. Picking up the M-14 rifle, I made sure the Safety Switch was set to ON, slid the bolt mechanism back and forth to make sure it worked smoothly and there was no round in the chamber. After which, I locked the fifth ammo magazine with sixteen rounds into the magazine slot in front of the trigger guard. Now, forty pounds heavier than when I entered the Armory, I left for the Motor Pool Office with the rifle slung on my right shoulder.

Walking out of the Company Supply/Armory building, I saw a ¾-ton truck parked on the near side of the roadway facing to my left. Standing beside the truck was Sgt. Potts talking to a medium built Thai man wearing a white cotton shirt and tan pants. Approaching the truck, Sgt. Potts faced me, and handing me a clipboard, said, "This is Winai, your driver. If you sign off on the Release Authorization and Trip Ticket, you can be on your way. There's a map with the Trip

Ticket, but Winai goes to the Green Hill Site regularly, so he knows the route."

Exchanging sáwátdiis with Winai, I introduced myself as "Sandii," and signed the forms, keeping the clipboard with the Trip Ticket. With Winai climbing behind the steering wheel, I unslung the rifle as I climbed in the passenger side, fastening the rifle into its bracket on the dashboard. Winai then started the truck's engine and we were on our way to the Green Hill Radio Site.

Turning left at the main street, Winai drove to the traffic light and turned right to Camp Friendship's South Gate, 100 yards past the gravel road to the Tropo Site. At the South Gate, we showed our ID cards and the Trip Ticket to the U.S. Army MP, who waved us through.

Just past the South Gate, Winai turned left onto a two-lane highway, which I saw was like Highway 2 that I travelled on to Phimai, lined with businesses and houses, and fields of rice paddies surrounding hamlets. About five miles later, we passed through the large town of Dan Kwáan, after which the highway turned southward. After another five miles, Winai drove across Highway 24 onto a small, two-lane country road with only rice paddies surrounding hamlets in the distance on either side of the road, which made for a pretty drive across the verdant country side.

After a half-dozen miles, Winai pointed at the water temperature gauge and, "wata too hot," as he pulled to the side of the road. Opening the hood, I saw the fanbelt wasn't tight, and Winai went to a toolbox behind the seat, got a wrench, and tightened the slack fanbelt.

Continuing down the road a half dozen miles, it teed with another two-lane country road, which Winai crossed over onto a one-lane, asphalt paved road. After a few miles, Winai again pointed at the water gauge and said, "wata too hot," as he stopped the truck. This time when we opened hood, I saw the cloth back of the rubber fanbelt was beginning to separate. Seeing a hamlet about 100 yards off the road to our left, I grabbed my rifle and we walked along a narrow, dirt road to it, in the hope they might have a spare fanbelt.

Locating the hamlet's headman, who was clearly intimidated at the sight of my rifle and uniform, I listened while Winai talked with him. Though I could understand much of what Winai said, I caught very little of what the headman said. As we walked back to the truck without a fanbelt, I asked Winai in Thai, "What did the headman say?"

He shrugged his shoulders and replied, "I don't know. He doesn't speak much Thai, mostly Khmer. But, they have no tractor, only water buffalo, so no fanbelt."

Returning to the truck, Winai took a roll of black mechanic's tape from the toolbox and wrapped it around the separating part of the fanbelt to repair it as best as possible, which worked for a few miles. By then, the road was winding up through the jungle alongside a babbling stream. Filling the steaming radiator every few hundred yards, we slowly proceeded on the winding asphalt road as it rose up through the dense jungle.

Finally, after one stop, the truck's engine would not turn over. With no vehicles having passed us since we started up this 1-lane, desolate, jungle road, we only had two options left as the sun began to set. Either spend the night in the truck on this jungle road or walk the rest of the way in the dark to the Green Hill Radio Site. As Winai assured me it was not much further to the Radio Site, I chose the latter. Grabbing my rifle from the rifle bracket and slinging it over my right shoulder, I saw Winai taking a tire iron from behind the seat and asked, "What's that for?"

He replied, "for sŭa."

I knew "sûa" meant "shirt" and "sùá" meant "mat," so I asked, "what is 'sŭa'?"

He lifted his hands like two big claws and growled loudly, and I exclaimed, "Tiger?"

Pointing to the dense, darkening jungle around us, he said "ye-sa, many ti-ga."

I rapidly unslung my rifle, pulled back on the bolt handle to chamber a round, flipped the Safety Switch to Off, and set the Selector Switch to Fully Automatic, as I thought, "the first sound of a growl or something big moving through the jungle, and I'll fill it full of holes."

Beginning our cautious walk up the jungle lined road with my rifle at the ready and Winai close behind holding the tire iron, the night became black. Tense with the fear of being pounced on at any second by a 300-pound Asian Tiger, two hours and two miles later, we came to bend in the road with a faint glow of light beyond it. Hurrying around the bend, I saw a shaded light over an 8-foot high, chain-link gate with rolls of concertina wire across its top, and yelled, "Hello, Green Hill. This is Specialist Lynch and Winai from Korat."

Hearing the order, "Advance and be recognized," I lowered my rifle, took out my ID card, walked under the light over the gate, and heard, "Where the devil have you been? They sent out a search party over an hour ago."

As the gate opened enough to let us in, I replied, "that piece of crap truck they sent us in broke a fanbelt about halfway here and broke down completely a couple miles back.

We were led to a one-story concrete barracks through the dark and each given a box of C-Rations with the explanation, "Sorry, but the mess-van isn't open after sunset, so this is the best we can give you."

After eating the Korean War vintage food, I was shown an empty bed and crashed onto it, as I only had an hour of sleep since getting off the night shift. When I woke the next morning one of the men pointed out the OD mess-van halfway between the barracks building and a 20-foot high, 80-foot square concrete building 50 yards away with VHF, UHF, parabolic microwave, and rotating radar antennas on top of it.

Carrying my combat gear and rifle with me, I entered the side door in the middle of the mess-van. To my left, I saw the food preparation and kitchen area, and to my right were several tables and benches extending from the far sidewall. Sitting at the first table, there was a PFC in jungle fatigues playing solitaire with a deck of cards. Looking up as I entered, he said, "Hi, I'm Fred, chief cook and bottle washer. You must be the guy who came in last night. What do you want for breakfast?"

I replied, "Hi, Fred, I'm Sandii, and two eggs over medium, some bacon and a glass of milk sure would hit the spot." Walking to the second table, I leaned my rifle against the sidewall, set my combat gear on the bench next to my rifle, and sat at the end of the bench facing the kitchen area. Several minutes later, Fred served me the bacon, eggs and milk I'd requested, and sat opposite from me at the table.

As we talked while I ate, I suddenly heard what sounded like someone throwing rocks at the side of the mess-van. I saw Fred drop to floor, and as I dumbly sat there, he yelled, "Sandii, we're under attack. Quick, get down and follow me to my firing position."

Dropping to the floor, I followed Fred as he scrambled to the kitchen area. As he grabbed his combat harness, he looked back at me and yelled, "Hey, you forgot your combat gear."

Rushing back to the table I snatched my combat harness and helmet. Turning to hurry back, he yelled, "And your rifle," and I yelled, "Yea, right," as I shoved the helmet on my head, slipped on the combat harness, and seized my rifle. When I returned to the door, Fred said, "When I open the door, you do what I do, and go where I go."

When Fred threw the door open, I watched as he ran in a low, serpentine manner to a small, sandbagged bunker 30 feet away, and dived into it as bullets kicked up dirt around him. Then, I held tight to my rifle with both hands, ran in a zig-zag, and dived headfirst into the small bunker as I heard bullets zing past me. Quickly chambering a round and flipping the Safety Switch to Off, I stood to return fire through the firing port. Fred grabbed my harness, pulled me back down and yelled, "What are you doing?"

I yelled back excitedly, "Returning fire."

He yelled, "Not like that, like this," lifting his rifle over his head, and fired blindly out the firing port. When his magazine was empty he yelled, "Now you fire while I reload."

Raising my rifle over my head, I began to blindly lay down grazing fire, and yelled over my right shoulder, "How long do we do this?"

Fred yelled, "Till the 50 Cal kicks in. It's the only thing that can hit anything through the jungle growth."

Then I heard the distinctive, rapid, "tud, tud, tud" of a 0.50 caliber machine gun. As the sound of bullets hitting our sandbag bunker stopped, I ceased firing my rifle. Then, when I heard "all clear" sound, Fred and I climbed up out of the bunker. As Fred looked down, he exclaimed, "Sandii, you're bleeding!"

Looking down, I saw a bullet hole mid-thigh, through the left inside pant leg of my jungle fatigues with some blood beneath the hole, and said, "Heck, now I've gotta shell out 12 bucks for another pair of pants," and thought, "Must of happened as I ran to the bunker and didn't feel anything because of the adrenal rush."

Fred led me to the barracks, where their Medic had an Aid Station set up. Dropping my pants before laying down on the stretcher on a waist-high stand, I saw a 3-inch long laceration to the skin on my left inner thigh. The Medic laughed and said, "6 inches higher and we'd be calling you Miss Lynch," as I thought, "Looks like the 'Lynch luck' has passed to the next generation."[134]

I winced as the Medic scrubbed the bullet wound with iodine, and said, "Guess I'll get a Purple Heart[135] for this."

The Medic chuckled and said, as he began to suture the skin together, "No Purple Hearts here. Remember, we all had to sign a National Security Non-Disclosure Form to not document any combat action in Thailand? Well, in order to get a Purple Heart, I'd have to enter 'wound received in combat action' on the Medical Report. The only thing I can write is, 'wound received in the line of duty'."

I lamented, "So, because I was wounded in combat in Thailand, I can't get a Purple Heart?"

He replied, "It may not be right, but that's the way it is. There are no Purple Hearts in Thailand."

---

134   In 1971, Eugene Womack, my first-cousin on Dad's side was a helicopter Crew Chief/Door Gunner in Vietnam; who later survived three Huey helicopters being shot down. In 2007, Jason Lynch, my son, was driving a new Stryker APC in Baghdad, Iraq, with the 4th Stryker Brigade, when the APC was exploded by a roadside bomb, injuring everyone in the vehicle's rear. Spotting the bombers on the wall of a near-by compound, he drove his APC through the wall, climbed into the twin-20mm gun turret, and raked the building, killing 26 insurgents. He was awarded a Bronze Star for this action.

135   A Purple Heart Medal is a heart-shaped military decoration hung from a purple ribbon awarded to members of the Armed Forces wounded or killed in combat action.

CHAPTER 36

THE MILITARY TAKES A DIM VIEW OF ADULTERY

While the Medic bandaged my leg wound with a 4 by 8-inch battle dressing, I asked, "So, do you guys get attacked up here very often?"

He replied, "Not really. Though we're only 50 miles from Cambodia, where the Thai Cong have safe haven, it's still a 3-day hump through dense jungle to get here, and 3 days back. And, a week in tat jungle full of tigers and poisonous snakes, is no picnic. Because of the tigers, they can't send out just a couple of snipers to pick us off. And, the Thai Army heavily patrols the jungles along the Cambodian border, so the trail of a large force can easily be found and ambushed. That means, they can only send a squad-size unit to attack us.

Plus, once they get here, they have to wait till daylight to attack, as we keep the area blacked out at night. Then, they can't get close to our heavily fenced perimeter, as the jungle's been cleared back for a 50-yard wide field of fire that's heavily mined. And, to carry a 60 mm mortar with enough rounds for ranging and then effective firing, is too much weight for a squad to carry for 3 days. So, every once in a while, they send a rifle squad to harass us, like this morning, and hope the Thai Army doesn't intercept them on their way back to Cambodia.

"Anyway, the Company's sent a tow truck up first thing this morning. They should be here by 10:00 to pick up you, your driver and the broke-down truck, and have you back to Korat by 1:00. Tomorrow, you need to go to Sick Call for the wound to be looked at and checked for infections. You can get dressed now and take this Medical Report Form with you when you go to Sick Call."

Sitting up on the stretcher and hopping down to the floor, I took the Medical form and said, "Thanks for the patch job, Doc," as I sat on the stretcher after pulling up my pants and fastening them. Folding the Medical form twice, I put it in my right breast pocket, and then smoked a cigarette to relax me before I laid down on the empty bed and fell asleep.

I woke to the Medic saying, "Hey, Lynch, your ride back to Korat is here."

Getting up from the bed, I put on my combat harness and helmet, grabbed my rifle, and went outside. There, I saw a 2½ -on flatbed truck with an A-frame tow-rig on the flatbed holding up the frontend of the broken-down ¾-ton truck. Walking toward the 2½-ton truck, I recognized John Williams, from my hometown, standing by the truck, wearing a combat harness and helmet, and yelled, "Hey, John, it's good to see you again."

John yelled back, "Hi, Sandii. How's it going? Heard you got shot!"

Pointing to the dried blood below the bullet holes in my left pant leg, I replied, "Luckily, it just broke the skin. How you doing?"

He laughed, "Just waiting on you, Sandii. It's a beautiful day for a drive through the countryside. So, if you climb in, we can head back to Korat, and with luck, be back in time for lunch."

Climbing up and into the passenger side of the cab, I saw a muscular young Private wearing a combat harness already seated there next to Winai, and said, "Sáwátdii," as I crowded in beside the Private. Fastening my rifle into the bracket before me and next to the Private's rifle, I saw that John's rifle was in a bracket next to the driver's door. I also heard the truck's engine was idling and ready to go when John put the truck in first gear and slowly rolled it forward.

Driving the truck around in a wide circle, John towed the ¾-ton truck inside Green Hill's compound, before exiting through the gate.

Once on the narrow, asphalt road, John put the truck in second gear to let the truck's engine act as a brake, while we went slowly down the steep, windy road through the jungle. When the road exited the jungle, and became straight and level on the verdant plain of the Korat Plateau, John sped the truck up to fourth gear on the narrow country road, and asked, "So, Sandii, what happened to that ¾-ton for the engine block to seize up?"

I explained the problems with the fanbelt, our repair efforts, and our frequent stops to put water in the radiator from the nearby stream. I went on to tell him about our walk in the dark through the jungle, the firefight, and being wounded, but can't get a Purple Heart for National Security reasons.

John responded, "I can understand why you kept going up the mountain, as you'd have to walk twenty miles back before you'd find a phone to call us. You're lucky you got as far as you did. And, it's political crap you can't get a Purple Heart for a combat wound because you're in Thailand. But, the CO's Infantry, so maybe he knows of a loophole for that."

I replied hopefully, "Hey, I hadn't thought of that."

John said, "After dinner this evening, why don't you swing by my hooch, it's number 531, and smoke gunsha with me? Thai weed is excellent stuff, and only costs $3.00 a pound."

I remembered Gunsha is Asian slang for marijuana, and replied, "I haven't tried weed before. I don't suppose it'll hurt to try some," thinking, "I'll have plenty of time, as I don't have to leave for Korat till 7:00 for my date to go dancing with Lompét."

When we reached the main two-lane road, John sped up to 45 MPH, and we made it back to the Company Area in time for lunch at the Mess Hall. After lunch, I went to the armory, and turned in my combat gear and rifle. I also had to fill out a report for the bullets I'd used in the firefight, and to field strip and clean the rifle because I'd fired it.

Leaving the Armory, I went to my hooch to drink a cold can of Bud and smoke a cigarette before going to HQ to give my report on the trip to Lt. Price. Arriving at HQ, PFC Schultz saw me and said, "the CO wants to see you right away, Specialist Lynch," as he led me to the CO's Office.

Entering the Office, I marched to the front of Lt. Price's desk, came to attention, saluted and said, "Specialist Lynch reporting as ordered, Sir."

He returned my salute, and looking past me to make sure the door was closed, he said, "Have a seat, Sandii, and tell me everything that happened."

As I reported to him everything about my trip, I showed him the bullet holes in my left pant leg and blood stains. When I explained why I wouldn't be able to receive the Purple Heart, he exclaimed, "That's ridiculous! I made sure every man in my platoon in Nam who received any kind of wound in combat, even just a scratch from barbwire, was awarded the Purple Heart. I'll see what I can do to straighten out this SNAFU. You can go, Sandii, and enjoy the rest of your time off, while I look into this."

Leaving the CO's Office, I returned to my hooch and drank another cold can of Bud and smoke a cigarette as I stripped to my skivvies, turned on my fan, and went to bed. Waking to the 5:00 bugle call for Mess, I dressed in a fresh set of jungle fatigues and went to dinner in the Mess Hall.

Going to Hooch NW-531 after dinner, I found John sitting on his bed, listening to some psychedelic music by Vanilla Fudge through headphones from a tape deck in his wall locker. Seeing me walk up to him, he pulled off the headphones and said, "Sandii, it's great to see you. You ready for some of the good stuff?" as he stood on the bed and took a one-pound coffee can down from the rafters.

I replied, "That's what the invitation said."

Removing the plastic lid from the can, he removed a small, white sheet of cigarette paper from a Z-Z Top packet and poured some chopped up green leafy material onto the paper. Then, rolling the material in the paper into the shape of a cigarette, he gave a little lick along the free edge to seal the rolled paper, and lit one end while he sucked smoke from the other end. Several seconds later, I smelled a distinctive, strong, earthy odor as he exhaled and said, "Oh yea, this is primo gunsha. Here, take a hit off this joint," as he handed it to me, remembering that "joint" was slang for a marijuana cigarette.

Taking the joint, I inhaled a lung full of the smoke, and holding my breath for a few seconds as the THC, which is Tetrahydrocannabinol, the active drug in marijuana, entered my bloodstream and went to my nervous system. Feeling a sense of euphoria, I exhaled and said, "Wow, John, that is some excellent stuff," as I handed the joint back to him.

After John and I had a second hit off the joint, he said, "That's all you should have, as it's your first trip."

I responded, "You're probably right, as I've got a date to go dancing tonight, and I don't want to be totally stoned[136] for it. But, I really appreciate and thank you for the experience, John."

Walking back to my hooch, I became very dizzy and nauseated, and stumbling onto the grass, I vomited my dinner. Still feeling dizzy, I regained my feet and managed to find my hooch. Laying down on my bed, I thought, "If only two hits of that stuff makes me feel like this, then one experience is enough for me, and I'll stick to drinking booze."

Leaving for Korat an hour later, I wasn't so dizzy anymore, but my mind was still in a confused state of euphoria. By the end of the half-hour bus trip, I was beginning to sober up pretty good. Returning to my Hotel room, I was thankful for the tepid shower before I dressed to pick up Lompét at the cafe. After my half-mile walk to the cafe, I felt like myself again.

Entering the cafe, I saw Lompét standing by the door, looking stunning in her revealing, form-fitting, red silk dress. But, an American had her trapped against the wall, trying to talk with her. Seeing me enter the cafe, she said forcefully to the American, "I say to you, I hafa boy fa-ren," as she ducked under his arm with a relieved look on her pretty face and ran behind me.

He said to me, "you're lucky to have such a hot looking tîi-lók panting after you like that."

I looked down at his 5-foot-9 stature with a stern expression and said, "She's not my tîi-lók, the *lady* is my girlfriend, and you've disrespected her. I *suggest* you apologize for your rudeness."

The man looked up at my 6-foot-2 unwavering gaze. After a few seconds, he looked down to the diminutive Lompét, standing defensively behind me, and said, "I apologize for my rudeness, ma'am," and then to me, "My mistake, sir," as he quickly left the cafe to the applause of the patrons.

---

136   Under the influence of a narcotic, hallucinogen, etc.

As Lompét and I exchanged sáwátdiis, she said in Thai, "Thank you for saving me from that not-good man[137], my darling."

I replied, "My honor to defend my girlfriend," as she followed me out of the cafe.

Arriving at the night club by săawm-law, we soon met up with Glen and Súpa at a table on the 3rd tier. When we danced, I very much enjoyed watching Lompét dancing in her seductively red dress, and by the time we dance sensuously to our last Tango, I was very much aroused with the sight of her happy movements as she danced.

Entering my Hotel room, it seemed we couldn't remove our clothes fast enough to free our pent-up lust in wanton lovemaking, like a cascading avalanche. But, when she saw the bandage around my left leg, Lompét shrieked, "My darling, you're hurt."

I replied soothingly, "It's nothing, my darling. Just a scratch from a piece of metal this morning. The Doctor put on a big patch, so it won't become infected. Don't worry, my darling. There's no pain."

After we'd unleashed our lust in unrestrained lovemaking, Lompét snuggled happily in my strong arms as we spooned in the afterglow and cooed, "My darling, I missed making love with you this morning. But, when you bravely defended my honor against that not-good man, my love for you soared like an eagle. I'm so blessed to be your girlfriend, my darling."

The next morning, we roused our desires and made love vigorously in the Kama Sutra position we'd planned two days earlier. After removing my bandage, we pleasantly showered together, and Lompét tenderly rewrapped the 3-inch gash on my left thigh. While we affectionately kissed goodbye, I enjoyed the feel of her luscious, petite body with my hands, and said, "Till tomorrow morning, my darling."

After I had breakfast in the Mess Hall, Jim told me at formation, "The CO wants to see you in his Officed following formation. When he's done, just catch a bus to work."

I responded, "I'm sorry, Jim, but I was shot in the leg during a firefight at the Green Hill Site and have to go to Sick Call for the bandage to be changed before I can go to work."

---

137   The word "bad" does not exist in the Thai language

Jim exclaimed, "You were shot?" and everybody looked at me with concern as I replied, "There was a firefight at the Green Hill Site while I was there yesterday, and a bullet grazed my left inner thigh. It's just a flesh wound so, no big deal. But, the Medic said I had to be seen by a doctor at Sick Call."

Jim responded, "How come I'm just finding out about this now?"

I replied, "The CO knows all about it, so you'll have to ask him about that. It's probably for National Security reasons, since any combat action in Thailand is not to be recorded or repeated, which means, I'm technically in violation for telling you. So, you shouldn't tell anyone else what I just told you," as I looked around and smiled at everyone who was listening intently.

In his Office, Lt. Price said, "Sorry, Sandii, but the Regulations are very specific. The Medical Record must say 'due to combat action' to be awarded a Purple Heart. And, the National Security Nondisclosure Form everyone in Thailand signs, clearly states the word 'combat' can't be used on any official or unofficial correspondence. So, you can't be awarded the Purple Heart for your combat wound. But, I'm putting you in for the Army Commendation Medal, which is the highest non-combat decoration you can be awarded."

I responded, "Thank you, Sir. To receive an ArCom is better than a poke in the eye with a sharp stick."

Catching a Thai bus to the Camp Dispensary, I entered and presented the Medical Record Form with my ID card to the white tunicked Medic behind the chest-high counter. Taking my Form he told me to have a seat in the Waiting Room. After a while, my name was called, and I was led to the first Treatment Room on the right. Sitting as directed on the exam table, the Doctor removed the bandage and asked, "A bullet wound in the line of duty? How'd that happen?"

I replied, "Easy. I was running to a bunker and got in the way of one of many bullets being fired at me."

He laughed and said, "And for National Security reason, the Medic couldn't write 'due to combat action' on the Medical Record. You aren't the first I've seen, and probably not the last. Well, the Medic did a good job cleaning and suturing the wound, and I don't see any sign of infection. I'm going to wrap this with a 4 by 4 gauze pad and a 4-inch Ace bandage and give you a half dozen more gauze pads. I want you to change the gauze pad daily, and if you see any redness or swelling or if it feels hot to the touch, you're to go directly to the Hospital's Emergency Room. Other than that, you're to return in a week to have the stitches removed. Any questions?"

I replied, "Sounds simple enough," as he finished wrapping the bandage and handed me six 4 by 4 gauze pads, which I put in the large waist pockets of my jungle fatigue shirt and left to catch a Thai bus to the Air Base Site.

Walking into the Operations Room, I saw everyone was busier than a one-legged man in a butt-kicking contest from the numerous outages reported from the late Friday afternoon Stateside traffic. As a result, I didn't get a chance to tell anyone that Lt. Price was putting me in for the ArCom Medal.

After a busy day at the Air Base Site, I was more than ready to be relieved by John and Larry at 6:45. Even though the Thai bus's seats were cramped and hard, it felt good to give my brain a half-hour break on the way to Korat. Returning to my Hotel room, I was happy to hear Súusîi's knock on my door as I was undressing.

Opening the door, Súusîi rushed into my arms, and we passionately kissed. When we'd stripped off our clothing, she threw herself backwards onto the bed and lifted her inviting legs wide to receive me. Climbing between her enticing legs, I mounted her, and as I began shifting her wanting body to a Kama Sutra position, she moaned anxiously, "No. Please. Like this. Love me like this, my darling."

Soon, I felt her luscious body convulse with her orgasmic rush, and she cried out, "Yes! Yes! I needed to feel your desire for me right away, my darling. I nearly died when I got your letter and found out I wouldn't feel your lovemaking for two more days," and when she felt my orgasmic thrust distending into her love canal, she cried out again, "Yes! Yes! My darling, I missed the feel of your sexual desire shooting into me."

After our quick shower together, she gently rewrapped the wound for me before we dressed. Then leaving for the night club, we had a fun evening dancing. By 10:00, I'd danced a seductive Tango with Súusîi, and we returned quickly to my Hotel room. There, she thoroughly enjoyed our energetic lovemaking in the Kama Sutra position I'd performed that morning with Lompét. Spooning together in the afterglow, with her happily cuddled in my arms, we went to sleep.

Waking at 3:30, we made love passionately in another Kama Sutra position I knew. While we playfully showered together, she readily agreed to be at my room at 4:00 on Tuesday for our lovemaking tryst before I worked the night shift, wanting to feel the love and desire we had for one another again before Thursday, when we'd meet for dinner and dancing. After Súusîi gently dressed my wound with a 4-by-4 gauze pad, wrapping it with 4-inch Ace bandage, we dressed and passionately kissed goodbye. She then followed me to the Hotel's entrance, where I hired a sáawm-law to take her home, and another to carry me to the Chainarong Gate.

Returning to the Company Area, I went to my hooch to drop off the laundry I'd brought in my shopping bag and changed into a fresh set of jungle fatigues. Putting on my bullet-holed jungle fatugue pants, I saw Maan-daa had patched the two holes in the left leg in such a way, they were barely visible. While Skip and I went to breakfast in the Mess Hall, I gave him a detailed description of my trip to the Green Hill Site, the firefight, why I couldn't be awarded the Purple Heart, and that Lt. Price had put me in for the ArCom Medal instead.

Arriving at the Air Base Site after formation, Jim had me go into the Site Office to give a brief account of what happened during my Green Hill trip and why I couldn't receive the Purple Heart to him, Bob, Red and Phizer, while Skip relieved John and Larry from their duties in the Operations Room. When I conclude that I was told to report for Sick Call the following Saturday to have my stitches removed, Jim stated, "That's what happens when politics enters a war. Inane decisions that screw the guys who actually fight the war. Sandii, you can join Skip in the Operations Room while we do the Shift Change Report. And, I'll try to arrange a replacement for you next Saturday while you're at Sick Call."

Fortunately, it was Sunday and things were relatively quiet. On my 10:55 meal run, I met up with Glen in the Mess Hall, and told him all about my trip to the Green Hill Site, the firefight, and not being able to get the Purple Heart, but the CO was putting me in for the ArCom instead. Glen responded, "Well it couldn't have been much of a wound, as it didn't affect your ability to dance Friday night."

I replied, "The only time it hurt, was when the Medic scrubbed it with iodine."

While returning to my hooch after lunch, I stopped at the Howard Johnson to buy three 6-packs of Bud that I put in my wall locker. Returning, I bought three more 6-packs of Bud and two cartons of Pall Mall to stockpile in my wall locker, as this was the last week of the month and some of the guys would be broke. Then, I put a couple changes of clothes in my shopping bag for when I returned to Korat.

At the end of my day shift, I made the 6:35 meal run and turned the truck over to John and Larry in front of the Day Room. After eating a filling dinner in the Mess Hall, I swung by my hooch to pass out some of the 6-packs of Bud and packs of Pall Mall to those who were broke, and were very thankful. Then, I grabbed my shopping bag and headed for Korat.

Returning to my Hotel room, I readied for Lompét's knock on the door. Since we had all evening to be together, and it had been Lompét's day off, we cuddled for a while in the afterglow of our vigorous love-making. Then, she leisurely looked through the Kama Sutra book and selected a new position. While we discussed the position, Lompét became frisky with some playful foreplay, and we made love again in the position we'd been discussing.

Spooning together in the afterglow of our second lovemaking session, with Lompét snuggled warmly in my arms, she cooed, "I love you very much, my darling, and your desire for my small body. I also love that you make our lovemaking lots of fun, not just to release your sexual desire."

I responded, "My darling, I love that you're fun to be with all the time we're together, not only when we make love. It's not just your beautiful body I desire, it's also the fun you have in your heart."

Sleeping blissfully, while holding Lompét's succulent body against me, I was aroused by her playful foreplay with the 3:30 wake-up call, and thoroughly enjoyed her energetic lovemaking as we released the lust we had for each other. After a fun shower, she tenderly bandaged my thigh with a new 4 by 4 gauze pad on my wound, which was healing nicely. When she'd helped me dress in my jungle fatigues, we affectionately kissed goodbye as I caressed the curves of her petite body, and said, "I'll return to you after my meeting, my darling."

Arriving at the Company Area, I ate a hearty breakfast in the Mess Hall before attending morning formation. After formation, I went to my hooch and made sure everyone was set with beer and smokes. Then changing into a fresh set of OD BDUs, I departed for Korat.

Returning to my Hotel room, I sensuously roused Lompét from her sleep on the bed. After our passionate lovemaking and an enjoyable shower together, she rebandaged my thigh before we lay on the bed side by side, as she picked out and we discussed our next Kama Sutra lovemaking position. When she'd dressed for work and we'd lovingly kissed goodbye, I went to bed and slept till 12:30.

Waking in a hungry state, I quickly dressed and walked to the cafe for lunch and then had fun teaching to Lompét till 3:30. Returning to my Hotel room, I changed into my OD BDUs and left for Camp Friendship.

Exiting the Thai bus at the Company Area, I made two trips to the Howard Johnson, each time buying three 6-packs of Bud and a carton of Pall Malls to add to the stockpile in my wall locker. I then rewarded myself with a cold can of Bud before leaving with Skip for dinner in the Mess Hall.

After eating dinner, we swung by the Howard Johnson, and giving $3.00 to Skip, I was able to buy two sets of three 6-packs of Bud and a carton of Pall Malls. As we walk back to our hooch, Skip asked, "How come you're buying so much beer and cigarettes already? You've got all week."

I replied, "I'll be gone all day everyday till Friday, and won't be able to buy anymore at the Howard Johnson till my lunch meal-run on Friday, which is four days from now."

Skip laughed in retort, "I'm sure glad we Jews know how to manage money."

At 6:40 Skip and I were in front of the Day Room when Tommy drove up in the truck and stopped before us. As Tommy exited the truck, I said, "There's a 6-pack of beer and a pack of smokes on your bed waiting for you, and the same for George."

He replied, "That's great, Sandii. Sorry I can't say the same for you. You two'll need to hustle, as the shit was already hitting the fan when I left."

Arriving in the Operations Room, I saw it was an 'all hands on deck' situation. Walking up to Frank in the Grand Canyon, he quickly told me which circuit he was working on, his progress on finding the problem. When I had a grasp on the situation, I told him he was relieved. Skip did the same thing with Jim, taking over on one of the two outages Jim was working on. I could hear Bob and Roger in the breakout circuit racks working on at least one outage there. It wasn't total chaos, but we did have a busy evening. It was after 9:00 before Jim and Roger left to catch a Thai bus for their separate homes.

We were still moderately busy till after midnight. So, Bob gave me $5.00 for a quick run to the NCO Annex to buy 3 orders to go of cheeseburgers, fries and beer for us to eat and drink. As Skip and I mopped up on a few low priority circuits, Bob began to work making entries in the Site Log from the quick notes made in the Temporary Log. When I left on the 6:35 meal run to deliver the truck to Jim in the Motor Pool, life in the Operations Room had been quiet for a few hours.

After eating breakfast, I went to the hooch and made sure everyone was set with beer and smokes for the day, before I changed into a fresh set of OD BDUs and left for Korat. Returning to my Hotel room, I had fun with Lompét as we made love and showered together. After she redressed the wound on my left thigh, she chose another Kama Sutra position, which we had fun discussing.

Getting several hours sleep after Lompét dressed and left for work, I again went to the cafe for lunch and to have fun teaching her English until 3:30. Returning to my Hotel room for my 4:00 tryst with Súusîi, we vigorously made love to satiate the pent up lust she'd built up for me since Sunday morning, and thought, "This should keep Súusîi happy with her love for me till Thursday, when we meet here for dinner, dancing and lots of lovemaking."

Returning to the Company Area, I went to the Mess Hall for dinner before going to my hooch to set out beer and smokes for George and Tommy. Hooking up with Skip, we left in time to meet Tommy in front of the Day Room on his 6:35 meal run, and drove to the Air Base Site. Relieving Jack so he could go home to his tîi-lók, I asked him why I didn't see Jim in the Site Office for the Shift Change Report. Jack replied, "Jim left early as comp time for the extra time he'd worked last night."

Bob was in the Operations Room with us after the Shift Change Report and making his initial entries in the Site Log. Hearing the front door slam shut, I saw Phizer run into the Operations Room shouting, "Quick, someone has to drive me to the Tropo Site."

Bob said, "Calm down, George, and tell me what's going on."

Phizer responded excitedly, "It's Jim. He came home early and found me alone with Mary in the bedroom. But, we weren't doing anything. Honest. Jim said he was going to kill me with a knife from the dining room and left their home in the Jomsurang Hotel. So, I ran out and caught a bus here as fast as I could. I need one of you to drive me to the Tropo Site, where there's enough people to protect me from Jim. Can you do that?"

Bob replied, "Okay, Skip. Drive George to Tropo and I'll call to give them a heads-up."

Phizer said, "Thanks, Bob, you're a pal," as he ran for the front door with Skip fast on his heels.

Bob picked up the phone, and I heard him say, "Ted, connect me with the Tropo Site… Let me speak to the Senior Sargent. … Listen, this is Bob at the Air Base Site. One of our guys is driving Spec-5 Phizer there for protection from Sgt. Smith, who may be intent on killing Phizer for diddling with his wife. You might call the MPs to take him into protective custody. … Yea. This is no bull."

A few minutes later, I heard the front door slam and Jim yelling, "Where's that son of a bitch, Phizer? Is he here?" as he ran into the Operations Room carrying a steak knife.

Bob replied calmly, "George was here, Jim. But, Skip drove him to the Tropo Site, where the MPs will take him into custody. Jim, why don't you come with me to the NCO Club, where you can tell me all about it over a couple beers. Sandii, if you need me, you know what to do," as he led Jim from the Operations Room.

Several minutes later, Skip returned and said, "The MPs were there and took Phizer with them. Where's Bob?"

I replied, "Jim showed up in a rage with a steak knife looking for Phizer. Bob's taken him to the NCO Club to cool down with a beer and some talk."

Then, Skip and I talked about this weird set of events and what it might mean. When Bob returned later without Jim, Skip told him about the MPs and asked, "So, what's going to happen now, Bob?"

Bob replied, "To Jim? Nothing, as he's the victim. To Phizer? He's due for discharge next month. They'll likely transfer him to Company A in Sattahip, give him an Article 15 for violating Article 134 of the UCMJ for 'adultery.' Then bust him to Spec-4, fine him for 1/3 of his base pay, and bar him from re-enlisting, which is better than a General

Court Marshall, and getting 10 years at the Ft. Leavenworth Military Prison and a Dishonorable Discharge. The military takes a dim view of adultery."

CHAPTER 37

THAT'S MY CONUNDRUM

I said, "Consensual sex between two adults isn't a felony crime. Adultery might be grounds for divorce, and in some States it's considered an immoral crime, like homosexuality, and a misdemeanor. How come it's a felony crime in the military?"

Bob answered, "it comes under the heading of Good Order and Discipline, like Officers can't date an Enlisted person. If a man is deployed overseas and his wife lives in Base Housing surrounded by thousands of single men, the military doesn't want the deployed man worried about if his wife is being hit on by his brothers-in-arms while he's fighting for his country. Also, the wife can be evicted from Base Housing if she's committing adultery in their home. By keeping a strong lid on adultery, it's a real deterrent for single Soldiers to stay away from another Soldier's wife, and the waiting wife from trolling for another man to satisfy her while the husband is deployed."

Skip responded, "With the thought of ten years in prison hanging over me, it'd certainly put a damper on my sex drive. So, with Phizer gone, who's going to take over as Site Engineer?"

Bob replied, "Good question, and something that'll be decided at Tropo, since Phizer's scheduled to go Stateside next month and Jim in January. The word that's come down to Tropo last month, is the 442nd is slated to receive more troops next month and January. But, they'll barely cover those rotating Stateside, which include John on Red's Team, Jack on Bill's Team, and a bunch from the outlying sites and Korat Tropo, many of whom are Spec-5s, and SSG Anderson, their site Engineer. My guess is, we'll have to do without a Site Engineer for a month or two."

For the rest of our night shift, a pall hung over us as we muddled through several reported outages. When I met with Glen in the Mess Hall on the 10:55 meal run, he wanted to be filled in on the details of Phizer's dalliance with Jim's wife. Also, there was a lot of speculation on who might be sent to the Air Base Site to replace Phizer, but the Tropo Site was so strapped for Spec-5s, or even Spec-4s eligible for promotion to Spec-5, that nobody came to their collective mind.

Making the 6:35 meal run to the Motor Pool, normally Phizer would've been there for the truck to be passed to, as it was supposed to be Jim's off day. Instead, there was a morose looking Jim standing at the end of the row for the ¾-ton trucks. As I parked the truck next to the end of the row, he said, "Sáwátdii, Sandii. How'd it go last night?"

I replied, "Sáwátdii, Jim. You know, SOSDD[138]. A few outages is all. It'll be nice to have a couple off days," as I handed him the Tip Ticket clipboard.

Jim responded with a sigh, "Wish I could say the same. Looks like Roger and I won't have any off days for a while. Not until we get a new Site Engineer, anyway. Well, have a nice day, Sandii."

Walking to the Mess Hall, I thought, "That lifer Phizer has really screwed things up for Jim in more ways than one. Well, at least he won't be able to re-enlist and become a real lifer."

After breakfast, I quickly went to my hooch to pass out beer and smokes to everyone. As I changed into a fresh set of jungle fatigues before going to Korat, Skip arrived and asked, "Sandii, will you be here for Thanksgiving Dinner tomorrow?"

---

138   Same Old Stuff, Different Day

I exclaimed, "Thanksgiving! I forgot all about Thanksgiving. Working 6-day weeks, I have trouble keeping up with what day of the week it is, much less the day of the month and holidays. I already have dinner plans, so probably not."

Skip laughed and said, "No problem. Thanksgiving Dinner will be at lunch time, so the guys who live off Base, like the CO, will still be able to go home when they get off at 5:00."

I replied, "Thanks for the heads up, Skip," as I walked out the front door and thought, "That means Christmas is only four weeks away, and I haven't even thought about getting anyone Christmas gifts, which'll have to be mailed in the next two weeks to get them Stateside by Christmas Eve."

Riding on an uncomfortable Thai bus to Korat, I thought of what to get. Fortunately, my list wasn't too long. Linda; my parents; two younger sisters, Margaret 10, and Nancy 19; and younger brother, Bobby, 16. The by time I arrived in Korat, I had it figured out. I'd get Linda, Margaret and Nancy each a Thai style dress, but none for mom because she hated wearing a dress. In fact, as soon as the Catholic Church decided a woman could wear a pantsuit to Mass, I never saw her wear a dress again.

Dad was a teacher, and at age 50, Mom was to receive a BS in Education, so getting them a set of wood carved elephant bookends, as the elephant was the National Symbol of Thailand, seemed reasonable. And for Bobby, a wood carved chess set would do nicely for him, since he was a brainiac on the High School Chess Tournament Team. I'd also get Linda a pretty ring, as jewelry was supposed to be really inexpensive in Thailand.

Arriving at my Hotel room, I was ready for Lompét when I heard her knock on the door. Enjoying our enthusiastic lovemaking in a new Kama Sutra position, and the rush from our orgasms, we spooned for a while in the pleasant feelings from our lovemaking and told of our love for the other. I then explained to her about Christmas, the tradition of gift giving, that I had two younger sisters, and asked if she would model for the dresses I'd like to get them for Christmas gifts.

She replied, "My darling, I'm very honored to do this for my beloved boyfriend."

After we happily showered together and she picked the next Kama Sutra position for our lovemaking, we dressed and left for Mrs. Poomsan's clothier shop. Entering the shop, I explained to Mrs. Poomsan in Thai what I wanted, and she said, "No problem. I make lots of formal Thai dresses for Americans to send their families. Let me show you some Thai fashion magazines."

Seeing a style of the formal Thai dresses desired, I said, "Mrs. Poomsan, would you make two of them to fit Lompét, as my two youngest sisters are her size, or smaller, and one dress to fit you for my other sister."

Selecting the colors of flowered embroidered silk for each dress and agreeing on the price for the three dresses, I arranged to have the fitting the next morning and paid her a deposit of 200 Bhat, $10, for half the cost. Leaving the shop, Lompét continued on to the cafe, and I returned to my Hotel room for a nap, thinking, "Fortunately, I've enough money in the Bank to buy everything now, when everyone else is broke and the shops are likely to make better deals before Pay Day next Monday. I can stop by the bank today, after I teach English to Lompét. Then after dinner at the Mess Hall, I can return to my room for another nap before I take her dancing. Then tomorrow morning, after the fittings at Mrs. Poomsan's shop, I can shop for the bookends, chess set, and ring for Linda before the Thanksgiving Dinner in the Mess Hall at noon. Then, on Pay Day, I can pick up the dresses and mail it all Stateside."

Waking after a couple of hours, I dressed and went to the cafe for lunch. After a fun afternoon teaching Lompét English, I left at 3:30 to catch a Thai bus to the Bank on the Air Base. Arriving there, I exchanged $75 for 1,500 Bhat before boarding a Thai bus to the Company Area, where I was able to take a short nap before the 5:00 bugle call for Mess.

After dinner in the Mess Hall, I returned to my Hotel room and slept till 7:30, when I dressed and left for the cafe to meet Lompét, and take her dancing. Entering the cafe, I watched her scurry from the back of the cafe, looking most becoming in her form-fitting, low-cut, light blue silk dress. As we exchanged sáwátdiis, she said, "My darling, I didn't wait by the front door looking pretty for you, as I don't want more problem with any not-good American man."

It being the Wednesday before Pay Day, there were few Americans to be seen on Mahat Thai Road and had no problem hiring a sǎawm-law for 2 Bhat to take us the half-mile to the night club. Arriving there, we met up with Glen and Súpa on the 3rd tier, and I told Glen about how Jim and Roger were having to work every day to fill in for Phizer until the new troops arrived in December and January. This was also a problem, as Jim, John and Jack were due to rotate Stateside in January.

I had a fun evening socializing with Glen and Súpa, and dancing with Lompét in her fetching light blue dress. After dancing our provocative Tango, we hurried to my Hotel room and feverishly made love to assuage our pent-up lust in climatic release. Then, in the afterglow of climax, we blissfully went to sleep as we spooned happily together.

Waking to Lompét's tantalizing body snuggled in my arms at 3:30 in the morning, we quickly felt our desires blossom into the lust we happily satisfied with our energetic lovemaking in the Kama Sutra position she'd previously chosen. After basking in our afterglow, we enjoyed teasing each other as we showered. Then she gently applied a new 4-by-4 gauze pad to the wound on my left leg and bandaged it. As I dressed in my jungle fatigues, she selected another position from the Kama Sutra, which we discussed before we passionately kissed goodbye, and I left for Camp Friendship to have breakfast and attend formation.

Returning to my Hotel room after formation, we had fun with our foreplay. Eliciting the desires we felt for each other into a raging lust, which we then satiated by our vigorous lovemaking in the position we'd discussed a couple of hours before. When she'd chosen our next Kama Sutra position and we'd discussed it, we dressed and departed for the dress shop.

Entering the shop, Mrs. Poomsan happily exchanged sáwátdiis with us, and took Lompét to the changing room. When they returned, each wearing one of the three dresses I'd ordered, I made approving comments and Mrs. Poomson made note of a few minor changes. Then, they went back and returned with Lompét wearing the third dress, beaming with pride at being chosen for this task, and Mrs. Poomsan said, "it is a great honor you give her to stand-in for your sister because she is seen as a member of your family during that time."

As Lompét went into the shop's rear to change into her clothes, I asked, "Mrs. Poomson, do you know where there's a good jewelry shop?"

She replied, "Yes, Mr. Sandii. If you walk up Wacharasrit Road, cross Chomphon Road and turn left, there's a reputable jewelry shop near the Bangkok Bank."

Leaving the dress shop, Lompét and I exchanged our sáwátdiis, before she walked on to the cafe for work, and I walked to the Jewelry shop on Chomphon Road. Entering the jewelry shop lined with display cases, and seeing no other customers in sight, I was greeted by the English speaking, Chinese proprietor. Asking him to show me his selection of women's rings, he took me to one of the glass display cases on the left side of his shop. There, I saw a very pretty, conical-shaped silver ring with at least 20 small precious and semi-precious gemstones, set in four circular layers. Asking to see several other rings first, I then asked to see the cone-shaped ring. Taking it out of the display case, he said, "Ah, yes. This is very popular with the ladies. It is called the Princess Ring because the 22 gems are in the shape of a Buddhist temple's stupa and worn by the Royal Princesses. It is only 2,000 Bhat, or $100 dollars."

I exclaimed, "That's too expensive!"

He responded smiling, "You're special American friend. Only 1,500 Bhat for you."

I replied, "It's the end of the month, so I have very little money."

He offered, "I understand, my American friend. For 1,000 Bhat, it's yours."

I turned to leave and said, "I know where I can buy this same kind of ring for 600 Bhat."

With no other customers in sight, he responded desperately, "You're a very good man. I'll sell it at a loss to you for 800 Bhat."

I replied, "You're an honest man. I'm happy to pay you more for the pretty ring," as I handed him eight red 100-Bhat bills from my left front pants pocket and thought, "Forty bucks, this is great. I know the size is too large for Linda's dainty fingers. But, as I don't know her ring size or which finger she'll like to wear it, it'll be easier to cut it down to fit than stretch it to fit."

Having purchased the Princess Ring, I walked up Chomphon Road looking for a curio shop selling wood carvings. Finding one, I entered it. After some diligent bargaining with the shop owner, I bought a set of 8-inch tall elephant bookends, Thailand's national symbol, for 60 Bhat, and a set of carved wood chess pieces in a 15-inch square, wood box containing felt lined depressions for each piece and an in-laid chessboard on its surface, for 200 Bhat.

After the shop owner wrapped and placed the bookends in one cardboard box and the chess set in another box, I put them in my shopping bag. Exiting the shop, I walked down Chainarong Road to its Gate carrying my hoard and boarded a Thai bus for Camp Friendship.

Exiting the bus at my Company Area, I toted the presents to my hooch, and drank a cold can of Bud as I emptied the shopping bag into my wall locker. Seeing nobody in the hooch, I left for the Mess Hall and the promise of a Thanksgiving Day meal.

Entering the Mess Hall, I saw it was nearly full of laughing, talking mean, some in OD BDU or jungle fatigue uniforms and some not, enjoying plate loads of roast turkey with all the traditional trimmings of a Thanksgiving Dinner. Grabbing a tray and set of flatware, and placing it on the waist-high counter, a Thai cook set a plate with an inch-thick mix of sliced dark and white turkey meat on it, covered with mashed potatoes and giblet gravy liberally poured on top. The next Thai cook put a second plate on my tray full of yams, coleslaw and two bread rolls. I saw behind the two serving cooks, the other two Thai cooks busy prepping plates full with food being served at the counter.

Picking up my heavily laden tray, I carried it to the beverage table, where I saw the tomato juice dispenser was filled with a dark red liquid labeled "Cranberry Juice," which I passed up for three glasses of chocolate milk. Proceeding to the dining area, I saw Skip smiling and yelling with a mouth full of food, "Hey, Sandii, over here."

Walking to where Skip was eating, and setting my tray on the table opposite him, I said, "I see you waited like one dog waits on another," as I sat down and dug into the scrumptious fare before me. Looking along the center of the table, I saw besides the usual condiments, there were quart jars of butter, honey and cranberry jelly for the bread rolls on my second plate.

Skip laughed and replied, "I just wanted to make sure this chow-hound got here soon enough to get seconds before they ran out of food."

I laughed in response, "Like, when have you ever seen the Army run out of food, and where are you going to put seconds in that skinny body of yours?"

Skip replied, "There's a first time for everything. Besides, my Mom always said I have a hollow leg."

After we had our second helping of the delicious feast, as my Mom also accused me of having a hollow leg, we went by the Howard Johnson, and I paid for two more sets of three 6-packs of Bud and a carton of Pall Malls. As we carried them back to our hooch, I proclaimed, "You can never have too much beer and smokes, Skip. Also, I have all my Christmas shopping done already. If you have enough money, you should go to Korat and get your Christmas shopping done now, because everyone's broke before Pay Day and the shop owners are hurting for business."

Skip laughed and replied, "It's Hanukkah shopping for me, not Christmas. And, it's a good idea."

Entering our hooch, I opened my wall locker to add the beer and smokes to my stockpile. Retrieving the Princess Ring, I said, "Look what I got for forty bucks to give Linda."

Skip exclaimed, "Forty bucks! That has to be worth at least 100 bucks Stateside. Where'd you buy it? I gotta get one of those for Judith."

As I gave Skip the directions to the jewelry shop, he took out the Bhat he'd stashed in his wall locker. Then, we left and boarded a Thai bus to Korat. As we rode the bus, I explained the bargaining techniques I'd used to get the 2,000 Bhat asking price down to the 800 Bhat selling price. Exiting the bus at the Chainarong Gate, I walked with Skip up Chainarong Road to Mahat Thai Road, where I turned left to walk to the cafe, as Skip continued up to Chomphon Road and the jewelry shop.

Entering the cafe, I exchanged sáwátdiis with Lompét. Explaining to her I'd just come from a big feast at Camp Friendship celebrating our Thanksgiving Day, and showing her my bulging stomach as proof positive why I wouldn't be eating lunch there today. Then, I proceeded to enjoy teaching her English till 3:30, when I left for my Hotel room.

At my Hotel room, I prepared for Súusîi's arrival. Opening the door at the sound of her knock, we quickly engaged in passionate intercourse using the Kama Sutra position I'd pleasured Lompét at 3:30 that morning, much to Súusîi's own pleasure. After a quick shower cleaning the crud from our bodies, she gently rewrapped my wound, and then we dressed for an enjoyable dinner at the Ming Ter.

Returning to my Hotel, we again relished the longing we had for each other in a different Kama Sutra position that suited our rapacious lovemaking. Entwining in the pleasant glow of our orgasmic release, we kissed and caressed the other's body with affection as we proclaimed our love. After a while we extricated our arms and legs from around our bodies for a playful shower together.

When we'd dressed for a fun evening, Súusîi properly followed behind me to the night club, where we met up with the usual dance group on the 3rd tier. Having been a month since they'd seen me, there were lots of questions in English about what I'd been doing in the interim. Not wishing to be rude, I gave short answers till our Pepsi's arrived, then quickly asked Súusîi to the dance floor, and enjoyed flirtatiously dancing with her.

After an enjoyable evening dancing with my enticing Súusîi, we danced a sensuous Tango to evoke our desires into a raging appetite to gratify our sexual senses. Going rapidly back to my Hotel room, we feasted on our pent-up lust until it was satiated in orgasmic release. Slipping from our Kama Sutra position to spoon our bodies in the afterglow of our lovemaking, we fell joyfully asleep.

In the morning, Súusîi took immense pleasure in our vigorous lovemaking knowing we'd be together the next evening fulfilling her need to feel my desire for her with more dancing and lovemaking without having to wait days to do so. After we had fun showering together, she rebandaged my thigh before I dressed in my jungle fatigues. Then, caressing her voluptuous body as we kissed goodbye, she cooed desiringly, "I love you very much, my darling, and will be thinking of your desire for me till we're together tomorrow night," as I left for Camp Friendship.

Exiting the Thai bus at the Company Area, I went to my hooch and drank a cold can of Bud as I set out a 6-pack of Bud and a pack of Pall Malls each on Dan, George and Tommy's beds, then changed into a fresh set of jungle fatigues before going to the Mess Hall for breakfast. After formation, as Phizer was now history, Skip and I rode in the truck's cab with Jim. As Jim drove us to work, he said, "Sandii, I discussed this with Roger, and tomorrow morning, instead of going to formation, we want you to go to the Dispensary and be there before they start Sick Call. That way, you'll be one of the first they see, and you can be to work before we're slammed with the usual Saturday morning outages, okay?"

I replied, "Mâi bpén raî. I can be there long before Sick Call starts at 7:00."

The morning went smoothly, and when I met Glen for lunch on the 10:55 meal run, he said, "The word from Sattahip is Phizer's been busted to Spec-4, will have $100 deducted from his pay this Monday, and is on barracks restriction for the remainder of his tour. Also, nobody'll have anything to do with him. I imagine Jim'll be happy to hear that."

I responded, "I imagine all Jim would be happy to hear is Phizer was shot by a firing squad, as he and Roger now have to work seven days a week to make up the slack he left."

After lunch, I made two trips to the Howard Johnson for beer and smokes, adding some to my stockpile, and giving Dan, George and Tommy each a 6-pack of Bud and a pack of Pall Malls, for which they were most grateful. Then, on my 4:55 meal run, I set out the same on Ronnie and Stony's beds, and packed my shopping bag with fresh clothes, which I took back to work with me.

Relieved of my duties by John and Larry at 6:45, I was off for Korat with my shopping bag like a cat with its tail on fire. Arriving at my Hotel room, I put away the clothes in my shopping bag, changed my attire to take Lompét dancing, and left for the cafe.

Entering the cafe, I saw my pretty Lompét quickly walk to me from the cafe's back wearing her form-fitting, low-cut, hot pink silk dress swaying enticingly around her shapely legs and felt my body flush with desire for her. Exchanging sáwátdiis, I said, "My darling, you look most beautiful tonight."

She replied, "I love your desire for me, my darling," as we exited the cafe.

Arriving at the night club by sǎawm-law, we met with Glen and Súpa as they also arrived by sǎawm-law. Entering the night club, I overheard Lompét tell Súpa, as they followed me and Glen to a table on the 3rd tier, about the honor I had given her to stand-in for my sisters at the dress shop. After enjoying the evening watching the enticing Lompét dance in my arms, and then my seductive Tango, I was enthralled with the ecstasy of our lovemaking when we returned to my Hotel room.

Spending a delightful night spooned tightly together, we woke and engaged in impassioned lovemaking in the Kama Sutra position she chose previously, and loosed our mutual lust in climactic release. Passing some time in its afterglow, we then had fun showering together before she wrapped a new 4-by-4 gauze pad onto my nearly healed wound and helped me dress in my jungle fatigues. When we passionately kissed goodbye, I enjoyed the feel of her tantalizing, petite body as I caressed it desiringly with my hands before I departed for Camp Friendship.

Exiting the Thai bus as the Company Area, I went to my hooch to set out the beer and smokes on Dan, George and Tommy's beds, and changed into a fresh set of jungle fatigues before going to the Mess Hall for breakfast. On leaving the Mess Hall, I boarded a Thai bus into Camp Friendship and got out across the street from the Camp's Dispensary. Crossing the street, I walked to the Dispensary's glass-fronted doors and became the first in line for Sick Call, watching several white-tunicked Medics milling around inside until one of them opened the front doors.

When the Entrance door was opened by a Medic, there were at least a dozen men in line behind me. Walking to the chest-high counter, I showed my ID card to a Medic behind the counter and said, "I was told by the Doctor to return this morning to have my stitches removed."

Going through a stack of Medical Records behind the counter, he said, "Yea. Here we go. Lynch, Sherman A. will you follow me, please?"

Walking around the counter to the right, I followed him into the 1st Treatment Room on the right, and he said, "have a seat on the exam table, Specialist Lynch." Then, handing my Medical Record to the Doctor sitting behind the desk, he said, "Sir, here's your GSW[139], from a week ago."

The Doctor said, "Thanks, Frank," as he took my Medical Record. Opening it as he stood, he said, "Oh yes. GSW left thigh, in line of duty. Could you drop your pants, Specialist Lynch, so I can examine it?"

Dropping my jungle fatigue pants to the top of my shiny black combat boots, I then sat on the exam table, as he walked to the stainless steel cabinet and removed a dark-green cloth packet sealed with one-inch wide masking tape that had dark stripes on it. Setting the cloth packet on the exam table next to me, I saw it was labeled "Suture Removal." He opened the cloth packet, and I observed it contained a pair

---

139   Gun Shot Wound

of tweezers, a small pair of scissors, and several iodine pads. He then opened a paper packet and pulled on the pair of latex gloves it contained and asked, "Any problems with the wound? Any redness, swelling or being hot to the touch?" as he began to unwrap the bandage.

I replied, "No problems, except it itches sometimes."

With the bandage and gauze pad removed, he said, "Itching is a good sign. It means the wound is healing. And, it looks like it's healing very well, so I'll go ahead and remove the sutures."

Swabbing the wound area with the iodine pads, he then lifted each suture in turn with the tweezers by knot, slipped the open tip of the scissors under the sutures, snipped it in two, and painlessly pulled the suture from the wound. Then placing a new 4-by-4 gauze pad over the wound and wrapping it with a fresh 4-inch Ace bandage, he said, "That'll protect the suture holes till they scab over today. Then you can remove the bandage and you're good as new, except for the scar."

Leaving the Dispensary, I crossed the street and boarded a Thai bus making its loop at the East end of the Camp. As it did so, I saw the H-type concrete buildings I'd seen under construction when I was doing my in-processing, were now finished barracks with soldiers living in them. I also saw beyond them other H-type buildings under construction. When the bus turned right onto the main street bordering the half-mile square empty field containing the Tropo Site in its far corner, I saw a huge hole had been dug in the ground near the main street and wondered, "What's with that big hole in the ground? It's too deep to be the foundation for a building."

Exiting the bus when it stopped near the Air Base Site, I went straight to the Operations Room, and found things in full swing with the usual large number of outages reported in as people Stateside were sending out final messages to the Vietnam Theater of War before they went home for the weekend. Entering the Grand Canyon, Jim handed me the Temporary Log and said, "Sandii, glad to see you made good time getting through Sick Call. We were just notified KEG-4 is down. It's on an A-2 circuit, so you've got ten minutes to get it back in service." And, so began my Saturday day shift at the Air Base Site.

On my 10:55 meal run, after eating lunch in the Mess Hall, I went by the Howard Johnson and bought the usual set of beer and smokes, which I carried to my hooch, and distributed it to Dan, George and Tommy. Then, packing my shopping bag with fresh clothes, I returned to the Air Base Site. When I made my 4:55 meal run, after eating dinner in Mess Hall, I again went by the Howard Johnson and bought a set of beer and smokes, which I carried to my hooch, and set a 6-pack of beer and pack of smokes each on Ronnie and Stony's beds. Then, I put the third 6-pack of beer and remaining packs of smokes in my wall locker, and returned to the Air Base Site.

When I was relieved by John and Larry after a busy day, I left quick as rattlesnake strike for Korat. Soon after entering my Hotel room, I heard Súusîi's knock on my room's door. Opening the door, she threw herself into my desiring arms, fervently kissed me, and said, "My darling, I've missed your desire for me very much," as she rapidly removed her clothes. After our rapacious lovemaking in the Kama Sutra position I'd experienced with Lompét that morning, we took a fun shower together, where she laughed, "My darling, I'm so happy with your desire to pleasure me in so many different lovemaking positions."

When she began to bandage my thigh, I said, "See, my darling, the doctor removed the thread from my wound and said it doesn't need to be bandaged after today." Then we dressed and left for the night club, where we had a delightful evening dancing together. After our sensuous Tango, we returned to my Hotel room and released our pent-up lust with a vigorous bout of lovemaking in a different Kama Sutra position.

After a wonderful night sleeping contentedly together in each other's arms, we woke with our passionate lovemaking fueled by the knowledge we wouldn't see each other again till Tuesday evening for dinner, dancing and more lovemaking. When we'd showered and I'd dressed in my jungle fatigues, we then passionately kissed goodbye. As I desiringly caressed Súusîi's sumptuous body, I thought, "Being with Súusîi is so much fun and loving her is so satisfying, why do I feel something is missing?"

After eating breakfast in the Mess Hall, I went to my hooch to make sure everyone was set for the day with beer and smokes, before changing into a fresh set of OD BDUs and going to formation. Then, leaving directly for Korat, I had a wonderful, fun filled day with Lompét, making love, studying English, having lunch at the Ming Ter, seeing a Samurai movie with Glen and Súpa, then more lovemaking before eating dinner at the Thai BBQ restaurant.

Once we'd made love again and showered playfully, she helped me dress in my OD BDUs to leave for the night shift. When I'd desiringly caressed her luscious, petite body as we kissed goodbye, I thought, "Being with Lompét is so much fun and loving her feels so satisfying, then why again do I feel something is missing?"

Riding a Thai bus to Camp Friendship, I pondered, "I'm loved by two very pretty, fun, sexually desirable and satisfying women, who I love and make me happy in return. But, I feel something is missing. I have my work, which I find enjoyable and challenging, and outside of my work, I have two women I find enjoyable. That's it! Neither of my love relationships, which take up all my time outside of work, are challenging.

"Aside from learning how to make love in different Kama Sutra positions, the only other thing I've learned is how to have great 'pillow talk' in Thai. It's like when I went to the night club the first time with Jintana and was looking forward to improving my Thai language skills with a group of Thais, only to learn they wanted to practice their English with me, which I found very disappointing. Then, when Súpa became Glen's tîi-lók, I lost my study buddy, and have not learned very much more Thai since.

"Tonight, I need to talk with Bob about where I can find a group of Thais to broaden my knowledge of the Thai language and culture, while keeping my love life enjoyable and satisfying. That's my conundrum."

CHAPTER 38

THEY DON'T GIVE ARCOMS FOR RIDING SHOTGUN

Exiting the bus at the Company Area, I walked to my hooch, and set a 6-pack of beer and pack of smokes each on George and Tommy's beds for them when they got off the day shift, thinking, "I'm glad tomorrow's Pay Day so I won't need to do this again for a few weeks."

Changing into a fresh set of OD BDUs, I left with Skip for the Mess Hall, where we had dinner before meeting with Tommy in front of the Day Room. When Tommy arrived with the truck, I let him know there was a 6-pack of beer and a pack of smokes on his and George's beds, to which he responded, "Thanks, Sandii. I'm sure glad tomorrow's Pay Day so you won't be burdened with keeping us in beer and smokes for a while. When I left the Site, it was quiet, so you should have a quiet night shift."

Driving to the Air Base Site, I asked Skip how things went at the Jewelry shop, and he replied, "It went really good. I was able to talk the shop owner only to $45 on a Princess Ring for Judith, but it's still a great deal. And, you're right about the shop owners being desperate to sell, and made some good deals that I was able to put a deposit on, before I ran out of Bhat."

Arriving in the Operations Room, Jack said everything was quiet, as I relieved him to go home to his tîi-lók. And, things remained quiet till 9:30, when Ted called from the PBX building to let us know he had a line through to Rosey for WATS calls Stateside. Talking to Linda and then my family, I told them I'd be mailing my Christmas gifts to them tomorrow, as it was Pay Day, so there would be plenty of time to get there before Christmas. And, to please not to open the packages till Christmas Day.

Meeting Glen in the Mess Hall on my 10:55 meal run, I asked, "As we don't study Thai together since Súpa has become your tîi-lók, have you stopped trying to improve your Thai language skills?"

Glen laughed and replied, "Heck no. Súpa finds learning English both too complicated and too many sounds she can't get her tongue around. So, we speak only Thai at home and she has me learn at least one new word or phrase each day. It's something Tom's tîi-lók does with him, and she suggested it to Súpa, and it works really well for me. Why? Is there a problem with Lompét?"

I answered, "Oh, no. there's no problem with Lompét. She's lots of fun to be with, both in and out of bed. It's just that we're so focused on her learning English, that my learning Thai has been stymied, and it's something I only realized today. So now, I'm trying to figure out what I can do to fix it, short of having Lompét for my tîi-lók, which she'd be more than happy to be, if I asked."

Glen responded, "And, other than asking Lompét to be your tîi-lók, I don't know what else to suggest."

While Skip was on his 11:55 meal run, I presented my conundrum to Bob, who replied, "So, you've two girlfriends who're learning English. One at her College, and the other from you, but you want to learn more Thai. Does that about sum it up?"

I answered, "That's pretty much it."

Bob responded, "Then it sounds to me that you need to find a place full of Thai men, so you won't look like a butterfly chasing other women to your two girlfriends. Have you thought about going to a Thai bar? And, I don't mean one that caters to Americans that's full of prostitutes. I mean a bar where Thai men hang out after work to relax before they go home to their wife or girlfriend."

I responded, "That sounds like a good idea, but aren't women there, too?"

Bob replied, "Thai social customs forbid that. You know as well as I do, that men and women socialize separately, even in their own homes. Of course, you'll have to go past where most of the American bars are to find a Thai bar. And, with the Thai you already know, it'll be no problem to be welcomed as a regular."

I said, "Thanks, Bob, I'll have to try that on my off day this Wednesday."

As things were slow at the Air Base Site, and it would be very busy Pay Day for me when I got off my night shift, I was able to get a couple hours of sleep before the breakfast meal runs started at 4:55. Making the 6:35 meal run, I delivered the truck to Jim before going to the Mess Hall for breakfast. Arriving at my hooch, I opened a can of Bud from the mini-fridge to drink while I changed into my Class-B khaki uniform for Pay Line. Skip and I left for the Pay Line early to get our pay as soon as possible, so we could go to Korat and pick up the items we had on deposit and mail them today.

When we arrived in front of the Day Room, there were only two guys ahead of us in the Pay Line. Waiting for the Day Room's front door to open I watched as the Pay Line grew longer behind me. Soon, I saw the Spec-4 Brown join the Pay Line wearing a pressed set of OD BDUs. Pointing this out to the guy behind me, I asked, "It's great to see Brown made Spec-4, but doesn't he know the uniform-of-the-day for pay is Class B khakis?"

The guy replied, "Unless you're on duty. It's part of the deal he made with the CO for his promotion to Spec-4. As the only lineman in the Company, he's 'on duty' 24/7, then he can wear his OD BDUs to receive his pay."

Collecting my $220.00 in pay, I then paid $7.50 for a $10.00 Savings Bond and $8.00 for Maan-daa's services, and exchanged $100.00 for 2,000 Bhat. Returning to my hooch, I drank a cold can of Bud as I put a 6-pack from my wall locker into the mini-fridge, changed into a fresh set of OD BDUs, and put fresh changes of clothes in my shopping bag. As I did so, George, Tommy, Ronnie and Stony came by and gave me $10.0 each for keeping them in beer and smokes while they were broke. A little while later, Dan stopped by and gave me $10.00 for the service.

Putting $100.00 into the tobacco can I kept on the top shelf of my wall locker, I picked up my shopping bag, and caught a Thai bus to the Bank on the Air Base. Depositing the $50.00 into my Savings Account, I then boarded another Thai bus to Korat. Returning to the Sri Pattana Hotel, I went to the Reception Desk and paid the 750 Bhat in advance for a month's rent on my room. After, going to my room, I put away the clothes in my shopping bag and changed into civilian clothes before I went to Mrs. Poomsan's dress shop. Entering the shop, I paid her the balance due on the three dresses I ordered, and she put each dress into separate cardboard boxes, which I labeled each accordingly to whom is was for, and then placed them in my shopping bag.

Returning to the Company Area on the Thai bus, I went to my hooch and wrapped the Princess Ring in the dress for Linda, thinking, "Won't this be a surprise when she discovers the ring wrapped in the dress."

Carrying the five packages to the Mailroom in HQ, I addressed each to its recipient and thought as I mailed them, "It's a good thing I only have to pay the postage from the APO[140] in San Francisco, otherwise it'd cost a fortune to pay the freight from Thailand."

Leaving the Mailroom, I caught a Thai bus to Korat and had at Lompét's cafe, where I enjoyed a fun afternoon teaching her English till 3:30. Returning to my Hotel room, I was able to nap for at least an hour before I had to dress in my OD BDUs and leave for Camp Friendship.

Exiting a Thai bus at the Company Area, I went to the Mess Hall for dinner, where I met up with Skip. After dinner, we walked to our hooch and each drank a cold can of beer before meeting Tommy with the truck in front of the Day Room at 6:40. As he exited the truck, Tommy said, "It looks like you're in for a very busy night, as it was really hopping when I left."

Ship laughed and said, "And that's news how? It's always like that on a Monday night. At least, it gives us something to do in our spare time."

Arriving in the Operations Room, I took over the outage Jack was working on in the Grand Canyon so he could go home to his tîi-lók, as Jim handed Skip the Temporary Log and assigned him an outage to

---

140   Army Post Office

work on. At 9:30, Bob told Jim and Roger, "You two go home before the busses stop running. If we don't get any of the outages back in service in a timely manner, I'll just Log that the delay was 'due to insufficient manpower,' and maybe the Quad-C A can pull enough power to have Army Personnel send us more people. Heaven knows they claim to have the power of God in this Theater of War."

Fortunately, we weren't overwhelmed with outages after Jim and Roger left. In fact, it had quieted down enough by our midnight meal runs, that afterwards, Skip and I could each get a couple hours sleep on the mattress in the back of the Operations Room by the time Skip left on his 5:40 meal run, when I made my 6:35 meal run and turned the truck over to Jim in the Motor Pool, I said, "no worries, Jim. Things calmed down after you and Roger left last night."

After eating breakfast in the Mess Hall, I quickly went to my hooch, drank a cold can of Bud, rapidly changed into a fresh set of jungle fatigues, and put some clean clothes in my shopping bag before leaving to catch a Thai bus for Korat. Arriving at my Hotel room, I stripped to my boxers, put my clean clothes away prior to resting on the bed, and waited with desire for Lompét's knock on my room's door.

Answering Lompét's knock on the door, she leapt up into my outstretched arms and passionately kissed me as I carried her petite, lusting body to the bed. As she speedily removed her clothes, she said eagerly, "My darling, we haven't made love for two days, and my body aches to feel your desire for me."

Throwing herself backward onto the bed with her enticing legs spread invitingly high and wide to receive me, I easily pushed my lusting shaft fully into her taut, wet love canal. Achieving the orgasmic release from our pent-up lust with wanton lovemaking in the Kama Sutra position she'd chosen, she cried out, "My darling, I love you very much and the desire you have for my small body."

Spooning together in the afterglow of our vigorous lovemaking, she mused, "I wish we could be together every day and night, sharing the love and desire we have for each other. Just think of how much fun we could have with each other all the time if I found a house for us to live together in," as she wiggled her luscious, little butt enticingly against my groin.

I wearily groaned at the words "a house for us to live together in," as I thought in a panic, "I've let this go too far with the ruse that I'm her 'boyfriend' to engender the envy of her workmates and stop them from teasing her. Yes, I've grown to love her and it's fun being with her, but if we lived together, I'd end up not wanting to end my love for her and want to take her Stateside as my wife, like so many other Americans do. I've no doubt she'd be a loving and attentive wife, but there's no way I can afford the dowry her father will demand for his permission to marry her, even if it was as little as $1,000. Besides, I have Súusîi, who is happy with the status quo and has no immediate aspirations to marry me. And even if she did, her father would most likely forbid it and send her away, like Julii's father did."

I responded, "My darling, I do love and desire you very much, and I enjoy every minute we are together, and if I lived with you, I'd want to be married to you. But to marry you, your father would want his dowry money for having raised you, which is a lot of money, and you're worth every Bhat. However, the money the Army pays me isn't enough for a the dowry. My darling, I'm your boyfriend, but first, I'm your teacher for you to learn and be a good 'tîi-lók' for an American man, like I did for Glûaimáaí.

"I also loved and desired Glûaimáaí very much, and she too wanted to be my tîi-lók, but she understood and accepted that I couldn't have her as my tîi-lók for the same reasons. And now, she's happily living with an American man, who says he wants to marry her and take her to America as his wife. You're very pretty, Lompét, and very good at ballroom dancing and lovemaking, and have learned enough English to easily attract an American man to desire you to be his tîi-lók, or even his wife. I'll be your teacher and boyfriend till an American man asks you to be his tîi-lók, which you're ready to be."

Lompét had been crying when she replied, "My darling, forgive me. I'm a foolish little woman who forgot why we're together. You're correct. I know you love and desire me very much, as I do you, but my father would want a large dowry from you to marry me, even though no Thai man wants to marry me. I'll begin to flirt with American men in English as you've taught me, and I hope you'll still be my teacher."

Holding her close in my arms, I said, "Of course I'll still be your teacher and your boyfriend, if you like."

Turning around in my rms and passionately kissing me, Lompét moaned, "Yes. Very much yes, my darling, I want you to still be my teacher and my boyfriend," and lifting her succulent breasts to my mouth, "and feel your desire for my little body with lots of lovemaking."

After vigorously making love again, we playfully showered together. Then, lying side by side on the bed, she happily picked a Kama Sutra position, which we enjoyed discussing how to perform, before she dressed to leave for work. When we had passionately kissed goodbye, she said, "I'm looking forward to seeing you at lunch and to your teaching me English."

With Lompét gone to work, I slept for a few hours before I also dressed and left for the cafe. After eating my lunch, I spent a couple of happy hours teaching Lompét English. Then, at 3:30, I returned to my Hotel room.

At 4:00, I heard Sûusîi's knock on my room's door, and opening it, I was met by an onslaught of her passionate kisses, as she rapidly removed her clothes. Soon, we were wrapped around each other, energetically making love in the Kama Sutra position I had experienced with Lompét that morning. Once our lust was expended in orgasmic copulation, she gasped, "My darling, your lovemaking is so marvelous, it brings me joy just to think of your lovemaking while we're apart."

When we'd bathed in the afterglow of our lovemaking for a while, expressing our mutual love for each other, we had a fun shower washing the crud from the other. After we dressed, she properly walked behind me to the Ming Ter for dinner, and there talked about what had happened while we were apart. She was impressed with my strategy to by my Christmas presents the week before Pay Day when most Americans were broke and the shop owners were desperate to sell their wares.

Returning to my Hotel room, we lovingly undressed each other and enjoyed caressing the other's bodies in sensuous foreplay, resulting in being consumed by our lust in vigorous lovemaking, and the rush from our orgasms. We then slept for an hour, entwined in the pleasure of our orgasmic release, and woke to enjoy a fun shower together, after which we dressed and left for the night club.

Entering the night club, we saw David and Mary, and spent an enjoyable evening socializing with them and dancing in each other's arms. After we danced a scintillating Tango, we quickly returned to my Hotel room, and wantonly made love to release our pent-up lust in orgasmic rushes. In the afterglow that followed, we slept joyfully wrapped in each other's arms and legs.

With the 3:30 wake-up call, our playful foreplay ignited the desires we had for each other into passionate lovemaking. In its afterglow, we looked forward to the time we'd have again the following evening before we went dancing at the night club with our friends. When we'd playfully showered together, I dressed in my jungle fatigues, and then caressed the luscious curves of her body as we passionately kissed goodbye.

Arriving at the Company Area on a Thai bus, I went to the Mess Hall for breakfast before attending morning formation. After the rigamarole of everyone being reported "present or accounted for," SFC Davidson announced, "There's a few things the CO wants passed to you before you're dismissed. First, our new CO arrived in country last night and will fly up to Camp Friendship today. The Change-of-Command Ceremony will be at morning formation next Monday. Second, everyone who has their off day today, will report to the Motor Pool for transport to the Tropo Site to rebuild the perimeter bunkers now that they've had a chance to dry out since the end of the monsoon season over a month ago. This is an annual PM everyone gets to participate in, regardless of rank. Those whose off day is this Friday or Sunday will be doing PM on the perimeter bunkers on those days. Third, Specialist Lynch, you're to report to the CO right after formation, before you go to the Tropo Site. Platoon, dismissed."

I looked at Jim, who looked at me and shrugged his shoulders to indicate he had no idea why I was to see the CO. Entering HQ, PFC Schultz said, "Go on in, the CO's waiting for you."

Entering the CO's Office, I marched to the front of Lt. Price's desk, smartly saluted, and said, "Specialist Lynch, reporting as ordered, Sir."

Returning my salute, he said, "Please, shut the door and have a seat."

After I shut the door and sat in a chair before his desk, he said, "I received a response this morning on my recommendation for you to receive the Army Commendation Medal. I'm sorry, Sandii, but it doesn't look like you're receiving the ArCom Medal. It was all I could do to talk the Battalion CO into it, as there's a limited number that can be awarded in each Battalion. Since there can't be any mention of combat action in the recommendation, Brigade denied it on the ground that riding shotgun on a broken down truck isn't substantial enough to award an AirCom to anyone. I'm sorry, and wish I could do more, but I've done the best I can do."

I responded, "Mâi bpén rai, Sir. I appreciate the effort. After all, it's just the way things are in Thailand. And you're right, they don't give ArComs for riding shotgun."

CHAPTER 39

AWARDED A PURPLE HEART FOR BEING STUNG BY A SCORPION

Leaving the CO's Office, I walked directly to the Motor Pool and climbed up the tailgate of a 2½-ton truck into its canvas cover back, noticing as I did so, that it was pulling a 1-ton, canvas covered trailer. Looking into the dark cave created by the canvas cover, I saw it was full of Soldiers wearing either OD BDUs or jungle fatigues, as combining the two different types of combat uniforms violated Army Regulation. Including myself, half the ten men seated in the back of the truck were from my hooch, and the only talk was angry gripes about the Army messing with their off day, especially those who had a woman waiting in Korat for them.

As soon as I sat down on the far end of the wood bench on my left, I heard the tailgate slam shut and the truck's engine start. When I heard the passenger door being closed and the air brakes released, I felt the truck roll forward. Because of the large, towed trailer, I could see nothing but, the trailer being towed behind the truck.

Glen was sitting next to me said, "Súpa is going to be worried about what's happened to me when I don't come home like I usually do. The least they could have done was give us a heads-up, like the other two shifts now have."

I responded, "Yea. Lompét's going to show up at my Hotel room and be really upset to find I'm not there, and then wait in the hallway for me a while before she finally goes back to the cafe. Heck, I didn't even know they have perimeter bunkers at the Tropo Site."

Glen replied, "I didn't either, and I work there. I guess they're defensive positions the Thai Army security guards use on our perimeter. I know we've been told not to leave the immediate area of the Tropo Site after sundown. Especially if a Red Alert's called, as the Thai Soldiers on perimeter duty tend to shoot first and ask questions later. But, I was told by a couple of guys that they went out once at 2:00 in the morning and found a pair of guards asleep on guard duty. They were able to remove a round from the magazine for one of the rifles and laughed at the thought of the guard trying to explain how he came up a round short when he checked in his rifle and ammo after guard duty."

I laughed, "I bet he never went to sleep on guard duty again."

I later noted from the crunching sound from under the truck's tires, the truck was on the gravel road to the Tropo Site. After I felt it stop at the guard shack, I could feel the truck pull off the gravel road to the left and drive onto the empty field. When the truck had bumped across the field for a while and the air in the rear had filled with dust, it stopped, and we clambered quickly over the tailgate and out of the dust filled air in the back of the truck.

Spec-5 Tom Lewiston, who'd been riding in the truck's cab, picked me and four others to follow him to a small sandbag bunker located twenty-five yards from the perimeter fence and fifty yards from the far corner of the field that bordered the main street transecting Camp Friendship. The other five followed the other Spec-5, a 6-foot-2-inch tall, gravel voiced man named Zuligich, to the back of the one-ton trailer.

The perimeter bunker was U-shaped, with 4-foot high walls made of sandbags stacked in staggered layers forming 2-foot thick walls. The 6-foot wide front wall had two firing ports through it three feet from the ground. The two sidewalls were three feet long with a firing port in each one, and then sloped at a 45-degree angle to the ground.

Tom said, "Okay, let's start taking this bunker apart. If the sandbag has started to rot, carry it a few yards toward the fence and bust it open with your foot. Otherwise, set it off to the side and we'll use it when we rebuild the bunker."

As the six of us dismantled the bunker, Spec-5 Zuligich and his 5-man team began to carry new bags of sand to the bunker's location and stack them in a pile. I found half the sandbags I picked up were starting to rot and easily broke open when kicked by my combat boot after I carrying it a few yards away. When we reached the bottom layer of sandbags, I grabbed the tide-off end of a sandbag with my right hand to lift it up, and felt like my thumb had been hit with a big hammer.

Screaming out in excruciating pain, "Something bit me," I squeezed around the base of my right thumb with my left thumb and forefinger to stop the blood from circulating to the rest of my body. This was something I was taught in the Boy Scouts while earning my Wilderness Survival Merit Badge, that if you're bit by anything unseen, then you automatically presume it's poisonous and try to cut off the poison from being passed throughout the body as quickly as possible.

Watching someone kick over the sandbag, I saw a green scorpion with an inch-long body crawling on the ground where the sandbag had been, and watched someone squashed it under their combat boot. Looking down in a fog of intense pain at the cause of my extreme agony, I saw Tom pick up the mangled scorpion's body with a piece of burlap from a busted sandbag and put it in the right cargo pocket of his jungle fatigue shirt as he urgently yelled, "Quick. All of you unhitch the trailer from the truck."

Feeling Tom grab me by the right arm and forcefully pull me to the passenger side of the truck, I heard him say, "I'll help you into the truck and take you to the Hospital's E.R. Those little green beggars are nothing to trifle with."

As Tom reached up to open the passenger door to the truck's cab and then pushed me up, helping me climb into the cab high above the ground, I could hear Zuligich's deep, graveled voice giving commands to coordinate unhitching the large, 1-ton trailer full of sandbags from the truck's tow hook. The truck's driver had already started the truck's engine when I heard Zwigich's deep voice yell, "Trailer's clear," and then Tom yell, "Get to the Hospital as fast as you can."

Through the agony radiating from my right thumb, I felt the truck bouncing over the rough surface of the empty field, as I desperately tried to cut off the circulation of blood from my right thumb with my left thumb and forefinger. Looking down at my right thumb, I saw it had swollen to twice its normal size already.

As the truck approached the gravel road to the Tropo Site, the driver started blowing the truck's horn repeatedly in a series of three blasts to signal an emergency, as Tom leaned out the passenger window and yelled to the Thai solders at the guard shack over and over, "Baak bprá-dtuu! Hét-gaan-chúk-châan!" Which means "Open gate! Emergency!"

Once the truck was on the gravel road and gaining speed toward the guard shack, the Thai guards quickly realized the truck was not going to stop for their red-and-white striped pole across the gravel road and rapidly raised it. When the truck had flown past the guard shack with its horn blaring it's series of three blasts, it made a right hand turn at the main street without stopping. But, on Tom's orders, the driver didn't crossover to the left hand lane. Instead, he drove the truck up the 12-foot wide shoulder of the road between the oncoming traffic and the deep drainage canal, as he continued making his three blasts with the truck's horn.

As the truck approached the traffic light controlled intersection, Tom told the driver to slow down, and then he leapt from the slow moving truck, waving his arms as he entered the intersection to stop the traffic and let the truck pass through without stopping. When the truck was even with Tom, he jumped onto the truck's running board as it sped on toward the hospital, continuing with its three horn-blast sequence.

Making the right turn into the left hand lane of the road that ran in front of the Hospital, I saw a group of people dressed in white standing at the E.R.'s entrance with a gurney. It appeared they had been alerted that some sort of medical emergency was en route to the Hospital. As the truck pulled into the E.R.'s entrance driveway, I heard Tom yell from the running board, "Over here. I've got a man that's been stung by one of those little green scorpions," and then yank open the truck's door.

Looking down at my right hand, I saw the thumb side of my hand to the wrist was very swollen and the skin was a mottled purple color. Also, I was beginning to feel dizzy, as I watched white clad arms pulling me out of the truck's cab. Rapidly lying me on the gurney, I saw a Medic put a tourniquet around my right forearm, an Army Nurse start an IV in my left hand, and another Medic put an oxygen mask on my face.

Once their medical tasks were rapidly completed, I saw the roof of the E.R.'s drive-through pass overhead as the gurney was maneuvered through a doorway. Then, watched as the 4-foot long, fluorescent lights in the white-tiled ceiling race past my eyesight until they halted the gurney in a green curtained alcove. On an adjustable bedside table below the level of the gurney, I saw a large stainless steel bowl that they put my very swollen right hand into, and then burying my hand in ice.

When the Doctor came in, I heard a woman's voice saying, "His vital signs are stable, Doctor. There appears to be only one small puncture wound on his right thumb, and his right hand has significant edema, and is mottled and discolored. His dog tags indicate he's allergic to penicillin and egg serums. Nothing else is contraindicated. I also gave him two grams of morphine IV to relieve the severe pain he is in."

Tom handed the Doctor the piece of burlap with the mangled remains of the small, green scorpion. The Doctor responded, "Very good, Specialist. Usually, we don't even get much of a description. With this, I know what kind of anti-venom to treat with," and turning to me, asked, "Do you have any other medical issues that you know of?"

I replied groggily, "I have a recent gunshot wound to my left thigh. The Doctor who removed the stitches last Saturday, said it was healing good. Also, I have hay fever allergies. But, other than that, I've no other medical issues."

Turning to the Nurse, he gave her instructions on the amount of which anti-venom to inject into my IV line. Then facing me again, he said, "The toxin of these little, green scorpions is very poisonous compared to the much larger black scorpions. Though not usually fatal, if not treated quickly, the swelling of the affected area can lead to necrosis and amputation. Fortunately, the quick action taken in your case has limited the damage. But, I'm also surprised because in the other cases I've seen where the person has been stung on the finger or toe, which is usually the case, the entire arm or leg is swollen by the time we give the anti-venom. Whereas, only your hand has any significant swelling. Were you ever bitten by anything poisonous before?"

I replied, "When I was four years old, we lived in Texas, and I was bitten by a small rattlesnake in our backyard that I'd picked up."

The doctor responded, "Well, the toxin in a rattlesnake's venom is similar to the toxin in the venom of these little, green scorpions. It looks like your immune system has produced an antibody that's somewhat effective against the toxin in the scorpions venom. So you're lucky the scorpion sting didn't cause any more damage than it did," then turning to Tom, he asked, "Are you his supervisor?"

Tom replied, "I was in charge of the detail when he was stung."

The Doctor said, "We'll need to keep him under observation for an hour in case there's any other adverse effects. In the meantime, I'm going to have compression bandages put on his hand and lower arm to reduce the swelling. If you're back in an hour, he should be good to go with a 48-hour light-duty chit. And, thanks for bringing the scorpion's remains. It was a big help in giving him the timely treatment."

Tom turned to me and said, "You hear that, Sandii? I'll be back in an hour to pick you up," then laughingly added, "You sure picked a stupid way to sandbag your way out of working on this sandbag detail."

As Tom left, the Doctor gave instructions for the Nurse to remove my right hand from the large basin of ice, and wrap my hand and lower arm tightly with 4-inch Ace bandages to help reduce the swelling. Then, to rewrap my hand and arm tightly every 15 minutes. When Tom returned an hour later with the 2½-ton truck to pick me up from the Hospital, after I'd been discharged with a 48-hour, light duty chit, I saw the swelling in my right hand was pretty much gone. But, it was a purplish color, like one big bruise.

Riding to the Company Area in the truck, Tom said, "I called Jim and let him know what happened to your hand with the scorpion, and how the scorpion lost the encounter. He's relieved to hear you'll be able to return to work with a 'light-duty chit.' But, I was told you're to report to the CO when you return to the Company Area."

I replied, "I'm sure Jim was glad to hear I'll be able to work the day shift tomorrow, as we're down a man with Phizer gone. I'm curious about Zuligich. He looks a little old for a Spec-5."

Tom responded, "You're right, as most of us Spec-5s are in our early 20's, and he's in his 30s. He was a Spec-4 in an MOS for 12 years that was being phased out, with no chance for promotion. He was told there was a huge shortage of Microwave Radio Repairmen with ample opportunity for advancement, and if he re-enlisted for the school, he'd make Spec-5 in seven months. So, he did. Then, he was transferred to the 442d, and came over with the replacement group that arrived 3 weeks before your group, and was made the Team Leader of the Microwave Team for the shift at the Tropo Site.

"Word is, when Anderon leaves next month, Zuligich'll be promoted to Staff Sargent as our new Site Engineer because he's the only E-5 in the 442d with the Time in Service to be eligible for promotion to Staff Sargent. It's not only that he meets the Time in Service requirement, he's also a really smart guy, and will do a good job as Tropo's Site Engineer. I'd say it's pretty good to go from Spec-4 to Staff Sargent in six months after being stuck as a Spec-4 for 12 years. But, then wars are always good for fast-tracking promotions."

After being dropped off in front of HQ, I entered the building and was told by PFC Schultz to proceed to the CO's Office. Walking to the office door, I knocked and heard a voice respond, "Enter." Entering the office and closing the door behind me, I marched to the front of Lt. Price's desk, saluted him and said, "Specialist Lynch, reporting as ordered, Sir."

Looking up from the documents on his desk, Lt. Price returned my salute, then exclaimed, "Good Lord, Sandii! your hand looks like it's been beaten with a stick. The word I received from the Hospital was, you'd been stung by a small, green scorpion, not that your hand was mauled shaking hands with a gorilla. What happened?"

I replied, "I was in a territorial dispute with an enemy scorpion over a sandbag bunker in which I was severely wounded as it aggressively attacked me with its offensive chemical weaponry. The enemy won the initial skirmish but was annihilated by the supporting elements of my unit, Sir."

Lt. Price laughed and responded, "if your Medical Record had said that in Vietnam, you'd have been awarded a Purple Heart for being stung by a scorpion."

CHAPTER 40

Now, I'm An Expert Frame Tech

L eaving the CO's Office, I walked into the Mailroom to check my mail slot and found a 3 by 5 inch pink form stating I had a package to pick up. Stepping over to the open top half of the Mailroom's Dutch door, I handed the pink form to the Mail Clerk. After a few seconds of looking through one of the several stacks of packages on the waist high counter across the far wall in the Mailroom, he selected a shoebox sized package and handed it to me. Looking at the return address, I saw it was from Linda and felt it was fairly heavy.

Carrying the package rapidly back to my hooch, I grabbed a cold can of Bud from the mini-fridge to drink as I ripped off the brown paper wrapping a shoe box sealed with masking tape. Using the sharp pointed end of my church key, I easily slit the tape to open the box. I found the contents were wrapped in aluminum foil over a dark brown mass wrapped in cellophane and a letter from Linda. The letter said how much she missed me, hoped I'd have a good Thanksgiving Dinner, and that the enclosed chocolate brownies would reach me by Thanksgiving Day. I thought, "Well, it's only a few days late, but better late than never with anything chocolate."

✦ 495 ✦

Carefully peeling back the clingy cellophane, I discovered the layers of ½-inch thick brownies, originally cut into 2-inch squares, had broken up into a mass of crumbs. This was the state for any care package[141] of baked goods received in the mail to have the brownies, cookies, cakes, etc., split into pieces from all the bouncing and jostling during transport. Though fractured into bits and pieces, the crumbs were still moist and tasty.

After eating a few handfuls of the chocolate nibbles, I carefully rewrapped the remainder in the clingy cellophane and set the open shoe box on the table. It's customary for anyone in the military who receives a care package of tasty treats to share the bounty with his mates.

Finishing my beer as I changed into a fresh set of skivvies and jungle fatigues, I left to catch a Thai bus to Korat. Arriving at the Chainarong Gate, I briskly walked up Chainarong Road to Mahat Thai Road, and then left a short distance to the cafe where Lompét worked. Entering the cafe just after it opened for business at 10:00, she saw me and ran up to me with a very happy smile on her pretty face. As we exchanged sáwátdiis, she saw the results of the scorpions sting to my right hand and exclaimed, "Ôo-hôo! Muu kaawng kon!" Which means, "Wow! Hand belong to you!" in Thai.

I began to explain her to her in Thai what had happened, but I was at a loss because I didn't know that I words for "scorpion," "sting," "swollen," "sandbag," and others to describe what had happened to make my hand look so bad. I tried to pantomime the experience, but that was too complicated and lengthy a process, and told her my hand was good and I'd explain it to her during our English lesson that afternoon.

Leaving the cafe, I walked to my Hotel room and took a tepid shower before laying on the bed to nap until 12:30. Returning to the cafe with my Thai-English Dictionary, I was able to explain to Lompét what had happened to my hand as I ate lunch, and to tell her my hand was fine now, despite the way it looked. I then spent a pleasant afternoon teaching her English till 3:30, at which time I ate dinner and left the cafe.

---

141   A euphemism in the military for any package received from family and friends.

Instead of returning to my Hotel room as usual, I decided to implement my plan to locate a suitable Thai bar to socialize with Thai men to improve my Thai language skills. With my Thai-English Dictionary in hand, I began a methodical search of the roads and lanes North of Mahat Thai Road. I figured most of the bars South of Mahat Thai Road would be set up to serve Americans due to their proximity to the Chainarong Gate.

Popping in for a moment at each Thai bar, I observed they were mostly the same small, 30-foot wide establishments, with a serving counter along a side wall, and a loose arrangement of wood tables and chairs. Though it was a while before the end of the normal workday, I could tell by the appearance of the few clients I saw there the social strata the bar served. Mostly, I was making note of those with middle class men wearing dress shirts and slacks. Finally, from several prospective locations, I selected a Thai bar on Manatt Road across from the Assadang Hotel, which was just an old concrete box with small cheap rooms with a jailhouse vibe endemic of so many cheap Thai Hotels, not like the Korat Hotel around the corner from it.

Returning to the time bar, which by now was half full of Thai men, I walked up to the waist-high serving counter and exchanged sáwátdi-is with the bartender. After buying a bottle of Sing Hăi Beer, I saw a table with several Thais sitting around at and a couple of empty chairs. Walking to the table, I exchanged sáwátdiis with them, told them my name was Sandii, and asked if I could sit at their table. Without a hint of any attempt by them to speak any English, they happily welcomed me to join them. After explaining I spoke only some Thai and they would need to speak in little slower so I could follow their conversation, they introduced themselves to me.

They were all in their 20s and 30s, wearing white dress shirts and brown or black slacks, except one who was wearing the khaki uniform of a police Sergeant with a Sam Browne belt and holstered pistol. At first they were intrigued as to why an American was in their social haunt, instead of chasing pûu-ying in a bar serving Americans. Once I explained who I was and what I did, and that I wanted to learn as much as I could about the Thai people, culture and language while I was in Thailand, they went on with their jocular camaraderie, accepting me as all equal in their group.

As we socialized, I soon found it was customary for one member of the group to buy a bottle of Sing Hăi Beer and pass it around the table until it was empty, then another one by the next bottle. This was because Sing Hăi Beer only came in quart bottles and was so potent that the typical Thai couldn't drink an entire bottle without passing out, as they were much smaller than the typical American. Besides, these men weren't here to get drunk, but to relax with other men socially after the drudgery of a day's work before going home to their wives or parents.

As we talked around the table, sometimes I'd get a confused look on my face, and they'd stop to explain a joke or colloquial phrase to me. Since all these men had graduated from a Thai College, then each of them spoke a medium amount of English to explain, or they would simply grab my Thai-English Dictionary to translate a less common word. By 7:30, I told the several men still at the table that I needed to leave, as I had a date to go dancing at a night club with friends.

Leaving the Thai bar and my newfound friends, I walked to the cafe and waited for Lompét to enter from the back. When she did, I saw she looked resplendent in her form-fitting, low-cut, red silk dress, that prominently displayed the tops of her apple-size breasts and her shapely legs beneath the thigh-high hem of her dress swirling around them. After exchanging sáwátdiis, I said in English, "Lompét, you look very beautiful tonight."

She responded with a laugh, "An you sa-me-la like bia, my boy-fa-ren. You go to fa-ren home wit Glín-dii and Súpa?"

I replied, "No, my girlfriend. I have beer with Thai men at bar and make new friends to learn more Thai to speak."

She nodded her pretty face in approval and said, "I like you wan talk moh Thai. It iss goot you know moh Thai, like it goot I know moh Angrit."

I asked, "How would you like walking to the night club and I can show everyone the beautiful girlfriend I have," and thought, "not that I want to get rid of her, but it's time to simplify my life and hers. And, as they say, it pays to advertise."

She replied happily, "Tat iss fun ting to do. I happy you wan so eba-ri-body you hap a beautifa gra-fa-ren."

Lompét walked behind me for the ten minutes it took to go from the cafe to the nightclub. I knew she was enjoying all the attention from the approving looks of the street full of American men, who were out in force because it was just after Payday, and thought, "This is a big confidence builder for her to see how desired she is by American men and make it easier to flirt with any who came in the cafe."

Arriving at the nightclub, Lompét was in high spirits from her walk because of the many compliments that she received from passing Americans. We quickly spotted Glen and Súpa, and joining them at their table on the 3rd tier, Lompét chatted in Thai to Súpa about my hand being stung by a little green scorpion, while I told Glen about what happened at the hospital and my talk with Lt. Price. I decided that telling Glen about my new haunt at the Thai bar could wait until another time.

After a fun evening socializing with Glen and Súpa, and holding Lompét's scintillating body in my arms, I performed my sensuous Tango with Lompét to heighten her lust for me. When we had consummated our pent-up lust in my Hotel room with rampant lovemaking, we blissfully fell asleep as we happily spooned in the afterglow of our climax.

In the morning, after our playful foreplay aroused our desires, we vigorously copulated in the Kama Sutra position previously chosen by Lompét, which resulted in the orgasmic release we craved. Enjoying the pleasant feeling from our lovemaking for a while, we then had fun showering together. As I dressed in my jungle fatigues, she happily chose our next Kama Sutra position, which we discussed before we affectionately kissed goodbye till Friday night.

After breakfast in the Mess Hall and morning formation, Skip and I road in the truck's cab with Jim to the Air Base Site. Jim looked at my discolored right hand with concern. But, when I held up my hand, showing my fingers curling and flexing without difficulty or pain, he smiled and nodded his head in approval.

Arriving in the Operations Room, as I relieved Jack from his night shift, I said, "Heard you're getting short, Jack."

He responded, "I sure am. Thirty-one days and a wake-up, and I've enjoyed this one-year all-expense-paid vacation very much. Almost wish I'd extended, it's been so good, and going to Ft. Huachuca from here is going to suck big time."

I asked, "Are you arranging to marry your tîi-lók And take her with you?"

He laughed and replied, "I'd love to do that, but I don't think my wife would appreciate my bringing home an á-nú-pan-rá-yaa," as he quickly left the Operations Room.

The morning went smoothly, and making the 1055 meal run, I told Glen about what happened after the scorpion stung me. When I finished, he said, "Well, I'm glad you survived in one piece, because I've heard some real horror stories about those little green scorpions. Whenever we do cable pulls under the Tropo Site's floor, most guys wear gloves because of the occasional snake or scorpion they find under there."

I responded, "the only thing I've seen under the Air Base Site's floor has been a few rodents Bob killed with his 'better mousetrap'."

On my returning to the Air Base Site, Skip left for lunch at the Mess Hall on his 11:40 meal run, and I took over his working with Bob to track down an outage on a low-priority teletype circuit that was called in. They'd connected the wayward circuit to one of our monitoring teletype machines, and I began to rapidly strike the R and Y keys on the QWERTY keyboard to create a square-wave signal for Bob to check with an oscilloscope.

Each letter, number or symbol typed on the QWERTY keyboard produced a series of on and off voltages in a digital code, which were then converted to high and low audio tones in the breakout circuits for a radio to transmit. It just so happens the on/off code series for the R key is the inverse of the code for the Y key, and if the circuits are properly tuned, then the alternate striking of the R and Y keys produced a series of on/off voltages is seen as square-shaped traces on the oscilloscope.

When the circuits are not properly tuned, the trace on the oscilloscope appear sloped instead of vertical, or as rectangular shapes instead of the required square shapes. So, while one person rapidly strikes the R-Y-R-Y series on the keyboard, the other person watches the trace on the oscilloscope as he slowly adjusts the variable resistors in the circuit till the shape appears square.

As we performed this tedious task, I told Bob about my locating a Thai bar in Korat for me to frequent with the type of clientele I'd like to hobnob with, how I went there last evening, and my favorable experiences with a group of men I met sitting at one of the tables.

Bob responded, "It sounds like you studied this out pretty good, and it doesn't hurt to have friends in low places to chase the worries of the day away with a bottle of Sing Hăi Beer. Especially to have a friend who's a Sargent in the local constabulary. The group sounds pretty much like our group that meets at Horn's home, though a bit more eclectic. And, it'll meet your need for an immersion environment to improve your Thai language skills. How often are you planning to go to this Thai bar?"

I replied, "At least once a week. But, as often as my time will allow with me balancing two women at the same time, which will be until Lompét becomes someone's tîi-lók."

That evening, I was relieved at 6:40 by John and Larry, and was gone like a flash of gunpowder to catch a Thai bus for Korat. Going to my Hotel room, I'd barely removed my combat boots when I heard Súusîi's knock on my room's door. Soon, we were enthralled in passionate lovemaking using the Kama Sutra position I experienced with Lompét that morning. As we lay in each other's arms, basking in the pleasure of our orgasmic release, she said as she tenderly held my discolored right hand, "My darling, your hand looks very bad, what happened to cause this injury?"

Now knowing the Thai words, I told her about being stung by the small green scorpion, but now my hand is okay, except for its color. She responded, "My darling, I know people who've been stung by this kind of scorpion and have lost a finger or toe, or more. You're lucky not to have lost your thumb."

After we took a quick shower to wash off the crud, we dressed and left for the night club. There, we met up with our ballroom dance friends on the 3rd tier, and I answered their questions in English about how my hand had been injured, but was okay now. Súusîi and I then had fun socializing with our friends and gaily dancing together. When the time came, and we'd danced an erotic Tango, we hastily returned to my Hotel room and engaged in rapacious lovemaking till the orgasmic release of the pent-up lust we had for each other.

When we'd blissfully slept in the pleasant feelings left by our lovemaking, we woke in the morning with the need to fulfill the lust we had reignited with vigorous lovemaking. After we had fun showering together and I'd dressed in my jungle fatigues, I caressed her enticingly as we passionately kissed goodbye. Then she moaned with desire,

"My darling, I can hardly wait till Saturday afternoon to feel your body loving mine."

Work on Friday was the calm before Saturday morning's storm of outages, which thankfully I'd not be working, but looking forward to the possibility of talking with Linda and my family that night, or on Sundays night shift. When I'd been relieved from my duties at 6:40 that evening, I left for Korat, and this time Lompét wore her hot-pink silk dress that enticed the eyes of many admiring Americans as she walked behind me to the night club. After I enjoyed the exuberance of dancing with Lompét in her hot-pink silk dress, we then expressed our mutual desires in vigorous lovemaking afterward, and then again in the morning.

Leaving after we'd passionately kissed goodbye, I returned to my Company Area for breakfast in the Mess Hall and the formation that followed. Then, going to my hooch, I drank a cold can of Bud as I changed into a fresh set of OD BDUs and put fresh clothes in my shopping bag before catching a Thai bus back to Korat. Entering my Hotel room I watched Lompét's enticing body asleep on the bed and became aroused as I quietly stripped. When she woke to my sensuous caresses of her silky smooth skin, she responded in kind, and soon we were enjoying the rapture of our lust in the Kama Sutra position she'd chosen before I'd left for Camp Friendship.

After we playfully showered together and she chose our next Kama Sutra position as we lay next to each other on the bed. Then, I helped her pronounce the English words she knew until she dressed and went to work at 9:30. When she'd left, I slept till 12:30, and then dressed and walked to the cafe for lunch, after which I enjoyed teaching Lompét English from the textbook until 3:30.

Returning to my Hotel room, I'd quickly stripped to my boxers before hearing Súusîi's knock on the room's door. Opening the door, I saw her blouse was unbuttoned, exposing her luscious, firm breasts, as she leapt into my open arms, wrapping her arms and legs around me, and began kissing me passionately. Carrying her writhing body to the bed, I felt her bare, wet crotch grinding with lust against my abdomen. Setting her feet on the floor, she rapidly shucked her blouse and skirt, as I dropped my boxers to the floor. Then, pushing her backward onto the bed, she cried out, as I thrust hungrily between her raised legs into her taut, inviting love canal, "My darling, I've missed your desire for me very much."

When our wanton lovemaking climaxed in the orgasmic release of pent-up lust, we embraced to enjoy the pleasure the rush of our vigorous lovemaking produced. Then she cooed, "I love you so much, my darling, and the joy of feeling your sexual desire filling me."

As we sensuously showered together later, she moaned, "Please, my darling, give me more of your sexual desire, it's going to be a long time before we're together again Tuesday," and enticingly presenting her luscious butt to me, I made love with her again.

When our short, sexual interlude ended, we dressed, passionately kissed goodbye, knowing we'd be together all evening and night on Tuesday. At the Hotel's entrance, we rode away in separate săawm-laws to our own destinations.

Returning to my Company Area, I met up with Skip our hooch and drank a cold can of Bud before going to the Mess Hall for dinner. By 6:40 we were in front of the Day Room when Tommy arrived in the truck, informing us it has been a hellish morning, but all was calm now. Arriving in the Operations Room, I relieved Jack so he could quickly go home to his á-nú-pan-ná-yua. While waiting for Bob to finish with the Shift Change Report, I read through the record of the mornings outages in the Site Log with Skip to see if there had been any an anomalous outages.

Bob arrived in the Operations Room and happily said, "Sáwátdii, Sandii and Skip. I've got good news. The PM scheduled for this weekend has already been done. Bill's team was bored Wednesday night, and with the report of Sandii's hand been severely damaged by a scorpion sting, they went through and vacuumed out all of the racks for bugs so we wouldn't have to do it tonight. Instead, I've decided you two can set up my special rat trap. So, Sandii, you go to the Supply/Repair Room and get the test cart. Skip, you pull up the section of floor over the rat trap. Then both of you carefully connect the wires to the oscilloscope, while I go to the NCO Club and get a fresh piece of meat for the bait."

By the time Bob returned with the bait, Skip and I had the oscilloscope wired to Bob's rat trap contraption. After I placed the bait in the center of the smaller tin can lid on the top layer of the rap trap, I turned on the modified oscilloscope, and thankfully there wasn't a mass of sparks from a malfunction.

Skip and I then replaced the section of floor, and we went about our normal routine, which was relieving our boredom while waiting for an outage to be reported. I'd periodically try to repeat tying a knot in a patch cord as Frank had shown me when I arrived four months earlier, without success. I'd described this feat to Skip, who after numerous failed attempts said it couldn't be done. That Frank had pulled some sort of illusion to convince me it could be done. Illusion or not, I'd occasionally tried to replicate the feat.

After several failed attempts, I finally asked Bob if he could do it, and laughed as he replied, "Of course. Any experienced Frame Tech can do it." Then taking the patch cord from my hand, he deftly flipped the bitter end up and it fell neatly through the coil in the cord, resulting in a knot in the cord.

Skip had been watching and said, "I don't believe it. It's some kind of illusion."

Bob said, "It's no illusion," as he flipped the end up again, made a second knot in the cord and handling it to Skip, added, "see for yourself."

Skip pulled on each end of the cord, tightening the knots, and responded, "Okay, it's not an illusion, but it's some kind of trick."

Bob replied, "Of course, there is a trick to it. It's figuring out the trick that's the fun, and nobody who knows the trick is going to tell it to you."

I responded, "Okay, Bob, if you're not going to tell us, then just let me watch you do it again, thinking, "I remember there was some sort of wrist action when Frank did it. I'll just watch Bob's hand closely as he does it."

Bob took the patch cord back from Skip, and untied the two knots in the cord. I watched Bob's hand intently as he flipped up the bitter end of the cord and it fell neatly through a loop in the cord, but this time, I saw it was more than a twist in his wrist. He'd done something with the tips of his fingers holding the bight of the cord, and I said, "Do that one more time, Bob."

When he put a second knot in the cord, I'd watch with my eyes firmly fixed on his fingertips, and I said, "I think I know the trick, Bob. Let me have the patch cord, so I can try it again."

Taking the patch cord from Bob, I untie the two knots. Then, flipping the bitter and into the air, at the apex of its flight, I did the usual twist with my wrist, but this time, I added a role of the bight with my fingertips making a perfect loop in the cord for the end to fall through, and yelled, "Now, I'm an Expert Frame Tech."

CHAPTER 41

I'M AN OFFICER MAGNET

After successfully tying an overhand knot in the patch cord with a single handed flip of its bitter end into the air, the act certifying me as an Experienced Frame Tech, Skip excitedly said, "Tell me how you did it, Sandii."

I replied, "No way, Skip. it took me four months to discover how, and I'm not going to just give it away. Besides, you heard Bob, 'nobody who knows the trick is going to tell it to you'."

Just then, I heard a muffled "snap" from the back of the Operations Room. We all ran to the back and quickly raised the 2-foot square section of the floor. Next to Bob's electric rat trap, I saw a 2-foot long snake constricted in a ball. Skip laughed and said, "It looks like the rat trap also traps rat killers."

Bob responded, "From now on, I'm not just going to grab cables under this floor willy nilly without wearing some heavy gloves. That's a cobra down there," as he walked to the desk and returned with a pair of adjustable, long handled pliers.

When he gingerly picked up the snake, he said, "First, we find a ton of insects. Then, we discover we're infested with rats. And now, we have the body of a cobra that's been slithering around down there. This building is supposed to be foolproof to infestation from the outside."

I laughingly responded, "My Mom says, 'it's impossible to make anything foolproof, because fools are so ingenious."

While Bob tossed the snake's remains out the side door, Skip and I made sure Bob's electric rat trap was working before replacing the section of floor and returning to the Grand Canyon. There, Skip fruitlessly attempted to tie singlehanded a knot in the patch cord by flipping the bitter end into the air, even after I demonstrated to him several times it could be done.

After a while, Ted called from the PBX building to let us know he had a line up to Rosie in St. Louis for us to make free phone calls via WATS to our families and friends Stateside. When it was my turn, I called Linda first to let her know I'd received the package of brownies in the mail, and that they were very delicious and appreciated, leaving out the disintegrated condition they'd arrived in. Also, to let her know that I missed her very much, and I mailed a Christmas package to her. I decided it was best not to tell her about my encounter with the scorpion or that we had just killed a cobra lurking in our sub floor space.

I then called my family to let my parents know I was safe and sound and had mailed Christmas packages to everyone. After talking to them, I talked with my sisters and brother, listening to the important things that were happening in each of their lives.

Finishing with my two phone calls, it was time for my 10:55 meal run for midnight chow in the Mess Hall. Meeting up with Glen there, I told him about Bob's 'better mousetrap' having killed a cobra in the subfloor of the Operations Room, and that Bob was puzzled by how any living thing, especially rats and snakes could get in there, because it's all supposed to be sealed from the outside world.

Glen responded, "The same question's been asked at the Tropo Site with all of the critters, especially snakes, having been found in its subfloor spaces. It turns out, there's lots of conduit pipes between the buildings and the MRC-98 vans that a small animal could use for ingress to the subfloor areas. I'm sure the Air Base Site has the same thing between it and its Generator Shed, and with the Air Force Comm Center buildings."

On returning to the Air Base Site, I told Bob about this theory, and he said, "I suppose it's also true here, but I'm not going crawling around under there to find out."

When Skip returned from his meal run, I said, "You know, after talking to Linda and my family about mailing the Christmas presents to them, I realized it put quite a dent in the money I was saving to buy a tape deck this month. I guess it'll be another month or two before I can buy one. How about you?"

Skip laughed and replied, "Same here. But, I was thinking my investment with my Hanukkah presents for Judith will pay better dividends in the long run than an investment in a tape deck will for me."

I respond to, "You're right there, Skip."

After Bob returned from his meal run to the NCO Club Annex, things were still slower than molasses in February, so Skip and I took turns getting some sleep on the mattress once we'd removed it from the subfloor with considerable circumspection. Leaving on my 6:35 meal run, I delivered the truck to Jim in the Motor Pool and ate a fast, but hardy, breakfast in the Mess Hall. Then going to my hooch, I drank a cold can of Bud as I quickly changed into a fresh set of OD BDUs and packed some fresh changes of clothes in my shopping bag, before leaving to board a Thai bus to Korat.

Arriving at my Hotel room, I prepared for a wonderful day with Lompét, teaching her English, eating at restaurants for lunch and dinner, and going to see the Samurai movie with Glen and Súpa, all interspersed with exhilarating lovemaking in various Kama Sutra positions. When our day of gaiety came to end, I lovingly kissed her goodbye at 5:30 with the knowledge she would be desirously waiting in bed for me when I returned the next morning, after I worked the night shift.

Getting off the Thai bus at the Company Area, I went straight to the Mess Hall for a quick meal to supplement the dinner I had with Lompét. There I hooked up with Skip prior to meeting Tommy with the truck in front of the Day Room. After a very quiet Sunday night at the Air Base Site, which afforded me the chance to get a few hours' sleep, I made the 6:35 meal run to deliver the truck to Jim in the Motor Pool.

Exiting the truck, I handed Jim the clipboard with the Trip Ticket, and he asked, "How'd it go last night?"

I replied, "Quiet as a church mouse. How's it going with you and Roger having to work seven days a week?"

He answered, "We've worked out a schedule where, except for Saturday mornings, he comes in at 10:30 to help cover the meal runs for lunch. I leave at 5:00 to have dinner with Mary, except for Monday nights. I suppose you're not hanging around for the Change-Of-Command Ceremony to see what our new CO's like?"

I laughed, "And miss all the folderol? I'm out of here on the first bus too Korat as soon as I've had breakfast. In fact, I prefer to stay away from Officers as much as possible. What happened with Lt. Price was a pure fluke of circumstances. Besides, I'll get a glimpse of him at tomorrow's formation," as I walked toward the Mess Hall.

Leaving the Motor Pool Area, I stopped in the Mess Hall for a quick breakfast and left to catch the first available Thai bus for Korat.

Returning to my Hotel room, I found Lompét peacefully asleep in the bed and quietly stripped, before slipping into the bed and spooning around her small, luscious body. When I had, she snuggled her delectable butt against my groin and moaned, "My darling, I missed the feel of your warm body around me as I went to sleep. But now, I want to feel your desire for my small body," as she sensuously turned over in my arms and offered her firm breasts enticingly to my mouth.

Soon, we were consumed in vigorous lovemaking, feeding on our lust in a Kama Sutra position. When we lay together in the afterglow of our orgasmic release, she cooed, "I love the way you always desire my small body and look forward to being in heaven with you after we go dancing."

After our usual fun shower together, we happily lay side by side as we briefly discussed our next Kama Sutra position. Then, I taught her English till 9:30, when Lompét dressed, and we lovingly kissed goodbye. When she'd left, I slept for several hours before I dressed and walked to the cafe for lunch and to teach her English till 3:30, then returned to my Hotel room to sleep for an hour.

Leaving my Hotel room at 5:00, I walked up the left side of Assadang Road the three blocks from the Sri Pattana Hotel to Manatt Road and turn left to the Thai bar. Entering the small Thai bar, I bought a large bowl of rice noodle soup with chicken and a bottle of Sing-High Beer, before I exchanged sáwátdiis with the familiar, smiling faces around the table as before, though a couple of the faces were new. Then I sat down and had an enjoyable evening with my new Thai friends, sharing in their jocular camaraderie as we passed bottles of Sing-High Beer around the table till 7:30, when I left to take Lompét dancing.

Walking the quarter mile to the cafe, and going two blocks up Manatt Road to Mahat Thai Road, where I turned right and entered the cafe. A few minutes later, Lompét appeared from the back wearing her light blue, form-fitting, low-cut silk dress that displayed the tops of enticing, apple-size breasts and her shapely legs. After we exchanged sáwátdiis, she laughed and said approvingly, "My da-ling, I can sa-may-la you been da-ring-king wit you Thai fa-ren again. Dit you ha-ba fun time?

I laughed and replied, "Not as much fun as I'll have with you, my beautiful girlfriend. Shall we walk to the night club?"

She answered, "Tat wi-la be fun, my da-ling."

Being a Monday night, there weren't as many Americans walking on Mahat Thai Road as there had been Friday, but I saw those who were there, were giving Lompét an approving once-over look. After a few minutes, I heard a male voice behind me say kindly, "Sáwátdii, sûai mâak pûu-ying[142]. A pretty lady like you shouldn't be walking alone. Can I escort you to where you're going?"

Hearing her reply, "Sáwátdii, ká. I not alone, I am wit my boy-fa-ren," I slowly stopped and turned, saw a 6-foot tall, slender, nice looking American standing next to Lompét, who said, "Sorry, Mac, I didn't know she was with you."

I pleasantly responded, "Mâi pbén rai. I guess you didn't know it's customary for a proper Thai woman to walk behind her man. Only a prostitute will walk beside a man. My name is Sandii. I work next to the Air Base Comm Center. And the lady's name is Lompét. She's a waitress at a cafe a little way back up the street," as I offered my right hand.

He replied, as he shook my offered hand, "A pleasure to meet you, Sandii and Lompét. My name is Steve. I'm one of the disc jockeys at the AFTN Radio Station. My apologies for interrupting your walk. Since you work near the Air Base Comm Center, you'll have to pop in sometime and I'll give you a tour of the place."

---

142   "Hello, very beautiful woman."

I responded, "That sounds great. I'll have to do that sometime. Well, you have a nice evening, Steve," as I turned to continue on to the night club with Lompét walking close behind me.

Entering the night club, we soon joined Glen and Súpa sitting at a table on the 3rd tier. After I told Glen about my encounter with Steve, he said, "If he'd been trying to chat up Súpa while she was walking behind me, I'd have punched him in the mouth. But, it's cool he turned out to be a disc jockey at the AFTN. It would be nice to know who the idiot is that writes all those stupid and annoying Safety and Security commercials they do between the Rock-N-Roll music sets they play. Are you going to take him up on his invite for a tour?"

I replied, "Yea. I was thinking about popping over when I work days on Wednesday or Thursday to see when he's scheduled to work, if we're not too busy."

After an excellent evening socializing with Glen and Súpa, and dancing with my enticing Lompét, till we finished our sensuous Tango. Then, walking impatiently to my Hotel room, we rapidly stripped and wantonly made vigorous love together. As we spooned in the afterglow of our climactic rush, Lompét cooed, "I love so much being in this heaven with you, my darling."

In the morning, we enjoyed our lovemaking in a new Kama Sutra position before we playfully showered together. Then I pleasantly watched Lompét's lithe, delightsome body as she helped me dress in my OD BDUs to leave for Camp Friendship and enjoyed the feel of her luscious body as I caressed it while we passionately kissed goodbye. She coyly said as I left, "I be he-ra wen you come back, ready for you bery goot lo-ba-making, my sa-weet hawt."

Exiting the Thai bus at the Company Area, I walked to my hooch and changed into a fresh set of jungle fatigues before going to the Mess Hall for a delicious and filling breakfast. Adequately satiated, I went to where the Tropo Platoon was organizing for formation. Joining the Air Base Squad in the last rank, Jim said, "You were right to skip the folderol of the Change-of-Command ceremony. You didn't miss a thing, except the usual claptrap about how honored and privileged he was to be the CO of such an exemplary Signal Corps Company."

After a few minutes, SFC Davidson call the Tropo Platoon to attention and went through the process of getting everyone in straight ranks and equally spaced. Then he checked to make sure the members of each squad were present or accounted for in preparation for the Company Report before ordering, "Parade . . . Rest!"

I watched as Spike marched in from the right to the flagpole in front of HQ, and went through the rigamarole for each Platoon to report, "All present or accounted for." Then, he made an about face and reported to our new CO standing on the steps to HQ.

When Spike had reported, "All present or accounted for, Sir," to the new CO, a 6-foot tall, medium built man wearing pressed jungle fatigues, with the crossed semaphore flags of the Signal Corps on its left collar and the twin silver bars of a Captain on his right collar. He said in a loud voice, "Company, stand at ease."

At these words, I thought, "This is not a good sign. It usually means bad news with a lengthy explanation."

He announced, "For those of you who weren't here yesterday, I'm Captain Markus Richards, Signal Corps, your new CO. I received a message yesterday from USAS-Thai that the end of January, next month, the 442d's Company C billet area will be moved to the H-type, concrete buildings nearing completion on the east side of Camp Friendship."

There was an audible groan throughout the ranks, as I thought, "This is just like the Army. Just when we have the hooches the way we want them, the Army's going to crowd us into big, concrete boxes with no privacy. Plus, we won't be eating in the General's Mess Hall anymore, but in an Army slop line."

He continued, "I know that you've all made yourselves cozy and comfortable in your little, wood hooches, but you know how much the Army hates for any of its Soldiers to be cozy, much less comfortable," which received a laugh from everyone, and I thought, "At least he's got a sense of humor."

He then went on, "There are some upsides to this new location. First, you'll have basketball, tennis and handball courts in the Company Area. Second, you'll have indoor showers and flush toilets, as well as full size refrigerators to keep your beer cold in, something dear to every Soldier's heart. Third, you'll be closer to the Camp's PX, Theater and Enlisted Club. Also, closer to the Camp's Dispensary, Education Center, Personnel and Finance Offices. Fourth, you'll be able to park your vehicles in front of the Mess Hall to eat, instead of having to park in the Motor Pool and walk to the Mess Hall. And fifth, and most important, the barracks are located right across from the new Swimming Pool that's currently under construction," and I thought, "So, that's what the big hole in the ground is for."

"As for the Company's Motor Pool, it will remain an integral part of the 442d, and will be allocated its own modern maintenance facilities in the Camp's POL Area. This was a hard won concession by the Battalion CO, and strenuously argued by the First Brigade's CO, General Rienzi, as U.S.AS-Thai's General wanted to integrate our Company's Motor Pool Platoon into U.S.AS-Thai's Transportation Regiment.

"The big downside for you is, you'll have to eat in the Camp's Enlisted Mess Hall, and eat the mass-produced crap it puts out, instead of the short order chow you are accustomed to. And now, you know everything I know. Later this week, I and the Senior NCOs of the Company will take a tour of our new Company Area to determine the billeting assignments for each Platoon and the transient troops that will be arriving over the next few months.

"There's one other thing. I'd like Specialist Lynch from the Tropo Platoon to see me in my Office right after formation. First Sargent, dismiss the Company."

I heard Jim smirk, "Sandii, I thought you told me that you 'prefer to stay away from Officers as much as possible.' It appears to me that Officers prefer to be with you as much as possible. It's like you're an Officer magnet."

I quipped, "I'm not responsible for the good taste an Officer has," and thought, "Now, what the heck does Capt. Richards want with me. We haven't even met yet, as far as I know," as I walked rapidly to the CO's Office to get this over with as soon as possible, and quickly return to my waiting Lompét.

Entering the CO's Office, I closed the door behind me as I marched to the front of his desk, saluted him, and said, "Specialist Lynch, reporting as ordered Sir."

Returning my salute, Capt. Richards said, "At ease, Lynch. Have a seat," and as I sat in a chair, he continued, "During my Change-of-Command briefing with Lt. Price yesterday morning, he said you speak Thai and lived in Korat, and the go-to man for shopping in Korat and learning to avoid the foibles in Thai customs. In fact, he helped me understand that, no matter how distasteful is sounds at first, it's just the way things are in Thailand for teenage girls as young as fourteen to become live-in lovers for a lot of men in my Company. I believe the word he used was 'tîi-lók for such women.

"He also told me that everyone here calls you 'Sandii' because Thai's can't pronounce your real name. Also, that 'Sandii' means 'extremely good' in Thai. Is it okay if I call you 'Sandii'?"

I replied, "That's fine with me, Sir," as I thought, "You're my CO, so you can call me whatever you want. And, why are you getting so chummy with a low-ranking Enlisted person like me?"

He continued, "None the less, I'm hoping you'd be willing to take my wife and I on a shopping tour of Korat some afternoon on one of your off days."

I thought, "Aha, there's the rub. It's not like I can say 'No' to him, because he's my CO, and a request is more like an order," as I took a moment to think of an off day that would best work for me, and said, "I'd be honored to do that, Sir, but my earliest, feasible off day is a week from Saturday. But, that's almost two weeks from now. There's lots of men in the company who speak Thai and live in Korat, who can take you and your wife on a shopping tour in Korat much sooner than I can. Besides, all of the shopkeepers speak English, as they study it for four years in High School."

He responded, "A week from Saturday will be perfect. That'll give me and my family time to get settled in at the Jomsurong Hotel, and our two kids started in school. So, if it's OK with you, my wife and I'll meet you in the Hotel Lobby at noon, a week from Saturday, Sandii."

I replied, trying to sound cheerful about losing my off day to this man and his wife, "That works for me, Sir."

He answered, "Good, we'll see you then, Sandii. You can go now. As you can see, I've a lot of work to do here."

I stood, saluted him, and said, "Thank you, Sir," thinking as he returned my salute and I quickly left his Office, "Maybe Jim's right that I'm an Officer magnet."

CHAPTER 42

Where Does The American Male's Libido Lie

Leaving the Company's HQ, I caught a Thai bus to Korat, where I found Lompét in my Hotel room eagerly awaiting my return, as she'd promised when I'd left for Camp Friendship. Being quickly aroused by the sight of her alluring body lying provocatively on the bed, I rapidly stripped off my clothes. Leaping between her inviting, upraised legs, we began our rigorous lovemaking in the Kama Sutra position we'd discussed before I left.

As we laid in repose, enjoying the climactic rush from our lust filled lovemaking, I told her in English, "My beloved, my new boss asked me to take him and his wife shopping two Saturdays from now, so I won't be able to teach you English that afternoon. I tell you now, so it won't be a surprise later."

She responded, "I happy you bo-sa gi-ba you ti-sa bik hon-na, my da-ling. An, I tank you fo say to me now, so I not tink you a but-ta-fa-ly."

After we playfully showered together, and she'd chosen and discussed with our next Kama Sutra position, we worked on her English until it was time for her to dress in her attractive light-blue silk dress and leave for work at 9:30. When she'd left, I slept till 12:30, and then dressed to have lunch at the cafe. After which, I taught her English till 3:30.

Returning to my Hotel room, I prepared for a very exhilarating evening and night with Súusíi, as we dined, danced and slept together between our several bouts of vigorous and satisfying lovemaking in various Kama Sutra positions. The next morning, when I lovingly ran my desiring hands over the silky curves of her luscious body, while we affectionately kissed goodbye, I said, "I will miss you very much, my darling, till we go dancing on Thursday night."

She responded, "I love you very much, my darling, and will ache for your excellent lovemaking till then."

Arriving at the Company Area, I thought while walking to my hooch, "There's another big downside with this move to a new Company Area on the east side of the Camp. it's going to add 5 to 10 minutes to my commute time for getting to and from Korat."

Entering my hooch, I drank a cold can of Bud as I dumped out the dirty clothes from my shopping bag and refilled it with fresh clothes to pick up at lunchtime. Then, changing into a fresh set of jungle fatigues, I went to the Mess Hall for breakfast. After formation, as I rode to the Air Base Site in the truck's cab with Jim and Skip, I said, "Have either of you thought about the fact that the move of our Company Area to the other side of the Camp will add 5 to 10 minutes for the bus ride to and from Korat?"

Jim replied, "I hadn't thought about that, but you're right, I'll have to plan on leaving the Hotel earlier." Then he laughed and said, "But, I'll be gone by then, as I'll be leaving for Stateside on January 20th. I need to talk with Sgt. Davidson about who he plans on replacing me with."

Entering the Air Base Site, Jim walked into the Site Office, where Bob and Bill were waiting for him, while Skip and I proceeded to the Operations Room. There, I asked Jack, "Guess you've heard about the Company Area being moved to the other side of Camp Friendship?"

Jack laughed and said, "That don't mean a spit to me. I'll be long gone by then," as he quickly left the Operations Room.

When Bob entered the Operations Room, he said, "Sandii, Skip and the others told us at the compound all about the Company being moved to the other side of Camp Friendship. Too bad you weren't there to join in the discussion. Horn lifted his 'no talk about the military' rule since it affects everyone so much. I guess you were at the Thai bar. How's that going for you?"

I replied, "It's going great. In some ways, it's like being at the compound with you guys, sitting around drinking Sing Hăi Beer and shooting the bull about what's going on in their lives, but in Thai, of course. I'm really learning to pick up more of the Thai language, and their slang terms for things. Like 'pâai-lom,' literally 'to release wind,' means 'to fart,' and 'dtit din,' literally 'to stick to the ground,' means 'to be a common man'."

Bob laughed and replied, "Which are things I didn't know. Nor, what they'd probably teach at the Military Language School at Monterey, California, and you'd probably be able to teach to the U.S.AS-Thai linguistic unit."

I said, "Bob, I bumped into a guy in Korat who's one of the DJ's at AFTN and invited me to take a tour of their Radio Station. If we're not too busy later on, is it okay to pop over for a minute to schedule a time with him for a tour?"

Bob replied, "Sure. If we're not too busy later. But, wouldn't it be easier to just call there?"

I answered, "That's a great idea," and after a while, I had Ted at the Base BPX patch me through to AFTN, and I set up with Steve to be there Friday evening after dinner at 6:00. This would give me plenty of time for a tour before I had to relieve Jack from duty at 6:45.

The rest of the day continued apace with several outages to keep it interesting. When I went to lunch at 10:55 and dinner at 4:55 the talk in the Mess Hall amongst the troops was all speculation about the pros and cons of the upcoming move, with a few guys who had the opportunity to go over and take a look for themselves. At 6:45, I was relieved by John and Larry, and thought, "The longer drive across the Camp will even delay my being relieved from duty by five minutes."

Arriving at my Hotel room, I changed clothes and left to pick up Lompét at the cafe. Entering the cafe, I watched as she entered from the back, looking ravishing in her red silk dress. And, even though it was a Wednesday evening, there were plenty of Americans out and about to give her desiring looks as she walked close behind me to the night club. As we walked, I thought, "This is very much like the musical 'Pygmalion,' where the professor takes a common, street girl to educate and clothe her, then is able to pass her off as a high society woman."

Entering the night club, she said with enthusiasm, "My da-ling, I fee-la like a cata-pi-la you make into a beautifu-la butta-fa-ly."

Meeting up with Glen and Súpa on the 3rd tier, Glen said to me after exchanging sáwátdiis, "You know, the change in the location of the company area might be good for some. But, for us who live off base, it's really going to mess with our travel time to and from home."

I replied, "Yea, I know. Jim and I talked about it as we drove to the Air Base Site this morning. But, since he's leaving for Stateside right before the move, it doesn't affect him."

I then had a fun evening socializing with Glen and Súpa, and dancing with the radiant Lompét. When it was time, I danced an erotic Tango with Lompét, after which we rushed to my Hotel room and expunged our pent-up lust for each other in unrestrained lovemaking. Lying breathless together in our state of orgasmic release, I gasped, "My beloved, Lompét, I enjoy very much that lovemaking with you is like your name, 'spicy wind'."

She responded, "An I enjoy bery mut tat lo-ba-making wit you iss like you name, 'et-sa-temely goot'."

After spending the night sleeping blissfully cuddled in our own little heaven, our desire for each other exploded into lust driven lovemaking in a Kama Sutra position that heightened our climactic release. When we had showered and she'd helped me dress in my jungle fatigues, we affectionately kissed goodbye, as I felt the silky curves of her lovely, small body with the happy knowledge we'd be together again after Friday morning's formation.

Arriving at the Company Area, I swung by my hooch to drink a cold can of Bud, as I dumped my dirty laundry out of my shopping bag and changed into a fresh set of jungle fatigues, before going to the Mess Hall with Skip for breakfast. After morning formation, we rode in the truck with Jim to the Air Base Site and spent the day in the Operations Room quickly dispatching the several reported outages we received.

At 6:45, John and Larry arrived to relieve me, and I blasted out of there like shot from a cannon, with my shopping bag of fresh clothing, to catch a Thai bus for Korat. Entering my Hotel room, I'd hardly began to undress, when I heard Súusîi's eager knock on the room's door. Quickly opening the door, I was assailed by her passionate embrace and kisses. As she rapidly removed her already unbuttoned blouse and her skirt, and then avidly helped me strip out of the rest of my clothes, she moaned, "I've missed your desire for me very much since yesterday morning, my darling. My body burns with desire to feel your big strong body and loving me."

When the fire of our lust had been consumed in furious lovemaking, we lay gasping in an euphoric state for a while before taking a quick shower and dressing to go to the night club. Arriving there, we socialize with our ballroom dance friends on the 3rd tier when we weren't happily enjoying the foreplay of our dancing together. After dancing a sensuous Tango that fanned the flames of our pent-up lust to a white hot crescendo, we quickly returned to my Hotel room to revel in our rampant lovemaking that crested with our orgasmic release. Then, wrapped together in its afterglow, we blissfully fell asleep.

With the 3:30 wakeup call, we reignited our desires with sensuous foreplay to again enjoy the climax of our frenziedly lovemaking. Then, we basked for a while in its afterglow, telling of our love and affection for each other, before we playfully showered together. After dressing in my jungle fatigues, I caressed her scintillating body as we passionately kissed goodbye and expressed how much we'd miss each other till we were again embracing each other tomorrow afternoon.

Leaving for Camp Friendship, I thought, "Súusîi is so exciting and fun to be with, that I'm enjoying the growing love we have for each other. I wish there was some way we could have more time together without drawing suspicion from her father."

Arriving at the Company Area, I went to my hooch and drank a cold can of Bud as I changed into a fresh set of OD BDUs, before going to the Mess Hall for breakfast. There, I met up with Skip, who said, "There are plans for a farewell party Sunday night for Dan, as he'll be leaving Monday morning for his flight Stateside. Could you meet us at 8:00 o'clock in a bar on Mahat Thai Road that he'd frequented, for the sendoff party the guys on his shift are holding after they got off their day shift?"

I replied, "Sure, after all, Dan's been a good hooch mate. Besides, I've never been in one of those bars for Americans, and it'll be interesting to see how different it is than the Thai bar I've been going to. I don't think there'll be any problem leaving Lompét for an hour on Sunday night."

After morning formation, I returned quickly to my Hotel room and prepared for Lompét's arrival at 8:00 o'clock. When she arrived, we passionately made love in the Kama Sutra position she'd picked to satiate our lust in its climactic release, and then thoroughly enjoyed its afterglow as we spooned affectionately together. After we had fun showering together, we lay side by side on the bed, while she chose our next Kama Sutra position, and had fun discussing how to perform it. The rest of our time together, I had fun teaching her English, till she dressed and left for work at 9:30.

Sleeping after she left till 12:30, I then dressed and walked to the cafe, where I ate a pleasant lunch. While teaching Lompét English, I told her about the party for Dan Sunday night at 8:00 o'clock, but I'd only be gone an hour, and then would return to her loving arms. At 3:30, I went back to my Hotel room, changed into my OD BDUs and left for Camp Friendship.

Exiting the Thai bus at the Company Area, I walked to my hooch and drank a cold can of Bud, while watching Dan and Skip play against Ronnie and Stony in a game of Double Deck Pinochle till the 5:00 bugle call for Mess. As we all ate dinner together, I said, "Skip, you'll be driving to the Air Base Site alone, as I'll be meeting one of AFTN's DJ's at 6:00 for a tour of their radio station. I've never been to a radio station before, so it should be pretty. Also, I want to find out where they come up with all those hokey commercials for STD prevention, Base Security, and other military subjects."

Finishing my dinner and a relaxing cigarette, I returned to my hooch to rest as I drank a cold can of Bud before catching a Thai bus to the Air Base. Exiting the bus at the NCO Club, I walked across the street to a group of white painted, elevated wood buildings that made up the Korat Air Base Comm Center. Off to its right, I saw sign over the door that read, "AFTN Radio Station, Armed Forces Thailand Network."

Walking to the door, I saw stenciled in red on it, "Authorized Personnel Only." Knocking on the door, I saw it open and an Air Force Cpl. in jungle fatigues asked, "What can I help you with?"

I replied, "I'm supposed to meet Steve here. One of your DJs. Is he here?"

The Cpl. answered, "Sure. Come on in," and as I entered, he yelled over his shoulder, "Hey, Steve. Your Army buddy is here to see you."

I heard Steve yelled back, "What Army buddy," and when he saw me, he said, "Sandii, I didn't know you were in the Army. When you said that you worked next to the Air Base Comm Center, I thought you were in the Air Force."

I responded, "I do work next to the Air Base Comm Center, in that light green, metal building across the parking lot from the Base Exchange. We're the Army Liaison to your Comm Center. We tend to keep a low profile. Right now, we're very short handed, as we were supposed to have a compliment of 19 troops working there. But, only seven of us Army types work there, plus a few Company Reps and a Thai from the C.A.T. It's really a boring job, but someone has to do it. So, what's this place like?"

Steve then led me on a tour down the hallway through several offices, and a soundproof room with a red light over its door that was turned off. Inside this room, there was a desk surrounded by turn tables, tape decks, microphones and shelving along the walls full of small, vinyl, 45 RPM records, which he called Broadcast Studio Number Two. Across the hall from it, I saw another door with a red light over it that was turned on, and he said, "That's our Broadcast Studio Number One, and the red light indicates it's currently on the air and no one's to enter, unless it's an emergency."

Steve then led me to a door at the end of the hallway, and opening it, I saw a large room that was under renovation, with what appeared to be a giant tape deck in the center of the room. The giant tape deck had a pair of 16-inch reels with an inch-wide magnetic tape in one of the reels. Steve proudly said, "This is our latest addition, a TV studio. Next month we'll be doing some test broadcast for a month before we start our actual TV broadcasts and be the only English language TV station in northern Thailand, with a license from the C.A.T. to broadcast on Channel 10.

"We got Channel 10, as no Thai TV station wanted the channel because, as you know, to be 'number 10' in Thailand means it's 'very bad.' But, we're only permitted to broadcast with a few hundred watts of power. Just enough power for TV reception on the Air Base and Camp Friendship. Beyond that, the signal strength isn't enough to be picked up by the civilian TVs and compete with the local, commercial TV stations. So, to the civilian population we'll be a 'Number Ten' TV station.

"We'll Be showing mostly reruns of many of the popular TV series from Stateside, like '*Star Trek*,' '*Twilight Zone*,' and '*Pete and Gladys*.' We're also contracting with one of the local TV networks for live TV news feeds to record for an up to the minute news show. But, our commercials will still be that dumb crap the military wants us to put out."

I exclaimed, "TV! We're going to get actual, Stateside, TV shows? That's great. But, who writes your dumb commercials?"

He replied, "We have a team that censors all the news we can broadcast from AP and UPI, who also writes the material for our Health and Security commercials to make sure it conforms to the needs of the military. Then, they just give it to us DJs for the recordings to be broadcast. If they'd let us write them, they'd have a whole different flair."

As Steve finished giving me the tour of AFTN, I asked, "So, Steve, the other evening, you seemed pretty interested in Lompét."

He responded, "Hey, Sandii, I'm really sorry about that. And yeah, she's really a pretty, little woman. But, she's your tîi-lók, and if things were reversed, I'd have punched you in the mouth."

I laughed and said, "Steve, she's not my tîi-lók, she's my student. I'm teaching her English and ballroom dancing to improve her chances to be a tîi-lók. We were on our way to a Thai nightclub, where they do ballroom dancing. She's really a smart little girl, and in the five weeks I've been teaching her, she's learned quite a bit of English. Though, she has problems saying our consonants, like most Thais. And, she likes going to Japanese Samurai movies. But, if you're interested in Lompét, you should know she's only 14."

Steve laughed and said, "Heck, yea. I'm interested. Besides, most of those girls they have hooking in those bars are young teenage girls. Can you introduce me to her?"

I laughed and replied, "Steve, I've already introduced you to her that evening on the street. If you go to the cafe on Mahat Thai Road where she works, you can ask for her to be your waitress. And believe me, she'll have remembered you."

Steve responded, "Hey, you're a real pal, Sandii. Just give me the directions to the cafe where she works," which I did, and also told him that Sundays were her days off.

Leaving AFTN, I thought, "It looks like I found a nice guy that Lompét can be a tîi-lók for, which will free up more time for me to spend at the Thai bar and time with Súusîi, if it becomes available."

Entering the Operations Room, I relieved Jack so he could go home to his tîi-lók, just as Skip arrived for work. When Bob entered the Operations Room, I excitedly said, "Guess what Bob, AFTN is going to start doing TV broadcasts along with their radio broadcast. And, they'll show stuff like *Star Trek*, *Twilight Zone*, and *Pete and Gladys*. But, you guys won't be able to receive it in Korat, as they are only going to put out enough power to cover the Camp and the Air Base."

Bob responded, "That shouldn't be a problem for us at the compound. Did you get what TV channel they'll broadcast on?"

I laughed and replied, "Sure. The C.A.T. gave them channel 10 because no Thai TV station wants to be 'Number Ten.' but, what does that matter?"

Bob answered, "Because knowing the frequency of their broadcast, then we can design and build a high-gain, directional antenna for that frequency to pull in enough signal and amplify it for our TV's to watch their shows. We've got too much electronic knowledge to let a little thing like low signal strength to deprive us from receiving their TV broadcasts."

Skip responded, "Hey, that'll be really great to sit on Horn's porch and be able to watch the *Star Trek* shows we've missed seeing Stateside while drinking Sing Hǎi Beer."

It was a fairly quiet night while we sat at the desk in the Operations Room and speculated about what having an English language TV station would be like under military management. On my 10:55 meal run, I met up with Glen in the Mess Hall. As we ate, I told him about the prospect of our having TV service in a couple of months, especially being able to catch up on the latest season of *Star Trek* that we've been missing while we've been in Thailand.

I said laughingly, "Do you remember on Friday nights at Ft. Monmouth, when they'd bring those three busloads of women down from the YWCA in Newark for us to dance with at the Rec. Center's Ballroom, and all the guys were holed up in the TV lounge watching *Star Trek* till it was over at 8:00?"

Glen laughed in reply, "And all of the women were pissed because they weren't allowed in the TV lounge, and they had to wait around like bumps on a log until we were finished watching *Star Trek*? Makes you wonder where does the American male's libido lie?"

CHAPTER 43

SPIKE'S LIFE AIN'T WORTH A PLUGGED NICKEL ANYWHERE

Driving the truck to the Motor Pool on the 6:35 meal run at the end of my night shift, as I handed the Trip Ticket clipboard to Jim, I asked, "When we moved to the new Company Area, how are we going to work passing the truck from the night crew to the day crew? I mean, the Camps POL isn't anywhere near where the new Company Area will be, or even the Camp's Enlisted Mess Hall, like it is here."

Jim replied, "Good question, Sandii. and you're right, the Camp's POL isn't close to the new Company Area or the Mess Hall. I'll have to bring that up with Sgt. Davidson."

After a quick breakfast in the Mess Hall, I walked rapidly to my hooch, and drank a cold can of Bud, as I changed into a fresh set of OD BDUs and grabbed my shopping bag with fresh clothes, before hustling out to catch a Thai bus to Korat.

Entering my Hotel room, I swiftly prepared for Lompét's arrival. Soon I heard her knock on the room's door, and thoroughly enjoyed our vigorous lovemaking in a Kama Sutra position. After our playful shower, we had fun studying English as we lay side by side on the bed.

When she'd dressed and we'd lovingly kissed goodbye as she left for work at 9:30, I then slept till 12:30. While dressing to leave for the cafe, I thought, "If Lompét becomes Steve's tîi-lók, I'm sure going to miss all those good times making love with her, teaching her English, and showing her how to ballroom dance. Súpa will probably already have another girl for me to teach, but I'm going to decline the offer, because I'll want more time to love and dance with Súusîi. Plus, I want more time to learn Thai and to experience the Thai culture with a few sightseeing trips, like the one to Phimai."

Arriving at the cafe, I tried a different meal of curried fried pork with rice for lunch. Of course, every meal that wasn't made fried rice, called "kâao-pát," was served with rice. In fact, the Thai word to eat a meal was "gin-kâao," literally "to eat rice." I thought, "it's not only time to expand my knowledge of the Thai language, but to expose my taste buds to the full range of Thai cuisine, because the food any people eat is a reflection of their culture."

Having had fun teaching English to Lompét till 3:30, I left for my Hotel room to enjoy my delectable Sûusîi in our lust filled tryst. When she and I had satiated our bodily appetites for each other in climactic euphoria, I dressed in my OD BDUs and lovingly kissed her goodbye with the thought that we'd have all of Tuesday night to be together.

Exiting the Thai bus at the Company Area, I quickly made my way to the hooch and enjoyed a cold can of Bud, before going to the Mess Hall for a delicious dinner. As I picked up my tray from the waist-high counter and looked at the large ceramic plate laden with the succulent, thick slices of spicey roast beef and big pile of mashed potatoes, all smothered in rich brown gravy, I thought, "This doesn't really compare in flavor with the many spices used in Thai food, but it was the mainstay of most of our dinners on the farm where I grew up."

Seeing Skip and others from my hooch sitting at a table, I set my laden tray on the table next to Skip. As I sat down, Skip said, "Sáwát-dîi. It looks like Spike is back to his old tricks with our getting a new CO. He kicked me out of bed this morning and told me to go and get a case of beer for the mini-fridge. Luckily, we were able to pool our resources and fill the fridge with beer. We're sure that when our new CO gets word of Spike's harassing tactics, he'll shut Spike down again. However, we're trying to figure out something that'll be a permanent solution."

I responded, "Getting that bomb from the flight-line bomb loaders was strictly a fluke and a one-off. And, we all know how that turned out. I've made friends with a Sargent on the local Police force who would be able to arrest Spike and throw him in their monkey house for a while, but that would take some time and planning to pull off at best. Besides, Spike'll be rotating Stateside in a few months, so it'll have to be something we can come up with and do quickly."

Everyone nodded their heads in agreement, but no one could think of anything sinister we could do to Spike. So, the topic switched to the more fun subject of tomorrow night's farewell party for Dan, and the others that were leaving with him, until we left the Mess Hall at 6:30 and walked to the front of the Day Room for our rides to work.

After a quiet, boring night at the Air Base Site, during which I was able to get a couple hours sleep on the mattress stored under the back of the Operations Room, I drove the truck on my 6:35 meal run to the Motor Pool and transferred it to Jim. When I'd eaten a fast breakfast in the Mess Hall, I rapidly walked to my hooch and drank a cold can of Bud, as I quickly changed into a fresh set of jungle fatigues. Then, grabbing my shopping bag full of clean clothes, I hastened to catch a Thai bus to Korat.

Returning to my Hotel room, I prepared to spend a fun filled day making love with Lompét, in addition to eating lunch and dinner with her at the Ming Ter and joining Glen and Súpa to watch a Samurai movie. That evening, after we'd playfully showered together and she helped me dress for Dan's party, I left at 7:45 for the American bar on Mahat Thai Road.

Entering the bar, I saw it was similar in size and layout to the Thai bar I went to on Mahan Road, but full of American men instead of Thai men. Also, instead of being devoid of women, there were lots of mini-skirted Thai girls sitting on or near American men. And, unlike the Thais, who passed around a quart bottle of Sing Hǎi Beer, each American had his own bottle of Sing Hǎi Beer, or bottle of the rot gut Leaping Deer Whiskey, sitting in front of him.

I quickly spotted Dan with the guys from my hooch, and from the Tropo Platoon in general, sitting at a couple of tables pushed together. Walking to the bar, I ordered a bottle of Sing Hǎi Beer for substantially more than what was charged at the Thai bar. While waiting for my bottle of beer, a young, pretty Thai girl walked up beside me, placed her two arms around my right arm, and asked, as she sensuously caressed my arm, "You wan party wit me tonight, G.I.?"

I responded in Thai, "'I've a jealous girlfriend who'll cut my eyes out if I look at another woman."

Collecting my bottle of beer and change from the bartender, I went to join my friends at the table to celebrate with Dan and the others leaving in the morning for Stateside. As I grabbed a chair and sat down next to Skip, he said, "We've come up with a great way to get rid of Spike. We're each kicking in 20 Bhat to put a contract out on Spike. Dan says he knows some guys that for 200 Bhat, you can get any American wacked. The price is 100 Bhat for a Thai, and they'll do in an Indian for free, as a favor. If everyone chips in, we'll have at least 400 Bhat. What do you say, Sandii?"

I replied, "I say, here's my 20 Bhat," as I pulled a blue 20-Bhat bill from my wallet, handed it to Dan, who already had a wad of them in his hand, and thought, "Why didn't Dan think of this earlier. This is a lot simpler than getting that 200 pound bomb to blow up Spike, which was a bust anyway."

A while later, I heard an uproar, as some big, brawny American kicked over a table and started cursing the Air Force, Thailand, and everything associated with the Vietnam War. Then, I watched a couple of guys, who had been sitting at his table, try to calm him down, and he threw them back, yelling, "get off me you gook[143] lovers," as he kicked over another table and some chairs.

Soon, I heard a siren approaching and then stop outside the bar's entrance, followed by two small Thai Police Officers dressed in khaki uniforms and Sam Browne belts with holstered pistols, entering the bar's front doorway. I watched them cautiously approach the much larger American, saying, "Pa-lease come wit us, krup."

The brawny American picked up a chair and threw it at the two small Police Officers, as he yelled, "Get away from me you gook pigs[144], I ain't going to your filthy hoose gow[145]."

The two Thai Police Officers looked at each other, shrugged their shoulders, and as they drew their 0.38 caliber revolvers from their hol-

---

143   A hostile and contemptuous term for an East Asian.

144   A derogatory term for a police officer.

145   Slang term for a jail.

sters, everyone in their line of fire ran for the sidewalls. Then, the air rang loudly with two ear shattering explosions, as each Officer calmly shot a bullet into the big man's thighs, which were easy targets from only ten feet away.

The large American fell forward like a big oak tree as the force of the two 0.38 caliber bullets knocked his legs out from under him. Then, the two small Thai Police Officers, with their large revolvers still drawn, stepped forward to either side of him, each grabbing him by his shirt, as he yelled, "You shot me! You shot me!" and dragged him, like a big bag of potatoes, out the front doorway, trailing two large smears of blood on the floor to the doorway.

Watching from my chair at our table, I saw them drop him on the sidewalk, like a bag of trash, and climb into the cab of a brown, ¾-ton truck. Then, four men dressed in the khaki uniforms of a U.S. Army MP, U.S. Air Force AP, Thai Army MP and Thai Air Force AP, picked up the wounded American by his arms and legs, and carried him into the back of the truck with them, as he squealed like a stuck pig.

As the truck pulled away with its siren blaring, I asked, "Dan, how come the military Police Officers didn't come into the bar to arrest the guy, or even help the local Police carry him out after they shot him?"

Dan replied, "The Military Police only have jurisdiction on their own Military posts, and are forbidden by the law to enter any place of business. In fact, their being allowed to ride in the back of the Police vehicle is a courtesy, so they can take the offender back to his base, if he's not arrested. Or to notify his CO, if he's arrested and put in the local jail, like this guy'll be, to have arrangements made to bring him food and water. It's interesting that the jurisdiction of the local Police extends on to all military bases, which is unlike the military bases Stateside, where the local Police can't officially go onto a military base without the Provost Marshall's permission, even if they're in hot pursuit of a suspect."

After all the excitement of the shooting was over and the blood had been mopped up, I decided it was time to return to my Hotel room and spend the rest of the night with Lompét, having told her I'd be gone only an hour.

Entering my Hotel room, I found Lompét had been anxiously wait-ing for my return. When she asked me if the party was fun, I told her in English, "There were many men he work with to say goodbye to him and drink Sing Hăi Beer with him. One woman ask me if I want to party with her, and I tell her that I have a beautiful girlfriend who will cut my eyes out if I look at another woman." I'd decided to leave out the part about the shooting, as she looked worried enough at the fact I had gone to an American bar, which have a reputation for fights between the Americans.

She laughed with relief and said, "I am happy you hat fun wit you fa-ren-sa, an hat no pa-ro-lem wit any fight. An it be te-ru, I cut her eye out to look at you, not you eye."

After she helped me undress, we had fun arousing our lust for each other with our affectionate foreplay, and enjoyed our vigorous lovemaking in a Kama Sutra position that enhanced the pleasure of our orgasmic release. Then, as we spooned in the afterglow of our fulfilled passion, we went happily to sleep.

With the 3:30 wake-up call, we again had fun with the foreplay prior to our invigorating lovemaking in another Kama Sutra position. Then, we playfully showered together before she helped me dress in my jungle fatigues. When we'd passionately kissed goodbye, as I desiringly caressed the silky curves of her luscious body, she said, "I be ready fo mo offa you goot lo-ba-making wen you come back."

Exiting the Thai bus at my Company Area, I quickly walked to my hooch, where I drank a cold can of Bud, as I dumped the laundry out of my shopping bag, replaced them with clean clothes, and rapidly changed into a fresh set of jungle fatigues. As I did so, Dan walked up to me dressed in his Class-B Army Khaki uniform and asked, "Hey, Sandii, you want to help me carry my duffle bag to the Day Room on the way to the Mess Hall for my last meal at Camp Friendship?"

I replied, "Dan, it would be my pleasure to do so."

With each of us picking up an end of his heavy duffel bag, stuffed with the last of the items he'd be carrying with him Stateside, we headed out the hooch's front door, and I asked, "Dan, what did you do with all of your stereo gear and tape recordings, as they're certainly not in this duffel bag?"

He answered, "They issue us a 4-foot square, 2-foot high, wood crate over at Company Supply that we can put up to 600 pounds of our personal items in, which they'll ship for free to your next duty station or to your home address of record. It's a really sweet deal, because it's not searched by U.S. Customs when it gets Stateside. Some guys buy up lots of gold and jewelry here really cheap, and then make a huge profit when they get home. I've known a few guys who've shipped a bunch of Thai weed home, because it's so cheap here. But, I wouldn't chance that, as I've heard they now have drug sniffing dogs, and it's not worth the possibility of spending 20 years at Ft. Leavenworth."

As we made it to the bottom step and started walking on the concrete walkway to the Day Room, I said, "That was quite the sendoff last night at that bar. Who'd have guessed there'd have been actual fireworks to celebrate your leaving Thailand for Stateside?"

Dan replied with a laugh, "More than you'd have guessed, Sandii. I don't know why it is, but there's always some guy who becomes stupid drunk and has to get into a fight. And, usually another moron who's willing to oblige him. Sometimes it's an argument over a pûu-ying. Occasionally, it turns into an all-out brawl that ends very quickly when the Thai Police shoot one or two guys in the leg. Haven't you ever been to a bar before, Sandii?"

I answered, "Not a bar here with Americans. There's a bar I do go to over on Mahan Road, across from the Assandang Hotel, and hang out with a group of Thai locals to improve my Thai language skills. But, it's very different as there's no pûu-ying in it, as it's socially not allowed. Just a bunch of guys kicking back, drinking Sing Hǎi Beer, and having few laughs together after work, before they go home."

Dan laughed and said, "Sounds like some of the bars I know back home."

Entering the back door of the Day Room, we propped the duffel bag upright with a few others along the right sidewall. After leaving for the Mess Hall out the Day Room's front door, Dan stopped me, looked around, and said in a low voice, "Just thought I'd let you know, we raised $25 last night for a bounty on Spike's head."

I exclaimed, "Wow! That's more than the average Thai earns in a month. With that much money on his head, his life won't be worth a plugged nickel in Korat."

Dan laughed and responded, "For that much money, Spike's life ain't worth a plugged nickel anywhere."

CHAPTER 44

YOU'VE SET OUR RECORD FOR SERIOUS INJURIES IN A MONTH

Entering the Mess Hall, there was a round of applause and many well-wishes for Dan as he walked down the center of the Mess Hall to the kitchen counter to order his last meal at Camp Friendship, and gave a few thumbs up with knowing winks along the way. As the Tropo Platoon gathered for morning formation, I saw Dan, and several others wearing Class-B Army Khaki uniforms, getting slaps on the back and handshakes from those around them. Several of those in khaki uniform were guys I hadn't seen before and thought, "They must be from the outlying Radio Sites. As shorthanded as the Company is, it's a good thing we're getting some replacements next week."

When SFC Davidson arrived, he said, "I want all of you shipping out today, to form up as a squad behind the Korat Air Base Squad, with Spec-5 Swenson as the Squad Leader."

Once they had formed up behind our Squad, SFC Davidson went through the process of having the Tropo Platoon's ranks dress right and cover down. When each squad had reported "all present or accounted for," he ordered the Platoon to stand at Parade Rest. Once the rigamarole had been finished that all the members of Company C were "present or accounted for," everyone was dismissed, except those that were shipping out, who were then marched to the Day Room to get their duffel bags and stand by for transport to the Air Base.

As for myself, I left with several others, walking quickly to the main street to catch a Thai bus to their homes in Korat. Entering my Hotel room, I saw Lompét lying provocatively on the bed, and soon we were enthralled in vigorous lovemaking to quench our lust using an exciting Kama Sutra position. After our playful shower, we lay side by side working on Lompét's English language skills till 9:30, when she dressed to leave for the cafe. Then, I lovingly kissed her goodbye, before I laid back down on the bed and slept till 12:30.

Upon my waking, I dressed and left for the cafe, where I had a plate of lâpgâi, a very spicy salad of diced, boiled chicken, for lunch with two bottles of Pepsi. Finishing my very spicy, but delicious meal, I enjoyed teaching Lompét English till 3:30, when I left for the Thai bar.

Walking the quarter-mile up Manatt Road to the Thai bar, I bought a large bowl of egg noodle and chicken soup with a side of rice, and a bottle of Sing Hăi Beer. Then sitting at the table with my Thai companions, I spent the next three hours immersed in their convivial atmosphere, expanding my abilities to follow and understand the tonal inflections of the Thai language, which is the most difficult thing for any Westerner to learn. When Sgt. Comkit of the Korat Police Force joined us, I asked in Thai, "Is it true, as a Police Officer, you can go into any military base without receiving their permission first?"

He cheerfully replied, "It's true. Enforcing the law is a most important job in Thailand. I'm a Police Officer every hour of every day. I only take off my uniform and pistol for sleep and for lovemaking. If a not-good person is on an Army base, I go onto the Army base to get them, and I shoot any person that tries to stop me."

I asked, "Have you ever been on the American Military bases?"

He laughed and answered, "Many times. Americans think, if he's on the American base, then the Thai Police can't get him. He thinks very wrong. I drive onto the American base straight to the Military Police Office. They give me Military Policeman to help me get the man I want with no problem. If the man not come with me, I shoot him, no problem. I always get the man I want, alive or dead."

I said, "Sometime, I'd like you to have a meal and beer with me at the American Air Force Sargent's Club."

He responded, "I'll like that very much, Sandii. I hear the American Air Force Sargent's Club is very good, but nobody invite me before. Sometimes we must do that," and I thought, "It'll be good to be in tight with a Thai Police Sargent, in case I ever get into trouble, which I hope never happens."

After a pleasant evening talking, laughing and drinking Sing Hăi Beer with my Thai friends, I left at 7:30 to meet Lompét at the cafe. On entering the cafe, I watched her walk from the cafe's back, looking very alluring in her revealing, hot-pink silk dress, and thought, "It's like Mom always said, 'you have to accentuate the positive,' and though Lompét's positives aren't very big, that dress sure does accentuate them very nicely."

As it was a Monday night, there wasn't a lot of Americans on the streets. But those that were there, were giving Lompét very approving looks as she walked close behind me. At one point, I spotted Steve from AFTN standing across Mahat Thai Road from us and saw him give me a big smile and a thumbs up, and I thought, "This is no chance greeting. He's letting me know he's been going to eat at the cafe, and things are going well with Lompét. I'd bet she even told him that we were going dancing tonight, and he staged himself there to watch her sashay behind me as we walked to the night club to signal me that things are going well. If he's smart, he'll follow us at a safe distance to see where we go dancing, so he can take her dancing there at a later date."

Entering the night club, we met up with Glen and Súpa for a fun evening of visiting with them when Lompét and I weren't enjoying each other on the dance floor. When the time came and we'd danced our lust provoking Tango together, we hastily retired to my Hotel room and were quickly enthralled in wanton lovemaking to achieve the climactic rush we eagerly sought. Attaining the ultimate ethereal state we desired, we happily spooned together and fell into euphoric sleep.

In the morning, the teasing caresses of our desires rapidly accelerated us into passion driven lovemaking, using a Kama Sutra position to increase the orgasmic release of the rampant lust we had for each other. After cooling down in its afterglow, we had fun showering together, during which she sensuously teased me with her enticing body to copulate with her again, as we wouldn't see each other again till we went dancing the following evening.

After Lompét helped me dress in my jungle fatigues, I desiringly caressed the silky curves of her sensuous, petite body, as I affectionately kissed her goodbye, before leaving for Camp Friendship with my shopping bag of laundry.

Arriving at my Company Area, I exited the Thai bus and went to my hooch, where I drank a cold can of Bud, as I emptied the laundry from my shopping bag onto the floor. I then filled the bag with clean clothes, before changing into a fresh set of jungle fatigues. Going to the Mess Hall for breakfast, I met up with Skip there. And, as I sat down opposite from him and began to eat, he excitedly said, "I saw Jack as he was leaving the Mess Hall for the Air Base Site. He told me that Tonsanut Tropo went off the air this morning after sending a message that they were under mortar. And that now, they've been busy with the Quad-C A ordering the reroute of high priority circuits. Also, we're to skip morning formation and meet Jim in the Motor Pool ASAP to leave directly for the Air Base. So, you need to eat up quick."

After I wolfed down my breakfast, we passed SFC Davidson as he entered the Mess Hall and yelled, "Tropo Platoon, listen up. Tonsanut Tropo's gone off the air. All of you on the day shift, drop what you're eating and let's get going. We have the trucks waiting to go right now."

I watched the mad scramble of a dozen men shoving food into their mouths as they jumped to their feet like their pants were on fire. Beating the rush out the Mess Hall's door, I saw Jim in the truck, parked on the Company's roadway, in front of the two 2½-ton trucks. As he frantically waved his left arm from the window for us to hurry and get in, I saw John sitting in the back of the truck. As Skip and I jumped into the truck's cab, he revved the truck's engine and propped the clutch, with the rapid acceleration slamming the passenger door shut behind us.

Focused on making the right turn into the left lane of the busy main street, Jim waited till we were safely travelling toward the Air Base before he said, "Sandii, as soon as we get there, I want you to run back and check the FRC-109 to make sure it's operating properly. Then, go to the Grand Canyon to take charge of the Temporary Log. Skip, most of the action will happen in the Grand Canyon. I want you to take over from Jack whatever he's working on. You are to ignore all outages lower than a Priority 2 and focus on the Priority 1 outages. Once things are semi-under control, I'll relieve John, and Sandii can drive him to the Company Area."

Arriving at the Air Base Site, I ran to the back of the Operations Room down the left sidewall and checked our FRC-109 microwave radio. Fortunately, I found all of the green lamps on the multiplexer cards were lit, and all of the amber and red lamps were not on. I had to do a minor tweak on the klystron box to get the frequency exactly correct, before logging the correction on the hourly log sheet.

Then, hustling up the far sidewall of the Operations Room, I saw Bill and Bob between two of the 5-foot tall stacks of racks for the breakout circuits with the test cart checking the circuits in a rack they'd pulled out. Reaching the Grand Canyon, I watched Jim, John and Skip between the two 7-foot tall stacks of racks busily plugging and unplugging patch cords among the maze of patch cords in monitor jacks for both the audio and teletype circuits.

Taking the Temporary Log notebook from John, I busily recorded the circuit outages they said as they were being pre-empted with other circuits that they were told to reroute. I also listened intently to the Order Wire and its rapid-fire chatter for orders given by the Quad-C A effecting any of our 252 in-house circuits and the responses by those Radio Sites affecting the changes, which I diligently recorded.

In a few minutes, Bill and Bod walked over from the breakout racks, and Bill said, "Okay, Jim, KEG-7 should be good to go. It was a wonky power tube. Also, the Quad-C A put the word out that it was a piece of shrapnel that dented the waveguide to their LRC-3 antenna. So, as soon as they have the damaged section replaced, they should be back to normal operations, and we'll begin to tear down all of this spaghetti."

By 9:00, our world was returning to normal operations, and I'd driven John to the Company Area. As this was already December 17th, and the third week after Pay Day, I decided it was a good time to start my stockpile of beer and cigarettes, especially since the guys had bought Christmas presents for their families and girlfriends, and would be broke a little sooner.

Entering my hooch with the three 6-packs of Budweiser and a carton of Pall Malls I'd bought at the Howard Johnson, I could hear a rapid, metallic squeaking sound from the back of the hooch. Setting what I was carrying on my bed, I walked to the end of the partition next to my bed. From there, I could see past the second partition on the right, and into Tommy's cubical. To my surprise, I saw Tommy on his bed, laying bare-bottomed between Súmat's upraise legs, vigorously making love with her.

Discretion being the better part of valor, I quickly and quietly left the hooch with the beer and cigarettes lying on my bed, knowing that no one would bother them. Returning to the truck I'd left parked in front of the Day Room, I drove back to the Air Base Site, and said nothing about Tommy and Súmat to anyone.

On my 10:55 meal run, I was eating lunch in the Mess Hall as Tommy placed his food laden tray opposite mine on the table. He said as he sat down, "Sáwátdii, Sandii. I take it from seeing the beer and cigarettes on your bed, that you've discovered my love interest in Súmat?"

I replied, "Sáwátdii, Tommy. I don't have any problem with it, so your secret is safe with me. How long have you had a love interest in Súmat?"

He answered, "Since I went through my bout with the clap right after we got here. She'd been showing some interest in me. Then one day, when there was no one else in the hooch and we were sitting on my bed, and the next thing I know is, we're boinking each other's brains out. I slip her a 100 Bhat each Pay Day, so she doesn't think I take her for granted. But, I appreciate you're willing to keep it quiet, or else she'd lose her job here."

I responded, "That's all well and good for now, but what are you going to do when we move to the new Company Area and you're living in a barrack with two dozen other guys?"

He replied, "Yea. That's something I've been thinking about. I guess we'll wait and see how that plays out after the move."

I said, "Why don't you just find a place to live together, or even make her your tîi-lók."

He answered, "Either way, she'd lose her job, and then what would happen to her after I leave? Guys only want a tîi-lók who's pretty and young, and Súmat is neither."

I replied, "You've got a point, there. Changing the subject. As you know Tonsanut was off the air for a few hours early this morning after a mortar attack damaged a waveguide."

I spent the rest of my lunch updating him about it, before going by the Howard Johnson to buy more beer and cigarettes to put in my wall locker, with those I'd left on my bed.

Returning to the Air Base Site, I spent the remainder of my workday busily getting most of our low priority circuits back in service as the high priority circuits that pre-empted them were restored to their normal routing. On my 4:55 meal run, I took another load of beer and cigarettes to my wall locker in the hooch. At 6:45, I was relieved by John and Larry, and flew from the Operations Room like a bat out of hell, to board a Thai bus for Korat.

Entering my Hotel room, Sûusîi arrived nearly on my heels for a torrid session of rampant lovemaking, before we went to the night club. After a couple of hours, with her dancing happily in my arms, we Tangoed sensuously together, increasing our lust to a fevered pitch. Returning to my Hotel room, we wantonly made love in a Kama Sutra position to infuse our lovemaking with a greater climactic rush, after which we succumbed to its afterglow expressing affectionately our love for each other, as we fell blissfully asleep.

With the 3:30 wake-up call, our loving caresses reignited our lust, which was satiated with vigorous lovemaking in another Kama Sutra arrangement of our bodies. As we basked in the euphoria of our orgasmic release, Sûusîi mused, "I love you so much, my darling, and your desire for me. I want to have more time with you , and sometime to go on another trip with you to have fun, like we did when we went to Phimai."

I replied, "I love you very much, too, my darling, and would really like to go again with you on another day trip. Maybe you can think of someplace interesting to go, and we can talk about it when we're together Thursday?"

After we had fun showering together, I dressed in my jungle fatigues, and as I caressed desiringly the luscious curves of her body and kissed her passionately goodbye, I thought, "We love each other so much, and it's nice to know there is more to our relationship than enjoyable dancing and great lovemaking."

Exiting a Thai bus at the Company Area, I went to my hooch to enjoy a cold can of Bud, as I changed into a fresh set of jungle fatigues. I then walked to the Mess Hall for breakfast, where I met up with Skip. After morning formation, we rode with Jim to the Air base Site, where we spent the day dealing with the reverberations of the Tonsanut outage.

During my 10:55 and 4:55 meal runs, I stopped by the Howard Johnson after eating lunch and dinner to buy three 6-packs of Budweiser and a carton of Pall Malls, which I added to the growing stockpiles in my wall locker. When John and Larry relieved me at 6:45, I flew from the Operations Room, like an arrow shot from a bow, straight to the Thai bus stop for a ride to Korat.

Arriving at my Hotel room, I changed clothes and left to pick up Lompét at the cafe. When I entered the cafe, she sashayed from the back looking very attractive in her alluring, light-blue silk dress. As we walked to the night club, she again drew the admiring eye of those Americans we passed.

On reaching the night club, we had a fun evening talking and joking with Glen and Súpa, when I was not enjoying the enticing view of Lompét gaily dancing in my arms. After we danced a seductive Tango, we rapidly left for my Hotel room, where we became enthralled in vigorous lovemaking. Attaining our desired climactic rush, we then slipped into a soothing cuddle and passed into heavenly sleep.

With the 3:30 wake-up call, we quickly aroused our desires into a lust that devoured us in passionate lovemaking with our bodies arranged in an exciting Kama Sutra position. After our fun shower, we lay side by side on the bed, and I enjoyed teaching Lompét English until she dressed and left for work at 9:30. Then, sleeping for a few hours, I also dressed and left for the cafe at 12:30.

Entering the cafe, I exchanged sáwátdiis with Lompét at the front door before she effusively said, "My goot tea-cha, I hap ba-ry happy new-sa. You fa-ren, Sa-tee-ba, he ass-ka me to be hiss tîi-lók. I am mut happy to say, ye-sa to him. You come quick. He wan to tan-ka you fo tea-cha me to sa-peak Angrit and to dan-sa like an A-me-ri-can."

She then happily led me to a table where Steve was sitting. As he stood with my approach, we warmly shook hands, and I said, "Congratulations, Steve. I'm very happy Lompét will be your tîi-lók, as she deserves a good man that she can take care of." And, as he and I sat down, I turned to Lompét and said, "Please, bring me and Steve the best meal in the cafe with a Pepsi. I want to honor your becoming his tîi-lók."

While she was gone to get our meals, Steve profusely thanked me for teaching her English and to ballroom dance, and especially for introducing her to him, though in a roundabout way. Then, Lompét returned with two large plates of bplaa-pôw, a grilled fish coated in salt and stuffed with pandanus leaves and lemongrass, with bowls of rice and two bottles of Pepsi. She also brought me the English textbook, thanking me for having been her wonderful teacher, and for finding her a handsome American man to be a tîi-lók for.

When we'd finished the delicious and filling meal, Steve graciously paid the bill, and I left the happy couple to make their plans to live together. Returning to my Hotel room, I stripped and went happily to sleep, knowing Lompét will have a good man to love and take care of, and with luck, to get married to.

At 4:00, I woke to Súusîi's knock on my room's door. After our passionate interlude, we lay happily entwined in the afterglow of our climactic rush, and she told me about Phanom Rung, an ancient Khmer site about 90 miles East of Korat. Also, how it was the largest Khmer monument in Thailand, and that there was a series of other ancient Khmer sights that stretched 20 miles further East. And, for 100 Bhat, I could hire a taxi for the all day excursion, which would be more comfortable and a lot faster than going by bus.

I responded, "My darling, it sounds like a perfect day trip to be with you. maybe we could do it on Sunday. But, won't we need another couple to go with us?"

She replied, "Sunday would be perfect my darling. And, we won't need another couple with us, as we'll have the taxi driver with us."

With that set, we happily took a quick shower and dressed, before we lovingly kissed goodbye and left for our separate destinations. As I rode a Thai bus to Camp Friendship, I thought, "This day has worked out perfectly. Not only did Lompét become Steve's tîi-lók, but that freed up Sunday to spend all day with Súusîi to see more of Thailand."

Exiting the bus at my Company Area, I quickly walked to my hooch for a cold can of Bud to drink, as I changed into a fresh set of jungle fatigues. Then, I left for the Mess Hall to have dinner, where I met up with Skip, before walking to the front of the Day Room to wait for Tommy. When he arrived with the truck, he said, "I read the Site Log for the last couple of days, and I can't believe all the chaos caused with the Tropo link between Tonsanut and Korat being down for a few hours. Well, today was pretty quiet, so you should have a quiet night."

After I relieved Jack from the day shift, it was a quiet evening till 8:00, when the phone rang. As Bob hung up the phone, he said, "That was a frantic call from Ted that there's a flying squirrel flitting around the inside of the PBX Room, and could we spare someone to come and help catch it. Sandii, you were raised on a farm and know about animals, why don't you go over and give them a hand?"

I laughed and said, "Yea. I've caught a few ground squirrels in my day, so catching a flying squirrel should be an interesting diversion from the boredom here."

Entering the 12-foot long, 16-foot wide PBX Room, with its PBX switch board full of jack holes and patch cords across the far wall, I saw one guy trying to work the PBX, while two others were chasing a darting, 6-inch long squirrel with a long tail, around the room with a 16-inch cube-shaped, cardboard box. I convinced them to stop chasing the little critter for ten minutes to give it a change to calm down, and then we could slowly herd it into a corner to reduce the number of directions it could fly in.

While we stood back from the flying squirrel, I asked, "Does anyone know how this flying squirrel got in here?"

One of the Airmen replied, "Yea. I bought it for 40 Bhat at the street market. The guy told me it was a baby, and I could raise it to be a fun pet. When I brought it in here to show the other guys, it got out of the box."

I laughed and responded, "Man, you've been duped. It might be young, but it's no baby."

A little bit later, we were able to slowly herd the flying squirrel into a corner by the door. Then, while the other two distracted it from the front, I was able to grab it from behind between my right thumb and forefinger by the scruff of the neck. With it twisting wildly as I tried to put it in the cardboard box, I could feel it slipping from my grip. As I tried to get a better hold on it with my left thumb and forefinger, it rotated its head around and sank its needle sharp, little incisors deep into my left thumb.

Tossing the flying squirrel quickly into the cardboard box, I pinched the bit areas on each side of my left thumb between the ends of my right thumb and forefinger to staunch the bleeding, and yelled, "It bit me! You," indicating the Airman who had bought the flying squirrel and was now holding it tight in the box, "bring that critter to the Hospital with us, so it can be tested for rabies. And, Ted, call Bob and let him know what's happened."

The Airman with the box, quickly followed me as I ran to our Air Base Site's truck. Then, driving the truck as I awkwardly shifted with my right hand while it held my left hand, we went to the Army's 33rd Field Hospital's Emergency Room. While the Doctor bandaged my left thumb, he said, "The Army Veterinarian here will quarantine the flying squirrel for two weeks to see if it has rabies, or not. According to your Medical Record, I see that four weeks ago, you were treated for a gunshot wound to your left thigh. Then, two weeks ago, you almost lost your right thumb to one of those little, green scorpion stings. Now, you've been bit by a possibly rabid flying squirrel. I think you've set our record for serious injuries in a month."

CHAPTER 45

HEY, ONE OF THOSE NEWBIES IS A BLACK GUY

Returning to the Air Base Site in the truck with a bandaged left thumb, and without the Airman's flying squirrel, I entered my Radio Site, while the Airman walked back to the PBX Room. Entering the Operations Room, Bob laughed and said, "You're becoming a regular at the Army Hospital, aren't you?"

I laughed and replied, "The Doctor said that I've set the record for their number of serious injuries in a month. Also, that the Veterinarian will quarantine the flying squirrel for two weeks to make sure it doesn't have rabies. Did I miss anything here?"

Skip replied dejectedly, "Just watching me fail at tying a knot in a patch cord. How about you show that to me again, Sandii?"

As he followed me into the Grand Canyon, I replied, "Mái bpén rai, Skip," and in a low voice added, "but, here's a hint. This time watch my fingers closely."

Grabbing a patch cord hanging from one of the hooks, I held its middle four feet from the loose end. As Skip watched my hand closely, I flipped the bitter end up into the air, twisted my wrist and rolled my fingertips at the apex of its flight, which made a loop in the cord for the plug on the end to fall down through the loop and make the knot. Skip said intently, "I think I see it. Do it again, Sandii."

When I did it again, Skip happily said, "Okay, Sandii. Now, give me the patch cord, so I can try it," and after a couple of near misses, he tied a knot in the patch cord with a single-handed flip of the cord and yelled, "Look, Bob, now I'm an official Frame Tech."

Leaving on my 10:55 meal run, I met up with Glen in the Mess Hall, and when he saw my bandaged left thumb, he asked, "What happened to your thumb? Did it get caught slamming a rack closed?"

I laughingly replied, "Nothing as mundane as that. I was bit by a flying squirrel," and told him about the incident in the PBX Room, and what the Doctor had said.

Finishing my tale of woe, Glen said, "I hope for your sake it doesn't have rabies. I've heard you have to get fourteen shots in the gut to be vaccinated against rabies. So, what else is new?"

In reply, I told him about Lompét becoming Steve's tîi-lók, and he said, "That's great news for Lompét. I suppose once they're settled, Steve'll bring her to the night club to ballroom dance. Do you want Súpa to set you up with another one of her pretty girlfriends?"

I replied, "Steve'd be a fool not to take Lompét dancing, as she really enjoys it. As to Súpa setting me up with one of her girlfriends, I don't think it'll be necessary. Some of the women in my Thursday night ballroom dance group have shown they're interested in me. Besides, this'll give me more time to spend going to the Thai bar to improve my language skills. Also, I don't want to get bogged down teaching another girl English and ballroom dancing so she can become some other guy's tîi-lók."

Returning to the Air Base Site, it was Skip's turn to leave on the 11:40 meal run. When he left, I told Bob about Lompét becoming Steve's tîi-lók, and my planned day-trip by taxi on Sunday with Súusîi to see the ancient Khmer sites at and near Phanom Rung. Also, that I'd be taking my new CO and his wife on a shopping tour of Korat at the suggestion of Lt. Price.

Bob responded, "Sounds like you've got a busy weekend ahead of you. I've been to see those ancient sites at and near Phanom Rung, and hiring a taxi is a great idea. Just be aware, you'll have to pay any of the expenses for the driver, like his meals, or if he hits and kills anything like a chicken. Under Thai law, whoever hires the taxi is responsible for any damages. And if he kills a chicken, it's not just the cost of the bird, but also the loss of profit from any eggs it might have laid. So, if he gets into any kind of car wreck, get out and run away as fast as you can from the scene.

"Now, with Lompét gone, do you have plans to take on another tîi-lók trainee?"

I laughingly replied, "I'm officially out of the tîi-lók training business. I now need the time to be with my main squeeze, Súusîi, which is a long-term relationship. Also, it gives me more time to go to the Thai bar and bone up on my Thai."

The night was pretty quiet, so Skip and I were able to get a couple of hours sleep each before the end of our shift. When I drove the truck to the Motor Pool at 6:35, I gave Jim a quick report on the flying squirrel incident before walking to the Mess Hall for breakfast. After eating breakfast, as I no longer had Lompét to spend the morning and afternoon with, I went to my hooch and drank a cold can of Bud, as I stripped to my skivvies, turned on my fan, took the blanket off my bed, and lay on the cool, white sheets to sleep till the bugle call for Mess sounded at 11:00.

Rising from my bed, I found it was not soaked with sweat, and thought, "That's right, this is Thailand's cool, dry season with the air mainly flowing South from the Himalayas, and the morning temperatures start in the 60s and only go up to the mid-80s, instead of the mid-90s, with very low humidity."

Getting a cold can of Bud from the mini-fridge to drink while I used the piss tube by the front door and to dress in my colorful civilian clothes, I then walked with Skip to the Mess Hall for lunch. After eating lunch, we went to the Howard Johnson, where I paid for six 6-packs of Budweiser and two cartons of Pall Malls before we returned to our hooch and added them to the stockpile in my wall locker.

When Ronnie and Stony returned from eating lunch in the Mess Hall, Skip and I partnered against them to play Double-Deck Pinochle for the rest of the afternoon, as we drank beer and smoked cigarettes in our skivvies. Hearing the bugle call for Mess at 5:00, we finished playing the hand we'd started before dressing in a fresh set of OD BDUs and leaving together for the Mess Hall to eat dinner.

After eating dinner, Skip and I again went by the Howard Johnson to load up with six more 6-packs of Bud and two more cartons of Pall Malls to add to the stockpile in my wall locker. At 6:35, we walked to the front of the Day Room and met Tommy with the truck. As Skip drove us to the Air Base Site, he said, "It was good having you around this afternoon, or we'd have been scrounging around for the fourth for Pinochle. Now that Lompét's gone, are you going to be around more, or is Súpa going to fix you up with another of her pretty, young girlfriends?"

I replied, "Yes and no. I already have a new girlfriend that Súpa didn't fix me up with. She's one of the girls who belongs to the ballroom group that I meet with on Thursday nights. Her name is Súusîi and is a College student. So, she takes classes during the weekdays, and I can't see her every night because she has to study most evenings. But, I do have a dinner and dancing date with her tomorrow evening, after I spend the afternoon taking our new CO and his wife on a shopping tour of Korat, like I did with Lt. Price and his wife. Plus, I'll be gone all day Sunday on a day-trip with Súusîi to see some ancient Khmer sites East of Korat. Also, I've some Thai drinking friends at a Thai bar in Korat I'll be socializing with at least once a week to learn more Thai from. But, I'll be around most afternoons to be your partner for Pinochle."

Skip responded, "I'm glad to hear you'll be around more, as life is kind of dull without you."

It was a pretty quiet night, which Skip and I spent part of trying to put a second knot in a patch cord to be an Expert Frame Tech. But, the first knot had somehow changed the dynamics of the patch cord to use the same wrist and finger action to tie a second knot. After we'd each made our midnight meal run, I was able to get a couple hours of sleep on the mattress. When I'd delivered the truck on my 6:35 meal run and eaten breakfast, I drank a cold can of Bud in my hooch as I changed into a fresh set of jungle fatigues and put clean clothes in my shopping bag before catching a Thai bus to Korat.

Entering my Hotel room, I immediately stripped to my skivvies and went to bed thinking, "It sure felt strange for Lompét not to have been here to make love with when I returned."

Getting up at 11:30, I took a quick shower and dressed in my civilian clothes before walking the short distance to the Jomsurang Hotel around the corner from the Sri Pattana Hotel. Entering the Hotel's Lobby, I didn't see Cpt. Richards, so I walked across the Lobby and flirted with Dhoi in Thai, who was still as beautiful and shy as before. Also, her friend Suumiî, was just as encouraging for Dhoi to talk with me and said in Thai, "Sandii, you speak the Thai language better than the last time you visited Dhoi. She told me she likes that you can speak to her in Thai because she only speaks English a little bit."

Soon, I saw Cpt. Richards enter the lobby with a 5-foot-2, pretty redhead, with a medium, almost plump build, and thought, "She was probably quiet a slender little fireball when they got married. But, after a couple of kids, she's having to work to keep the pounds off. I've heard women say, 'I got fat with my last baby,' and my Mom always joked, 'under this fat, I still have my girlish figure'."

Walking over to the couple, I said gallantly, "Capt. And Mrs. Richards, I'm Sandii, at your service."

Cpt. Richards responded, "Sandii, this is my wife, Sue. And in this informal setting, you can call me Mark. Sue, this is Sandii, the man from my Company I told you about, who's very knowledgeable of the local language and customs, and will be showing us around Korat this afternoon."

Sue said, "It's a pleasure to meet you, Sandii," as she put forth her right hand to shake mine.

I made the wâai, bowed slightly, and said, "I'm sorry, Sue, but Thai custom forbids any physical contact between a man and woman in public, even if they're married. However, I'm honored to make you acquaintance, Sue. I see your children must have received their good looks from Mark, because you still have yours," thinking, "a little humor should lighten any awkwardness from her faux pas."

Sue laughed as she quickly withdrew her hand, and said, "Thank you for noticing. Mary did tell me how the Thao culture looks down on any PDA between a man and a woman in public. And, that I should walk between you two and slightly behind while we're out and about. Also, how women are treated like second-class citizens, who at age 14, either have to get married, find a job or be sold into prostitution by their fathers, if he doesn't have the money for them to go to High School," she added with disgust.

Mark chimed in, "Actually, Sue, that's the way things are all over Asia, not just in Thailand. I saw the same thing when I was in Vietnam. But, back to the subject at hand. Steve said there's a really good Thai BBQ place up the street from here, where their 'little bit spicy' chicken is plenty spicy and good. So, shall we be on our way because I'm a little hungry?"

Leaving the Jomsurong Hotel, I guided them up Rajadamnern Road to the Gáí Yâang Sâang Thai restaurant, pointing out the same landmarks and places I had with Steve and Mary. Then, after we ate lunch, I showed them the same shops, and helped them with the bargaining for good prices, as I had done for Steve and Mary, but adding the jewelry shop, where Sue bought a beautiful emerald ring. When we returned to the Hotel, Mark said, "Thank you so much, Sandii, for the tour of Korat and the help with getting the prices down so much. You certainly know how to speak the lingo here. If there's anything I can do for you, just let me know, and I'll see what I can do."

I replied, "It was my pleasure, Mark. And, there's one thing you might be able to do for me. Tomorrow is my second off day, and my girlfriend and I have planned a day-trip to see some ancient Khmer religious sites about 90 miles East of Korat. It would be helpful if you could excuse me from morning formation tomorrow, which would allow us to get an earlier start."

Mark laughed and responded, "A little *quid pro quo* would certainly be in order for having given up your afternoon to take Sue and I on a shopping tour of Korat, especially since tomorrow is Sunday. I'll tell SFC Davidson you're on a special recon detail for me and are 'accounted for.' So, you two have a safe and fun day-trip. But, I'd like a report from you, as it sounds like something my family and I would enjoy, also."

Walking back the few hundred yards to the Sri Pattana Hotel, I thought, "It'll be great for us to sleep in a little in the morning and still get an early start on our day-trip, instead of wasting all that time travelling to and from morning formation."

Returning to my Hotel room by 4:00, I stripped to my boxers and napped till 5:00, when I woke to Súusîi's knock on my room's door. After our vigorous lovemaking satiated the pent-up lust we had in an orgasmic rush, we took a quick shower together, before dressing and going to the Ming Ter for dinner. Over dinner, I told Súusîi about my success in taking my new CO and his wife on a shopping trip around Korat, for which I was allowed to be absent form tomorrow morning's formation.

With this happy news, we made our plans for the day-trip to see the ancient Khmer sites that were ten miles Southeast of Nâng Rông[146] and stretched twenty miles between Bâan Ta Pek and Bâan Kruat[147]. Leaving at 6:00, we could eat breakfast in Nâng Rông before going on our tour of the locations in the cool of the morning, and then eat lunch in Bâan Kruat. After lunch, we should be able to make the one-hundred mile trip back to Korat via Prakhon Chai in three hours, to leave us plenty of time for dinner and a movie.

Having finished eating our dinner and making our plans for Sunday, we walked back to the Sri Pattana Hotel, where the Hotel's concierge made arrangements to have a taxi waiting in front of the Hotel at 6:00 for a daily rental fee of 100 Bhat and changed my wake-up call from 3:30 to 5:00.

Returning to my Hotel room, we took pleasure from sensuously undressing each other with enticing kisses, and then enjoyed our passionate lovemaking in an erotic Kama Sutra position. With the climactic release of our lust, we lay happily entwined in the afterglow of our orgasmic rush, speaking of our love for each other and the fun we'll have on our day-trip. After a while, we disengaged from our loving position and took a playful shower together, before we dressed and walked the few hundred yards to the night club.

Entering the night club, I saw sitting with Steve and Mary on the 3rd tier were Mark and Sue, who were signaling for us to join them. As Súusîi followed me happily up the stairs to join Steve and Mary, I explained to her the other couple at the table was my new boss and his wife. Arriving at their table, they stood up and we exchanged sáwáwt-diis in the Thai manner, and I introduced Súusîi to Mark and Sue.

As Súusîi sat with the two women, it was obvious Sue had been given some background on Súusîi when Sue asked, "I understand you're a College student. What's that like for you?"

While Súusîi answered their questions in what English she knew, Steve and Mark asked me about our plans to see the ancient Khmer sites East of Korat, until Súusîi's and my Pepsi's arrived. Once we had a sip of our drinks, then Súusîi and I excused ourselves to the dance floor, where we had a lot of fun dancing together and took occasional

---

146   Which means Teach Path
147   Bâan meaning village, house or home.

breaks for a dink of Pepsi. When a Tango was played later in the evening, we danced a sensuous Tango, then said goodbye to the other two couples, as we made our hurried exit from the night club.

Returning to my Hotel room, we passionately and eagerly removed our clothes, before we hastily threw ourselves onto the bed and began feverishly making love in a Kama Sutra position I placed her in. After our stored up lust was satisfied in orgasmic release, we lay in the euphoria of its rush, lovingly wrapped in our arms and legs, and happily slept till 5:00.

Aroused from our sleep by the 5:00 wake-up call, our affectionate foreplay soon spurred our desires into the lust filled lovemaking we enjoyed with vigor, and the climactic rush we craved. After having a fun shower together, we dressed and left for the Hotel's front entrance, where I found a well-dressed taxi driver waiting for us.

After exchanging sáwátdiis, he introduced himself as Potkim. I gave him our names and paid him the expected 100 Bhat. As he opened the back, left door of an old green, 1949 Desoto, I enjoyed the view of Súusîi's shapely legs as she climbed into the back seat and slid to the other side of the worn, brown leather seat. Climbing in after her, I sat on the smooth, plush leather and thought, "Oh yes. This is so much better than having to spend the day riding on the hard, cramped seats of a Thai bus. Why didn't we do this for our day-trip to Phimai?"

Leaving the Hotel, Potkim turned right onto Rajadamnern Road and then left onto Ratobanikun Road, which ran the outside length of Korat's southern moat. Passing the Chainarong Gate at the end of the road, he turned right onto Tagosura Road that led to the highway passing around the South side of Korat Royal Thai Air Base and Camp Friendship's South Gate to Dan Kwain. Driving through the large town of Dan Kwain, we proceeded South between the eight miles of rice paddies and small hamlets, to Highway 24 and turned left.

Though it was relatively early in the morning, Highway 24, which is the major East-West highway between Korat and Ubon on the Laos border and ran about 15 miles just North of the Cambodian border, was busy with traffic. After travelling 40 miles through the verdant countryside, full of rice paddies and small hamlets, we arrived about 8:00 in Nâng Rông, a large town of about 10,000 people in the Buriram Province. Stopping at the Phop Suk restaurant, near the Bus Station on Highway 24, Súusîi recommended the "kûh mûu," the town's famous pork-rump roast.

After the three of us finished a filling, delicious breakfast, we went another ten miles on Highway 24 to Bâan Ta Ko, where Potkim turned South onto Route 2117, a 2-lane country road. Four miles later, Route 2117 veered Southeast at Bâan Ta Pek, and four miles further, we arrived at the Phanom Rung historical site.

As we began to climb up, Súusîi explained that the Prasat Hin Phanom Rung was a Hindu temple built on the summit of an extinct volcano, 650 feet above the rice paddy fields surrounding it, between the 10th and 13th centuries when the Khmer empire extended West from Angkor, in Cambodia, into present-day Thailand. Also, that "Phanom Rung" is derived from the Khmer words for "big mountain."

Walking up the 520-foot processional walkway, I saw it was flanked by sandstone pillars with Angkor style lotus-bud tops. We continued up some steps and across the three bridges flanked by 16 five-headed mythical serpents guarding each of the three dirt terraces that represented passage from the earthly realm to the heavenly leading to the temple proper. The temple was built of sandstone with a tall, central tower containing beautifully carved lintels and pediments depicting Hindu gods. The lintel above the main entrance to the central tower showed a dancing Shiva, who is the most important of the Hindu gods, followed by Vishnu and Brahma.

Súusîi explained that the temple complex faced East, toward Angkor, and four times a year the sun shines through all fifteen of the sanctuary doorways. That the correct solar alignment happens during sunrise from April 3 to 5 and September 8 to 10, and at sunset from March 5 to 7 and October 5 to 7. And, the locals celebrate around the April alignment with ancient Brahmin ceremonies.

After spending some time wondering around the temple, we walked down to the Kuti Reusi Nong Bua Rai site[148], that sits right below Phanom Rung. Returning to the taxi, Potkim drove us several miles down Route 2117 to Muang Tam, "Town Lower," where the Hindu temple Prasat Muang Tam lies. There, I saw the five "prangs," or towers, of the temple standing on a low base, surround by four ponds. The deeply

---

148   Nong Bua Rai literally means "Younger Lotus Field."

carved sandstone lintel over the temple's entrance depicted the god Shiva and his wife, Uma, riding on the bull Nandin above a demonic face, surrounded by an elaborate garland.

We then rode another ten miles down the road to Prasat Thong, another ancient Hindu temple near Bâan Kruat, where I bought each of us a bottle of Pepsi and a bowl of fried rice with grasshoppers for lunch. I found that in the rural areas, insects were the main protein source added to fried rice.

Finishing our surprising, tasty lunch, we went several miles South of Bâan Kruat to the widely scattered Lan Hin Dtat[149] Bâan Kruat, where the sites for cutting the sandstone used to build these ancient structures came from.

Having seen these few of the many ancient sites around Phanam Rung, Potkim drove us North on Route 2075 the 15 miles to Prakhon Chai. There, he turned left onto Highway 24 for the 90-mile ride back to Korat. On our return trip to the Sri Pattana Hotel, Súusîi and I slept most of the 3-hour ride from Prakhon Chai. Arriving at the Hotel refreshed from our nap, we thanked Putkim for driving us. As I paid him a 20 Bhat tip, for which he was very grateful, I thought, "I'm sure this is the amount the taxi company paid him for driving their taxi all day."

Entering my Hotel room, I sensuously kissed Súusîi's mouth, neck and breasts, as I seductively removed her clothes and caressed the luscious curves of her body. After our passionate lovemaking crescended in the orgasmic release of our lust, we lingered for awhile in the afterglow of our climactic rush. Then, we happily showered and dressed before going to the Ming Ter for dinner.

Having brought some Hotel stationary and a pen with me, she helped me write an account of our day-trip as we ate dinner. I did this to give Cpt. Richards so he could plan a similar trip for his family. Finishing our dinner, we then went to the Action Theater to watch a Japanese Samurai movie that showed at 7:00. During the movie I enjoyed the feel of Súusîi's hands holding my left arm and squeezing it tight when there were scenes of bloodbaths and carnage.

Returning to my Hotel room after the movie, Súusîi enjoyed the feel of my loving desire for her with my sensual foreplay that aroused

---

149   Literally "Open Stone Cut."

her longings to an insatiable lust. This was fulfilled by the climactic rush from our unrestrained lovemaking in a Kama Sutra position she favored. Then, lying encircled by our arms and legs around each other, we enjoyed the pleasant feeling of our requited lust, and spoke of our love for the other and what a perfectly wonderful day we'd had together, as we fell asleep.

With the 3:30 wake-up call, we again enjoyed the passion of our lovemaking in a different Kama Sutra position to enhance the pleasure of our orgasmic release. After we had cleaned each other as we frolicked in the shower, we spoke happily of our planned reunion to go dancing Tuesday night, as I dressed in my jungle fatigues. Caressing the delectable curves of her desirable body, I kissed her lovingly goodbye, and said, "My darling, I'll miss you very much till I see you Tuesday night."

Exiting the Thai bus at my Company Area, I walked happily to my hooch feeling the pleasure of just having had spent thirty-six wonderful and uninterrupted hours with my very pretty and loving Súusîi. Entering my hooch, I grabbed and opened a cold can of Bud from the mini-fridge, as Skip asked, "Sandii, we missed you Sunday morning. How'd you get excused from morning formation?"

After taking a swig from my can of Bud, I replied, "I was on a secret recon mission for the CO yesterday," and pulling the notes I'd made of the day-trip from my jacket pocket, I added, "And here's my written report for him."

Finishing my Bud, as I changed into a fresh set of jungle fatigues and dumped the laundry from my shopping bag on top of the jungle fatigues I'd left lying on the floor, I then left with Skip for the Mess Hall. As we walked there and over breakfast, I told him about taking the CO and his wife on a shopping tour of Korat. And how at the end of the tour, he gave me permission to skip Sunday's morning formation, so I could take my "new" girlfriend, Súusîi, on a day-trip to see some ancient Khmer temple sites 90 miles East of Korat. As he'd expressed an interest in taking his family on a day-trip to the same sites, I'd written a report on the trip for him.

When we went to join morning formation, I gave Jim a quick description of why I was not at yesterday's formation and asked if he'd pick me up from in front of HQ after morning formation, as I'd written a report of my trip to give to the CO, at his request. After formation,

I quickly walked to HQ and handed the report on my day-trip to Cpt. Richards. Then, I went and stood by the flagpole in front of HQ to wait for Jim to pick me up with the truck on the way to the Air Base Site.

After a comfortably busy morning working on a few reported circuit outages, I left on my 10:55 meal run. Over lunch with Glen, I told him I'd hooked up with one of the girls from the ballroom dance group named Súusîi, and how we'd spent Sunday seeing the ancient Khmer temple sites East of Korat. Then, after lunch, I swung by the Howard Johnson to buy three 6-packs of Budweiser and a carton of Pall Malls, which I added to the stockpile in my wall locker.

While Skip was gone on his meal run, I chatted with Bob about my Sunday day-trip, and we compared my experiences to his, as he and Gúlapp had previously made a similar trip there. And, after a quiet afternoon, I left on my 4:55 meal run and chatted with Glen over dinner about the need for the prospective replacements scheduled to arrive today.

Leaving the Mess Hall with Glen after finishing our dinner, we stopped on the steps at the sight of three 2½-ton trucks parked in front of the Day Room. As we watched the newbies, clad in OD BDUs with shirts tucked in and their pant legs bloused at the top of their black combat boots, exiting from the back of the first two trucks and walking to the back of the third truck to heft a heavy OD duffel bag from its open rear, and then carry it into the Day Room, Glen exclaimed, "Hey, one of those newbies is a black guy!"

CHAPTER 46

You're Allergic To The One Thing That Might Save Your Life

Watching the lines of three dozen newbies walking to the rear of the last 2½-ton truck to get a duffle bag and carry it into the Day Room, I did see that one of them was Black and said, "Yea. I see him. You know, in my 90-man Microwave class, we had a German, an Iranian, a Japanese and a Hispanic, but not one Black guy. Though there were several in my five week Basic Electronics class, none of them passed it."

Glen responded, "Yea. Pretty much the same with my 90-man Frame Tech class, except we did have one Black guy in our class. I've seen lots of Blacks around the Camp and the Air Base, but there's not one in our Company, nor in the whole Battalion that I've heard of. I was told that most of the Blacks couldn't pass Basic Electronics, even after taking it three times, because they didn't take trigonometry in High School. Heck, in the Black High School at my hometown in Texas, I don't think it was even offered, and you have to know Trig to do the calculations for electronics. But, you only need an 8th Grade education to enlist in the Army."

As we walked to the Motor Pool for our rides, I said, "Where I went to Elementary School in Honolulu, Hawaii, all of the other kids were either Chinese, Japanese or Filipino, and on Ford Island, where I lived, there were no Black kids. Then, when we moved to Fremont, California, eighty percent of the kids in my school were Portuguese, and none were Black. And in Oregon, seventy-five percent of the counties had Sundown Laws on Blacks until 1955, when such laws were made illegal. Even then, it was still being enforced by the Jackson County Sheriff's Department, where I lived. And in Josephine County, just to the West, there was only one Black student in Grants Pass High School. But, at Klamath High School, ninety miles to our East, about a third of the students were Black, because Kingsley Field Air Force Base was located there. So, growing up, there weren't any Blacks in the schools I went to or the neighborhoods I lived in. Do you know what happens to the guys who don't graduate from Basic Electronics?"

Glen replied, "Mostly, they're sent to schools to be Clerks, Cooks or Truck Drivers. But, if they can't pass those courses, then they become an MP because there's no school required to be one."

Arriving at the Air Base Site, I told Bob and Skip, "I saw the newbies arrive, and one of them's a Black guy."

Bob responded, "Well, that'll make two in the Battalion, as there's one with Company B in Ubon. If he's lucky, they'll send him to Ubon, so they can be together," as he left to have dinner at the NCO Club.

While I'd been on my meal run, things had started to get busy as people Stateside were returning from their weekend off. By the time I was relived at 6:45, the pace of outages had picked up, but were not out of control as Jim and Roger had planned to remain.

Leaving the Operations Room when John and Larry relieved me, I caught a Thai bus to Korat. Exiting the bus at the Chainaong Gate, I walked directly to the Thai bar, and spent the evening drinking Sing Hăi Beer and smoking Pall Malls, which I shared with the others because American cigarettes were a lot better than the local brands.

After a fun evening talking and joking with my Thai friends, I left for the Sri Pattana Hotel, where I changed the time for my wake-up call to 5:00. Going to my room, I stripped and took a shower, before I went to bed. With the 5:00 wake-up call, I thought as I quickly put on a fresh set of skivvies and my jungle fatigues, "I sure miss the lovemaking with Lompét, and watching her luscious, petite body as she'd help me dress, and caressing her body as we kissed goodbye."

Exiting the Thai bus at the Company Area, I went to my hooch and drank a cold can of Bud as I changed into a fresh set of jungle fatigues. Leaving the hooch with Skip, we went to the Mess Hall for breakfast and saw lots of newbies there, most identified by the Signal Corps Orange, diamond-shaped patch on their left sleeves.

Leaving the Mess Hall after finishing our breakfast, I saw three ranks of those newbies forming in front of an SSG at the far end of the Company formation, as we walked over to join the Air Base Squad at the back of the Tropo Platoon. As Jim walked back to our Squad after talking with SFC Davidson, he said, "Listen up Air Base, I've just learned that of the thirty-six newbies who arrived, we'll get a Frame Tech, a Microwave Repairman and a Spec-5, who'll be our new Site Engineer."

Arriving at the Operations Room after formation, I said, "Hey, Jack, we've got good news for you. We'll be getting a new Microwave Repairman to replace you next month."

Jack laughed and responded, "Make no difference to me if you get a replacement for me or not. I'm out of here in twelve days and a wake-up."

Bob walked into the Operations Room and said, "I heard that, Jack, and as you're being transferred and not discharged, if we didn't get a replacement for you, then the Army could delay your transfer to meet the needs of the Army."

Jack laughed and responded, "I wouldn't mind the Army keeping me here. But, the Army would meet the wrath of my wife in doing so. And believe me, she really knows how to skin the hide off anyone with her tongue who crosses her. You all have a Merry Christmas."

After Jack left, we had a nice, quiet Christmas Eve for the rest of our day shift. As I ate lunch with Glen, he said, "An SSG that came in with the newbies will be sent to Ubon Tropo, which'll secure Spec-5 Zuligich's promotion to SSG and be Korat Tropo's next Site Engineer. But, with the number of Spec-5s shipping out, there'll be lots of promotions to fill those Team Leader vacancies, and the lifers are fishing around to see who they can snag for promotion to Spec-5. Most guys want to be passed over, so they won't be having to tell their friends what to do."

After lunch, I went to the Howard Johnson and bought three 6-packs of Budweiser and a carton of Pall Malls. Then going to my hooch, I placed a 6-pack of Bud and a pack of Pall Malls each on George and Tommy's beds, before adding the rest to my stockpile. On my 4:55 meal run, I did the same thing after eating dinner, except this time I put the beer and smokes on Ronnie and Stoney's beds.

Being relieved at 6:45 by John and Larry, I was gone like a rocket to catch a Thai bus for Korat to spend my Christmas Eve lovemaking and dancing with my lovely and luscious Súusîi. The next day was Christmas Day, which was like any other day in our Theater of War and in Thailand, and began with Súusîi's voracious appetite for loving me. After we had fun showering together, I dressed in my jungle fatigues and affectionately kissed her goodbye, as I lovingly stroked the silky skin of her curvaceous body, before saying, "I love you, my darling, and will miss you very much till tomorrow afternoon."

After a hearty breakfast with Skip, who I met up with in the Mess Hall, we joined the Air Base Squad in the Tropo Platoon and I saw the Platoon had three more ranks of ten men each behind our Squad, which more than doubled the size of our Platoon. As I looked back at the thirty newbies, I said to Skip, "It may look like a lot of guys, but out of those thirty guys, our Company will only get ten, which isn't close to what's needed to plug the holes in our manpower shortage."

Skip responded, "Yea. As we saw with Phizer, if something happens to any one of us, some of us'll have to do extra shifts for a while to take his place, like Jim and Roger had to do."

After formation, Skip and I head for our hooch with Ronnie and Stony, where each of us drank a cold can of beer, before going to bed. With the 11:00 bugle call for Mess, I got up and drank a cold can of Bud as I used the piss tube, dressed in my colorful civilian clothes, and then walked with Skip, Ronnie and Stony to the Mess Hall for lunch, which was a special affair for Christmas with roasted turkey and all the trimmings. After eating lunch, we returned to our hooch, and I gave Ronnie and Stony each a 6-pack of Bud and a pack of Pall Malls, before we spent the rest of the afternoon playing Double-Deck Pinochle, as we drank beer and smoked cigarettes.

When the 5:00 bugle call for Mess sounded, we finished the hand we were playing and settled the debts from the game, before we dressed in fresh OD BDUs and went to the Mess Hall for dinner. Returning from the Mess Hall I saw a guy busily unpacking his duffel bag into Dan's old wall locker. After we each grabbed a cold can of beer from the mini-fridge and opened them, I opened a second one for the newbie.

As we approached the newbie, I handed him the open can of Bud and said, "Welcome to hooch 525 and Merry Christmas. I'm Sandii, and this here is Skip, Ronnie and Stony."

The 5-foot-10, blond haired, slender built newbie responded with a big smile and said, "Thanks, Sandii, I sure can appreciate cold brew after today. I'm Charlie Sutton from Orange County, California, a 26-Lima assigned to Korat Tropo. I was told to go to work with you guys for the first half of the night shift. You sure have a sweet setup here with a mini-fridge and your own cubicles. And, the weather here is just like home."

Ronnie laughed and responded, "Enjoy it while you can, Charlie, because we're being moved to a concrete barracks next month. And, this California weather will end in April when the Monsoon Season starts with its hot, humid and rainy weather. Also, you can stop empty-ing your duffel bag and leave it in front of your wall locker tomorrow morning, as your house girl will launder all your clothes and put it all away tomorrow. What you need to do now is secure your stuff, get your shirt on, and finish your beer, then go with us to the front of the Day Room to catch a ride with me and Stony to the Tropo Site. Sandii and Skip both work at the Air Base Site."

As we finished our beers and Charlie secured his wall locker, I quickly set a 6-pack of Bud and a packed of Pall Malls each on George and Tommy's beds. When Charlie put his shirt on, I saw from the chevron with rocker stripes on the sleeves that he was a PFC. As we all walked to the front of the Day Room, Ronnie and Stony told him what it was like to work at Korat Tropo.

When Tommy arrived in the ¾-ton truck, he gave us a quick run-down on our two new PFCs and the new Spec-5. And, that John would be taking them to the Motor Pool for their driver's test after tomorrow morning's formation. Also, that it had been a busy morning, with all the Christmas Eve traffic from Stateside. But now, it was pretty quiet with it being Christmas Day.

Arriving at the Operations Room, I relieved Jack so he could go home to his tîi-lôk, and we settled in hopefully for a nice, quiet Christ-mas night. As 9:30, Ted called to let us know he had a line up to Rosie at the WATS center in St. Louis, but not to take too long, as he had a long list of people who wanted to call home for Christmas.

When we had the Lynch handset jacked into the circuit to the Philippines, Bob made the first call to his family and spent several minutes exchanging Christmas wishes with his family, before passing the handset to me.

Calling Linda first and wising her a Merry Christmas, she told me how surprised she was to find the gorgeous Princess Ring wrapped in the very beautiful pink silk dress. And, how she'd have the ring size cut down to fit her right ring finger, which she wore currently with some tape wrapped through it for a temporary fit. Also, that the silk dress felt wonderful against her skin when she tried it on. Though she'd have to take it in at a couple of places for it to fit properly. Then she asked, "Did you get the Christmas brownies I sent you?"

I replied, "Not yet, Honey, but they'll be very much appreciated when they do get here. We have to hang up now, as there's a lot of other people waiting to call home for Christmas. I love you and miss you, Linda, and am glad you liked the Christmas presents so much. Give everybody there my love," and waited for her to hang up so I could call my family in Oregon.

When Rosie put my call through to my family, I reassured my parents that I was doing well, and no harm had befallen me. They said they really like the elephant bookends, which they'd used to replace their old, plain metal ones in the living room. Then, Maggie and Nancy each told me how much they loved their exotic silk dresses, and would wear them to church on Sunday, after they'd been taken in a little bit to fit. And, Bobby told how he loved the great chess set and could hardly wait to take it to his next Chess Club meeting to show it off.

Finished talking with my family, I passed the handset to Skip for his Hanukkah calls to Judith and his family, who lauded him on the wonderful presents he'd sent them. As he signaled Bob to let Ted know we were finished with our phone calls, he gushed, "Judith said she's going to wear the Princess Ring on her left ring finger as a Promise Ring for me till I get back from Thailand."

During our nice, quiet night shift, Skip and I each managed to get a couple of hours sleep. When I delivered the truck to Jim in the Motor Pool on my 6:35 meal run, he said, "Sandii, I've just been told the Bob Hope Christmas Tour will put on their show at Camp Friendship on Saturday, the 28th. Also, everyone in the Tropo Platoon who's off day is Saturday, will be detailed to help set up and take down the Show's sound system. So, any plans you have for Saturday'll have to be cancelled."

I responded excitedly, "The Bob Hope Show'll be here Saturday, and I'll get to work backstage setting it up and taking it down? That's amazing."

Jim added, "And, there's a perk for those who work with the Show, the first three rows in front of the stage will be reserved for them to see the Show."

I exclaimed, "Front Row Seats! That's incredible, Jim. I'll be there for sure, come Hell or high water," as I walked away on cloud nine to the Mess Hall.

After breakfast, I went to the Mailroom to see if Linda's package had arrived. Seeing nothing in my mail slot, I continued to my hooch and drank a cold can of Bud, as I stripped to my skivvies and went to bed, sleeping till the 11:00 bugle call for Mess. After I'd drank a cold can of Bud while using the piss tube and dressing in my colorful civilian clothes, the five of us went to the Mess Hall for lunch. Over lunch, Charlies asked, "Where can I go to get some great clothes, like you guys here? I didn't see anything like them in the PX."

I replied, "In Korat. All the clothing there is custom made and costs very little. Tell you what, Charlie, I have to go into Korat to see my girlfriend this afternoon. If you want, I can take you there and introduce you to my tailor and shoemaker, and you can order some."

Charlie responded, "That'll be great, Sandii."

Finishing our lunch, Charlie followed me to the Howard Johnson, and we each bought three 6-packs of beer and a carton of cigarettes before going back to our hooch. After I gave Ronnie and Stony each a 6-pack of Bud and a pack of Pall Malls, I showed Charlie how the Thai currency system worked. Not having enough spare Bhat on hand to sell enough to him for shopping, we caught a Thai bus to the Bank on the Air Base.

Exiting the Thai bus at the Bank, I point out our Korat Air Base Radio Site and the Base Exchange, where they sold jungle fatigues. At the Bank, Charlie bought 800 Bhat for $40, assuring him it was more than enough to get him through till Pay Day, next week. Then, we boarded another Thai bus for Korat.

Getting off the bus at the Chainarong Gate, I led Charlie up Chainarong Road the short distance to the Sikh's tailor shop. There, he made a 120 Bhat deposit on three silk shirts and two pair of cotton pants, with an appointment for a fitting on the following Tuesday. Then, I led him up the road to Mahat Thai Road and the cobbler shop, where he paid 100 Bhat for the plaster mold of his feet and lower legs, and a 40 Bhat deposit for the pair of shoes he ordered to be ready on Tuesday.

Giving Charlie the simple direction for him to return to the Chainarong Gate bus stop to board a Thai bus back to Camp Friendship, he thanked me profusely. When we'd parted ways, I headed for the Sri Pattana Hotel. Entering my Hotel room about 2:00, I stripped to my boxers and went to sleep, as I waited for Súusîi.

Waking to Súusîi's knock on the door a couple of hours later, I quickly rose and opened the door. Aroused by the desire in her eyes and her exposed breasts from her unbuttoned blouse as she threw her arms around my neck, we passionately kissed while I carried her to the bed. Motivated by our lust, we hastily removed the few clothes we had on. As I thrust fully into her hot, wet love canal, she cried out with pleasure, "Châi dâai, my darling, I missed your desire for me so much."

When our vigorous lovemaking culminated in the orgasmic release of our lust, we lay enjoying the ephemera of our climactic rush, speaking fondly of our love for a while. Then I said, "My darling, I have to work all day Saturday on a special project and don't know when I'll be finished. Can we have dinner together and go dancing tomorrow, instead of Saturday, and maybe spend Sunday evening together too?"

She responded enthusiastically, "That would be excellent, my darling. Then, we'd be able to have two nights loving each other this weekend, instead of one."

After we'd happily showered, dressed and lovingly kissed goodbye, we cheerfully walked to the Hotel's entrance knowing we'd be together on Friday and Sunday. Riding a săawm-law to the Chainarong Gate, I thought, "This is perfect. Now that Lompét is with Steve, I am spending more time with my loving Súusîi like I wanted."

Returning to my hooch, I drank a cold can of Bud, as I rapidly changed into a fresh set of Od BDUs and set a 6-pack of Bud and pack of Pall Malls on each of George and Tommy's beds. Then leaving for the Mess Hall, I met up with Skip, and we discussed over dinner the prospect of being on the setup crew of the Bob Hope Show on Saturday, with front row seats to the Show to boot. On the way to the Day Room, I stopped by the Mailroom and saw my mail slot was still empty.

When Tommy arrived with the truck in front of the Day Room, I saw a short, plump PFC exit the passenger side of the truck. Tommy said, "This is Chuck Butler. He's Jack's replacement and came back with me because things are beginning to pop at the Site with post-Christmas traffic from Stateside, and Jim didn't want you to be bothered with bringing him back."

Arriving at the Operations Room, I saw Jim and Jack busy in the Grand Canyon. As Skip took over from Jack, I went to check the FRC-109, and noticed Bob and Roger were working on a rack in the break-out circuits. Seeing and recording that all was good with the micro-wave radio, I returned to the Grand Canyon and began taking notes in the Temporary Log.

By 9:00, things were still busy, but manageable, so Jim and Roger left for their homes in Korat. At midnight, Bob gave me a 5-Dollar bill and sent me to the NCO Annex to get each of us a burger with fries and a cold can of beer to eat as we worked. A couple of hours later, things became quiet, and Bob began transcribing from the Temporary Log to the Site Log, as Skip and I monitored the Order Wire chatter for any more circuit outages for our Radio Site.

Skip made his 4:55 meal run, and then I made my 6:35 meal run. As I passed the truck to Jim in the Motor Pool, he introduced me to Spec-5 Tim Larson, our new Site Engineer, who was a 5-foot 10, slender, brown haired guy I remembered being a microwave repair instructor at Ft. Monmouth. After breakfast in the Mess Hall, I went to my hooch, and drank a cold can of Bud as I stripped to my skivvies, turn on my fan, and went to bed.

Waking to the 11:00 bugle call for Mess, I went through my routine of drinking a cold can of Bud, as I used the piss tube and dressed in my colorful civilian clothes. Walking to the Mailroom, I found in my mail slot a card envelope from my family and a notice there was a package for me in the Mail Clerk's Office. Opening the envelope as I waited for Linda's package, I found a Christmas card with their individual messages for me to have a Merry and Safe Christmas.

Returning quickly to my hooch, I left the card and the unopened package on my bed, since I already knew what was in it, and walked rapidly to the Mess Hall with the others for lunch. After eating lunch with the guys from my hooch, we went back, and I shared the shoe-box full of broken, mint flavored Christmas brownies with my hooch mates. I also gave Ronnie and Stony each a 6-pack of Bud and pack of Pall Malls, and set the same on George and Tommy's beds. With those chores done, I left to catch a Thai bus to Korat.

Entering my Hotel room, I stripped to my boxers and slept till 5:00, when I heard Súusîi's knock on my room's door. We then spent a wonderful evening and night dining, dancing and sleeping happily together, interspersed with vigorous lovemaking in various Kama Sutra positions.

Over dinner, Súusîi proposed some day-trips we could take together to: Ayutthaya, the ancient capital of Thailand, 120 miles West of Korat; the Khâo Yái (Big Hill) National Park, Thailand's oldest and most visited animal reserve, 65 miles Southwest of Korat; and, the Elephant Study Center at Bâan Ta Kiang, 120 miles West of Korat, where we could ride an elephant.

In the morning, after we'd satisfied our sexual desires in passionate lovemaking and had playfully showered together, I dressed in my civilian clothes and lovingly kissed her goodbye, with the feel of her sensuous body in my hands. As I left for Camp Friendship with my shopping bag of laundry, I thought, "My life here is great, with a pretty Thai woman who loves me emphatically, knows where we can take day-trips to show me Thailand, and is flat-out fun to be with. And now, I get to help set up and then watch the Bob Hope Show on the front row."

Exiting the Thai bus at the Company Area, I rapidly walked to my hooch, where I drank a cold can of Bud, as I emptied my shopping bag onto the floor and quickly changed into a fresh set of jungle fatigues. Then, setting a 6-pack of Bud and pack of Pall Malls each on Ronnie, Stony, George and Tommy's beds, I left for the Mess Hall.

As I joined the others sitting at a table and eating their breakfast, Ronnie laughed and said, "You want to hear something funny, Sandii? Spike tried to sign out a 45 pistol from our Armory claiming he needed it for self-defense against assassins. The Armorer told him that no one could sign out a weapon without a written order from the CO. And

Schultz said he overheard the CO tell Spike that, unless he could document such a threat existed, he would not sign an order for him to sign out a pistol, and added that the only people allowed to carry a pistol on Camp Friendship are the MPs and the Paymasters on Pay Day."

I laughed and responded, "Sounds like some lifer must have tipped him off about the 500-Bhat bounty."

After morning formation, the dozen of us in the Tropo Platoon on our off day, including Jim, boarded a 2½-ton truck for a ride to the Bob Hope Show's location, which was a 100-yard square area near the Camp's East perimeter fence, across the road from the 33rd Field Hospital. Exiting the truck, I saw we were joined by a platoon from the Construction Battalion, tasked with building the Show's stage, setting up the tents for changing rooms, and raising scaffolding at several key spots for the big movie cameras to record the Show and the audience's reaction to the Show.

There was also a platoon from the Engineer Battalion setting up large portable generators, and running thick power cables to the Stage, camera scaffolds and changing rooms. Meanwhile, those of us from the Tropo Platoon were helping the Show's sound crew set up the sound system and cables that ran from the large distribution/mixer panel at the right end of the Stage.

In the process of running a phone line into Bob Hope's tent, I saw a 16-by-24-inch picture frame with a character sketch of Bing Crosby, dressed in golfing attire and leaning on a golf club with his legs crossed, attached to the center pole of the tent. I asked the Show crewmember I was with, "Isn't that a drawing of Bing Crosby?"

He replied, "Yea. Bob takes it with him on every tour for luck."

By the time we left on the truck for lunch, the large field in front of the Stage was already filling with Soldiers and Airmen, except for a 12-foot wide area directly in front of the Stage reserved for those who worked setting up for the Show. When we returned an hour later, we helped the Show Crew run continuity and sound level tests on the myriad of microphones, cables, amplifiers, speakers and recording devices for the Show.

When all the sound systems had been checked and rechecked, we were thanked and dismissed to go sit in the reserved area in front of the Stage. Of course, the Construction and Engineer Battalion guys had already sat on the ground in front of the Stage, leaving only the back of the reserved area open to the Signal Corps personnel. But, this was a boon for us, as the Stage was elevated four feet above the ground, and its front edge actually blocked the view to most of the stage. So, sitting twelve feet from the Stage gave me a full, panoramic view of the entire Stage.

Very happy with having a perfect view for the Bob Hope Show, my heart dropped when I heard over the sound system, "Will Specialist Sherman Lynch of the 442d Signal Battalion, report immediately to the 33rd Field Hospital Emergency Room," fifteen minutes before the Show started.

As I stood up to leave, Skip said, "Don't worry Sandii, I'll save your space."

Jim stood up as I moved to my left passed him and asked, "What's going on, Sandii?" and I replied, "I've no idea, Jim."

Cpt. Richards, standing next to the sound system controls at stage right, asked, "What's going on, Sandii?" and when I replied, "I've no idea, Sir," he ordered, "You're to report here, to me as soon as you return."

Walking rapidly passed the Stage, Bob Hope's tent and through the Show's perimeter gate, I turned right and ran the fifty yards to the Hospital, where patients in wheelchairs were lined up along the sidewalk across the road from the Show with the Medics, Nurses and Doctors. Passing through their lines, I entered the Emergency Room, and said breathlessly in a loud voice, "I'm Specialist Lynch of the 442d, what do you want?"

A Doctor replied, "Follow me and strip to your waist. The flying squirrel that bit you has been reported missing by the Veterinarian. So, we have to start the 14 shot series for Rabies vaccination on you right away. And, I don't want to miss any of the Bob Hope Show. Now, lay on the exam table and we can get this over quickly."

Lying on the exam table, I saw the Doctor pick up a vial full of clear liquid and a syringe with a needle, and asked, "Excuse me, Sir, but what kind of serum is that?

He replied, "It's the Rabies Vaccine."

I said, "I realize that, Sir. But, what is the culture medium for the vaccine, as I'm allergic to vaccines made with chicken egg serums?"

He looked at the vial and answered, "It says 'Duck Egg Serum.' Well, maybe you're not allergic to duck egg serums. But, to be safe,

I'll do a wheal test. Normally, we inject a 100 to 1 dilution under the ski, and if you're allergic, then a red area of inflammation about the size of a Quarter appears. Since you may already be allergic, I'll make a 1,000 to 1 dilution."

Watching as he slid the needle's point beneath the skin of the underside of my left forearm, I saw a small bump appear under the skin, as he injected a small amount. Within a minute a red area the size of a Half-Dollar appeared around the small bump, and the Doctor stated, "Well, that cuts it for sure. Lynch, you're allergic to the one thing that might save your life."

CHAPTER 47

WHAT IN THE DEVIL HAPPENED LAST NIGHT?

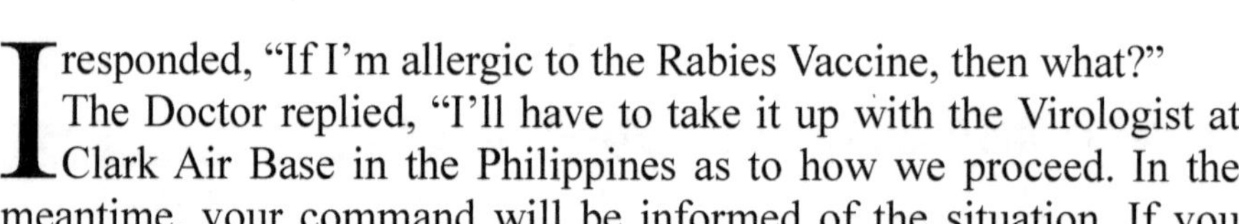

I responded, "If I'm allergic to the Rabies Vaccine, then what?" The Doctor replied, "I'll have to take it up with the Virologist at Clark Air Base in the Philippines as to how we proceed. In the meantime, your command will be informed of the situation. If you develop any fever, or cramping of your muscles, you are to report to the Emergency Room immediately. Now, let's go and enjoy the Bob Hope Show."

Leaving the Hospital, I ran back the way I came, and seeing my CO, I saluted and said, "Reporting as ordered, Sir. They flying squirrel that bit me got away, and it turns out I'm allergic to the Rabies Vaccine. The Virologist in the Philippines will be consulted on how to proceed, and you'll be notified."

Returning my salute, he replied, "Very well, Sandii. I suggest you return to your seat and enjoy the Show."

Going back to my reserved spot on the ground, I told Jim and Skip what I'd told the CO just as the Show began.

The Bob Hope Show was great, as I watched from my close-up seat on the ground his several comedy routines, a magic act, a guy doing great aerial feats on a trampoline, eight members of the Rockets from Radio City Music Hall in New York City showing off their long, shapely legs with high-kicking dance routines, and the appearance of Ann Margaret, the redheaded actress who was the heartthrob of all the military men at that time. At the end of the Show, Bob Hope led everyone in his hallmark song, "Thanks for The Memories."

When the Show was over, we in the Tropo Platoon, quickly helped the Sound Crew disconnect and roll up all the audio cables and place them in airtight containers for transport to the next Show on their tour. Once everything was properly stowed, we climbed into the 2½-ton truck, still feeling jubilant at having seen the Bob Hope Show, and especially Ann Margaret, so close up.

Returning to our hooch, Skip, Charlie, Glen, Ronnie, Stony and I each celebrated with a cold can of beer as we stood in a circle, laughing and recounting our memories of the Show till we heard the 5:00 bugle call for Mess. Then, quickly changing into civilian clothes, we all left en masse for the Mess Hall, except for Glen, who went home to Súpa and said he'd meet us later at the compound.

Leaving the Mess Hall after dinner, we all caught a Thai bus for Korat, and went to the compound, inducting Charlie into Jim Horn's strange House Rules. There, we escaped from the rigors of work, military life and Vietnam's Theater of war. Tom was already there with his tîi-lôk, Renu, and Glen soon showed up with Súpa. When Glen left with Súpa at 7:45, he told me that they were meeting up with Steve and Lompét at the night club, and I thought, "It's a good thing Súusîi and I went dancing last night, as it would've been a little awkward there tonight. I need to keep tabs with Glen as to when they go to the night club to prevent any future awkward encounters."

At 9:00, after a fun evening of camaraderie and drinking Sing Hăi Beer, during which the talk focused on the Bob Hope Show, the party broke up, and I returned with others to the Company Area. Entering our hooch, we each had a cold can of beer, as we readied for bed, more than ready to get some sleep after our busy and exciting day.

Waking to the 5:00 bugle call for Mess, I went through my routine of drinking a cold can of Bud, as I used the piss tube, dressed in my jungle fatigues, and set a 6-pack of Bud and pack of Pall Malls each on George and Tommy's beds, before walking to the Mess Hall with Skip. After casually eating a scrumptious breakfast and leisurely smoking a cigarette, we left for morning formation. As our Air Base Squad waited for the formation to begin, John introduced Skip and me to PFC Mark Daniels, John's 6-foot tall, slender, black haired replacement.

After the formation's rigamarole, Skip and I rode in the back of the ¾-ton truck to the Air Base Site, while Jim and Tim rode in the truck's cab. Entering the Operations Room, we relieved Jack and Chuck from the night shift. Then, Skip drove Chuck back to the Company Area, while I manned the Operations Room alone till the Shift Change Report ended and Bob came to the Operations Room.

Being a Sunday, life in the Operations Room was pretty slow. After reading the Site Log about the outages during the two days I was off, Skip and I fruitlessly spent part of the day trying to figure out how to tie a second knot in a patch cord single-handed to relieve the boredom. During my 10:55 meal run, I'd brought a set of clean skivvies back with me and took a hot shower, which was quite a change from the tepid showers in my Hotel room.

When I was relieved at 6:45 by John, Larry and Mark, I was gone like a flash of lightening to catch a Thai bus to Korat. Arriving at my Hotel room, I was beginning to strip to my boxers, when I heard Súusîi's knock on my room's door. Opening the door, I was instantly engulfed by her passionate hugs and kisses, as I picked her up with my arms around her and carried her to the bed. When we'd ravaged each other in wanton lovemaking to satiate the two days of pent-up lust with our orgasmic release, we lay together in the euphoria of our climactic rush expressing the love and missed desire we had for each other while we were apart.

After our playful shower together, we lay side by side and excitedly discussed the preliminary plans for our next day-trip in four weeks, which would be my next Sunday off day on January 26th. We decided to go to the Khôa Yái National Park first, as there would be plenty to do and see there on a Sunday. Then two weeks later, we'd go on a day-trip to Ayutthaya on Saturday, February 8th, when everything will be open for business.

At 8:30 we left to walk to the Action Theater for the 9:00 showing of a Japanese Samurai movie. Returning to my Hotel room after watching the movie, we enjoyed our affectionate foreplay that aroused our lust filled need for the vigorous lovemaking. In a sexually enhancing Kama Sutra position, we culminated our copulation in the orgasmic rush we desired. Wrapped in its euphoric afterglow, we fell happily asleep.

Roused from our slumber with 3:30 wake-up call, we reengaged our lust filled lovemaking in another Kama Sutra arrangement. Elevating our enjoyment of the love we had for each other, we relished the crescendo of our climactic rush. After we had fun showering together, I dressed in my jungle fatigues and affectionately kissed her goodbye, while caressing her silky smooth skin and thinking, "Great sex, lots of fun, and now two day-trips planned. Súusîi, you're the perfect girlfriend for me."

Returning to the Company Area, I walked to my hooch and drank a cold can of Bud, as I dumped the laundry from my shopping bag onto the floor, hastily changed into a fresh set of jungle fatigues, and quickly set a 6-pack of Bud and pack of Pall Malls each on George and Tommy's beds. Then going to the Mess Hall, I met up with Skip and told him about the two day-trips I had planned with Súusîi while we ate breakfast. As we walked to morning formation, Skip said, "This Súusîi sounds like the perfect girlfriend for you, Sandii. She's educated, smart, lots of fun to be with, and she knows some great places for you to travel together with. And, you don't have to pay the expenses of having a tîi-lók. I'd say you have it made in the shade."

After formation, we rode in the back of the truck to the Air Base Site. When Skip and I relieved Larry and Mark from the night shift, it was my turn to drive them back to the Company Area. Enroute, Mark asked, "Sandii, why were you in such a hurry to leave when you were relieved last night?"

I replied, "Because, like a lot of guys here, I have a place in Korat. And though I don't have a tîi-lók, I do have a pretty girlfriend who loves me, and likes to do fun things with me, like ballroom dancing, going to the movies and taking day-trips to interesting places. We've already been to the Festival in Phimai and the ancient Khmer temple sites at Phanom Rung. And now, we've two day-trips planned for Khôa Yái National Park, sixty-five miles Southwest of Korat, and to Ayutthaya, the ancient capital of Thailand, 120 miles West of Korat."

Mark responded, "So, where'd you meet this great girlfriend of yours? In a bar, like most guys?"

I laughed and replied, "First of all, most of the guys with a tîi-lók, met them were they worked as a waitress, or some other menial job, not in a bar, which is a bad idea. Second, my girlfriend is a College Student I met ballroom dancing at a night club. If you check around the Company, I'm sure someone's tîi-lók would be happy to introduce you to one of their friends, who'd be glad to date an American," and arriving at the Day Room, I said, "Here you go. Have a nice sleep."

Returning to the Air Base Site, I spent the morning working with Skip and Bob on several outages we had called in. On my 10:55 meal run, I met up with Glen and told him over lunch about the two day-trips I had planned with Súusîi and asked when he and Súpa were going dancing again. He replied, "Tonight, and again Thursday, as that's our next off day, and you know how I love the effect that dancing has on Súpa. How about you? Are you two going dancing tonight?"

I answered, "We went dancing last Friday, and last night we went to the movies. As much as she'd like to spend every night with me, we have to keep it low-key, so her father won't think our relationship is serious and keep her away from me."

On my 4:55 meal run, after I ate dinner with Glen, I quickly went to my hooch and set a 6-pack of Bud and pack of Pall Malls on each of Ronnie and Stony's beds before driving back to the Air Base Site. When John, Larry and Mark relieved me at 6:45, I caught a Thai bus to Korat.

Exiting the bus at the Chainarong Gate, I walked the mile up Chainarong Road to Assadang Road and my Thai bar. Buying a bottle of Sing Hăi Beer from the bartender, I joined my friends sitting at our usual table. I'd found, like myself, most of them didn't come every night, but often enough to maintain continuity with those who regularly sat at the table. During our course of the evening, I regaled them about my "girlfriend." As the Thai word for "girlfriend" also means "fiancé" or "wife," it gives more significance that its English counterpart used for casual relationship between a man and woman. Informing them of the love we shared, the fun we had going dining, dancing and to the movies, the two trips we'd taken together, and the two trips we had plans to take. They all thought it was really good I had a Thai "girlfriend" to love and do fun things with, instead of going to the American bars and dealing with prostitutes, who could give me an STD.

After a few hours, I said, "Sáwátdii," to my Thai comrades, left the bar feeling happy about the friends I'd made there, and walked to my Hotel, as it was too late to get a Thai bus to Camp Friendship.

Changing my wake-up call to 5:00, I continued to my room, stripped to my skivvies, and fell asleep on the bed. With my 5:00 wake-up call, I showered and shaved before I put on a fresh set of skivvies and my jungle fatigues.

Returning to my Company Area, I went to the Mess Hall for a leisurely breakfast and cigarette before going to morning formation. After formation, I walked with Skip back to our hooch for a morning's sleep, thinking, "Tonight's New Year's Eve, and though I'll be at work, I'd have already set off my fireworks with Súusîi this afternoon. Yea, 1969 will start off pretty good for me, with a girlfriend Stateside who may love me, a girlfriend here who does love me and I enjoy doing things with, a job I really enjoy, a great bunch of hooch mates, and a group of Thai friends I enjoy spending time with while I improve my Thai language skills."

Waking to the 11:00 bugle call for Mess, I did my usual routine before dressing in my colorful civilian clothes and going with my hooch mates to the Mess Hall for lunch. En route back to my hooch after lunch, I stopped at the Howard Johnson to buy three 6-packs of Budweiser and a carton of Pall Malls, before going by the Mailroom to check my mail slot, which was empty.

Entering my hooch, I gave a 6-pack of Bud and pack of Pall Malls each to Ronnie and Stony, before adding the remainder to the stockpile in my wall locker. I then left with Charlie for Korat, to make sure he made it to the correct tailor shop for his fitting, and cobbler shop to get his new shoes, on the way to my Hotel for my afternoon tryst with Súusîi.

As Charlie and I rode a Thai bus to Korat, he said, "I've noticed several of the guys I work with have tîi-lóks, like Tom and Glen, but I'm so busy getting up to speed learning my job, that I never have a real chance to talk with them about how to find a tîi-lók for myself."

I responded, "The simplest way is for one of them to ask his tîi-lók to fix you up with one of her girlfriends and go on a couple of dates to see if things click. Glen's tîi-lók has set me up with a few of her pretty girlfriends. I usually eat my midnight meal with Glen. If you want, I can talk to him about it, then they could double-date with you to meet her at a cafe for a meal together before you go on an actual date to a movie or dancing."

Charlie responded, "That'll be great, Sandii. I want to be in a steady relationship with a girl, rather than going to bars and blowing my money on drinking and whores, and probably get the clap."

Exiting the bus in Korat, I helped Charlie with his shopping before I went to the Sri Pattana Hotel. Entering my Hotel room, I stripped to my boxers and slept for a couple of hours before I woke to Súusîi's knock on my room's door. Opening the door, I braced myself as she lept into my arms with her blouse unbuttoned, and her arms and legs wrapped possessively around my neck and waist, as she feverishly kissed me all over my face. She cried out, "I love you so much, my darling. Hurry and make love to me with all your desire for me," while I carried her to the bed.

When our wanton lust had been satiated in unrestrained lovemaking that reached its zenith in the explosion of my orgasmic thrust distending fully into her love canal, she cried out, "Yes, my darling. Fill me with your sexual desire."

As we entwined our arms and legs around each other in the afterglow of our climactic rush, Súusîi began to sob against my chest, "My darling, I love you so much, but I've terrible news. My father told me yesterday, he has been promoted to an office in Bangkok, and we're moving there tomorrow. I've no idea when we can be together again. If you give me your address, I can write to you, and we can make plans to meet here or in Bangkok. At least now, I have your sexual desire in me to carry always in my body."

I was stunned by this news and thought, "Again, I'm in love with a woman and we're torn apart by the father. That's it. I'm done with dating girls under the thumb of their father. I have to find an emancipated woman I can love, have fun with and travel places together," and said, "Of course, my darling, I'll give you my address and find a way to be together. But, as you know, I'm limited to how far I can travel to a day-trip, and it takes half a day by train at best to go from Korat to Bangkok, and there's no civilian airport her to quickly fly to Bangkok. However, our love is strong enough to find a way to be together."

She responded, "Yes, my darling. Our love for each other is very strong. I'd marry you in a heartbeat, but my father would never allow it, even if I was going to have your baby."

We cried together for a while, and when we showered, she enticed me to make love with her again. Then, we dressed and lovingly kissed goodbye, hoping it wasn't the last time, but knowing it probably was, barring some miracle.

Returning to the Company Area, I walked morosely to my hooch and drank a cold can of Bud as I dumped the laundry in my shopping bag on the floor, changed into a fresh set of OD BDUs, and set a 6-pack of Bud and pack of Pall Malls each on George and Tommy's bed. Leaving for the Mess Hall, I met up with Skip and told him over dinner my tale of woe, to which he said, "Well, at least you still have a girlfriend Stateside and haven't received a Dear John letter, like a lot of the guys here."

I responded, "You're right, Skip, and there's plenty of fish here in the Sea of Thailand. But, it's just that things were going so perfectly with Súusîi. Anyhow, I've made up my mind not to become entangled again with any woman here whose father has a legal claim on her, and look for one who's no longer financially obligated to her father."

Finishing our dinner, we walked across the roadway to the Day Room, and waited for the truck. When Tommy arrived with the truck, we exchanged sáwátdiis and drove to the Air Base Site. Entering the Operations Room, we relieved Jack and Chuck, and I drove Chuck back to the Company Area.

Returning to the Operations Room, we dealt with a couple of reported outages before I left on my 10:55 meal run. Meeting up with Glen, I told him what happened with Súusîi as we ate, and Glen said, "Partner, that's a tough break. You want me to talk with Súpa to meet one of her girlfriends?"

I replied, "I appreciate the offer, but I've had it with women who are indebted to their fathers. I want to find someone who's emancipated and not subject to the whims of their father. If Súpa knows a woman like that, then I'd be interested. But, Charlie's looking for a tîi-lók. Maybe you two could arrange for him to meet some of Súpa's girlfriends."

He responded, "I'll see what Súpa can arrange for you and Charlie. But, most all the girls she knows are young and still belong to their fathers, so I doubt there's much she can do for you."

When I returned to the Operations Room, Skip left on his 11:40 meal run, and I told Bob about Súusîi having to move with her father to Bangkok, and my decision to find a woman who was not under the control of her father. Bob responded, "I see your dilemma, and you've had a bad run of luck with losing your girlfriends due to their fathers.

The only women I can think of who meet your criteria are those who are divorced or widowed. I don't know about the divorce rate in Thailand, but with the reckless way men drive in Thailand, there are a number of fatal car accidents that result in quite a few widows left behind.

"I imagine the best thing to do is find a matchmaker. A 'mâay-súu,' which means 'purchase mother,' or a 'tâo-gáa,' an old person who knows everyone that's available for marriage, that you can pay to find a suitable 'faan,' a girlfriend or fiancé, for you. Also, you can check with our friends at your Thai bar, as they'd certainly know of a local matchmaker, or even a divorcé or widow they can introduce you to."

I responded, "Hey, that's a good idea, Bob. I'm sure some of my friends at the Thai bar will know a divorced or widowed woman they can introduce me to. I'll do that when I go there Thursday night. Maybe this New Year won't be so bad after all."

At the end of my night shift, I drove the truck to the Motor Pool and said, "Happy New Year" to Jim, as I passed it to him. While eating breakfast, Charlie sat down to eat his breakfast with me, and said, "Happy New Year, Sandii, and thanks for talking with Glen to help me find a tîi-lók. He said it shouldn't be a problem and might be able to introduce me to some girls I can choose from over lunch and dinner at a cafe on our two off days this Thursday and Friday. The sooner I can get a tîi-lók to love the better, as I'm as horny as the Devil."

Leaving the Mess Hall, Charlie and I walked to our hooch, where I drank a cold can of Bud, while I passed a 6-pack of Bud and pack of Pall Malls each to Ronnie and Stony as we exchanged "Happy New Year" greetings. Then, stripping to my skivvies, I turned on my fan, lay on my bed, and went to sleep with the hope my Thai friends could fix me up with a suitable emancipated woman.

About 9:00, I was rousted from my bed by PFC Schultz telling me, "Sandii, you've been ordered to report immediately to the Hospital's E.R. The CO's ordered a jeep to drive you there from HQ. So, you need to put on a uniform and get there ASAP."

Quickly dressing in a fresh set of jungle fatigues, I thought, "What do they want this time?"

Arriving at the Hospital's E.R. in a jeep, a white tunicked Medic met me and said, "Specialist Lynch, you and your driver are to follow me," as he led us to a treatment area in the E.R.

The Doctor who treated me when I was called away from the Bob Hope Show, said, "I just got back from a Medical Conference in the Philippines on your case, and it was decided it is best to begin the Rabies Vaccine Series in the E.R., where we can quickly treat any life threatening reaction you might have. Or, you can wait till you develop symptoms and hope for the best. Your choice."

I replied, "Well, let's get started and see what happens," as I stripped to my waist.

Lying on the exam table, the Doctor put a 10-inch diameter, white paper circle on my abdomen with the numbers "1" through "14" in an irregular order around its edge. Then the Doctor drew an "O" with a pen next to the number "1" on the circle at the upper left quadrant of my abdomen, and gave me an injection in the center of the "O".

I felt a pinch as the small ¾ inch needle broke the skin and into my abdominal muscle, and half a cc of the vaccine was injected. A Medic watched me closely and took my vital signs every ten minutes as I lay on the exam table for two hours. But, nothing else happened. I felt a little woozy as I sat up when the Medic said, "Okay, you can get up now. And driver, you're to bring him back at 0700 tomorrow morning for his second injection."

Returning to the Company Area, I went to the Mess Hall and joined by hooch mates for lunch, telling them as we ate about what happened at the Hospital. Then we all went to our hooch, except for Charlie, who wore his new shoes to Korat to pick up his new clothes.

Entering our hooch, we each grabbed a cold can of beer from the mini-fridge. As I drank mine, I stripped to my skivvies and went to bed, where I slept till the 5:00 bugle call for Mess. After dressing in a fresh set of OD BDUs, I set a 6-pack of Bud and pack of Pall Malls each on George and Tommy's beds, before I walked with the others to the Mess Hall for dinner.

Having eaten our dinner and casually smoked a cigarette, we walked to the Day Room and waited for our rides to work. When Tommy arrived with the truck, he told Skip and me there'd been an increase in reported circuit outages with people Stateside leaving on New Year's Eve, but it had quieted now. At the Operations Room, Skip and I relieved Jack and Chuck, and Skip drove Chuck back to the Company Area.

Bob received a call from Ted at 9:00 to inform us he had a connection through to Rosie at the WATS Exchange in St. Louis. With the Lynch handset jacked into the audio circuit to Rosie, Bob passed on calling his family, so Skip went first with a call to his Judith and wished her a "Happy New Year," and told her how much he loved and missed her. Then, I called Linda and wished her a "Happy New Year," and let her know I'd received the box full of mint-flavored brownies. Also, that I'd helped set up the Bob Hope Show, and was able to sit in the third row from the Stage as payment for my work. So, she should be able to spot me easily in the audience when the 1968 Bob Hope Christmas Tour was later televised in the States.

Linda said, "Sweetheart, I can't possibly accept the Princess Ring from you because it's so expensive. When I took it to the jeweler to be resized, he appraised it at $200, which is way more than you should've spent on me for a Christmas present."

I laughed and said, "Honey, the asking price by the jeweler here was only $100, and believe me, I bargained the price down to much less than that. Thailand is one of the leading gem producers in the world, so jewelry costs a lot less here. So, please, Dear, just keep it for me."

After Linda had acquiesced to my arguments and agreed to keep the ring, we expressed our mutual love and absence from the other, and she hung up. Then, Bob called Ted to let him know we were finished with our phone calls, and I removed the jack plugs from the audio circuit.

Leaving on my 10:55 meal run, I hooked up with Glen in the Mess Hall and he said, "Súpa doesn't know any girls like you want, as all the girls she knows are all young and work at menial jobs. However, Charlie's happy to hear Súpa's made arrangements with four of her girlfriends to meet him for lunch and dinner at a cafe on our off days. Then, whichever he chooses, they'll double-date with us on Monday afternoon to see a Japanese Samurai movie."

When Skip returned from his meal run, I told him I'd have enough money now to buy a tape deck, as I won't have to shell out $37 for the monthly rental of my room at the Sri Pattana Hotel, since I no longer have a girlfriend to share it with. We then planned on going to the Base Exchange tomorrow afternoon, the day after Pay Day, to miss the crowds of guys that would be there on Pay Day spending money on things they'd been unable to buy when they were broke.

Delivering the truck to Jim on my 6:35 meal run, I went to the Mess Hall for breakfast before being driven to the Hospital's E.R. for my 2nd injection of Rabies Vaccine. The number "2" was in the lower right area of my abdomen on the opposite side of the number "1" on the circle. Soon after the injection, the Doctor said, "That's interesting. The site of yesterday's injection has turned red with inflammation."

After sleeping for two hours on the exam table while the Medic checked my vital signs every ten minutes, he woke me and said I was to return at 7:00 the next morning for my third injection. Being driven back to the Company Area, I went to my hooch and changed into my Class-B Army Khaki uniform to get paid in. As I changed, Charlie came into the hooch all jazzed up as he thanked me for helping with the plans to have him meet four pretty Thai women to choose from to be his tîi-lók. I also collected $10 each from Ronnie, Stony, George and Tommy for the beer and butts I'd supplied them with while they'd been broke.

I then left for the Pay Line in front of the Day Room. After I'd been paid my $220, and spent $7.50 on a $10 U.S. Savings Bond, $8 for Maan-daa's services and $50 for 1,000 Bhat. Going back to my hooch, I changed into my civilian clothes, and put all but $50 and 400 Bhat in the tobacco tin can I kept in my wall locker, before leaving to catch a Thai bus to the Bank on the Air Base.

Having deposited the $50 in my Savings Account, I boarded another Thai bus to Korat. Exiting the bus at the Chainarong Gate, I walked to the Ming Ter for a delicious lunch of "gaangórm," a typical Isaan curry meal that's heavy on herbs and only mildly spicy, before going to my Hotel room and to bed for some much needed sleep.

Waking about 4:30, I dress again in my civilian clothes and walked to my frequented Thai bar, ordering a large bowl of rice noodle chicken soup and a bottle of Sing Hăi Beer from the bartender. Sitting at my usual table, I ate a spoonful of my soup and took a large swig of the potent beer before it was passed around the table. While my friends commiserated with me as I morosely told them my tale of woe in the loss of my beloved girlfriend, I'd take another large swig of the potent beer each time the bottle came to me.

As I was often buying the next bottle of Sing Hăi Beer to be passed around the table, they made no complaints as to my inordinate large swigs of beer each time it was passed to me. After a while, I vaguely remember them escorting me out of the bar through the haze of my drunken stupor, and to a place full of beautiful Thai women.

Waking with a killer hangover the next morning, I found myself lying on my left side, on a lumpy bed, in a very cheap looking Hotel room. Rolling over to my right side, I looked into the very uncomely face of a Thai woman in her 30's with a large scar across her left cheek, who happily said, "Sáwátdii, tîi-lók."

As I quickly jumped up from the bed and rapidly pulled on my clothes, I thought, "What in the Devil happened last night?"

CHAPTER 48

They're Having Me Promoted To Spec-5

Leaving the homely, older woman wrapped in the bedcovers with a very disappointed look on her scarred face, I exited the cheaply decorated room into a stark and stained hallway. Locating the stairwell, I walked down to the main floor, crossed its Lobby, and exited its front doors. Recognizing the building I'd just left was the Assadang Hotel, I looked at my wristwatch, and seeing it was almost 6:00, thought, "If I move fast, I can make it back in time to change into my jungle fatigues and get some coffee in the Mess Hall before morning formation."

Flagging down a sawm-law, I paid the drive the exorbitant price of 10 Bhat to rush me to the Chainarong Gate, where I boarded the next Thai bus to Camp Friendship. Nursing my splitting headache as I rode on the crowded and cramped bus, I thought, "I'd kill for a gallon of coffee right now."

Exiting the bus at the Company Area, I ran to my hooch, stripped off my civilian clothes, threw on a fresh set of jungle fatigues, quickly pulled on my combat boots, and without lacing them up, I buttoned up my fatigue jacket as I rushed to the Mess Hall. Entering the Mess Hall,

I walked rapidly to the large, stainless steel coffee urn, and filled a mug with hot coffee, which I quickly drank.

Refilling the mug with hot coffee, I sat at the nearest table to lace up and tie my boots as I drank the hot coffee. With my boots tied, I refilled and drank two more mugs of hot coffee before going to morning formation, where Skip said, "Sandii, you look like something the cat drug in. What happened to you?"

I replied, "And I feel like something the cat drug through a dung pile before throwing me on a garbage heap. Long story short, I got plastered on Sing Hăi Beer last night with my Thai friends over my loss of Súusîi, who kindly put me into bed with the ugliest Thai woman I've ever seen."

After formation, I was driven to the Hospital's E.R. and received my 3rd Rabies Vaccine shot in the lower left part of my abdomen, as indicated by the numbered circle. A few minutes later, the Doctor and I observed the location of the previous day's injection became red with inflammation, and the Doctor said, "Well, it looks like your strange allergic reaction yesterday was no fluke."

Having slept on the exam table for two hours, the driver took me back to the Company Area, where I caught a Thai bus to Korat because it had occurred to me that Suumii, the Receptionist at the Jomsurong Hotel, had told me that Dhoi was a widow. Exiting the bus at the Chainarong Gate, I hired a săawm-law to carry me to the Sri Pattana Hotel, where I went to my room, stripped of my clothes, and took a liberating, tepid shower.

Feeling almost human again, I shaved, and dressed in fresh skivvies and civilian clothes. Being ravenous as I left my room, I went to the Ming Ter for a large plate of fried rice with chicken and a Pepsi. With my hunger now assuaged, I walked the short distance to the Jomsurong Hotel.

Entering the Hotel's Lobby, I crossed to the Reception Desk, and with no pretense, began a friendly conversation in Thai with Suumii and Dhoi, focusing mostly on Dhoi. With Suumii's encouragement, Dhoi lost most of her shyness toward me and we had an open discourse of ideas and opinions, during which I affirmed she was indeed a widow. And a young widow at that, being only twenty. Her husband had been a Major in the Thai Army with Thailand's Black Panther Division when he was killed in the Vietnam War. Also, she lived with her parents, so her mother could tend her two-year-old daughter while she worked, which her mother was very happy to do, as all of her children were now grown and gone.

I learned she was fifteen when her father had arranged for her to be married to a handsome Army Captain. Then a year ago, he had been promoted to Major, and was a Battalion XO when he was killed in a firefight during the Viet Cong's Tet Offensive, leaving her a widow with a one-year-old daughter. I then thought, "So, she's not a new widow and may be ready for another relationship. And, the fact she has a young daughter isn't a problem because I like kids, being the oldest sibling in my family. Also, she is very beautiful."

Asking her if she liked to go and dance formal Thai dancing at night clubs and watch Samurai movies, she replied, "Yes. But, I've done none of those things since he died."

I looked at Suumii and said, "Don't you think it's time for Dhoi to go dancing again and have some fun? Maybe you and your fiancé could ask Dhoi and I to double-date to a night club, so Dhoi could go dancing."

A big, sly smile appeared on Suumii's pretty face as she turned to her friend and said, "Dhoi, would you like to go dancing with Somsak and me tomorrow night, and maybe this kind man would like to go with Somsak and me to be your dance partner?"

My ploy had worked perfectly with Suumii, as I'd seen from the beginning how Suumii pushed Dhoi to talk with me, especially since I could speak decent Thai. Then looking at Dhoi, I watch her laugh as she replied, "Suumii, of course I'll help you go dancing with Somsak by going on a double-date with you. I'm your best friend from when we were children, aren't I?"

I said, "I too, am willing to help a friend in need. Maybe I could have dinner tonight with Somsak, so we can become acquainted before we are on a double-date together."

Suumii replied, "That is a good thought. I'll call him on the phone now, and we can make the plans before you leave," as she picked up a phone and made the call. Soon, it was agreed we would all meet at the Ming Ter, since it was close by, and have dinner at 6:00 when Suumii and Dhoi got off work at the Reception Desk.

After chatting a little while longer, I returned to my Company Area and took $120 from the tobacco can in my wall locker. Then Skip and

I caught a Thai bus to the Air Base Exchange and looked over the tape decks they had on display. The most popular brand was Teak[150]. What caught my eye was an Akea model that not only had the 8-inch reel-to-reel tape deck, but also had an 8-track tape player that was a popular device being installed in the dashboards of cars. Plus, it also had a self-contained, stereo speaker system, so I wouldn't need to buy a pair of speakers or a headset to hear what was recorded on a magnetic tape. An additional feature was it had a power source conversion switch that allowed it to run off the Camp's local 50-cycle, 120-volt source or the Air Base Site's 60-cycle, 110-volt source. The sticker price on the floor-demo was $86.

Deciding the Akea model was the tape deck system for me, I went to the counter clerk and asked for one to be brought form their stockroom. The clerk replied, "I'm sorry, but we sold the last one in stock this morning. But if you like, I can sell you the floor demo for 40% off."

Doing the math quickly in my head, I exclaimed, "That's at least 34 bucks off. Heck, yea, I'll take your floor demo for 52 bucks."

The clerk responded, "Then just give me a minute to get its box and packing material from the stockroom," as she left the counter and quickly returned with the Akea's original box containing the Styrofoam packing and documentation. With the Akea tape deck safely repackaged, I gave her three, crisp 20-Dollar bills for the slightly used tape deck and eight 8-inch reels of blank magnetic tape that cost $1.00 each, and she gave 40 cents in change. Now, I just had to wait for Skip to buy his tape deck.

Once Skip finally selected and purchased the Teak tape deck model he wanted, with five reels of blank magnetic tape and a headset, we hauled our new possessions across the parking lot to the Air Base Site. There, we talked Red into letting Larry drive us back to the Company Area. As it was a slow Friday afternoon, Larry was happy to have a reason to leave the Operations Room for awhile.

Returning to our hooch, we excitedly unpacked and set up our tape decks, only to realize we didn't have any recorded tapes to listen to. I told Skip, "I've a dinner date in Korat and need to return there to get ready for it, so I'll see you later at the compound."

---

150   Pronounced "Tee-ack."

Skip responded, "Then I'll go to the Air Base Library and check out some taped music we can listen to here and copy later while we're at work Monday and Tuesday night."

Leaving our hooch, with me carrying clean clothes in my shopping bag, we boarded a Thai bus for Korat. Skip got off the bus on the Air Base, while I rode on to Korat. Exiting the bus there, I then walked to the Sri Pattana Hotel to stretch my legs after riding the cramped bus. Arriving at 3:30, I went to the Reception Desk and asked for 5:30 wake-up call, which would allow me time to get a good nap before I went to the Ming Ter for my dinner date. Going to my room, I put away the clothes in my shopping bag, then stripped, took a shower and shaved before taking my nap.

Waking to the 5:30 wake-up call, I dressed in a fresh set of skivvies and clean clothes, and walked to the Ming Ter, where I asked for a table for four and ordered five bottles of Pepsi, one of which I drank strait away to quench my thirst. A little bit later, I saw a young, handsome, 5-foot-8 man enter the front door, closely followed by Suumii and Dhoi, who recognized and pointed me out to the man.

Having only seen the beautiful Dhoi sitting at the Hotel's PBX board, I was very pleased to see she was 5-foot-5 and had a slender, shapely figure, easily discernable in her form-fitting, light blue silk blouse and dark blue skirt that modestly reached three inches below her knees. I stood as they approached, and when we had exchanged sáwátdiis, Suumii introduced Somsak to me.

When we'd had sat down, with me and Somsak one side of the table and the two women on the other, he thanked me very much for having already ordered the Pepsi, as he was quite thirsty. Over dinner, we all spoke in Thai as Dhoi's conversational English was limited. Because I'd been going to the Thai bar, my ear was used to the nuances and inflections of spoken Thai, so had little problem following the conversation.

By the end of the meal, Somsak had warmed to my good natured humor and lack of pretense. Also, in the course of our discussions, I'd found that Suumii's father owned the Jomsurang Hotel, which explained how Dhoi got her job there, and that Somsak's father was a major construction contractor with U.S.AS-Thai, which accounted for how such a young man could afford the large dowry for a prize as Suumii, who's English indicated she'd graduated from college.

At the end of the meal, it was agreed we'd meet tomorrow night in the Lobby of the Jomsurang Hotel at 8:00 to go dancing. When Somsak said we'd ride to the night club in his car and he'd pay the check for the four meals, I thought, "Sandii, you've moved into the upper crust of Thai society."

When we left the Ming Ter, I decided to walk with Somsak as he led the women back to the Jomsurang Hotel. With my warm acceptance of his walking arm in arm with me as a sign of our camaraderie while we talked, I was sure it impressed him as most American men would've cringed form such familiarity with another man. At the driveway to the Hotel, we exchanged parting sáwátdiis as I continued on Phokiang Road to Buarong Road and the compound.

Arriving at the compound, the armed guard passed me through the main gate's door. When I replied "No" to Horn's query to having any booze with me, I entered the gate to his home and exchanged sáwátdiis with the usual gang of guys sitting on the porch's wall, drinking Sing Hăi Beer. Crossing the porch, I entered Horn's home and exchanged sáwátdiis with the four pretty tîi-lóks sitting at the table, before I grabbed and opened a cold bottle of Sing Hăi Beer from the refrigerator.

Exiting onto the porch, Tom said in an angry voice, "Sandii, I'm not supposed to leave to go Stateside for two more months, but I received my travel orders today that I'm scheduled for a departure flight to Bangkok on the 27th. The Army be damned if it thinks I'll leave before my extension expires on February 24th for my discharge Stateside. What're they going to do? Court Marshall me and kick me out of the Army?" To which everyone laughed.

Of course, Horn's House Rules forbade any discussion on the innateness of the Army's orders to discharge Tom a month early, and I thought, "There must have been a SNAFU in Army Personnel Stateside for this order, considering the major manpower shortage in the 442d, especially for Spec-5s."

I happily announced, "As some of you know, my girlfriend was forced to move to Bangkok with her father's transfer there. And, that I've sworn never again to date another woman under the control of her father. Well, I've just had dinner with a beautiful, 20-year old-widow, who's agreed to go dancing with me and her friends tomorrow night."

Bob toasted, "To Sandii, who has more bad luck than anyone I know with losing beautiful women to the wiles of their fathers, and the good luck to find other beautiful women to replace them."

Everyone raised their bottles of beer and cheered, "To Sandii."

Then Charlie told everyone how Glen and Súpa had set it up for him to meet four different beautiful Thai women interested in being his tîi-lók, and one of them will go dancing with him tomorrow night, to which he toasted, "To Glen and Súpa, the best matchmakers in Korat."

Again, everyone raised their bottles of beer and cheered, "To Glen and Súpa."

At 9:00, the friendly camaraderie of the party broke up, and I walked with the others returning to Camp Friendship the short distance to the Chaophaya Inn and hired a săawm-law with Skip for the one-mile ride to the Chainarong Gate. En route, I gave Skip the backstory on how I met Dhoi and had remembered she was widowed.

Returning to our Company Area in a crowded Thai bus, we went to our hooch and drank a cold can of beer as we readied ourselves for bed. Waking to 5:00 bugle call for Reveille, I went through my morning routine and dressed in a fresh set of jungle fatigues before leaving with everyone for the Mess Hall.

After eating our breakfasts and smoking our cigarettes, we left the Mess Hall for morning formation, where I reminded Jim that I had to go to the Hospital's E.R. right after formation for two hours to get my 4th Rabies shot. Jim responded, "Thanks for reminding me, Sandii," and turning to Larry, "Sorry, Larry, but Sandii has to go to the Hospital for two hours to get his 4th Rabies shot, so I'll need you to come with us this morning for a couple of hours to replace him, okay?"

Larry sourly replied, "Sounds like a pretty lame way to get out of work for a couple of hours. But, I'd rather be at work for a couple of extra hours, than have to get 14 Rabies shots in the gut."

After formation, I was driven again in a jeep to the Hospital's E.R. to receive my 4th Rabies shot. This time the numbered circle showed it was to be given in the upper right quadrant of my abdomen. Right after the injection, I saw the site of the previous injection become red with inflammation, and the Doctor marveled, "I've never heard of anything like this. If this phenomenon happens again Sunday and Monday, I'll give the Virologists a call for an explanation."

As I began to sit up after my 2-hour nap, I felt the assaulted muscles in my abdomen ache and thought, "After ten more of these shots in the gut, will I even be able to sit up?"

When I'd been driven in the jeep to the Air Base Site. I asked the driver to stand by for a minute to take Larry back to the Company Area with him. Entering the Operations Room, I saw things were in the usual busy Saturday morning mode, and Larry was very happy to hear the jeep was waiting to take him back to the Company Area when I relieved him. Then, I joined the foray with Bob, Skip, Jim and Tim to get the many reported circuit outages restored to service.

Tim joined me on my 10:55 meal run, and I asked, "So, how are things settling in for you?"

He replied, "This is the best duty I've ever had. With the possibility of an early promotion to Staff Sargent, I'm going to HQ Monday to request a 6-month extension of my tour. The only thing I need is a tîi-lók. I've heard you live in Korat and speak Thai. Maybe you can give me a little help with that?"

I answered, "In the circles of Thai society I'm in, there are few, if any women looking to be a tîi-lók. But, a guy at the Tropo Site I usually eat with is likely to help you find a tîi-lók."

When I met up with Glen in the Mess Hall, I introduced him to Tim. When Tim posed his need to Glen, he told Tim that he'd just done the same thing for a newbie on his Team at Tropo, and will see what could be arranged for Tim. When I told Glen and Tim the story on how and why I met Dhoi, and that we'd be at the night club tonight with Dhoi's affluent friends, Tim laughed and said, "Maybe Dhoi has another rich, single girlfriend she can set me up with as her lover and save me the expense for the upkeep of a tîi-lók."

I responded, 'I'll keep you in mind, but just be aware, unless you're married to her, the father can sell her for a dowry at any time." I then told him my stories of how I'd lost Jintana, Julii and Súusíi, to which he exclaimed, "Pay a dowry! I thought that's what went with a bride from her family when she got married."

Glen laughed and responded, "Maybe in the Western World. But in Thailand, the father expects to be compensated for what it cost to raise his daughter, and she's treated as chattel until she or the groom pays it. Heck, five dollars of the fifty I give Súpa each month for her living expenses as my tíi-lók goes to her father, and I'd have to pay him over 1,000 Dollars to marry her."

Tim responded, "Then forget what I said about finding me a high-society Thai woman, Sandii, I'll wait to see what Glen can find for me."

Returning to the Operations Room after lunch, I continued to work on our circuit outages for the rest of the afternoon. As I was leaving on my 4:55 meal run, Jim told Skip and I, "When you're on your meal runs, if you see Jack, Tommy or Chuck, give them a heads up that at 1300 tomorrow, there'll be an all-hands meeting here to discuss an issue that's been raised by the Air Force."

While I was on my meal run, I saw Tommy in the Mess Hall and passed the message to him. When Tommy asked what it was about, I had to say, "I haven't a clue," and asked Bob when I returned from dinner, "Do you know what the issue is with the Air Force that requires an all-hands meeting?"

Bob replied, "Because of last year's Tet Offensive in Vietnam, the Air Force wants to prepare for another Tet Offensive this year by the Thai Cong. They plan to put up an 8-foot tall, chain-link fence topped with concertina wire around the Comm Center in case the Air Base is overrun, to include our Radio Site. We need to decide whether we want such a fence to include this Army facility."

When I was relieved at 6:45 by John, Larry and Chuck, I told them as I left the Operations Room the purpose of tomorrow's meeting, and John laughed as he responded, "That doesn't mean a hill of beans to me. Tonight's my last night working here, and tomorrow night's my last in Korat, because I fly out of here first thing Monday morning."

Catching a Thai bus for Korat, I went to my Hotel room to shower and shave before I went on my double-date with Dhoi to the night club. Arriving in the Jomsurang Hotel Lobby at 8:00, I saw Somsak, and as we exchanged sáwátdiis, he asked, "Are American women ever late?"

I laughed and replied, "Always. It's their way to show who's really in charge."

Soon, Dhoi and Suumii entered the Lobby, and Dhoi looked very fetching in her form-fitting, short-sleeve, pink silk dress with a full skirt that modestly hung three inches below her knees. After exchanging sáwádtiis, we exited through the Hotel's front doors, where Somsak led us to a blue 1965 Ford Thunderbird. When I climbed into the front passenger bucket seat, he said, "My father gave me this car for my College graduation present so I can drive to my classes at Suranarii University of Technology, where I'll receive a degree in Mechanical Engineering," as the two women sat in the back.

Arriving at the night club, he parked the car in a parking lot on its far side. Exiting the car, Dhoi and Suumii followed us into the night club, where I saw Glen, Steve and Charlie sitting at a table on the 3rd tier with Súpa, Lompét and another very pretty Thai girl. As we were led by the maître d' up the steps to the 3rd tier with Suumii and Dhoi following us, I saw them give me a friendly wave, which I returned and Somsak asked, "Are those friends of yours, Sandii?"

I replied, "Yes. Those are three of the men I work with and their girlfriends."

Somsak directed the maître d' to stop at their table, where we exchanged sáwátdiis and made cursory introductions before continuing to a table with a placard in Thai Script. When the maître d' removed it as we sat down, I presumed it said "Reserved" in Thai. Then, Somsak asked me what I'd like to drink, I replied, "A Pepsi, please. I don't like to mix drinking alcohol with my ballroom dancing, as it confuses my feet."

Somsak laughed and responded, "A very wise philosophy, Sandii," and ordered a bottle of Pepsi for each of us. When the Pepsi's quickly appeared in front of us, I noticed the waiter didn't' wait to be paid, but rabidly retreated a few steps from the table. When Somsak and I pulled a cigarette out to smoke, the waiter instantly had a lit cigarette lighter before our cigarettes to light them, and I thought, "Somsak must have a running tab here, so he doesn't have to be bothered with producing money to pay for anything at that time, with a precent of gratuity factored in for the maître d' and waiter for this first-class service."

Having a sip of our Pepsi, we took to the dance floor. I soon found that Dhoi knew very little about ballroom dancing, whereas I saw Somsak and Suumii were quite adept at it, probably from learning it while in college. Fortunately, Dhoi was a quick learner as I added to the rudiments of the basic steps she knew for the Waltz, Cha-cha and Tango.

Of course, the tables were turned when the orchestra played the music for the Thai ram dances, the formal dance style of Thailand. Though I'd watched it numerous times in the night club before, and even tried dancing to it with Jintana a few times, I performed it awkwardly with the stylized movements as the women danced in one line while the men danced in a contra line. Even then, I enjoyed watching the smile very much on Dhoi's beautiful, oval face and the movements of her slender, shapely body, and thought, "Dhoi, I'm going to enjoy every chance I can have to be with you."

Before we left at 11:00, Dhoi agreed to have lunch with me at the Ming Ter on Monday at noon, and we all agreed to have dinner and go dancing on Wednesday night. After Somsak drove us to the Jomsurang Hotel, he and I escorted Dhoi and Suumii to the Lobby and exchanged parting sáwátdiis with them. As Somsak drove me to my Hotel, he said seriously, "I think you're a very good man, Sandii, and Suumii told me that you are the only man Dhoi has been interested in since the passing of her husband. I hope your intentions for Dhoi are honorable, because she is very important to me and Suumii, as she's Summii's friend and will be, as you say, the Maid of Honor at our wedding next month."

I responded, "As the widow of a fellow fallen Soldier, I have the upmost respect for Dhoi. And, I also like her very much. I've already requested an extension of my tour of duty in Thailand, and expect to be here for another year. If, during that time we fall in love, then I may ask her to marry me. Do my intentions sound honorable enough for me to continue to date her?"

Somsak laughed and replied, "Very honorable indeed. Not many men would be willing to raise another man's child, especially a girl child. But I must warn you that, because Dhoi's husband was an Officer in the Thai Army, her mother will not like that you're an Enlisted man, and will think you're unworthy of her daughter."

Exiting his car at the Sri Pattana Hotel, I responded "Sáwátdii, Somsak and thank for the warning about Dhoi's mother. If I meet her parents, I'll be sure not to bring it up."

Entering my Hotel room, I quickly stripped to my skivvies and went to bed thinking, "So, Dhoi's mother is a social bigot against Enlisted men. That might prove to be tricky. I wonder what her father's attitude on the subject is."

Rising to my 5:00 wake-up call, I dressed in my jungle fatigues and left for Camp Friendship. Exiting the Thai bus at my Company Area, I walked to the Mess Hall, where I met up with Skip, and had a delicious breakfast and leisurely smoked a cigarette, before going to morning formation.

After morning formation, I rode in the jeep to the Hospital's E.R. for my 5th Rabies shot. This time, the numbered circle showed it was to be given on the left side of the abdomen, between the locations of the 1st and 3rd shots. Shortly after it was administered, I saw a red area of inflammation appear around the point where the 4th shot was given, and the Doctor said "I wonder what the Virologists are going to say about this strange reaction."

Sitting up after my 2-hour nap, I felt my abdominal muscles complain about this repeated insult them, which was only going to get worse each morning. After being driven in the jeep to the Air Base Site, I spent a quiet day in the Operation Room until 1:00, when everyone who worked at the Air Base Site crowded into the small Site Office, except Bob who manned the Operations Room.

It was the general consensus that we wanted no 8-foot tall security fence around the Air Base Site for two reasons. First, if the Air Base was overrun by the Thai Cong, then a fence around an otherwise nondescript building would only invite attention to it, and an attack on it as a place requiring protection. And second, it would be a royal pain to our backside having to unlock and relock its gate every time we entered or exited our building.

When Skip and I get off work, we changed into our civilian clothes and went to a bar in Korat for the send-off party for Jack and John, with several others from the Tropo Site, and outlying Radio Sites in Company C, leaving in the morning for their flight Stateside. However, this time there was no disturbance in the bar like the last send-off party three weeks before.

After formation the next morning, at which I bade Jack and John a safe trip home, I rode in the jeep to the Hospital's E.R. for my 6th Rabies shot, which was given in the left side of my abdomen between where the 2nd and 4th shots were given. Again, I had an allergic reaction at the site of the previous day's location. The Doctor said, "I gave the Virologist in the Philippines a call first thing this morning and described your allergic reactions to each Rabies shot. He said your strange allergic reaction was new to him, and would call some of the leading Virologists Stateside to find out the cause of your phenomenon."

Rising later from my 2-hour nap with an increasingly painful abdomen, I rode back to the Company Area in the jeep and went to my hooch. Drinking a cold can of Bud as I changed into my civilian clothes and put some clean clothes in my shopping bag, I then caught a Thai bus to Korat. Entering my Hotel room, I stripped to shower and shave before I lay on the bed and took a nap.

An hour later, I woke up and dressed, and then walked to the Jomsurang Hotel to meet Dhoi for our lunch date. Entering the Hotel's Lobby, I crossed it to the Reception Desk. Leaning over the Desk, I was greeted by Dhoi's beautiful smile and her happy "Sáwátdii, Sandii," as she rose quickly from the PBX switchboard.

Enjoying the view of Dhoi's nicely endowed, slender figure as she walked from behind the Desk, I said, "Sáwátdii, Dhoi and Suumii," to which Suumii replied happily, "Sáwátdii, Sandii," with a big smile for me, and I thought, "That smile is for the happiness she feels for her best friend's resurgence into a life of joy again after the loss of her husband."

Following properly behind me, we walked the short distance to the Ming Ter, where we had a wonderful lunch together as we learned more about each other, our likes and dislikes. Having finished our lunch, we talked a little longer, enjoying each other's company, before walking back to the Jomsurang Hotel. When I'd exchanged farewell sáwátdiis with Dhoi and Suumii, I could hear Suumii excitedly pumping Dhoi about how her luncheon date with me went.

Returning to my Hotel room, feeling very happy with how well my lunch with Dhoi had gone, I stripped to my skivvies and slept on the bed for a couple of hours. Waking in a very good mood, I dressed and put my dirty clothes in my shopping bag before walking to the Chainarong Gate to board a Thai bus to Camp Friendship.

Exiting the bus at the Company Area, I walked to my hooch, where I found Skip, Ronnie and Stony sitting at the card table in the middle of the hooch teaching Charlie how to play Double-Deck Pinochle, while they drank beer and smoked cigarettes. Grabbing a cold can of Bud from the mini-fridge, I stood and watched them play Pinochle till the 5:00 bugle call for Mess.

Once they'd finished playing the hand, we all changed into our OD BDUs and headed to the Mess Hall for dinner. As we satiated our appetites with fried chicken and mashed potatoes smothered in country gravy, and leisurely smoked our cigarettes, Charlie and I talked about how well our dates at the night club on Saturday night went, and our hopes and plans for advancing the relationships with the new women in our lives. Then we all walked across the Company roadway to wait for our rides to work in front of the Day Room.

When Tommy drove up in the ¾-ton truck and stopped it in front of Skip and I, he angrily railed as he exited the truck, "Can you believe those lifers at Tropo? They're having me promoted to Spec-5."

CHAPTER 49

DEAD OR ALIVE

Skip said, "Congratulations on your promotion, Tommy."
I responded, "Skip, it's more like condolences."
Tommy bitterly agreed, "Condolences is right, Sandii, because I'll be leaving my sweet gig at the Air Base Site and moving to the Tropo Site to be a Team Leader, having to boss guys around, and having to deal with all that lifer crap there."

I asked, "Why you, Tommy? Surely, there's guys at the Tropo Site they can promote to Spec-5 and be a Team Leader?"

Tommy replied, "Heck, I even purposely flunk the Frame Tech Spec-5 Exam they made me take last month. But, they told me that taking the Exam was only a requirement to be promoted to Spec-5, whether you pass it or not. It's because I was rooked into going to that Combat Engineer School before going to Ft. Monmouth to be a Frame Tech, giving me the time in service to be promoted to Spec-5. But don't worry, I'll think of something to stop them from promoting me to Spec-5 at tomorrow morning's formation."

As Tommy stomped off toward the Mess Hall, Skip and I drove to the Air Base Site to relieve Chuck from the day shift. In the Operations Room, Chuck informed us that he didn't need a ride back to the Company Area because he was now living with Jack's ex-tîi-lók, who he described as "a hot little number." As Chuck quickly left to catch a Thai bus for Korat to be with this "hot little number," I thought, "Well, that keeps things simple for everyone concerned. Jack doesn't have to worry about his ex-tîi-lók being cared for, now that he's gone. She didn't have to find job to support herself and pay her father to keep from being sold into prostitution. Chuck doesn't have to go through the hassle of meeting and dating a girl with the hope she'll agree to become his tîi-lók. And, Skip and I don't have to leave the Operations Room shorthanded on a busy Monday night to drive Chuck back to the Company Area."

And it was the usual busy Monday night, with Jim and Roger working through till 9:30, when things slowed down enough for them to catch a Thai bus home to Korat. On my 10:55 meal run, I met up with Glen in the Mess Hall, and told him about having lunch with Dhoi, and Tommy's unfortunate promotion to Spec-5, to which Glen responded, "Yea, the word going around Tropo is they're promoting a dozen guys in the Company to Spec-5, because so many of the Team Leaders and NCOICs here, and at the outlying Radio Sites, are rotating Stateside. And, those I know at the Tropo Site, they're not happy about it either. Also, when you see Tim again, have him contact me, so we can set up times and places to meet some of Súpa's girlfriends. As he's a Spec-5, they consider him quiet a catch, sight unseen."

As work slowed through the night, I later told Bob about my lunch date with Dhoi today, and that I'd have lunch again with her tomorrow. To which Bob responded, "It looks like you've found the perfect woman to put an end to the dilemma you've had with the fathers of your other girlfriends."

While Skip was on his 4:55 morning meal run, at 5:30, I heard the Site's front door slam shut and saw Tommy stagger into the Operations Room. Still dressed in his jungle fatigues, he announced in a loud, slurred voice, "When I show up at morning formation drunk, there's no way they'll promote me to Spec-5, and I can stay here in this wonderful place."

Bob looked at me and said, "Where there's a will, there's a way," as we sat him down in a chair.

At 6:25, Skip helped me stand Tommy up from the chair, guide him outside to the truck, and put him onto the passenger side of the cab's seat, where he toppled over across it. Climbing into the driver's side of the truck's cab, I managed to push Tommy back enough on the seat to make room for me to drive. Arriving at the Motor Pool, Jim sent me to tell Tim to come and help him get Tommy to the Mess Hall and get some coffee in him before morning formation, as I went to the Mess Hall for my breakfast.

As I ate breakfast, I saw Jim and Tim guiding Tommy into the Mess Hall and to the large coffee urn. There, they managed to get a couple mugs of hot, black coffee into Tommy while he repeatedly sang happily, "I ain't get'n promoted. I ain't get'n promoted." Then, I watched as they guided Tommy out of the Mess Hall and to formation.

Finishing my breakfast quickly, I thought, "I have to see this," as I exited the Mess Hall and stood on the concrete walkway by the Tropo Platoon. After everyone had been reported "present or accounted for," Spike read out thirteen names to "report front and center." When Tommy's name was called, I watched as Tim guided Tommy to the line of Spec-4s being promoted to Spec-5.

As the CO proceeded down the line of Spec-4s, awarding each a pair of Spec-5 patches to be sewn on their uniform, he said, "Congratulations on your promotion to Spec-5." When the CO came to Tommy, the CO said, "I know what you're trying to do, Meirhouser, and it's not going to work. I have thirteen Spec-5 stripes to hand out, and you're getting one of them, even if it's posthumously."

After formation, I climbed into the jeep waiting for me, and rode to the Hospital's E.R. for my 6th Rabies shot. Before I was given the injection between the 2nd and 4th locations on the right side of my abdomen, the Doctor said, "I talked again to the Virologists in the Philippines this morning. They told me that they couldn't find any medical publication documenting this pattern of allergic reaction to a Rabies Vaccination Series before and want me to take photographs of your abdomen before and after each of your remaining injections for visual documentation and send them a copy of the complete medical history of this once you've completed the fourteen-shot series. Then, they'll probably submit the findings to some Medical Journal for publication."

I responded, "And what do I get out of this?"

He laughed and responded, "Eight more Rabies injections in your abdomen and a very sore gut."

After my 6th Rabies shot, with before and after photographs of the same novel allergic reaction, and a 2-hour nap, I sat up on the exam table, with some pain to my abdomen. Then, exiting the Hospital, I rode the jeep back to the Company Area. Walking to my hooch, I drank a cold can of Bud as I changed into civilian clothes, and then left to catch a Thai bus to Korat.

Arriving at my Hotel, about 10:00, I requested an 11:30 wake-up call and went to my room for a quick shower and shave before laying on my bed for some much needed sleep. Getting up at 11:30, I dressed and walked the 400 yards to the Jomsurang Hotel. Crossing the Hotel's Lobby, I exchanged sáwátdiis with Dhoi and Suumii at the Reception Desk. As Dhoi got up from the PBX switchboard to go with me to lunch, Suumii asked, "Sandii, would you be available to go with Som-sak, Dhoi and I to dinner and the night club on Thursday night?"

I replied, "I would be available and most honored to go with you," as I thought, "Suumii really wants to push my relationship with Dhoi, or they've collaborated to do so. Either way, is just fine with me."

With Dhoi walking behind me the short distance to the Ming Ter, we arrived and had a fun time talking over our lunch. At one point Dhoi asked, "Sandii, my parents are curious as to what kind of man I've been spending time with. If you'd like, could you have dinner with us Sunday? It's not necessary, as I'm free to spend time with whoever I want."

I replied, "I would like very much to meet your parents and your daughter on Sunday for dinner. But, it must be early, as I work that night and must be at work by 6:45," as I thought, "Might as well get this meeting with her socially bigoted mother over with, before I become attached to this beautiful woman, and she decides I'm not good enough for Dhoi."

Agreeing to meet on Sunday at 4:00 where she worked, I returned Dhoi to the Reception Desk by the end of her 1-hour lunch break. Then, I went back to my Hotel room to get a few hours' sleep before leaving to board a Thai bus to Camp Friendship.

Exiting the bus at the Company Area, I went to my hooch for a cold can of Bud to drink and to change into a fresh set of OD BDUs, before going to the Mess Hall for dinner with Skip. After dinner we went and stood in front of the Day Room with the others who were working the night shift.

As Tommy arrived with the truck, I could see he was still defiantly wearing his Spec-4 stripes, and exiting the truck, he happily said, "I've been given a reprieve from having to wear the Spec-5 stripes until next week, when a newbie will replace me at the Air Base. And guess who I'm replacing at Tropo? Frank! He's putting on Sargent stripes next week to be the new NCOIC of the Korat Air Base Site, as Jim's leaving the flowing Monday for Stateside. Who knows? Maybe when Frank leaves in the Spring, I'll be the Air Base Site's NCOIC. Wouldn't that be a hoot and a half?"

Arriving in the Operations Room, I relieved Chuck and watched him happily leave to be with his new tîi-lók in Korat. After a nice quiet evening, Skip and I brought our tape decks back with us on our respective midnight meal runs and made copies of the two taped albums Skip checked out of the Air Base Library. Then, Skip brought his tape deck back to our hooch on his 5:40 meal run, and I brought my tape deck back to our hooch on my 6:35 meal run before delivering the truck to Tim in the Motor Pool.

When I'd eaten my breakfast in the Mess Hall and the morning formation had ended, I rode in the jeep to the Hospital's E.R. for my 7th Rabies. Receiving the shot near my abdomen's top midline after a photograph had been taken and seeing the peculiar allergic reaction at the location of the previous injection, of which another photograph was take, I slept for two hours. After I woke and endured the pains in my abdomen when sitting up to leave, I rode back to the Company Area and drank a cold can of Bud in my hooch, as I changed into my civilian clothes.

Catching a Thai bus to Korat, I went to my Hotel room to shower, shave and take a nap. Being woken from my slumber by an 11:30 wake-up call, I dressed and walked to the Jomsurang Hotel to take Dhoi for lunch at the Ming Ter. Having enjoyed another delightful lunch with Dhoi, I escorted her back to the Hotel before walking to my room at the Sri Pattana Hotel, where I went to bed and slept till 5:00.

When I woke and dressed again, I walked to the Thai bar and enjoyed a large bowl of egg noodle chicken soup, as I shared a bottle of Sing Hǎi Beer being passed around the table. At first they joked with me about being so drunk that, for some mysterious reason, I picked the ugliest woman in the brothel to spend the night with. Then, I told them about meeting Dhoi by chance and later remembering she was a widow, which was the type of emancipated woman I was looking for to be my girlfriend, and now I was having lunch with her regularly. Also, that I would have dinner with her parents and 2-year-old daughter on Sunday. I purposely left out the affluent circumstances of her best friend, as that may sound like I was bragging, which is socially looked down on in Thai society.

Sgt. Comkit said, "Speaking of going to lunch, you once invited me to have lunch with you at your NCO Club. I'm still interested in doing that with you if the invite is still open."

I responded, "Of course it's still open to you, my friend. Would tomorrow be too soon? And, where would you like for us to meet, so I can take you there?"

He replied, "Tomorrow will be good, and I can meet you at noon in the NCO Club's parking lot."

After a pleasant evening of jocular camaraderie with my Thai friends, I left the Thai bar at 9:00 and walked the half-mile to the Jomsurang Hotel. There, I left a note for Dhoi at the Reception Desk that I'd be unable to meet her for lunch tomorrow but was very much looking forward to having dinner and going dancing with her and her friends that evening. Then, I walked to the Sri Pattana Hotel and went to my room.

Getting up with my 5:00 wake-up call, I dressed and walked the one mile to the Chainarong Gate to catch a Thai bus to my Company Area. Going to my hooch, I drank a cold can of Bud as I changed into a fresh set of jungle fatigues, and then walked to the Mess Hall for breakfast. Meeting up with Skip, and the others from my hooch, I told them about my invite to have dinner with Dhoi and her family on Sunday. Also, I'd be taking a Thai Police Sargent, who was my friend from the Thai bar, to the Air Base NCO Club for lunch today.

After morning formation, I went to the Hospital's E.R. by jeep and received my 8th Rabies shot near the bottom of my abdomen's mid-line, with before and after photographs to document the same strange allergic reaction at the prior day's vaccination site. The Medic then gave me a bottle of Aspirin and said, "The Doctor instructed me to give these to you to take two of these pills three times a day with food. They'll help reduce the pain to your abdominal muscles."

Swallowing two of the pills with water, I took my usual 2-hour nap on the exam table. When I woke, there was still pain to my abdominal muscles, but not as sharp as before. Returning to the Company Area in the jeep, I went to my hooch and drank a cold can of Bud, while stripping to my skivvies, turning on my fan, and going to bed.

At the sound of the 11:00 bugle call for Mess, I got up slowly form my bed, feeling the generalized pain in my abdominal muscles, and drank a cold can of Bud as I dressed in my civilian clothes. Then walking to the Mailroom, I found a letter from Linda and one from my parents and returned to my hooch.

With everyone else gone to lunch, I sat at the table and drank a cold can of Bud and smoked a Pall Mall, as I enjoyed a nice quiet read of their thanks again for their Christmas gifts, how much they missed and loved me, and their wishes for me to have a "Safe and Happy New Year."

Finished with reading the letters, I put them in my wall locker with the other's I'd received and left to catch a Thai bus to the Air Base. Exiting the bus at the NCO Club, I walked to the East end of the building to stand in its shade as I watched the parking lot's entrance for Sgt. Comkit to arrive in his Police vehicle.

After several minutes, I saw a brown ¾-ton military type truck pass in front of the NCO Club and make a right-hand turn into its parking lot. Seeing Sgt. Comkit sitting behind the driver's wheel, I quickly walked over to his truck, exchanged sáwátdiis, and welcomed him to Korat Air Base and its NCO Club. I saw he was dressed as usual, wearing his tan, short-sleeve Police uniform with the Sam Browne belt, and his pistol on his right hip.

We amicably chatted in Thai as we walked to the front of the NCO Club. Entering the Club, I saw a six-foot tall, medium built man, wearing a white shirt and red tie, with a dark blue sport coat and tan slacks, walking toward us with his left arm extended and the palm of his hand raised up. Indicating we were to stop, he said, "Hold it right there, you two. You can't come in here wearing that pistol. The Club has a strict 'No Weapons Policy,' so you'll have to surrender it to me."

Seeing the brass name plate over the left breast pocket of his sport coat read MAA MITCHELL, I calmly said, "Master At Arms Mitchell, Sargent Comkit is a Thai Police Officer and is entitled to wear his pistol everywhere he goes, including this NCO Club."

Lowering his extended left hand slightly and turning it palm side up, he reached toward Sgt. Comkit's pistol and said, "I don't care who he is, the NCO Club has a strict 'No Weapons Policy,' and he must surrender that pistol to me, or leave."

Sgt. Comkit quick drew out and raised up his 0.38 caliber revolver, and fired one shot into the ceiling, with a loud, resounding "boom" that could be heard throughout the NCO Club. Then, pointing the business end of his revolver at the MAA's face, Sgt. Comkit calmly said in English, "You take one step to me, and I choot you dead."

Looking down the bore of the 0.38 caliber revolver, the MAA, with his left hand still extended, said with resolve, "You will not enter this NCO Club with that pistol."

Sgt. Comkit responded with equal resolve, "I come in NCO Clup wit my gun. You can choo-sa if you dead or alive."

CHAPTER 50

NOTHING LIKE KNOWING PEOPLE IN HIGH PLACES

Having stepped back a few steps when Sgt. Comkit drew his pistol and fired it at the ceiling, I looked at the equal resolve in the faces of the MAA and the Sgt., and thought, "This is a real Mexican standoff. The MAA is not going to let Sgt. Comkit enter the NCO Club without giving up his pistol, and Sgt. Comkit is going to enter the NCO Club with his pistol and shoot the MAA if he makes any attempt to stop him. But, probably in a leg, like I saw the other Thai Policemen do to that guy at the bar in Korat."

After a very tense minute, I saw four U.S. APs run in through the front entrance of the NCO Club with their automatic, 0.45 caliber pistols drawn and ready for action. The AP SSG in the lead quickly assessed the situation and yelled, "Master At Arms, stand-down!"

The MAA replied, "He can't come in here with that pistol."

The AP SSG calmly responded, "If you don't stand-down, he can legally shoot you dead. The Thai Police have legal authority to enter any building on this Air Base, fully armed, any time they want, and can shoot dead anyone who tries to stop them."

The MAA persisted, "But, the NCO Club has a strict 'No Weapons Policy'."

The AP SSG said, "I suggest you go read that Club Policy again, and you'll see a disclaimer that says, 'This policy does not apply to Thai Police Officers, who have legal law-enforcement authority.' So, please, stand-down before he shoots you. And, if you survive being shot, you'll be Court Marshalled under Article 37 of the UCMJ for disobeying a legal order."

Looking incredulous, the MAA lowered his hand, stepped back, and said, "I'm going to look at the NCO Club Policy Manual to verify what you said," as he turned around and walked in a huff to the NCO Club Office.

Placing his pistol in his left hand, the AP SSG walked to Sgt. Comkit with his right hand extended in friendship and said in Thai, "I apologize, Sargent, for the misunderstanding with my associate. He must be new to his work. Please, let me buy you a drink," as he gave his pistol to the AP behind him.

Sgt. Comkit replied as he holstered his pistol and shook the man's hand, "I'm here at the invitation of my friend, Sandii, for lunch. Maybe you can buy him a drink, too."

Entering the NCO Club's ballroom area, which looked very much like the one at Camp Friendship's Enlisted Club, the three of us sat at a circular table. When a pretty Thai barmaid came to our table, I ordered a Scotch with one ice cube to chill it, Sgt. Comkit ordered a Tom Collins, and the AP SSG asked for a Pepsi, saying, "I'm on duty, otherwise I'd have a Bourbon whiskey."

For lunch, Sgt. Comkit and I each ordered a double cheeseburger and fries, which he said he loved to eat, but weren't served anywhere in Korat. When the AP SSG finished his Pepsi, he excused himself and returned to his duties. A little while later, MAA Mitchell came to our table and said, "My apologies, Sargent, for my ignorance of the Club's 'No Weapons Policy' as it applies to the Thai Police. You and your pistol are welcome here any time. And to show you my sincerity, both of your lunches are on the house," and I thought, "Wow! This is great. I got a free fireworks show, drinks and lunch today, because this clown didn't know the limits of his authority."

After Sgt. Comkit and I enjoyed our free lunch together, he gave me a ride in his truck to Korat, dropping me off at the Sri Pattana Hotel.

Giving instructions at the Reception Desk to wake me at 5:00, I went to my room, took a couple of Aspirin on top of my lunch, stripped to my skivvies, and fell asleep on the bed.

With my 5:00 wake-up call, I rose gradually from the bed. Even though the Aspirin took the edge off my abdominal muscle pain from my eight Rabies shots, it still felt like someone had punched me in the gut. After I'd showered, shaved and dressed, I walked to the Jomsurang Hotel's Lobby, where I exchanged sáwátdiis with Somsak while we waited for our women to arrive.

When Suumii and Dhoi entered the Lobby, we all happily exchanged sáwátdiis. Somsak told us that he wanted to take us someplace different for dinner, as we exited the Hotel and climbed into his car. He then drove us up the wide Assadang Road, and crossed the wide Prajak Road intersection, where I saw to my right a large, sandstone temple that Somsak told me was the Wat Phra Narai Mahurat, and that just passed it was the Wut's church, the Naranya Temple, which sat on an island where some enormous monitor lizards lived in the surrounding water.

Turning to his left 100 yards past the Naranya Temple, Somsak drove down a 2-lane road to Yom Marat Road, where he turned left twice into a parking space in front of the Rabieng Kaeu Restaurant. On entering its antique-filled dining room, I saw a large, leafy garden in the back. As we were led to a large table for four, Somsak told us the entree dishes were meant to be shared.

Unable to read Thai, I let the others select the items from the menu to order. When we each had a place setting put before us, and several large bowls of entrees and rice, I took some of everything to eat and found the meal to be simply excellent. However, I'd noticed the menu price for each item on the menu to range from 40 to 150 Bhat and was very happy this was Somsak's treat.

After we'd eaten our sumptuous and delicious meals, we went back to Somsak's car and travelled all the West on Yom Marat Road and crossed over the parallel Chumphon and Rajadamnern Roads, on either side of Korat's West moat, to Vatmung Lane and the night club. Stopping in the parking lot next to it, we entered the night club, and were again given the VIP treatment by the maître d' and by the waiter on the 3rd tier assigned exclusively to our table.

I had a wonderful evening, socializing with Somsak and Suumii, when I wasn't dancing with Dhoi, who was quickly learning the new steps I taught her and to follow my leads as we danced a Waltz, Cha-cha or Tango. Later in the evening, as we danced a romantic Waltz, Dhoi looked at me with her exotic, almond-shaped eyes and hesitantly said, "I like you very much, Sandii, and hope it will be acceptable to you for my desire to sleep with you tonight."

Managing to contain my surprise, I replied, "I'd be honored for you to sleep with me tonight."

Looking relieved, she responded, "I was worried, because of your Christian beliefs about unwed sex to be wrong, that you might not be able to sleep with me. With all of this dancing in your arms, my urges to sleep with you have become very strong."

We soon took leave of Somsak and Suumii, with Dhoi saying, "Sandii has agreed to take me home early, as I'm very tired. So, thank you for the wonderful dinner, Somsak. And, I'll see you tomorrow at work, Suumii."

With a knowing smile, Suumii responded, "Yes, Dhoi, you look very tired. Sandii, thank you for taking Dhoi home, so Somsak and I can continue to have fun dancing together."

Leaving the night club, Dhoi walked behind me the short distance to the Sri Pattana Hotel, where I left a request at the Reception Desk for a 3:30 wake-up call. Entering my room, we passionately kissed as we quickly removed the other's clothes and Dhoi moaned with desire, "Sandii, I've been with no man, other than my husband, and have missed very much the feel of a man making love to me."

With our clothes removed, Dhoi pulled me with her as she lay back onto the bed, eagerly ready to receive me between her shapely, wide-spread and upraised legs. As I slid fully into her hot, wet love canal, she happily moaned, "Oh, Sandii, you're so much larger."

I feverishly responded, "Only because I find you so desirable to love, Dhoi," as I shifted her into the Kama Sutra position my other lovers had found most sexually stimulating to release our pent-up lust. Soon, I felt her spasms as her climactic rush flooded through her body, and she yelled, "Dâai! Dâai!" And when my orgasmic thrust distended fully into her love canal, she gasped, "Sandii, that's amazing."

Pulling my arms tightly around her and rubbing her slender, sensuous body against the front of my torso, she happily cooed, "I'd like to be your girlfriend very much, too, my darling, as you're also the answer to my prayers to again have a man in my life to love me and my daughter."

When we were woken in the morning, we roused our desires for each other with passionate foreplay. Then shifting Dhoi's luscious body into another sexually enhancing Kama Sutra pose, we wantonly made love to satiate our lust with the orgasmic release we strived for. Lying together in the ephemeral pleasure of our climactic rush, Dhoi cooed, "My darling, you've made me so happy, I can hardly wait to be with you again. I know you have to work today and tomorrow, but when can we be together again?"

I replied, "My darling, I understand you must spend time with your daughter, or I'd ask you to be with me every night. Maybe we can go dancing again Saturday night?"

She answered, "I'm glad you're so understanding of my daughter. And yes, my darling, I'd very much like to dance with you again Saturday night, as it makes me desire your lovemaking even more."

When we enjoyed our shower together, I noticed for the first time the stretch marks on her taut abdomen from having been pregnant. And her breasts, though still lovely to see and caress, sagged a little form once being filled with milk for her daughter. But, I still found her 5-foot-5 tall, slender body very sexually desirable with her round, sensuous hips and tight butt. Also, I could now enjoy seeing the full length her shapely long legs that I found very appealing.

After we'd dressed and lovingly kissed goodbye, I escorted Dhoi to the Jomsurang Hotel. There, we exchanged farewell sáwátdiis and that we'd miss each other until we met again at 7:30 in my Hotel room before going dancing. Walking to the Chainarong Gate and boarding a crowded Thai bus for Camp Friendship, I thought, "Now I've the perfect girlfriend, who's beautiful, tall, fun to be with, has a lovely body and enjoys lovemaking with me. Next time we're together, I'll see if she's willing to take day-trips with me, which will have to include her daughter, of course."

Exiting the bus at the Company Area, I walked to my hooch and drank a cold can of Bud, as I changed into a fresh set of jungle fatigues before going to the Mess Hall for breakfast. Meeting up with Skip and my other hooch mates, I told them over breakfast about the incident at the Air Base NCO Club with Sgt. Comkit, to which they all laughed uproariously.

After morning formation, I boarded the jeep for my ride to the Hospital's E.R. and my 10th Rabies shot, having prepared for it by taking two Aspirins with my breakfast. With the before and after photographs taken of the injection and its weird allergic reaction, I took my usual 2-hour nap.

When I'd gingerly sat up, inducing the dull abdominal pain of having been beat with a big stick, I rode in the jeep to the Air Base Site. Arriving in the Operations Room, I said, "Bob, could you call Jim, Tim and Pramoon in here? I have to report a very serious incident I was involved in at the Base NCO Club yesterday afternoon."

With everyone gathered in the Operations Room, I could barely keep a straight face as I told them about the tense Mexican stand-off between the NCO Club's MAA and Sgt. Comkit after he'd fired a shot into the ceiling. Then, how the AP SSG had defused the standoff by telling the MAA he was in the wrong, and that Sgt. Comkit and I each received a free drink and lunch out of the mishap. They all laughed about the MAA's stupidity to confront an armed Thai Policeman, and Tim asked, "Do you really think Sgt. Comkit would've shot the MAA?"

Pramoon replied, "It iss no doubt a Thai Policeman will shoot anyone who not follow his commant. Maybe not in the head, but in the leg or the body."

Then Skip and I told how we saw two Thai Policemen shoot an unruly American in each leg at a bar in Korat when we'd gone to a farewell party there. To which Tim responded, "I'll sure make it a point never to get on the wrong side of a Thai Policeman. And, Sandii, how'd you get so cozy with a Thai Police Sargent to invite him for lunch at the Base NCO Club?"

I then told them how I went to a Thai bar to improve my Thai language skills by immersion, and that Sgt. Comkit was one of the many Thai friends I'd made there.

When I went on my 10:55 meal run with Tim, and we met up with Glen in the Mess Hall, I told him about the NCO Club incident, to which he had a hardy laugh. I also told Glen that Dhoi and I were now officially boyfriend and girlfriend, to which Tim asked, "So, is Dhoi going to become your tîi-lók?"

I replied, "I doubt it. I think Dhoi's mother would not only resent not being able to care for her granddaughter, but also the loss of social status by her daughter being a 'kept woman' by an American, especially and Enlisted American. Unless Dhoi decides she wants to live with me, I think she'll be perfectly happy having me as a boyfriend, which in the Thai culture is basically the same as being engaged."

Then, Glen and Tim talked about making arrangements to meet some of Súpa's friends until it was time for us to return to work.

When I entered the Operations Room, Bob said, "I don't know if either of you follow the pro-football games Stateside, but AFN has just sent a teletype message to AFTN that this Sunday afternoon's Super Bowl IV game between the New York Jets and the Baltimore Colts will be sent to them live to be copied here Sunday night and be re-broadcast Monday morning to the troops here, just like they did with the World Series. We've just been handed another sure thing to bet on when we get off work Monday morning."

Skip responded, "I could sure use some more money to buy a good power amplifier and a pair of speakers to go with my new tape deck."

And I said, "I'm always game for some easy money."

Bob continued, "Unlike the World Series, where there were seven games to bet on and couldn't make large bets or give point spreads on the games to not be found out, the Super Bowl is a one-shot deal. But, don't get too wild with your bets and draw a lot of attention to yourselves, and don't make any bets with the guys you live with, if possible."

After work, I caught a Thai bus for Korat and went to the Thai bar, where Sgt. Comkit and I regaled our bar mates with hilarious reenactments of the incident with the NCO Club's MAA as we drank from the bottles of Sing Hǎi Beer that were passed around the table. Leaving at 9:30, I boarded a crowded Thai bus to Camp Friendship and went to my hooch for a good night's sleep.

Rising painfully from my bed after the 5:00 bugle call for Reveille, I did my usual routine of drinking a cold can of bud, as I used the piss tube and dressed in a fresh set of jungle fatigues. Then, I walked to the Mess Hall with my hooch mates and took two Aspirins with my breakfast.

Before morning formation began, Tommy was told he was needed to work at the Air Base Site for a couple of hours to help with the expected increase in circuit outages typical for a Saturday morning, while I was at the Hospital getting my Rabies shot. After formation, I rode in the jeep to the Hospital's E.R. to receive my 11th Rabies shot. By now, I'd been given Rabies shots in so many different locations in my abdomen, that the Doctor discarded the numbered circle and looked for the least tender spot on my abdomen to give it.

After my 2-hour nap, I carefully sat up from the exam table and left in the jeep for my ride to the Air Base Site. In the Operations Room, I relieved Tommy so he could ride back to the Company Area in the jeep, while I took over the circuit outage he'd been working on. At the end of a busy day in the Operations Room, I quickly left for Korat when I was relieved by Larry at 6:45.

Having showered and shaved at the Air Base Site before being relieved, all I had to do when I arrived at my Hotel room was change into my civilian clothes and to be ready to go dancing with Dhoi when she came to my room at 7:30. Exchanging sáwátdiis and an affectionate kiss with each other, she walked properly behind me to night club, where we were treated no differently than the other patrons. Not seeing Glen and Súpa, or any others I knew that frequented the night club, I led Dhoi to an empty table on the 3rd tier and order Pepsi's for us.

We had fun dancing together through the evening, as her skill with the dance moves I taught her to the Waltz, Cha-cha and Tango improved. During one of our breaks from dancing to sip on our Pepsi's, I asked, "My darling, how would you feel about you and your daughter going with me for a day to the Kâo Yái National Park in two weeks and see the animals there?"

She replied pleasantly surprised, "Really, my darling? You would want to spend a whole day on a trip with me *and* my daughter?"

I answered, "But of course, my darling. I've wanted to go to the National Park, and wouldn't it be a fun place to take your daughter? Besides, you're my girlfriend, and I can't think of anyone else I like to share the experience with. And, if the trip goes well with your daughter, then maybe we can take her to Bâan Tôa Klong and see the elephants next month."

She responded agog, "Your name does fit you very much, my darling, because you are an 'extremely good' man, and the Lord Buddha has blessed me greatly to give me you to be my boyfriend. Yes, my darling, I'd like very much for me and my daughter to spend the day with you at Kâo Yái National Park."

Now, as Dhoi danced with me, I saw she was not only enjoying dancing with me, but also enthused with the prospect of having a future with me that embraced her daughter. As the evening progressed, the orchestra played a Tango, to which I applied my erotic techniques. When the Tango finished, she gasped passionately, "Now I desire you more than ever."

Leaving the night club quickly, Dhoi followed me as I rapidly walked to my Hotel room, where we hastily stripped off our clothes. Leaping onto the bed, our bodies collided in rampant lovemaking driven by our pent-up lust. Her gyrating body strove with unbridled desire that soon exploded in a climactic rush that was quickly followed by my own eruption of sexual desire distending deeply into her love canal. As she clasped my body with her arms and legs pulling me into her still undulating hips, she moaned breathlessly, "I love you very much, my darling, and I've never felt so loved in my life."

Rolling onto my right side and spooning Dhoi desiringly against my body within my arms, I said lovingly, "I love you also, my darling, and that I'm able to bring you so much pleasure." Then, we fell blissfully asleep in the euphoria of our afterglow.

With the 3:30 wake-up call, I sensuously caressed and kissed the womanly curves of Dhoi's luscious body, arousing from her desire for me the hot lust for lovemaking contained in the bowels of her being. When we'd peaked our lust driven lovemaking in the climactic rush we sought, we lay happily together for a while engulfed in the ephemeral state of our orgasmic release.

When we'd enjoyed the feel of each other's body as we washed in the shower and then dressed to leave, Dhoi felt wonderful in my arms as I lovingly kissed her sweet lips before accompanying her to the Jomsurang Hotel. There, we exchanged parting sáwátdiis with the promise to meet in the Hotel's Lobby at 4:00 to go to her parent's home for dinner.

Proceeding to the Chainarong Gate in the fresh morning air to board a crowded Thai bus to Camp Friendship, I thought, "Loving and being with Dhoi is so different that being with my other lovers. There, they had a zest and youthful lust for life, and lots of lovemaking. Whereas Dhoi's lovemaking was just as vigorous, she was more serene and mature in the passion she has for me. Probably the loss of her husband to war and the responsibility of raising her daughter has made her more contemplative in her approach to life and love. Whatever it is, I very much enjoy the change in pace."

Exiting the bus at my Company Area, I enjoyed drinking a cold can of Bud, as I changed into a fresh set of OD BDUs, before walking to the Mess Hall. There, I joined my hooch mates and took two Aspirins with my breakfast. After morning formation, I rode in the jeep to the Hospital's E.R. for my 12th Rabies injection, with the before and after pictures taken of my abdomen. Roused from my 2-hour nap on the exam table, I cautiously got up and walked painfully to the jeep for my ride back to the Company Area, where I slept in my hooch till the 11:00 bugle call for Mess woke me up.

Slowly rising from my bed, I drank a cold can of Bud as I dressed in my civilian clothes, before going to the Mess Hall with my hooch mates to eat lunch and take two more Aspirins. Finishing our lunch, we returned to our hooch, and while the three others left to find a fourth for a game of Double-Deck Pinochle, I put some clean clothes in my shopping bag, as I drank a cold can of Bud, and then left to catch a Thai bus to Korat.

Entering my Hotel room, I stripped to my skivvies and slept for several hours, before I showered, shaved and dressed to have dinner with Dhoi's family. Walking to the Jomsurang Hotel, I met Dhoi in the Lobby at 4:00, where she directed the săawm-law I hired to take us to the Chainarong Gate. When I asked why we were going there, she replied, "To ride a bus to the Thai Army Base, where my father has his home as a Colonel in the Thai Army."

I exclaimed, "A Colonel! You didn't tell me your father is in the Army, much less that he's a Colonel."

She responded, "My darling, you never asked what my father did. Is it a problem?"

I laughed and replied, "No. It's not a problem, my darling. Just a surprise."

Boarding a Thai bus to Camp Friendship, we exited it in the middle of the Thai Army Base. Not knowing where to go, Dhoi gave me directions to her father's home as she walked behind me. We arrived at a large wood bungalow, in the midst of similar bungalows, where she led me into a simply furnished large room called the "háwng-ráp-bprátaan-aa-hâan," translated as the "living room," which literally means "room receive people eat food."

I saw to my left that the end of the room contained the kitchen and food preparation area, in the center was a large wood table with chairs around it, and at the right side wall was a TV with several cushioned chairs in front of it. Across the back wall were three doors leading to the master bedroom, the bathroom and a bedroom for children. Like my hooch, the top half of the outside walls had long, screened windows with large shutters that were propped open for ventilation.

Greeting us at the door was a 5-foot-8 man, in his late 40s, looking very imposing in the khaki uniform of a Thai Army Colonel. Standing slightly behind and to his right, was a very beautiful, 5-foot-5, slender woman in her late 30s, dressed in a light-green silk blouse, and the Thai style long skirt with horizontal green and red stripes, who looked like an older version of Dhoi. Being held on the woman's right hip was a very pretty, 2-year-old girl in a simple brown shift.

Pushing herself from the woman's arms, the little girl slid to the floor and ran to Dhoi, happily yelling, "Maan-dad, maan-daa." As Dhoi scooped her up, she said, "Sáwátdii, Mii-kâa," which means "Hello, Precious."

After exchanging sáwátdiis and introductions, the Colonel and I sat at the table to talk, while the women walked to the kitchen area, with Dhoi's mother asking her questions about me. Sitting at the table, I saw it already had four places set to eat, as the Colonel asked me questions about my unit and what I did in the U.S. Army. Soon, Dhoi and her mother brought bowls of cooked food to the table, and as they sat down, the mother asked, "Dhoi tells me you're in the U.S. Army at Camp Friendship. What is it you do?"

Fortunately, the Colonel answered, as I was not familiar with the Military terms in Thai, "Sandii is an electronics expert, like one of our Warrant Officers," and hearing the Thai word for "Officer," she was placated that I was not an Enlisted man. I thought, "It seems the Colonel is not as concerned about my rank as his wife, and is more pleased that his bereaved daughter has a man in her life to make her happy again. And, even as a lowly Spec-4, I probably earn as much or more than he does."

As we ate dinner, I saw Mii-kâa sat on the floor between the women, playing contentedly with some toys. When the delicious meal was finished, the women cleared the table and brought a bottle of Sing Hăi Beer and two glasses to the table, as the Colonel offered me an American menthol cigarette to smoke, which I graciously accepted. Though I didn't care for menthol cigarettes, the Thais were crazy about them, even to the point of putting mint oil on their rolled cigarettes.

While the Colonel and I drank beer and smoked cigarettes as we talked at the table, Dhoi and her mother stayed and chatted in the kitchen, as tradition required. During my talk with the Colonel, I found he was the CO of the Thai Infantry Regiment responsible for the perimeter security of Korat Air Base and Camp Friendship. Also, after my Company was moved into the concrete buildings, another Thai Infantry Battalion would be moved into the vacated wooden hooches.

At 6:00, the Colonel escorted me to the main road through the Thai Army Base, during which he was deferred to and saluted by everyone we met, and I was eyed as a VIP for future deference, should I be seen again on the Army Base. Reaching the bus stop, he waited and talked with me till a crowded Thai bus to Camp Friendship arrived. Boarding the bus, I paid the 1-Bhat fare to the driver, and two Thai soldiers quickly stood and gave me their seat, having seen me talking with Colonel as the bus stopped. Sitting in the now empty seat on the crowded bus, I thought, "Nothing like knowing people in high places."

CHAPTER 51

MÍI-KÂA, THIS IS YOUR AA SANDII

When the Thai bus arrived at my Company Area, the two Thai soldiers who had given me their seat, now exited before me. As they stood by the bus waiting for it to leave so they could cross to their Battalion Area, they came to attention and saluted me as I exited the bus. Returning their salute, I thought, "So goes the Army maxim, 'When in doubt, if it doesn't move, paint it, and if it moves, salute it'."

Walking to my hooch, I heard a familiar voice behind me say, "Sandii, what's with the Thai soldiers giving you their seats and saluting you when you got off?"

Turning to look behind me, I saw Glen. As we walked along the Company's roadway, I explained, "I just had dinner with Dhoi's family on the Thai Army Base. As it turns out, her father is a Colonel there, and he's the Regimental CO of Camp Friendship's perimeter defense troops, which includes that Thai Battalion across the street. Those two guys must have seen me talking with their CO as we waited for the bus to arrive, and must have thought that I was an Officer, also. So, to be on the safe side, they gave me their seats as I got on the bus and saluted me as I got off behind them.

"I also found out from Dhoi's father, that when we move to our new Company Area in a couple of weeks, another Thai Infantry Battalion will be moving into our old hooches. I imagine our old wood hooches will be a step up for the Thai Soldiers, as the house Dhoi's father lives in as a Colonel, isn't much better than the hooch we live in, except it has indoor plumbing, with a bathroom and two bedrooms."

As Glen turned right for the Mess Hall and I turned left for my hooch, Glen said, "You better tell the others you're dating a Thai Colonel's daughter, because they won't believe me."

I laughed and responded, "That's the truth."

Entering my hooch, as I drank a cold can of Bud and changed into a fresh set of OD BDUs, I told my hooch mates the same things I'd told Glen, which they found hardly credible. We then walked to the front of the Day Room to wait for our rides to work. And, when Tommy arrived with our truck, Skip and I then drove to the Air Base Site.

Walking into the operations Room, I relieved Chuck, who quickly left to be with his tîi-lôk. When Bob entered the Operations Room after Shift Change Report, I told him about my dinner with Dhoi's family on the Thai Army Base. And, despite her father being a Colonel, his home was little different than our hooches, except for the indoor plumbing. Also, that our hooches will be taken over by another of his Infantry Battalions when we vacate them.

Bob responded, "I can believe they're moving another Thai Infantry Battalion there, as there's a major military buildup for all U.S. Military Bases in Thailand in preparation for a Tet Offensive, that may extend into Thailand for the Chinese New Year on February 17th. In fact. I've heard they may do a preemptive Red Alert and lockdown all the Military Bases on the 15th of February, allowing only essential Thai workers onto the Base."

Skip quipped, "I hope they count our mây-bâan as 'essential Thai workers,' as I can't imagine how we'd survive without them for three days," to which we all laughed, as we settled in for a hopefully quiet night in the Operations Room.

When Ted called at 9:00 to let us know he had a line up to Rosie in St. Louis, for free phone calls to our families and friends Stateside, we each gratefully declined, as we'd just called them on New Year's. Returning from my 10:55 meal run, I reported to Bob and Skip, "There's a lot of excitement about the Super Bowl Game being broadcast by AFIN. The odds-on favorite is Johnny Unitas for the Baltimore Colts, as he is more experienced as a Quarterback than the young Joe Namath for the New York Jets."

We later listened to the Super Bowl Game's live feed from the AFN audio circuit on our set of test speakers and were jubilant to hear the Jets beat the Colts 16 to 7, as it would be easier to make bets against the Colts as the odds-on favorite. Skip and I and flipped a coin to see who would take the 4:55 meal run to get first crack at bets on the Game, which he won. I then made the 5:40 meal run to make my bets because, by the time I'd arrive at the Mess Hall on my 6:35 meal run, most everyone would've eaten breakfast and gone to morning formation.

As I'd taken my two Aspirin on my 5:40 meal run, I was able to skip eating another breakfast on my 6:35 meal run and make a few more bets before the Mess Hall cleared out for morning formation. When formation ended, I left the Mess Hall and rode in the jeep to the Hospital's E.R. for my 13th Rabies shot. After my usual post-injection 2-hour nap, as I carefully sat up on the exam table, I could hear the play-by-play announcer on a radio of the Super Bowl Game. Hearing the Colts were ahead 7 to 0, I quietly told the Medic escorting me to the jeep, "If you want to make some easy money, bet the Doctors that the Jets will win."

The Medic asked suspiciously, "How do you know the Jets will win?"

I replied cynically, "The Super Bowl Game was played Stateside early this morning our time, and I'm in the Signal Corps. You don't think some of us haven't heard the score already?"

Riding the jeep back to the Company Area, I went to my hooch and drank a cold can of Bud as I stripped to my skivvies, turned on my fan and went to bed. Rising slowly from my bed at the sound of the 11:00 bugle call for Mess, I took two Aspirin with my cold can of Bud, as I dressed in my civilian clothes before going to the Mess Hall. As I leisurely ate my lunch, I happily collected over $100 from the bets I'd made and thought, "This is like having a second Pay Day in the middle of the month."

Before returning to my hooch, I stopped by the Howard Johnson to buy three 6-packs of Budweiser and a carton of Pall Malls to start my stockpile, as this weekend was the third one of the month, and most of the guys will be broke next week. Putting the beer and cigarettes in my wall locker, I also put my 'easy money' in the tobacco can I kept on the top shelf of my wall locker. Then, I spent the afternoon drinking beer and smoking cigarettes, as Skip and I played Double-Deck Pinochle against Ronnie and Stony for the usual stakes. When the bugle call sounded Mess, we finished the hand we were playing and settled the debts, before changing into our OD BDUs and walking together to the Mess Hall for dinner.

Walking out of the Mess Hall after we ate dinner, into the dimming light of the setting sun, I walked to Howard Johnson to buy more beer and cigarettes for my stockpile, before it closed. As I did so, I saw four 2½-ton trucks parked on the Company's roadway, and OD clad troops climb from the first three trucks and walk to the rear of the fourth truck. Passing in front of the first truck on the way back to my hooch, I saw a line of newbies carrying OD duffel bags on their right shoulder into the Day Room with their shirts tucked in and boots tightly bloused.

Entering my hooch, I heard Ronnie say as he drank from a can of beer, "They sure sent us a shitload of FNGs[151]. You think they finally got the word Stateside how shorthanded the 442d is?"

I replied, "Don't forget, there's a bunch of guys rotating Stateside, and this lot will probably barely fill the empty slots that they leave."

Then, there was considerable discussion as to how many of them were actually Signal Corps, as we had noted several were Pvts and PFCs not wearing the Signal Corps Orange School Brigade patch on their left sleeve, and would be replacing the Battalion's clerks, mechanics and armorers who were rotating Stateside. As we finished our beers and left for work, Stony said, "I guess we'll see Wednesday morning how many of them will join us with the Tropo Platoon."

Skip responded, "Well, however many are Signal Corps, I know that one of them will be replacing Tommy at the Air Base Site."

Walking to the front of the Day Room to wait for our rides to work the night shift, groups of eight carrying duffel bags passed us in the dark going in the opposite direction to the transient hooches, and I had a flashback to when I had arrived in the dark and thought, "With luck

---

151   F..king New Guys

they won't get caught up in a Red Alert only to find there's not enough weapons to go around."

Arriving in front of the Day Room, I saw the four 2½-ton trucks were now gone. When Tommy drove up with our truck, I said, "A large number of newbies arrived earlier, and many of them weren't Signal Corps."

He replied sourly, "Yea, I know. Jim got word that a lot of them are support personnel. He also told me that after I work Wednesday night, I'll only get one day off and start working at Tropo on Thursday's day shift. Well, at least I'll still be in the same hooch with you."

I responded, "But, only for two more weeks. When we get moved to the new Company Area, we'll see then how they plan to arrange the housing for us, and even if we keep the same mây-bâan. How's things at work?"

Tommy replied, "Heck, I hadn't thought Súmat might not be my mây-bâan after the move, and she could even end up in a different building. As for work, it looks like you're in for the usual busy Monday night."

Arriving in the Operations Room, I saw it was busy, and Chuck was very happy to be relieved from the beehive of activity he was in. Jim and Roger helped keep things under control till about 9:00, when most of the circuit outages had been resolved. The work had slowed to a crawl after our meal runs, so Skip and I managed to get an hour's nap each before Skip's 4:55 meal run.

On my 6:35 meal run, as I turned the truck over to Tim, I asked, "How's the tîi-lók hunt going with Glen and Súpa?"

He replied, "Really great. They set me up to meet four girls for lunch and dinner on Sunday and yesterday. They're each so pretty, it's hard to choose between them. But, one has such an infectious smile, I chose her to go dancing with us tonight. Hopefully, it won't take long for her to agree to be my tîi-lók."

I laughed and responded, "If you treat her good tonight, I'm sure by tomorrow night she'll be making living arrangements with you," as I went to the Mess Hall for breakfast. Taking two Aspirin as I ate, I then rode in the jeep to the Hospital's E.R. for my 14th and final Rabies shot. Easing myself up from the exam table after my 2-hour nap, the Medic said to me in a low voice as he helped me to the jeep, "Hey, man.

Thanks for that hot tip yesterday. I made sixty bucks off those arrogant Doctors. So, here's a fiver for the tip," slipping me a 5-Dollar bill.

I responded, "Hey, what goes around, comes around. You've been taking care of me, and I had a chance to take care of you."

Returning to the Company Area in the jeep, I went to the Howard Johnson and bought more beer and cigarettes for my stockpile. Going to my hooch, I drank a cold can of Bud, as I added the purchase to my stockpile, changed into civilian clothes and put clean clothes in my shopping bag, before catching a Thai bus to Korat. Leaving a wake-up call for 11:30, I went to my Hotel room to shower, shave and have a good nap, before going to get Dhoi at the Jomsurang Hotel to take to lunch.

Walking to the Ming Ter, we had fun as we talked over lunch and made plans for our day-trip with Mîi-kâa to the Kâo Yái National Park. After escorting Dhoi back to work, I returned to my Hotel room and slept for several hours before going back to the Jomsurang Hotel to take Dhoi to dinner when she got off work.

Asking Dhoi where she'd like to go to dinner, she replied, "To the Anago. It's a Japanese restaurant by Chaophaya Inn. It's easy to go to from here, out the Hotel's back."

Showing me passed the Hotel's dining room, we walked out the back of the Jomsurang Hotel to a walkway crossing the back of the Chaophaya Inn to its lane on Jomsurangyat Road. The Anago was located on the Road's left-hand corner, next to a Post Office.

Entering the Anago, we exchanged sáwátdiis with a Japanese woman wearing an obe, who led us to a table in an alcove and handed us menus as we sat down. There was a huge list of Japanese dishes, and one page of Italian pastas, from which Dhoi chose the lasagna meal. Liking lasagna myself, I ordered two of them with Pepsi's. Though I saw the menu prices were expensive, ranging from 30 to 300 Bhat, or $1.50 to $15.00, I thought, "What the heck, I just won over $100 from the Super Bowl Game and can afford to splurge a little on Dhoi."

Asking her why she didn't choose a Japanese meal, she laughed and answered, "My darling, I don't care for Japanese food, as it's not spicy like Thai food. But, I really do like Italian food."

After a pleasant evening talking with Dhoi as we ate the delicious lasagna, I hired a sǎawm-law to carry us the half-mile to the night club. As we entered, I saw Glen and Tim sitting at a table on the 3rd tier with Súpa and another very pretty Thai girl. When Dhoi said she wouldn't mind joining my friends at their table, I led her there, where we exchanged sáwátdiis and were invited to sit with them. I soon saw that mixing Dhoi with the other two women was like mixing oil and water, as she had very little in common with them. Though they were polite enough to each other, and Dhoi didn't act condescending toward them, their conversations soon became stilted and Dhoi looked relieved when we all got up to do dance.

Dhoi and I had a fun evening as we danced happily together. Later, I led a sexually stimulating Tango with her to heighten our lust for each other, without doing any deep dips because of my abdominal pain. Then, we quickly went to my Hotel room and enjoyed the passionate release of our pent-up lust with vigorous lovemaking in a different Kama Sutra position that intensified our climactic rush. As I lovingly spooned with her in my arms, enjoying the euphoria of the afterglow, Dhoi cooed, "My darling, you make me very happy. I wish we could do this every night, but I must be able to spend time with my Míi-kâa, too. It's enough for me now to be with you two or three nights a week."

I softly responded, "My darling, I wish we could be together every night, too. I understand you must have time with Míi-kâa, also, and look froward with longing for those nights we can enjoy together," as I thought, "Since at least two nights a week I have to work anyway, that'll leave me at least one night a week at the Thai bar to improve my Thai language skills," and went happily to sleep.

With the 3:30 wake-up call, we pleasured one another with our sensuous foreplay and energetic lovemaking in a Kama Sutra posture that increased the joy of the orgasmic release of our lust. As we lay together sexually spent, Dhoi said breathlessly, "It is wonderful to wake up and feel your desire to love me, and to enjoy your different ways of lovemaking is very exciting."

After a fun shower together, we dressed and lovingly kissed, before we walked to the Hotel's entrance, as I carried my shopping bag of dirty laundry. There, I hired a săawm-law to take us to the Chainarong Gate bus stop. As she boarded the Thai bus behind me, I saw an empty bench seat where we could sit together. I sat by the window, as Dhoi would exit first, and found it a real pleasure to have her to talk with as we rode to the Army Base. And, even though there could be no PDA between us, I enjoyed the feel of her lovely body next to mine as we chatted in Thai.

As I exited the bus at my Company Area, the few Thai soldiers who'd exited before me, came to attention and saluted me. Having recognized their CO's daughter and that we were clearly friends, they again presumed I must be an officer. Returning their salute, I walked my hooch, and drank a cold can of Bud, as I emptied my shopping bag, changed into my jungle fatigues and took 2 Aspirins, before walking to the Mess Hall.

Joining my hooch mates for breakfast and a cigarette, we talked about the newbies, and if Tommy's replacement would crash and burn on Saturday with the large number of circuit outages expected. Exiting the Mess Hall, I saw three ranks of newbies, with 10 in each rank, forming up behind the Air Base Squad, and heard Ronnie say, "It looks like a bunch of the FNGs are going to Crypto, or other support jobs as clerks or mechanics, which doesn't really leave that many for us."

Falling in with Air Base Squad, I thought, "Sure am glad I'm done with those Rabies shots, though my abdomen's still tender form getting 14 of them there."

After formation, I returned to my hooch and drank another cold can of Bud, as I changed into civilian clothes and put some clean clothes in my shopping bag, before leaving to board a Thai bus to Korat. Arriving at the Sri Pattana Hotel, I asked for an 11:00 wake-up call as I went to my room, where I put away my clothes and went to bed.

Waking at 11:00, I showered, shaved and dressed in clean clothes, before walking to the Jamsarang Hotel and taking Dhoi to the Ming Ter for lunch. After an enjoyable lunch with Dhoi, I escorted her back to work, before returning to my Hotel room and going back to bed for some more sleep.

Several hours later, I woke and dressed, and then walked to the Thai bar to eat a large bowl of rice noodle chicken soup, as I shared bottles of Sing Hăi Beer and talked with my Thai friends. After a couple hours of their comraderies, I walked the mile to the compound, and spent a couple of hours joking, talking and drinking Sing Hăi Beer with my workmates. At one point Bob asked, "So, Sandii, when are you going to bring Dhoi to the compound so we can meet her?"

I replied, "I don't think she'd enjoy coming here."

Glen interjected, "I agree, after we met her last night. Don't get me wrong. I think Dhoi's beautiful and friendly, but she has practically nothing in common with our tîi-lóks. She' not snooty or uppity, or anything like that. But, having been a Thai Army brat, whose father is a Colonel, and a widow with a child, her background is entirely different than our tîi-lóks. What was really fun to watch, is how the Thai troops acted around Sandii. After seeing him with their CO when he got on the bus, they gave him their seat, and then saluted him as he got off the bus at the Company Area."

I added, "And after I rode on the bus with Dhoi to the Thai Army Base this morning, when I exited the bus at our Company Area with some Thai soldiers, they also saluted me. I figured, since I was riding the bus with their Regimental CO's daughter, they believed I was an Officer, also," to which everyone laughed at the mistake in identity by the Thai soldiers.

Returning with everyone to our Company Area after the party broke up at 9:00, I went to my hooch and drank a cold can of Bud, as I readied myself for bed. Waking to the 5:00 bugle call for Reveille, I went through my normal morning routines, before leaving for the Mess Hall with my hooch mates dressed in our jungle fatigues. After breakfast, we left for morning formation, where Skip and I met Tommy's replacement as the Air Base Squad formed up. He was a 6-foot tall, skinny PFC named David Lewis. Jim detailed Mark, John's replacement, to take David to the Motor Pool to get his Military Driver's License before he started work that day with Bill, Skip and I at the Air Base Site to begin learning his duties in Operations Room, which he would need to know to hit the ground running when he joined Bill's Team with Saturday's cacophony of circuit outages.

During my 10:55 and 4:55 meal run, I bought more beer and cigarettes for my stockpile. While working our 12-hour day shift, we put David through his paces to be up to speed as much as possible for his baptism of fire in Saturday's usual mayhem. When I was relieved at 6:45, Mark drove me back to the Company Area, where I went to my hooch and spent a quiet evening playing Double-Deck Pinochle with Skip as my partner against Ronnie and Stony, while we drank beer and smoked cigarettes.

The next day, Friday, was spent much like Thursday, getting David up to speed on his familiarity with our 252 in-house circuits in preparation for the usual firestorm of circuit outages he'd be dealing with on Saturday. We also had a small change-of-command ceremony after the Shift Change Report in the Site Office, with Sgt. Frank Howell replacing Sgt. Jim Smith as the Site NCOIC, to which Frank happily said, "It's really great to be back in our home away from home."

On my 10:55 meal run, after I added the beer and cigarettes to my growing stockpile, I brought back fresh clothes in my shopping bag, and took a hot shower and shaved that afternoon in preparation to take Dhoi dancing after work. Relieved by Larry at 6:45, I rapidly left to catch a Thai bus to Korat, dressed in my civilian clothes to be ready for Dhoi when she came to my Hotel room at 7:30. After we'd lovingly greeted each other with a passionate kiss, and she was walking behind me to the night club, I thought, "This is very different than being with Julii and Súusîi, as they would've been eager for a bout of rapacious lovemaking when they entered my room to satisfy the pent-up lust within them before we went dancing."

Entering the night club, I led Dhoi to an empty table on the 3rd tier. While waiting for our Pepsi's to arrive, I saw Glen, Charlie and Steve arrive with their tîi-lóks behind them, and walk to our table, where we pleasantly exchanged sáwátdiis before they went to an empty table. When our Pepsi's came, we took a refreshing drink and went to the dance floor, where I had a delightful time watching my beautiful Dhoi as we gaily danced the evening away.

After we later danced an erotic Tango, we hastily returned to my Hotel room, where we impatiently removed our clothes as we passionately kissed. With Dhoi's luscious body exposed to me, I embraced her desiringly as I laid her back onto the bed, sliding fully into her hot, wet love canal as she eagerly raised her shapely legs wide to receive me. Undulating her voluptuous hips in anxious anticipation, I shifted her into a Kama Sutra posture, and we energetically made love until the orgasmic release of the lust we held within us.

Spooning with my strong arms lovingly holding her gratified body against me in the afterglow of our climactic rush, we passed blissfully into sleep.

Waking to the 3:30 knock on the door, we rejoined the desires we had, and rekindled our lust with passionate kisses and enticing caresses to enjoy the fevered lovemaking we ignited. With our renewed lust satiated with orgasmic release, we playfully washed each other in the shower. Dressing in my civilian clothes, I thought, "I can't ever let anyone in Korat see me again in my uniform, as someone will see that Dhoi is dating an Enlisted man, which will surely get back to her mother and put a major damper on our relationship."

Leaving my Hotel room, we lovingly embraced and kissed before walking to the Hotel's entrance, where I hired a săawm-law to carry us to the Chainarong Gate bus stop. Riding a Thai bus together, we made plans to have lunch that afternoon. And, as Sunday was her day off, she'd spend the morning with Mii-kâa before we met in my Hotel room at noon to go to lunch and see a Japanese Samurai movie. Then, we'd have dinner at her home so Mii-kâa could get used to seeing me before she travelled with us for a day at the Kâo Yái National Park the following Sunday.

Exiting the bus at the Company Area, I had the same encounter with the Thai Soldiers saluting me as I stepped off the bus. Going to my hooch, I went through my routine of drinking a cold can of Bud, as I dumped laundry from my shopping bag and changed into a fresh set of jungle fatigues before walking to the Mess Hall for breakfast and attending morning formation.

Returning to my hooch after formation, I changed into clean civilian clothes and left for Korat. Entering my Hotel room, I stripped to my skivvies and slept for several hours, before getting dressed and taking Dhoi to lunch at the nearby Ming Ter. After enjoying lunch with Dhoi and escorting her back to work, I returned to my Company Area, and had an entertaining afternoon playing Double-Deck Pinochle with Skip as my partner against Ronnie and Stony, while drinking beer and smoking cigarettes.

When the bugle sounded Mess at 5:00, we finished playing the hand and settled our debts before changing into our OD BDUs and leaving for dinner in the Mess Hall. As Mark stopped the truck in front of the Day Room, he told Skip and me, "I really appreciate all the work you two did trying to get me up to speed, because all hell broke loose this morning with circuit outages."

Getting into the truck, Skip and I laughed when Skip responded, "Well, don't think you're over the hump on Sunday, because Monday nights are usually busier, with everyone Stateside getting back to work after having the weekend off," as we left for the Air Base Site.

Arriving in the Operations Room, I relieved Larry and took over the circuit outage he'd been working on, while Skip drove him to the Company Area. As we remained moderately busy through most night, so we weren't able to get any nap time in. When I delivered the truck to Frank in the Motor Pool on my 6:35 meal run, he said, "To bad you have to work tonight and miss the farewell party for Jim and the others leaving tomorrow. However, I really appreciate the work you and Skip did getting Mark up to speed for Saturday. For a newbie, he did pretty good helping with the circuit outages yesterday."

After eating breakfast, I took three 6-packs of Bud and packs of Pall Malls from my stockpile, and passed them out to Tommy, Ronnie and Stony, who were thankful to have some beer to drink and cigarettes to smoke while they played Double-Deck Pinochle that afternoon. Then I drank a cold can of Bud as I changed into civilian clothes and put clean clothes in my shopping bag, before I left to catch a Thai bus to Korat.

Leaving a wake-up call for 11:30 at the Hotel's Reception Desk, I went to my room. There, I stripped to my skivvies and slept till I heard the knock on my door. As my abdomen was now healed from the fourteen Rabies shots, I was able to rise quickly to shower, shave and be dressed by the time Dhoi knocked on my door.

After we lovingly embraced and kissed, she followed me to the cafe where Lompét had worked on Mahat Thai Road, as it was near the Action Theater on Wacharasrit Road, and it added variation from the Ming Ter for eating lunch. When we'd finished our delightful, little lunch, it was a short walk to the Theater, where I enjoyed Dhoi holding my left upper arm, while we watched the action packed, Japanese Samurai movie.

When the lights came on as the movie ended at 2:30, Dhoi coyly said, "My darling, we have two hours before we need to catch a bus to my home for dinner. Maybe we can return to your room and relax while we wait."

I responded with a knowing smile, "What a very good idea, my darling," as I led the way out of the Action Theater and back to my Hotel room."

With plenty of time before we needed to leave, we playfully kissed and caressed each other leisurely with our foreplay, and thoroughly enjoyed our lovemaking in a fun Kama Sutra position. When we'd experience the thrill of our climactic rush, we spooned together in our euphoria, and Dhoi cooed, "My darling, you really know how to make my afternoon with you perfect."

After enjoying our fun shower together and had dressed, we lovingly embraced and kissed, before leaving to ride a săawm-law to the Chainarong Gate bus stop. As we rode the half-empty Thai bus to the Thai Army Base, we discussed what Mii-kâa should call me, since she would be with us frequently, and it was inappropriate for a child to call an adult by their name.

The problem was, because the Thai culture was highly structural and family oriented, the family relationship titles depended not only on their age relationship, but also on which side of the family lineage one belonged. For instance, there wasn't a Thai word for "brother" or "sister," but "pîi-chaai" for an older brother, "náawng-chaai" for a younger brother, "pîi-sâao" for an older sister, and "náawng-sâao" for a younger sister. We decided the most proper title for me would be an uncle who was Mii-kâa's father's younger brother, or "aa."

When we arrived at the home of Dhoi's father, and Mii-kâa ran happily into her mother's arms to greet her, Mii-kâa looked at me suspiciously and Dhoi said, "Mii-kâa this is your Aa Sandii."

CHAPTER 52

BEING WITH DHOI AND MII-KÂA, IS LIKE BEING A FAMILY

After a delicious, home-cooked Thai dinner, the Colonel and I talked at the table, as we drank the bottle of Sing Hăi Beer from glasses and smoked his American menthol cigarettes. As he always wore his uniform, I could only think of him as "the Colonel". Meanwhile, Dhoi and her mother cleared the table, washed the dishes and had their own gabfest in the kitchen part of the large front room of the home. When we exchanged sáwátdiis as I left, little Mii-kâa made the wâaí, bowed and said, "Sáwátdii, Aa Sandii."

The Colonel again escorted me to the bus stop, and I said, "You honor me with your presence to walk with me to the bus stop, Father," as in the Thai culture, an older man is often addressed as "Father".

He laughed and responded, "Thank you, Sandii, but it's just an excuse to get out of the house and away from the clucking of two hens. Besides, now that you'll include my granddaughter in your activities with Dhoi, I'd like to know your intentions with Dhoi, though she's free to do what she wants, with whoever she wants. And, I'd like an honest answer."

I replied, "Truly, Father, my intentions are honorable. I've been here six months and have fallen in love with three other Thai women. The first woman, the father married her to another man. The second woman, the father didn't want her married to an American and go to America to possibly not be seen again. And the third woman, the father moved to Bangkok due to business, and she had to go with him. After those bad experiences, I decided to find an independent woman, whose father couldn't take away from me, and Dhoi's that woman.

"I've requested a 6-month extension of duty here. So, I'll be here for another year. If I reenlist, I'll be here an additional year. If I don't reenlist, I'll go to University on the GI Bill to earn a 4-year degree in Electrical Engineering, and if I can find a job here, I'll move back to Thailand. As for whether or not we get married, that'll be Dhoi's choice."

He responded seriously, "And her mother's choice. If she finds out you're an Enlisted man, that will be intolerable to her, and she'll find some way to separate you two. Well, here comes the bus. Thank you for your candor, Sandii. And, like I said, Dhoi's free to do what she wants, with whoever she wants," as we exchanged sáwátdiis before I boarded the Thai bus.

Exiting the bus at my Company Area, I exchanged salutes with the Thai soldiers who got off the bus before me, and walked to my hooch. There, I drank a cold can of Bud, as I changed into a fresh set of OD BDUs, and set the beer and cigarettes on George's bed, before carrying my tape deck to the front of the Day Room to wait with Skip and his tape deck for our ride to the Air Base Site.

When David arrived with the truck, he told us everything had been thankfully quiet in the Operations Room, as he exited the truck and we carefully set the tape decks in the middle of the cab's bench seat. Carrying our tape decks to the back of the Operations Room, I relieved Chuck, who rapidly left for his home in Korat, while Skip set up the tape decks and began the process of copying the taped albums he'd brought from the Base Library. After Bob finished with Shift Change Report, things were quiet with nothing happening in the Grand Canyon, except for Skip or I going to the back of the Operations Room to check on the progress of copying the albums.

About 4:00, Ted called to let us know he had a line up with Rosey, and we each had a turn to call our families and girlfriends Stateside. It was really great to talk with Linda, and then my parents, to hear how everyone was doing, and telling them about the changeover in staff, with guys rotating Stateside and the few newbies arriving, which was still leaving us shorthanded with people who needed to learn the ropes on how things were actually done at a Radio Site.

Returning from my 10:55 meal run, I discussed with Bob that my room rental at the Sri Pattana Hotel expired tomorrow night and was deciding whether to keep it simple and rent the room for another month, which would cost me $37.50, or just on a needed basis, which would be on my off days and when I worked the day shift. The latter method would be a hassle, as each week I'd have to register with the Reception for four nights and get a different room each time, but would save me about $12.50 a month. Bob recommended, "If I were you, and being paid only $200 a month, I'd be more fugal, as $12.50 can go pretty far in Thailand. Plus, what if something happens to you or Dhoi? Then, you'd be out for the cost of the remaining days when we won't be using the room."

After taking my tape deck back to my hooch and delivering the truck to Tim in the Motor Pool on my 6:35 meal run, I ate breakfast in the Mess Hall and returned to my hooch. There I drank a cold can of Bud, as I changed into civilian clothes, and passed out beer and cigarettes to George, Tommy, Ronnie and Stony. Then packing some clean clothes in my shopping bag, I left the hooch to catch a Thai bus to Korat.

Arriving at the Sri Pattana Hotel, I rented the room for two more nights, as I planned to use it Tuesday to nap between when I took Dhoi to lunch and going to the Thai bar, and on Wednesday, after I took Dhoi dancing. Requesting an 11:00 wake-up call, I walked to my room, unpacked my shopping bag, stripped to my skivvies and went to bed.

Waking at 11:00, I showered, shaved and dressed, before walking to the Jomsurang Hotel and taking Dhoi for a delightful lunch at the Ming Ter. There, she agreed to go to dinner with me before we went dancing at the night club, which would save her the time to go home for dinner and return to Korat. After escorting Dhoi back to work, I went to my Hotel room and slept till 5:30.

After several hours of sleep, I took a quick, refreshing shower, dressed and waited for Dhoi's knock. On opening the door, we embraced and kissed passionately. Then, she pushed me gently away and said, "My darling, I desire you very much," and looking down at the bulge in my pants, she laughed and added, "and I see it is the same with you," as she unfastened my pants.

When our vigorous lovemaking climaxed in the release of our lust, we happily washed the crud off the other, dressed and walked to the Thai BBQ Chicken restaurant at the North end of Rajadomnern Road. Having feasted on the "little bit spicy" bird, we strolled to the near-by night club, and happily spent the evening gaily dancing together, until I performed my sensuous Tango with Dhoi. Then, we anxiously returned to my Hotel room, rapidly stripped off our clothes, and thrust ourselves passionately onto the bed in a torrent of lovemaking. With the orgasmic release of our consuming lust, we happily spooned in its afterglow and passed contentedly into sleep.

With the 3:30 wake-up call, Dhoi and I again aroused our lust, as we enticingly pleasured each other in sensuous foreplay, and enjoyed a sexually stimulating Kama Sutra position that increased our climactic rush. After we'd enjoyed the pleasant feeling of our orgasmic release for a while, we showered playfully together and dressed, before we lovingly embraced and kissed as we left. Walking to the Hotel's front entrance with Dhoi and carrying my shopping bag of laundry, I hired a sǎawm-law for our ride to the Chainarong bus stop. Boarding the crowded Thai bus, two Thai Soldiers quickly stood and offered us their bench seat, and thought as I sat down, "Dating the Colonel's daughter sure has its perks."

Exiting the bus at my Company Area after the two Thai Soldiers and returning their salute, I thanked them for being generous to their CO's daughter, as I walked to my hooch. There, I changed into my jungle fatigues and emptied my shopping bag, while I drank a cold can of Bud, before going to the Mess Hall for breakfast and then to morning formation.

After formation, I returned with Skip to our hooch, and dank another cold can of Bud, as I changed into civilian clothes, put some fresh clothes in my shopping bag, and passed out beer and cigarettes to George, Tommy, Ronnie and Stony, before leaving for Korat. Entering my Hotel room, I put my clothes away, stripped to my skivvies and went to bed for a few hours of sleep.

Upon my waking, I showered, shaved and dressed, then took Dhoi to the Ming Ter for a delightful lunch. Escorting Dhoi back to work,

I then returned to my Hotel room for my regular nap before going to the Thai bar. There, I had my usual large bowl of rice-noodle chicken soup to eat, while I shared bottles of Sing Hăi Beer and enjoyed the camaraderie of my Thai friends. At 6:00, I exchanged sáwátdiis with them, as I left to spend the rest of the evening with my compatriots at the compound. As we talked and drank Sing Hăi Beer, we mostly listened to Tom grousing about his early orders to fly on a military transport to Bangkok.

Leaving at 9:00 with everyone else, I returned to our Company Area and my hooch, where I drank my usual cold can of Bud, as I got ready for bed. Rising at 5:00 to the bugle call for Reveille, I went through my usual process of drinking a cold can of Bud, as I used the piss tube and dressed in a fresh set of jungle fatigues, before going to the Mess Hall with my hooch mates for a leisurely breakfast and cigarette, as we waited till it was time to go to morning formation.

After formation, Skip and I rode in the back of the ¾-ton truck to the Air Base Site. There, we spent a comfortably busy Wednesday in the Operations Room tracing several circuit outages as they were called in. On my 10:55 and 4:55 meal runs, I bought more beer and cigarettes for my stockpile. And during my 4:55 meal run, I set a 6-pack of Bud and pack of Pall Malls on George, Tommy, Ronnie and Stony's beds, bringing back with me a change of civilian clothes to wear after I showered and shaved before being relieved at 6:45.

When I was relieved, I quickly left to catch a Thai bus to Korat and meet Dhoi at my Hotel room to go dancing at the night club. After a wonderful and fun evening dancing together, we danced a sensuous Tango and left quickly for my Hotel room. When we'd quenched the flames of lust the Tango had ignited in us with our climactic rush, we blissfully slumbered in the afterglow of our passionate lovemaking.

Roused by the 3:30 wake-up call with the feel of Dhoi's warm, sensuous body snuggled in my arms, I enticingly kissed the nape of her lovely neck and caressed desiringly the womanly curves of her voluptuous body. Rolling over in my arms, she moaned with delight as I pleasured her round breasts with my mouth. When our lust was fully aroused, we enjoyed the vigorous lovemaking that ensued in a Kama Sutra arrangement, resulting in the climactic rush through our beings. Basking in the afterglow of our lovemaking, we expressed our growing love.

After we playfully showered together and dressed, I filled my shopping bag with the possessions I had in the room. Then, we lovingly embraced and kissed, before leaving the room and walking to the Hotel's entrance, where I hired a săawm-law for our ride to the Chainarong bus stop. Riding together on a Thai bus, we chatted happily till she exited on the Thai Army Base. Getting off the bus at my Company Area, I returned the salute of the Thai soldiers who left before I did, and walked to my hooch. There, I drank a cold can of beer as I emptied my shopping bag, changed into a fresh set of jungle fatigues, and put a 6-pack of Bud and pack of Pall Malls on George and Tommy's beds. Then, I left for the Mess Hall to have breakfast with my hooch mates prior to morning formation.

After formation, Skip and I rode in the back of the ¾-ton truck to the Air Base Site, where we spent a routine day in the Operations Room running down the few circuit outages that were called in during my 10:55 and 4:55 meal runs, I bought the usual beer and cigarettes from the Howard Johnson to add to my dwindling stockpile. When I was relieved at 6:45 and driven back to the Company Area by Mark, I went to my hooch and drank a cold can of bud, as I gave a 6-pack of Bud and pack of Pall Malls each to Ronnie and Stony. Taking off my fatigue shirt and combat boots, the rest of the evening was spent with Skip and I partnered against Ronnie and Stony, playing Double-Deck Pinochle, as we drank beer and smoked cigarettes. At 10:00, the debts from the game were tallied and we went to bed.

Waking to the 5:00 bugle call for Reveille, I went through my routine of drinking a cold can of Bud, as I used the piss tube and dressed in a fresh set of jungle fatigues, before going to the Mess Hall with my hooch mates for breakfast, and then to morning formation. After formation, we returned to our hooch to each consume a cold can of beer, as I gave a 6-pack of Bud and pack of Pall Malls to Tommy, Ronnie and Stony. Then, I stripped to my skivvies, turned on my fan and went to bed.

Rising to the 11:00 bugle call for Mess, I drank a cold can of Bud, as I put on civilian clothes and left to catch a Thai bus to Korat. Walking to the Jomsurang Hotel, I then took Dhoi to the Ming Ter, where we enjoyed each other's company over a delicious lunch of náam dók, a spicy salad with sliced meat.

Finishing our lunch, I escorted Dhoi back to her work, where I chatted with Dhoi and Suumii for a while. While walking to the Chainarong bus stop, I thought, "The cost of this round-trip excursion and to take Dhoi to lunch is less than a Dollar, and well worth the pleasant hour I get to spend with Dhoi."

Returning to my hooch in the Company Area, I was told by Tommy that Skip had gone to the Air Base Library to check out some taped albums for us to copy at work that night. So, I spent the rest of my afternoon enjoying Tommy as my partner against Ronnie and Stony playing Double-Deck Pinochle, as we drank beer and smoked cigarettes. When the bugle call sounded Mess at 5:00, we finished the card hand and counted the debts for the games played to be settled on Pay Day, as everyone was broke but me. Changing into a fresh set of OD BDUs, I went to the Mess Hall for dinner with my hooch mates.

After dinner, Skip and I returned to our hooch and lugged our tape deck to the front of the Day Room, to take them with us to the Air Base Site. While in the hooch, I'd also set a 6-pack of Bud and pack of Pall Malls on George's bed. When David arrived with the truck, we carefully set the tape decks on the cab's bench seat between us to protect them, as I drove us to the Air Base Site.

Entering the Operations Room with our tape decks, we carried them to the back, as we relieved Chuck to go home to his tîi-lók. When Bob entered after Shift Change Report, we exchanged sáwátdiis with him and quickly returned to the back of the Operations Room to cross-connect our tape decks for the process of copying the taped albums Skip checked out from the Air Base Library, as Bob made the initial entries in the Site Log.

After a quiet Friday night, we left our tape decks at the back of the Operations Room when we were relieved, so we could copy the other taped albums Skip would check out when he returned the copied ones to the Air Base Library. Delivering the truck to Frank in the Motor Pool on my 6:35 meal run, I then had breakfast in the Mess Hall, before walking to my hooch and drinking a cold can of Bud, as I readied for bed.

Waking to the 11:00 bugle call for Mess, I drank a cold can of Bud, as I quickly dressed in civilian clothes, and gave Tommy, Ronnie and Stony a 6-pack of Bud and pack of Pall Malls each. Then wrapping some clean skivvies in a bundle, I caught a Thai bus to the Air Base

Site for a quick hot shower and shave, before boarding another Thai bus to Korat.

Riding a sáawm-law from the Chainarong bus stop to the Jomsurang Hotel, I met Dhoi at the Reception Desk and we walked to the Ming Ter for lunch. Making our final plans over lunch for our day-trip by taxi to the Kâo Yái National Park, she explained, "I think you should know how raising a small child in a Thai family works. As you may have seen, except for when Mii-kâa wants to play, one of us is always holding or carrying her. In the family oriented Thai culture, a child is always held by someone, so they can feel safe and wanted, until they're too big to be carried. If a child misbehaves, we simply put the child down until they agree to behave.

"This is unlike what I've seen with American children, who always shout 'no' to get their way. As you know, there is not a Thai word for 'no' that a Thai child can say if they want to be contrary. If they're not obliging, we set them down and ignore them until they decide to do what's expected of them. Also, we never scold or tell a child they can't do something. We might show them how it's unsafe to do somethings or call them back from a danger, but mostly they learn the limits of their surrounding from their experiences.

"I just want you to know these few things before we have my Mii-kâa with us on our day-trip. As a 2-year-old, she'll run around some of the time and not want to be held or carried. If you should want to carry her some of the time for me, it'll be most helpful, as she is now too big for me to carry all the time. Also, she'll be more accepting of you, if you carry her some of the time."

I cheerfully responded, "I'd be more than happy to carry our Mii-kâa most of the time, so you can better enjoy our day-trip together."

When we'd finished talking over lunch, I escorted Dhoi back to her work at the Jomsurang Hotel. There, the Hotel's concierge arranged the hiring of a taxi for our day-trip at 100 Bhat for the day, plus expenses, and to meet us at 8:00 in the morning in front of the Hotel.

Before returning to my hooch in the Company Area, I walked to the Sri Pattana Hotel to pay in advance the rent for the following four nights to have a place for Dhoi and I to spend the night after our day-trip and Tuesday night after dancing at the night club. Entering my hooch when I returned to the Company Area, I drank a cold beer and smoked cigarettes with my hooch mates, as I watched them play Double-Deck Pinochle until the bugle call for Mess at 5:00.

While they finished the hand they were playing, I changed into a fresh set of OD BDUs, and set a 6-pack of Bud and pack of Pall Malls on George's bed. After eating dinner in the Mess Hall with my hooch mates, I went to the Howard Johnson and bought beer and cigarettes to replenish the stockpile in my wall locker before going to the Day Room to wait with Skip for the Air Base Sites' truck.

Receiving the truck from Dave, we rode to work, where I relieved Chuck and took over tracing the circuit outage he'd been working on in the Grand Canyon. Meanwhile, Skip went to the back of the Operations Room with the new taped albums he'd brought with him and began the process to copy them before he came to the Grand Canyon. When Bob entered the Operations Room after Shift Change Report, he said, "Frank wants me to remind you that Monday morning you'll need to have all your personal gear packed for the Company's move to its new Area. Also, to get plenty of rest Sunday night, as the move'll probably be an all-day event for you. The guys working the night shift will only have to move their own beds, wall lockers and personal gear to their new digs, so they can get some sleep before they work the night shift again."

Skip cynically responded, "Well, at least that'll give us something to do Monday besides sleep and play cards all day, as most of us are too broke to do anything else."

We had a few residual circuit outages to work on through the evening, and after our midnight meal runs, Skip and I were able to get a couple of hours sleep. During my 10:55 meal run, I ate a quick meal with Glen, before we went to our hooch and quietly packed most of our personal gear into our duffle bags for Monday's move. I also filled my shopping bag with changes of clothes to take with me when I went to my new room at the Sri Pattana Hotel.

Skip and I decided to leave our tape decks at the back of the Operations Room until after Monday's move, to reduce the chance of being damaged during the move. Having showered and shaved first, I delivered the truck to Tim in the Motor Pool on my 6:35 meal run, and quickly ate breakfast in the Mess Hall. Then, walking rapidly to my hooch, I drank a cold can of Bud, as I hastily gave a 6-pack of Bud and a pack of Pall Malls to George, Tommy, Ronnie and Stony. After changing into civilian clothes, I grabbed my packed shopping bag, and left to catch a Thai bus for Korat.

Hiring a săawm-law at the Chainarong Gate, I soon arrived at the Sri Pattana Hotel, where I picked up my waiting room key, went to my new room, and put away the clothes in my shopping bag. Then, walking to the Jomsurang Hotel's Lobby, I saw Dhoi holding Mii-kâa on her left hip and a large bag of treats in her right hand. After we exchanged sáwátdiis, we went to the Hotel's front entrance and found the taxi driver standing next to a two-tone blue, 1950 Studebaker sedan.

Exchanging sáwátdiis with the driver, he said his name was Bancha, as I handed a red 100-Bhat bill for the day's rental. Then, I introduced Dhoi to Bancha as my "faan," which he could interpret she was either my girlfriend, fiancé or wife. As Dhoi was carrying a toddler, he'd naturally presume she was my wife, since what American would have a girlfriend with a small child. Also, he was picking us up in front of the Jomsurang Hotel, whose residents were all American families.

After my "family" climbed into the spaciously cushioned back seat, Mii-kâa moved onto Dhoi's lap, where she could see out the windows. Then, Bancha drove up Rajadamnern Road to its end at the wide Mittaphap Road that bordered Korat's northern moat. There, he turned left and drove on Mittaphap Road, which became Hwy 2 as it went West from Korat. It wasn't long before I saw Mii-kâa peacefully asleep in Dhoi's arms, and the next thing I knew, it was two hours later. Waking up when the car stopped at Kâo Yái National Park's Visitor Center, I paid the 10-Bhat parking fee and the 20-Bhat entrance fee for each adult.

In the Visitor Center, I learned the Park was huge. Covering 864 square miles in parts of four Provinces, it was one of the largest intact monsoon forests in mainland Asia, and was a UNESCO World Heritage Site. Rising to 4,432 feet at the summit of Kâo Rom, the Park's terrain covered four vegetation zones: evergreen rainforest, semi-evergreen rainforest, deciduous forest, and hill evergreen forests at the top. And besides the herds of elephants that roamed the Park, there were tigers, leopards, bears, gaur (the world's largest type of cattle), barking deer, otters, various gibbons and macaques, and large Burmese pythons. The Park's bird list boasted 392 species, including one of Thailand's largest populations of the colorful hornbills. Purchasing some leech socks at the Visitor Center, we hiked the 3-mile trail to the

Nong Pak Chi observation tower that overlooked a small lake and salt lick, reportedly the best wildlife-spotting place in the Park.

Fortunately, Dhoi had brought a bag full of snacks to fortify ourselves before we started our hike up a well-maintained trail. Dhoi carried Mii-kâa a half-mile up the trail before she became a little tired from carrying the extra twenty pounds and told Mii-kâa she could let me carry her or walk. Looking at me skeptically, Mii-kâa decided to walk. But after 100 yards, she held up her little arms to Dhoi to be carried. Again, Dhoi gave her the choice between walking or being carried by her Aa Sandii.

Mii-kâa hesitantly turned to me and held up her arms. Reaching down, I turned her around, placed my two large hands under her armpits from behind, and lifted her easily up and over my head, setting her on my broad shoulders. She gave a startled squeal as I did this, firmly grasping her arms around my head and her legs around my neck, when her bottom settled on my shoulders. Then, I heard her happily say, "Mother, look at me. I'm bigger than you."

From then on, Mii-kâa was very happy with her elevated point of view atop her Aa Sandii, as we continued up the trail, looking at all of the colorful birds flying around, monkeys sitting in the trees, and a few other animals on the ground and in the trees. Reaching the observation tower, we had fun for a half-hour watching the various birds and mammals coming to drink at the small lake, and a few elephants and deer attracted to the salt licks. Because of the altitude and being the end of January, the weather was sunny and pleasantly warm, which made our outing quite comfortable and enjoyable.

Three hours after we left, we returned to the taxi, sufficiently tired from our 6-mile walk with an appetite to match. Climbing happily into the taxi, Bancha drove us to Pak Chong, the District Capital, fifteen miles from the Park's Visitor Center, and stopped at a nice cafe for a sumptuous lunch. Then, driving us the fifty-five miles back to Korat and the Chainarong bus stop. I gave Bancha a 20-Bhat tip as we exited the taxi.

As the three of us had slept in the comfortable back seat of the taxi most of the 2-hour ride back to Korat, we were quite refreshed when we board a Thai bus for the Thai Army Base. Dhoi's parents were relieved we'd had a safe trip to and from the Kâo Yái National Park, and listened attentively to Mii-kâa as she excitedly babbled about what she'd seen at the Park, from her perch on top of her Aa Sandii.

After we'd had a typical Thai dinner of fried rice, cook with fresh vegetables, varied spices and chicken, Dhoi and I excused ourselves to leave and see a Japanese Samurai movie at the Action Theater. Actually, it was a ploy we'd discussed to go to my Hotel room for a relaxing evening of lovemaking, pillow talk and a comfortable night's sleep together, after a fun day as a family with Mii-kâa.

Waking to the 3:30 wake-up call, I enjoyed the appeal of Dhoi's sensuous body against mine, as we passionately kissed and desiringly caressed each other with enticing foreplay that aroused a firestorm of lust. After being consumed with wanton lovemaking in a sexually exciting Kama Sutra position that peeked with our orgasmic release, we enjoyed its ephemeral afterglow, holding and caressing each other with affection. A while later, we had fun bathing one another in the shower, before we dressed, and desiring hugged and lovingly kissed before we left.

Leaving my Hotel room, Dhoi walked behind me to the Hotel's entrance, where I hired a săawm-law, so we could talk some on our way to the Chainarong bus stop. Boarding a Thai bus to Camp Friendship, we sat on a bench seat and chatted happily about the success of our day-trip with Mii-kâa, how well she has now accepted me as part of the family, and our upcoming day-trip with Mii-kâa in two weeks to see the elephants in Bâan Tâa Klang.

Watching the enticing sway of Dhoi's slender, sensuous body as she exited the bus at the Thai Army, I mused, "Being with Dhoi and Mii-kâa is like having a family."

CHAPTER 53

IF YOU CAN ROLL IT, YOU CAN SMOKE IT

Exiting the Thai bus at the Company area, I walked to my hooch and drank a cold can of Bud, as I changed into a fresh set of jungle fatigues and put as much beer from my stockpile into the mini-fridge as it would hold, figuring the more we drink here, the less I'll have to carry later to the new barracks. Then walking to the Mess Hall for breakfast, I met up with my hooch mates, where all the talk was rumor and speculation about today's move, what life'll be like at the new Company Area, and how lousy the food's going to be at Camp Friendship's Enlisted Mess Hall.

Finishing breakfast, we went to morning formation where I saw Tom dressed in his Class-B Army khaki uniform, fuming about his orders to fly to Bangkok this morning and then Stateside tomorrow. After the usual rigamarole of each Platoon Sargent reporting "all present or accounted for," SFC Davidson faced us and said, "At ease, men. The plan of the day is, when I dismiss you, everyone working the day shift will have already emptied their wall lockers and will go directly to work. The rest of you, as the night shift has already been instructed to do, will go to your hooch, empty your wall lockers, place all of your personal gear against a sidewall, strip and breakdown your beds, and carry the bed frames, mattresses and mosquito netting out to the roadway, and load them onto the trucks. Then you'll load all of the tables and chairs. After you've unloaded them in the new barracks, you'll return to load all the wall lockers and mini-fridges onto the trucks. When those have been unloaded in the new barracks, you'll be shown your billet location and return to move your personal gear.

"Then, those who are working the night shift will have the rest of the day to get their personal area squared away and get some sleep before you go to work tonight. The day shift will be given a fifteen minute longer meal break to move their personal gear to their new billets. The rest of you will then be divided into work details to help move the Company's Supply, Armory, Motor Pool, HQ and Day Room to their new locations. Anything that's not moved today, will be moved tomorrow by today's day shift.

"As for meals. Lunch will be in this Mess Hall. After that, all meals will be in Camp Friendship's Enlisted Mess Hall. So, enjoy our lunch as much as possible, as from now on, you'll be eating Army chow. Platoon, dismissed."

Returning to my hooch with all my hooch mates, except Tommy, who was working the day shift, we all drank a cold can of beer, as we took off our jungle fatigue jackets and placed all of our personal gear against a sidewall. Then, we all drank another cold beer, as we stripped the bedding from the mattresses, which we piled by the front door. Next, we removed the mosquito net and supports from each bed frame, folded the bed's ends under the mattress support frame, and stacked them all by the pile of mattresses. We all then dank another cold beer, before we began the parade to carry the table, chairs, bed frames, mosquito netting, mattresses and bedding to the Company's roadway, where we loaded them into the back of one of the waiting 2½-ton trucks, from which the heavy canvas covers had been removed and the wood bench seats folded up, and the same items from other hooches were being loaded.

When that was finished, we returned to our hooch and drank another cold can of beer, before pairs of us carried the heavy, steel, double wall lockers out to the roadway and loaded them, with those from other hooches, into another 2½-ton truck, as those loaded with the beds had left to be unloaded. After which, we were directed to go to a transient hooch and do the same thing.

En route, we stopped at our hooch and drank another can of cold beer, as I refilled the mini-fridge with the rest of the beer in my stock-pile. After we had disassembled all the bedding, mattresses, mosquito netting and bed frames in the transient hooch, and carried it all to another truck, we stopped at our hooch and drank cold can of beer each. Then, we carried the heavy, steel, double wall lockers from the transient hooch to another truck on the roadway. With all of the hooches now stripped of everything but personal gear and mini-fridges, we were directed to bring our personal gear and the mini-fridge out to be loaded into a truck, where it and we would be driven to the new Company Area and shown where each of us was to be billeted.

Returning to our hooch for the last time, we drank a celebratory can of cold beer. As we carried our personal gear to load into the back of a truck, I took a 6-pack of Bud and a packet of Pall Malls and set it on top of George's duffel bag for him to get when he moved his personal gear during his extended lunch break. Before we carried our mini-fridge to the truck, we each drank a farewell can of cold beer to our hooch, and I put my several remaining cans of Bud into the cargo pockets of my jungle fatigue pants.

With our mini-fridge loaded in the back of the 2½-ton truck, I stood in the back, holding onto the top of the topside rack, and watched as the truck drove out to the main street, turn left and drive through the traffic-controlled intersection to the end of the street. There, it turned left onto the road that paralleled the perimeter fence, and then left again onto the wide strip of ground between the big drainage canal, and the basketball and hand ball courts, stopping across the concrete courtyards from the last H-type concrete building to my right.

There, SSG Zurligich approached us and said in his deep graveled voice, "Okay, men. Follow me to building NE402-A, where the Tropo Platoon is billeted. Each shift is housed together by their shift, and in their Teams, with the Team Leaders berthed at each end. This is to help with team cohesion, as most Team Leaders prefer to be housed with their Teams. The Air Base Team for each shift will be berthed between the Tropo's Microwave and Frame Tech Teams."

Entering Building NE402-A, which was the West Wing of an H-type building on a concrete base one foot above the ground, I saw a 30-foot wide room, with a 12-foot ceiling, that was 84 feet long. Six inches from the concrete floor, along each concrete wall, was an 8-inch high, wire-screened gap for ventilation as there were no windows in the walls. The same type of wire-screened gap ran along the top of the walls. At the far end of the room was a double-wide doorway to a 30-foot wide space with another double-wide doorway leading to an identical barracks room.

In our barracks room, I saw six pairs of opposite facing wall lockers extending from each sidewall, making semi-private, 2-man areas, except for a 1-man area at each end of the room for the Team Leaders. In each 2-man area, there were two stacks with a bed frame, mosquito netting, and bedding ready for assembly. Down the center aisle were three tables with four chairs each, and I thought, "So, they're fitting three 8-man hooches into one 24-man barracks room."

SSG Zuligich said, "Okay, men. Those of you who are off today, are on the right, and those of you working tonight are on the left. The first five beds on each side are for the Tropo Frame Tech Teams, the next two beds are for the Air Base Teams, and the last five beds are for the Microwave Teams. The night shift will have the rest of the day off to square away their gear and get some sleep before going to work tonight. The rest of you will be returning with the truck to HQ when your personal gear has been off loaded from the truck. Any mini-fridges you brought with you will be put in one of the spaces for the Team Leader's use. If there's no questions, then let's get going."

When I'd finished unloading my personal gear from the truck next to my unassembled bed, I helped Tommy carry the mini-fridge from our hooch into his space, we plugged it into a wall outlet, and put the several cans of Bud I had in my cargo pockets into it. Then, we went to the 30-foot square common room between the two barracks rooms, where there were four full-size refrigerators, each to be shared by the men of each shift. Looking to my right in the common room, I saw the Shower Room with porcelain sinks for shaving, the Latrine with porcelain flush toilets, and I thought, "At least I don't have to wait till I get to the Air Base Site to take a crap."

Returning to the Company's HQ with those who had the day off, we were divided into work details, and I was sent to Company Supply. There, I helped palletize stacks of boxes, crates and spools of wire, and secure them with rope, before they were forklifted onto the back of a 2½-ton truck and pushed forward on the truck's bed. While the truck was gone to be unloaded at the new Company Supply Room, another ruck backed up to the large doorway at the end of the Supply/ Armory building to be loaded with prepared pallets from the Company Armory, and we'd dismantle the emptied steel shelving onto pallets and fill other pallets with boxes, crates and spools of wire to be loaded when the truck returned.

Hearing the 11:00 bugle call for Mess, the Supply NCOIC gave us an hour for lunch. While eating our last meal in the General's Mess Hall with my old hooch mates and Frank, we talked about how the move was going on the work detail they'd been assigned to.

Skip described how he'd been moving the HQ and Day Room into one wing of an H-type building, with the HQ in the front area of the building that was divided into four rooms for the Mailroom, CO, XO, and even Spike having his own room for an Office. Also, the large room in the back area of the building not only had the Ping Pong, pool and card table, but a place with a large TV with new cushioned couches to watch it on, as AFTN would also begin broadcasting TV in a couple of weeks.

Then, Frank told how the other wing of H-type building that contained the HQ and Day Room, had been partitioned with 8-foot high walls into 2-man rooms for Sergeants and Spec-5s, and 1-man rooms for the Senior NCOs, with each room having its own mini-fridge. And, the 30-foot square room in the middle of the wing that led to the Shower Room and Latrine, was a TV lounge for the NCOs. Also, Spike had received permission from the CO to remain in his old doghouse, with a personal jeep to drive between HQ and his doghouse, as he'd be leaving in a month.

Ronnie said, "That's because he's afraid someone could easily whack him if he was living in the NCO barracks, even if he's living in his own partitioned room," to which we all laughed.

Glen groused, "You know what's really dumb, is the drive to the Tropo Site is still the same distance, even though we can see it from our new Company Area a half-mile away. To get there, we still have to ride the half-mile to the Camp's main intersection, the half-mile to the gravel road leading to the Tropo Site, then the half-mile to the Tropo Site. Why didn't they just build a half-mile road from the new Company Area to the Tropo Site and save us the extra mile to drive there?"

I replied, "That's because, if they did that, then you'd be driving straight into 50,000 watts of microwave energy and be cooked alive before you get to the Tropo Site. The one big problem we have is, I won't be able to continue providing beer and cigarettes to George, Tommy, Ronnie and Stony, without having to do the same for a everyone else in the Tropo Platoon living in the barracks. Doing it in an 8-man hooch is one thing, but in 48-man barracks is something entirely different."

Skip added, "The real pain in the butt for us working at the Air Base Site, is we'll have an extra mile further to get to and from work for meal runs, going to and from the Air Base Library to check out taped albums, and to and from Korat."

After eating lunch in our old Mess Hall, we went to the Howard Johnson, and each bought two cans of cold beer. Then, we walked to our old hooch, where we sat on the floor, leaned against a wall and rehydrated ourselves, before returning to our work details at noon.

When the bugle call sounded Mess at 5:00, we all climbed into an empty 2½-ton truck and rode to the Camp's Enlisted Mess Hall, which was a huge facility, designed to feed over a thousand troops at each mealtime. After the truck backed into a space in the parking lot at the front of the Mess Hall, I climbed down with the others, and walked to the Entrance doorway at the middle of the Mess Hall's front.

Entering the Mess Hall, I saw the dining area was at least 150 feet wide and 50 feet across, filled with square, white linoleum topped, metal tables with four chairs around each table. There were Exit doorways in each sidewall, and two chow lines down the center of the Mess Hall to two food service lines, enabling them to feed over a thousand troops in a timely fashion. At the food service line, I picked up a stainless steel tray, with the usual depressions to divide the food portions served, and a set of steel flatware. I also saw all of the food servers were Thai men, as were the cooks in the kitchen area under the supervision of the Army cooks.

Sliding my tray on the waist-high counter of the left-hand food service line, I saw the food selection was significantly varied and the portions served were substantial, and thought, "Though this is not as good as the short order meals at the General's Mess Hall, they do have stacks of sliced roast beef, ham, turkey and chicken, baked and mashed potatoes with gravy, a variety of cooked vegetables, and fresh salad materials and dressings to choose from. So, the win-loss columns in regard to food are about the same."

After filling my tray with a stack of sliced beef, ham and turkey, baked potato covered in brown gravy, and a fresh green salad smothered with Italian dressing, I poured three glasses full of chocolate milk from a long beverage bar at the end of the food service line, and sat at a table with Skip, Ronnie and Stony. Finishing our sumptuous meals, we each pulled a cigarette from our packs for a relaxing after dinner smoke. As we did so, several guys from the surround tables bummed cigarettes from us, and Skip said, "This is going to be a real problem with having a relaxing smoke after I eat a meal at the end of the month, as most everyone here will be bumming cigarettes because they can't manage their money and are broke."

I responded, "You're right, Skip, and I have a perfect solution from my Junior High School days. My PE teacher was a retired Marine Gunnery Sargent, who treated his boys PE classes like we were in bootcamp. He divided each class up into platoons of three 10-man squads each, like they did in the Marine Corps, and spent the first part of the school's term teaching us how to march around the gym. He said it provided us with the discipline to work as a team we'd later need when we were either drafted or enlisted into the military. We even had drill competitions between the platoons, executing all kinds of regular and complicated column and flanking maneuvers that we were graded on.

"Anyway, I belonged to a rather rowdy bunch of guys in my grade level, and he caught some of us one day out behind the school smoking cigarettes. After he chewed our butts about the harmful effects smoking would have on our physical performance in his class and in any sport we chose to play, he told us he knew he couldn't prevent us from smoking illegally. But if we were going to smoke, he wouldn't turn us in to the Principal for smoking on school property if he caught us again, providing we rolled the cigarettes ourselves, saying, 'if you can roll it, you can smoke it.' And, I became very adept at rolling my own cigarettes in Junior High School. Of course, when I graduated to Senior High School, I went back to smoking store-bought cigarettes.

"After we finish here, I'm going to our new barracks for a cold can of Bud, before going to the PX to buy some beer for my guys, and some paper and tobacco to roll cigarettes with. Then, when I light up a cigarette here in the Mess Hall, or anyplace else, and someone asks me for a cigarette, I'll just pull out the paper and tobacco, hand it to them and say, 'If you can roll it, you can smoke it'."

CHAPTER 54

WE TREAT THE GIRLS FOR THE BABIES THE GUYS GIVE THEM

When we'd finished smoking our cigarettes, the others went to our new barracks, while I walked to the nearby PX, and bought twenty-three cans of Budweiser, a packet of Z-Z Top cigarette paper, a tall, thin, 3-ounce can of Prince Albert Tobacco. Entering my new barracks room, I saw in the 1-man space to my right, Spec-5 Lewis Hopkins, who'd been promoted to replace Spec-5 Tom Lewiston as the Frame Tech Team Leader at Tropo for the X-shift, and was leaving for Korat, having just finished assembling his bed.

In the 1-man space to my left, I saw Tommy relaxing on his bed with his OD BDUs on, waiting to leave for his night shift, and I said, "Sáwátdii, Tommy. I've got five cans of beer to put in your fridge. How's it going?" as I put the beer in his mini-fridge and removed a cold can, which I opened with my church key and took a swig from.

Tommy replied, "Just waiting to go to work, Sandii. You know, this place might be set up for twenty-four men, but we're so short-handed, there's only sixteen occupied beds here, and that's if you count the half dozen guys who live in Korat with their tîi-lóks, like Lewis over there. I'm supposed to have four other men on my Frame Tech Team, but I've only got two, Scott Jones and Mike Williams, just like Lewis only has Glen and Stony on his Team. And, it's the same with the two Microwave Teams at the other end of our barracks. Hopefully, we'll get some more when the newbies arrive next week, as some of these guys rotate Stateside over the next several months, and we actually didn't get that many from the last two groups of newbies that arrived."

I replied, "I knew Tropo was short-handed, but not that much. The Air Base is okay for now, but that's only because everyone but Frank has arrived in the last six months, and Frank's leaving in four months. God forbid any of us get sick or injured and can't work. Well, I need to get this beer to Ronnie and Stony, and get my area squared away. Maybe we'll get a chance to talk tomorrow."

Taking a 6-pack of Bud and pack of Pall Malls each to Stony, who was alone in the first 2-man space on the right, and to Ronnie, who was alone in the fourth 2-man space on the right, I then took my last 6-pack of Bud in the full-size refrigerator on the same side of the doorway in the common room, which was labeled "X-SHIFT." Opening its door, I saw the top two shelves were labeled "MICROWAVE TEAM," the middle shelf was labeled "AIR BASE TEAM," and the bottom two shelves were labeled "FRAM TECH TEAM," as I put my 6-pack of Bud on the middle shelf.

The refrigerator on the other side of the doorway was labeled, "Y-SHIFT." Looking across the common room, I saw the refrigerators to the left and right of the doorway to the other barracks room were labeled "GEN OPS" and "Z-SHIFT," respectively, and thought, "Looks like every 2-man barracks space has their own refrigerator shelf assigned to it."

Walking back to the middle, 2-man space I shared with Skip, I helped him finish tying the mosquito net support poles to the ends of his bed and tie the netting to the supports, before we did the same to my bed. Then, we helped the others in our X-Shift area put together the spare bed their spaces. Returning to my bed, I unpacked my duffel bag into my wall locker, hugging my clothes on the hangers there, and asked, "Skip, do you think we'll still have Maan-daa as our mây-bâan?"

Skip replied, "It'd be convenient if we do, as I like the way she looked after us, and she has my key. But I doubt it, as everyone's been shuffled around. It'll be simpler for Porntit to assign the mây-bâan to a specific set of beds and let the chips fall as they may. I guess we'll find out tomorrow from the Y-Shift, as they'll be here while we're working the day shift."

Finished getting my area squared away, I took a hot shower, and then Skip and I partnered against Ronnie and Stony playing Double-Deck Pinochle, as we drank beer, and I practiced rolling cigarettes to smoke till 10:00. We then tallied our account to be settled on Pay Day, and got ready for bed. Turning off the lights to our barracks, I saw at each end of the room was a junction box with a tiple set of three-way switches controlling the three rows of fluorescent light fixtures that ran the length of the room, and that a light fixture at each end of the middle row remained on, so the room did not go completely dark.

Waking to the bugle call for Reveille at 5:00, I walked to the common room in my flip-flops and got a cold can of Bud from the middle shelf of the X-Shift refrigerator to drink, as I used the Latrine and then dressed in a fresh of jungle fatigues, putting the pack of Z-Z Top papers and thin can of tobacco in the left breast pocket of my fatigue jacket. Leaving with all the other X-Team members, I walked to the Camp's huge Mess Hall for breakfast. There, I saw the food service line had a large variety of fried and cooked breakfast foods in large, stainless steel food warming pans.

Ronnie, Stony, Skip and I sat at the same four-chair table to eat our breakfast. Finishing my meal, I pulled the papers and tobacco from my jacket pocket and began to roll four cigarettes. As I did so, a pair of MPs came and stood over me. When I'd passed the hand-rolled cigarettes to the others and we lit them, the MPs sniffed the air like a couple of bloodhounds in hope of a marijuana drug bust, to which we all laughed at their disappointed looks, as they walked away, including those siting at the tables around us. I also saw nobody tried to bum a cigarette from us as we leaned back and comfortably enjoyed my flavorful, hand-rolled cigarettes.

Finishing our cigarettes, we walked back to our Company Area and joined the Tropo Platoon as it formed up on the basketball court in front of SFC Davidson, who was facing away from our wing of the H-type building. After morning formation, the Y-Shift, who were now on their off day, and the Z-Shift, who had worked the day shift yesterday, were told to report to HQ for work details to finish moving all the material in the Company's Supply, Armory and Motor Pool that had not been moved yesterday. Meanwhile, those of us on the X-Shift were dismissed to board the vehicles parked behind us on the other side of the basketball court.

As Skip and I looked for our familiar ¾-ton truck to ride to the Air Base Site, Frank laughed and said, "I never liked driving that old, ¾-ton truck, and was able to talk our new Motor Pool NCOIC into issuing us a jeep as we'd be driving two miles further round trip to and from our Air Base Site, twelve times a day on our meal runs. And, as a jeep burns half as much gas as a ¾-ton truck, the lower amount of fuel used would decrease the amount his Motor Pool fund had to pay the POL for the gas we used."

Looking at the jeep Frank let us to, I said, "What a sweet ride," as we piled in. With Frank driving, he yelled, "Yahoo!" while he burned rubber from the rear tires on the basketball court's concrete surface, as he made a U-turn to drive in the direction of the Air Base, and said, "I better not hear of either of you doing that."

Entering the Operations Room, I relieved Chuck, who rapidly left for Korat. On my 10:55 meal run, I made a quick stop with the jeep at our old Company Area to buy twenty-three cans of Budweiser, and finding the Howard Johnson closed up, I drove to the PX thinking, "Of course, it's closed. There's nobody living here to buy stuff from it."

After buying the beer at the Camp's PX, I drove to the front of my barracks and quickly put some of the beer in my wall locker. Then, I walked to the Z-Shift's area, where I identified George's bed by the personal gear by the bed and left a 6-pack of Bud and pack of Pall Malls on his bed. As I walked passed Tommy's bed on my way out of the barracks, I left the same on his bed.

Driving the jeep to the Mess Hall's parking lot, I expertly backed the jeep into a parking space. Entering the Mess Hall, I joined the left of the two quickly moving chow lines to its food service line. Picking up a tray and set of flatware, I saw the warming pans were piled with cheeseburgers, hot dogs, French fries, and fried onion rings, and the ice-chilled pans were full of various sliced meats and sandwich toppings, and I thought, "Even if not the made-to-order food of the General's short order Mess Hall, the selection here is so much larger and you don't have to wait for it to be cooked."

Skipping my favored cheeseburgers, I got the fried onion rings, the makings to build myself a large Dagwood sandwich, and three glasses of chocolate milk. Spotting Glen sitting at a table with Ronnie, I joined them. As I sat at their table, Glen said, "You'll never guess who showed up at the Tropo Site for work this morning. Tom Lewiston. Not that anyone was surprised, as he's been saying since he got his departure orders that he's not leaving for Stateside till February 24th, at the end of his approved extension of tour. SFC Davidson wasn't even angry with him, as we're so short-handed. Tom said he didn't even board the C-130 for the flight to Bangkok. And now, he already has orders for departure next Monday, with SFC Davidson to personally escort him to the flight line and make sure he boards the C-130 to Bangkok."

When we'd finished eating, I saw Glen begin to take out a pack of cigarettes from the breast pocket of his fatigue jacket. As I took the makings for a hand-rolled cigarette from my pocket, I said, "Don't do that Glen. Half the smokes in your pack'll be gone before you can get one lit from all the broke guys sitting around us bumming them from you. Here, let me roll one for you."

Rolling three cigarettes for us to smoke, a pair of MPs appeared on either side of me. When I'd finished rolling them, and handed one each to Glen and Ronnie, we lit them and laughed at the MPs, as they disappointedly walked away after smelling the sweet odor of the pipe tobacco as it rose up in the smoke from our cigarettes.

Leaving the Mess Hall, I showed Glen and Ronnie the jeep we now had for the Air Base Site. As they marveled at the Army's version of a sports car, I said, "Wish I had time to drive you two to the Tropo Site, but I have to get back in time for Skip to make his meal run."

Returning to the Operations Room, I took over from Skip, as he quickly left for his turn to drive our little hot rod to the Mess Hall on his meal run. Talking with Bob, as we tested a suspect breakout circuit, I told him how I came to my decision to hand-roll my cigarettes, how well my ploy worked in the Mess Hall to stop others from bumming my cigarettes, the disappointed looks on the MP's faces when they didn't smell any marijuana after I lit them, and "even at ten cents a pack for cigarettes, I've already figured it costs half as much to roll my own cigarettes."

On my 4:55 meal run, I again made a quick stop at the Camp's PX to buy another twenty-three cans of Budweiser. Stopping at my barracks, I put a 6-pack of Bud and a pack of Pall Malls on Ronnie and Stony's beds. Putting the rest of the beer in my wall locker, I placed a change of civilian clothes in my shopping bag, which I hid under the jeep's driver's seat, before driving to the Mess Hall. After Glenn, Ronnie and I finished eating dinner, we again enjoyed seeing the disgruntled looks on the MP's faces when we lit my hand-rolled cigarettes. Ronnie laughed and said, "You think they'll ever get tired of watching you roll cigarettes and then be disappointed you're not using marijuana?"

I replied, "I hope not. I really enjoy watching them every time they make fools of themselves in front of everyone in Camp Friendship."

Driving back to the Air Base Site, I took a quick shower and shaved before Skip left on his 6:35 meal run and gave Larry and Mark the jeep at the basketball court. As soon as they relieved me, I quickly changed into my civilian clothes, before leaving to board a Thai bus for Korat to spend the evening happily dancing with my beautiful Dhoi at the nightclub, and then sleeping contently with her after our passionate lovemaking.

When we woke to the 3:30 wake-up, Dhoi exclaimed, "Your body's too hot! I think you're sick, my darling."

I laughed and responded, "My body is hot for lovemaking with you, my darling."

Dhoi said seriously, "That may be true, my darling. But, as much as I'd enjoy lovemaking with you now, I think you're sick, and should take a shower to cool your body, then see a Doctor at Camp Friendship. There are too many illnesses in Thailand that we survive easily, but your people die from. I love you too much to see you die. So, you see a Doctor right away, my darling, okay? If not for your sake, then for mine."

I replied, "I feel good, my darling. But, for your sake, I'll do as you say," and thought, "My dad always said, 'A man can never win an argument with a woman,' so why try and do it now. Besides, I do feel a little warm and crummy."

After Dhoi washed me down good in the shower, we dressed and lovingly kissed, before leaving my Hotel room for Chainarong bus stop to board a Thai bus. When she exited the bus on the Thai Army Base, I said, "If I'm sick, I'll let you know. I'm sure I'll be well enough next Saturday to take you and Mii-kâa to see the elephants at Bâan Tâa Klang."

After riding the bus all the way across Camp Friendship to my new Company Area, I exited the bus and walked to the Tropo Platoon barracks. Drinking a cold can of Bud, I set a 6-pack of Bud and pack of Pall Malls on George and Tommy's beds, and then changed into a fresh set of jungle fatigues. While Skip and I walked to the Mess Hall, he said, "Sandii, are you feeling all right? You look a little flushed this morning."

I replied, "Not you, too, Skip. Dhoi told me this morning I felt too hot to her, and I needed to see a Doctor."

Skip responded, "So, it's not just me, then. After we eat breakfast, you go straight to the Camp Dispensary, so you can be seen first at Sick Call, and I'll tell Frank what's going on. And, if you're sick, we'll be able to cover for you easy enough on the day shift."

I said, "You treat me like you're an old Jewish mother. But, I won't argue with you about it, and I'll see you after Sick Call."

Skip laughed and responded, "I learned from the best."

Entering the Mess Hall, I ate a large, healthy breakfast, before teasing the MPs with the hand-rolled cigarettes I made for Skip and me. Finishing my cigarette, I left the Mess Hall and walked the short distance to the Entrance door of the Camp Dispensary, which was adjacent to the Mess Hall. There, I was by far the first in line for Sick Call.

When the Entrance door to the Dispensary opened at 7:00, I was the first to give the white tunicked Medics at the chest-high counter my name, service number and medical complaint. Then, one of them went to their Record Room with my information. A moment later, the Medic returned with my Medical Record and led me to a Treatment Room. There, he handed my Medical Record to the khaki uniformed Doctor sitting behind the desk, as I sat on the exam table.

After the Doctor put a thermometer in my mouth, checked my blood pressure and my pulse, he removed the thermometer and said, "Looks like your temperature is a little high, at 101 degrees, but not bad. Your pulse and blood pressure are fine. Do you have any aches, pains or nausea?"

I replied, "No, Sir. I feel just fine."

He asked, "Have you recently been anywhere, other than Korat?"

I answered, "I went to the Kâo Yái National Park last Sunday to see the wild animals there."

He responded, "Maybe you picked up a flu bug there. Since you have no other complaints and a low grade temperature, I'll give you some Aspirin to bring the fever down and return you to duty. If you get any other symptoms, don't hesitate to return here for a reevaluation. If you still have a fever tomorrow, then report back for Sick Call. Any questions?"

Having no questions, he gave me a packet with a dozen Aspirin, telling me not to take more than two pills every six hours, and I left to catch a Thai bus for the Air Base. Exiting the bus at the Bas Exchange, I walked to our Radio Site, and reported for duty with Frank in the Site Office, telling him what the Doctor had said. Frank responded, "There's a lot of diseases in Asia we don't have Stateside, and I don't want you passing anything around to the rest of us here. So, I'm having Skip drive you back to the Company Area, where you'll be on bed rest for the remainder of the day. And, regardless of how you think you feel in the morning, I want you to report first thing to Sick Call to be medically evaluated. If you're still running a fever, I want you to call me from the Company HQ and remain on bed rest. Are there any questions?"

I didn't have any questions, so Frank led me to the Operations Room and told Skip to drive me back to the Company Area, and he'd cover in the Operations Room till Skip returned. Putting my jungle fatigues and other clothes in my Latrine wall locker into my shopping bag that I'd left there the day before, I left with Skip to drive me back to our barracks.

Entering my barracks, I drank a cold can of Bud, as I dumped out my shopping bag, stripped to my skivvies, turned on my fan and went to bed, where I soon went to sleep. Waking to the 11:00 bugle call for Mess, I drank a cold can of Bud as I dressed in civilian clothes, and then walked to the Mess Hall for lunch.

Entering the Mess Hall, I filled my tray with cheeseburgers and fried onion rings, and seeing Glen and Ronnie, I joined them at their table. While we ate, I explained to them why I wasn't at morning formation, and asked Glen if he could have Súpa go to the Jomsurang Hotel and let Dhoi know I'll probably be on bed rest for a couple of days before I can have lunch with her again. Glen said it was not problem, and after finishing our meals, we took great delight in my enticing some MPs into public humiliation with my hand-rolled cigarettes for each of us to smoke.

Before returning to my barracks, I walked to the Camp PX to buy twenty-three cans of Budweiser, of which I set a 6-pack with a pack of

Pall Malls each on Ronnie and Stony's beds when I returned. Then, I spent the afternoon with Tommy as my partner, playing Double-Deck Pinochle against two other guys from the Tropo's Y-Shift, while drinking beer and smoking cigarettes.

Later in the afternoon, six mây-bâan came into our barracks room, carrying armloads of clean and pressed clothes. I found the name of Skip and my new mây-bâan was Aida and gave her the combination to my padlock. She'd already received the key to Skip's padlock from Maan-daa. In a brief talk in Thai with her, I learned she was 24 years old, the mother of three children, and lived with her husband and his family, who took care of her children while she worked, which was the norm in the Thai culture.

Hearing the 5:00 bugle call for Mess, we finished the hand and tallied the debts, before they changed into their OD BDUs, and we all walked to the Mess Hall for a dinner. When we'd finished dinner, I watched guys at the nearby tables bum cigarettes from them, while I took out my cigarette makings and rolled a cigarette. As I rolled my cigarette, Tommy said with concern, "Sandii, are you crazy? You can't roll a joint in here," eyeing two MPs coming to our table.

I replied cynically, "Crazy like a fox. I'm not rolling marijuana but tobacco. As the guys from the nearby tables are broke and bumming your cigarettes, nobody has asked me for one. And, it's become a game I play with the MPs, who come over in hope of a marijuana bust and leave in humiliation, when the only thing they can smell, as I light my hand-rolled cigarette is tobacco smoke and not gunsha. So, I'm saving money and having a good laugh at the same time I'm smoking my cigarette."

When I lit my hand-rolled cigarette, the others at our table laughed with me at the disappointed looks of the MPs walking away from us. As Tommy and the others walked back to our barracks and waited for their ride to work the Tropo night shift, I walked to the Camp PX and bought 23 more cans of Budweiser, a box full of Z-Z Top packets of paper, and a 1-pound can of Prince Albert tobacco.

Returning to my barracks, I put a 6-pack of Bud in my wall locker, a 6-pack of Bud and pack of Pall Malls each on Ronnie and Stony's beds, and the remaining five cans of Bud in the refrigerator, as I removed a cold one. While drinking the cold can of Bud, I sat on my bed facing my wall locker, opened the 1-pound can of tobacco and refilled my 3-ounce tobacco can I'd been carrying around. Then, taking an apple I'd picked up from the Mess Hall's food service line and put in my pants cargo pocket, I cut half of it up into slices that I put in the 1-pound can to keep the tobacco moist, and ate the other half.

Though I felt the 101 temperature I was running all day, I didn't feel any of the aches or pains I normally had with the flu or a cold. After smoking a hand-rolled cigarette and finishing my cold can of Bud, I turned on my fan, stripped to my skivvies and went to sleep thinking, "Though it's a bit of a hassle to hand-roll a cigarette, I don't get the harsh chemical taste or smell of the store-bought cigarettes."

Waking when my day shift returned from work at 7:00, I told Skip about our new mây-bâan, Aida, and that Maan-daa, Súmat and Nitnói were also working in our barracks. Then Skip told me, "If you can't work the two night shifts, Frank said not to worry, as Larry can cover tomorrow night and Tim can cover the following night. So, how you've been doing?"

I replied, "I've been feeling warmer than normal, but none of the other symptoms I'd normally have with the flu or a cold. However, I am sleeping more. Probably from the energy I'm burning up with having a fever. You up for playing some Double-Deck Pinochle?"

Skip answered, "Sure, just give me a minute to get a beer and round up Ronnie and Stony."

After a pleasant evening playing Double-Deck Pinochle, drinking beer and smoking cigarettes, we went to bed at 10:00. Waking to the 5:00 bulge call for Reveille and still feeling warm from my fever, I drank a cold can of Bud, as I dressed in a fresh set of OD BDUs, and went directly to the Dispensary after eating breakfast in the Mess Hall. Being first in line for Sick Call, I was quickly seen at 7:00, but by a different Doctor, who told me the same thing as the previous Doctor, when the thermometer again showed my temperature was 101, and returned me to duty.

Taking the packet of a dozen Aspirins I was issued, I walked to the HQ and called Frank to let him know my temperature was 101 degrees. Cpt. Richards, seeing I was using the telephone in his HQ, asked me what was going on. When I told him a brief medical history of my current health, he said, "I agree with Sgt. Howell. You're to remain in your barracks on bed rest, so you're not spreading whatever bug you have to my other troops. If you still have a fever tomorrow morning, and you're not admitted to the Hospital, you're to report back to me. Do you understand? I don't want you around my Company Area day after day, spreading who-knows-what to everybody, and have my whole Company down sick."

I spent that day like the previous day, sleeping, eating lunch and dinner in the Mess Hall, after which I walked to the PX and bought twenty-three cans of Budweiser, giving George, Tommy, Ronnie and Stony each a 6-pack of Bud and pack of Pall Malls, and sometimes playing Double-Deck Pinochle, as I drank beer and smoked by hand-rolled cigarettes. The next morning, I went to sick Call and saw a third Doctor, who found I still had a 101 degree fever with no other symptoms and discharged me back to duty with a packet of a dozen Aspirins.

Following Cpt. Richards' orders, I walked to my Company's HQ and told Cpt. Richards what had happened at the Dispensary. He responded angrily, "This is intolerable! Sandii, you're just getting the runaround at the Dispensary. You come with me, and I'm going to straighten this out."

Leading me out of HQ and to his jeep, he drove me to the Dispensary, where he demanded to see my Medical Record. Under which the UCMJ, a Commanding Officer has a legal right of access to any Record of a person under his Command. Demanding to see the Doctor who'd treated me, the Medics, flustered at having to deal with an irate Captain, quickly produced my Medical Record and ushered the Doctor from the Treatment Room, who said, "What seems to be the problem, Cpt. Richards?"

He replied, as he shoved my Medical Record across the chest-high counter to the Doctor, "This man has had a 101 fever for three days. Why isn't he in the Hospital?"

The Doctor answered, "I'm sorry, Captain, but the Hospital Admission Regulations in a Theater of War is very specific. If a patient's temperature isn't 102 degrees or higher, we can't refer him to the Hospital for admission, we must return him to duty."

Cpt. Richards grabbed my Medical Record back from the Doctor and said, "I'll see about that, as he turned, and I followed him out of the Dispensary and to his jeep.

Driving to the Hospital, I followed him into the E.R., where he told the first white tunicked Medic he saw, "I want to see whoever's in charge here."

The Medic responded, "That'd be Dr. Chambers, Sir. I'll get him right away, Sir," as he scurried away.

Soon a Medical Officer, wearing the gold oak-leaf of a Major on the left collar of his khaki uniform, appeared and said, "I'm Major Chambers, Captain. What can I do for you?"

He replied politely, as he handed my Medical Record to the Major, "Specialist Lynch has been sick for three days with a 101 degree fever. All the Doctors at the Dispensary seem to be able to do is return him to duty with some Aspirin, which is supposed to reduce his fever, but hasn't done so. I've been putting him on bed rest to limit the possible spread of whatever tropical disease he has to the other men in my command. Now, I want to know what you're going to do about it."

The Major responded, "I agree with you, Captain. And Stateside, he'd have been admitted to a Hospital and put in isolation. But, we're in a Theater of War, and our Medical Regulations are designed to keep as many men as possible on duty. If you request it, I'll write in his Medical Record that I've determined his temperature is 102 degrees and have him admitted to our Hospital. But, I must advise you that this is an Army Field Hospital, which has a limited patient capacity that may require us to Medevac him to Tripler Army Hospital in Honolulu, Hawaii."

Cpt. Richards requested, "If that's what it takes for my man to get proper medical attention, then I'm asking you to determine he has a 102 degree temperature."

The Major responded, "Consider it done. Besides, I admitted a man several days ago with the same symptom of running a low grade fever for several days, and he's still on the Ward with a low grade temp, and we've no idea what's causing it. If this is the beginning of some Asian bug that's going around, then I'm giving the Doctors doing Sick Call a heads-up to refer patients with this symptom to the E.R., so we can find out what it is and the course of the infection."

As Cpt. Richards left, I was escorted by a Medic with my Medical Record down a hallway to the West side of the Hospital complex. At the end of the hallway, I saw to my left a large, windowed room with rows of white hospital beds extending from the windowed walls, most of which contained men. On the wall in front of me, I saw a large sign with an arrow pointing to the room that read "Ward A." To the right of this sign was another large sign with an arrow pointing to the right that read "Ward B."

Looking into Ward B, I saw the same hospital bed arrangement lining the windowed walls. But, instead of the beds containing men, many of the beds in Ward B had very pregnant Thai women in them, and I asked the Medic somewhat confused, "What's with all the pregnant women in Ward B?"

He laughed and replied, "That's the result when you have lots of horny, young American men mixed with lots of obligating, pretty women. As you know, from your first Health and Safety lecture, this Hospital Command regulates the prostitutes for Camp Friendship's STD Prevention Program, which includes providing birth control pills to the prostitutes. But, just like the STD Prevention Program doesn't prevent some of the guys from getting an STD, the birth control pills we issue to the prostitutes don't prevent some of the girls from getting pregnant. And, just like we treat the guys for the STDs the girls give them, we treat the girls for the babies the guys give them."

CHAPTER 55

Dhoi's Father Now Thinks Of Me As His Son-In-Law

Entering Ward A, we stopped at the Nurse's Station to the right of the Ward's entrance from the hallway. There, an Army Nurse, wearing an Army issued white dress and nurse's cap, took my Medial Record from my escort, opened it and said to the Medic sitting next to her, "Take Specialist Lynch to the Shower Room for a good scrub down, and put all his clothes in a Bio-Hazard bag and send them to the Laundry. Then, give him a hospital gown and slipper socks to wear, escort him to Isolation Room 2, and get his Intake Vital Signs. Be sure to wear your PPE[152], and use good isolation technique, as we don't know what he has or how contagious it is. But, whatever it is, you don't want to be exposed to it, or pass it around to our other patients."

The Medic put on a yellow paper gown, face mask and latex gloves, before escorting me to a room across from the Nurse's Station, where there was a small shower room. Holding out to me an open red plastic bag, I stripped and put all of my clothes in the red bag, except my com-

---

152   Personal Protective Equipment

bat boots, which he sprayed thoroughly with an aerosol disinfectant, and my personal effects that were inventoried, placed in a large manila envelope, and sealed closed.

Watching to make sure I lathered myself from head to toe in the shower with a small, green bar of soap, which he had me throw away before I rinsed off. He then handed me a towel, large open-backed hospital gown and pair of rubber-soled slipper socks to dry off with and wear when I finished with taking the shower.

Feeling half naked dressed in the gown and slipper socks, he led me down the aisle between the two rows of hospital beds, full of guys watching me, to a glass-enclosed room on the left at the far end of Ward A, with lettering on the glass door that read "Isolation Room 2" in large red letters. Entering the 12-foot square room, I lay on the hospital bed, and he checked my temperature, pulse and blood pressure.

As he left the room, he said, "I'll be back in a minute with the book cart. It has a good selection of books on it to choose from, which'll help with the boredom of being stuck in this room, if you need anything, there's a button on a wire by the headboard. Breakfast is at 6:00, lunch at 11:00, dinner at 5:00, and a bedtime meal at 10:00. You can walk around in the room, but don't leave the room at any time, unless told to do so. If you need to piss or crap, there's a bedpan under the bed. Also, there's a sink with soap and paper towels to wash with, and a glass to drink from."

Soon, the Medic returned with a 4-foot tall, library book cart, with three rows of books on each side. Opening the inward swinging door, he asked from outside the door, "What's your favorite type of book?"

I replied, "Mostly science fiction. You have anything by Isaac Asimov?"

After looking for a minute, he said, "Yea. I've got *I Robot* and some from the *Foundation* series."

I responded, "Give me *I Robot*, that'll be good for starters. Then I'll read the *Foundation* series," and thought, "It's a good thing I'm dyslexic, which makes some letters appear backwards or upside down if I try to read fast, or I'd just burn right through them."

While I spent the rest of my morning reading, Skip came dressed in civilian clothes for a visit, and asked through a speaking vent in the door, "Sáwátdii, Sandii. How's it going in there?"

I got up and replied, "Sáwátdii, Skip. It's great to see you. I'm able to catch up on my reading, though I could really go for a cold beer and a smoke."

He laughed and responded, "They actually patted me down to make sure I didn't smuggle anything in to you."

I said, "Could you do me a favor? My girlfriend, Dhoi, knows I'm sick, but would you have Frank go by the Jomsurang Hotel, where she works at the Reception Desk, and let her know I'm in the Hospital and doing okay. It'd be nice for her not to worry, as it'll be a few days before I can see her again."

Skip responded, "Mâi bpén rai. In fact, I'll go to Korat after lunch and do it myself."

I then gave Skip the combination to my padlock and asked him to divide up the beer and cigarettes in my wall locker between George, Tommy, Ronnie and Stony. After a little while, Skip was told he had to leave, and I went back to reading *I Robot* on the bed. For lunch, I was served a tuna fish sandwich and a green salad on a covered thermal plate. At 5:00, the Medic brought in thermal plate loaded with roast beef, mashed potatoes and gravy, and mixed vegetables. And, for my bedtime snack, it was a thick, turkey sandwich, and I thought, "At least the Hospital food here is plentiful and good."

Before each meal, they checked my vital signs, and gave me two Aspirin to try and reduce my persistent 101 degree temperature. I also found out the guy in Isolation Room 1, across the way from me, had the same problem of running a low-grade temperature as I did, and had been admitted a few days before me.

I was woken at 5:00 in the morning by a Medic dressed in PPE, who checked by vital signs before giving me two Aspirin with a break-fast of scrambled eggs, sausage patties and a glass of white milk. As he did this, I saw other Medics and a Nurse wearing PPE, who were carrying blankets and heating pads into Treatment Room 1, and asked, "What's going on with the guy next door?"

He replied, "He's been running a low-grade fever, like you, but when I checked his vitals this morning, he was lethargic, and his temp was only 93 degrees. They're trying to warm him back up before his temp drops much more and he dies from hypothermia. I guess, we'll be keeping a much closer watch on your temp in case the same thing happens to you."

Later, after watching the activity with Medics, Nurses and Doctors dressed in PPE going in and out of the room across from mine, a Doctor wearing PPE came into my room and said, "Mr. Lynch, I'm sure you've seen all the activity with the patient in the room across from you. As you may be aware, he was admitted to the Hospital a few days before you, complaining of having a low-grade fever for several days, just like you had. Not bad, but certainly not good, either. It appears the part of his brain for controlling his body temperature had caused his body temperature to rise a few degrees to fight an infection in his body, which is normal and good.

"Now, it seems the continued elevated temperature has caused the brain's control mechanism to fail, and his body temp dropped dangerously low over night. I've ordered, from now on, to have your temperature checked every hour, and if it drops below normal, we'll be able to treat it sooner, and stop it from dropping too low, like his did.

"Since this appears to be some sort of local epizootic disease of unknown etiology to us, we're bringing in a local doctor to help us get a more specific diagnosis. And, as you both recently visited the Kâo Yái National Park, we're putting out a Health Warning to all military commands that the Park is 'Off Limits' until further notice."

I laughed and said, "So, you're telling me that I've got 'a touch of the epizootic.' When I was a kid and sick with the flu or a cold, my Mom always said that I had 'a touch of the epizootic.' I can't wait to tell her it's an actual disease."

Later that morning, I saw a Thai Army Doctor go in an examine the patient in the room across from mine. Then, he came into my room and begin to examine me, and I asked in Thai, "Doctor, what kind of sick do I have?"

He replied in perfect American English, "You speak pretty good Thai, Mr. Lynch. And, to answer your question, it appears you and your neighbor have an avian or bird flu. It's not uncommon around here and have a few cases around Korat occasionally. It can be fatal, but fortunately it doesn't appear to be easily transmitted between humans, just from birds, usually in the wild. The Doctors here want to keep you in isolation to be on the safe side, though I told them it's not necessary.

"I'll be back every day to check on you and make sure you don't have any other of our local diseases. Your fever should break in a day or so, and after you've stabilized, you'll be discharged back to your normal duties. Sáwátdii, Mr. Lynch."

I responded, "Sáwátdii, Doctor, and thank you for the encouraging news."

After lunch, Frank stopped in to see how I was doing, and to let me know he was keeping Dhoi appraised of my condition. Also, that today was Pay Day, and the CO was keeping my pay in his Office Safe till I was discharged from the Hospital. Then, I told Frank what the Thai Army Doctor had said, for which he was happy to hear it wasn't contagious between humans, and would pass that to the CO. I also thanked him for keeping Dhoi informed, and that I should be back to work in a few days.

The next day, I watched the guy in the other room happily dress in his jungle fatigues and leave.

After having my temperature checked every hour, on the hour, for two days, on Tuesday, my temperature dropped to 97 degrees. They put a surgical, full length, heating pad under me and another one over me, with several blankets on top of that, and used an electronic rectal monitor to keep a close watch on my body's core temperature, which stopped dropping at 95 degrees.

On Wednesday afternoon, I was declared "stabilized" and happily dressed in my OD BDUs, as I was discharged from the Hospital. On my way to HQ to get my pay from the CO, I stopped in my barracks and drank a celebratory cold can of Bud with Skip, Ronnie and Stony, as they were playing Double-Deck Pinochle with Larry, who was very happy he wasn't going to need to cover for me the following night.

They told me that SFC Davidson had escorted Tom Lewiston to the Air Base, and made sure Tom was on the C-130 when it flew to U-Tapao Air Base. But, the following morning Tom showed up at the Tropo Site, ready for work, explaining he rode the bus to the Hotel in Bangkok with the others on the flight, and then boarded a train back to Korat that afternoon. Now, he'll be taken by an MP under guard on the C-130 to U-Tapao Air Base and then driven to Bangkok next Monday, who'll put Tom on the plane Stateside the following morning to make sure he leaves.

I asked, "Do you think he'll fly Stateside then?"

Stony laughed and said, "Tom's been my Team Leader since I arrived here, seven months ago. And, knowing him all that time, I'll give five to one odds he'll find a way to be back at work the next day," and he had no takers.

Ronnie said, "Speaking of people leaving last Monday morning, that night, a big bunch of FNGs arrived here. We must've had two dozen of them fall in behind our Tropo Platoon at formation this morning. With any luck, we'll be getting some to fill the holes in our Teams at Tropo."

I replied, "Well, it's about time if they do. But, I need to go to HQ and get my pay."

Finishing my Bud and a hand-rolled cigarette, I reported to HQ that I was back to full duty and signed for my $220 in pay that Cpt. Richards brought from his Office. Paying Miss Porntit my $8.00 monthly housekeeping fee, I returned to my barracks, where Ronnie and Stony each gave me $10.00 for the beer and smokes I'd provided while they were broke, and Skip handed me $20.00 from George and Tommy for the same service.

Stripping to my skivvies, I showered and shaved, before I drank another cold can of Bud, as I dressed in civilian clothes. Putting $200 in my tobacco cash can, and left to catch a Thai bus to the Bank on the Air Base. There, I deposited $50 in my Savings Account and exchanged another $50 for 1,000 Bhat, before walking across the road to the Air Base Site to let Frank know I'd been discharged from the Hospital and would be working my shift that night. With this news, Frank said, "Tim'll be glad to hear he doesn't have to work a night shift on one of his off days."

Leaving the Air Base Site, I caught a Thai bus to Korat, where I walked to the Jomsurang Hotel and happily surprised Dhoi. After chatting with Dhoi and Suumii about my hospital experience for awhile, and letting Dhoi know I'd meet her tomorrow for lunch to make final plans for our day-trip with Mii-kâa on Saturday to see the elephants at Bâan Tâa Klang, I left to catch a Thai bus back to Camp Friendship.

Exiting the bus at the Camp's PX, I bought 23 cans of Budweiser, which I carried to my barracks. Putting the 5-pack of Bud in the refrigerator, I opened a cold can of Bud to drink, as I put the three 6-packs in my wall locker and changed into a fresh set of OD BDUs, before walking to the Mess Hall for dinner.

Seeing Skip, Ronnie and Stony in the Mess Hall, I joined them with a tray of meat and potatoes from the food service line. When we'd finished eating, I rolled myself a cigarette, and we all laughed watching the chagrin on the MP's faces when I lit the tobacco in my cigarette.

Walking to the basketball court in front of our Tropo barracks, we watched a beautiful sunset as we waited for our vehicles to arrive for work. When David drove up with the jeep, Skip drove us to the Air Base Site, where it felt good to be back at my home away from home, as I relieved Chuck in the Operations Room. Working on a few circuit outages that had been called in through the night, with none of the problems found in our Site, Skip and I also made copies of the taped albums he'd checked out of the Air Base Library. Skip told me he'd left our tape decks at the Air Base Site and made copies of other albums for both of us while I was in the Hospital for which I thanked him.

On my 10:55 meal run, I met up with Glen and Ronnie, who excitedly told me they'd each had an FNG assigned to their Team, and each of the Teams on the other two shifts also had FNGs assigned to them. returning to the Air Base Site, I shared the news with Bob and Skip, and Bod said, "But, that's only a temporary fix, as it will only replace guys who are leaving over the next few months. You guys will need a massive influx of men, if the Army's going to fully take over from us civilian Tech Reps by the end of the Government's Fiscal Year, when our contract expires in October."

On my 6:35 meal run, I delivered the jeep to Frank by our basketball court and told him about all the newbies assigned to the Tropo Site from the batch that arrived last Monday, before I walked to the Mess Hall for breakfast. After I ate a filling breakfast and relaxed with a hand-rolled cigarette, I strolled to the Tropo barracks, where I drank a cold can of Bud, as I stripped to my skivvies, turned on my fan, and went to bed for some much needed sleep.

Waking to the 11:00 bugle call for Mess, I drank a cold can of Bud, before I showered, shaved and dressed to take Dhoi to lunch at the Ming Ter in Korat. During our lunch, we enjoyed making plans to go dancing the following night and for our day-trip with Mii-kâa to Bâan Tâa Klang on Saturday. Returning to the Jomsurang Hotel, the Hotel's concierge made arrangements for a taxi to meet us at 8:00 on Saturday morning in front of the Hotel for our day-trip. With everything set for Saturday, I left to catch a Thai bus back to my Company Area, where I went to the Tropo barracks and slept till the 5:00 bugle call for Mess.

After drinking a cold can of Bud, as I dressed in a fresh set of OD BDUs, I went to the Mess Hall with Skip, Ronnie and Stony for dinner. Returning to our barrack, we waited on the basketball court with the rest of the X-Shift for our rides to work. At the Air Base Site, Skip and I again made copies of the taped albums Skip had checked out that day, while we worked on the circuit outages as they were called in. On Skip's 4:55 meal run for breakfast, he carried his tape deck and tapes back to his wall locker, and I did the same with my tape deck and tapes on my 6:35 meal run. Then, I turned the jeep over to Tim, before going to the Mess Hall for breakfast.

Finishing my breakfast and hand-rolled smoke, I walked to the Tropo barracks and drank a cold can of Bud, as I changed into civilian clothes and filled my shopping bag for my stay at the Hotel. Then, catching a Thai bus to Korat, I went to the Sri Pattana Hotel and rented a room for four nights. Requesting an 11:00 wake-up call, I walked to my room, unpacked my shopping bag, stripped to my skivvies, and went to bed thinking, "Bob's idea to rent a Hotel room on an as needed basis sure saved me a lot of money from when I was sick for a week."

Roused by my wake-up call, I showered, shaved and dressed, before walking to the Jomsurang Hotel to take Dhoi to lunch at the Ming Ter. After an enjoyable lunch, and happily talking about our day-trip with Mii-kâa to see the elephants the next day, I escorted Dhoi back to her work at the Hotel. Then, I walked back to my Hotel room, where I stripped to my skivvies and slept till 5:00.

Dressing in fresh clothes, I then walked to the Jomsurang Hotel and had fun talking with Dhoi and Suumii about Summii and Somsak's wedding in six weeks, on the propitious occasion of the Spring Equinox. When they got off work at 6:00, as Dhoi and I walked out the Hotel's front door, she asked, "Can we go to your Hotel room first, so I can freshen up before we go to dinner?"

I replied, "But of course, my darling. You've been working all day and need a little time to refresh yourself before we go out for the evening," as she walked behind me to my Hotel room.

Entering my room, Dhoi through her arms around my neck, kissed me passionately, and said eagerly, "My darling, I've missed your love so much," as she began to unbutton her dress.

With my hormones now aroused, I responded with desire, "My darling, I have also missed your love."

Soon, we were stripped of our clothes and vigorously making love in an arousing Kama Sutra position that enhanced the explosive release of the pent-up lust we had from our ten-day separation. As my orgasmic thrust distended full into her love canal, Dhoi's sensuous hips continued to vigorously undulate against my groin as she breathlessly gasped, "Yes, my darling. Fill me with your sexual desire that's been stored up inside you."

Lying together in the afterglow of our climactic rush, I moaned with satisfaction, "My darling, I love you so much and am happy you desire my love for you," and she cooed in response, as she caressed my body desiringly, "As do I, my darling, as do I."

After we showered and dressed, we lovingly embraced and kissed, before leaving for our walk to the Thai BBQ Chicken Restaurant for a filling meal to sustain us during our fun evening of dancing at the night club. Later in the evening, when we'd danced our sensuous Tango, we returned to my Hotel room for the climactic release of the raging lust we'd enticed from each other as we danced our provocative Tango. Holding Dhoi's sensuous body lovingly enclosed by my arms, as we spooned, enthralled in the afterglow of our lovemaking, we happily went to sleep.

Waking to the 3:30 wake-up call, we enjoyed our enticing foreplay to arouse the lust contained within us and wantonly copulated in vigorous lovemaking. With the climactic rush engendered by our lust, we laid for a while in the ephemeral joy of our orgasmic release. We then relished our tender caresses, as we washed one another in the shower before we dressed and lovingly kissed as we left my room. Hiring a săawm-law, we rode together in our little bubble of love to the Chainarong bus stop, happy in the thought we'd be spending the day with our sweet, little Mii-kâa on our outing to see the elephants.

Returning to my Company Area on a Thai bus, I walked to the Tropo barracks and was introduced to the four new faces I encountered there, as the X-Shift and Y-Shift prepared to go to the Mess Hall for breakfast, before morning formation. Now, all the beds in our 24-man room were occupied. Drinking a cold can of Bud, as I changed into a fresh set of jungle fatigues amongst the hubbub of twenty-four men getting ready for breakfast, Tommy approached me and happily said, "Sáwátdii, Sandii. How does it feel to be over the hump?"

I replied confused, "Over what hump?"

Tommy laughed and answered, "Our tour hump. As of last Monday, we've been deployed 183 days. We now have 176 days and a wake-up left of our 1-year tour of duty, providing your extension isn't approved."

I responded, "Are you kidding? We've already been here for over six months? I haven't been counting down the days, like some guys. It's amazing how time flies when you're having fun," as I thought, "I sure hope my request for extension of my tour of duty gets approved, as I'm having the best time of my life here. I need to check with HQ and see why I haven't heard back on my request yet."

Walking en masse to the Mess Hall, there was a festive air to our large group as we entered the Mess Hall. After a filling breakfast with most everyone in our cluster of tables enjoying an after meal smoke, we proceeded as a whole to the basketball court in front of the Tropo barracks to await morning formation. After formation, I walked quickly to HQ and found PFC Schultz was now Spec-4 Schultz, and said, "Congrats on making Spec-4, Schultz. I guess I missed out on tacking them on," thinking, "To bad you can only tack on new stripes the day of promotion."

As he protectively covered his tender arms, he replied, "Thanks, Sandii. And yea, you missed out on tacking them on. What can I do for you?"

I answered, "I was wondering if my request for extension of tour has been approved."

He responded, "Over seventy-five percent of the Company has requested an extension of tour, and with the recent influx of FNGs, only the first half of the requests have been approved. The rest will depend on how soon and how many FNGs we get. But, with all the buildup of forces that's been going on, it'll most likely be on a case by case basis, based on the needs for your MOS. If you were in the first half, you'd have received your extension orders by now."

I said dejectedly, "I guess I wasn't in the first half, then. Well, congrats again on getting Spec-4, Schultz." And quickly left the HQ thinking, "If you snooze, you lose. I should have submitted my request when I first heard about all that was happening at Ft. Huachuca."

Walking rapidly to the Tropo barracks, I hastily changed into civilian clothes and hustled to the bus stop across the street from our basketball court. Boarding a Thai bus to Korat, I rode to the Chainarong bus stop, where I hired a sǎawm-law to carry me quickly to the Jomsurang Hotel. There, I found Dhoi holding Mii-kâa on her hip, as she patiently waited in the Lobby for me. After we happily exchanged sáwátdiis, we exited the Hotel and saw Bancha standing by his 1950 Studebaker taxi.

When we'd all exchanged sáwátdiis, my "family" scooted onto the plush back seat, as I gave Bancha a red 100 Bhat bill. With Mii-kâa sitting happily on Dhoi's lap, Bancha drove to the right down Rajadamnern Road, crossing over the train tracks to the Road's end. He then turned left, alongside the train tracks, passing in front of the Chira Train Station. The road we were on became the 2-lane Hwy 201 to Buriram, and old provincial capital, 60 miles East of Korat. Proceeding another 25 miles on Hwy 201, we came to Surin, a larger, more modern provincial capital. As we travelled to Surin, I saw that Hwy 201 paralleled the train tracks most of the way, and several old steam locomotives pulling freight or passenger cars chugged passed us in the opposite direction.

Since we'd followed the train tracks all the way to Surin, I asked Dhoi why didn't we take the train. She laughed and replied, "The trains running East from Korat, though frequent, are famously unreliable, taking two to four hours to get to Surin, or back again."

In Surin, Bancha turned North onto Hwy 214, and crossed over the train tracks. Driving another twenty-five miles to Route 3027, he turned left and followed the elephant signs for 18 miles to Bâan Tâa Klang, which was a Suai village, an ethnic people, indigenous to the southern Korat plateau, where the people and elephants lived side-by-side.

Bancha parked his taxi near the village's open market, where Dhoi fiercely negotiated the price for the food items each of us had selected from the vendors to eat for lunch. After lunch, we watched a half-hour talent show with the elephants doing tricks with balls, among other things. There was also a small museum, where we watched a cobra show for 5 Bhat each. Then I paid a mahout 20 Bhat for a 20-minute elephant ride with Dhoi, Mii-kâa and I sitting on a riding platform high up on the elephant's back, while the mahout sat on the elephant's neck giving it directions.

With little else to see, I bought Mii-kâa a small, woodcarving of an elephant, before Bancha drove us the 4-hour drive back to Korat. While Bancha drove, the three of us slept comfortably together in the back seat, with me holding Dhoi in my arms and Mii-kâa snuggled on Dhoi's lap. When Bancha stopped at the Chainarong bus stop, I gave him a 20-Bhat tip, as we exited his taxi and boarded a Thai bus to the Thai Army Base.

Exiting the bus on the Thai Army Base, I put Mii-kâa on my shoulders, where she happily rode, as we walked to Dhoi's home and enjoyed a Thai dinner with her mother and father. After dinner, Dhoi and her mother cleared the table and remained in the kitchen for their hen fest, taking turns holding Mii-kâa, while the Colonel and I sat at the table for our after dinner smoke. Refusing his offer of an American cigarette and removing the makings for a hand-rolled cigarette from my shirt pocket, I explained to him the reason I now rolled my own. He then said amazed, "With all the money you Americans are paid each month, I find it hard to believe any American Soldier, except maybe a Private, could be broke in three weeks."

Explaining to him my own thriftiness, taught to me by my parents, where each Pay Day, I put $50 into my Savings Account, buy a $10 U.S. Savings Bond and then collect additional money from my friends for providing them with beer and cigarettes when they were broke at the end of the month, he responded, "Lûuk-kâyi[153], I'm impressed with your frugalness, and how well you treat my daughter and granddaughter. I look forward to seeing you often."

Finishing our cigarettes, Dhoi walked passed us to the bathroom and said, "excuse me, Father, but I must get clean and change clothes to go dancing with my 'faan' tonight."

As the Colonel and I continued to talk, I saw Dhoi exit the bathroom a short while later wrapped in bath towel and walk into her and Mii-kâa's bedroom. When Dhoi walked out of the bedroom, she looked absolutely beautiful in her form-fitting, pink silk party dress. Making our parting sáwátdiis, Dhoi and I walked to the bus stop on the Army Base's main street to catch a Thai bus to Korat, as I perfunctorily returned the salute of every Thai Soldier who crossed our path, when they saw I was walking in front of the Colonel's daughter.

Exiting the bus at the Chainarong bus stop, I hired a sawm-law to carry us to the Sri Pattana Hotel, where I showered, shaved and

---

153   Son-in-law

dressed in fresh clothes before we walked to the night club. After a wonderful evening of ballroom and Thai rom dancing, at which I was becoming proficient, we performed our salacious Tango and quickly returned to my Hotel room. There, we satiated our pent-up lust with the orgasmic release from the vigorous lovemaking we engaged in.

Lying snuggled together, as I lovingly spooned her in my strong arms, enjoying the pleasant feeling of our climactic rush, I happily thought as I fell asleep, "The perfect ending to a day, especially as Dhoi's father now thinks of me as his son-in-law."

CHAPTER 56

BECAUSE OFFICIALLY THERE'S NO COMBAT IN THAILAND

Waking in the morning to my 3:30 wake up call, Dhoi and I expressed our love for each other as we lovingly kissed and desiringly caressed the erogenous areas of the other's body. Arousing our passions to frenzied lust, we wantonly engaged in vigorous lovemaking, having positioned Dhoi in a Kama Sutra arrangement that increased the fulfillment of our climatic rush.

As Dhoi spooned her luscious body in my warm embrace, enjoying the ephemeral glow of our orgasmic release, she cooed, "I love you, my darling, and in a way so different from my husband. I loved him because he was my husband and my daughter's father, who disappointed him for not being a son. Our marriage was arranged, and only met him a few times before we married, when I was 15. Also, he was the only man I'd made love with, before I met you. And, though his lovemaking was enjoyable, it was perfunctory, as I was his wife, and it was my duty to please him when he came home from his many Army duties. Plus, when we went dancing, it was to military balls, as part of his duties, not just for fun.

"But, it's very different with you, my darling. You love and enjoy spending time with me and Mii-kâa, as much as possible. And, your ways of lovemaking seem to be aimed at bringing me as much pleasure to me, as it does to you. Also, dancing with you is great fun and sexually enticing. Plus, my father appreciates the way you treat me and Mii-kâa, which makes him happy. But, though my mother likes you, she's afraid you'll marry me and take Mii-kâa, away from her, as Mii-kâa fills her days with joy."

I responded, "I love you, too, my darling, and you bring me much joy when we're together, whether it's just having lunch, or fun dancing and lovemaking, or on a fun day-trip with Mii-kâa. And, speaking of daytrips, next month, I'd like to see Ayutthaya, Thailand's ancient capital."

Facing me, she exclaimed, "Mii-kâa, too? That would be wonderful."

I replied, "Of course with Mii-kâa. To me, you're a package deal. But, I'd like to go by train. It'd give us a chance to move around, and more time there, by catching a night-train back to Korat."

While we showered and dressed, and then rode a Thai bus to the Thai Army Base, we began to plan for the train trip, and the things to do and see in Ayutthaya, which she'd only been to once as a young girl with her family. As I continued on to my Company Area, I thought, "This trip is going to be so much fun. But, with so many things to see, it is too bad we'll have to cram it into one day."

After drinking a cold Bud, as I hastily changed into a fresh set of jungle fatigues, I walked rapidly to the Mess Hall for a quick breakfast, before needing to return in time for morning formation. When Frank, Tim, Skip and I arrived at the Air Base Site, they went into the Site Office for Shift Change Report, while Skip and I relieved Chuck in the Operations Room, so he could rush home to his tîi-lók in Korat.

Subsequent to a quiet Sunday in the Operations Room, I spent an entertaining evening in the Tropo barracks, drinking beer, smoking my hand rolled cigarettes, and helping Skip, Ronnie and Stony teach Spec-4 Bill Shaw and PFC Miles Trashinsky, the two newbies on Tropos X-shift, how to play double pinnacle.

Bill had moved into Ronnie's 2-man space, and Miles, who everyone called "Trash," had moved into Stony's 2-man space. When Skip met the two newbies, he asked, "So, Trash, is Trashinsky Polish for air pollution, as it literally reads 'trash in sky'?"

Trash retorted, "I don't speak Polish, so I wouldn't know," and everyone laughed.

The remaining two men on Tropo's X-shift, Spec-4 Ray Daws, who shared Charlie's 2-man space, and Spec-4 Greg Lyon, who shared Glen's 2-man space, who had extended their tours, lived in Korat with their tîi-lóks. So, the only time I saw Ray and Greg was at morning formation and waiting for rides to work the night shift. Also, they were slated to replace Spec-5s Dan Nichols and Lewis Hopkins as Team Leaders when they rotated Stateside in several months, and their Teams would be as short-handed as before the newbies arrived.

It was hoped other arrivals of newbies would begin in several months to replace not only those leaving by then, but also those of us leaving in six months or less, and the Tech Reps, whose contracts expired in eight months. Of course, if newbies didn't start arriving in several months, then the large number of Tour Extension Requests now in limbo, would be approved, which is what many of us were praying for.

Waking to the 5:00 bugle call for Reveille, I grabbed a cold Bud on the way to the latrine to drink as I emptied my bladder. Since the Y-shift was working the night shift, and the half the X-shift and Z-shift were living in Korat with their tîi-lóks, then there was little competition to use the shower room. After I showered, shaved and dressed in a fresh set of jungle fatigues, I walked with Skip to the Mess Hall. After we leisurely ate breakfast and smoked a cigarette, we returned to the Tropo barracks and drank another cold beer, as we waited till it was time for morning formation.

Joining the Air Base Squad at the back of the Tropo Platoon, I saw Tom Lewiston dressed in his Class-B khaki uniform standing in the midst of the Platoon. But, standing behind us, I saw two MPs also dressed in their Class-B khaki uniforms, wearing white web pistol belts with white holsters and black pistols, and thought, "Those must be the MPs detailed to make sure Tom gets on the plane Stateside tomorrow morning in Bangkok. I'd give good odds that he'll be back for morning formation Wednesday and still not have any takers."

After working a quiet Monday in the Operations Room, the calm before the Monday night rush of circuit outages, I quickly changed into civilian clothes when I was relieved at 6:50 by Larry and Mark, and caught a Thai bus to Korat. Entering my Hotel room, I hastily showered and shaved before Dhoi arrived, and we left to go dancing at the nightclub.

Spending an enchanting evening watching my beautiful Dhoi dancing in my arms, or across from me in the Thai rom dances, we lastly danced our sensuous Tango. Rapidly departing for my Hotel room, we quickly stripped and became enthralled in energetic lovemaking to satiate our stored-up lust in the explosion of our climactic rush. Then, spooning in the ethereal joy of our afterglow, we happily went to sleep.

Roused from our sleep by the 3:30 wake-up call, we expressed our love with sensuous foreplay and engaged in vigorous lovemaking for the orgasmic release of our lust. When we'd had fun showering together and had dressed, I packed my belongings in the shopping bag. Then, we lovingly embraced and kissed, before leaving to ride a săawm-law to the Chainarong bus stop.

After Dhoi exited the Thai bus on the Thai Army Base, I continued on to my Company Area. Entering the Tropo Barracks, I drank a cold Bud, as I hastily emptied my shopping bag and changed into a fresh set of jungle fatigues. Walking rapidly to the Mess Hall, I had a quick breakfast, before swiftly returning to join the Tropo Platoon for morning formation. As I joined the Platoon, Ray and Trash asked, "Sandii, we both know half our X-shift are never around in the barracks as they have tîi-lóks in Korat. Why is it, you're gone most nights, if you don't have a tîi-lók?"

I replied, "I have a girlfriend, named Dhoi, who works in Korat and lives with her father on the Thai Army Base, which is located between the Air Base and Korat. Dhoi's father is a Thai Army Colonel, who is the CO of the Thai Army Regiment providing the perimeter security for the Air Base and Camp Friendship. Anyway, I rent a Hotel room on my off days and when working the day shift, so I don't have to deal with catching the last bus from Korat at 10:00. I don't spend every evening with Dhoi, as some evenings I go to the Tech Rep's compound, which you'll probably go to on Thursday and Friday this week with Skip, Ronnie and Stony."

They exclaimed, "You're dating a Thai Colonel's daughter! How'd that happened?"

I replied, "It's a long story, and we don't have time to get into it now, as formation is about to begin."

After formation, I told them how I met Dhoi, why I decided to date her, and some of our history together, as we returned to our barracks and each drank a cold beer, while getting ready for bed. Ray responded, "Are you sure Dhoi's only 20 years old? With her being a widow with a 2-year-old kid, I'd figure she's several years older."

I replied, "You mean to tell me there's no underage marriages where you live? Heck, back home in Southern Oregon, I knew a woman who was a widow with five kids by the time she was 21, and another woman who was twice divorced, with a kid by each husband, when she was 19. Also, one girl who was a divorcee at 14. Plus, it's normal here for a girl to marry at 14, so yeah, it's easy to believe Dhoi's a 20-year-old widow with a 2-year-old daughter."

Waking to the 11:00 bugle call for Mess, I drank another cold beer, as I dressed in civilian clothes to take Dhoi to lunch. When I was leaving, I saw Tommy and said, "Sâwâtdii, Tommy. How're things working now with Súmat?"

He replied, "Pretty good, actually. On my off days, I ride on the bus with her when she leaves and go home with her to Korat, where she lives with her family. After we eat dinner and spend the evening with her family, we sleep together in her bedroom. Her family's fine with it, as they're hoping I'll marry her. Also, I give the old man a lói Bhat each week to pay for the food I eat and to sleep with Súmat. It's better than trying to sneak in a quickie here and hope we don't get caught. How's things going with Dhoi?"

I answered, "Really good. Her father has fully accepted me as a future son in law, and Dhoi's daughter recognizes me as her Uncle Sandii. The only holdout is her mother. If she finds out I'm an Enlisted man, she'll try to kibosh our relationship."

Boarding a Thai bus for Korat, I exited at the Chainarong Gate, and walked to the Jomsurang Hotel. There, I exchanged sáwátdiis with Dhoi and Suumii, before Dhoi and I walked to the Ming Ter for lunch. As we ate, Dhoi produced a train schedule for passenger trains to and from Bangkok, which stopped at Ayutthaya, and a map of Ayutthaya, showing the locations of Hotels and sites to see. Given the number of places we'd like to see in Ayutthaya, which was the capital of Siam from 1350 to 1767, when it was sacked by the Burmese Army and the capital moved to Bangkok. In 1932, when Siam's last slave was freed, the name of the country was changed to "Bprá-têt Thai," which literally means "Land of the Free." We lamented we'd only have one afternoon and evening to see them, before we had to leave on a sleeper coach, so I could return in time for morning formation.

After escorting Dhoi back to the Jomsurang Hotel, I chatted for a while with her and Suumii about our plans for the daytrip to Ayutthaya on Saturday, March 15th. Then, we talked about Suumii and Somsak's wedding day plans the following week, on Friday, March 21st, and found it was a series of dawn to dusk ceremonial events. The final wedding vows and the reception would be held at the Saranari College Auditorium, where Suumii had graduated from. Since Dhoi was the bride's escort for the daylong event, then I was invited to the wedding and the reception afterwards as Dhoi's "faan."

Returning to my Company Area on a Thai bus, I entered the Tropo barracks and drinking cold Bud, as I stripped to my skivvies, turned on my fan and went to bed for a little shuteye, before working the night shift. This was possible because of the dry, 80-degree weather of winter, versus the humid, mid 90-degree weather of summer.

Waking to the 5:00 bugle call for Mess, I quickly drank a cold Bud as I used the latrine, and then readied myself for a hot shower and shave. Dressing in a fresh set of OD BDUs, I then walked to the Mess Hall with Skip for a leisurely dinner. As I smoked my hand-rolled tobacco cigarette, much to the disappointment of the hovering MPs, Skip laughed and said, "You think those MPs'll ever stop fretting over a joint filled with tobacco, instead of marijuana?"

I laughed in reply, "I hope not. It's the high point of my eating in this Mess Hall."

Returning to the Tropo barracks, Skip and I wrapped our tape decks in the OD Army blankets from our beds and carried them with the blank tapes and taped albums out to the basketball court. When David drove up in the dark with the jeep, we carefully loaded and tide them on to the jeep's cushioned back seat. As we drove into the Air Base Site's parking space, I saw in the jeep's combat dimmed headlight beams, the glint of steel from an 8-foot-high chain-link fence, topped with concertina wire, surrounding the Air Base Comm Center, and Skip said, "It looks like the Comm Center's paranoia has been acted on."

I laughed in response, "The irony is, Ted told me the Comm Center guys aren't happy about that fence. Now, they're going to have armed

APs at the locked gates, checking their IDs as they enter, to make sure only 'Authorized Personnel' enter the Comm Center's area. And, that working there will turn into a real pain in the butt with all the heightened security."

Skip laughed and said, "What do they think somebody's going to do, sneak in a bomb, like we did? Sure am glad we voted that idea down."

When Bob entered the Operations Room, he said, "It was passed to me at the Shift Change Report, that because it's Lincoln's Birthday Stateside tomorrow, they're expecting an uptick in traffic outages tomorrow morning. So, we need to be prepared for that. Also, since the Chinese New Year's Day is on Wednesday the 19th, then all military bases will be locked down from the 18th through at least the 20th, in preparation for another Tet Offensive this year.

"In general, that means all perimeter gates will be closed to civilian traffic. So, no mây-bâans for you two, and all of us Tech Reps will be housed in BOQs. And, there'll be restricted travel between the military bases. So, me and the other Air Base Tech Reps'll be in the Air Force BOQs, and you guys will be eating in the Air Base Mess Hall while you're on shift, as your movements will be limited to 7:00 o'clock in the morning and evenings.

"Those coming on shift, will drive your jeep from your Company Area to here. Then, those going off shift, will drive your jeep back to your Company Area, after you've eaten in the Air Force Mess Hall. Also, there'll be no formations, or other massing of troops, and your movements will be restricted to your Company Area and going to and from the Mess. So, I suggest you begin stocking up on beer and cigarettes before then, as the Camp's PX and the Air Base's BX will be closed during the lockdown.

"If you have any questions, you'll need to call whoever's in charge at Tropo, as you now know as much as I do about the lockdown."

Well, things were slow in the Operations Room, so Skip and I had plenty of time to make copies of the taped albums from the Air Base Library. We even managed to each get a couple hours sleep after the midnight meal runs. On my 6:35 meal run, I enjoyed the cool morning air of Thailand's winter, as I drove the jeep to the basketball court in front of the Tropo Barracks and handed it over to Frank.

Entering the barracks after I ate breakfast in the Mess Hall, Tommy greeted me cheerfully, "Sáwátdii, Sandii. Guess who showed up at morning formation?

I laughed and replied, "Tom Lewiston. But, how did he get back so soon after the MPs put him on the Stateside flight with his duffel bag in the plane's cargo hold?"

He answered, "Tom told the MPs since he was being discharged when he arrived Stateside, he tossed his uniforms and only had a couple of changes of clothes in a small carry-on bag. When the MPs put him on the jet later at Don Muang Airport the next morning, he simply walked to the rear of the plane, and exited out the door, where they were loading food. Then, he boarded a train back to Korat spent the night with his tîi-lók, where he left his duffel bag. Now, he's not scheduled to leave for two more weeks, which is when he wanted to leave in the first place."

Drinking a cold Bud, I stripped to my skivvies and went to bed, without turning on my fan, as the temperature was a comfortable 65 degrees. Waking to the 11:00 bugle call for Mess, I showered and changed, before drinking another cold Bud, as I dressed in civilian clothes and left to catch the Thai bus to Korat, for a fun lunch with Dhoi at the Ming Ter.

Returning to the Tropo barracks, I slept for a couple of hours with the fan on, because it was now 80 degrees. Waking to the 5:00 bugle call for Mess, I drank a cold Bud with Skip, as we dressed in our OD BDUs and left for the Mess Hall to eat dinner. Afterwards, we walked to the PX, and each bought twenty-three cans of beer for our stockpiles to prepare for next week's lockdown.

After stowing the beer in our wall lockers, we walked out to the basketball court and waited for David to arrive with the jeep. During our night shift, we again made copies of the taped albums then packed up our tape decks to take back with us on our breakfast meal runs. When I'd been relieved by Larry and Mark, Larry drove me back to the Tropo barracks. There, I drank a cold Bud, as I changed into civilian clothes and fill in my shopping bag with changes of clothes, before leaving to catch a time bus to Korat.

Arriving at the Sri Patana Hotel, I paid the receptionist 100 Bhat to rent a room for four nights. Requesting an 11:00 wake-up call, I went to my room and slept till I heard the wake-up call knock on my door.

After I'd showered, shaved and dressed, I walked to the Jomsurang Hotel and took Dhoi for a pleasant lunch at the Ming Ter. Escorting her back to work, I then returned to my Hotel room to get some more sleep, before my busy evening with Dhoi.

After several hours of sleep, I dressed and walked back to the Jomsurang Hotel, where I chatted with Dhoi and Suumii till they got off work at 6:00. Then, hiring a săawm-law for a ride to the Chainarong Gate, Dhoi and I rode a Thai bus to the Thai Army Base. Exiting the bus, I escorted Dhoi to her father's home for dinner.

While eating dinner, Dhoi and I discussed with her parents our plans to take Mii-kâa with us on the train for a day-trip next month to Ayutthaya and do some sightseeing of the old Siam capital. When the Colonel commented there was too much to see in just one day, I agreed and told them it was because I had to make the morning formation every day that I couldn't get a 48-hour pass. Otherwise, I'd stay another day to take in all the sights at a leisurely pace to absorb the historical significance of Ayutthaya.

As Dhoi was getting ready to go dancing, the Colonel and I discussed the pending lockdown of all the military bases in expectation of a second Tet Offensive, Therefore, I wouldn't be able to have dinner with them next week. He told me how his entire Regiment would be deployed around Camp Friendship's perimeter for the lockdown, but personally doubted there would be much, if any, of a Tet Offensive, as the one last year severely depleted the Viet Cong's numbers for such massive attacks again. Also, the Thai Cong's forces weren't enough to mount any significant attack on any Thai Air Bases, especially at Korat, as it was too far from the Cambodian border for any large force to cross the wide expanses of rice paddies and get to Korat, without being spotted and destroyed by the Thai Army.

When Dhoi was ready to go, we made our parting sáwátdiis, and walked in the dim light to the bus stop. Exiting a Thai bus at the Chainarong Gate, I hired a săawm-law for a ride to the night club, where we happily danced till 10:00. With the pent-up lust from the foreplay we enjoyed while ballroom dancing, we went to my Hotel room and vigorously made love in a Kama Sutra position that elevated our climactic rush. Relishing the afterglow of our orgasmic release, we blissfully fell asleep, as I desiringly spooned Dhoi in my arms.

With the 3:30 wake-up call, we lovingly reignited our lust with sensual kisses and caresses, resulting in wanton lovemaking to satiate the passionate desire we had for each other. For a while, we cuddled in the ephemeral joy of our experience, before we playfully showered together and dressed to leave. With a loving embrace and tender kiss, we left and road a săawm-law to the Chainarong Gate, where we boarded a Thai bus to take Dhoi to the Thai Army Base and me to my Company Area.

After drinking a cold Bud, as I changed into a fresh set of jungle fatigues, I had breakfast in the Mess Hall, before attending morning formation. There, I congratulated Tom for successfully hoodwinking the MPs. When formation was over, I returned to the Tropo barracks and consumed another cold Bud, as I changed into civilian clothes. Then, catching a Thai bus to Korat, I went to my Hotel room, where I slept for several hours.

On waking, I dressed and walked to the Jomsurang Hotel. There, I pleasantly visited with Dhoi and Suumii, before taking Dhoi to the Ming Ter for a delightful lunch. After escorting Dhoi back to her work, I chatted happily with her, while Suumii went to lunch with Somsak. Returning to my Hotel room I took a nap before going to the Thai bar to share Sing Hăi Beers and jocular camaraderie with my Thai friends, as I ate a large bowl of chicken-noodle soup for dinner.

At 6:30, I left the Thai bar and walked the mile to the compound, observing the evening air seemed cooler than usual. As I sipped on my bottle of Sing Hăi Beer, others on Horn's porch commented on the coolness of the evening air. But, nobody ever bothered to follow any weather forecasts, as every day was a pleasant repeat of the warm and dry weather of the day before. After a fun evening of shared comradeships, the party broke up at 9:30, and I returned to Camp Friendship with the group of guys who didn't have a tîi-lók.

I spent the night sleeping bundled up in the blanket on my bed. When I got up with the 5:00 bugle call for Reveille, I kept my blanket wrapped around me, as I quickly fished out my long thermal underwear from the bottom drawer of my wall locker. Rapidly pulling them on, before dressing in a fresh set of the heavier OD BDUs and putting on my OD field jacket, while I shivered in the cold air. I commented, "It's colder than a well-digger's butt this morning," and heard Skip retort, "More like, colder than a witch's tit in the brass bra."

After going to breakfast in the Mess Hall with Skip, who was similarly attired, and then morning formation, Tim, Skip and I piled into the jeep, as Frank drove us to the Air Base Site as fast as possible. Entering our air-conditioned building to get warm, I saw Bob and Bill standing outside the Site Office and said to them, "Man, it's freezing out here. Do either of you know what the temperature is?" as I thought, "How ironic. In the summertime we hurry into this air-conditioned building to escape the heat and now we hurry in to escape the cold."

Bill replied, "AFTN said it's 55 degrees, because a rare Artic front has come in over the Himalayas down from Mongolia. It's a good thing it didn't' get any colder as Thais here, have been known to die of exposure at 50 degrees."

While I quickly removed my thermals and jacket in the Latrine, and put them in my wall locker, along with Frank and Tim, Skip relieved Chuck so he could go home to his tîi-lók. After the usual very busy Saturday morning, dealing with large numbers of reported circuit outages, I left on my 10:55 meal run. Leaving my thermals and jacket in the jeep, I walked quickly across the parking lot to the Air Base's BX. There, I bought 23 cans of Budweiser, a box of Z-Z Top paper, and a one-pound can of Prince Albert tobacco to add to my stockpile in the Tropo barracks.

Stowing everything I brought in the jeep in my barracks wall locker, I then put a change of civilian clothes and skivvies in my shopping bag, and placed them under the seat in the jeep, before driving to the Mess Hall for lunch. Returning to the Operations Room after lunch, I had a busy afternoon, as we caught up on the outages reported in the morning.

Prior to being relieved by Larry and Mark at 6:30, I'd taken a quick shower, shaved and dressed in civilian clothes. Quickly leaving the Air Base Site, I carried my shopping bag with me to catch a Thai bus to Korat. Entering my Hotel room, I set my shopping bag in the wardrobe and rested on the bed, while waiting for Dhoi.

When Dhoi arrived at 8:00, we walked to the night club and enjoyed each other immensely, as we gaily danced together. Returning to my Hotel room at 10:00, we expunged our pent-up lust in vigorous lovemaking, and then went happily to sleep in the afterglow of our climatic rush.

Roused by the 3:30 wake-up call, we expressed our love and desire for each other in sensuous foreplay and ecstatic lovemaking, before we playfully showered together and dressed to leave. Because I worked Monday night and nobody was sure how long the military bases would be on lockdown due to a possible Tet Offensive, we agreed to meet that evening in my Hotel room to spend the night together.

Having lovingly embraced and kissed, I grabbed my shopping bag and we left for the Chainarong Gate to catch a Thai bus to our separate abodes on the Thai Army Base and Camp Friendship. After an uneventful Sunday at the Air Base Site, with the weather returning to its normal warmth, I went back to my Hotel room for a very enjoyable evening of loving foreplay and energetic lovemaking with Dhoi.

After sleeping happily through the night, as we spooned lovingly together, we woke to the 3:30 wake-up call, and had another bout of sensuous foreplay and vigorous lovemaking. Then, we showered, dressed and affectionately kissed, prior to leaving for the Chainarong Gate to catch a Thai bus to our respective residences. After I had breakfast in the Mess Hall and went to morning formation, I slept till the 11:00 bugle call for Mess. Then, I drank a cold Bud, as I showered, shaved and dressed, before leaving for Korat and taking Dhoi to lunch at the Ming Ter.

Returning to the Tropo barracks, I slept a few hours, before Skip and I left to eat dinner in the Mess Hall. Then, we wrapped our tape decks in blankets to take with us in the jeep to work. But, there had been no opportunity to copy any of the taped albums Skip had bought this Monday night. Not only did we have to deal with the usual uptick in circuit outages due to the amount of post-weekend message traffic from Stateside, but there was the added message traffic in preparation for the pending Tet Offensive.

Because the lockdown was being initiated in the morning, we decided to pack up our tape decks and take them back to our barracks on the mid-night meal runs. Also, as the lockdown went into effect at 0600, and there was no morning formation, we were instructed by Tropo for both of us to separately eat breakfast at the nearby Air Force Mess Hall. Then, Skip was to drive the jeep to the Company Area at 0640, where the Y-shift would drive it to the Air Base Site, and I'd drive it to the Company Area and turn it over to the Z-shift for them to drive to the Air Base Site at 1850 to relieve the Y-shift.

When Frank, Tim, Larry and Mark arrived at the Operations Room to relieve me, Frank said, "Sandii, when you arrive at the Company Area, remember, you're not to leave your barracks for any reason, except to go to the Mess Hall, unless you're told otherwise."

Driving through the gate to Camp Friendship, I had to show my ID and let the MPs search the jeep, before I could proceed to the Company Area. There, I went to where the Z-shift were housed and told Chuck and David the jeep was parked by the basketball court, before I went to bed.

Waking to the 11:00 bugle call for Mess, I drank a cold bud as I dressed in a fresh set of jungle fatigues. Seeing the OD BDUs I'd worn last night were still piled on the floor, I remembered we'd have no mây-bâan to clean our clothes and dug my old laundry bag out of my wall locker to put my laundry in, and tied the bag to the end of my bed's frame, before leaving with Skip for the Mess Hall.

Walking to the Mess Hall, I saw to my right the mass of Thai Army troops along Camp Friendship's perimeter fence. Pointing them out to Skip, I said, "Dhoi's father told me his entire Regiment would be deployed along our perimeter for the lockdown," and Skip responded, "Well, I hope they're not needed, as then we'll be joining them in the firefight, if there's enough rifles to go around. And, if we're shot, we can't be awarded a Purple Heart, like what happened to you, because officially, there's no 'combat action' in Thailand."

CHAPTER 57

MY LIFE IN THAILAND WITH DHOI EVOLVED INTO A HAPPY ROUTINE

Entering Camp Friendship's Enlisted Mess Hall for lunch, I saw it was fuller than usual and nobody was in civilian attire. In fact, many were wearing a combat harness and helmet, and some even had a rifle. I also noted, there were no Thais on the serving lines or in the kitchen areas. Rather, it appeared those working the serving lines on KP duty consisted of non-essential troops from the Personnel and Finance Offices, and those with rifles were from the Transportation Regiment, who were hauling the never-ending stream of bombs to the Air Bases.

After Skip and I finished eating and laughing at the despondent look in the MP's faces walking away when I lit my hand-rolled cigarette, we picked up our eating utensils and carried them to the Exit door to be disposed of. En route, I saw several men on KP duty, busily wiping vacated tables.

Exiting the Mess Hall after a leisurely lunch, we rapidly walked to the Tropo barracks, not wanting to be caught in the open when any shooting started. Entering the North end of the barracks, housing Tropo's Z-shift and Generator Operators, I saw every bed was unmade and had a white laundry bag tied to its end. Also, there was practically nobody there, as the Z-shift was working that day, and I thought, "Obviously, nobody is enforcing any military standards during this lockdown."

In the lounge area between the two barracks rooms, Skip and I each retrieved a cold beer from our shelf in the X-shift refrigerator, and opened them with our church keys. Entering our barracks room, I saw it was full of guys, as there were now 24 men in the room from our X-shift and the Y-shift, since it was their off day.

Skip and I were immediately challenged to a Double-Deck Pinochle for the usual money stakes, by a pair of guys from the Y-shift looking for fresh competition from the X-shift. Soon, all three tables in our barracks room was filled by six 2-man teams, all of whom were ardent Double-Deck Pinochle players, and a round-robin tournament was organized between the 2-man teams. The winner of the tournament would be the team that had won the most money from the five other teams. The non-participants observed these money-stakes games, not only to cheer on the guys from their shift, but also to pick up on their advanced strategies.

In this way, our afternoon quickly passed, as Skip and I enjoyed our team strategies against other teams we'd not heretofore played against, while drinking beer and smoking cigarettes. When the 5:00 bugle call for Mess sounded, there was no clear-cut champion, as a 500-point game often took an hour to play. Every team agreed to pick up where we left off tomorrow evening, as the X-shift had to work the night shift, and the Y-shift would be working days, tomorrow.

Before going to dinner with Skip I quickly showered, shaved and dressed in a fresh set of OD BDUs. When we returned from the Mess Hall, we drank a cold beer, while waiting till 6:50 and drove in the jeep to the Air Base Site to relieve those who worked the 12-hour day at 7:00.

After Shift Change Report, Bob entered the Operations Room and said, "Things have been busy here today running down reported circuit outages. But, none were traced to here. We can expect more reports of outrages tonight, because of the increased message traffic to prepare for this second Tet Offensive. So, there won't be any catnapping tonight, no matter how slow it gets, as the shit can hit the fan at any time, and we must be fully awake to deal with it."

Though we were fairly busy through the night with reports of circuit outages due to the increased message traffic, the proverbial fecal rotating device wasn't employed. At least, not at Korat. We did hear of some minor skirmishes early in the morning at some of the Air Bases near the Laos and Cambodian borders. Even in Vietnam, there was no reports of large-scale assaults, like those in 1968.

Bob speculated, "With the near destruction of the Viet Cong in their all-out attacks to drive out the 'Yankee devils,' the NVA[154] had to take over control of the war against South Vietnam and its allies. Learning a lesson from the Viet Cong's debacle, I guess they're not as willing to sacrifice their troops on massed attacks against heavily fortified positions, especially with the massive American buildup of troops this last year. No, I think their goal with the '69 Tet Offensive is to rouse the locals in an uprising against the governments of South Vietnam and Thailand. Failing that, their objective would be to draw the American forces out of their well-protected bases and bleed us into leaving in the jungles."

For my mid-night and meal runs, I walked to the nearby Air Force Mess Hall, which was much like Camp Friendship's, except the food seemed fresher and of better quality. At 7:00 Larry and John arrived in the Operations Room to relieve me and Skip. Then, we waited till Shift Change Report ended and dropped Bob off at the air Base BOQ, before driving the jeep to the Tropo barracks. There we each drank a cold beer, as we quickly stripped and went thankfully to bed.

Waking to the 11:00 bugle call for Mess, I showered, shaved and then drank a cold Bud as I dressed in a fresh set of jungle fatigues and put my dirty clothes into my laundry bag. With that done, Skip and I rapidly walked to the Mess Hall for a relaxed lunch and smoke, before quickly returning to the Tropo Barracks. There, we rejoined the money-stakes Double-Deck Pinochle Tournament with the Y-shift and spent the afternoon playing the round-robin games, while drinking beer and smoking cigarettes.

When the 5:00 bugle call for Mess sounded, we'd played against nearly all the teams in the tournament. As the Y-shift was now working the night shift, we agreed to finish our competitions the next afternoon.

---

154   North Vietnam Army

Everyone then rapidly walked to the Mess Hall for dinner in a straggled order, so as not to be a large group to easily target for any Thai Cong who might be in the area.

Returning to our barracks after dinner, most of our X-shift slept, as the y-shift waited to leave at 6:50 to relieve the Z-shift. When the Z-shift arrived, we woke up and started a separate round-robin tournament with them. So, Skip and I remained busy through the evening, until 10:00, playing money-stakes Double-Deck Pinochle, while drinking beer and smoking cigarettes.

With the 5:00 bugle call for a Reveille, Skip and I decided it was prudent to wear the same jungle fatigues, as there was no telling how long the lockdown would last, or when our mây-bâan would be allowed to return to work and wash our clothes. When Skip and I returned from eating breakfast at the Mess Hall, we each drank a cold beer, as we stripped to our skivvies and went back to bed. The Double-Deck Pinochle tournament with the Y-shift wouldn't resume till after lunch, because they'd be sleeping after working the night shift.

Waking to the 11:00 bugle call for Mess, I showered, shaved and then drank a cold Bud, as I dressed in a fresh set of skivvies and old jungle fatigues, before walking to the Mess Hall with Skip for lunch. Returning to our barracks after lunch, we were preparing to resume the tournament with the Y-shift, when Spec-4 Schultz came through our barracks saying loudly to everyone, "The lockdown is over, and we've returned to normal operations."

Skip responded, "With lots of the guys leaving to go home to their tîi-lóks, there won't be many left to finish the tournament. Besides, with all the money we've won, I imagine we came out near the top."

Drinking a cold Bud, as I rapidly changed into civilian clothes and packed several sets of civilian clothes in my shopping bag, I then caught a crowded Thai bus for Korat, which became jampacked as it crossed the Air Base. Exiting at the Chainarong Gate, I hired a săawm-law for a ride to the Jomsurang Hotel, where I surprised Dhoi, who was overjoyed to see me again. We quickly made plans for me to go home with her for dinner and then go dancing, before I left to rent a room for four days at the Sri Patana Hotel.

After taking a nap for a couple of hours, I returned to chat with Dhoi and Suumii, while waiting for Dhoi to get off work at 6:00. Riding a săawm-law to the Chainarong Gate, we boarded the Thai bus and rode to the Thai Army Base, where I had dinner with her family. While Dhoi readied herself to go dancing, I chatted with the Colonel about what we each did during the lockdown, with him telling me it had been a good opportunity to evaluate the combat readiness of his Regiment and identify weaknesses in Camp Friendship's perimeter defenses.

When Dhoi was ready, we left to catch a Thai bus back to Korat and rode a săawm-law to the night club. After a splendid evening dancing sensuously with my beautiful Dhoi happily in my arms again, we rapidly walked to my Hotel room and enjoyed the climactic release of our stored lust with vigorous lovemaking in a Kama Sutra position. While spooning in the glory of the afterglow, we spoke of our love for each other, as we fell contently to sleep.

Roused by the 3:30 wakeup call, we pleasured one another with enticing foreplay that culminated in wanton lovemaking and the orgasmic satisfaction of the lust we'd engendered. Lying for a while to regain our breath and calm our racing hearts, we then enjoyed our loving caresses in the shower, as we washed each other. When we'd dressed and affectionately held one another as we kissed, Dhoi and I then left to ride in a săawm-law and a Thai bus to our respective abodes, agreeing she'd come to my Hotel room Saturday evening to go dancing again.

Entering the Tropo barracks, I drank a cold Bud, as I changed into a fresh set of jungle fatigues, before walking to the Mess Hall for breakfast. Returning to the Company Area for morning formation, I then rode the jeep to the Air Base Site with Frank, Tim and Skip. Relieving Chuck from duty in the Operations Room, he quickly left for his tîi-lók in Korat. The morning was very busy with reports of circuit outages, due to the increased message traffic from people Stateside leaving for a 3-day weekend celebrating George Washington's birthday.

After work I returned to the Tropo barracks to find my bed made, and my laundry cleaned and put away, thinking "Life is finally back to normal," as I removed my jungle fatigue jacket. Then, I settled into a pleasant evening playing Double-Deck Pinochle with Skip against a couple of guys from the Z-shift, while we drank beer and smoked cigarettes till 10:00.

Waking to the 5:00 bugle call for Reveille, I went through my usual routine of showering, shaving and drinking a cold Bud, as I dressed in a fresh set of jungle fatigues. Then, I walked with Skip to the Mess

Hall for a breakfast, before returning for morning formation, and rode in the jeep to Air Base Site to enjoy my work there with Skip and Bob.

Before being relieved at 6:50, I changed into civilian clothes, and left for my Hotel room to meet with Dhoi, and spent a wonderful evening dancing together at the night club. Then, returning to my Hotel room, we enjoyed our wanton lovemaking, before we slept in each other's arms. Upon our waking, we began our day with vigorous lovemaking, and then happily shower together, before we dressed. After we lovingly embraced and kissed, we travelled together to our respective abodes, bring my clothes in the shopping bag with me.

After breakfast and formation, I slept till the 11:00 bugle call for Mess, then dressed in civilian clothes for lunch in the Mess Hall. As it was Sunday and Dhoi's day off, I rode a Thai bus to the Thai Army Base and spent a pleasant afternoon visiting and having dinner with Dhoi and her family. Returning to the Tropo barracks at 6:00, I drank a cold Bud, as I dressed in a fresh set of OD BDUs and packed my tape deck to take with me in the jeep to work.

At the Air base Site, Skip and I spent our entire night shift copying taped albums with our tape decks. And, when Ted informed us he had a line up to Rosie, we talked with our girlfriends and families Stateside, telling them we were fine, but not mentioning anything about the lockdown for the 1969 Tet Offensive. The only disappointment with working this night shift, was missing the big farewell bash for Tom Lewiston's actual send off, Also, I was not able to see him off at morning formation, before I went to bed.

After the 11:00 bugle call for Mess, I showered, shaved and dressed to take Dhoi to lunch at the Ming Ter in Korat. Returning from Korat to the Tropo barracks, I found a message on my bed to report to the CO's Office in HQ at my earliest opportunity. As I had no idea why the CO wanted to see me I quickly changed into a fresh set of jungle fatigues and had Skip check over my uniform for any visible defects, before walking rapidly to HQ.

Entering HQ and stepping to the wait-high counter, I asked Spec-4 Schultz if he knew why the CO wanted to see me. As the Company Clerk, he knew everything happening in his HQ, even before the CO knew. He replied, "He's not happy about receiving a TELEX from the First Brigade's CG requesting you to be given a temporary duty assignment for two day to the Thai's Second Army. So, look sharp."

Walking through HQ to a door marked "CO's Office," I knocked and heard the order, "Enter."

Entering the CO's Office and closing the door behind me, I saw it was not much different than his old office, except the external wall was concrete, instead of wood, and had no windows, only the gaps at the top and bottom of the wall. Stepping to the front of his desk, I saluted smartly and said, "Specialist Lynch, reporting as ordered, sir."

He looked up from a stack of papers, returned my salute and said kindly, "Lynch, I was all set to chew your butt for violating your chain-of-command when I received this," as he passed me a typed TELEX message, "but realized you probably didn't know anything about it. Could you explain this to me, please?"

Looking at the message in my hand, I saw it read:

FROM: BG RIENZY, CG 1ST SIG BGDE
TO: CPT RICHARDS, CO C-CMPY, 442D SIG BN
SUBJT TDY LYNCH, SHERMAN A SPEC-4 RA19860451
CG 2D ARMY THAILAND REQUESTS LYNCH ASSG TDY
ON MAR 15-16, 1969, FOR LIASON DUTY WITH 52D INF
REG THAILAND.

I stammered in shocked reply, "Sir, I don't know anything about this. All I can say, is March 15th is when I plan to take a day-long trip with my girlfriend, Dhoi, to see Ayutthaya, the ancient capital of Thailand. And, that Dhoi is the daughter of a Thai Army Colonel, who is the CO of the Thai Infantry Regiment responsible for Camp Friendship's perimeter security and is aware of our planned day-trip to Ayutthaya. It's possible the Colonel would like for his daughter and I to have two days to take in all the sights, instead of trying to cram it into one day. That's the only connection I can think of, Sir."

He responded, "You're dating the Regimental CO of this Camp's defenses? How'd that happen?"

As he listened intently to my explanation, he shook his head amazed, and said when I'd finished, "Sandii, I'm impressed. But, the next time you plan a day-trip with this Colonel's daughter, please give me a heads-up. And, if it looks like two days off would better suit your trip, tell me about it, and I'll see what I can do. It's nice to have high-placed friends, but don't ever let me think you're abusing their influence, okay?"

I replied, "Understood, Sir. Does this mean you're approving the Thai Army's request for TDY duty for March 15th and 16th, Sir?"

He laughed and answered, "Barring the needs of the Army, I'm giving you the 2-day TDY. But, don't mention this to anyone. I don't want it getting around you're receiving special privileges because you're dating a Thai Colonel's daughter. And, I'll tell Sgt. Howell about the TDY, so it doesn't go any further than here. Dismissed."

Saluting him as I left his Office, Spec-4 Schultz gave a sidelong look when I passed him leaving HQ, and I gave him a thumbs-up to signal all was okay. Returning to the Tropo barracks, as no one asked about my visit with the CO, I said nothing about it. Drinking a cold Bud, I hung my jungle fatigues back up in my wall locker, and readied to get some shut-eye for an expected, very busy night at work following the Stateside's 3-day weekend.

Waking to the 5:00 bugle call for Mess, I drank a cold Bud, as I dressed in a fresh set of OD BDUs, and left with Skip for a leisurely dinner and smoke in the Mess Hall. Returning to the barracks, I waited in the dark on the basketball court for David to arrive with the jeep. Driving the jeep to the Air Base Site, we found things going full tilt in the Operations Room when I relieved Chuck. When things had slowed a bit, Skip slipped to the back and began copying with our tape decks one of the taped albums he'd brought. Before Skip's 4:50 meal run, we'd wrapped up our tape decks for transport in the jeep back to the Tropo barracks.

When I'd handed the jeep over to Tim on my 6:35 meal run, I quickly carried my tape deck into the Tropo barracks and left it on my bed, as I rapidly walked to the Mess Hall for breakfast, before the serving line closed at 7:00. Returning to the Tropo barracks via it's North door, I saw considerable celebration with the Z-shift yelling happily at me, "We're getting a new First Sargent tomorrow, and we'll never see that lowdown, dirty dog, Spike again, as he's to leave for Stateside Monday morning, next week."

I responded happily, "That's great news," as I walked to the lounge area, and got a cold Bud to drink in celebration with the remanent of X-shift, before changing into civilian clothes and leaving to catch a Thai bus to Korat with my shopping bag full of clothes.

I'd previously told George, Ronnie and Stony, since we're now living in 24-man barracks rooms, and not an 8-man hooch, it was not feasible for me to supply them with beer and cigarettes, without doing the same for everyone else in the Tropo barracks. But, if they like, I'd loan them $20 to be paid back $25 on Pay Day. This they thought was a good idea and readily agreed to it. I didn't make this offer to Tommy, as he was now a Spec-5 and making considerably more money. Besides, with his new arrangement Súmat, he was spending less money.

While I was leaving, the three of them each hit me up for a $20 loan, which I promptly provided from my tobacco can of cash, and then left for Korat. Arriving at the Sri Patana Hotel I rented a room for four nights and requested an 11:00 wakeup call. Entering my room, I put away the clothes in my shopping bag, stripped to my skivvies and went to bed.

With the wakeup call, I showered, shaved and dressed, before leaving to take Dhoi to lunch at the Ming Ter. There I told her the good news that I'd be given two days off for our trip to Ayutthaya. She was overjoyed with the news, and said she'd bring the map and train schedule tomorrow for us to plan our longer trip and reservations for a place to spend the night while we were there.

Escorting Dhoi back to her work, I went to my Hotel room for a long nap, before returning at 6:00 to go home with Dhoi, and have dinner with her family, which had become our routine for my off day when we went dancing. While Dhoi was getting ready to go dancing after dinner, I told the Colonel about my getting the two days off, and thanked him for making it possible. But, to please not do it again, as it put me in a difficult position with my Company CO, to which he understood and agreed.

When Dhoi was ready, we left for the night club, as we routinely did on my first off day, where we had a fun evening dancing, before leaving for my Hotel room to glory in the release of our pent-up lust with vigorous lovemaking in a sexually enhancing Kama Sutra position. Spooning in the afterglow of our climactic rush, went happily asleep. Then, again in the morning we express our desire for each other with wanton lovemaking, before we affectionately showered together, and dressed to leave. After we lovingly embraced kissed, we left for the Chainarong Gate to board a Thai bus for the Thai Army Base and Camp Friendship. There, I drank a cold Bud, as I dressed in jungle fatigues, and went to the Mess Hall for breakfast. So ended what became the routine for my first off day.

On my second off day, it became my routine, after breakfast and morning formation, to change into civilian clothes and return to my Hotel room to sleep till 11:00. Then, I'd shower, shave and dress, before walking to the Jomsurang Hotel and take Dhoi to lunch at the nearby Ming Ter. After which, I'd escort Dhoi back to her work and return to my Hotel room for a few hours of sleep. After my nap, I'd go to the Thai bar for dinner and to share bottles of Sîng Hâi Beer in the jocular camaraderie of my Thai friends till 6:00. Then, I'd walk to the Tech Rep's compound to drink one of Horn's Sîng Hâi Beers, while spending a relaxing evening with my compatriots till 9:00. Returning with my barracks-mates to our Tropo barracks, I'd be in bed by 10:00.

On my first workday, I normally woke to the 5:00 bugle call for Reveille, perform my usual ablutions, then drink a cold Bud, as I dressed in a fresh set of jungle fatigues, before walking with Skip to the Mess Hall for a breakfast. Returning for morning formation, we'd then ride in the jeep to the Air Base Site. After a productive day working in the Operations Room and enjoying lunch with Glen on my 10:50 and 5:40 meal runs, I'd shower, shave and change into civilian clothes, before I was relieved at 6:50 and caught a Thai Bus to Korat. Returning to my Hotel room, I'd meet Dhoi at 8:00 for a tantalizing evening of dancing with my beautiful Dhoi in my arms, before we returned to my room, engaging in various Kama Sutra positions to enhance our vigorous lovemaking. Then, we'd sleep happily together in the afterglow of our orgasmic release.

On my second workday, Dhoi and I were roused by the 3:30 wake-up call. Reigniting our lust for each other with sensuous foreplay, we enjoyed the loving desires of our hearts in wanton lovemaking. Then, we lay for a while in the afterglow of our climactic pleasure. When we'd playfully showered together, dressed to leave, and lovingly embraced and kissed, I'd pick up my shopping bag full of dirty clothes, as we left to catch a Thai bus to our separate abodes.

Returning to the Tropo barracks, I'd drink a cold Bud, as I changed into a fresh set of jungle fatigues and leave for breakfast in the Mess Hall. After morning formation, I'd ride the jeep to the Air Base Site for another productive day working in the Operations Room. At the end of the workday, I'd spend the evening with Skip as my partner, playing Double-Deck Pinochle for money-stakes, while drinking beer and smoking cigarettes till 10:00, usually going to bed with some extra money from our winnings.

During my two days working the night shift, I'd sleep till the 11:00 bugle call for Mess, then shower, shave and drink a cold Bud, as I dressed to leave for Korat and take Dhoi to lunch at the Ming Ter. After an enjoyable lunch with Dhoi, I'd escort her back to work and chat for a while, before returning to the Tropo barracks and sleep till the 5:00 bugle call for Mess. Then, I'd drink a cold Bud, as I dressed in a fresh set of OD BDUs and walk with Skip to the Mess Hall for a dinner.

On our first night, we'd pack up our tape decks to take with us in the jeep to the Air Base site, and make copies of the taped albums he'd brought with him in the back of the Operations Room. On my 10:50 meal run, I'd meet with Glen and talk about what was happening with us, and afterward I wrote letters to Linda and my parents.

After our second night, we'd pack up our tape decks and take them back to the Tropo barracks on our breakfast meal runs. The only variation was when my night shift was on a Sunday, I spent the afternoon on the Thai Army Base with Dhoi and her family, before returning to the Tropo barracks to get ready for working the night shift, or take Dhoi to the Action Theater and my Hotel room.

The only regular change to my 6-day schedule was the monthly Pay Day. Then, I'd dress in my Class-B khaki uniform, get in the Pay Line at the Day Room by 8:00 to receive my $220 in pay, buy a $10 Savings Bond for $7.50, pay $8 for Suda's services as my mây-bâan, and exchange $100 for 2,000 Bhat. The, while I was changing out of my Class-B khaki uniform in the Tropo barracks, I'd collect the $25 from those who borrowed $20 from me when they were broke at the end of the month. Then later, I went to the Bank and deposited $50, or more in my Savings Account.

I still cared about my Linda in New Jersey, who I wrote to regularly and called periodically when I worked a night shift. But, being assuaged by the old adage, "If you can't be with the one you love, then love the one you're with," then my life in Thailand with Dhoi evolved into a happy routine.

CHAPTER 58

WE'D NEVER BE ABLE TO SEE EVERYTHING IN JUST ONE DAY

It was a reassuring feeling to believe my life here in Thailand now had a sense of stability and routine to it for a least the next five months. Hopefully longer if my request for extension of my tour of duty was approved. Of course, unwanted things in life happened to upset the apple cart, like with Frank and Tommy being promoted to Spec-5, transferred to the Tropo Site, and made to work with those lifers there. But, Frank lucked out and was made the Air Base Site's NCOIC, and maybe the same thing could happen to Tommy. In the meantime, I'm as snug as a bug in a rug, with a good job I enjoy, a beautiful woman to be and do things with, a fun bunch of guys at the Thai bar to hone my Thai language skills, and a relaxing place I can retreat to and discuss the issues of the day that didn't have anything to do with work or the military, while drinking free Sing Hai Beer.

My second off day began with seeing our new First Sargent leading the morning formation rigamarole, and happily not seeing Spike any-where within view. Though I'd see this new 1SGT, a tall, well-built man with a business-as-usual demeanor, at all the morning formations

I attended, and in the Pay Line on Pay Day, I was happy not to see him otherwise for the rest of my tour of duty.

Saturday was March 1st, Pay Day. Since it was when I worked by first night shift, I went immediately after morning formation to the Tropo barracks to shower, shave and drink a cold Bud, as I dressed in my freshly starched Class-B khaki uniform. When Skip and I thoroughly searched each other's uniform to make sure everything pinned on the uniform was centered and level, and there were no visible loose threads, we walked through the barracks, out the back door and turned right toward the Day Room, which occupied the back half of the building housing HQ.

Joining the end of the Pay Line, and it being a while till the payout began, I rolled and lit a cigarette. The man in front of me, smelling my tobacco smoke, turned and asked, "Hey, can I bum a cigarette from you?"

Pulling the makings from under the front of my khaki shirt, I handed them to him and replied, "Mâi bpén rai."

He looked at me dumbfounded and replied, "Man, I'm dying for a smoke. Can you roll one for me?" And, knowing if I rolled it for him, then I'd have to roll one for everyone else who asked, I sympathetically replied, "Wish I could, but according to my PE teacher's rule, 'If you can roll it, you can smoke it.' So, I can't help you there," and he turned away disgruntled.

Eventually, the Pay Line began to move. Entering the Day Room, I saw our new 1SGT sitting next to Lt. Willis at the Savings Bond table, scrutinizing each Soldier as he stood in front of the table, and thought, "Sure am glad Skip looked over my uniform for defects, as I sure don't want to get on his shit-list the first time he sees me."

After being paid my $220, I walked to the Saving's Bond table, came to attention and handed Lt. Willis a new 20-Dollar bill to purchase a $10 Savings Bond for $7.50. Noticing the 1SGT was looking intently at my face, after taking a cursory look at my uniform, he said, "Thank you for supporting the war effort, Specialist Lynch," as he handed me the $12.50 in change.

I replied, "Just doing my duty, First Sargent," and thought, "He's not checking our uniforms for defects, as he's trying to memorize the face of every man in his company." As I went to the next table to pay for Aida's services.

Returning after Pay Line to my bed in the Tropo barracks,, I drank a cold Bud, as I changed into civilian clothes, and collected $25 each from George, Ronnie and Stony. Plus, $25 from a guy on the Z-shift who George had explained how he'd borrowed $20 from me after being broke, with the expectation to pay $25 on Pay Day. When I'd collected the $20 extra on my four payday loans, I thought, "This is a pretty good, tax free, side business, which will be expanding by word of mouth. I'd better buy a little notebook, so I can keep track who's borrowing money from me."

I'd no doubt everyone I loaned money to, would repay me, as one of the things not tolerated by Soldiers in their ranks was a Soldier who welshed on a bet or loan with his fellow Soldiers. Such an act was cause for a "blanket party," where the offender was wrapped in his blanket while he slept and soundly beaten. There was on appeal from this form of barracks justice, as to report to an authority that your black-and-blue body was other than the result of accidently slipping on a bar of soap in the shower, was cause for a "GI shower," Then, your fellow Soldiers dragged and stripped you in the shower room, and scrubbed your black-and-blue skin off with stiff bristle brushes.

The afternoon after working my first night shift was on Sunday which I spent on the Thai Army Base with Dhoi and her family. While going over Dhoi's map of Ayutthaya, her parents provided invaluable information on what to see and where to stay, since Dhoi had only been there once before as a young girl. Having helped us work out an itinerary of what sights to see, they suggested we stay at the Bâan Are Gong, an imposing 50-year-old teak guesthouse close to the train station, and overlooking the Krûngsîi River[155]. It also had reasonably priced double bedrooms, which would be good, since we'd have Mii-kâa with us.

After my two off days, I went to work my first day shift on Wednesday, March 5th, at the Air Base Site. After Shift Change Report Bob entered the Operations Room and excitedly said, "The Apollo 9 Mission to the moon successfully lifted off on Monday, and is now halfway there, with Jim McDivit, Dave Scott and Russ Schweichant. Their 10-day mission is to orbit the Moon several times, while test flying the

---

155   Half Good Fortune River

Lunar Module for the first time in space. So far, the only thing the Russians have been able to do successfully is launch Soyuz 4 and 5, and then have one of their Cosmonauts transfer from one capsule to the other via a spacewalk. If this Apollo mission is successful there's no doubt we'll be the first to put a man on the Moon in a few months."

Though AFTN was now broadcasting TV, it was not getting any of the live TV feeds coming from Apollo 9. Also, AFTN's after dinner news programs were at 7:00, right when we had shift change, so I didn't have a chance to watch any of the news footage shown later of the Apollo 9 Mission, even as exciting as they may have been to watch. However, over the next week, I did follow the AP and UPI teletype news feeds updating the Mission's progress until its splashdown on March 13th, when I was working my first night shift.

When I was relieved after my second night shift, the morning of March 15th, I'd already showered, shaved and dressed in civilian clothes, before I quickly left with my clothes and toilet kit in a small suitcase I'd bought at the BX. Boarding a Thai bus to Korat, I hired a săawm-law to rapidly carry me to the Sir Patana Hotel, where I rented a room for four nights, before continuing to Korat's Main Train Station. There, I found Dhoi and Mii-kâa waiting on the station's platform with their baggage and our First-Class tickets for the 8:15 train to Ayutthaya. I'd purchased the First-Class tickets two days earlier via the Jomsurang Hotel's concierge when I'd taken Dhoi to lunch. These tickets were for compartments with beds and cost only $100 Bhat each way.

Soon I heard the whistle, and then saw an old, black steam locomotive coming from the left, pulling five passenger cars. I saw the first car was labelled "First Class" in English under some Thai script. When the train stopped, and after some people exited the First-Class car, I handed our First-Class tickets to a Thai porter. Taking our tickets, he then picked up our suitcases and carried them, as he led us down a narrow hallway along the left side of the car to our compartment, and I thought, "At least we'll be riding on the shaded side of the car to Ayutthaya."

The compartment was comfortably furnished with facing cushioned seats that could be made into a double bed. Above a large window was a pull-down bed, and to the right of the entrance door was a door to the lavatory. When the porter placed our luggage under the seats, I tipped him a One-Bhat coin as he left. We then promptly sat in the right-hand seat so we were facing the direction of travel, with Dhoi snuggled happily against my left side, as no-one would expect we weren't a married couple, since we were travelling with a toddler.

Mii-kâa climbed into my lap and pressed her little nose against the window to get a good view of the doings outside. Shortly, I felt a small jerk as the train began to move. Soon the train was moving down the tracks at 40 MPH and it wasn't long before the gentle rocking of the train car and the repetitive "click-clack" of its wheels crossing the joints of the steel rails had lulled us to sleep.

After 90 minutes, I woke as the train jerked to a stop at the Pak Chong Train Station. When it pulled out several minutes later I watched the view through the window of the passing jungle, as the train for the next 90 minutes passed through a low pass in a mountain range separating the Korat Plateau form the alluvial plain of central Thailand, before the train reached the Provincial Capital of Saraburi. There, the train stopped for several minutes, before leaving for Ayutthaya.

An hour later, having watched miles of rice paddies with small hamlets scattered amongst them and the occasional town along the way, the train made a long turn to the left and headed south. By now, Dhoi and Mii-kâa were awake and also watching out the window as the train approached the outskirts of Ayutthaya, which were not unlike those of Korat.

Before the train came to a stop the porter knocked on our compartment door and collected our bags from under the seats. Leading us out of the train car and onto Ayutthaya's Train Station platform, he set them down, and I gave him another One-Bhat tip. Then, gathering up our suitcases, and Dhoi placing Mii-kâa on her left hip, we walked the 100 yards down a lane due west of the Train Station to the Bâan Are Gong guesthouse, where the concierge at the Jomsurang Hotel had made a reservation for a room with two beds.

Entering the Bâan Are Gong, an imposing 50-year-old teak guesthouse, we were cheerfully welcomed by the Chinese-Thai family who ran it. After paying 260 Bhat for two night, a son carried our bags as he led us to an upstairs room. Entering the room I saw it was a well-furnished, spacious room made of teak that looked out over the Krûngsîi River.

Looking down at the river, I saw a boat dock beneath me at the end of the lane. When I asked him about it, I had trouble fully understanding him, as my ear was tuned to the Isaan dialect. I asked Dhoi to talk with him, and learned the dock was for a ferry across the river to the island where Ayutthaya is located for the cost of one Bhat per person. He also recommended when we went to Ayutthaya, to eat at the Lung Lék[156] cafe, as it was everyone's favorite noodle emporium, and on the way to the Ayutthaya Tourist Center. This was the best place to get information to tour with. He also explained that the the full name of Ayutthaya is "Paá Ná-Kaaywn Sii Yuu-Tayaa," or "Buddha Image City Dignity Yuu-Taya".

Giving the young man a 2-Bhat tip we then unpacked our suitcases into a chest of drawers before walking down to the boat dock. Paying the 3-Bhat fee we rode the ferry up the wide Krûngsîi River a quarter mile to the Châo Prom[157] Pier, at the end of Naresuam Road. There I hired a săawm-law to carry us to the Lung Lék cafe, which was a mile away on Chiikun Road, or "Chinese Person Road".

Arriving at the Lung Lék, we were seated and given a menu. See-ing the large selection of noodle meals on the menu, I let Dhoi select several for us to share. After a delicious variety of spices and flavors assaulted my pallet, and we'd finished eating, I hired another săawm-law for the 1-mile ride to the Ayutthaya Tourist Center. Though not familiar with the Central Thai dialect, I didn't let that affect my bar-gaining abilities using the Isaan dialect to brow beat the driver to a price substantially lower than his asking price, having taken the driver by surprise with my Isaan dialect

After taking in all the information at the Tourist Center's excel-lent upstairs exhibition hall, I had a good understanding of the ancient city's former magnificence. Collecting a map, brochures and some good advice, we left and walked North a few hundred yards up Sîi Sânpét Road and turned left into the Ayutthaya Historical Park, we came to the three magnificent stupas of the Wat Prâ Sîi Sânpét, or "Temple Buddha Image Dignity Choose Diamond."

According to our literature, these three stupas were the most iconic images in Ayutthaya. Built in the late 15th century, this temple was the city's largest and used by several Emperors. It once contained a 53-foot-tall standing Buddha, the Prâ Sîi Sânpét, covered with 550

---

156   Uncle Small
157   Rent Brahma

pounds of gold, which was melted down by the Burmese conquerors in 1767.

When we'd finished walking through this ancient ruin, we walked South to the adjacent Wihaan Prá Mongkon Bophit, the Temple Buddha Image Auspicious Sign Chapel, a sanctuary hall that housed one of the larges bronze Buddha images in Thailand. The 56-foot-high figure had undergone several facelifts due to lighting strikes and fires. In 1955, the Burmese Prime Minister donated 200,000 Bhat, $10,000, to restore the building, an act of belated atonement for his country's sacking of the city 200 years before.

By this time little Mii-kâa was getting cranky. Though she'd been happily riding on my shoulders, it was past her nap time. Walking the few hundred yards back to Sîi Sânpét Road, I hired a săawm-law for the 1½-mile ride down Naresuan Road to the Châo Prom Pier, and then rode the ferry down the Krûngsîi River to the guesthouse, where the three of us took a nap.

After our refreshing nap, we walked the short distance to the Train Station. There I hired a săawm-law to carry us the ¾ miles South down Watkluay Road, beside the Krûngsîi River, across the Pridi Damrong Bridge to Ûu Thong Road, or the "Harbor Joined Road." This road followed the edge of Ayutthaya's island made by a system of natural and man-made rivers, then south to the Pae Krûng Gáo, or "Houseboat Half Old," a well-established riverside restaurant serving top-notch Thai food.

Finished with our delicious dinner, we walked West a short distance across Ûu Thong Road to Wat Suwannaram, the "Temple Gold Naram," to see its different architectural style. The exterior, designed by Rama I, was in the older style "uposatha," with the slightly bowed line along the Temple's edge. Its plain interior finish, typical of the Ayutthaya period, was attributed to Rama III. Next to it, was a sanctuary from Rama IV's reign, resplendent with a glittering exterior mosaic.

Walking South, we crossed Ûu Thong Road again, to the ruins of the Pom Phet Fortress, which sits in the bend of the Krûngsîi River, a quarter mile before its confluence with the Châo Phraya River bordering Ayutthaya's southern and western edges. There, the Krûngsîi River turned south.

From a pier at the Fortress' ruins, we rode a ferry across the Krûngsîi River to Wat Pánan Choing, or "Temple Large-Hammer Pedestal." Despite the hectic nature of this Temple from the merit-making ceremonies and ritualistic fish feeding, we were impressed by the 63-foot wide Prá Pánan Choing statue in the sanctuary. The statue's broad shape was typical of the Ûu Thong period when it was built in 1324. Lining the walls were 84,000 Buddha images surrounding the huge statue.

Leaving Wat Pânan Choing, I hired a săawm-law to carry us the 1½-miles north on Watklaay Road back to our guesthouse. Readying ourselves for bed, there was no way around the fact that Mii-kâa was not going to sleep alone in a strange bed in a strange room. So, Dhoi and Mii-kâa slept in one bed, while I slept in the other. Later, I woke to Dhoi slipping into my bed, and we began our sensuous foreplay. When our lust overcame us, we quickly moved some of the bedding onto the teak floor, where we consummated our vigorous lovemaking as quietly as possible. With most Thais living in one-room dwellings, it was common for a couple to make love with their children in the same room.

Early the next morning, I showered, shaved and dressed before Dhoi got Mii-kâa up for their shower prior to dressing. After eating breakfast in the guesthouse we rode the ferry to the Châo Prom Pier, where I hired a săawm-law to carry us one mile up Naresuun Road to the ruins of Wat Prá Máhátáat, or "Temple Buddha Image Great Element ruins," on the south side of the road.

This Temple site contained the most photographed image in Ayutthaya, a huge sandstone Buddha head peering out from within a tree's entwined roots. Nobody knows for sure how the Buddha head ended up in the tree. Some say it was abandoned after the Burmese Army sacked Ayutthaya because it was too heavy, and the tree grew around it. The Temple was built in 1374 during the reign of Borom Rachathirat I. I saw the central "prang," a Khmer-style stupa, had rows of headless Buddha images.

Crossing to the North side of Naresuan Road, we walked the short distance to Wat Râtburaná, or "Temple King Repair." The prang of this Temple is one of the best extant versions in Ayutthaya with detailed carvings of lotus blossoms and mythical creatures. The Temple was built in the 15th Century by Borom Rachathirat II on the cremation site for his two brothers, who died while fighting each other for the throne. Looters raided the site in 1957 and stole many of its treasures. A subsequent excavation of the site uncovered many rare Buddha images in the crypt.

We then walked west one-third of a mile across the Ayutthaya Historical Park to the ruins of the Wat Tan Mikáradt, or "Temple Buddha Teaching Mikáraat." Its most prominent feature was a central stupa surrounded by "singha," its guardian lion sculptures. Finding a pleasant place to sit among the ruins, we relaxed for a little bit and let Miikâa play around the singha sculptures, before continuing a little further west to the ruins of the Old Royal Palace. Though it must have been resplendent in its day, it was little more than a foundation with tumble downed wall from when it was sacked and burned by the Burmese Army in 1767.

Just beyond the Palace ruins was Klong Tháw Road, or "Canal Connect Road," a wide avenue through the Ayutthaya Historical Park connecting the Lopburi River to the north and the Chao Phraya River to the south. Walking a few hundred yards South, we came to a lane that led west to the ruins of Wat Lókáyásútharam, or "Temple Discard Rubbish Highest Temple." Lying out in the open amongst the ruins was a huge 138-foot-long sandstone Buddha, reclining in the "para nirvana" posture, covered with a saffron robe.

Having hiked across the Historical Park, we walked back to Klong Tháw Road. There, I hired a săawm-law to carry us the 3.5 miles across Ayutthaya's island, crossing Pridi Damrong Bridge, then north up Dusit Road to the Floating Market near the ruins of Wat Kûdi Dao, or "Temple Park Good Star," and Wat Ayutthaya. Then, I hired a longtail boat to carry down the large canal that paralleled Dusit Road, going between the wooden platforms that were just above the water. Though a little kitsch, the Floating Market venders sold fresh fruit and vegetables, cooked snacks, clothes, and artwork, with traditional performances showing all day.

Touring down the canal through busy wooden platforms looking at the varied activities and items for sale, Dhoi bought some fresh fruit and cooked food. Then the boat driver took us West on a canal emptying into the Krûngsîi River, just below our guesthouse. Returning to our room we feasted hungrily on the food Dhoi bought, before lying together on a bed for a nap.

Waking refreshed from our nap we walked down to the boat dock, where I hired a long-tail boat for 20 Bhat to carry us to the sites along the 8 miles of rivers surrounding Ayutthaya's island. Travelling South on the Krûngsîi River to where it turned West, passing between the Pom Phet Fortress ruins on our right and Wat Pánan Choing to our left, we went straight onto the Chao Phraya River, where the Krûngsîi River turned South. A mile up this river, we stopped at the Wat Pûut Thai Sáwân, or "Temple Speak Climb Heaven," to see the reclining Buddha in its Khmer-style prang. Just past this temple, we stopped on the river's outer bank to see the Muslim District's Mosque.

Continuing up the river, where it made a wide bend to the north, we stopped on the outer bank at the Wat Chai Wâttangraam, or "Temple Pierce Proper Temple," Though it was immersed in jungle, we could still see its impressive, 117-foot high, central Khmer-style prang, built in 1673 by Prasat Thong. A half-mile further upriver we passed under a wide bridge and saw Wat Kâasátthrát, or"Temple Value Truth Speak" on the river's outer bank.

Reaching the northwest corner of Ayutthaya's island, the driver followed the Chao Phraya River to the left a half-mile to the Jaadii Puu Kâao Tong, or "Pagoda Earth Mountain Gold", built by the Burmese during its 15-year occupation. The top part of its stupa was later added by the Thais. At the front I saw the statue of Naresuan, a memorial to the all-conquering Emperor, surrounded by dozens of statues of fighting cockerels. The legend is, when Naresuan was a hostage in Burma his invincible fighting cockerels secured his fearsome reputation. Entering the Pagoda, we clambered up the 79 steps of the stupa for a splendid view of Ayutthaya.

Returning to the boat, the driver went back down the Chao Phraya River to its confluence with the man-made Lópburi River that traversed the northern edge of Ayutthaya's island. This was dug to connect the Krûngsîi River to the East with the Chao Phraya River to the west. Traveling a mile up the Lópburi River, we stopped at a bridge leading North to Wat Nîa Prá Mayrú, or "Temple Face Buddha Image Cremation Tower". This temple escaped the wrath of the Burmese Army's 1767 invasion, as it was used as their base. Inside the Temple was a magnificent 1500-year-old green sandstone Buddha from Sri Lanka. Proceeding into the central sanctuary, I saw a carved wooden ceiling showing the Buddhist heaven.

Continuing on the Lópburi River, we passed Wat Kuti Tang, or "Temple Ditch Gold", on our left, and a large Chinese Shrine to our right, before we reached the river's divergence from Krûngsîi River. There we exited onto a dock for the Hûa Raw Night Market, or the "Head Stay Night Market", which offered riparian seating to enjoy a wide range of Thai and Muslim dishes, the latter indicated by a green star and crescent.

Having eaten our fill of a variety of delicious foods and enjoyed a beautiful sunset, I hired a long-tail boat for the mile ride to our guesthouse dock. Returning to our room we let our very tired Mii-kâa nap for a bit, while we sensuously showered and made love, before drying each other off, dressing and packing to leave on the night train to Korat. Then, Dhoi gently woke Mii-kâa and carried her behind me the short distance to Ayutthaya's Train Station, as I ported our suitcases.

When the big, black steam locomotive noisily arrived, pulling five passenger cars, I handed our tickets to the porter for the First-Class car, who picked up our suitcases and led us to our compartment. On entering it I saw he'd already made the upper and lower beds. Tipping him 2 One-Bhat coins, he left, and we all stripped to our underwear and lay on the larger lower bed with me comfortably spooning Dhoi as she cuddled Mii-kâa in her arms. While happily falling asleep I thought, "Thank you, Colonel, for a wonderful two-day trip, as we'd never be able to see everything in just one day."

CHAPTER 59

HOW SIMILAR THE TEACHINGS OF JESUS AND THE BUDDHA ARE

Having slept on the train for four hours, I woke to a knock on our compartment's door and a voice announce loudly, "Korat, sîp-hâa naa-tii. Korat, fifteen minute."
Rising from the bottom bed, Dhoi and Mii-kâa went into the compartment's lavatory first, while I dressed and pulled our suitcases from under the bed. When they exited the lavatory, I entered to relieve myself and freshen up. Leaving the lavatory I saw Dhoi and Mii-kâa were dressed with Dhoi sitting on the bed, holding Mii-kâa on her lap, and brushing her black hair. When Dhoi finished with Mii-kâa, she began brushing her own luxurious, long black hair.

Feeling the train slowing and then jerking to a stop I opened the compartment's door and the porter scurried in to pick up our suitcases. We then followed him to the Train Station's platform where he set the luggage down, and I tipped him a One-Bhat coin, as I said thankfully, "Kup koon mâak, krúp."

No sooner had the porter set our baggage down, than two sǎawm-law drivers, the first two in a queue at the end of the platform, ran over, seized our baggage and began to carry them to their sǎawm-laws.

Their ploy was to get our suitcases into their vehicles before a negotiated price was made, and bargain from a stronger position.

When I yelled in Thai for them to stop, and they failed to do so, I yelled again in Thai, "Stop. Thief," to which they immediately froze with fear on their faces. Having drawn the attention of two Thai Policemen talking on the platform, and I said in a low voice to the drivers, "Five Bhat each to go Sri Pattana Hotel, or you go to the monkey house."

Being a reasonable price to carry us and our luggage the 1.3 miles to the Sri Pattana Hotel, they sheepishly nodded their heads, and I waived my hand and yelled to the Policemen, "Mâi bpén rai, krúp," and thought, "That sure simplified things."

Following the two cowed drivers to their saawm-laws, I climbed into the first one with our suitcases, and Dhoi boarded the second one with Mii-kâa. Ten minutes later, we arrived at the Hotel, and I left a 5:00 wake-up call request at the Reception Desk, before we went to my Hotel room and to slept on the bed fully clothed.

Roused by the wake-up call several hours later, we quickly went down to the Hotel's entrance with our suitcases, where I hired two saawm-laws to carry us to the Chainarong Gate. There, we boarded a crowded Thai bus for Dhoi and Mii-kâa to ride to the Thai Army Base, and for me to go to my Company Area.

Entering the Tropo barracks, I drank a cold Bud, as I dumped the clothes from my suitcase onto the floor, put the toilet kit in my wall locker and hurriedly changed into a fresh set of jungle fatigues, before rapidly walking to the Mess Hall for breakfast. Having quickly eaten my breakfast, I rushed to the basketball court in front of the Tropo barracks, and made it in time for morning formation.

After the 1SGT reported to the CO, "Company all present or accounted for, Sir," the CO said, "Company, stand at ease. I've got some good news, bad news and fun news for you this St. Patrick's Day morning. The good news is, I've been informed that starting the first week of April, new personnel will be arriving every four weeks for the foreseeable future, so the Battalion will be fully manned by the beginning of the fiscal year on October 1st. The bad news is, all of you who've requested an extension of tour not already approved, will be denied. The fun news is, next week, the Company is scheduled for your annual weapons familiarization on the Thai Army Base's rifle range on Monday, Wednesday and Friday mornings, with the Z-shift on Monday, the Y-shift on Wednesday and the X-shift on Friday, which is your second off day. First Sargent, dismiss the Company."

With the announcement denying any more extensions of tour, I heard a lot of groans from the people the around me and thought, "Why'd the Army have to send all of those replacements now to mess up our plans to stay happily in this heaven on earth, verses sending us to that hellhole at Ft. Huachuca, AZ."

In the Operations Room that morning, there was considerable chatter on the Order Wire about getting new replacements every four weeks, the bleak expectation a lot of us would be sent to Ft. Huachuca, and how men from the outlying Radio Sites would come here for a morning of target practice next week. Also, the Tech Reps were griping about the non-renewal of their contract the next fiscal year, and how some would seek Warrant Officer commissions to fill the billets for Radio Site OICs that would be needed, so they could remain in Thailand. There was even some work that was done amongst all the chatter.

Because Dhoi and I had spent the weekend together in Ayutthaya we decided to wait till after my second day working to go dancing at the night club and spend the night lovemaking. During our lunches together, when I worked my two night shifts, the conversations were all about the preparations for Suumii and Somsak's wedding and how busy they'd be all day performing the Buddhist rituals for a successful life together.

Getting off work after my second night shift, I ate breakfast and spent the morning sleeping in the Tropo barracks. After lunch in the Mess Hall, I went to the Sri Pattana Hotel and rented a room for four nights, where I slept till 4:00. When I woke, I showered, shaved and dressed in a form-fitting, dark-grey silk suit Mr. Sing had made me two weeks ago for this occasion. I then went down and hired a săawm-law to carry me to Saranarii College, where I followed the signs in Thai and English to its auditorium.

Entering the designated doorway, I walked into a large hallway and saw cases of beer, assorted liquors and wine stacked six feet high all along the right sidewall. Showing my wedding invitation to a Thai man in white livery, he consulted a chart in his left hand and led me through a double doorway to my left. Following him, I entered a large, box-like room festooned with lotus blossoms and Buddha images hanging from yellow curtained walls. At the front of the room was a large, raised stage, and the room was filled with rows of large, round tables covered with yellow cloth. I also noted those seated in the left half of the room were all Thai men wearing suits, and those seated in the right half of the room were all Thai women in their colorful Thai finery.

Proceeding to a table toward the front, near the left sidewall, my usher indicated an empty place at the table with a folded placard containing Thai script, which I presumed was my name. Making my sáwátdiis and giving my name to the five men seated there, I sat down. My usher asked in Thai what I'd like to drink, and I replied in Thai, "Scotch whiskey on ice."

While he was gone to get my drink, those sitting at the table introduced themselves to me, and in the process, I found these men were all corporate and banking executives. And gazing quickly at the other tables around me, I saw no other "farang," Thai for a Caucasian from the Thai pronunciation of "French", within my sight. When the liveried Thai returned shortly, he set an empty glass in front of me, and then a fifth of Hundred Pipers Scotch and a pitcher of ice cubes.

Looking at the drinks before the others at my table, as I poured three fingers of Scotch and a couple of ice cubes into my glass, I saw they each had a fifth of a high-end brand of liquor in front of them. Remembering Dhoi telling me a Thai wedding reception lasted until the couple returned from their honeymoon, I realized we were each provisioned for the long haul. And, from the lackadaisical manner these high-powered men interacted with me, and as I was the only farang around, I thought, "They must believe I'm some high-level American business friend of the bride or groom's family. Boy, would they be surprised to find out I was actually some low-level enlisted Army puke."

As it's bad manners in Thai culture to impress others with your social status, I was never pressed about my background, or how I knew the bride and groom. And, when the final nuptial ceremony was concluded at sunset on the stage by an elderly Buddhist monk wearing a red-orange robe, and mounds of food was served to everyone, Dhoi did not come over to greet me, for to do so would violate the Thai proprieties that separated the sexes socially.

While celebrating till early in the morning, for to leaving before the bride and groom returned from their honeymoon any sooner would be construed as an insult, each man at my table, and several from sur-rounding tables, had given me his business card with an invite to have lunch or dinner with them sometime to discuss the terms of my em-ployment with them, and I thought, "Clearly, to have a Thai speaking American working with their firm would be quite a jewel in the in corporate crowns."

When Suumii and Somsak returned from their honeymoon, I quick-ly made my sáwátdiis and hurriedly left to return to my Company Area for morning formation. Luckily I'd been served plenty of food with my Scotch through the night, so I'd no need to eat breakfast in the Mess Hall before formation.

Returning to my Hotel room after formation, I was totally exhaust-ed and slept until 4:00 in the afternoon. After I'd showered, shaved and dressed, I went to the Thai Army base for dinner with Dhoi's family as Dhoi had the day off from work after the wedding festivities. When Dhoi had readied herself after dinner, we went dancing at the night club, before we retired to my Hotel room for a repast of lovemaking to satiate our pent-up lust for each other.

When we boarded the săawm-law I'd hired for our ride to the Chain-arong Gate, I saw a considerable amount of preparations happening along Rajadamnern Road, as we turned right onto it, and asked Dhoi what was going on. She replied, "It's for the Táao Suranerii Festival, when Korat celebrates its namesake heroine from March 23rd to April 3rd. it features theatre performances and other events on Rajadamnern Road, passing in front of her monument across the road over there."

The following week I went through my normal daily routines, ex-cept on Friday. Everyone who worked the X-shifts from the Tropo and Crypto Platoons, a third of the Motor Pool and Headquarters Platoons, and those on their off day from the outlying Radio Sites, were formed up after morning formation and marched to the Company Armory. There everyone was filed in to be issued a combat harness with two canteens of water and five magazines of ammo, a steel helmet with liner, and an M-14 rifle, before climbing into one of the four waiting canvas covered, 2½-ton trucks.

From the canvas cave of the truck I rode in, the most I could see was the front of front of the truck behind me, as we rode West across Camp Friendship and the Air Base, onto the Thai Army Base. There, I felt the truck turn right, going north on an asphalt road. After about ten minutes, I hear the truck's wheels crunch onto a gravel surface, as it turned right and then stopped.

Clambering out of the back of the second truck, I saw we were in a gravel covered parking lot, next to a tall wood tower with a flagpole on top flying a red flag, surrounded by wide-open, dry yellow grassy fields. Beyond the tower was the usual 3-foot high berm of dirt for the firing line, with a 100-yard wide field of fire to the large, white bullseye targets in front of a 20-foot high dirt wall to stop the bullets fired at the targets.

When everyone had piled out of the trucks, Lt. "Brucy-poo" Willis was trying to get everyone organized into ranks behind the trucks, but was being defeated by his high squeaky voice, which everyone tended to laugh at and ignore. The next thing I heard was SSG Zuligich's deep, gravelly voice say, "You better let me handle this Sir," and in his booming voice of command yell, "Everyone, form up in two ranks behind your truck at attention," which was promptly obeyed.

Familiarizing with a weapon is different than "qualifying" with one. To qualify, one fires at one or more types of targets at different distances to score points. The number of points scored determines your level of qualification as either a Marksman, Sharpshooter or Expert. To be familiarized, you only need to demonstrate you can operate the weapon safely, without shooting yourself or another accidently.

The firing range we used had 30 firing positions spaced 8 feet apart, and the four trucks had brought about a dozen men each, including the driver, who also had to familiarize with the weapons. After the Range Safety lecture was given by SSG Zuligich, those from the first two trucks were marched onto the firing line berm, and ordered for each of us to stand behind a small wood sign, with what must have been a number in Thai script written in red on it.

When SSG Zuligich saw from the Range tower each man was behind a sign, he boomed, "Lock and load one magazine of ammo, set the Selector Switch to Single Fire, and raise your right hand when you've done so," which made you remove your finger from the trigger. With everyone's right hand raised, he ordered, "Set the Safety Switch to Off, and from the standing position you will fire at your target. When you've emptied the magazine, clear and lower your weapon, then raise your right hand. You may commence firing."

I immediately was inundated with the staccato of explosions from bullets being fired by the two dozen M-14 rifles filling the air around me, as I fired methodically at the black center of the large, white target 100-yards down range. It was a matter of personal pride that I grouped my 16 shots from when I was awarded the Top-Shooter-of-the-Week Award at Boy Scout Summer Camp in 1965. As we'd been given no opportunity to zero-in my rifle's sights, then the closer my shots were grouped together, the better my aim would prove to be.

After everyone on the firing line had emptied their 16-round magazine, cleared their rifle and raised their right hand, SSG Zuligich ordered us to set the Selector Switch to Semi-automatic, which fired three rounds with one pull of the trigger. When everyone indicated with his raised right hand he was ready, we were ordered again to commence firing from the standing position. Then, he had us repeat the process with the Selector Switch set to the Full Automatic position, which allowed the magazine to be emptied with one pull on the trigger. To empty a 16-round magazine of an M-14 on Full Automatic without spraying bullets in a wide upward arc into the air, which could kill someone miles away, was nearly impossible. So, we fired in four to six round bursts to keep from shooting bullets over the back wall.

Having had fun firing the M-14 rifle from the standing position in each of the three firing modes, we were then instructed to fire one magazine in the kneeling position and one magazine in the prone position. When we had emptied all five of our magazines, we were told to pick up all of the empty cartridges and put them in an empty ammo can, as we filed off the firing line to several long tables. There, we were told by the armorers to field-strip our rifles and clean them thoroughly with the equipment stored in the rifle's butt.

While I broke my rifle into its three main components, the stock, firing mechanism, and barrel, to clean them with the oil, cloth patches and three-part cleaning rod with changeable tips contained in the rifle's butt, the other half of the men were marched to the firing line and went through the same familiarization process with their M-14 rifles that we had. Before we were each allowed to reassemble our rifle, an armorer would carefully inspect each of the three parts to make sure they were cleaned to their standards, which required everyone to clean their rifle at least two or three more times, before being allowed to reassemble their rifle. Once the rifles were reassembled, we stood them on their butt end in pyramids of three or four.

When the second order of men finished their familiarization process with their M-14 rifles, and while they were cleaning their field-stripped rifles, we unloaded the six M-60 machine guns and their ammo cans from the first truck and carried to the firing line. There, they were placed at every other firing position, and three of the armorers set them up. As the M-60 is a 2-man crew-served weapon, we were told to pair up for our familiarizations with the M-60, which most of us had never fired before.

Skip and I teamed up, and when it was our turn an armorer meticulously went over the loading and firing of the M-60 with us. Then we were each given a turn to load and feed the belt of bullets into the firing mechanism, while the other lay behind the M-60 and had fun spraying bursts of bullets into the 20-foot high dirt berm 100 yards away, watching every third tracer bullet burn through the air and explode like a firework when it hit the dirt wall of the berm. The poles holding the targets up had all been removed, so they wouldn't be chewed up with the machine gun bullets.

When everyone in our firing echelon had fired the M-60 machine gun, we all had to go around picking up the hundreds of empty cartridges and metal cartridge links, and put them into separate empty ammo cans. Then, the second echelon of shooters were marched onto the firing line to familiarize with the M-60. While they familiarized with the M-60, we stood around the trucks for an extended smoke break till they were finished. Afterward, the armorers tore down the M-60 machine guns, and loaded them onto the first truck.

Then, we each retrieved our M-14 rifle from the pyramid stacks, and boarded the trucks for our ride back to the Company Armory. There, we each checked in the equipment and rifle we'd been issued, before going to our barracks for a cold beer. After showering off the dirt and gun powder residue from our bodies, we dressed in civilian clothes to go to the Mess Hall for lunch.

Since I'd gone dancing and spent last night with Dhoi, and told her this morning I'd be gone to the rifle range on the Thai Army Base, with no idea when we'd be finished, then we agreed just meet in my Hotel room on Saturday night and go dancing. Therefore, when I'd dressed in civilian clothes, I went with everyone to the Mess Hall for lunch, before catching a Thai bus for Korat.

Arriving at my Hotel room, I stripped to my skivvies and slept for a couple hours, before dressing and going to the Thai bar for my usual large bowl of chicken noodle soup for dinner and to share bottles of Shin Hai Beer with my Thai friends. As we talked I told them about my trip to Ayutthaya, how amazed I was that there were over 400 temples and temple ruins in, and around Ayutthaya's island. I also commented that constructing all those temples and lavishing them with huge Buddha images, many of which were, or had been, covered with gold, must have been a severe burden on the Thai economy.

They responded that such a large expense was of little consequence to them, as giving so much physical recognition and personal sacrifice for the essence of their lives and culture was of little matter. Each described how they'd dedicated two years of their youth as a Buddhist monk, living the whole time in a monastery, studying and meditating on the teaching of the Buddha, and eating only once a day from their alms bowl the food they'd gone out each morning and begged for from the people they passed on the street, as they'd sworn to a life of poverty, wearing only the orange robe they been given by their family when ordained.

When they asked about my religion, I admitted in the Roman Catholic Church I was raised in, that we'd also constructed huge cathedrals and large churches, lavished with gold, silver and precious gems, containing many large statues of Jesus, his Mother Mary and our many Saints. Also, that I'd gone all of my life as a child to private Catholic schools and graduated from a Catholic High School. Impressed with my extensive Christian education, and believing I was certainly an authority on my Christian faith, they began to ask me many questions about the life and ministry of Jesus, with intense curiosity.

Having to teach them in a bar about Jesus and his teachings, while drinking from bottles of Sing Hai Beer being passed around, I found to be quite the counter intuitive circumstance. But, even Jesus deemed it acceptable to teach His Gospel to publicans while drinking, for which he was condemned by the Sanhedrin, the highest court and council of the ancient Jewish Nation.

When they had finished their poignant questioning one of them surmised, "It sounds like the teachings of your Jesus are very much like the teachings of the Buddha. But, where Jesus taught that people were to turn the other cheek when struck by someone, the Buddha taught us to live in such a way as not to be struck in the first place."

It now being time to leave for the compound, I thanked them for the opportunity to express my religious beliefs to them, and we exchanged sáwátdiis as I left. En route to the compound, I thought as I walked, "As Jesus and the Buddha both espoused a lifestyle that is loving, charitable and compassionate, it never occurred to me before how similar the teachings of Jesus and the Buddha are."

CHAPTER 60

DISASTER DICK'S JONES HAS BEEN COUNTERED BY YOUR IRISH LUCK

On Monday, March 31st, after two days of working the day shift, the CO announced at the end of morning formation, "Due to the projected influx of men we're to receive next week, and the following months, there'll be a reorganization of the current housing for the Tropo and Crypto Platoons to accommodate the increase of personnel. Your Platoon Sargents'll pass along to you those who'll be moving and to where. Also, all of these moves *will be* made by the end of this week, to be ready when the FNGs arrive next week. First Sargent, dismiss the Company."

When the 1SGT ordered, "Platoon Sargents, take charge of your Platoons," SFC Davidson made an about face and said, "At ease men. To make things as simple as possible, the moves in the Tropo will proceed as follows: All Spec-5s will move to the NCO barracks today and tomorrow, as will all the Generator and HVAC men be moved to a different barracks building you'll be shown after formation. The Tropo barracks will then be rearranged into six 2-man spaces. On Wednesday and Thursday, all the Air Base Site personnel will move to the space vacated by the Generator and HVAC personnel. And, to keep it simple, the X, Y and Z Tropo Shifts will remain in the areas you currently occupy, with some minor adjustments. You'll be given specific instructions by your Team Leaders later today. Platoon, dismissed."

Frank then faced his Air Base Squad and said, "I'm sure I'll get a call later this morning from Davidson about their plans for your moves. I imagine each Team will have their own two 2-man spaces, which'll eventually comprise a Frame Tech, Microwave man, Generator man and HVAC man, with Team Leader living in the NCO barracks. As I'll be leaving in six weeks, I'll only see the beginning of our Site's conversion from being led by Tech Reps, to being fully manned with Army Personnel."

I asked, "So, what are your plans for after you leave, Frank?"

He replied, "I've already had one year of College, and since I get out mid-May, it'll give me time to get settled before starting Summer Semester to get back into the routine of going to classes. After my pre-med degree, I'll go to Dental School. I've a brother who's a Dentist and told me he clears enough to retire by the time he's thirty-five and will travel around the world for a while. And, if he runs low on money, he'll make a pile more as a Dentist, and retire again. So, that's what I plan to do, too."

I responded, "Sounds like a good plan to me," as I headed for the Tropo barracks to get a cold Bud and some sleep, before going to Korat and taking Dhoi to lunch at the Ming Ter. Later over lunch, Dhoi and I discussed where we'd go on our next. At first, we talked about going to Chiang Mai, in northern Thailand near the Burmese border, because it was a scenic city surrounded by beautiful mountains, and her mother's side of the family lived there. But, we found from the train schedule, it was a 12-hour trip each way, and even if I was able to wangle a 2-day pass from my CO, we'd spend most of the time traveling on the train, which would be very boring.

So, we settled on Khon Kaen, a University city, 125 miles North of Korat, and only a 3½-hour ride by train. Then, we'd spend the afternoon touring the various religious sites around Bueng Kaen Nakhon, or "Large Pond Kaen City", a half-mile diameter lake at the south end of the city, about one mile from Khon Kaen's Train Station. As the Dtá-láat Rim Bueng, or "Market Edge Large Pond", was at the north end of the lake, we'd eat lunch there before going to the nearby Tourist Center to collect information on the many sites around the lake. And, as the city's Night Market was en route to the Train Station, we'd eat dinner there, amid its many stalls, before riding the train that evening back to Korat.

Returning to the Tropo barracks, Skip and I had forgone taking our tape decks to work, because our first night shift was a Monday night, and we knew it'd be a very busy night with reported circuit outages due to the increased message traffic from Stateside after their weekend off.

In the morning, having had a busy night in the Operations Room, I delivered the jeep to Frank on my 6:30 meal run, and had breakfast in the Mess Hall. Returning to the Tropo barracks, I drank a cold Bud, as I changed into my Class-B khaki uniform to go to the Pay Line and get paid. Then, Skip and I checked each other over to correct any deficiencies in our uniforms.

Walking through the other barracks room for the Pay Line, we saw the Generator guys had moved out and the left side of the room was vacated. Also, there were index cards taped to many of the wall lockers with a name written on each. Seeing our names were on the first pair of wall lockers in the first space on the left, Skip said, "This is perfect. We'll be closest to the refrigerator to get our beer, and to the Shower Room and Latrine. We couldn't have a better location, even if we picked it ourselves.

After we'd been paid and drank a cold beer while changing out of our Class-B khaki uniforms, we began moving to have it done before our two off days. I also saw Larry and Mark moving to the third pair of lockers for the Y-Shift and noted Chuck and David would be moving to the fifth pair of lockers for the Z-Shift. I thought, "The second, fourth and sixth pairs of lockers will eventually be filled by our Radio Site's Generator and HVAC repairmen for their respective shifts as they arrive."

As I moved my gear to my new living space, including my bedding, George, Ronnie, Stony and the five others I'd loaned $20 to the previous week, each stopped by to pay me $25. Checking their names off in my little notebook as they did so, I collected $200 and thought, "This is $40 extra, easy bucks I can put into my Savings Account. At this rate, it won't be long before I'll bank my entire pay each month and live off the monthly penury of those who can't manage their money."

Once I'd moved, showered and shaved, I drank a cold Bud while dressing in fresh civilian clothes and boarded a Thai bus to the Air

Base. There, I happily deposited $90 into my Savings Account. Catching another Thai bus to Korat for lunch with Dhoi, I later returned to the Tropo barracks and slept in my new location till the 5:00 bugle call for Mess. Fortunately, it was a fairly quiet night in the Air Base Site's Operations Room, so Skip and I were able to get some taped albums copied.

On my 10:50 meal run, I'd met up with Glen and Ronnie in the Mess Hall for our midnight meal. Sitting at a table next to ours were four guys from the Transportation Regiment we'd struck up a conversation with. Soon, they were bragging to us that they were the best drivers in Thailand, because they drove their vehicles nearly every day in convoys to and from Bangkok delivering bombs for the Air Force. We then derided their claims and challenged them to a quarter-mile drag race on the restricted road between the Tropo Site and its guard gate at 2:00 in the morning with two our 2½-ton trucks and jeeps.

Returning from my meal run, I received permission from Bob to preserve the honor of the Signal Corps in a quarter-mile race at the Tropo Site between our jeep and one from the Transportation Regiment. At 2:00, I met up with our adversaries at the Tropo Site's entrance gate, and in front of some bewildered Thai Soldiers. We measured and marked off a quarter-mile strip of the gravel road to the Tropo Site. The Transportation guys may have had more time driving vehicles in their convoys on hard-surfaced roads, but Glen and I had been raised driving on dirt country roads in Texas and Oregon, and we had no problem besting them in two-out-of-three races with his 2½-ton truck and my jeep against them on a gravel road.

Late the following Monday afternoon, the newbies arrived. And at Tuesday morning's formation, I saw some forty men in a Transient Platoon at the Company's far end. As Tuesday and Wednesday were my off days, it wasn't till Wednesday night, when I returned with the others from the compound, that I'd learned three of the newbies were assigned to the Air Base Site. All three were Generator Repairmen, with one each assigned to a shift and sleeping in their individual 2-man spaces. Of course, none of this was mentioned at the compound, due to Horn's rule against talking about anything work related.

I saw at next morning's formation, not only had the Air Base Squad's rank increased by three, but there were new men in each of the Tropo's X and Z-shift ranks. Of course, none of the Air Base Site's newbies were going with us to work, as they first need to get their Military Driver's Licenses at the Motor Pool.

Later that morning, Tim went in the jeep to get them. And having already toured our Operations Room the day before, they all went directly to the Generator Shed. There, they began their training by the Generator Tech Rep on the maintenance and repair of our Site's three generators, as those models were not standard, Army issue generators. So, it wasn't until I took my 10:50 meal run, that I met PFC Pedro "Pete" Hernandez, and affable Hispanic, who was born and raised in Houston, TX.

I learned from Pete, he'd been assigned to our X-shift Team, but wouldn't be working our Team's rotation for at least two weeks. Not until the Generator Tech Rep was satisfied he, and the two others, could adequately repair the generators and in-house electrical systems without his supervision. Meanwhile, they'd work ten-hour days from 7:00 to 5:00, Monday through Saturday, like those in the Motor Pool and Headquarters Platoons.

Meeting up with Glen and Ronnie in the Mess Hall, I introduced Pete to Glen as a fellow Texan. They quickly began arguing how much better West Texas was than the Texas Gulf, and vice versa, soon becoming friendly antagonists. Their only points of non-contention was the greatest battle fought in U.S. History was at the Alamo, and Texas was the best State in the U.S. By the end of lunch, Glen offered to help Pete find a tîi-lók, which he quickly accepted.

After our meal runs, Bob explained to me and Skip, "Saturday is the beginning of Thailand's three-day Songkran Festival, celebrating their New Year and the beginning of the Monsoon Season. It starts out as a respectful affair, with morning visits to the Temples with involved colorful processions and water-sprinkling ceremonies of sacred Buddhist images. Then, everyone fills their squirt guns with water, and head out to the streets to douse everyone else to wish them to be blessed with enough rain in the Monsoon Season. It's considered an insult to pass by someone and not spray them water, if you have any. So, I suggest you both go to the BX or PX and buy a big squirt gun."

During the afternoon, Skip and I separately went to the nearby BX and bought the largest squirt guns we could find, and stored them in our Air Base wall lockers till we went on our meal runs and stored them in our barracks wall lockers.

The next morning in the Operation Room, while Skip and I were fine-tuning the squarewave signal for one of our teletype circuits in the Grand Canyon, I heard both of the AP and UPI teletype monitors sound the "ding, ding, ding" alarm for an urgent news report. I watched as Bob casually rose from his chair at the desk, and mossy over the AP and UPI news-wire teletype machines.

After a moment, I heard Bob exclaim, "Holy crap! The shit's hit the fan at Harvard University. It's nothing new for their students to go on strike. But, this time a group of students were able to break into the Dean's Office and made off with boxes of documents. Some showed that Harvard had contracts with the CIA to do research to find weakness in North Vietnam that the CIA could exploit. Now, all of Boston is in an uproar, with large demonstrations at Boston Commons, because Universities are supposed to be politically neutral and the CIA is forbidden from any activity in the U.S. Boy, this is a big blow to the Government's dealings in the Vietnam war."

At the compound that evening, there were considerable heated discussions about this major *faux pax* by the CIA, and about the CIA's direct and clandestine operations in the Vietnam War. Many of us were of the opinion the CIA's actions at Harvard University were not only illegal, but also politically hurting the war effort, and casting a disparaging shadow on those of us actually involved in fighting the Vietnam War.

The following morning, on our second day shift, while Skip and I were waited for Bob to finish with the Shift Change Report, we read the news-wire clippings the night shift had saved on the fallout from the fiasco of the CIA's illegal dealings with Harvard. When Bob finally arrived, he announced, "There's been a big bust of a smuggling-ring operation between Thailand and Travis Air Force Base, in California.

"It seems, when the air crew of one of those huge C5-A cargo planes had offloaded their cargo in Thailand, they innocuously used some of the emptied shipping containers they were returning Stateside to be filled with products made in Thailand, like electronic devices, silk cloth, gold and precious gems. Once loaded on their cargo plane for their return flight, they flew the empty and contraband filled containers to Travis Air Force Base. There, the supposedly empty containers were offloaded onto transport trucks, like the other empty containers were, and taken to a civilian import-export company to be emptied before being sent onto the manufacturers that owned them.

"With no transport cost to ship the goods from Thailand, and in bypassing the U.S. customs inspectors, who were not inclined to examine empty containers, they avoided having to pay the large import tariffs on the merchandise, and their overall profit margin was substantial. Also, the smuggling ring was comprised of a few senior-ranking officers and NCOs on each end, who could unsuspectingly control the manifest to get the untaxed goods onto the cargo plain in Thailand, off the cargo plane at Travis, and onto the transport trucks to their import-export company. By keeping their operation small and contained with only one aircrew and a few people on each end, the racket was impregnable.

"Apparently, a red flag was raised when a senior NCO was seen driving a very expensive sports car. The Air Force CID began an investigation into how an Enlisted man, who's monthly pay wasn't nearly enough for him to afford such an expensive car, was able to buy one, even with monthly installments. As the smuggling ring was small and self-contained, and involved close-knit, high-ranking individuals, it took the Air Force CID six months to ferret out all the members.

"Other smuggling rings have been easier to find. But, those all involved drugs, which the FBI traced back to Army and Air Force personnel, and street dealers and civilian suppliers the FBI and local police had busted, then snitched on to make deals with prosecutors. If the senior NCO hadn't had an itchy proclivity to own an expensive sports car, that smuggling ring probably would've never been discovered."

I responded, "It's like my Mom always said, 'No matter how strong a chain is, it only takes one weak link for it to break.''

Over Saturday, Sunday and Monday, I carried my big squirt gun full of water everywhere I went on and off base. By mutual agreement, the barracks was declared a water-free zone, as well as all workplaces. Otherwise, I was drenched with water everywhere I went for three days. Even when boarding a Thai bus, as all the drivers had a large bucket of water tied to their seats and a large serving spoon to bless their passengers with water as they boarded his bus. And, no matter how stuffy the air inside the bus was, the windows were kept tightly closed to not be doused with water as the bus passed people on the streets and walkways.

I'd heard the Air Force General had been drenched with a bucket of water tossed through an open window of his staff car, and ordered no water was to be thrown or sprayed at, or from, any moving military vehicle on his Air Force Base as a Safety Policy. But, the order was mostly ignored because it was considered to violate the religious freedom and significance of Thailand's Songkrang Festival. Also, everyone was having too much fun soaking each other in this largest water fight in the world.

As the following Tuesday, April 15th, was Tax Day, the word was put out, with the IRS extension Forms provided by HQ, that we didn't have to file our Federal Taxes returns until 90 days after our tour in the Theatre of War ended. Not that I'd have much to pay in taxes to the IRS, because my taxable income for 1968 was less than $2,000.

When the morning of Saturday, April 26th, arrived on my second night shift, I told Skip and Bob, "Today, I'm officially a two-digit midget. Ninety-nine days and a wake-up, I should be flying out of Bangkok in the big silver bird going Stateside."

Loading my tape deck into the jeep for my 6:30 meal run, I drove to basketball court in front of the Tropo barracks, and turned the jeep over to Tim. Carrying my tape deck quickly into the barracks, I put it in my wall locker. Then, having already showered and shaved at the Air Base Site, I drank a cold Bud, as I rapidly changed into civilian clothes before my swift walk to the Mess Hall. After a hasty breakfast, I quickly left to catch a Thai bus to Korat.

Exiting the bus at the Chainarong Gate, I hired a sǎawm-law to first quickly carry me to the Sri Pattana Hotel, where I ran in and rented a room for four days, before taking it down to the Chira Train Station. There, I met Dhoi, who had our round-trip First-Class tickets to Khon Kaen, and was holding Mii-kâa on the Station's platform, where we waited for the 8:20 train to Khon Kaen.

Boarding the First-Class car when the train arrived, I had the porter lower the upper bed, so I could sleep during the 3½-hour trip to Khon Kaen, while Dhoi and Mii-kâa could sit comfortably on a seat and watch the scenery through the window as it passed by. When I tipped the porter two 1-Bhat coins, I tiredly stripped to my skivvies and climbed onto the bed for some much needed sleep, though I'd previously managed to nap for a couple hours in the back of the Operations Room.

When the porter sounded the 15-minute warning for the train's stop at Khon Kaen, I found Dhoi and Mii-kâa were asleep, and woke them before I dressed and then refreshed myself in the lavatory. After the porter escorted us from our compartment to the Train Station's platform, I still tipped him the customary One-Bhat coin, even though we had no baggage for him to carry.

Walking to the platform's South end, away from the noisy steam locomotive, I hired a săawm-law to carry us the 1¼-miles to the Rim Bueng Market at the north end of Bueng Kaen Nakhon, or "Large Pond Kaen City". While eating a delicious assortment of snacks from the food vendors, we wandered through the Market, which was much like a flea market back home, dealing mainly in cheap secondhand goods, and handmade articles and art.

Stopping at a paint-your-own pottery stall, we each picked out a mythical religious creature to decorate, and then have them glazed, while we toured the sites around the large pond. Mii-kâa, of course, had slathered her ceramic image in pink paint.

Crossing west to the outside of the lane encircling the large pond, we went to Wat Tâat, or "Temple Element", an old Temple complex with a soaring chapel and stupa in its compound. We were told by one of the cloistered monks, the stupa was built in 1789, and we went inside to see the many Buddha images featured there in 72 different meditation positions.

Leaving the Wat Tâat compound, we followed the lane south for 200 for yards to the Tourist Center, situated between the lane and Glaang Muang Road, or "Middle City Road", where we received information and brochures on the religious sites around the pond and places in Kohn Kaen proper. The large city of Khon Kaen had Northeast Thailand's largest University, and was an important hub for all things commercial. It was currently riding Isaan's economic boom for all it was worth, as nearly all the U.S. Air Bases in Thailand supporting the Vietnam War were in the Issan area of Thailand.

Walking 100 yards south, on the treelined space between the lane and Glaang Muang Road, we came to the Mahesak Shrine. It's modern Khmer-style prang was dedicated to the Hindu god Indra and contained many Hindu images.

Leaving the Hindu shrine, we proceeded south almost a half-mile along the lane to the south edge of the pond, to Wat Nong Wang, or

"Temple Swamp Latitude". In its compound, we saw the Prâ Mahatâat Kaen Nokhon, or "Buddha Image Great Image Kaen," inside the stunning stupa at the heart of this important Temple. It featured illumination murals showing the Isaan culture and various historical depictions, and on its fourth floor was a collection of rare Buddha images. From its nineth floor observation deck, I saw an amazing panoramic view of the large city, its surrounding countryside, and the mountain range twenty miles West of Khon Kaen.

Descending from the magnificent view, we continued a few hundred yards east to the Chao Wung Pûu, or "Intelligent Palace Male," a cloistered monastery noted for its meditative ambience. We then walked another 300 yards north amongst the tranquil trees to the Sâan Jâaesâao Diiyua, or "Court Princess Diiyua," known locally as the One Pillar Pagoda. This was a replica of an iconic Hanoi Temple, built by Kohn Kaen's Vietnamese community on the east side of Bueng Kaen Nakhon.

Continuing several hundred yards further up the pond's east side, we came to Wat Poe Noontan, or "Temple Intelligence Noontan," a peaceful, tree-filled Temple compound. It was a famous meditation center that predated the city, with a "sâa-laa," a rest-house, reported to be like no other in Thailand. The ground floor was covered with ingeniously sculpted trees, animals and village scenes of people acting out old Isaan proverbs.

Leaving this Temple, we crossed over the Poe Tisan Road to the Saan-jâao Bueng Tao Gong Ma, or Court-Lord Land Tao Gong Ma, also called Saan-jâao Bueng Kaen Nokhon. This was Kohn Kaen's biggest and most beautiful Chinese Temple. We then walked across the lane to see the Guan Im statue, or "Chinese Goddess of Mercy" statue, in the nearby park, before returning to the Bueng Rim Market to pick up our glazed artwork.

Famished after our 2-mile tour around Bueng Kaen Nokhon, I hired a săawm-law for the ¾-mile ride west on Ropbung Road and north on the Busy Glaang Muang Road, to Khon Kaen's Night Market on Reunrom Road, located between Glaang Muang Road and Nâa Muang Road, or "Front City Road." There, we enjoyed the awesome noshing atmosphere, eating our fill of the various vendor cooked foods, as we feasted our eyes on the large number of stalls hocking all kinds of goods and foods.

When we'd seen and eaten enough, I hired a săawm-law to carry us West on Reunrom Road the half-mile to the Train Station. There, we relaxed on the platform's benches, while waiting for the south-bound train to Korat. Hearing the long-way-off mournful whistle of the steam locomotive from the north, to safely warn people as it slowly crossed Khon Kaen's many roads, on its way to Khon Kaen's Train Station. Then, we got up and joined the throng of people on the plat-form waiting for the train, either to board or to greet family and friends who'd exit.

As the train came to a chugging and squealing stop, we walked the First-Class car. When a porter had finished assisting people from the car, I handed him our First-Class tickets and he escorted us to our com-partment. There, I asked him to make up the lower bed for us. When he'd done so, I tipped him 2 One-Bhat coins as he left, and then we stripped to our underwear and happily went to bed and got some sleep after a fun, but exhausting day.

Arriving in Korat at the Chira Train Station, I hired a săawm-law to take us to the Sri Pattana Hotel, as the Thai busses to Camp Friendship had long since stopped running at 10:00. Waking to the 5:00 wake-up call I'd requested, we dressed and left the Hotel in a săawm-law to the Chainarong Gate. There, we boarded a crowded Thai bus to take Dhoi and Mii-kâa to the Thai Army Base, while I continued to my Company Area.

Entering the Tropo barracks, I drank a cold Bud, as I hastily show-ered, shaved and dressed in my jungle fatigues, before rapidly walking to the Mess Hall for a quickly eaten breakfast. Swiftly walking to our basketball court, I had time enough to smoke a hand-rolled cigarette before formation started. After which, I went to bed and slept till the 11:00 bugle call for Mess.

Drinking a cold Bud as I dressed in civilian clothes for lunch, I was hit up by several guys for a $20 payday loan. Returning from the Mess Hall after I'd eaten lunch , several more guys asked me for $20 payday loans, all of which I recorded in my pocket-sized notebook. Putting changes of clothes in my shopping bag to take with me, I caught a Thai bus to the Thai Army Base, where I spent a relaxing afternoon with Dhoi's family. After dinner with the family, Dhoi and I went to see a Japanese Samurai movie at the Action Theater, before going to my Hotel room to spend the night lovemaking. And, so ended a perfect weekend with Dhoi.

The following Thursday was Pay Day, and after I collected $55 in usury from the eleven guys who'd borrowed money from me, I deposited $100 in my Savings Account, before going to Korat and taking Dhoi to lunch.

Monday, the next week, I worked my second day shift. As I ate dinner in the Mess Hall with Glen and Ronnie on my 4:50 meal run, I saw a bunch of guys enter with the Signal Corps orange, diamond-shaped patch on the left shoulder of their tucked in OD BDU shirts and bloused pants, and said, "I wonder which of that group of newbies is the Microwave man who'll be replacing Larry on our Site's Y-shift, as he's being promoted to Spec-5 and'll be our new Site Engineer, because Frank's leaving next week. Also, Tim will not only replace Frank as the NCOIC, he's being promoted to Staff Sargent in anticipation that number of guys working at the Air Base Site will significantly increase over the next few months. In fact, today I've got ninety days and a wake-up left in country. Ronnie, it looks like you've been putting on some bulk. What've you been up to lately?"

Ronnie replied, "When the Camp's new Swimming Pool opened a month ago, I found it had a large Weight Room attached to it. So, I've been sleeping poolside every morning I'm not working days to get a good tan before I leave for Stateside. Then, I lift weights in the afternoon to work on, building up some muscles to attract the women when I get back home. Maybe even enter some body-building com-pe-ti-tions. What about you, Glen?"

Glen laughed and answered, "The only body building I plan to work on is with Súpa. But, hitting the poolside every morning to get a good tan before going back Stateside, sounds like a good idea. One thing the cowgirls hate back in Texas is a pasty looking cowboy. What about you, Sandii?"

I responded, "Getting a tan sounds like a good thing to work on in the mornings. Besides, it's too hot in the afternoons to lay out in the sun now days. Also, the Monsoon Season'll be starting soon, and you certainly don't want to be caught in the afternoon sunbathing poolside when those hit."

Sure enough, two days later, as I was eating lunch with Dhoi at the Ming Ter, a monsoon downpour drenched Korat, and we had to be careful where we walked on the way back to the Jomsurang Hotel.

When I returned to the Tropo barracks, I saw Larry packing up his gear. When I asked what he was doing, he replied, "Since I'm being promoted to Spec-5 on Friday and today's my off day, I have to move into the NCO barracks now. Besides, I've told my shift replacement he'll need to move into the Tropo barracks this evening after the 4:50 dinner meal run. Sure am going to miss living here with you regular guys, instead of with all those lifers in the NCO barracks."

When Bob arrived in the Operations Room that evening after Shift Change Report, he said to me and Skip, "This'll be my last weekend working with you two. I, and several other Tech Reps who applied for Warrant Officer commissions, will be leaving next week for Ft. Leonardwood, Missouri, to re-enlist as Spec-5s from our Inactive Reserve Army Status and sent to an 8-week Warrant Officer Course. Once we've finished the course, we'll be commissioned as CWO-2s[158] and transferred to the 442d to fill one of the OIC billets for those Radio Sites that will hopefully be fully manned by Army personnel before Philco's contract for Tech Support expires.

"My replacement here, will be Richard Dankers from the Tropo Site, who is commonly referred to as 'Disaster Dick,' because any equipment he comes in contact with, often seems to have the propensity to mysteriously break down. Not that he does anything to cause it. But, he's like a 'Jonas,'[159] so you'll need to be on your toes when he's around."

Friday was my second off day. Being in a rush to be in and out of the Company Area after spending the night with Dhoi and getting poolside for some sleep and to begin work on my tan, I hardly took notice of the four new PFCs in our Air Base Squad at morning formation. Also, after Saturday's morning formation, I was surprised to see we were back to riding a ¾-ton truck to the Air Base Site, as out of the last big batch of newbies, besides Larry's replacement, we'd also been assigned our three HVAC Repairmen. So that morning, while Skip and

---

158   Chief Warrant Officer – Pay Grade Level 2

159   Any person said to bring bad luck by being present, based on the Bible story of the Prophet Jonah thrown overboard in a storm because he had disobeyed God.

I rode in the cab of the truck with SSG Tim Larsen, Pete was riding in the back with our three new HVAC men.

That weekend, Bob spent his last two day shifts with us, orienting Richard to the Air Base Site's Operations Room. Even though Saturday morning was its usual chaos from numerous reported circuit outages, there was nothing untoward about any of the outages At the end of our day shift, I said, "Skip, I think all this talk about Disaster Dick may be bogus."

Skip laughed and retorted, "Or, maybe Disaster Dick's Jonas has been countered by your Irish luck."

CHAPTER 61

SHOOT YOURSELF IN THE HEAD WHEN YOU GET TO FT. HUACHUCA

Driving the jeep from the Air Base Site to the Tropo barracks on my 6:30 meal run, I was met by Mark, who had been promoted to Spec-4, and introduced to Larry's replacement, PFC Phil Jenkins. Phil said, "Good to meet you, Sandii. The last two days I've been working with Mark in the Operations Room. He said you're the one to talk with about hooking up with a tîi-lók."

I responded, "How about you check with me tomorrow in the Mess Hall at 11:00, and I'll introduce you to Glen. He works at the Tropo Site and has the best connections for you to meet some girls looking to be a tîi-lók. Okay?"

Phil replied happily, "Great, Sandii. Then, I'll see you in the Mess Hall at 11:00 tomorrow."

After a relatively quiet Sunday, which further dispelled Richard as a Jonas, everyone went to the Tech Rep's compound in Korat for a big send-off party for Bob and Frank. And though my Monday night shift was its usual busy self, by the end of Tuesday's quiet night shift, Skip and I were convinced the hoopla about Richard's moniker as "Disaster Dick" was pure bunkum.

Returning to work in the Operations Room on Friday, after my two off days, Richard told Skip and I, "The Generator Tech Reps decided the three new HVAC guys are ready to get into the guts of one of our two air-conditioners, having gone over all the mechanical and electrical diagrams during the last week and a half. So, there'll be a lot of commotion in the Air Conditioning Room later this morning, as the four of them squeeze into that small room for an overdue PM on an air-conditioner."

Sure enough, an hour later, I heard a lot of tramping on our hollow floor between the side door to the Generator Shed and the hallway to the Air Conditioning Room. A half-hour after that, I heard Richard exclaim, "Oh shit!" as the cool air blowing down on us from the overhead air vent stopped. A half-minute later, the Operations Room went totally black for a second, before the emergency battery-powered lights came on.

I saw Richard grab the phone on the desk and yell into it, "Ted, we just lost power, connect me with Quad-C A immediately," then turning to me and Skip, he said, "Quick, set all of the Power Switches to Off, so the equipment isn't damaged by a power surge when the backup generator comes online."

Running to the microwave radio, I rapidly toggled the Power Switches to the Off position on the Klystron and multiplex cards, before quickly going to help Skip turn those on the breakout circuits to the Off position by the time the overhead lights came on. A half-minute later, they went out again.

While our overhead lights were going on for a half-minute and then off again a half-minute later, Richard explained, "The air-conditioners draw 80% of the power from the generators. With them off-line, there isn't enough load from the electronic gear to keep a generator from running away. When a runaway generator hits a certain RPM[160], it automatically shuts down and the next generator come up online. When it spins up, the overhead lights come on until that generator runs away and shuts down, with the cycle repeating until an air-conditioner comes online.

---

160   Revolutions Per Minute

"Also, with no air-conditioning, even if the generators didn't runaway, the heat generated by the electronic gear, added to the outside temperature, would quickly heat our Operations Room to over 80 degrees, at which point some electronic components will begin to go out of tolerance and cause outages. Meanwhile, each time a generator spins up and then goes offline, we have to record each power outage in the Site Log. But, that's the easy part for us.

"When our air conditioning is finally fixed and we can safely turn the equipment back on, then comes the hard part for us, making sure each of our 252 in-house circuits are up and operating properly, which could take all afternoon."

I responded, "And, they can't blame this power outage on you, because you weren't in any way connected with the HVAC people, who obviously caused this power outage."

Richard laughed and said, "Thanks for the moral support, Sandii. But, I've no doubt others'll say it was my presence that caused the air-conditioner to go offline when the back-up was down for PM."

An hour later, the HVAC guys had the air-conditioner they'd been doing the PM on put back together and online. With the cool air again blowing down from the air vents and the overhead lights not going on and off every minute, we'd recorded 57 power failures in one hour. Richard said, "I'll bet that's a world record for power failures in one hour at a radio site. Okay, you two get everything turned on and this Site back online again, while I call Quad-C A, and pray nothing was broke."

We spent the rest of the day, with the rest of the Radio Sites in the Theater of War, getting all of our 252 in-house circuits rerouted back through their normal communication routes and back in service.

The next day was Saturday, and we had the usual, very busy day working in the Operations Room. We then had a nice quiet night shift on Sunday and were happy to call our families and girlfriends Stateside, via Rosie with the WATS lines. Also we were excitedly reading the AP and UPI newswire updates for the Apollo 10 launch, NASAs third flight to the Moon, this time with Stafford, Young and Cernan crewing the flight.

Again, the manned Moon mission was not to land on the Moon, but to fly the Lunar Landing Module, the LLM, relatively close to the Moon's surface and photograph possible landing sites. Three days later, I was working my two day shifts, and intently read every teletyped news report about the fifty hours Apollo 10's LLM orbited within 50,000 feet of the Moon's surface, before docking with the Command Module and beginning their three-day flight back to Earth.

Also, it being the fourth weekend after Pay Day, lots of guys were hitting me up for $20 payday loans, and I needed to withdraw $100 from the Bank to provide for the loans and to cover my own weekend expenses with Dhoi.

The following Monday was Memorial Day Stateside and the start of my two off days. While the Apollo 10 crew was successfully splashing down and being safely recovered, I was again hit with tragedy. When I'd gone to the Jomsurang Hotel to pick up Dhoi for lunch, I was given a letter via Suumii explaining that Dhoi's mother had somehow discovered I was not an Officer. Therefore, she had packed Dhoi and Mii-kâa off to Ubon to live with Dhoi's father, who was part of an inspection team examining and expanding the Thai Army's defenses around Ubon Air Base. Ubon Air Base contained a large portion of the huge B-52 Bombers, which had increased the number of bombing missions launched on Hanoi and Haiphong Harbor in North Vietnam, which were the Capital and the main import/export locations of the country.

Crushed again by an interfering parent, this time a socially bigoted mother, I thought, "Never again will I become emotionally involved with any Thai woman. Thankfully, I've only got seventy days and a wake-up left in country."

That evening at the compound, I told Glen about what had happened with Dhoi, he responded, "I'll talk with Súpa and see if she can fix you up with a tîi-lók on a short-term basis," for which I was thankful, as I had no desire to be celibate for my last two months in Thailand.

At formation the next morning, Glen told me, "Súpa says she has a friend named Song, who might be available for a short-term arrangement to be your tîi-lók. And, knowing you're willing to date a widow with children, she may be perfect for you, as she's a 23-year-old widow with five kids."

I responded, "Sounds fine with me. See what Súpa can do about a meet-and-greet, and we'll see how it goes from there."

After spending the morning sleeping poolside till I heard the 11:00 bugle call for Mess. I thought while dressing for lunch, "This is the week before Pay Day next Monday, and businesses will be starving for customers. As I'll be leaving in two months, this'll be the perfect time to buy some new clothes and shoes cheap, and maybe some jewelry for presents and investment purposes, before leaving for Stateside."

When I'd finished lunch and after the monsoon downpour, I boarded a Thai bus to the Air Base Bank to withdraw $200 from my Savings Account and exchanged it for 4,000 Bhat. Then, I caught another Thai bus to Korat, where my first stop was the short walk up Chainarong Road to the tailor shop. There, I ordered one tan and one light-blue three-piece silk suit, with an extra pair of pants each. Plus, five silk shirts and two pair of cotton pants, for which I was easily able to argue the price down to what was lower than usual. Then, I arranged for a fitting in three days, as I'd be working the day shift for the next two days, and paid a 340 Bhat deposit.

My next stop was the cobbler shop on Mahat Thai Road. There, I ordered a pair of patent leather black shoes, so I wouldn't have to spit-shine my black dress shoes when I went Stateside. Also, a pair of dark-brown leather shoes and a pair of tan, square-toed, suede plainsmen boots with three-inch long, leather fringes hanging from the top, a popular western-style boot at that time.

Paying my 200 Bhat deposit, I walked up to Chomphon Road, to the jewelry shop, to see what could be arranged in the way of solid gold items for investment, and precious gem jewelry for presents in the form of rings, necklaces and earrings. Entering the shop, I exchanged sáwátdiis with a young Chinese woman standing behind a glass jewelry case.

Though the Siamese people are of Sino-Tibetan decent from when they were driven South out of China by the Han Chinese a millennia before, there are several, distinctive, physical characteristics that differentiate the Siamese from other Chinese linages, like the Vietnamese and Laos. I recognized this young woman was clearly not of Siamese decent, as her face was considerably more square than the typical oval face of a Thai, her eyes and nose had a different shape, and her body had a stockier build than the Thai women I knew. And, though she was good looking in a Chinese way, she didn't have the naturally pretty features of most Thai women.

Introducing myself in Thai and stating what I was interested in buying, she responded in perfect American English, with a slight Southern drawl, "Sandii, my name is Sompit, and though you speak very good

Thai, it might be easier if we transacted your business in English, as I recently graduated High School in Raleigh, North Carolina, as an exchange student, and speak very good English."

I responded, "Sompit, that sounds good to me, as my vocabulary for jewelry is fairly limited." And, as we talked about what I was looking for, I also began to flirt with her, to which she responded favorably. When I'd decided on what I was interest in purchasing, she said I'd have to settle on the price with her father, who owned the shop and would be back shortly.

While we waited for him, I asked, "Would you like to go to dinner and dancing with me on a double-date sometime?"

She replied, "I would like that very much. But, before I can have a date with you, you will need to receive my father's permission. When I was attending High School in Raleigh, I did not go on any date, as I did not have my father's permission to do so. Perhaps you could ask my father to have dinner here with my family here this Sunday, as our home is on the top floor of this building. The floor above us, is where our jewelry is made, and the floor above that is where the artisans who make the jewelry live."

A moment later, Sompit's father arrived, the same man I'd bought Linda's ring from last November. After we settled on a more than reasonable price for a large, heavy, solid gold cross and chain, and a matching set of a ruby ring, necklace and pair of earrings, to impress Linda with on my return Stateside, I gave him a 3,000 Bhat deposit, which was nearly all the Bhat I had left on me, with the balance to be paid on Saturday, which happily surprised him because he knew Pay Day for the Americans was the following Monday.

With business out of the way, I formally asked him if I could come to dinner on Sunday, for the purpose of asking him permission to date Sompit. With his impression I was a prosperous American, he readily agreed and informed me they had dinner at 5:00.

Leaving the jewelry shop, I thought, "I won't need to pay any import or excise tax on the first two personal items I declare, which'll be the gold cross with chain, and the ruby jewelry set for Linda. Then, I should be able to turn a 40% profit on that cross and chain when I sell it Stateside. As for Sompit, she'll make an interesting distraction for the next two months, if things don't pan out with Súpa's widow friend," as I walked up to Assadang Road and the Thai bar for dinner and several rounds of Sing Hai Beer with my Thai friends, before going to the Tech Rep's compound.

At the compound, Glen told me discretely, "Súpa's arranged for you to meet with her widowed friend, Song, for lunch on Friday, since we'll be working the day shifts on Wednesday and Thursday. Also, the scuttlebutt is that Sargent Zuligich will be promoted to Sargent First Class and be the Tropo Site's next NCOIC, as Davidson is rotating Stateside next week, and Zuligich is the only person in the Company, and the Battalion for that matter, who has the time-in-service to be promoted to SFC."

I responded quietly, "Talk about being in the right place and the right time. This means, after twelve years service in the Army, Zuligich will have gone from a lowly Spec-4 to a high-powered SFC in less than two years."

After sleeping poolside on Friday till the 11:00 bugle call for Mess, I showered, shaved and drank a cold Bud, as I dressed in civilian clothes before catching a Thai bus for Korat. Exiting the bus, I walked the short distance up Chainarong Road to my fitting appointment with the tailor, before meeting Song at the agreed upon 1:00 time for lunch, where Súpa formerly worked.

Entering the cafe, still busy with the lunchtime crowd, I exchanged sáwátdiis with the waitress at the door, who then led me to the table where I exchanged sáwátdiis with Glen, Súpa and Song, who I saw was a very pretty, slender Thai woman, and thought, "Song doesn't look like she's the mother of five, nor any older than Súpa, who's now eighteen years old," as I sat down.

After a very pleasant lunch, during which Song tried to impress me with her limited English, but appeared relieved that I spoke Thai, she invited me to her home, so I could see it and discuss the living arrangements. On leaving the cafe, she gave the sǎawm-law driver I hired the directions to her house, which was nearby, in a southern suburb of Korat.

When we arrived at her modest 2-story wood home, she introduced me to five children, of which the oldest was an 8-year-old girl holding a toddler on her hip. I quickly deduced Song must have married when she'd graduated from the eighth grade at fourteen. Then, giving me a tour of her well-kept home that ended in her bedroom, I enjoyed her experienced and our vigorous lovemaking in a Kama Sutra position that I knew was particularly pleasing for women.

While we showered together, Song complemented me on my love-making style and said she'd very much enjoy being my tîi-lók for the two months I had left in Korat. As we dressed, she said I wouldn't have to give her any money, only to buy her a full-size refrigerator, which I could purchase through the PX to avoid the 100% import tax. I responded, "That sounds acceptable, but I'll have to check that out first and let you know."

Leaving Song's home with a passionate kiss from her and her becoming smile, I walked the short distance to a bus stop and boarded a Thai bus to Camp Friendship. Exiting the bus at the Camp's PX I entered and found the cheapest full-size refrigerator I could order was $128, plus the cost of delivery from the PX to Korat. I thought, "First, I'm going to see how things work out with Sompit's father on Sunday, because this is pretty expensive for just two months of STD-free sexual gratification."

Leaving for the Air Base's Bank on Saturday after lunch in the Mess Hall, I carried my large shopping bag with me onto a Thai bus. Withdrawing $200 from my Savings Account, which I exchanged for 4,000 Bhat, I then boarded a second Thai bus for Korat, and went to the tailor shop. There, I paid the balance of my bill and filled my shopping bag with the new clothes. Then, I walked up Chainarong Road to the cobbler's shop on Mahat Thai Road. After I tried on the two pair of shoes and pair of boots and found they all fit like a glove and were very comfortable, I paid the balance due, and the owner happily wrapped them up and placed them in a large, paper shopping bag for me.

Walking up to the next main street, Chomphon Road, I went to the jewelry shop, where Sompit and her father happily greeted me at the door. After exchanging sáwátdiis, I paid the 3,000 Bhat due on my large order. While they helped me pack the costly items in the midst of the packaged clothes in my large cloth shopping bag, I reassured them I'd be there tomorrow evening at 5:00 for dinner. As I left, Sompit showed me the side entrance to the building, since the jewelry shop was closed on Sundays, and thought, "Sompit's father must think I've loads of money, not only from my large cash purchase, but also that I'd two large bags full of other items bought the Saturday before Pay

Day, when most other Americans were flat broke. So, he'll be more than happy for his daughter to date a rich American."

The next evening at 5:00, after spending the morning sleeping poolside, and then the hot afternoon playing Double-Deck Pinochle for money-stakes with Skip as my partner, I arrived at the side entrance door of the jewelry shop's building. Sompit's father greeted me there, as it would've been inappropriate for Sompit to greet me there, because I'd not received her father's permission to be her suitor.

During dinner with Sompit's father and mother, who was also of Chinese decent, and her five younger siblings, all of whom spoke English, I found Sompit also had two older brothers attending Universities in the U.S. Though Sompit had been an exchange student and graduated from High School in the U.S., she'd not be going to a University in the U.S., or anywhere else, as it was doubtful her father could recoup the expense with a dowry when she married. Whereas, such investments in a son was expected to have a manyfold return for the family.

When I talked with Sompit's father alone after dinner, I had no problem receiving permission to date Sompit. He wasn't concerned that if I married her, she'd be living in the U.S., as it was expected that with whomever she married, she'd be leaving his family to be the property of her husband's family, as was the tradition of most Oriental cultures. Besides, the quicker Sompit married, the sooner he'd recoup the cost of raising her.

Receiving her father's permission, Sompit agreed to meet me for dinner the next evening at the Ming Ter. When I asked if she'd like to go dancing afterward on a double date with Glen and Súpa, she declined because she had started a lucrative business teaching Thais English at 8:00 during the evening in a room she'd leased at a nearby building. Hearing this, I thought, "Well there goes any plan to sexually enthrall her on the dance floor, and then easily seduce her in my Hotel room afterward. I'll need to come up with another way for her to become my lover."

Seeing my disappointment, Sompit offered, "If you'd like to spend more time with me, you could come and help me teach my English class for an hour at 8:00."

I responded, "That sounds like fun, and it'll lend credence to your class to have an American be there. But, I can't every night, as I do have to work some night shifts," and thought, "then after class lets out, who knows what fun we could have together."

Before formation the next morning, I met with Glen and told him about Song's requirement to be my tîi-lók for two months, which he agreed was a little steep, but to have guaranteed STD-free sex for two months, it might be acceptable. Then, I told him about Sompit and not being able to go dancing with her and Súpa because I'd agreed to help her teach English to Thais in the evenings as a little side business, with my hope of some hanky-panky afterward that could lead to her becoming my lover.

Glen said he'd have Súpa pass to Song my decision for her not to be my tîi-lók, as I'd found someone else less costly, which should soften the rejection. Then, he told me it was in the works to set Phil up with a tîi-lók, but couldn't coordinate anything with him till after we'd been paid today, as Phil had been working the night shift.

At formation, the CO announced to everyone's shock, "I'm sorry to inform you that Spec-4 Richard Johnson, from one of the Company's outlying Radio Sites, was killed in a motorcycle accident last night. It's believed, from his smashed speedometer, he was doing 100 kilometers per hour, or 65 miles per hour, on a country road at dusk, when he ran into the back of an ox cart and died instantly. As far as I know, this was the first death in the 442d since its formation. We'll now bow our heads in silence for a minute of respect for his passing."

A pall was over the Company when it was dismissed for duty, or to get ready for Pay Line. After I'd received my $220 in pay and allowances, bought a $10 Savings Bond, paid my $8 mây-bâan tab, and exchanged $50 for 1,000 Bhat, it took a while to collect the $400 from the sixteen payday loans I'd made, of which $80 was profit. Putting $500 in my tobacco cash can, most of which I planned to reinvest in several weeks, when these same guys, and others, were broke again. I then caught a Thai bus to the Air Base's Bank and deposited $50 in my Savings Account.

Returning to the Tropo barracks, I napped under the breeze of my fan till I heard the 11:00 bugle call for Mess. After eating lunch in the Mess Hall, I returned to the barracks, and settled into playing money-stakes Double-Deck Pinochle with Skip as my partner, while drinking beer and smoking cigarettes throughout the hot, muggy afternoon.

At the sound of the 5:00 bugle call for Mess, we finished the hand we were playing and settled the accounts. While the others left for the Mess Hall, I quickly showered, shaved and drank one more cold Bud as I dressed to have dinner with Sompit at 6:00 in the Ming Ter. As I rapidly walked across the basketball court to the bus stop, I saw a bunch of newbies in their tucked-in and boot-bloused OD BDUs, climbing out the backs of three 2½-ton canvas covered trucks, walk to the back of the fourth truck, heft a heavy OD duffle bag on their right shoulder and carry it to the far side of HQ toward the Day Room, and I thought, "Welcome to the Land of Smiles and heaven on Earth."

Arriving at the Chainarong Gate, I saw there was time for a ¾-mile walk to the Ming Ter in the setting sunlight. Walking West along moat beside Ratchanikun Road, I'd just crossed over and turned right up Rajadamnern Road, when a săawm-law pulled alongside me, and the driver offered to carry me to my destination. Pointing at the Ming Ter a quarter-mile away, I stopped and told him in Thai I didn't need a ride for that short distance. He argued that a rich American shouldn't walk any distance and offered to carry me there for only 3 Bhat. Five minutes later, a small crowd had gathered to watch an American arguing deftly in Thai with a săawm-law driver over a 5 sá-taang difference in price. The driver finally gave in, and for 60 sá-taang, I allowed him to carry me the 400 yards to the Ming Ter, which I could easily have walked in the five minutes we'd haggled.

Dropping me off at the Ming Ter, I handed him a One-Bhat coin, and thanked him for the ride, and told him to keep the 40 sá-taang as a tip. Still a little early, I entered the restaurant and was seated at a table. Waiting for Sompit's arrival, I thought, "Bargaining with that driver was an entertaining way to kill some time."

When Sompit arrived and we'd exchanged sáwátdiis, we talked in English about how our day had gone, while waiting for our orders to arrive. While talking over dinner, she was impressed with my previous experience at having taught two young waitresses English so they could become tîi-lóks for Americans, and said she'd employ some of my techniques with her class.

After over an hour talking while we ate, we left to go to her classroom, and I was surprised she had a little Vespa scooter sitting inside the entrance way to ride there on. The Vespa was a brand of popular moped that one sat on to drive, much like sitting on a chair, versus the person's legs straddling a motorbikes' frame. Sitting behind her, and holding her firm, rounds hips with my hands, we rode to a lane off Mahat Thai Road, and thought, "This is sure better than her having to walk there behind me, plus the physical contact is enjoyable, and I'll bet she feels the same."

Arriving at the 4-story building, I pushed the Vespa through a side door for her, and we climbed up two flights of stairs. Entering the twenty by thirty-foot room she'd leased, I saw it was full of wood chairs for her students to sit on. On the front wall was a black chalkboard behind a small wood table that she set her teacher's textbook on. The two sidewalls had 8-by-11-inch signs, each with an upper and lowercase letter of the English alphabet on it.

Several minutes later, her students began to arrive with their textbooks. I saw there were both men and women, mostly in their thirties and forties. And as expected, the men sat on the right side of the room and the women on the left.

We spent the next hour in focused learning, as these students were intent on learning English to improve their livelihood, having spent their hard-earned money to do so. With them deferring to my opinion on how to say words, the class ended, and the students left quickly for their homes. closing the door when the last pupil exited, I said with a smile to Sompit, "Does the teacher's helper get a little reward for his assistance?" as I walked to her and held her by the waist with my hands.

Sompit smiled hesitantly and held her face up for me to kiss her trembling, puckered lips. Though she was unsure at first, she quickly responded to my affectionate kiss on her lips with some enthusiasm, and I thought, "I'll bet this is the first time she's ever been kissed, given she didn't date anyone while going to High School."

After a minute, she gently withdrew and said, "That was very enjoyable, but it will be inappropriate for us to be alone here for any longer," and giving me a quick kiss on the lips, she put her textbook in a book bag, before we left.

Having pushed Sompit's Vespa out of the building, I climbed onto it behind her. Squeezing her lovely round hips between my thighs and hands, and giving them a firm massage with my fingertips, she gave a little moan as she straightened her back to lean against my chest and said, "That is enjoyable, too, Sandii. If you want, you can sit a little closer," and used her hips to pull my groin sensuously tight against her succulent butt. As we drove away, she gave me an enticing wiggle, and I thought, "Woman, are you signaling that you want our relationship to become sexual?"

Giving me a ride to the Chainarong Gate, I assured her I'd meet her at the classroom tomorrow night by 7:45, after I got off from working my 12-hour day shift. From then on, it became routine on my off days for us to meet for dinner at 6:00, before riding on her moped to where class was held. And after I worked the day shift, to meet her in the classroom by 7:45. Then, after class, we'd shut the door and make out for about ten minutes, limiting the time to keep the appearance of propriety.

Soon, our make out sessions evolved to include heavy petting. But, Sompit refused my offers to get a Hotel room, where we'd be more comfortable and have more time, explaining, "If we did that, then I would make love with you, which I really do want to do. But, knowing the value Americans place on virginity, I will not do that with you, unless we are married, which is what I hope you will eventually want."

On my second night shift after the first week of my helping Sompit teach her English class, Richard told me and Skip, "I'm going to the NCO Club at 8:30 for dinner and to watch the Friday night floor show. If you need me, just have the club page me and I'll be back immediately."

As this was something Bob occasionally did, we thought nothing of it. About 10:00 we received a call on the Order Wire from Korat Tropo that a 5-man inspection team from the Quad-C A had just left there and were on the way to our Air Base Site. I immediately placed a call to the NCO Club to page Richard Dankers. When he didn't return to the Operations Room in two minutes, I requested a second page for him, and then a third.

When the Quad-C A inspection team arrived, they asked why Richard was not present. It fell to me, as the senior military person on the Site, to tell them what I knew about Richard's absence. Then, two of them left for the NCO Club. One returned in two minutes, requesting on the Order Wire that Korat Tropo immediately send an experienced Frame Tech to Korat Base. After the request was acknowledged, he explained they'd found Richard passed out drunk in the NCO Club.

At the following Monday morning formation, after my two off days, Skip and I were introduced to Spec-5 Sean Tucker, as Richard's replacement and our new Team Leader. It turned out Sean had arrived last week with the large batch of newbies. But, we could hardly consider him as a newbie, as he'd already finished one tour with the First Signal Brigade in Vietnam. Having been transferred to Ft. Huachuca, AZ, after one month there, he'd reenlisted to return to the First Brigade just to get out of that "hell hole" before committing suicide as his other means to leave Ft. Huachuca.

Two weeks later, just after celebrating my twenty-first birthday by getting a Liquor Ration Card, I received my transfer orders to depart on August 4, 1969, for a 30-day leave, before reporting to the 11th Signal Group at Ft. Huachuca, AZ. When I showed my transfer orders to Sean, he laughed and said, "I recommend, if you're not going to reenlist, then just shoot yourself in the head when you get to Ft. Huachuca."

CHAPTER 62

I'LL NEVER FORGET THIS MOMENT FOR THE REST OF MY LIFE

Actually, my transfer orders were in four parts, starting with a departure time of 8:00 on August 4, 1969, from Korat RTAFB[161], to U-Tapao RTAFB, en route to USAS-Thai, Bangkok, for debriefing. Then, orders for an August 5th flight on Tiger Airways Flight 12 from Don Muang Airport to Travis Air Force Base, with orders for a 30-day Post Combat Leave, beginning August 6th, which was incidentally Linda's birthday. Finally, an order to report on September 5, 1969, to the "11th Sig Grp, StratCom",[162] Ft. Huachuca, AZ.

As it turned out, the three groups who'd arrived sequentially with Glen, me and Skip's groups to the 442d Signal Battalion, and did not receive an extension of tour, had all received their orders on the same day. Also, not everyone was being transferred to Ft. Huachuca. Skip, with a large number of others, were surprised with orders to Germany. But, Tommy had orders back to Ft. Monmouth, NJ, where his family's political connections had arranged for him to be a General's driver, to

---

161   Royal Thai Air Force Base
162   Eleventh Signal Group, Strategic Communications Command

which I said, "Sometimes it's good to have friends in high places, so you could get such a skate job,[163] you lucky dog."

My daily routines had also shifted for my last 41 days in Thailand. After spending my mornings poolside napping on my off days and those I worked nights, Skip and I spent the hot, muggy afternoons in the Air Base's air-conditioned Library, using its tape decks to listen to and make copies of taped albums. In the evenings I didn't work nights, I went to Sompit's classroom to help teach her English class, and then have our ten to fifteen minutes of passionate kissing and heavy petting.

During the evening of my two off days, I'd take Sompit out to dinner on one of them, then go to her classroom to teach for an hour, before our short make out session. On the other evening, I went with the guys to Horn's home in the compound for a relaxing evening with my compatriots, drinking Horn's Sing Hai Beer. There, I saw Bob's tîi-lók, Gúlapp, sitting with the other tîi-lóks, and learned Bob would still support her while he went to Warrant Officer School, before returning to the 442d with a commission and posting as a Radio Site OIC.

To my surprise, shortly after arriving with the other guys from X-shift, I watched as Spec-5 Dan Durkins from Tropo's 2-shift declared at Horn's gate that he had no booze with him and received permission to enter Horn's home. Dan was a 5-foot-7, homely looking, medium built guy, who walked with a slouch and wore glasses, giving him the appearance of being a nerd. Also, with the misfortune of having the last name "Durkins," he'd acquired the handle of "Dork Durkins." As everyone affectionately called him "Dork," because of him warm and friendly demeanor, he felt the moniker made him an accepted member of his Microwave Team. This was especially important to him now to still be identified as "one of the guys" with his recent promotion to Spec-5 to replace his Team's Leaders, who'd transferred Stateside.

Dork had a bemuddled look on his face when he exited from the house onto the porch with a bottle of Sing Hai Beer in his right hand. Glen asked, "Why so glum, Dork? Did you get into a fight with your tîi-lók, cause you normally don't come here alone?"

163　Slang word meaning to ride or move along easily, as on a pair of roller skates.

Dork replied, "No. Everything's fine with her. Great, as a matter of fact."

I responded, "So, what's happened? You get a 'Dear John' letter, like most of the other guys?"

Dork answered morosely, "Not a 'Dear John' letter. I got a 'Dear Dan, I've had a little girl' letter from my girlfriend Karen, back home."

Stony said cheerfully, "Well, congratulations on becoming a Dad, Dork. I imagine you're just disappointed it wasn't a boy."

Dork responded angrily, "Come on, Stony. Do the math. We came here together eleven months ago, so I couldn't possibly be the father. No, Karen wrote that after I was gone two months, she'd become really depressed missing me, and her girlfriends took her out to a bar to cheer her up. Long-story-short, she got drunk and horny, and she had a one-night stand with a guy she met at the bar. When Karen found she was pregnant, she'd hoped the baby was early enough to make it sound plausible I was father. She said that she still loves me very much, and wants to marry me as soon as I return after my 6-month extension of my tour of duty.

"I'd be a hypocrite, if I faulted Karen for having sex while I've been gone, as I have a tîi-lók here. Besides, I still love her and want to marry her when I get back. It's just that I don't know if I can accept raising a kid that's not mine."

We then spent the evening consoling Dork, and telling him that girls tend to look like their mothers, so he should have no problem loving the baby girl and accepting her as his own once he got back home and married Karen. By the time the gang broke up, Dork was feeling much better, especially after drinking a quart bottle of the potent Sing Hai Beer.

On Wednesday morning, when I got off my second night shift and eaten breakfast in the Mess Hall, I went to our Company Supply and showed a Supply Clerk my transfer orders. Upon seeing them, he led me to the rear of their large Supply building, where I saw stacks of 4-foot square, 30-inch deep wood crates with pallet skids. After helping him take one down, he used a stencil making machine to produce a stencil with my name and service number in 1-inch letters.

After stenciling in black my name and service number, and "Fragile, This End Up" on all four sides, he said, "Okay, Specialist Lynch, this is your box in which you can send up to 600 pounds of your personal belongings to your home-of-residence address or to your next duty station. I suggest you don't put any drugs in it, as they're checked with drug sniffing dogs when they arrive at Travis Air Force Base. Other than that, you can ship anything you want," laughingly adding, "including your tîi-lók, if you've a mind to drill some air holes for her."

Leaving Company Supply with the stencil temple of my name and service number, I went to the Tropo barrack and drank a cold Bud, as I changed into my swimsuit and headed out for my poolside nap. Hearing the 11:00 bugle call for Mess, I returned to the Tropo barracks and drank another cold Bud, as I changed into civilian clothes for lunch. Entering the Mess Hall, I saw Spec-5 Tim Reynolds, my old LRC-3 classmate, sitting alone at a table. After getting a tray of cheeseburgers and fried onion rings, I sat down to join him and said, "Tim, you're looking pretty glum. Did you get orders to Ft. Huachuca, too?"

Tim replied despondently, "No. Actually, I received orders to Germany. But, I've a different problem to deal with. I just came the JAG[164] Office, where an attorney told me I'm being sued by a collection agency for $25,000. Before leaving Stateside, I'd signed a Power-of-Attorney for my mother to handle paying off a few thousand dollars in student loans for my Associates Degree. It turns out she opened some credit card accounts in my name and ran up $25,000 in debts, for which I'm now liable.

"The attorney told me I can sue my mother for fraudulently using my Power-of-Attorney and have her charged with embezzlement. But, under the Soldiers and Sailors Act, as long as I'm in a Theater of War, my pay cannot be garnished or be charged interest on the balance due. The attorney has arranged with the 442d to have my transfer to Germany cancelled, if I reenlist for three more years. If I do, they'll add one year to my tour here and promote me to Staff Sargent, since I meet the one-year-time-in-grade requirement and the 442d is short on Staff Sergeants. Plus, I'll receive a $10,000 reenlistment bonus as a Staff Sargent, versus the $8,000 bonus as a Spec-5.

"So, I'm going to reenlist, which'll give me the money and time to pay the $25,000 debt and not have to sue my mother. The hard part for

---

164   Judge Advocate General

me is, it hurts so much to have been stabbed in the back like that by my own mother."

The following Sunday, I worked the night shift and was able to call Linda and my family to let them know I'd received my transfer orders to fly out Tuesday morning, August 5th, from Bangkok, and arrive about 24 hours later at Travis Air Force Base, California, in the evening of the same day, having gained a day by flying East over the International Date Line. Linda was excited to hear I'd arrive in New Jersey on August 6th, her twenty-first birthday, having told everyone I planned to spend the first two weeks of my 30-day leave in New Jersey with Linda.

Leaving the Tropo barracks the next evening to work my second night shift, I saw three truckloads of newbies arrive, and wondered if any contained my replacement. Getting off work in the morning, which was Pay Day, July 1st, I drank a cold Bud, as I dressed in by Class-B khaki uniform. After receiving my expected $220, buying a $10 Savings Bond and paying my $8 mây-bâan tab, I only exchanged $50 for 1,000 Bhat, and thought, "One good thing about dating Sompit is, it costs me next to nothing to date her. Only the cost of taking her to dinner every six days, which is less than a buck."

Returning to the Tropo barracks, I drank another cold Bud, as I changed into civilian clothes and waited to collect $525 from the twenty-one guys I'd made payday loans to. Realizing a profit of $105 and seeing how our next Pay Day was Friday, August 1st, the week before my leaving for Stateside, I thought, "I'll put $300 in my tobacco cash can, as seed money for the payday loans, and deposit $375 in my Savings Account to draw interest on until any of it's needed for payday loans in three weeks."

As today was my first day off and Pay Day, I'd asked Sompit last Saturday evening in the classroom, if she'd like to have dinner tonight at the Anego restaurant for an Italian pasta meal. I figured my breaking the news of my transfer orders to leave Korat on August 4th over an expensive dinner would soften the blow of the bad news. Sompit had excitedly replied, "I like Italian food very much and am most happy to dine with you at the Anego on Tuesday evening. In fact, if you come to the jewelry shop's side door, I would be pleased to give us a ride there, so we may arrive together."

Wearing my new brown three-piece suit, I arrived at 6:00 and knocked on the side door, which was immediately opened by Sompit. I saw she'd also dressed up for our dinner date at the spendy Anego Japanese restaurant, wearing a form-fitting, light-blue silk bouse, revealing the round contours of her small breasts that were lifted up by the wide, corset-like bra worn by most Thai women. Unlike the bras with a half-inch wide chest-strap with two hook-clips worn by American women, the breast-cups of the bras worn by Thai women were held in place with a 3-inch wide chest strap with six hook-clips, which defeated my one-handed technique to unhook a bra.

Sompit was also wearing a mid-calf long, dark-blue and gold, horizontally stripped formal Thai-style skirt with a 3-inch wide, white belt around her waist, which nicely enhanced her luscious round hips.

Pushing her Vespa out the doorway for her, she then sat on the seat, which I mounted behind her. Holding her voluptuous hips tight in my hands, I pulled my groin firmly against her sensuous butt between my wanting thighs. When she gave me a little moan of desire, as she enticingly wiggled her lovely round bottom against my loins, I became aroused and thought, "What I wouldn't give for us to be heading to a Hotel room to feast on the lust we have for each other with vigorous lovemaking, instead of going to dinner."

As we ate our delicious Italian pasta at the Anego with a carafe of red wine, I said, "My darling, I'm sorry to say that I've received transfer orders to leave Korat on August 4th and fly Stateside. I'd hope my request for a 6-month extension of tour would have been approved. But we're now receiving enough replacements, my request was denied."

I saw tears begin to form in her pretty slanting Chinese eyes and roll down her lovely checks, as she said in shock, "Oh no, my darling Sandii. I had hoped you brought me to this beautiful restaurant to propose marriage to me because you have clearly shown your love and desire for me, as I have shown mine to you with our lovemaking. Maybe that can still happen before you leave, and I could go to the United States with you?"

I replied, "My beloved Sompit, if my tour of duty had been extended for six months, that may have been possible. But, with only one month, there is no way it could happen now. First, I'd have to get permission from the Army to marry a foreign national, and that alone could take a month or more. And then, it'd take several months to get you a Green Visa Card to go as my wife to the U.S. I still have one year left on my Army enlistment before I could return here to marry you, and we've only been dating for a month. So, you may not want to wait a year apart from each other to marry me. Besides, I don't even have a job here to return to for me to make a living and to pay your father a dowry to marry you."

Wiping away her tears, she responded, "Yes, my darling, you are right. You will need to pay my father a dowry to marry me, and need to have employment to do it. But, in this month I have known you, I have grown to love you very much, and am very willing and able to be apart from you for a year, before we are happily wed," and with a bright smile she added, "And, who knows what can happen between now and then to let that happen."

That evening, after we taught her class, our make-out session was very passionate, as our hands and kisses freely caressed over our partially removed shirts. Sompit even unhooked her bra to allow me to suck small breasts into my mouth, as we lowered ourselves to the floor. Then, she took my right and slid it up, under her dress, along the silky smooth skin of her inner thigh, to her pantiless, wet crotch. As I used my fingers to pleasure her, she stroked me desiringly, and I again offered to take her to a Hotel room, where we'd be more comfortable.

She moaned in reply, "I want to do that with you very much, but I won't copulate with you until we are married. So, this will have to do until then," as she grasped me, and I felt her body shudder with a climactic rush. Then, leaning over me and taking my manhood into her mouth, Sompit reciprocated the release I'd given her.

After restoring our clothes and again looking presentable, we stoicly left the classroom and rode happily together on her Vespa to the Chainarong Gate. As I dismounted, Sompit smiled lovngly and said, "I love you so very much, and the taste of your sexual desire. I am looking forward to teaching again with you tomorrow night," to which I responded, "As am I."

I happily thought while riding a Thai bus to Camp Friendship, "Maybe being able to have a Thai wedding will be enough for Sompit to go to bed with me, as I don't need the Army's permission for that. Then, I could work on getting the marriage legalized by the Army for her to get a Green Visa Card to live with me at Ft. Huachuca, as I've been told there are practically no women to be had around there, and Linda may not agree to marry me before I go to Ft. Huachuca.

"Besides, I've really had fun with Sompit while teaching her English class, and very much enjoyed making out with her, especially tonight, which is a good indicator of how good she could be in bed. Also, she clearly loves me, and I like her very much and could easily fall in love with her. Plus, I know that Thai women do make the perfect wives and lovers, which I'll certainly need when I'm at Ft. Huachuca for a year. The big drawback with Sompit is, I don't know if she can dance, or even likes to do dance, which is a key element for me. I wish Bob was still around to help talk me through this, as I don't trust myself to make a rational decision while my hormones are raging."

The next evening, I first went to the compound with Skip to relax and socialize, as those who didn't have tîi-lóks were hitting the bars to drink and chase pûu-ying. Then, leaving at 7:30, I walked the ¾-mile to Sompit's classroom. When I entered the room and closed the door, she ran into my arms and gave me a passionate kiss, as no students had arrived yet. After we had a fun hour together teaching her class, Sompit quickly shut the door behind the last student, and said, "I love you so much, my beloved," after she'd passionately kissed me.

While we wantonly kissed each other, Sompit rapidly unbuttoned her blouse and hastily unhooked her bra, a task that confounded me, but she did easily. Then, lifting up her bra, she pulled my hungry mouth down to feast on her tasty, small breasts, and moaned with desire as we laid down on the floor. Taking my right hand, Sompit slid it up under skirt, between her hot thighs, and placed it eagerly on her wet, pantiless crotch, and moaned, "Please, pleasure my lust for you, my beloved," as she unfastened my pants and begun to desiringly stroke my fully engorged shaft.

A moment later, Sompit stifled her ecstatic cry, as her climactic rush filled her aroused body. Then, she anxiously pushed me onto my back and gasped, "Now, I must taste your hot sexual desire," and sucked me hungrily into her mouth. As she brought me to my own orgasmic release, I thought, "You may still be technically a virgin, Sompit, but in every other way, you certainly are not, which suits me just fine."

The next morning after formation, Tim stopped Sean, Skip and I, and said, as he pointed to a skinny, 5-foot-8 kid, "This is PFC Sam Goodman. He's a microwave man that'll start working on your X-shift

Team today and will be Sandii's replacement when he leaves in four weeks. So, you'll have plenty of time to bring him up to speed before then."

I laughed and responded, "Sam, that's a lot better than the no time I was given when I started at the Air Base Site, as the guy I replaced had left two days before I started. Also, I was given only three weeks to cross-train as a Frame Tech, before Skip arrived to replace our Team's Frame Tech, who was transferred to Tropo. But, don't go get yourself shot in a firefight, like I did, as there's no Purple Hearts in Thailand."

Taking Sam with me on the 10:50 meal run to meet Glen, and hope Súpa could fix him up with a tîi-lók. Joining Glen in the Mess Hall, he introduced me to his replacement, PFC Dan Hoffsteader. Not seeing Ronnie with him, who usually made the same meal runs with Glen, I asked, "So, where's Ronnie? He's always here with you."

Glen shook his head and laughed in reply, "Ronnie got the creeping crud and was medevac'd to the Clark Air Force Base Hospital in PI. He'd noticed some kind of fungus on his crotch last week and went to Sick Call, where they gave him an anti-fungal cream. But the fungus must've thought it was fungal food and spread like crazy. When his skin started to crack open and bleed, he was hospitalized here. However, they don't have a Mycologist here. So, they medevac'd him to Clark, where they have a Mycologist to treat him. Hopefully, he'll be back soon, as he's slated to be promoted to Spec-5 in a couple weeks to be the next Microwave Leader on our shift."

For the next week, my life went by quickly with my being busy cross-training Sam to be a Frame Tech and orienting him to our 252 in-house circuits. Also, being busy having "virgin" sex with Sompit after we taught her English class in the evening, when I wasn't working the night shift. On Thursday, July 10th, when I arrived at Sompit's classroom, she gave me a passionate kiss and excitedly said, "We both have Sunday off. How would you like to ride with me to have lunch with a family friend, who has a jute plantation just outside of Bâan Prasat, about 30 kilometers north of Korat?"

I quickly calculated that to be about 18 miles and replied, "An 18 mile ride through the countryside, holding your sexy hips, sounds like fun to me. When do you want to leave?"

She answered, "That is wonderful. If you meet me at my home by 10:00, we could be at the plantation about 11:00. That would give us enough time for a tour, before we ate lunch. Then, after the monsoon rain, we could ride back to Korat and have dinner with my family, if that is acceptable to you?"

I replied, "Sounds like a perfect way to spend Sunday with you. And after dinner, maybe we could go to a movie."

During my second night shift on Saturday, I was able to call Linda again, and she told me arrangements had been made for me to stay for free in a student dorm-room at the nearby Drew University, as they were empty before the start of the Fall Semester. Also, she'd bought tickets for us to go see an outdoor Rock Concert on August 15th through 17th at a place in up-state New York called Woodstock, with reservations for us to stay at a nearby motel. I responded, "That sounds great to me," and thought, "Especially the part about our spending the weekend together in a motel. Maybe she's looking to make our relationship a committed one, or even to get married, which would be perfect timing for my being stationed at Ft. Huachuca."

Getting a couple of hours sleep afterward, I showered and shaved before driving the truck to the Company Area on my 6:30 meal run. Eating a quick breakfast in the Mess Hall, I then napped a couple of hours poolside and took a dip in the pool, before drinking a cold Bud in the Tropo barracks, as I dressed in civilian clothes to spend a fun day with Sompit.

Leaving for Korat shortly after 9:00, I arrived at Sompit's home by 10:00. After we flirtatiously exchanged sáwátdiis, I pushed her Vespa out the doorway and sensuously situated myself behind Sompit's luscious butt, holding her lovely hips possessively in my hands. As she accelerated west down Chomphon Road to the Suranarii Monument, I felt her warm back press desringly against my broad chest.

Turning right at the Monument onto Rajadamnern Road, I felt Sompit's voluptuous butt wiggle enticingly against my loins, as she went with the flow of traffic to Mittaphap Road and turned left. A half-mile further, she followed the directions of the traffic cop to turn right onto Hwy 2, and a couple of miles later, she followed the traffic left onto Route 205 for several miles.

Waiting for a break in the oncoming traffic, she turned right and sped quickly onto a dirt country road, where I enjoyed the feel of her firm, round butt jostle between my desiring thighs and pleasurably against my wanting groin, as the Vespa bounced along the uneven surface of the dirt road. With no traffic on the road and wanting to show my desire for her, I slid my right hand up under the waist of her flapping blouse, and cupped her firm jostling breast. Sompit leaned her breast longingly into my massaging hand and moaned, "Oh yes, my dearest, that does feel good. But, it is quite distracting, so please stop."

Reluctantly, I slid my hand back down to her luscious hip, still enjoying her firm, round bottom jostling between my wanting thighs. After a little while, Sompit turned left on to a lane leading to a large, one-story, European-style white house, and stopped in the shade, under a large banyan tree. Climbing off the Vespa, I heard a man's loud voice with an Aussie slur say from the direction of the house, "Allo, Sompit. It's good to see ya. Is this strapping big lad, the Yank ya wanted me ta meet?"

Turning toward the house, Sompit took me unabashedly by my left hand and led me to a tall, well-built man with a weather-beaten face, who looked about 50-years-old, and said proudly, "Hello, Uncle Jim. This is my boyfriend, Sandii," as she affectionately squeezed my hand, "and am very pleased to introduce him to you. Sandii, this is James MacPherson, my uncle on my father's side."

Reaching out with my free right hand, I said, "Glad to meet you, Jim. You're not related to the James MacPherson who translated Ossian's poetic prose from the old Gaelic manuscripts, are you?"

He laughed and replied, "No, I'm not related to that scoundrel who falsely claimed were his translations of Gaelic folklore by the bard Ossian from his third century writings. But, it's a pleasure to meet a young man who is so well-read, Sandii. I'd like you to meet my wife of twenty-two years, Lu, the younger sister of Sompit's father," as I espied a Chinese looking woman about forty-years-old. "We met shortly after my release from a Jap POW camp here about, and her family helped me set up this jute plantation to make burlap cloth and ropes with. Well, come on inside for some lemonade, and then I'll give you a quick tour of my operation here before we tuck in some grub."

After refreshing my dry mouth and throat with some delicious, ice-cold lemonade, he led me and Sompit on a tour of his large machine processing facilities, extoling the versatility of the jute plant, and thence its commercial demand. Over lunch, he explained how he intended to expand his operation and modernize his production, which led to the practical purpose of my visit. While he and I sat in the cooling breeze on the veranda and drank cold Sing Hai Beer, he explained how he needed to have a partner knowledgeable in electronics and with farming experience, before investing in the new equipment he wanted to install, and offered me a one-third partnership.

I responded, "Jim, I'm very tempted by your offer, but I still have a year left on my enlistment, and can't possibly consider accepting it till I'm discharged," and thought, "Surely, this generous offer is contingent on marrying Sompit, which is a possibility. Besides, if I've a mind to return to Thailand, and things don't pan out with Sompit, I've a stack of business cards from corporate executives who will hire me. Either way, I'd be set for life."

After our nice visit with Jim and Lu, and the monsoon downpour had past, we rode back to Korat, enjoying the view of the verdant countryside. With my sensuous hold of Sompit's luscious bottom being enticingly jostled against my loins, Sompit could feel my rising desire for her. She said to me as we entered Korat, "My beloved, would it be acceptable to you, if we stopped at the classroom for a few minutes and made things ready for tomorrow night's class?"

I replied readily, "What an excellent idea, my dearest."

Entering the classroom, that was our clandestine love nest, Sompit threw her desiring arms around me, and we passionately kissed. When our pent-up lust had been subsumed in virgin intercourse, we regained our composure and left for Sompit's home. There, we had a wonderful dinner with her family, before leaving to see a Japanese Samurai movie. As Sompit's parents now considered me to be her "faan," and our having spent the day alone on our visit to her Uncle Jim, they had no compunction with us leaving by ourselves to see a movie at the Action Theater, for which I hired a sǎawm-law to carry us there, as it had no place to leave Sompit's Vespa.

After watching the action-packed, bloodletting movie, I took Sompit home via a sǎawm-law, which then carried me to the Chainarong Gate. Returning to the Tropo barracks, I heard considerable grousing from those who'd just been to the Camp's Theater and seen the new Clint Eastwood movie, *Hang Em High*. Skip explained, "We'd gone to see *Hang Em High* with the full expectation it would follow the mantra of his three spaghetti westerns, *A Fist Full of Dollars*, *A Few Dollars More*, and *The Good, The Bad, and The Ugly*, as a rugged individualist with no name, who lived outside the law, and was not involved with any woman. The first thing those American idiots did was to make him an honest cattleman with a name, then pin a badge on him and throw him in bed with a woman. They've ruined his whole persona the Italians had imbued in their movies."

I responded vehemently, "Those jerks. Leave it to the Americans to screw-up a perfectly good image. I'd planned to see that movie tomorrow. But now, I'll skip it in protest of their idiocy."

The next morning after formation, I went with a bunch of guys to the Air Base and bid a good farewell to Glen, George, Stony and the others that were there to board the old C-130 for U-Tapao Air Base and Bangkok, before flying Stateside. Especially to say "so long" to my boon companion, Glen, who'd helped me learn Thai, and introduced me to and then commiserated with me, on my ill-fated relationship with the exotic Jintona. But, I was happy to know we'd be stationed together again in two months, even if it had to be in that hell-hole called Ft. Huachuca.

Two days later, while working my second day shift, I read the continuous spew of AP and UPI teletyped updates leading up to the launch of the Apollo 11 Moon mission, manned by Neil Armstrong, Mike Collins and Buzz Aldrin. The historic goal this time was to successfully land and walk on the Moon, and then to return safely to Earth. Though there was considerable hope in their success, there was quite a few bets made on the success or failure of the mission's launch, landing on the Moon, and/or safe return to Earth. There were even some claiming it was all a big hoax to spoof the Russians.

The next day, before leaving to work the night shift, I saw Ronnie sitting in the Mess Hall eating dinner and sporting his new Spec-5 stripes. Sitting at his table with my tray full of food, I said, "High, Ronnie. Congrats on getting your Spec-5. Too bad you missed out on saying goodbye to Glen, George and Stony's leaving the other morning. How'd things go for you at Clark Air Base?"

He replied, "Thanks for the congrats, Sandii, but I'd rather the lifers had left me as I was. Yeah, it sucked big time not being able to say goodbye before they left, as I'd know them since we flew here together. Living in the same hooch together and working at Tropo on the same shift as Glen and Stony for a year. It would've been great if Glen's extension had been approved, then we could've been Team Leaders together, too.

"Also, he could've gone with us on the big trip we've planned. There's a bunch of us who'll be discharged from here about the same time, and plan to buy motorcycles for a road trip from here, across Burma, Nepal, and India, and continue West across the Middle East, as far as we can get in a year. Then, we'll go to the nearest U.S. Embassy and show them our discharge papers. According to Army Regs, no matter where you are in the World within one year of your discharge, you're entitled to a free flight back to your home Stateside. It's a once-in-a-lifetime change to take the ride-of-a-lifetime.

"As for the Hospital at Clark, it took a while for their Mycologist to figure out what it was I had and how to treat it. I was lucky to leave there with my nuts still attached. By the time I was cured, I was left with a mass of scars from my naval down to my mid-thighs due to all the cracked open and bleeding of my skin. With all that scarring, I'll never be able to compete as a body builder and be appealing to women. So, that's really depressing."

I responded compassionately, "Sorry to hear that, Ronnie. And speaking from experience, they've got some really bizarre diseases here. But, that motorcycle trip sounds like it'll be amazing. Wish they'd have let me extend, so I could've gone with you, instead of to that hell-hole, Ft. Huachuca."

For my two night shifts, I followed the teletype reports intently of Apollo 11's progress to the Moon. I even stopped in the Operations Room on my two off days after lunch, on my way to and from the Air Base Library to copy taped albums, and read the teletyped news of this momentous trip that was being saved.

Having read the news on Apollo 11 after leaving the Air Base Library on Saturday, I left my dubbed tapes in my Air Base wall locker before leaving to have dinner and go teaching with Sompit. On Sunday, I went with Sompit to a beautiful Chinese Buddhist Temple before we had dinner with her family. Afterwards, I went to the compound and talked with the others about the impending Moon landing that was set to happen in the next twelve or so hours.

At Monday morning's formation, there was considerable excitement in the ranks about the imminent Moon landing to happen any hour now, and how everyone would be listening to AFTN's live radio broadcast to hear what happened the moment of the landing. In our Operations Room, we'd plugged a speaker into our in-house circuit carrying the live audio to AFTN, and thankful it was a relatively slow Monday morning for circuit outages.

At 9:00, I received a call from Steve at AFTN-TV, telling me they had a live video feed from a local TV station, and if I could get to a TV set, I might be able to watch the Moon landing. When I left on my 10:50 meal run, I drove directly to our Company's Day Room. There, I joined a dozen guys occupying the TV area's lounge couches, as everyone else was at work.

I was amazed to be in a Theater of War, halfway around the world from the U.S., watching the grainy black-and-white images that were coming all the way from the Landing Module, supposedly on the Moon. Then, I saw a form in a spacesuit descend several steps, and hear a voice say, as a foot extended to the surface, "One small step for a man. One giant leap for Mankind." The room erupted in cheers, with everyone jumping up and down, as I thought, "I'll never forget this moment for the rest of my life."

CHAPTER 63

I'VE NEVER SEEN SO MANY LIGHTS

As my last two weeks in Thailand dwindled down, and I went through my usual daily routines, and began to fill my large, wooden shipping crate in Company Supply with all of my belongings. Except for the few uniforms I'd need in transit to New Jersey, and all my civilian clothes I'd carry in my duffel bag, which was the only thing allowed for me to take on my flight Stateside.

Three days after Apollo 11 landed on the moon, and had spent 28 hours and 38 minutes collecting 47.5 pounds of rocks and soil samples from its surface, I listened on my second night shift as it safely returned to Earth.

Having sorely missed being with Sompit during my two night shifts, and wanting very much to take her to bed and have her be with me at Ft. Huachuca, the next evening over dinner at the Ming Ter, I proposed, "My beloved, will you marry me in your Chinese Temple? Then, once our marriage is consummated here and I have permission from the Army, you could fly to America and to live with me at Ft. Huachuca."

She replied joyfully, "Yes, my dearest. I accept your proposal of marriage, but I will only marry you in America, when you receive permission from the Army. I have heard of many women getting married and living with an American here, only for the Army not to recognize Thai wedding and never see their American husbands again after they leave. I would hope that would not happen to me. But, it is possible your Army might not later give its permission. Besides, you might not be able to pay the dowry my father will require, which would be over $3,000, because of the cost of my education in America."

I responded, "Thank you for accepting my proposal, and when I get to Ft. Huachuca, I'll ask the Army for permission to marry you. Now that we're officially engaged, then we can celebrate our engagement in a Hotel room after class tonight."

Sompit laughed and responded, "You know I'd love to do that with you. But, you know my rule, 'No marriage, No intercourse.' However, we can enjoy each other after class, as usual."

The following Monday, on my 6:30 meal run for dinner, I watched four empty 2½-ton trucks leave the Company Area, presumably after dropping off a bunch of newbies. Two days later, when we left for our night shift in our truck for the Air Base Site, I met Skip's replacement, Mike Jessop, who rode in the back with Sam and our two Generator Shed guys. Then, Skip and Sean put Mike through his paces to replace Skip when he left for Stateside in three weeks, while I continued to work with Sam to replace me this weekend, before I left on Monday.

Friday was Pay Day, and after receiving my $220 in pay, I bought a $10 Savings Bond and paid $9 for Aida's services through the weekend. Bypassing the Bhat-exchange table, having enough Bhat for my last weekend in Korat, I went to the Tropo barracks, where I collected $625 from the 25 guys I'd made payday loans to. I could've received another $400 in advance pay for August and September, but decided I had plenty of money already for my 30-day leave Stateside. Besides, I might need that $200 in pay when I arrived at Ft. Huachuca on September 5th.

After collecting my payday loans, I spent the rest of my morning out-processing and collecting my Military Records from the Dispensary, Personnel and Finance Offices, which had to be done in uniform. When I'd gone to lunch in the Mess Hall, I then caught a Thai bus to the Air Base's Bank and closed out my Savings Account, putting $1,000 of my cash into Traveler's Checks for safe keeping.

Returning to the Tropo barracks, I collected up the last of my personal items I wanted shipped Stateside. Having individually wrapped each of my hundred plus recorded magnetic tapes in aluminum foil to protect them from any X-rays that might be made of the contents in my wood crate as it transmitted to my home in Oregon, the crate was topped off with styrofoam packing, the lid sealed and screwed closed, with a shipping label attached to the lid.

Returning to the Tropo barracks, I showered, shaved and drank a cold Bud, as I dressed in civilian clothes. Hearing the 5:00 bugle call for Mess, I left with the guys from my X-shift for dinner in the Mess Hall, before going to the compound in Korat with them for my last evening of relaxing camaraderie. Leaving the compound at 7:30, I walked to Sompit's classroom for a fun time helping teach her class, and then thoroughly enjoying our brief interlude of passionate, virgin sex, before returning to Camp Friendship.

After morning formation on Saturday, I went to the Air Base Site's Operations Room, enjoying the usual hustle and bustle of a busy Saturday morning, while I supervised Sam as he troubleshot the in-house circuit outages assigned to him. With the feeling of a job well-done during my year of working here, I showered and shaved, before reluctantly leaving the Air Base Site for the last time on the 6:30 meal run, thinking, "I'm certainly going to miss this home-away-from-home."

Having a quick dinner in the Mess Hall, I drank a cold Bud as I changed rapidly into civilian clothes and caught a Thai bus to Korat, where I hired a săawm-law to Sompit's classroom. At the end of the English class, she told her students this was the last time I'd be helping her teach them, to which I received a thunderous applause of thanks. As we made ourselves presentable after our passionate virgin love-making, Sompit asked, "Will you work again tomorrow before leaving on Monday?"

I replied, "No, as I'll be packing to leave. But, I'm expected to attend a big party in Korat for everyone leaving Monday morning."

She responded hopefully, "Would you be available to come to dinner at 5:00 in my home, and them come here to help me set up my classroom before you attend your farewell party?"

I replied lovingly, "My beloved, it would bring me great pleasure to have dinner with you and your family, and greater pleasure to spend time loving you, before going to my farewell party."

The next morning after formation, I spent poolside one last time, before eating lunch in the Mess Hall one last time. Then, packing nearly everything I had left in my duffel bag, I showered, shaved and drank a cold Bud, as I dressed in civilian clothes. Boarding a Thai bus to Korat for the last time, a lump rose in my throat as I rode past my old Company Area, now full of Thai Soldiers. Looking at the General's Mess Hall and the old, raised, dark-brown, wood hooches, I fondly reminisced about all the crazy things that happened while I lived there for six months. The same thing happened as I looked longingly at the light-green steel building on the Air Base, my home-away-from-home, and all the fun times I had working with Skip, the best workmate ever, and with Bob, my mentor on all things Thai.

Exiting the bus at the Chainarong Gate, I hired a săawm-law to carry me to the jewelry shop on Chomphon Road, enjoying the last time I'd be haggling with a drive over the cost of a ride. Arriving at the jewelry store, I thoroughly enjoyed my last Thai meal in Korat, and that it was with Sompit's family. Before I left with Sompit on her Vespa, her family bade me a tearful farewell with prayers for a safe trip to America and my return to Thailand.

Sitting close against Sompit, with her enticingly firm butt held between my desiring thighs and my hands sensuously holding her luscious hips, I asked, "Why don't we just go to the nearby Korat Hotel, where I can discreetly rent a room for us to comfortably love each other before I leave tomorrow," thinking, "It doesn't hurt to ask."

She replied, "My dearest darling, I really do want to do that with you, but I do not trust my passion for you enough to not stop me from taking you between my aching legs and your desirable manhood fully into me. I hope you will continue to accept the pleasure of my love for you within the bounds we have been enjoying. Believe me, when we are married, I hope you can handle the amount of lovemaking I want to have with you."

After our passionate love fest in our love nest, Sompit cried profusely while we made ourselves presentable again, and asked me to leave her alone to regain her composure when we lovingly embraced and kissed goodbye. Leaving Sompit as she wished, I walked to the bar on Chainarong Road where the farewell party was being held, thinking, "Sompit, when we're married, I'll very much enjoy handling all the lovemaking you want to have with me."

The send-off party was a large, raucous affair, with the drinking deliberately held to moderation, because nobody wanted to get too drunk and rowdy, as to cause the local constabulary to be called in and end up missing tomorrow morning's flight, or worse.

With a slight hangover the next morning, I drank a cold Bud while dressing in my Class-B khaki uniform, before going to the Mess Hall with the eight guys in the Company who'd arrived in the 28-man group I was part of. After happily eating my last meal at Camp Friendship, I returned to the Tropo barracks and carried my heavily laden duffel bag to the Day Room.

When morning formation ended, the eight of us were escorted to the Day Room by some of our former workmates. There, a 2½-ton, canvas-covered truck was waiting to carry us and our duffel bags to the Air Base's flight line. After being helped by Skip to climb into the cave-like back of the truck and heafting my heavy duffel bag on my back, I rode with others in the dark cave to the flight line. Exiting the back of the truck with my duffel bag, I saw a bunch of the guys from the X and Y-shifts, in various attire, standing near the open rear of the old C-130 that would fly us to the U-Tapao Air Base, before our bus ride to Bangkok.

Passing them with many farewell hugs and handshakes, I then joined the left single file of two 4-man lines being directed by the C-130s Load Master. Having made sure I was behind Tommy, I sounded off with my name and service number. He made a check on his clip boarding list, and I entered the plane's cavernous belly.

As I entered the plane's cargo hold, I saw three more 2½-ton trucks pull onto the tarmac, stop and disgorge khaki uniformed men carrying OD duffel bags on their backs. From the unit abbreviations on the truck's front bumpers, I recognized they were from the Transportation Regiment, Construction Battalion and USAS-Thai's Headquarters Company.

Walking to the cargo hold's front end, I sat in the web seat next to Tommy. Strapping myself firmly into the web seat with its shoulder and lap harness, I placed my duffel bag upright, firmly between my legs, and watched as the large belly of the C-130 was nearly filled with khaki-clad men. When the plane's large rear ramp began to lift up and close, I saw the Cargo Master walk up the cargo hold's center, checking that each passenger was firmly strapped into his seat with his duffel bag tight between his legs.

Reaching the ladder up to the flight deck, he yelled, "Cargo secure. You can spin 'em up, Sir," as he climbed the ladder and strapped himself into the jump seat. I then heard the loud whine, cough and bang from each of the four engines in succession, as they roared to life. When they'd warmed up for a minute, I felt the plane jerk forward, as it began taxing to the end of the runway. Then, feeling the front of the plane spin to the right, it stopped for a moment, as I heard the engines gunned to full throttle, before feeling the sudden thrust forward when the brakes were released.

Experiencing the acceleration of the old C-130 down the runway, rattling like the giant bucket of nuts and bolts it was, I saw those around me fervently praying like I was, for the rickety old plane not to fall apart and crash on takeoff. Suddenly pushed down into my seat for a second, before feeling my stomach drop like a rock with a sudden lift upwards, like being on a roller coaster, I realized I'd just been tossed up into the air by the up-slope at the end of the runway. Then, the rattling subsided, as I heard the wheels retract into the belly of the plane, and felt the plane bank to the left, as it turned to a southern heading for U-Tapao Air Base.

Once we'd safely landed at U-Tapao, and thankfully exited the old C-130, I boarded one of the two waiting Air Force busses, with my duffle bag in hand. After a 2-hour ride to Bangkok, the bus arrived at the same Hotel I was in the year before. When I was issued my room key and meal voucher for lunch, I was told to be in Conference Room 220 by 1:00. Also, that for no reason was I to leave the Hotel, which could be cause for my transfer orders to be revoked and be punished under Article 15 of the UCMJ. I thought, "What are they going to do? Cut my hair and send me to Ft. Huachuca?"

After carrying my heavy duffel bag to my room, which looked just like the one I had the previous year, I met up with Tommy and we went to the Hotel's restaurant for lunch. When a very pretty Thai waitress with a scintillating smile came to our table, we didn't even take the menus she proffered, but ordered our favorite Thai meals in Thai.

Having finished eating lunch, I pulled the makings for my cigarette from under my shirt front and began to roll a cigarette. As I did so, Tommy pointed me to the restaurant's entrance, and watched two MPs in khaki uniforms enter and sit at a table next to ours. Looking at them with a smirking smile on my face, I lit my hand-rolled cigarette, and we laughed at their disappointed faces, as they stood up and left.

Having leisurely finished our cigarettes, we each left a 1-Bhat tip on the table and moseyed up to the Conference Room directly, having recognized its number from the year before. A khaki-clad SSG standing just inside the doorway, directed us take the next available seats toward the front of the room. After doing so, we began to chat and joke with those around us, as the room filled with the others we'd flown down with from Korat.

At 1:00, the SSG closed the door and walked to the lectern at the room's front. Introducing himself in a monotone voice. He began his debriefing lecture by emphatically emphasizing that under no circumstance could we say, mention, discuss our write about any combat action in Thailand that we'd seen or heard of. Also, if we'd had sex with anyone, male or female, within the last two months, to report to Sick Call at the nearest military installation and be examined for STDs, before having sex with anyone Stateside. Then, for the remainder of our 2-hour debrief, he went into detail and answered questions on the political, economic and social unrest in the U.S., and under no circumstance were we to participate in any kind of demonstration while wearing our uniform.

When he'd finished our debriefing, he called out our names and service numbers, and passed to each person his red Military Passport, a plane ticket for the flight to Travis Air Force Base in California, and two meal vouchers. One for dinner tonight, and one for breakfast in the morning. Then, we were instructed to assemble with our duffle bags only and dressed in our Class-B khaki uniforms at 0800 in the Hotel's front Lobby. He said in parting, "Remember, you are not to leave this Hotel for any reason. And, tonight's movie in the Hotel's theater is the newly released musical, *Camelot*, which is free to those who show their orders and plane ticket. Tomorrow morning, you'll have a wake-up call at 0500 to make sure you have plenty of time to clean up, eat breakfast and be at the Hotel's Lobby by 0800. Good luck, gentlemen."

Looking at the seat numbers on our plane for Tiger Airlines' Flight 12, Tommy and I were happy to see we'd again be sitting next to each other on our flight Stateside, because of the close alphabetical order of our names. Returning to my room, I took a hot, luxurious bath, my first in a year. As I shaved and dressed in civilian clothes. I missed having a cold Bud to drink as I did so, and sent my rumbled khaki uniform out with the valet to be cleaned and pressed. Then, I met up with Tommy in the Hotel's bar and drank a cold bottle of Sing Hai Beer before going to dinner together and again laughing at the disappointed look on the MPs faces when they smelled the burning tobacco from my hand-rolled cigarette.

After watching the 7:00 showing of the musical *Camelot*, I returned to my room and politely turned down the valet's offer to fix me up with a woman for $15.00, when he brought back my uniform. Stripping to my skivvies, I went to bed and fondly remembered the good times I'd had with my succession of girlfriends, as I went to sleep.

With my 5:00 wake-up call, I again had a luxurious hot bath, before I shaved and dressed in my freshly cleaned and pressed Class-B khaki uniform, wishing again I had a cold Bud to drink as I did so. Walking down to the restaurant for breakfast, I met up with Tommy, and we both ordered a full-on American breakfast, and stuffed ourselves, not knowing how long it would be till we were fed on our flight Stateside. Then, I lit up a hand-rolled cigarette and we had another good laugh at the disgruntled MPs, as they left.

Returning to my room, I packed the last few loose items into my duffel bag, made sure I had my transfer orders, Passport and plane ticket under the front of my shirt with my cigarette makings, and tucked my dark-green garrison cap over the right side of my black web belt. Looking around the room one last time to make sure I'd not missed anything, I hefted my heavy duffel bag over my right shoulder to hang by its strap down the center of my back, and left for the Hotel's front Lobby.

There, I waited for Tommy, before joining the long line of khaki-clad men flying Stateside with us. Sitting on my upended duffel bag, I enjoyed a hand-rolled cigarette, while waiting for our busses to arrive. Soon, I saw three U.S. Air Force busses arrive, with a 2½-ton truck behind each bus, to carry the mass of khaki-clad Soldiers and Airmen, and their duffel bags to Don Muang Airport.

As we began to file out the Hotel's Lobby door, each man stated his name and service number to the three Air Force Sergeants holding clipboards. When one of them located the man's name and service number, the Sargent checked the name on his list and parsed the person to one of the three busses.

When it was my turn, I was directed to the middle bus, where another Air Force Sargent check my name on his list, verifying I was boarding the correct bus, told me to put my duffel bag in the truck behind the bus and then to sit in the first available seat on the bus. Thankful I didn't have to carry my duffel bag on my lap all the way to the airport, I did as instructed. Climbing up into the bus, I saw Tommy waving me to the seat next to him.

After the bus was loaded, the Sargent did a head count to make sure he had the right number of bodies on his bus. Then, the busses and trucks convoyed to Don Muang Airport, where I saw the trucks drive onto the tarmac to transfer our duffel bags into the cargo hold of a waiting Boeing 707 with "Tiger Airlines" on the fuselage.

Meanwhile, the busses continued to the passenger terminal, where my name on the Sargent's list was check again, as I exited the bus. Entering the terminal, I was told to position myself in the line to the boarding gate in the seating order shown on my ticket. Once Tommy and I had arranged ourselves accordingly, I rolled a cigarette and said, "Tommy, this is the last cigarette I'm going to smoke. I've promised Linda I was going to quit smoking when I left Thailand."

Tommy laughed and said sarcastically, "Good luck with that. I'll bet you five bucks you don't make it to Travis Air Force Base."

I responded, "That's a bet. Besides, it's like my Mom always said, 'If at first you don't succeed, failure may be your thing.' And, I don't intend to fail at this."

To which he laughed and said, "But, my Mom told me, 'the road to hell is paved with good intentions.' And, I'll be collecting that five bucks from you before we land at Travis."

Boarding the plane in seating order, and after being greeted at the plane's doorway by a pretty, round-eyed stewardess, I saw again the first-class section of the plane was filled with Officers and Senior NCOs. After Tommy and I sat in our assigned seats, this time on the plane's right side with Tommy sitting next to the window, I fastened my seat belt and watched the parade of Soldiers and Airmen walking down the aisle to the seats behind me.

Soon, I heard the whine of the plane's four jet engines starting in sequence, and then felt the plane roll down the taxi way, turn right at the end of the runway, and stop. Hearing the pitch of the engine's whine increasing to a roar, I was suddenly pushed back into my seat by the acceleration of the plane to achieve take-off speed. When I felt the nose of the plane tilt upward and heard the rumble of the wheels on concrete stop, I thought excitedly, "I'm actually going home."

Once the plane was safely airborne, I heard on the overhead speakers, "This is the Captain speaking. Welcome to Tiger Airlines Flight 12 to Travis Air Force Base. We'll be flying over Da Nang, South Vietnam, at 36,000 feet. Then, across the South China Sea to Okinawa, Japan, where we'll land at Kadina Air Force Base. There, you'll be able to exit the plane, stretch your legs and shop at the Duty Free Store, while the plane is refueled, and the crews changed. Then, the fight continues to Elmendorf Air Force Base in Alaska, where the plane is refueled again, before you finally land at Travis Air Force Base about twenty-four hours from now. I hope you enjoy your flight home, men. And, thank you for your service."

A short time later, the pretty, round-eyed stewardesses distributed lunch. A half-hour after eating my lunch, I saw Tommy pointing down out the window and exclaim, "I can see flashes on the ground, Sandii! Sure am glad I'm up here and not down there."

Several hours later, having slept as we flew over nothing but water, the plane landed at Kadina Air Force Base. There, I exited the plane as the sun was setting, and entered a huge hangar, where I saw rows of vending and change machines, and black telephone boxes lining the walls. I also saw on the left sidewall, a large sign that read, "Duty Free Store," and walked straight for it.

Arriving there, I read a large notice informing everyone we were limited to buying a half-gallon of liquor, or a case of wine, or a case of beer, and was surprised to see they had Sing Hai Beer. I bought a half-gallon of Haig-and-Haig Scotch whiskey to give Linda's family, as I watched Tommy buy a 12-bottle case of Sing Hai Beer in quart bottles, explaining, "This might be my last chance to buy this good beer, as it may not be available Stateside."

The clerk packaged and sealed our purchases in padded cardboard boxes, explaining, "Do not break these seals until after you've gone through Customs, or you'll have to pay the Import Tax. Also, you'll need to fill out this yellow Declaration Card and present it to the Customs Officer when you arrive Stateside."

Returning to the plane, Tommy and I stowed our packaged booze in an overhead bin and placed the yellow Declaration Cards inside our Military Passports, which we kept under our shirt fronts. After the plane took off from Okinawa, we were severed dinner, and tempting though it was to smoke after dinner, especially when Tommy lit his cigarette, I resolutely refrained. A couple hours later, the plane's Captain announced, "We've just crossed the International Date Line, and it is now again August 5th, 12:33 AM local time."

Several hours later, we landed in the bright light of Alaska's long Summer day at Elmendorf Air Force Base. There, they spent a half-hour refueling, while we sat in the plane. By now, my internal clock was completely out of sync with the local time zone, which was eighteen hours behind Thailand's time zone. Of course, it now being night in Thailand, I had no problem falling asleep after we were served another dinner following takeoff.

Five hours later, I woke as the plane landed at Travis Air Force Base, where it was announced the local time was 8:12 PM, Pacific Daylight Savings Time. Tommy dug his wallet out of his right hip pocket, extracted a 5-Dollar bill and said as he handed it to me, "I didn't believe you could do the whole twenty-four hours without smoking a cigarette, and I hope you can do it for the rest of your life, good buddy. God knows I couldn't."

Responding as I took it, "I admit it's been a tough twenty-four hours to go cold turkey with everyone around me smoking. But, like they say, 'Quitting is something you have to do one minute at a time,' and I think I've the willpower to quit for the next minute."

Exiting the plane, and carrying my package of Scotch whiskey down a portable stairway in the fading light of sunset, I was directed to the plane's cargo hold door. There, the duffle bags were being systematically brought to the door by Airmen in OD BDUs, who read the name and service number on each loudly. As each man stepped forward and showed ID card to claim his duffel bag, it was lowered onto the claimant's right shoulder, who then followed the procession to a glass-walled terminal building.

Hearing my name and service number, I quickly stepped forward to the cargo door, took my duffel bag onto my right shoulder from the Airman who handed it down, while I hugged the box containing the Scotch under my left arm. Then, I hastily followed the rapidly moving file of men carrying duffel bags and boxes of booze to the terminal building. There, joining the end of the shortest line I saw, I waited to be seen by one of a half-dozen uniformed U.S. Customs Officers standing behind tables, as men placed their duffel bag, and whatever box of booze they were carrying, on the table.

When it was my turn, the Customs Officer helped me lower my duffel bag down onto the table. Then, setting my box of Scotch whisky on the table, I removed my red Military Passport and the filled out yellow Declaration Card from under my shirt front, and handed them to him. After answering several questions, he stamped my Passport and Declaration Card. Hefting my duffel bag onto my shoulder, I picked up my package and walked to an exit doorway with a sign over it reading "San Francisco Intl. Airport." I saw over another exit doorway a sign reading "Sacramento Bus and Train Terminals," and thought, "That must be for the guys who are going somewhere in central California, Nevada or Oregon, which I'd take, if I weren't flying first to see Linda in New Jersey."

Exiting through the doorway, I was directed to store my duffel bag in the baggage hold at the bottom of a large Greyhound bus. When I'd done so, I carried my package to the bus's doorway, climbed the few steps up into the passenger area, and saw Tommy waving to me from a row of seats he'd saved for us on the right side of the bus.

Walking down the aisleway to Tommy, I sat down in the aisle-seat next to Tommy in the window-seat. Though it was now dark outside, there was enough light from the huge hangars on the flight line for me to see a couple of the gigantic C-5A Globemaster cargo jets with their ten-story high tails protruding skyward, as the Greyhound bus drove toward the Air Base's Main Gate.

Exiting the Main Gate and following the road to Vacaville, I watched in amazement the mass of cars and semitrailer trucks on the six lanes of Interstate 80 passing below, as the bus drove across the overpass, before it turned right and circled around under the overpass to the Interstate's on-ramp to head West on I-80 for San Francisco. There, I saw on my left, the huge Anheuser-Busch brewery and said to Tommy, "That's where all the Budweiser beer we've been drinking in Thailand is made."

Soon, the bus was climbing and weaving up to the low mountain pass separating the San Francisco Bay Area from the San Juaquin Valley. As the bus ascended to the pass, I saw the iconic Red Roof Restaurant on the frontage road outside the bus's right window.

Reaching the summit of the pass, the bus picked up speed as it descended and weaved down the other side toward the city of Vallejo at the North end of San Francisco Bay. As the bus passed between the tops of two hills before I-80's final decent to Vallejo, I heard Tommy exclaim, "Look at all the lights, Sandii!"

I looked out the window to our right at the panoramic view of San Francisco Bay. After having experienced a year in the dimly lit Camp Friendship and the city of Korat, I was amazed at all the lights blazing brightly around San Francisco Bay, and softly said, "Sweet Jesus, I've never seen so many lights."

EPILOGUE

February 1987, seventeen-and-a-half years later, I stood on the top deck of the USS Cayuga, LST-1186[165] looking for the first time since August 1969 at Thailand from the Sea of Thailand. Stretched a mile away was a beautiful, white sand beach in front of a verdant jungle on the Southeast coast of Thailand in the Chanthaburi Province, which bordered Cambodia. I was now a U.S. Navy Hospital Corpsman First Class, an HM1 and Leading Petty Officer, the LPO, of the U.S. Marine Corps' 3/1 BLT BAS[166], consisting of 37 Corpsmen and a Navy Surgeon. We were here for a 2-week combined-op with the Thai Marines. Standing next to me was my Thai counterpart, a 5-foot-9, handsome Thai Hospital First Class named Govit Thatarat.

---

165   Landing Ship Tank. LSTs are named after counties, in this case, Cayuga County, NY.

166   3rd Battalion, 1st Marine Infantry Regiment, Battalion Landing Team, Battalion Aid Station.

On the USS Cayuga, was its ship's complement of 196 Officers and Sailors, the 125 U.S. Marines of the 3/1's India Company, a platoon of five LAAVs[167], to carry the two companies of U.S. and Thai Marines on the LST to the beach. Also, there was a a platoon of U.S. Navy Seabees with their four pontoon docks attached to the side of the LST for the LKA[168] ship to off load supplies brought with a Company of Marines from the First Service Support Group at Camp Pendleton Marine Corps Base, California.

The LST and LKA were two of the four U.S. Navy ships that comprised the 3/1 BLT flotilla. The flagship of the flotilla was the huge aircraft carrier/troop ship, the U.S.S Bellawood, LHA-3. The Landing Helicopter Assault ship was named for the 5th Marine Regiment's bloody battle of WWI at Bellawood in France. The 5th Marines doggedly held their ground when the other Allied Forces on both its flanks retreated. That left the Marines surrounded by the Germans, and they suffered 80-percent casualties.

The BLT's Corpsmen claimed LHA stood for "Largest Hospital Afloat," as it contained a 300-bed hospital with three surgical units. Besides the rest of the 475 Marine Infantrymen of the 3/1 BLT, the LHA also carried a two Marine Squadrons of CH47 and CH53 helicopters and a Marine Squadron of Harrier jets, a Marine Recon Platoon and a Marine Transportation Company, whose vehicles were carried to the beach in LCMs[169] stored in the LHA's well-deck, which could be flooded by sinking the aft portion and lowering the LHA's stern ramp.

The fourth ship in the flotilla was the USS Ogden, LPD-5[170], which carried five 105 mm howitzers and five 155 mm canon from the 11th Marines Artillery Regiment. Each gun was towed by a 2½-ton truck, which carried their ammunition.

The USS Cayuga's slogan was "Are We Having Fun, Yet." It also had the unenviable moniker as the "Death Ship," as on each of its pri-

---

167   Landing Amphibious Assault Vehicle, a lightly armored, tracked vehicle, capable of carrying twenty combat equipped Marines.

168   Landing Kargo Assault

169   Landing Craft Medium, capable of carrying a 2½-ton truck with a one-ton trailer or artillery piece.

170   Landing Portable Dock. LPDs are named after county seats, in this case, the City of Ogden, Weber County, Utah.

or 6-month-long West Pac cruises, at least one member of the ship's small crew complement had died. In the first month since leaving its home port in Long Beach, CA, two people had died. The first week out, a Navy Lieutenant died of a massive heart attack, which an autopsy aboard the LHA showed it resulted from, an 80- percent blockage of his coronary arteries. The second death was at the Subic Bay Naval Station in the Philippines, when a drunk Sailor stumbled at the foot of the Cayuga's gangway, falling headfirst onto the logs fendering the ship from the pier, and broke his neck. Out of the 4-ship flotilla, these were the only deaths so far[171].

I went ashore in the third LAAV, riding in the 20-mm machine-gun turret at the front top. As the BAS's LPO, I had the option to ride in the topside turret with a sea-level view of the beach landing, versus sitting in the windowless, cramped space below. When the LAAV rolled onto the white sand of the pristine beach and dropped its rear ramp, I climbed out the back of the turret, grabbed my combat gear, which included my large AB-1 Bag[172], and a 0.45 caliber pistol for defensive purposes. Exiting the rear of the LAAV, I made my way with HM1 Thatarat, who'd ridden in the turret of the fourth LAAV, along the busy beach, and joined the BAS when it landed with its 2½-ton truck and one-ton trailer in an LCM.

After the BAS landed, Thatarat and I crowded into the truck's cab with the Surgeon, and rode from the sandy beach, across the beach frontage road, and onto a narrow dirt road into the verdant jungle, behind the advancing Thai and American Marines. Four miles later, we crossed Thailand's Hwy 3, a 2-lane country road, and found a wide wayside to stop and set up the two 30 by 40-foot Medium Tents that comprised our BAS.

One tent was for triage, to sort the dead and dying from those who could be quickly treated and returned to combat. Then, those who were seriously wounded were passed through to the surgical tent. There, we had four surgical tables to stabilize the seriously wounded, before

---

171   The only other death in the flotilla occurred several months later, during combined operations with the Australian Marines, when a Marine from the USS Cayuga fell from a rubber boat during a landing and drowned.

172   Aid Bag, No. 1, a large, cloth bag containing all my First Aid equipment, including narcotics and a surgical kit to perform emergency surgery in the field.

being medevac'd to the LHR by helicopter. As I, another HM1 and our HMC[173], had been trained to perform major surgery on combat wounds, we manned the four surgical stations with the Battalion Surgeon in mass casualty situations.

Though Govit Thatarat spoke fair English, he was grateful I had retained a good portion of the Thai I'd learned during my Vietnam War tour of duty. This eliminated the need for him to translate when I spoke with his Corpsmen, Marines or Thai locals who wanted to do business with our BAS.

I'd told the Corpsmen assigned to the BAS to bring some money with them and I'd buy food from the locals, so we wouldn't have to subsist our MREs, or Meals Ready to Eat. Fortunately, at the crossroad a quarter mile West of our BAS, there was a farmer's market. Collecting 15 cents from each of the 30 Corpsmen manning the BAS, they were surprised when I returned with two large flats full of cooked food and fresh fruit, on which they feasted with gusto.

Of course, MREs weren't the only food we brought to eat. The BAS Supply Petty Officer, HM2 Richards, a huge 6-foot-4 man, weighing 240 pounds, and capable of tossing our heavy 8-cubic-foot cans effortlessly up into the back of our 2½-ton truck, had standing orders from me and our Surgeon, that regardless of where we landed in the world, we'd have a substantial amount of salsa and tortilla chips to snack on. Not only did he fill an 8-cubic-foot can with large bottles of Pace Picante Sauce and bags of tortilla chips, he'd also filled an eight-8-foot can with sealed haunches of ham, bricks of cheese, loafs of bread, and bottles of condiments he commandeered from the LHA's Mess Deck for everyone in the BAS to feast on.

It'd been determined beforehand, that when the BAS was fully established, which only took us a half hour to do, we'd run a clinic in our downtime to treat the ailments of the locals living in the area. When I'd gone to the farmer's market, I'd noticed catty-corner from it was the local Medical Clinic. Returning with Govit and our Surgeon, we climbed the steps up to the Medical Clinic, which was a 25-foot square, wood building on 5-foot high support poles. There, we intro-

---

173   Hospitalman Chief Petty Officer

duced ourselves to the Clinic's pretty Thai Nurse, who provided Thailand's free medical care to those who lived in the surrounding area.

The Medical Clinic was one large room, very much like my hooch at Camp Friendship. The front part was the Clinic, containing an exam table, stainless steel cabinets with glass doors filled with medical supplies, and a large filing cabinet to keep the Medical Records of her patients in. The back part was clearly her living quarters, with a bed, table and chairs, chest of drawers with a mirror, and a small bathroom.

She explained to us in Thai, that she'd wanted to be a doctor, but her father didn't want to spend money on a daughter to attend College, much less a University's Medical School. However, the Government did pay for her two years of Nursing School for her to provide minimal medical care in a rural clinic. Here, the serious cases were transported to the District Hospital in Non Khia, several miles east of the Medical Clinic. After hearing her story, I thought, "That sounds just like Sompit's father not sending her to University like her brothers, as she was not a son."

We arranged with her to spread the message that at certain times of the day the BAS would hold medical and dental screening clinics for the locals, as the LHA's Dentist had agreed to come ashore for dental exams and treatments. Also, one of the many skills taught to be an HM1, was to do emergency dental surgery. Of course, the purpose of our medical/dental clinics was not purely altruistic, as our clinics could entitle us to be awarded the military's Humanitarian Service Medal.

For ten days, I had fun at the BAS eating Thai food, bargaining with Thais on the services they wanted to provide, like doing our laundry, and talking in Thai with those who came to our medical/dental clinics. I also heard reports from my frontline Corpsmen in the jungle with their Infantry Platoons about how much fun they were having. Not only were the local Thais selling them tasty local food and souvenirs, but the local Thai men were also selling their young teenage girls to them for sex at $2 a pop, and I thought, "Well, that part of the Thai culture sure hasn't changed in the last seventeen years."

At the end of our 10-day combined operation along the Cambodian border with the Thai Marines, we packed up the BAS into the 1-ton trailer and climbed into the 2½-ton truck for the 4-mile ride back to the beach. As February was in Thailand's dry season and the daytime temps were in the mid-80s, we were all quite dirty and sweaty, and ready to get back aboard ship for a nice, hot clean shower.

Arriving at the sandy beach, looking at the beautiful calm Sea of Thailand beyond, and seeing the beach contained only the Thai and American Marines, we quickly climbed out of the truck, stripped to our boxers, and ran to cool down and clean off in the inviting surf. Jumping into the Sea of Thailand, I was surprised there was no cooling effect, but found it was like entering a warm tub of water, as the Sea was eighty degrees.

After splashing around for a while to wash off ten days of grime, I air-dried and put my smelly Marine Corps camouflage BDUs back on. Then, I returned to the LST in the turret of an LAAV.

During my time with Govit, I'd learned his assignment with the Thai Marines was temporary, unlike my 3-year sea-service tour with the U.S. Marines, and he was the Supply Petty Officer at their Naval Hospital in Bangkok. Also, the Hospital's supply system was in the process of being computerized with the Lotus 1-2-3® spreadsheet program, which I'd used to organize the BAS's medical and supply information.

Telling this to Govit, he invited me to spend my 6-day liberty at Pattaya with him in Bangkok, helping him computerize his Hospital's supply system. I quickly accepted, because it'd give me something to do with my 6-day liberty, as I was now married with children and wouldn't be whoring around like some of the Staff Sergeants I lived with on the LST.

Once the BLT had reembarked on the 4-ship flotilla, it sailed 85 miles west past Kó Chûung and Kó Kâam Yái[174], then thirty miles north to anchor off Pattaya Beach. There, we were given six days of liberty, with a skeleton crew to remain aboard ship. Having five Corpsmen with me for six 24-hour watches in the LST's Sick Bay, I took the first watch on Monday. The next morning, I packed a suitcase with clothes, rode the LST's LCP[175], to Pattaya Beach. Walking across Pattaya Beach Road to Pattaya's Bus Terminal, I passed many bars and shops, and numerous young pretty prostitutes trolling the streets in mini-skirts to attract customers.

---

174   Translated as Island Docile and Island Across Big.
175   Landing Craft Personnel

At the Bus Terminal, I bought a ticket to ride an air-conditioned bus the eighty miles North to Bangkok's Eastern Bus Terminal in the Sukhumvit District. Two hours later, I exited the bus and hired a taxi to take me two miles West on Sukhumvit Road to the Sheraton Grande Sukhumvit Hotel, which had a generous array of amenities and spacious rooms for 600 Bhat per night and paid 3,000 Bhat for five nights.

With the value of the Bhat having dropped to 42 Bhat per Dollar, it cost me less than $75 to spend Tuesday thru Saturday nights in this luxury Hotel. Also, its close proximity to the Eastern Bus Terminal and the Thai Naval Hospital only five miles away, made it a good location for me. Plus, a lot of the Officers and Staff NCOs were staying there, as it was close to Sukhumvit's shopping and entertainment areas.

After settling the things I'd bought with me in my spacious room, I went down to the Hotel's Restaurant for a delicious Thai lunch. Then, I walked for several hours searching through the many shops and stores along Sukhumvit Road, looking for souvenirs to by for my wife and kids, and other family members. En route, I met up with two of my Corpsmen from the LST, who asked me to go with them for dinner in the entertainment area along Soi 11. Stopping at one of the numerous lounges along the busy lane, we ate dinner. Before I returned alone to my Hotel room, I helped them negotiate the price for two of the young prostitutes, of the many that habitated the lounge, for them to spend the night with.

After breakfast Wednesday morning in the Hotel's Restaurant, I hired a taxi, which was a newer Toyota Corolla, and rode five miles through the bustling, congested large city of Bangkok's million-plus population to the Thai Naval Hospital near the Chao Phraya River. The front entrance to the Hospital's large, white one-story main building, led to a large lobby with many people in white or khaki uniforms scurrying to and from large hallways that went in several directions. Walking across the lobby to an information counter, I spoke in Thai to the Thai Navy Corpsman in a khaki uniform that I was there to see HM1 Govit Thatarat, who worked in Hospital Supply.

Several minutes later, Govit appeared, and after exchanging sáwát-diis, he escorted me down the hallway to the left, along the front of the Hospital, to the Hospital Supply Office. There, he introduced me to a Thai Naval Medical Corps Service Lieutenant, who was the Supply OIC, and a Thai Naval Nurse Corps Lieutenant, who was the Nursing

Service Liaison Officer, both wearing khaki uniform and who spoke good English.

I spent the day going over the spreadsheet program's layout and the numerous cell functions that could be performed. Their Lotus 1-2-3® program was the same as used by the U.S. Government, except it used the Thai Script instead of English. At the end of the day, Govit asked if I'd like to have dinner at his home, which I gratefully accepted. As his home was on the Thai Naval Base the Hospital served, we didn't have to drive far in his car to get to his home.

Govit's dwelling was very similar in layout as Dhoi's home on the Thai Army Base at Korat. After eating an excellent Thai meal with Govit's very pretty wife and two handsome young sons, he and I sat at their dining table, sharing a bottle of Sing Hai Beer, as he smoked cigarettes. We discussed our varied military careers, particularly laughing at the inane experiences I had with the 442d Signal Battalion during the Vietnam War. Having had a fun evening talking with Govit, while his wife watched TV with their two sons, he drove me back to my Hotel. There, we agreed he'd pick me up at 7:30 on Thursday morning and drive me to the Naval Hospital.

I spent Thursday helping them set up the various templates for the data to be entered into the spreadsheets of the different types of equipment and supply items used by their Hospital. Over lunch in the Hospital's Mess Hall, the Liaison Nurse invited me to have dinner with her German husband, who was a Doctor at the Bumrungrad International Hospital on Soi 3, just off Sukhumvit Road, which was near where they lived, and not far from where I was staying at the Sheraton Grande Sukhumvit Hotel.

After work, she drove me to their spacious three bedroom, two bathroom home, over a 3-car garage and servant quarters, contained within a high-walled compound. While eating a superb Thai meal prepared by their housekeeper/cook, the Doctor told me it only cost him $400 a month for the house, including their housekeeper/cook and guard/gardener, who lived in the servant quarters. Finishing a pleasant dinner with the Doctor, his wife and two children, he drove me in his Mercedes-Benz to my Hotel.

An hour or so after returning to my Hotel room, I heard a knock on my door. Upon opening the door, I saw two Marines I recognized from

India Company in civilian clothes holding up a third Marine between them and asked, "What's the problem, Corporal Sanders?"

He replied, "Sorry to bother you HM1, but Pvt. Dennison here, is sick. He's been throwing up and complaining of stomach cramps. Doc Sallis said you were staying here and to bring Dennison to you."

Looking at Pvt. Dennison, I saw he looked pale and clammy, and touching his forehead, I could feel he was running a high fever. Knowing how insidious tropical diseases were, I quickly dressed and had them help Dennison down to the Hotel's entrance. There, I hired a taxi waiting in the queue to take me and Dennison to Govit's home on the Thai Naval Base, dismissing the other two Marines, with my thanks. I knew Govit could help cut through the red tape to have Dennison examined by a Doctor at the Thai Naval Hospital.

Arriving at Govit's home, he quickly helped me transfer Dennison from the taxi to his car and rapidly drove us to the Naval Hospital's E.R. There, an attending physician hastily had a nurse start an IV in Dennison's arm and draw blood for analysis. It wasn't long before the Doctor had diagnosed Dennison had an intestinal bacterial infection that was not contagious, and had him admitted to a Medical Ward. Satisfied Dennison was in good hands, Govit drove me back to my Hotel.

Friday, after spending the morning with Govit entering data into the spreadsheet program and debugging errors that inevitably popped up, Govit led me to the Medical Ward during our lunch break. There, I found Dennison laying in the midst of the hospital beds lining the left side of the Ward. The Nurse on duty informed me he was recovering well with the IV antibiotics he'd been given, and would likely be discharged that afternoon, or tomorrow morning at the latest. Asking Dennison how he felt, he replied, "I'm feeling great, HM1, with all these pretty Thai nurses looking after me. And, with my new Thai buddies offering to introduce me to their sisters, I'm in hog heaven."

When Govit and I left after work in his car for his home, I saw his wife and children waiting outside for us when we arrived there. Climbing into the car's back seat, Govit drove us to a local street market, where we bought from the various venders tasty, cooked foods and fresh fruit to eat for dinner. Govit explained as he drove us back to his home, "It's cheaper and more fun to buy our dinner at the street market, than it is for my wife to make it at home."

Saturday morning, Govit had his family in the car when he picked me up at the Hotel. He then drove us to Silpakorn University on Maha Rat Road, where he parked his car. Crossing Na Prâ Lan Road to the South, we entered the Wat Prá Kaew and Grand Palace grounds. There, we spent the morning touring Bangkok's premier monuments to Thailand's religion and regency. At noon, we crossed Maha Rat Road, and I treated them to lunch at the nearby Khunkung Restaurant of the Royal Naval Association. With one of the few coveted riverfront locations along this part of the Chao Phraya River, I enjoyed the combination of river views and cheap, tasty seafood-based meals.

After our delicious lunch, we walked the quarter-mile South along the Maha Rat Road and crossed over to the Wat Pho compound. It's often referred to as Thailand's first University, as it has the traditional Thai School of Medicine that continues to this day. We first went to the main Temple to see its huge Reclining Buddha. Molded around a 151-foot long, 49-foot high brick core, was the finished plaster and gold leaf covered statue, which was an imposing reminder of the Buddha's passing into Nirvana. On the soles of the Reclining Buddha's feet, I saw depicted the 108 auspicious physical characteristics of the Buddha.

Walking out the gateway of the Temple's East wall, I saw the two stone giants who guard the gateway to the rest of the Wat Pho compound. Govit told me these huge granite figures depicted Chinese characters from the time of Marco Polo, and originally arrived in Thailand in the Nineteenth Century as ballast aboard Chinese junks.

Looking to my right, I saw the four tall Royal Chedi. Decorated with colorful inlaid tiles in the classic Ratanakosin style, they were meant to represent the first four Emperors of the Chakri Dynasty founded in 1782 with Bangkok as the new capital.

Continuing East, we passed through two consecutive long galleries of Buddha statues linking the four temple buildings comprising the exterior of the Prá Ûbosót, or Holy Buddhist Building. The immense ordination hall is Wat Pho's second-most noteworthy structure. Walking through two of the four passages linking the temple buildings, I saw 394 gold-gilded Buddha images displaying the Ayutthaya-era features. Entering the Prá Ûbosót, I saw an impressive 3-tiered pedestal holding the Prá Buddha Deva Patimakorn, an Ayutthaya-era Buddha statue originally brought to the Temple by Rama I, who's ashes are entombed in the pedestal.

Leaving through the Western Temple, we walked South around the four Royal Chedi and past a crocodile pond, to one of the compound's portals onto Maha Rat Road. There, we walked North past the Wat Prá Kaew and the Grand Palace grounds, and crossed Na Prá Lan Road back to Silpakorn University, where Govit had parked his car.

On the way to Govit's home, we again stopped at the street market to buy cooked food and fresh fruit for dinner. After eating dinner and my evening conversation with Govit, I bid goodbye to his family when he drove me to my Hotel, as I was returning to Pattaya and the USS Cayuga in the morning.

On Sunday morning, I packed my suitcase and had breakfast at the Hotel's Restaurant, before taking an enjoyable 2-mile walk along Sukhumvit Road to the Eastern Bus Terminal. There, I boarded an air-conditioned bus for the 2-hour ride to Pattaya, enjoying the coastal view of the Sea of Thailand. From Pattaya's Bus Terminal, I walked North past the numerous bars, shops and young prostitutes along Pattaya Beach Road to where the USS Cayuga's LCP docked on the beach for my ride back to the Death Ship.

The following morning, 4 four-ship flotilla sailed at sunrise for its 2-day cruise back to the Subic Bay Naval Station in the Philippines. As I stood on the port-side of the LST's exposed top-deck, watching the sunrise over Pattaya as we sailed South into the Sea of Thailand, I was joined by the big, burly form of the Company Gunny for India Company, and heard him say, "You know, HM1, this is my fourth West Pac cruise, and of all the countries we do combined ops with, Thailand is by far my favorite. Heck, we have more fun in the bush here, than on liberty anyplace else. Also, Pattaya is the only liberty port we visit where guys jump-ship to spend more time ashore. Of course, everyone returns before we sail. But just the same, guys are willing to lose a stripe, pay a fine and have extra-duty, so they can have an extra day or two chasing those young, pretty Thai women."

I responded, "You know, I was here for a year during the Vietnam War, and a lot of guys went crazy then, too, chasing the young, pretty Thai women," and thought, "and the women are still treated as second-class citizens, and the fathers are still just as willing to sell their 14-year-old daughters into prostitution now, as they did seventeen years ago, despite the fact that AIDS is now raging through Thailand's population."[176]

---

[176]   Several years later, Thailand's Parliament passed anti-prostitution laws in an attempt to curb the pervasive Pedophilia Tourism business prominent in Thailand with the exploitation of it's 14-year-old girls.

✦ 787 ✦

Be sure to watch for Sherman Lynch's upcoming sequel:

TAKING IT IN THE REAR AGAIN: THE VIETNAM WAR'S REAR ECHELON STATESIDE.

After Sandii's 30-day post-deployment leave following his year-long tour-of-duty with a rear echelon support unit in the Vietnam War that secretly extended as a second front in Thailand, he and his brothers-in-arms end up at Ft Huachuca, Arizona. There, he found they were to provide a wholly different type of rear-echelon support for the Vietnam war.

Ft. Huachuca was a remote, former all-black outpost in the high desert along the Mexican border, eighty miles from any significant city. This was completely different from the jungles and rice patties of Southeast Asia, where there was the nearby city of Korat for Sandii and his buddies to spend their off-duty time. Now, their duty assignments shifted from mission critical direct support of frontline combat units, to the macabre duty of being on burial details for the many slain in the Vietnam War, riot-control squads for the frequently violent anti-Vietnam War demonstrations, or radio strike teams for instant deployment to replace destroyed radio sites worldwide.

Ft. Huachuca also posed dangerous dilemmas for Sandii and his friends, from nefarious drug dealers and driving fast cars, to dalliances with willing, waiting wives of deployed soldiers, because there were few single women to date. Plus, there was the increased use of drugs and alcohol that went from recreational use to constant abuse for coping with Post Traumatic Stress Disorder (PTSD) from the Vietnam War, an unknown condition at that time. These led to numerous deaths and maimings among Sandii's comrades. Of course, there was still the ongoing confrontations between the antagonistic short-timers and the power-tripping lifers that provide many anecdotal situations.

About the Author

Sherman Lynch was born in 1948 at Millington Naval Air Station in Tennessee, where his father was a Navy Chief teaching Aviation Electronics. As a Navy brat, he lived in San Diego, California, from 1951 – 1953; on Ford Island, Hawaii, from 1953 – 1957; and in Fremont, California, from 1957 – 1961. His father then retired and moved the family to Oregon.

In 1967, he graduated from high school and enlisted in the U.S. Army for three years, going to bootcamp at Fort Lewis, Washington and then to Signal Corps School at Ft. Monmouth, New Jersey, for nine months, before going to the 1st Signal Brigade in the Vietnam War in 1968 – 1969. Then he went to the 11th Signal Group at Fort Huachuca, Arizona, and discharged in 1970 to go to college.

Bored with college, he reenlisted in 1973 for the Air Defense Missile School at Redstone Arsenal, Alabama, where he graduated from Fire Control Repair as a Spec-5, became an instructor and promoted to Staff Sergeant before his discharge in 1976 to attend the University of Alabama School of Nursing. After being forced out of Nursing School in 1977 by faculty that believed men should not be nurses, he enlisted as a Navy Hospitalman, rose to Hospitalman First Class, and served his three-year sea duty tour with the 1st Marines at Camp Pendleton, California, before his discharge in 1988 to attend college. In 1991, he received a BS in Computer Science, with a Minor in Writing. After the dot-com bust in 1999, he returned to medicine, and retired from the VA Hospital in Salt Lake City, Utah, with a twenty-five-year pension in 2007. He is now living in Utah.